THE APOSTASY

HYMN OF THE SUN AND THE MOON

ALLISON PAIGE

FINNEGAN PUBLISHING GROUP

ISBN: 9798986559377 (Paperback) | ISBN: 9798986559360 (Hardback)

Cover art by India-Lee Crews

www.finneganpublishinggroup.com
www.authorallisonpaige.com

TRIGGER WARNINGS

Assault, Blood, Death, Explicit Sexual Scenes, Gore, Graphic Violence, Manipulation, Religious Elements, Sexual Assault, Torture, and everything else that comes with the dark fantasy genre. Everything within the story is a work of fiction and in no way disregards or is meant to disrespect anyone's beliefs.

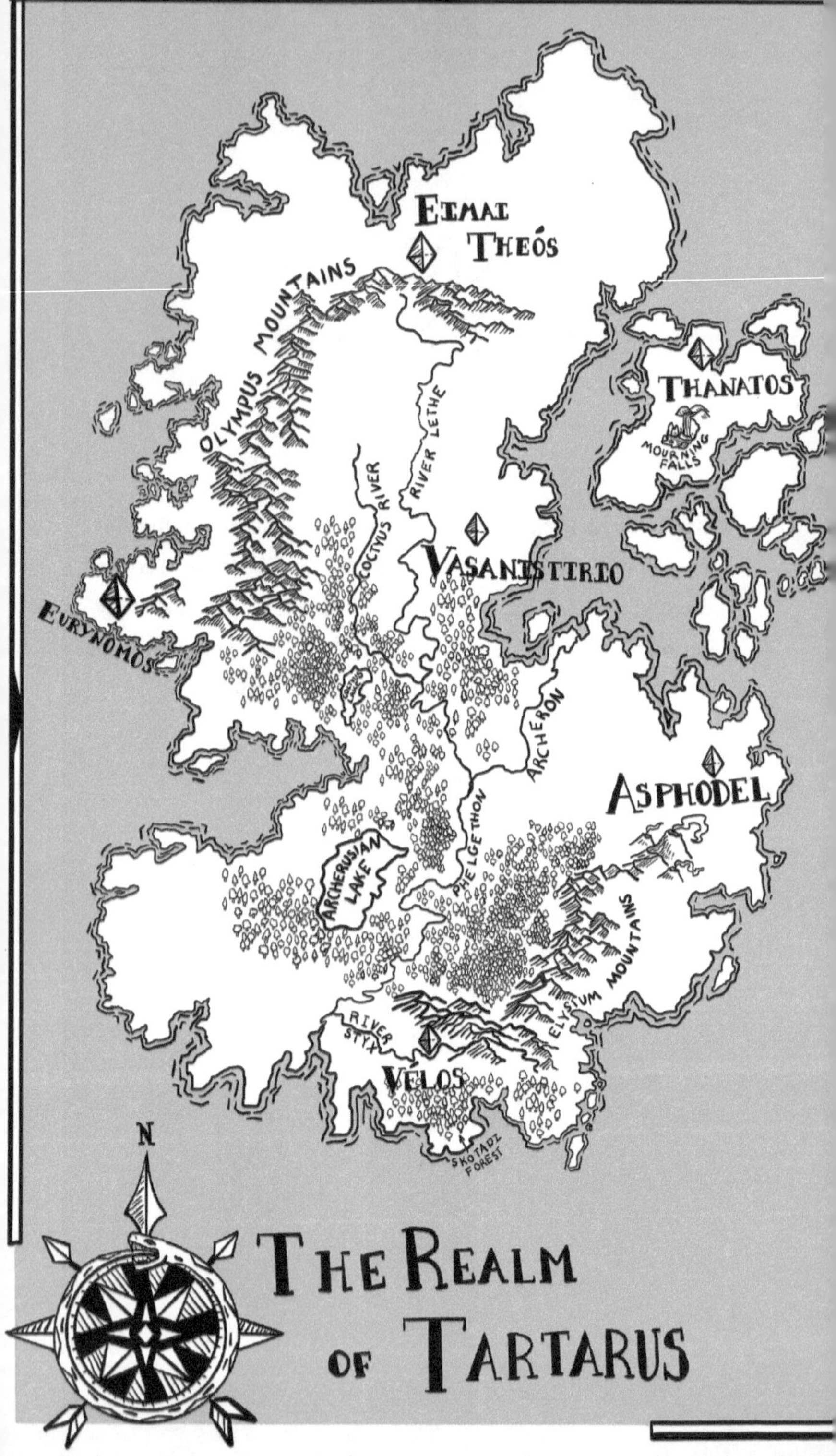

EIMAI THEÓS
OLYMPUS MOUNTAINS
RIVER LETHE
COCYTUS RIVER
THANATOS
MOURNING FALLS
VASANISTIRIO
EURYNOMOS
ARCHERON
ASPHODEL
ARCHERUSIAN LAKE
PHLEGETHON
ELYSIUM MOUNTAINS
RIVER STYX
VELOS
SKOTADI FOREST
N
THE REALM OF TARTARUS

EIMAI THEÓS

NO OTHER GODS

EURYNOMOS

DEATH AND VALOR

THANATOS

FEAR THE DRAGON

ASPHODEL

TO THE GRAVE

VÉLOS

HEART AND FIRE

GLOSSARY

ARCHANGEL Pronounced: arch-an-gel

Is the title given to the fiercest angels of great honor and wisdom. They are the most powerful of angels regardless of race and have an affinity for lightning. They are easily distinguished by their shared banded arm tattoos. They are the only known angelica to mark their bodies with ink. Each archangel is gifted two swords of holy light at their initiation.

AMORINI Pronounced: am-or-een-ee

Angels that were once behind making people fall in love. They would shoot their arrows into the hearts of soulmates once they were close enough to find each other, binding them. At the height of the Fall, they were cast out. Since then, they now kill a mate from each pair, always leaving the weaker victim behind to rot in despair and loneliness; never to feel whole. The amorini have pockets at the back of their necks where they keep their whistling arrows and are often seen with black longbows. They are the most human in appearance of all angelica.

ASPHODEL Pronounced: As-fo-del

One of the five courts of Tartarus ruled by Cyn Anzu. It is located in the west of Tartarus. Wide open silver grass plains make up the majority of this territory with a smaller mountain range and volcanos. It is home to the powers and even some amorini and seraphim.

CHERUB Pronounced: Chair-ub

Angels that bear three faces: a lion, ox, and human. They are able to switch between their faces, wearing one at a time or all at once. Cherubs are known to change their appearances often, even shifting forms to bear the body of a serpent. They have eagle wings covering their shoulders and feet.

CYN Pronounced: kin

A ruler or king of Tartarus that is distinguished by the invisible crown of thrones they wear around their brow. Each cyn is granted a significant amount of power. They hold the responsibility of ensuring Vasanastrio remains guarded.

DEMON Pronounced: Dee-mon

Any angel that has Fallen from Heaven and rejected and the Holy Trinity.

DHAMPIR Pronounced: Dam-peer

A creature crossed between a vampire and a human with witch's powers. Though they are not immortal, dhampir's need to feed on blood in order to survive. They can be created by demons and vampires.

EIMAI THEÓS Pronounced: Ee-my They-os

One of the five courts of Tartarus ruled by Cyn Maalik. It is located in the northern most part of Tartarus. The golden kingdom is said to be a replica of Heaven with is pristine and polished appearance. It sits high in the clouds behind the Olympus Mountains. It is home to the seraphim and thrones.

ESKA Pronounced: es-ka

A demonic slur to angels.

EURYNOMOS Pronounced: Ury-no-mos

One of the five courts of Tartarus ruled by Baal. It is located in the southeast of Tartarus in the ice-capped Olympus Mountains. It is home of to the Fallen keras.

HELLFIRE Pronounced: Hell-fi-ure

Fire that can only be wielded by the Fallen. Its distinct green flames can only be seen in Tartarus, though it is often wielded on Earth in the form of aggression, fury, and rage.

INCUBUS Pronounced: ink-u-bus | Plural: incubi (ink-u-bi)

Is the term given to angels that are able to dream walk. Dream walking is a dead custom lost centuries ago after the Fall. As demons, those taught in the ways of the incubi, often torture the dreamer with nightmares. They are also known to bring sexual arousal to the dreamer and feed on their energy at climax.

KAZA Pronounced: Ka-za

The second circle of Heaven. Here higher archangels deal out orders, fulfill prayers, and execute judgement.

KERAS Pronounced: ker-es

Angels behind violent deaths. They favor torture and "mercy kill" victims with extreme pain and suffering. They have the ability to bend their victim's will to their own, often making them forget the word "no". All keras have the ability to shape-shift.

MONET Pronounced: Mow-nay

Angels hat deals in emotional pain. They are in charge of dealing anguish, depression, and misery.

NEPHILIM Pronounced: Nef-il-im

A child born of mortal women and angels (typically Fallen angels). They are of great size and power and known as "gods of the world", though they are seen as abominations in the eyes of Heaven. It is suspected many of the gods from mythologies around the world were, in fact, nephilim.

ODONNOS Pronounced: o-don-us | Plural: odonni (o-don-ee)

An equine creature of Tartarus with the front legs and beak of an eagle.

OZIEN Pronounced: oze-yen

The demonic/angelic word for "mine".

PROMETHEUS Pronounced: pro-meeth-ee-us.

Best known as Heaven's flame. The silver flames can only be wielded by Heavenly hosts. These flames are deadly to the Fallen and much like a holy weapon, will leave permanent white scars on those lucky enough to survive them.

SERAPH Pronounced: sare-af | Plural: Seraphim (sare-a-fim)

Angels of the highest order with six wings. They are the most powerful of angels being created from fire itself. Typically, their bodies are covered in multiple eyes and split irises. They all bear red attributes.

THANATOS Pronounced: Than-at-os

One of the five courts of Tartarus ruled by Cyn Nakir. It is composed of a set of sunny islands made up of caves and channels. They are known to trade metals, ideas, and dreams.

TITHE Pronounced: t-eye-the

Angels created in the 21st century to replace the keras after the Fall. They are cruel in the judgements. Often human in appearance with lavender eyes.

VASANISTIRIO Pronounced: Va-san-is-tear-ee-o

A giant pit of never-ending pain that lies in the center of Tartarus. The most wicked of the Fallen are imprisoned here by Prometheus as their crimes are too great to walk free in the Underworld. Those within will remain as such until their Judgement.

VÉLOS Pronounced: Vey-lose

One of the five courts of Tartarus ruled by Cyn Bishop, Cyn Valen, Cyn Diriel, and Cyn Jinn. The white romantic kingdom is located in the southwest of Tartarus at the edge of the Skotadi Forest. The largest archive recounting the Falls across time and Creation can be found in their library as well as a vast knowledge of magic, history, and names. It is home of the amorini.

PRONUNCIATION GUIDE

ATTICUS

At-tuh-kus

BAAKO

Ba-ko

BAAL UKAI

Bale You-ky

BISHOP SORRINSE

Bish-op Sore-in-see

CALIX

Cal-ix

DAGON

Day-gon

DIRIEL

Deer-ee-el

ELENA (LANE) RIVERA

Ee-lane-a Riv-air-a

EZRA HOLLEN

Ez-ruh Hol-len

GLADR

Glade-err

JAVAN

Jay-van

JINN CALVANTAI

Gin Cal-van-tay

KASIYA

Kaz-ee-ya

MAALIK

Mal-ik

NAKIR

Na-keer

ORIAS

O-ry-us

RAGUEL

Ray-g-eh-l

RAMIEL

Ram-ee-el

RAUM

Rom

SABRIEL

Say-bree-el

SAMYAZA

Sem-ja-zuh

TORAH

Tore-uh

URIEL

Yur-ee-el

VALEN

Val-in

ZEPHYR

Zey-fir

To those who believe true love exists. This one is for you, though it might hurt a bit.

A LOST TEXT OF THE BOOK OF EZRA

Hymn of the Sun and the Moon

In the days of war of mankind, a woman is born clothed with the sun. Upon her head she shall bear a crown of seven five-pointed stars. At her axis, another woman is born clothed with the moon. Upon her head she shall bear a crown of three six-pointed stars.

A great sign appeared in the heavens: every light in the sky went dark. A loud cry was heard, shaking the earth. Out of its belly crawled the twelve earls of Hell. In their wake was a great army and on their lips was a battle cry: Death to mankind.

And another sign appeared: a great famine befell the land and a plague of death upon the people. Another army rose from the ground led by six dukes of Hell. Beneath their feet was the red flow of blood. Their tales swept out a quarter of mankind.

The woman who was the sun sat upon the throne of the underworld. An eighth star was added to her crown. At her back were great black wings. In her eyes was the Fury of Hell.

But behold came the night, swift with her vengeance. The key to the lock that would shut the gates of Hell. Within her hand she bore a blade of Heaven. She knew the names of the demons. And it was with their names that she cast them back to their depths.

Therefore rejoice, your salvation is here. But woe to you who, O earth and sea, for the great dragon has been awakened. And he knows his time is short.

And the woman who was the sun and the woman who was the moon fought with great strength. But none could say for which side they fought for.

I say to you, this is the Hymn of the Sun and the Moon.

CHAPTER ONE: UNDERWATER

Ezra

Death had followed me my entire life. It stole my mother before my first breath. It stole any friends I made through sickness and hapless accidents. And, just last week, it stole my father. One second we were talking on the phone, and the next there was the sound of screeching tires and he was gone.

I have no more surviving family.

Killian hadn't exactly pleaded when I broke up with him, but neither did he stop me from going. We had been on the rocks for a while. It was always that way when someone loved the other more. Or maybe he was afraid of the curse that surrounded me too.

I was alone.

I feared death had followed me into the forest. Its presence grew the deeper I hiked into the mountains. Some might say I was running from my problems. I might agree with them. What I really wanted was a moment of peace, a moment where death couldn't touch me. And yet I could feel it lurking.

I'd been two miles each way of my campsite. All telltale signs said I was alone, yet I could feel the pressure of someone watching me. I'd picked that spot specifically because it was a well-kept secret. It was just me and the wildlife. I intended to stay five nights beside the lake, but as the sun set on the second night, I'd already decided I would leave in the morning. At the very least, I would find somewhere closer to civilization.

The last of the sun's light slipped behind the mountain ridge, giving way to darkness and the cicadas' music. I'd always found their sound peaceful instead of shrill. It gave me comfort. But I couldn't hear if anyone approached my fire over their noise.

For someone so independent, I was easily spooked. That's why I had convinced myself to stay another night, to talk myself out of the irrational fear that stalked me, even if I was cutting my trip short. There wasn't anyone in those woods with me. There wasn't anyone for miles.

I picked up my phone and frowned at the No Service signal. It's fine. Everything was going to be fine. The car was ten miles away on the side of the road. If anything did go wrong, all of my information was in there. Someone would come looking for me.

You have no one.

I pushed the harrowing thought from my head. "Fuck's sake. Get it together," I whispered.

I crawled in my tent, rifling for my headlamp. I needed to go for a walk. Sitting there, letting my mind play tricks on me, was driving me mad. The lantern that illuminated my campsite beside the fire would be plenty, but I preferred having my hands free in case I lost my footing and needed to catch myself. In case I needed to run.

Every hair on the back of my neck stood on end. I whipped around, shining the little lamp through the forest. I held my breath, listening. Waiting.

I dove back into my tent and grabbed a can of bear spray. I fumbled around in my bag until I found a hunting knife my dad had given me. I stuffed it in my waistband, covering it with my shirt. There was still nothing as I crawled back out.

The cicadas had stopped. There wasn't a lick of sound in that forest save for my shallow breathing. I held it, straining to hear anything that would give away the location of my stalker.

It had to be an animal. But why couldn't I hear the damn thing? There should at least be the noise of something snuffling. Coyotes calling to each other. Birds typically sang if there was a predator.

Nothing.

Something pale moved between the trees directly in front of me. I cannot describe the utter terror that shot through me as it morphed into the silhouette of a man. How long had he been standing there? As if he realized I'd spotted him, he stepped forward, the orange glow of the light highlighting his sharp features. He was twice my size in height and build. I summed up the odd gold sheen of his pale skin to the fire.

"I'm sorry, I didn't mean to scare you," he said. His pleasant smile didn't reach his lavender eyes that had a feline slant. His light hair was cropped over slightly pointed ears. He cocked his head. "I'm set up about half a mile away. I was out for a stroll when I saw your fire. I thought I'd say hey to the neighbors."

Liar.

His eyes darted to the two pairs of shoes sitting outside my tent. They were a safety precaution. His eyes flitted to my hands. I was still gripping the bear spray.

I realized then I hadn't said anything. "You did scare me," I admitted. "Where did you say you were set up?" I knew he was the shadow that had been lurking at my back. He might not be death, but he was close enough to it. Even if he was by a slim chance telling the truth, I should have seen his portable light bobbing through the woods toward me.

A light he wasn't carrying. He had been moving through the darkness, or perhaps waiting until the shadows grew to come out from his hiding place.

"Over the hill." He thumbed over his shoulder. "Do you mind?" He motioned to the ground. I almost told him I don't, but reason prodded me.

"I do, actually. My boyfriend will be back shortly. He's funny about strangers."

There was something inhuman about his too perfect smile. Fake, even. He crouched on the other side of the fire, bringing us eye to eye across the flames. "We both know it's just you and me. Killian—isn't it?—is a long way from here."

I stood slowly, trying not to move too fast. He didn't stand, just looked up at me with his wrong-colored eyes. Every bit of him was poised to strike. I could run. I still had the headlamp gripped in my fist, the phone in my back pocket, the knife and spray. I would only need to keep away from him until I reached cell service... six miles away.

"I want you to leave. Now."

"You're not a very gracious host, Ezra." The dangerous look in his eyes had trickled into his voice.

Every instinct within me screamed to run. "How do you know me?"

"I know all about you. I know that you were abandoned as a

child and taken in by a man you called father. My condolences, by the way." There was nothing sincere within the drip of his voice. "I know that Killian of yours doesn't love you half as much as you love him. You take these little trips to make you feel better about yourself. It makes you feel strong and independent." He spun his finger through the air, motioning to the trees above us. "It's dangerous for a woman like you to be all alone."

"That's enough," I said, my voice shaking. How could he have known any of those things? I lived a private life. I had social media but posted once a year. There wasn't anything about my personal life someone could know unless they were close to me. And those people were dead. "Who are you? What do you want?"

The smile that had been plastered on his face fell suddenly. The light of his eyes grew dark and everything about him became unnaturally still.

"You." The single word hung in the air like a death knell. "I came all the way down here for you."

In a half second of deciding if I should run or fight, I shot the spray at him. Part of it caught fire as it cut over the flames, but it hit its mark. He let out a vicious snarl that sent me running into the forest that I begged to swallow me whole. His fierce roar made me run faster than I ever had.

His overbearing presence pursued me through the dense trees and overgrowth. The only thing I could hear was my crashing footfalls. I ran blindly. I didn't want to make myself an easier target in case he had a gun.

I didn't know how he could possibly have known those things. I'd never seen him before.

Creature, my mind screamed. A predator excited about chasing down its prey. The purple hues of his eyes had lit up when I bolted.

Pain erupted in the back of my right shoulder with the force of a punch. It struck me like a flaming rod, burrowing to the front of my chest.

I screamed and stumbled into a tree, nearly losing my footing when the pain intensified. Don't stop. Keep going! I pushed off with my good arm. The lake came into view faster than I thought it would and I turned right, cutting across the fine sand of its bank.

Don't stop!

He stepped out of the tree line ahead. I looked behind me to be sure. There was no one chasing me. I could have sworn he was right behind me, just about to grab me. My nostrils flared and I took a hesitant step back as he turned out his palms and walked toward me.

He laughed. It was music, rising high and then abruptly cutting off as he snapped his teeth together and breathed, "You're fast."

"Leave me the fuck alone," I growled. The burrowing sensation crawled, expanding what felt like little legs across my back. I held the spray out with my good arm, but he was too far away for it to hit him again.

He waved his hand and my wrist jerked of its own accord, slinging the aluminum can out of my grasp.

How did he *do* that? A new wave of fear roiled in the pit of my stomach.

He approached me casually, letting his hands fall to his sides. "That spray is a bitch, but it is not going to stop me. Do you think you can take me?"

I was as surprised as he was by the challenge that came out of my mouth. "Why don't you find out?" I sounded braver than I was. The adrenaline was pumping heavily through my blood. Running hadn't stopped him from materializing before me, so I would fight if I had to.

The pain made me strangely lucid as I broadened my stance. I held my right arm close to my chest and the other fist in front of my face.

In the time that I blinked, he was standing in front of me. He cracked his forehead against mine. I stumbled back and then abruptly dropped to my knees. There were three of him when he scooped me from the ground and tossed me over his shoulder. I blinked until the world stopped spinning. Blood ran down my face and into my eye.

There was no splash when he entered the water. I pressed my palms against his back to look up. We were already well away from the shore. A gasp lodged in my throat when I saw the ripples left by his feet on top of the water.

Wrong. Wrong. All of it.

A moment of clarity hit me, and I reached for the knife still wedged in my waistband. I pulled it free, gripped it with shaking hands, and stabbed him in the back. I gritted my teeth, fighting the way my right shoulder tried to lock. I pulled the bloodied blade free and slid it as hard as I could between his ribs. Bone met metal as I thrust a third time with a grunt and twisted.

"You little witch," he snarled.

He hunched forward, throwing me over his shoulder. I flew through the air, the sky falling away from me as I landed on my back with a smack. Ripples peeled away from the impact and splashed against his ankles. The grip he latched to my forearm constricted. His face was twisted into a monstrous snarl when he said, "I also know you can't swim."

Ice cold water swallowed me whole, enveloping me like a black blanket when he let me go. The knife was lost in my panic as I clawed for the surface. When my face broke, I screamed.

"Help!"

Searing pain latched hold of the back of my scalp as he dug his fingers in my hair. I sucked in as much air as I could before he pushed my head under. I gripped his wrists in an attempt to free myself, but his was iron clad. When he pulled me up, I screamed again.

He hoisted me on top of the water and leered. "Scream all you want. No one is coming to save you. You are alone. You are unwanted. And you are at my mercy." Each sentence was a blow. An impact to the fight boiling within my blood.

The water wasn't completely solid beneath me, but it was firm enough to kneel in while he touched me. With one hand still fisted in my hair, he slammed the other into my back. My face smacked against the water like it was concrete.

"You pathetic little waste. Did you really think you could fight me and win?"

The cool kiss of steel sliding up my shirt made everything else around me incredibly vivid. The soft scent of lavender mixed with the metallic tang of blood. The stars were bright. The water was as clear as the sky. Everything was strangely beautiful. In that moment, I knew I was going to die.

Death had finally caught up to me.

Iron pain cut into me as the top of my shoulder was sliced open. A second lashing crisscrossed the first, down to the curve of my hip. This time when I screamed, every star in the sky winked out.

The scream rang across the mountains, calling back to me. Over and over again I screamed as the blade dug into me, flaying me. My cries were muffled as I sank farther into the water. The blows didn't stop. Not even when I started to choke on my broken sobs.

Something landed behind us. I felt it the same way I had felt the presence of the monster tearing into me. The water rippled from a void of darkness that had expanded across the water. It lapped against my face as I lifted my chin. The lashings came to an abrupt halt.

A high-pitched whistle cut through the air, keening like the night wind. It drew closer, hurtling towards us from the shadows. I dug my bloody, shaking hands into the water to gain some sort of leverage to scramble to my feet.

I made it as far as a single knee before keeling over. But not before the distinct sound of flesh being pierced registered.

An arrow anchored into the side of my assailant's neck. He let me go, reaching for his throat. Blackness consumed me once more as water crashed over my head. It burned its way into my throat like razors.

I gasped when I surfaced. I swam away from the monster, but my face ducked under the water as I struggled to stay afloat. My arms were screaming in protest, my back tried its best to seize, but if I didn't move, I would drown.

My face barely broke the surface as I thrashed.

A figure stepped out of the darkness, their hand reaching for me. I latched hold, and they pulled me out of the water against their body.

A swirl of smoke and ash flitted before my eyes. Solid ground met me as I stumbled on the shore, my rescuer holding firm on my elbow.

"Help me," I choked. It came out as a garbled slur. I fell to the dry ground at his feet, the world spinning. I was going to be sick. The man—I could tell by his broad shoulders—turned me over, and that's exactly what happened. Lake water blew out of my lungs. I struggled to breathe again as fresh, sweet air burned its way in.

My teeth snapped together as the frigid water seeped in. It was *so cold.*

He stood, stepping over me so that I was between the shield of his legs. I leaned into his shin as I shuddered, desperate for the little warmth his presence provided.

The monster with the lavender eyes and pointed ears stumbled over the top of the water. He was maybe ten feet from us, his face curled into a mask of rage. He snapped the arrow clean, ripping it from one side of his throat and then the other, discarding both ends with a flick of his wrist. With a wound like that, he should have been like me—on the ground bleeding out. It fazed him no more than a scratch.

He gripped a curved golden sword with a pommel that wrapped around his hand. The edge was tinged crimson. My blood.

"She is not yours to take," the monster snarled.

The man, his figure covered in jet black clothes, strung the bow at his side and aimed it at the creature. He looked between us, his dark features unreadable beneath the shadows covering his face.

"What does an angel want with a mortal?" he asked.

Angels weren't real, and if they were they certainly didn't have wicked faces and cruel eyes. They didn't murder people. I closed my eyes, trying desperately to hold onto reality that was quickly slipping away. When I looked again, the angel was still standing on top of the lake, the water beneath his boots a giant black mirror.

I was losing too much blood. That was the only explanation.

"She does not have an adelfi—" the angel started.

"What does an angel want with her?" the man growled. His voice was too smooth and even. Rage rolled from him in waves. Wisps of smoke coiled down his back and up the length of his arm to that taut bowstring. The shadows around us crawled closer to my rescuer with outstretched hands and tapered, gnarled fingers. "You are no keras, and yet you slaughter her."

"You have no right to her, Valen." The angel looked between us, probably gauging if he could get to me before he took another arrow. His tongue darted between his lips.

"I have every right to her so long as her heart beats. Your race puts you outside of your limits."

"She is not what you think she is," the angel pleaded, his voice cracking in rage and desperation. He raised his blade, taking a step forward before whatever look Valen gave him made him halt.

I saw the man smirk in the dim light. "Oh, I know exactly what she is," he said, his voice sinister. He looked down at me with golden eyes burning bright as fire. "She's mine."

He released the arrow and dropped to a crouch. The sharp keen of the arrow's whistle rang through the air.

Smoke swirled as he took me into his arms. "Don't let go," Valen said against my ear. He tucked my head beneath his chin, and then he was all around me. Like the water, I could feel him everywhere, enveloping me like a giant black cloud. There were ashes in the air and then everything was aflame.

CHAPTER TWO: CHILD OF STARS

Ezra

Vélos, Tartarus

A powerful wind ripped the breath from my lungs. Then we landed, cold stone slamming into my knees. The air that had been ripped from my chest now barreled into me. I gasped. It only took a second for my mind to register that we weren't by the lake but in a room.

I leaned forward, still clinging to the man caged around me. I opened my eyes, immediately shutting them when everything spun. Smoke crept into my eyes, forcing fresh tears to roll down my cheeks.

I took another deep breath. We had been in the mountains and, though the image was blurry, gray walls surrounded us now. I shuddered as I let go to press one of my hands to the smooth surface beneath my boots.

Pain wracked my entire body. I made a sound somewhere between a gasp and a cry as I fell against the stone floor. My back felt like it was gone entirely.

I flinched from a warm touch that splayed across my torn flesh. At once, I wanted to bite down on something hard to stifle the scream building within my chest. There was nowhere I could go, no way to curl away from him. I bit my lip as the heat of Valen's scalding touch intensified.

"Shh," he crooned as I whimpered. "I'm fixing your back. Keep still."

It only lasted a minute, but it felt like an eternity as he worked his way over my shoulders, down the length of my spine, and then to my hips. It was only after he stopped that I could finally breathe again. I shuddered as he withdrew his touch and gritted my teeth against the pain.

Whatever he had done allowed me to shift and ease to my hands and knees. My shirt fell loose on my shoulders as I looked back at him. And then all thoughts ceased.

"Killian," I gasped.

He *wasn't* Killian, yet the resemblance was uncanny. He didn't have his crooked nose or short hair. He didn't have his gray eyes. But their faces, their build, their height... they could be twins.

Something struck me in the chest when I met his burning gaze. Though it was still dark, I could see him more clearly. His tight coiling black hair was cropped at the sides. The longer part of his fringe cut across vibrant gold eyes framed with thick lashes and, above them, thicker brows. His full lips were still parted like he wanted to say something else but was waiting for me instead. Though his skin was dark bronze, like the desert sands at nightfall, it had the same iridescent glow as the attacker's. The... angel.

He was the fiercest creature I had ever seen. His irises glowed, heated and hungry. Possessive.

She's mine, he had said.

A chill trickled down my back. The powerful urge to flee still pounded through my blood, but I couldn't move under his gaze. He kept a firm grip on my hand, as if he could sense that I would bolt the second he let me go.

He's not Killian.

He was something more.

He had asked me a question. My name, I think? "Ezra," I said, clearing my throat. My voice was raw, my mouth dry. "What's happening?" I looked past him, my eyes going wide as I took in the stone walls and massive pillars that separated floor-to-ceiling windows. It must have been an elaborate dream. Perhaps my paranoia created a terrible nightmare while I slept safe by my fire.

Everything felt wrong. The air was brisker, the night sky—what I could see of it—clearer and more vibrant. Despite the beauty that came to me in flashes, it felt like a warning sign. *Get out*, it seemed to hiss at me.

Valen scanned my face as he held out his other hand to help me to my feet.

He was barefoot, his jeans rumpled and his long-sleeve shirt worse off, though it fit a bit tighter than the pants. He leaned his long bow against one of the pillars. Beyond them were mountains, far different from the ones we had been in. These were black and cavernous peaks that shadowed an even darker forest beneath.

And the sky! I had never seen so many stars, so many colors. It was a cosmos.

"What is happening?" I repeated, my voice shakier. I did another take of the room now that it had leveled out. We were in a bedroom. His, maybe? I couldn't see much in the darkness save for half a bed with sheets thrown on the ground like someone had been in a hurry to get up. "Who are you? Why did you take me?"

"I took you because whatever that angel was going to do to you was much worse than being in my company." There was a subtle edge in his voice. Something sinister.

Why did he look so much like Killian?

Valen circled me. He examined me from toe to head, taking his time. There was a predatory shift in his composure that implied he wasn't just assessing me but stalking me.

I had to get out. Something was incredibly wrong.

"Ezra." The way he said my name drew my eyes to him and away from darting around the room for an escape. "Did he say anything before he grabbed you?"

"He knew who I was." I shook my head. "He knew things he shouldn't have. I tried to outrun him and then he was just there." I motioned to the spot in front of me, flinching as it pulled the taut flesh of my back. He had appeared before me like magic. "He said fighting was a waste."

The corner of his mouth curled. His eyes shifted, glowing brighter. There was no denying hunger stared back at me. "You tried to fight him?"

"I stabbed him, but that's when he threw me in the water."

I pressed a hand to my forehead. Hot pain stretched out its fingers, seeking the front of my chest. I gritted my teeth. "I think he shot me." He must have. If the bullet got any closer, it would worm into my heart. "In my shoulder. It keeps moving."

Valen cocked his head, his eyes dropping to my chest and then to something behind me. "The burns will take a few hours to heal."

"No, it's something else. He shot me before he cut me." I tried to point at it, but it only aggravated the pain.

Valen stepped behind me before sliding the scraps of my shirt aside. His fingers crawled over my shoulder, stopping when a flash of heat made me tense. "Fuck," he growled. "Brace yourself. This is going to hurt."

I leaned against the pillar as he instructed and nodded.

His finger delved into the wound. I gritted my teeth, stifling a sound of pain that rumbled in my chest.

It didn't feel like a bullet. It was like a cord, a string. He tugged and, inch by inch, drew it out from the place in my chest. My nails bit into the stone. Fresh tears spilled across my face as he gave another tug, ripping the needling tendrils and all its agony with it.

Sweet relief rushed through the length of my arm.

When I looked back, it wasn't a bullet at all but a silver tendril of light between his fingertips. In a flick of flame, it went up in smoke, disintegrating into nothing.

He ran a hand through his thick hair. By the hard press of his lips, whatever he pulled out wasn't good. I didn't like the way his eyes skirted over my body again or the way their fire burned a little brighter.

"What was that?" I rolled my shoulders, trying to rid a new ache that was starting to settle in my bones.

"I'm going to get someone." He held up his hands. "There are wards that guard the entire tyre, and more guard this room specifically. He will not come for you. He knows it would be a death sentence to even step in Tartarus." The coolness of his voice made me flinch.

I couldn't have heard him correctly. Tartarus wasn't a real place, but the meaning of its name couldn't have been clearer.

I cowered into one of the pillars. "What are you?" I blurted.

He slowed in his cross of the room. He looked at me, his gold eyes darker than they were before. "An angel," he said slowly.

The smoke, the ash, the wrongness that reverberated through the air of wherever he had taken us. I shook my head. "You're not."

"Think of me as your guardian angel," he purred, flashing a dark sneer that stood every hair on my body straight up. "I saved you, remember?"

He didn't wait for me to say anything. The latch closing was another warning signal to my brain. *Run!* I spun around the room, looking desperately for anything I could use as a weapon. But I was in no condition to fight. I barely had energy to remain standing. There was something wrong with this place. What was worse, there was something wrong with Valen.

It couldn't be a coincidence that he looked so much like Killian.

Had one monster been traded for another?

This isn't real. I dropped to the ground with my fists pressed into my temples. *Breathe. You're going to wake up soon.*

Wind moved through the room, cutting through my wet shirt and making me shiver. I looked down at the mud on my hiking boots, the blood on my arms. It was real. All of it.

Get. Up.

An intense pain shot through my back and grabbed hold of my arms. I winced, thrashing from the invisible assault. I hunched forward as another wave hit me, then settled just as quickly. This wasn't the same thing as the tendril. It made the lashings of the angel's blade bearable. It was everywhere and startlingly violent.

A few seconds passed before I could catch my breath. *What the hell was that?* I ran my hands over my back and arms, feeling for another wound the angel might have inflicted. There was nothing save for tender, charred flesh.

When Valen did return, it was with a thin framed man with skin as dark as soil and a shaved head. I retreated farther when he approached me, his stride fast and direct. I knew I couldn't jump without falling to my death, but they didn't know how desperate I was. I hopped on top of the balcony ledge and he stopped. The moon shining behind me illuminated his round face. Like Valen, one of his eyes was a vibrant amber, but the other was a dark blue. Those eyes dropped down to the candlestick in my grasp.

It was the closest thing to a weapon I could find in the unornamented room. One more step and I would use it to bash his brains in.

"Easy, Diriel," Valen crooned. "She's a fighter."

I never took my eyes off the newcomer as I tightened my grip.

"I'm not going to hurt her," the man said. He looked up at me with the same frown Valen still had plastered on his face. After a long moment his eyes widened, and he took a couple of steps back. He turned to Valen and hissed something. Whatever it was, Valen didn't seem all that surprised.

"Get down," Valen whispered firmly.

I wasn't brave enough to jump, but I wasn't going to let them know that. "I can hear you just fine from here."

The other man—Diriel—cursed and something like a smirk touched Valen's lips. "You did right in taking her, but she'll serve us no purpose if she's dead." To me he said, "Get. Down." The two words were issued like a thunderclap.

I hugged the pillar tighter. That's when it hit me. The smoke and ash that flitted around their bodies. The sheer power of their wrongness.

"You're Fallen."

Hearing the title didn't faze him. "And you're going to wind up just like us if you do not put both feet on the ground," Diriel growled.

"We are not going to hurt you," Valen added, his gaze fixed on me like a hawk on a rabbit.

Fallen angels. Demons. Evil.

My nails scratched over the stone surface as I struggled to make sense of what was happening. Bad. Wrong. All of this was wrong. *They* were wrong.

A candlestick wasn't going to do shit if they really wanted to hurt me. I had barely survived the first angel. What the hell was I going to do against two of them?

Neither of them moved. They might be annoyed, but they stood by, waiting patiently.

He saved you. The little voice in my head nudged my foot forward and, before I knew it, I was standing in front of them. Valen wouldn't have protected me to kill me. But he was Fallen. And he saw everything. Every time my chest rose, or my hands quaked, his eyes were there, drinking up everything I gave him. Rescuer or not, he was still a predator.

I held my breath when Diriel turned his hands out to me. It took everything in me not to hit him over the head and bolt. Fear rooted me. I knew there was nowhere for me to go. I could hardly comprehend the manner in which Valen had brought us here.

Diriel took hold of the candlestick. "Let go. Neither of us is going to hurt you."

My breath hitched as Diriel slid his other hand under my wrist.

The candlestick dropped as soon as he touched me. I couldn't move as a current raced through my body and Diriel took hold of my other hand. His coarse fingers curled over mine.

His bi-colored eyes held me in a trance as all feeling drifted away. The need to run was a distant hum in the back of my mind. The fear, pain, and desperation I had felt moments before vanished.

With a sudden twist of his hand, the darker male had my wrists ensnared in an iron hold. A powerful current bolted through my fingertips, lighting every nerve ending in my body. I stood rigid, my body tensing, freezing.

"Diriel!" Valen snarled. He sounded far away, as if I was trapped beneath the ice I could feel frosting over my skin.

"Do you have any idea how reckless you are?" Diriel bit back. His grip tightened as he looked between us. A lick of frosty wings brushed down the length of my body, cooling the pain slithering in my back. Tiny snowflakes formed over my clothes as they froze.

I clung to the little bit of heat left in my body. I held it close like my life depended on it. Maybe it did. I tried to blow into it, fan the flames. Fog slipped from my lips.

"Let her go." Valen's voice was as quiet as death.

"Did you know what she was when you took her?" His lips curled, his fingers tightening to the point where I could feel the bones of my wrist strain beneath his grip.

"No. My curiosity got the better of me, and be glad of it. Let her go, Diriel. She is our salvation." Reverence reverberated through the hollow of Valen's voice.

The icy tendrils hurt. They slithered down my arm, through my shoulder, and across my back to the other side. Even after Diriel let me go, throwing my hand away like he had been burned, it still radiated through me.

He stepped away as Valen came to my side. As soon as he touched my face, the fire within caught and feeling returned. I shuddered in his embrace. Desperate for the warmth his body provided, I clung to him. I focused on the heat and dragged what I could into me, though he offered it willingly.

"It wasn't an archangel or keras that had her. Though he tortured her like a keras would." To me, he said, "You're going to be all right." He spoke to me like you would a frightened animal. I still clutched Valen as I met his impenetrable gaze. The little bit of familiarity eased my urge to run, if only for a second.

Diriel let out a long, heavy sigh. He pinched the bridge of his nose as he tilted his face back. "Fuck."

"Let's get you changed," Valen said.

I didn't question when he pulled the scraps of my shirt away and handed me a pair of black sweats out of thin air. It struck me a little too late that I was half naked, my shirt hanging on by the collar. I held them to my chest. He turned his eyes away and fixed them on Diriel. I changed as quickly as I could, noticing that Valen had placed himself between me and the other male when his bi-colored eyes fell to me.

Diriel hissed. It started as a whisper and rose until he was laughing. It was silver bells and thunderous wooden drums. His laugh was a symphony. More joyous than the monster's.

"You have damned us or saved us."

Valen flashed a dangerous grin, yet his eyes, those wicked eyes, never lost their edge. "Fortune has finally graced us."

"I want to go home," I finally managed. I took a couple of steps back, putting three feet between me and Valen before he caught me in that bright stare.

"If I take you back, you will be slaughtered."

"Why?" My eyes darted between them.

"You are a nephilim."

"A gift," Diriel clarified.

"That angel was one of many that would kill you," Valen said.

Fear is a funny thing. It had paralyzed me before but, as the heat finished winding its way through my body, feeling returned to me. The subtle pain grounded me, and I found the fight that had been within me before.

"You just tried to kill me." My voice had lost its tremor.

"I was cooling your fire," Diriel argued.

"What is that? A nephilim." I looked to Valen.

"A child of angels and mortals," he said, his lips curling into a genuine smile. He was breathtaking when he smiled.

I shook my head, clearing my mind of whatever spell he was trying to cast. "I'm adopted," I said, irrationally. What they said was impossible. This entire situation was impossible.

Valen shook his head, still smirking. "Your father would not have been an angel. Whoever you got your blood from passed eons ago."

"Or perhaps he lies in chains," Diriel suggested. "I could not see him."

"Take me home," I interrupted. Even as the words left my mouth, I knew it wasn't what I wanted. What was there to go back to except death? I had nothing to go back to. But I didn't want to be *here*.

"You are home. You should have been here all along," Diriel said matter-of-factly.

I shook my head. "I'm not what you say I am. He was wrong and so are you. I am no one."

Valen's passive countenance narrowed as he said, "You are everything."

Diriel crossed his arms. "We need to tell the others. We can hold off on the other courts for now, but Bishop and Jinn need to know."

"Jinn is with the Murder."

"Valen."

He cut a fiery look at Diriel.

"The rest of Tartarus will come looking as soon as they catch wind of her. We need to prepare. We don't know how much time we have before this gets out. And who is to say the angel won't bring an army and break through? They're not likely to let her slip away."

"Enough," Valen growled.

"You would save me from a monster to hold me hostage?" I needed to make my case if they were to let me go. "I'm not a nepha-whatever. I'm human."

"We have made no error," Valen said firmly.

"What makes me so much safer with fallen angels?" As much as I wanted to disbelieve them, the harsh reality of it hit too hard. They *were* angels. Strikingly beautiful in physical features and the sound of their voices. Even the way they gestured and walked was flawless. My attacker had been too. But it was their power I was so certain of. It emanated from them like a beacon in the midst of shadows, hugging close to their presence. They curled around Diriel's feet like a cat and draped along Valen's shoulders, tied about his throat like a cloak.

Diriel's eyes narrowed the same time his lips curled, flashing white pointed canines. That mouth of his made him look more vampiric than the human costume he wore.

A new thought raised bumps along my skin. *Is this what demons really look like, or are they more monstrous underneath?*

"Heaven sees you as an abomination. Here, you are nothing short of a miracle. We protect our own," Valen said. His gold eyes were incredibly dark and, when his teeth flashed, he had the same sharpened points as Diriel. He turned to Diriel. "Leave us. We say nothing of this until I have decided what to do with her."

Diriel sucked the back of his teeth. "Your Majesty," he said in a mocking lilt. He turned on his heel, throwing a wary look over his shoulder at me. "At least she's got one thing right. Those bastards are monsters."

CHAPTER THREE: THE MIRACLE

Valen

The spell had taken longer to work its way into Ezra's system. No doubt her bloodline had something to do with that. Her eyes fluttered as she walked the room, her limbs growing heavy. Her questions came out slurred and broken.

"What did you pull from... back?" She yawned, her eyes going wide and shutting again as she fought against me.

Powerful little thing.

The spell I had crafted wasn't intricate, but it would knock any mortal on their ass within seconds. Ten minutes had come and gone.

"A dread knot."

"Whah," yawn, "are you?"

"An amorini." She wouldn't remember half of our conversation in the morning, but humoring her sated my curiosity. It gave me the opportunity to study her.

Her pacing and darting eyes was enough to get my blood pumping. My lust for blood was clawing for freedom, writhing desperately in the pit of my belly. The sheer sight of her, of what she was, stirred a desperate hunger I had not felt in ages.

She was terrified, and rightfully so. What she didn't know was that she now lay in a nest of vipers. Each one coiled and ready to strike as soon as she was within reach. I knew she sensed it; her fear grew stronger as fatigue seeped its way into her bones.

I coaxed her into bed, gently taking her arm as she climbed across the mattress.

"I'm not going home." There it was: acceptance. Or defeat. She clutched the sheets beneath her chin, her nostrils flaring. Even as she tried to stay awake, her body betrayed her. The tension in her muscles eased. Her eyelids fluttered.

Could she feel the heat of my gaze? How hard it was for me to keep my fangs from her throat? "You are home," I said gently. I leaned forward, my face hovering over hers. Such a rare and precious treasure she was. Unable to deny myself, I pressed my lips to her temple. I spoke against her skin, whispering another spell into her body that pulled her into a sleep so deep she would not wake until I willed it.

Beneath the sweat, blood, and fear, another scent wafted from her skin. One that made my stomach flutter and my throat constrict. She wasn't just any nephilim.

I forced myself back, my heart quickening.

"Ah, he emerges." Diriel smiled ruefully from his place on the lounge as I slipped from the bedroom. "I wanted to see what you would do with her."

"I did not take her to ruin her," I said, irritated. Despite the hunger clawing at my throat, I wasn't a total monster. I looked to the roaring hearth and let out a heavy sigh that shook loose the tension in my body. I shut my eyes as I tipped my head back.

"Right, because you didn't know what she was." Diriel's mouth curled into a half smile. "You feel it now, don't you? I can smell it on her."

My jaw clenched. "I could feel her power then, but it was not as loud as it is now."

"That'll change." Diriel nodded. "Do you smell what is *different*?" The hue of his eyes turned milky. In a blink, his waxy haze vanished.

I could feign ignorance, but lying wouldn't do me any favors. As a seer, Diriel knew the truth. And if he didn't, he soon would. "She does not bear the curse. I didn't notice it until she was in bed," I confessed. I wouldn't be able to let go of that scent. That glorious perfume that was now burned into my brain.

I flopped down next to Diriel and pressed my chin into my hands. I turned, cupping my cheek, to look at my brother. Not in the true sense of the word, but Diriel was my closest companion.

Diriel sat forward and clasped my shoulder.

I looked the other way, to the fire whose flames licked the stone frame. Unease, hunger, desire. These were all climbing their way back into my mind. "You know we cannot tell Bishop."

"Think of what he will do to her if it does not come from you." Diriel was always the voice of reason.

"I myself am tempted," I said.

"But you are wiser than Bishop and so you will not," Diriel said with a cluck of his tongue.

"And what of the Murder? It will be difficult hiding her until they leave."

"Difficult," Diriel agreed, "but not impossible."

"Gods," I cursed. I cut a look at Diriel. At Diriel's smile, I could not refrain one of my own. I laughed. Diriel joined in until we were both singing music. "This is a disaster."

"But this is our chance," Diriel answered, nodding. "Whatever you decide, I am with you. I will protect her, or I will help you coerce her. But she is what we have been waiting for. She is the key in winning this war. She is our way to freedom."

He was right. About all of it. But I couldn't wrap my head around it.

"She should not exist. Everything about her is impossible." Humans were never meant to wield the power burning within her blood. Even fewer of those that could were female. Certainly, no angelica had ever been a woman.

How had she slipped through the fingers of the Enemy? How had she come into existence? How had she reached me?

There were too many questions I didn't have answers to.

Her scream had been like a gunshot. Its power had ripped through worlds, throwing me out of bed so hard I swear my face had bruised as soon as it smacked against the stone floor. Its color was faint now, already healing, but I was grateful Diriel hadn't asked about it. He probably summed it up to the altercation with the angel.

"She is a miracle," Diriel said.

That she is. I slipped off into silence, as the glaze of the fire took hold of me.

Ezra couldn't be older than twenty-eight. If her power had truly been suppressed for so long, there was a chance it would come hurdling to the front with vicious intent. There was something sharp about her that lurked just below the surface. Beneath all the fear and sweat was something dangerous.

If she was pushed too far, or not properly trained in her power, she could easily become the destruction of Tartarus. If she was to be our salvation, she needed to be on our side.

"We will use her, but I'll not subject her to bearing children,"

I finally said. "If the others find out she isn't cursed...." I couldn't bring myself to finish. She would be torn apart just so every angel could have a shot at leaving his mark on her. I had my perversions, but I would damn myself again if something as precious as she was shattered.

"I'll have a tea prepared." Diriel stood, brushing his palms across his thick thighs. "Better to get it in her sooner than later."

I held up his hand. "Something temporary."

One of Diriel's brows arched.

I shrugged. One nephilim was more than enough to change the tide of this war. Multiple would bring Heaven to its knees.

"It would be foolish to limit our options."

Diriel nodded then paused. He bowed. "Your Majesty."

I scowled. "Cut it with the bullshit. Any louder and Bishop will have my head."

Diriel grinned, his demeanor teasing. "The truth has always left him heated. I will stand with you in the morning."

"The four of us must come to an agreement. Though, I am not worried about Jinn having a hand in this matter."

Jinn might be bitter, but he would do as he was told.

Diriel shoved his hands in his pockets. "What happens when Bishop demands her?"

It would happen sooner or later. Bishop expected everything when he deserved nothing. He would not let Ezra pass him by without a fight.

I ran my tongue over my lower lip. "Then you steal her away and I will end what I should have a long time ago."

CHAPTER FOUR: PERFECT TIMING

Ezra

The subtle pink sky was the only evidence that time had passed and a new day was creeping in. Even still, the room was shrouded in darkness. The white glow of three moons cascaded across the mountaintops. There were too many colors and too many lights in the sky for it to be so dark in the room.

But it wasn't just starlight that twinkled in the distance. No, those were city lights. Some flickered like flames, but others were still and bright as halogens.

The room had a historic, gothic feel, yet technology was evident in the light glowing from the table at my bedside like molten lava and the whirring of a jet engine somewhere in the distance.

Any hope I had that last night had been nothing more than a dream vanished. I turned my face into the pillow, but as much as I wanted to cry, I couldn't. The reality of what had happened was too surreal. And I was scared. Fucking hell, was I scared.

Fragments of events came back.

Angels.

Angels were real.

I'd grown up in church understanding they were messengers and warriors of God. While I believed most of what I read, I didn't actually believe *they* were real. Who had actually seen an angel? The grainy videos posted on the internet were clearly a hoax. For that matter, who had ever seen God?

I scoffed. I had been to church off and on in the last three years and, while I believed in God, I wouldn't exactly call myself a Christian. We all have our vices.

All that being said, I knew angels didn't kill people and fallen angels weren't good. Whatever Valen's and Diriel's intentions were, I couldn't help but wonder if their tolerance would come with a price. I wasn't stupid enough to believe last night had been a kindness. Not when Valen's predatory gaze had seared into me until the moment my eyes closed. Even then, I had felt the heat of them on me.

Wanting, yearning. Hungry.

A rich scent like sandalwood and vanilla eased the tension from my body. There was a subtle hint of sage pressed deep within the silk sheets. I curled my fingers together, relaxing and—let go. I jolted back, realizing whose bed I was in and why it shouldn't be so familiar. I jumped free of the bed as if it would keep me snared.

I shivered at the image of his burning eyes. Killian's eyes.

My palms sank into the mattress that had a light fog over it. Clouds, I realized. The bed was made of clouds, though there was no dampness or chill to them. It felt like an ordinary bed. The sheets reminded me of silk but were softer and thinner than anything I had ever felt.

I let my eyes wander across the room. Intricate carvings marked the doors' archways. They presented hieroglyphs and scenes of battle and glory. Death and destruction.

A large screen projected an assortment of maps, galaxies, and files on the opposite wall.

My brow furrowed. Advanced technology wasn't what I imagined when I contemplated Hell.

Valen was waiting for me in the next room. His face was aglow with firelight that made his eyes more entrancing. He was more beautiful than before, now that I could see him more clearly. In this light, he looked less like Killian. He appeared crueler and somehow, shamefully, that made him more attractive.

On top of a side table was a 3D projection rendering of mountains and a large castle.

I'm in that castle.

It was vast with four white towers, four pillars guarding the center steeple. Surrounding it was a river and what appeared to be a town. Tiny movement bustled about the city.

I blinked. Were those people?

"I expected you to sleep longer," he said. Was he frowning?

I took the seat across from him, easing my way down. My entire body ached, but I took my time out of caution rather than soreness. "I probably could."

I had so many questions that I didn't know where to begin. The more my mind raced, the tighter my chest became.

Valen's gaze was unwavering.

"Stop looking at me like that," I snapped.

"Like what?" A lazy smile fanned across his mouth, piercing a dimple in his right cheek.

He was even more beautiful when he smiled. His smile was perfect, but not in that faultless way that looked fake and unsettling. There were thin laugh lines around his mouth, and his teeth were stark white and straight. Killian had a crooked smile.

"Like I'm a piece of meat."

"You confuse my gaze with admiration. It has been a long time since I have seen a nephilim. I cannot help myself."

I hated that word. *Nephilim.* "How do you know that's what I am?"

"Diriel is a seer. I needed him to confirm my suspicions and, as it were, his visions have never been wrong. The angel's power overwhelmed what little of yours was evident. It has grown significantly in the time you've been here. Your kind is unmistakable."

I couldn't feel whatever power he was talking about. The only thing that had remained was the incessant ache in my back and arms. And I *knew* how power felt. His moved through the air like languid fingers along the lines of my body, not touching me but getting close enough to keep me on edge.

"And an amorini?" I vaguely remembered him speaking the word.

The corner of his mouth quirked. "It's what I am. Do you want something to eat?" He moved to rise.

"Answer my questions." I hesitated when his gaze heated. "You owe me that much," I said softly. Maintaining some control would keep me sane, though I knew who was really in charge.

He looked at me for a breath before turning. He crossed the room to a small table where dishes of fruits and bright greens blossomed across the china. He plucked a few things onto a plate before moving to a tea kettle. There was the slightest hesitation in his reach before he poured it into a cup. Even as my stomach growled, I refused to take it as he set it in front of me.

I doubted he had slipped anything in it. He could probably snap his fingers and command me to do anything he wanted. My better judgement kept my hands firmly clasped in my lap all the same.

"You should put something in your stomach. At the very least, drink the tea. It'll ease your nerves."

I looked at him expectantly.

Valen's face hardened before giving way to an exasperated sigh. "We are hunters. The most famous, albeit insolent, of us is Eros."

"Like, Cupid? The little baby who makes people fall in love?" I scoffed. I handled the cup, letting the heat soak into my palms. The scent wafted against my nose as I took a sip. It warmed its way down my throat and steadied my shaking hands. I drank another large swallow.

"Something like that." His mouth quirked. "He is only depicted as a child because of his foolishness. Mankind was originally created of one body with two heads, four arms, four legs, four eyes. One heart." When he grinned, it was a devilish upturn of his lips. "God became jealous of them. Their love was a powerful thing and He feared they would not look to Him for it. Or worse, they would grow too great for their mortal skin and overthrow Heaven. So, He split them apart. Cast them across the world.

"My kind was created to reunite them. He felt He had made a mistake. It was our job to seek out the mates and bind their souls—"

"Soulmates," I said softly.

Is that why he looked so much like Killian? Was this some sick joke? I didn't believe in soulmates, but I knew I loved Killian, was *in love* with him. Even if I had been the one to end things. I had never loved anyone the way I loved him.

Valen nodded, casting stray curls across his eyes. "Our hunting tactics have changed since the Fall. It sates the blood lust of being grounded. And it keeps Heaven riled up."

I blinked, not quite grasping what he was saying.

"We kill them," he clarified. "We leave the weaker mate behind to fall. Earth is so full of corruption that it doesn't take much to ruin them. Alcohol, drugs, sex." He waved his hand. "The list is endless. Taking their mate away ensures they drown themselves in whatever poison they can get their hands on. It keeps them from Heaven."

I was in a room with a murderer. I was in a world with thousands of them.

The simplicity of his explanation was too casual. In fact, there seemed to be a sense of pleasure behind his words.

"Don't look so surprised," he said. "Tartarus is a prison, after all."

Hell was Hell no matter which way you said it.

"You've made it very clear where I am. So why, if you are so wicked, am I stuck here instead of Heaven? Why would an angel be sent to kill me? I haven't done anything to be damned. I'm a good person." I set the cup back to its saucer.

I'm not a murderer like you.

Valen stretched his arm along the back of the couch. "Your kind is wicked. It wouldn't have mattered if you were a saint. There was nothing you could have done to prevent what has happened," he said, the last bit softer than the rest.

I broke his gaze long enough to press my hands against my face. Tears and screams rose within me. I swallowed all of them. *Rein it in, girl.* "This is really happening," I said, more to myself.

"Yes." He reached behind his neck and pulled out a long black arrow. It clacked against the table before the arrowhead landed in the plate of food. "Every amorini has a pocket behind their neck fitted along their spines to hold these. I find it strange that the angel used a dread knot so close to your heart. A weapon like that is typically reserved for my kind. I looked for a seam and you don't have one." He held up his hand. "I only checked on you once to heal that head wound of yours. Nothing more."

I touched my head. "Thank you," I forced. Nothing about him sneaking in while I slept made me feel any better. I should have checked the door for a lock. But what if he hadn't come in? What if I had slipped off and couldn't wake up?

I shut my eyes again. *Breathe.* "You want me to trust you and you're Fallen. You're a murderer and you snuck into my room while I was unconscious—"

"Technically, it's my room. By nature, you are Fallen too."

My eyes flew open. "I am not like you. I don't for one second believe Heaven would have sent someone to kill me to be saved by someone like you."

The gold glint of his eyes flashed, flickering like candlelight. Every trace that he might have been Killian's twin was snuffed out. "Like it or not, you are like me. Your blood damns you. Believe what you want, but you never had a choice in where your salvation lay. Besides, now you have been given an opportunity for something better. Those beliefs they spin on Earth are childish and better left forgotten."

I stood, not wanting to be sitting when he exploded. I could feel it building like a storm cloud. It shifted behind his eyes. My rage scented was building too. I bit back the ache in my still healing back.

"Better? You call this better? My entire life has been ripped away. And you, how can you sit there so casually and say that I-I-I am some sort of monster?"

His eyes narrowed. "What life?"

The question jarred whatever was going to come out next. "What?"

"Misery clings to you. What are you so desperate to run back to?" Genuine curiosity laced his voice, not contempt.

I couldn't give in. I couldn't tell him the truth. It didn't matter if there was nothing left for me. I couldn't live with this new hand I had been dealt. And damn him for throwing it back in my face.

"I'm a good person," I finally said.

The corner of his jaw ticked. He stood slowly, approaching me with such casual grace. I took a step back, and another. He followed. It was only when my back met the flat of a wall did he stop pursuing me. A thin haze of shadows I hadn't noticed evaporated around him as he shifted his weight back.

His eyes roved over my face. "I know you are. That too radiates from you. It does not matter though. You need to accept that." He hesitated, his lips thinning.

We stood like that for a long moment. I knew then I was never leaving. I was trapped in literal Hell. Tartarus.

Valen tipped his head to the side. "Who is Killian?"

I blinked. Had he been reading my mind?

"It was as if you knew me, when you said his name last night."

"He's...." I didn't want Valen to know who he was. Killian was the only person to come out unscathed in the turmoil that was my life. The least I could do was ensure nothing terrible befell him. "He's someone I used to know. You look like him."

His brow arched. "A boyfriend?"

I must have hesitated too long because he smirked. "Now I am intrigued."

"There's nothing to be intrigued about. We broke up and that was that."

"That is rarely ever just *that*. I told you what I am. I'm quite skilled in the ways of the heart and body." His eyes dropped to my mouth and then quickly back to my eyes. If I had blinked, I would have missed it. "In which ways do we favor each other?"

I didn't like that he was homing in on Killian. But he seemed less predatory and more curious than anything. "You both have a single dimple in your cheek. Your hair has more curls. His isn't as curly." I swallowed a little laugh. "Honestly, you're nothing like him. You favor each other, but it sounds ridiculous now that I'm saying it out loud."

"Please, continue," he pressed. There was something dancing behind his eyes. Mischievousness, maybe?

"His eyes are brown. His skin does not have the gilded sheen. We weren't a good fit, but he wasn't as…"

"As what?"

"Intimidating."

Valen's mouth quirked. "Do I frighten you, Ezra?"

Yes. "No," I forced out. Admitting my fear would only make matters worse.

Valen hummed dismissively. "We will see about that." He eased away, ending the conversation as quickly as it had started by turning on his heel. "I'll have a bath drawn," he said with a curl of his nose. As if I stank. I probably did. Dried blood and dirt still crusted my hair and nails. "You can tell me more about this Killian when I return."

Fat chance I was going to tell him anything else about my personal life. Killian included.

I followed him into the bedroom. "Where are you going?"

He looked over his shoulder. "To discuss what I have decided to do with you."

That didn't sound promising. "Take me with you." He might be scary, and I imagined his plans were even worse, but sitting around would only further drive my nerves wild. I wanted more proof that this wasn't still some sick part of my imagination playing tricks on me.

"No."

"Why not?"

"Because Tartarus does not treat pretty things kindly." There was something almost suggestive in his voice. As he said it, a hunger flashed across his eyes that was quickly replaced with impassivity. "When I introduce you to the court, to this world, I don't want there to be any surprises. There are five courts, each ruled by a cyn, a king. Except for Vélos. Here we rule with four. Bishop, Jinn, Diriel, and me." He ticked their names off one finger at a time. "Though Bishop would pretend he is the sole ruler. If he finds out about you before I've laid my claim, then you will be at his mercy. Something he has not exhibited in ages."

Not just any fallen angel, but a king. What were the chances? There was nothing regal about him save for his arrogance.

"If anyone has the opportunity to lay a hand on you before I can set boundaries, then there is nothing I can do to keep you safe. You are a rarity that will be used to its fullest extent if given the chance."

"Please." A voice in my head, reason, told me to let it go. "At the very least, tell me what you intend." I *needed* to know.

Valen's eyes darted between mine. His lengthy hesitation told me that whatever was going to happen was bad. "You will not like what will be said."

"I don't like anything you've told me."

He smirked at that. "If I bring you with me, you must do as I say. This will either go very well or very wrong. If I tell you to run, you run. Diriel will see to your safety until I can come for you."

I swallowed hard. He was serious.

"Alright."

"Good," he said with a nod. I followed him hesitantly into the adjoining room. He leaned over the edge of a large stone basin. He pressed two buttons and water surged from the arched faucet. I stared at it.

"Is there any way I can shower?" I wasn't in a hurry to have any part of me submerged. The rush of the dark blanket covering my head was still too fresh.

Valen paused, his hand hovering over the knob. It took only a second for him to realize what I meant. "Of course," he said quickly. He stood and motioned to a low trickling waterfall. "Lay your hand on it and the water will flow faster. I'll have clothes set out for you once you've finished."

"One more question," I said.

He turned his head slightly, pausing at the doorway.

"How did you know I was in trouble? Were you there... for me? You said you kill mates."

He faced me, his gaze appraising me once more, except this time there was a question in his eyes.

"You do not have an adelfi, Ezra." The sadness in his voice caught me off guard. It made his admission more painful. The knife it twisted in my chest was wrenching. "I happened to be in the right place, at the right time."

CHAPTER FIVE: THE CHOSEN ONE

Ezra

A lick of pain scuttled down my back as I slipped the dark red dress over my head. I kneaded the echo of it as another bite of pain entered my shoulders. It grew worse by the hour, lashing beneath my skin with violent intent. I ran my hands over the healing, stark pink lines.

My stomach fluttered at the sight of them. I had expected my back to still be flayed, or burnt after Valen's healing, but seeing this, seeing the scars forming, was somehow worse. I would carry the truth, that an angel tried to kill me, for the rest of my life.

Tears bit into the back of my eyes. He had ruined me.

I dabbed my sweaty palms to the thighs of my dress. I took a deep breath, shoving down the turmoil that threatened to overpower me. The satin was cool against my touch. This dress was the least revealing option Valen had given me. He had smirked when I stepped out, glowering at him.

"Is this really necessary?" I motioned to the scarlet fabric that pooled down at my sandal-clad feet. At least it covered the hideous hide that was my back.

His eyes narrowed into a devil's slit. "It is for my own pleasure to see you in something so fine.”

“You’re disgusting.”

His smirk widened into a smile. “You find me repulsive? I can hardly believe that if you were dating someone who looks like me.”

“I find your *actions* repulsive,” I corrected. *Is he flirting with me?*

I shouldn’t have clarified that bit, because it only further amused him. If he thought looking like Killian gave him the upper hand or would win me over somehow, he was wrong. His sense of entitlement was starting to piss me off. Just because he saved me, and looked like my boyfriend, didn’t mean he owned me.

“Hmm,” he purred. “The dress will make a statement upon our entrance.” His tongue flicked over his lower lip.

The tall arches he led me through looked like something straight out of a fantasy movie. They were so high, in fact, that there were clouds on the ceiling. Between them, at the top, was what could only be described as starlight.

I let my eyes wander down to the moving paintings of war and carnage decorating the walls. I swear I could hear the clash of metal. A few were more carnal, naked humans intertwined with winged creatures. I shouldn’t have expected to find anything better in Tartarus.

Valen directed me through another arch to an enclosed room that expanded the farther we walked into it. There was a round table in the center shaped like a ring with a large opening in the middle. Four chairs hugged the edges with high backs that twisted up like crooked thorns. Three of which were already occupied.

Diriel took in the dress with a suppressed smirk before meeting my eyes and smiling. The other two, who I suspected to be Bishop and Jinn, looked less than pleased.

“Take a seat,” Valen said, motioning to the single chair.

Valen said Bishop saw himself as the sole ruler. With an air of entitlement draped across his shoulders, I knew exactly which one he was.

His back was straight even as he lounged in his seat. His black hair was long and braided in a single twist, though both sides of his head looked recently shaved. He stretched out an arm banded in tattoos across the table, where he splayed his fingers, drumming them lightly over the top. They sparked every time they struck the wood. His face was sharp, angular, and defined with singular black lines tattooed across both cheeks. Another line ran vertical from his lower lip down the slope of his chin to his throat, disappearing beneath the black leathers he wore. Beneath his arched brows were silver eyes.

He didn't miss anything, continuing to assess me as I sat down. He didn't even have the audacity to flinch when I caught him staring at my chest. His eyes lingered on mine after he worked his way back up to my face.

Beside him, Jinn stared back just as cruelly. He had golden skin and red, straight hair that cut off at the top of his chest. His jade eyes narrowed with contempt. "Whatever joke you are playing is done," he snapped. "Get her out of that seat."

Before I could rise, a soft weight pressed on my shoulders, staying me. Valen's hands dangled above my head as he leaned over the back of the chair. Though he hadn't moved, I knew it was his touch that settled me.

"Since when is it appropriate to bring a whore to counsel?" Bishop's gaze lifted to Valen.

"I'm not a whore," I snapped.

A white glimmer shifted in his irises as he flashed his teeth at me. "You must be brand new."

"What does that matter?"

I recognized the look in his eye. I'd seen it before in men who liked to toy with women they thought were easy. Prey. I knew then it was dangerous to goad him, but I had never been one to sit by and take insults lightly.

"Easy," Valen whispered. It was so quiet, I wasn't sure if I heard him at all. I wasn't sure anyone else had either.

"Then you have yet to be broken in," Bishop goaded.

Heat rushed faster to my face than I could register the meaning of Bishop's words. The satisfactory grin on his face only made it worse.

"No, she has not." Valen's words were trailed by a hiss. "Her advent is due to a rescue, not a capture."

Jinn gave him an odd look. "Rescuing from whom?"

"From an angel."

"They would not dare come here," Bishop growled. His countenance shifted from teasing (*had he been playing with me?*) to serious as he sat forward.

"Earth," Valen corrected. "As it happened, I was already looking for Ezra." He pulled his eyes from me, but I got their warning. Why was he lying? Or had he lied to me, and he *had* been looking for me? "I caught him as he was mutilating her. He intended to kill her."

"You interfered with a keras' mercy." Bishop scoffed.

"Not a keras, not an archangel. Something lesser, or new. I couldn't tell."

The drumming of Bishop's fingers ceased. No longer appraising me, his gaze was curious as he looked me over.

Jinn nodded. "Who is she?"

Valen's eyes slid to Jinn and held them before he said that dreaded word. "Ezra is a nephilim."

Uncomfortable silence shifted through the room. The drastic change in the air set my nerves on fire. I straightened at Valen's response behind me as he stepped forward, leaning his hip against the chair. It was a casual move, but it put him between me and Bishop.

The heightened interest swelled in the air like a cold breeze as something *dropped*.

Though Bishop directed his gaze to Diriel, I could sense every bit of his attention was still focused on me. It was in the subtle lift of his chin as he inhaled, like he was smelling me. "It is true," Bishop breathed.

Diriel nodded. "And not just any nephilim. Whoever her sire was left her with what might have been the entirety of his power. The only thing to compare it to would be a seraph."

"What is that?" I asked, shifting in my seat. I cast a wary eye to Bishop before looking back at Diriel.

Diriel cocked his head slightly. "The seraphim are the most powerful of angels. All fire and fury."

"And a keras?"

"Nasty creatures. They torture the worst of men before killing them. Well, mercy killing is what they call it. They're even crueler as demons. They were made with a lust for blood. Funny, isn't it?"

There was nothing funny about it, but I understood his meaning. It was perfectly acceptable for them to be killers because that is what they were made for. Yet an accident like me was an abomination.

"How did the angel find you?" Jinn's voice had an unsettling edge to it. The heat behind his eyes had shifted to something darker. "Have you exhibited signs of your sire?"

"I don't know. I still don't believe what everyone says I am." I looked at Valen. He nodded for me to continue as I licked my lips. I leaned back into the chair and wrapped my arms around myself. "I don't have any powers. The only thing special about me is that I maybe heal quicker than most, but I still bleed, and I've broken plenty of bones." I flinched inwardly, remembering the very large, very vicious scars that mauled my back. I should be dead.

"The angel would have killed me if Valen hadn't been there," I said softly.

"If your power has been suppressed, I would not expect less," Jinn grumbled.

I looked at Diriel. "Why would the other courts want me? Last night you said they might steal me."

"To fuck you," Bishop said. He settled back in his seat, as if what he just said wasn't as crass as it sounded. "That is why it is the four of us in this meeting and the other cyn were not invited, isn't it? She's not barren."

Diriel frowned. "Some blessings are still withheld. I've done what I could in hopes to change that, but the curse still clings to her. Knowing that will not stop the other courts from wanting to test her limits. We need to convince them. Invite their own seers to test her, but if they attempt to use her, it could be the catalyst that sets her off."

My entire stomach twisted until bile rose in my throat. My chest was too tight. I forced it all down, swallowing hard.

"What are you talking about?" I breathed, heat staining my face. Raw fear coiled within me. And that's when I recognized the look in Jinn's eye. Lust.

A hot pain spider-webbed along my back and arms. I shifted, rolling my shoulders in an attempt to shrug it off. It was insistent this time, and the ache stayed. These scars would be the death of me. The pain dug against me with hard fingers, trying to tear its way out. I tried to shove it as far from my mind as I could and grasp some sort of hold of what was happening.

Valen tapped the top of my chair with the flat of his palm. "The Enemy purged the nephilim because men saw them as gods. They were wicked with Heaven's power and, unlike those of us who fell, they could not be controlled. Even the Fallen have rules that we must follow, but your kind abides no law. A curse was placed on women so no angel could ever get them with child again. If it were found out you can bear children, more nephilim, and they were released into the world, it would force the Enemy's hand to destroy your world sooner than foretold."

"She can set us free." Jinn's voice was deep with longing.

"And multiple could tear through the other realms," Diriel said. "But, it is just Ezra. We need to make that very clear to the other courts. We must be in accordance that she is to be kept safe." Diriel looked at each of them with his steady gaze. "All we really need is one."

The pressure building in my chest expanded. I couldn't do this. I was on the brink of tears. Or maybe I would scream first. It was taking every bit of strength I had left not to fall apart in front of them.

If it were not for Bishop's sharp laugh breaking into my despair, I would have lost it. It was one of the most beautiful sounds I've ever heard. Sweet like music, but as deep as the ocean.

"We are in accordance," Bishop said. And this time, when he smiled at me, it reached his eyes.

CHAPTER SIX: YOU DON'T OWN ME

Valen

What a creature.

Even with her damp hair matted and her face tear stained, I understood what the angel had that night, what might have drawn his attention. Ezra was unnaturally beautiful. Not in the way that some mortals could be, but angelic. In fact, humans probably found her odd. Pleasing enough that you might have looked at her more than twice but could never figure why she caught your eye to begin with. There was no real explanation why she pulled your gaze back again. That's how it was with angels. Even demons had a startling allure.

Her human traits made it easy for her to pass as mortal. Her evident curves and height were human. In contrast, she was too short by our standards. There was only the slightest point to her ears that peaked through her light gold hair. And, of course, she had blunt teeth.

I could not fathom how she had reached me. Even with her bloodline, it was impossible to break through the veil separating Tartarus and the mortal world. You couldn't shout into the void and be heard. And yet–

My thoughts came to an abrupt halt as Jinn leaned forward. If it were not for the barrier of the table between them, Jinn would have been leering inches from Ezra's face. His interest caught me off guard, but I was not nearly as worried about him as I was Bishop, who was quick to act and rarely contemplated the consequences. He would try and sway her to his side the first chance he got. And, if that didn't work, Bishop would force her. Because it would be for the good of Vélos.

I knew exactly what he was thinking because we were all thinking the same thing. Ezra could free us from our prison. She *would*.

The amorini had waited years for judgement or rectification, only to be ignored and further forsaken. Our saving grace had come.

I suppressed the idea of her having children, as much as it had been warring against me. It was hard lying to those who could read my mind. One slip up and they would see past the lie Diriel and I were spinning. It wasn't wise to invite other seers to peer at Ezra, but it would sate Bishop's curiosity long enough that he wouldn't try to bed her immediately.

Even if he did, as long as she drank the tea, she would be fine. Not that I had any intention of letting him get that close to her. No. I just needed a little bit of time to bind her to *my* side.

Which would not be difficult. The angel was right in that she did not have an adelfi, though I don't know how he could have known. All humans have an adelfi, but being half angel likely ruined any chance she might have had for true love.

A pity. But it would work in my favor. It was one less link to the mortal world.

And Killian might give me an advantage, being he was someone she had cared deeply for. Perhaps still did.

Bishop caught my eye. "We should get word to Maalik."

That wasn't happening either. In fact, that was the worst idea yet. Telling the cyn of Eimai Theós about her would breed chaos.

I bristled. "I am not putting her at the whims of Maalik until she is ready for that attention. Ezra has only just learned what she is. She does not understand the gravity of it. She needs time."

Ezra ran a hand over her taut face. She looked more pained by the second. The longer she sat, the more she rolled her shoulders and shifted in her seat. Her fear was like a perfume, laden with the sweet scent of her sweat. But behind that was boiling anger.

How far can she be pushed before her fire comes to a head?

Jinn scoffed. "We could turn the tides of this war, and we're really debating what we should or should not do with her? The Enemy cannot keep His word if the nephilim return." He jerked his attention to Diriel. "We could try. We should. Now. Pin her down, tie her to the table and—"

"You will not tell me what I will do with *my* body," she seethed. "You will not lay a finger on me."

There she is.

Her fear was sweet sugar. So honeyed that it made my teeth ache. I admired the brave front, but I could not resist sliding my tongue over my fangs as they lengthened.

"You do not get a say," Jinn said, eyes flashing. "We have been trapped here, left to rot, and you would refuse us the opportunity to rectify that?"

"Jinn," Bishop warned through the mind link.

Silence stilled around her, heated and deafening. "If you even think about touching me, I will tear you apart." She shoved up from her chair.

I grabbed her by the shoulder, forcing her back to her seat. She jolted and whirled around, her eyes as wide as her flared nostrils.

"You wanted to be here, so now you get to sit and listen." I let the venom trickle into my voice.

"My body—my life—is not up for debate," she bit. The fear in her eyes was so raw she was practically bleeding.

"Of course it is."

"You don't own me." There was a quiver in her voice. I ignored the way Diriel drummed his fingers over the tabletop, trying to draw my attention from her.

"I do own you, Ezra. As does Bishop and Jinn and Diriel. You are within our kingdom and therefore belong to all of us. What we decide is law." I tried to keep the satisfaction from my face as all color drained from hers. I let the moment sink in for a few seconds. "However, nothing shall be forced upon you." I looked away slowly, away from her parted lips to the others. More pointedly to Jinn.

"You're supposed to protect me." Her lips curled back like she might bite anyone who came too close. A desperate animal.

There was no doubt her bark was bigger than her bite. That didn't mean she wouldn't learn to use those teeth properly. We needed to play this very carefully. As unnatural as it was, she was stronger than everyone in the room. The sooner she found that out, the more dangerous she would become.

"I am," I said.

She gathered herself long enough to push my hand away. Crimson stains collected at the top of her cheeks and light danced within her eyes. I swear there was fire in them. In the end, she shut her mouth and twisted away from me, a visible shudder running down her spine. She was trying to keep us all in her line of sight. As if someone would pounce on her when she wasn't looking.

"Our first priority is getting you acclimated. I want you educated in the laws of Tartarus and this court. You will also need to learn strategy and combat." I looked again to Jinn who mumbled under his breath. "Once she has a grasp of things, we can get word to Maalik. She will not meet anyone outside this court defenseless. Her bloodline gives her the right to stand with us, not beneath us. Having the curse lifted would be incredible, but she will not be subjected to torment out of spiteful curiosity. She will not be subjected to anything unless she wills it."

The weight of Bishop's stare bore into me. A fierce strike of his power struck the wall around my mind. I lifted a single finger, a warning. It only heated the cyn's stare. He should have known I was not going to coddle her. She just needed to feel safe.

"You are not going to school me in anything. You are *not* going to touch me," she growled.

"Your education will be just one layer of protection in the event someone cannot get to you in time," I said softly. "Trust me, Ezra."

Chills spread along her skin.

I glanced at Diriel who had become oddly quiet as the flashes of images he saw passed before him. His eyes had glazed over, clouded by a milky white haze. He was gifted with the Sight, a formidable power that allowed him to see events before they happened. More powerful seers were able to distort and change time and events. It had been long suspected that Diriel was one of the first to wield such a power, though he had never admitted to it.

Bishop said something I couldn't hear. Not while I was looking at the woman before me.

"How can I?" she asked, her voice breaking.

"Because you are under my protection. I will not let anything happen to you," I said for her ears. And, in that moment, I meant it.

Something stirred in my chest as I held her eyes. For a brief instant, I considered telling her the truth of what would eventually happen to her. So long as she existed, she would be hunted. She would either lose the light of her humanity coming to our side or die in a war she knew nothing about while clinging to her hopeless faith.

She turned away, stretching her arms across the table before abruptly pulling them back to clench her fists in her lap.

"Ezra, you move so much," Diriel said. His words rang in the air, shaking me from my daze.

She paused mid-stretch. "The scars, where the angel cut me, hurt like hell. It grows worse by the minute."

Scars don't hurt.

"It's not the scars." Diriel let out a breath. He was the only one smiling in the room, his dual-colored eyes wide. "She has wings."

CHAPTER SEVEN: NAMES HAVE POWER

Ezra

It was my turn to laugh. It half came out as a snort and then bubbled out of my chest before I could contain it. "You really do have the wrong woman." I shook my head, my lips still parted in amazement. "I can promise you that I don't have wings." I motioned to my back and grit my teeth as liquid heat coursed through me.

"Our wings lie against our bones, beneath our skin," Valen said. He ran a finger from his elbow up, showing me where they were and how they ended at the small of his back. "Yours will have to be pulled."

Their words faded into the background. This was absolute madness. What was so hard to believe about me being normal?

"You'll pull them tonight." Bishop looked at Valen expectantly. "I'd like to see if there are any signs of her sire within her feathers."

Valen nodded in agreement.

That's all it took to push me over the edge.

I shoved up from my seat, forcing Valen to take a couple of

faltering steps back. I had to get out of there. If there was a way into this place, there was a way out. I needed to find it before they did any of the unspeakable things already mentioned.

"Ezra," Valen warned.

"I'm leaving."

He stepped in my path, and I shoved against his chest. I could feel him at my heels as I made my exit. His strong grip wrapped around my arm and spun me to face him.

"*This* is not a choice," he growled. "This is who you are."

"I'm not who you think I am! Neither am I some child you can tell what to do." I stepped back, bearing his weight as I shoved against him again, but he wouldn't let go.

A wave of heat struck me as Valen's quiet composure went up in flames. "You *are* a child! I was there at the Creation of all those before you, witnessing worlds live and die. You have not glimpsed a blip of life." He snapped his fingers in front of my face. There was ancient power in his voice he had kept hidden until then. It reverberated against the walls. An even greater force flowed from him into me. It singed my flesh and burned me to my bones; if my skin had not remained bare, I would have believed he really was burning me.

"What could have been on Earth is meaningless. There is nothing for you to go back to, no one. You have the opportunity for more and you would try to deny it simply because it's not what you want. You were born of angels and men. I will rip out your wings myself if I must, to prove it to you." The volume of his voice didn't waiver, but his point was as polished and sharp as a double-edged sword.

"You just said you would not force me into anything."

"We are not forcing you to be a nephilim, you are one. I am giving you the facts and offering protection and guidance."

Haze surrounded us. Already I could see the ash starting to sift around him as his temper rose. It should have been a warning sign, but I was too far gone. I was not going to be backed into a corner.

"Take me home. Now." My fingers twitched at my side.

"No."

"Valen."

"No," he growled.

I slapped him. The crack echoed down the hallway. The sound of it wasn't half as loud when he struck me back. Though he did not touch me, the force of his power sent me reeling as it stopped an inch from my face.

I blinked away tears and pressed my hand against the swell of my cheek. I looked up at him, my face burning with heat and pain. "So help me God, you better hope I am not a nephilim. If I am, as soon as I come into my power, I will burn this entire place to the ground. Starting with you."

Valen let me go. He took a step back and opened his mouth to say something. Anger, contempt, and something like pity raced across his features.

Movement caught my eye, and I turned to see that all three of them had stepped out to watch our quarrel.

"You're going to fit right in," Bishop purred. He tipped his head down, looking at me with a shining stare beneath dark lashes.

I turned on my heel before the smile had time to grace his cool features. I didn't know where I was going, but I needed to put as much distance between us as I could.

The dark presence of someone following me chased me as I went, but I didn't look to see which one it was. My entire body was shaking. I knew if I stopped moving I would fall, and I wouldn't let them see me cry.

I found myself standing in the middle of a bridge that connected the castle to an insidious mountain. The sun still hadn't broken the cloud cover. Its light was a burnished copper unlike the gold I was used to. Small aircrafts moved through the clouds, cutting through the mist like white-winged birds. Between the breaks in the sky were stars. But these stars didn't twinkle; they were more like a million little holes that had been punched out.

At least this Hell wasn't all fire and brimstone. It had appeal. Even with the looming dangers, it was oddly beautiful. And so advanced. The architecture and crafts were unlike anything I had seen before.

Two other bridges crossed over a river beneath the one I stood on. Several glittering towers with shelters beneath them lined the riverbank. The sound of a bustling community came and went on the wind. This wasn't the horror I had anticipated.

I looked over my shoulder. Diriel was standing on the opposite side of the bridge, inspecting his nails like he'd just had them done. I turned to face him, leaning my back against the stone railing. He looked up, his eyes widening, as if he was as surprised to see me as I was him.

"I think your power is already at work," he said as he approached. He leaned into the railing beside me, leaving a couple of feet between us.

I rolled my eyes. "What are you talking about?"

"It is not easy to get beneath Valen's skin."

I touched my swelling cheek and shuddered. What would have happened if he had made contact? "Could have fooled me." I looked down the way we had come. Shadows moved through the archways and windows of the castle. Tyre, Valen had called it. It was a monstrous thing with tall spiral towers and loftier steeples. "Does he have a habit of hitting women?"

Diriel snorted. "Not particularly."

"Where is he?"

"With the others. There's something I want to show you."

"What's that?" I made a quick scan of his body. There was nothing outright that he might have on his person.

"I have the Sight. It is a gift that allows me to see events throughout time. I can share my visions with others." He held out his hand, waiting. "I think it'll make things a little easier."

"Is that what you used on me when you tried to freeze me to death?"

"I wasn't trying to kill you," he said irritably. "I had no idea what control you had over your power and was dampening it."

I eyed him warily. They'd made it clear enough that I had nowhere to go. I could take comfort in knowing I was better alive than dead to them. At least Diriel didn't seem interested in testing unsavory theories.

And I was curious about this power I couldn't feel.

I stepped in front of him and laid my hands in his.

My vision tinged red, then black. Not unlike a smoke curl, it filled everything around me. Diriel gripped me as I fought it, holding me steady when I tried to retreat.

"Easy," he said, his voice like a whisper, caressing in and around my ears.

My blonde hair was more red than gold, and my light blue eyes were alight with gold-edged flame. There was fire all around me. It burned everything except the large, black, membraned wings folded at my back in molten obsidian. It dripped from my lips when I spoke and oozed when I opened my wings. Then my mouth grew wider, and I was screaming a wordless cry as fire shot out around me, burning everything in my path.

The scream tore from my throat, shattering the vision.

Diriel kept hold of me as the world righted itself, slamming the tyre and everything around us back into place. "I've got you," he said. His thumb brushed over the top of my hand. "Do you understand now?"

"I don't want that," I breathed. I could feel what he showed me was true, but I didn't want to believe it.

"All of that power, that fire and fury, will rot you from the inside out if we do not pull your wings." He ran his thumb over the top of my knuckles.

"That's not me!" I wrenched my hands free. "What if your vision is wrong? What if that is what I am to become if my wings are opened?"

"Ezra—"

"I'm not like you." As soon as the words left my mouth, I regretted them. The flash of hurt across Diriel's face was enough to put me in my place.

His eyes darkened and his mouth pulled back into a sneer. He flicked his wrist as if to rid himself of my touch. The edge of his tongue ran over his bottom lip, cutting between his teeth.

"I think you will find we are not so different. Not every demon sentenced to this prison has been put here rightfully. We are not all evil. And neither are you."

"*That* was evil." I pointed.

"It was power," he grated. "Left unchecked, it can be destructive."

I kept my hand up, turning from him. Tremors raked through my body. The tears I had tried so hard to suppress burned the back of my eyes. The dark presence of Diriel moved closer and I flinched.

"We want to help you."

"You want to devour me." I skimmed my hands down the thighs of my dress again, feeling vulnerable. It was the only thing between me and whatever the amorini wanted.

His jaw clenched. "Jinn is already being dealt with. What Valen said was true. Nothing shall be forced on you. Let us show you who you are meant to be."

I shook my head. "That's not me."

He sighed. "We can argue about this as long as you want, but nothing is going to change." He paused. "How about we make a deal?"

"What sort of deal?" I tilted my head back and breathed in, pushing the tears away. Wasn't it ill luck to make deals with demons?

"We leave this, for now. I will keep the others from pressing the issue of your wings until you are ready. But, Ezra, you will be lucky if you make it to tomorrow without them trying to rip free. The power of Tartarus calls to you. It is growing quickly, and we cannot allow you to die because you refuse to accept who you are. We will not."

I glared at him, nostrils flaring. The dark look in his eye hadn't lifted though, and I knew he was right; we could go around in circles, and nothing would change. They would get what they wanted regardless. I didn't want to die, but I was scared.

"You swear you won't force me? You won't r..." I choked on the word.

Diriel tilted his head downward so he could hold my gaze steady. "I swear it. None of us shall."

I held that unwavering gaze for a long while. Waited for the ball to drop and for him to hurt me. But he never did. Diriel was still as a statue, waiting.

"Fine," I said, my voice breaking.

Diriel let out a sigh of his own. "Let's take a walk."

"You're not going to take me back?"

"You could use the breather." He didn't wait for me as he strolled back the way we had come. I cast a glance over my shoulder before following him.

He walked with intent, leading me farther into the tyre. I tried to keep track of our path in case I needed to find my way back alone.

The castle was bold, though the farther we wound our way inside, the less menacing it became. The singe marks receded, the clouds thinned at the height of the arches, and white light filtered in through the windows. We passed hallways that seemed to go on for miles. Every stone was polished ivory, cut in perfect squares and fitted together. It was a thing of perfection.

"It is not as you imagined it," Diriel mused.

I shook my head. "Not at all." It was more beautiful than anything I could have pictured. Nothing could hold a candle to Vélos, not even the castles I had seen once in Scotland.

"I thought Hell was fire and brimstone. Not this." I waved my hand.

"When you die, the mortal soul does not come to us, nor does it go to Heaven. You fall into a state of nothingness until your judgement. Those who dwell here have been stolen."

My stomach clenched at the thought. It hadn't crossed my mind that there would be other humans here. "And the fire?"

Diriel turned out his hand and a lick of flame darted across his fingertips. "We are the fire."

The thrum of his power brushed against the front of my chest. The flames moved across his hand with ease. I had a sense to reach out and touch them but curled my hand into a fist in restraint.

"And why do you call it Tartarus? Is it different than Hell?"

"It is the same place but a different name. Hell became something simpler while Tartarus," he motioned, "has always been this. It is a prison, there is fire and pain. That much is the same. But there is beauty despite how much Heaven has tried to convince you all otherwise."

"And so advanced," I murmured.

What he was saying went against everything I had been taught. What struck me the most was that everyone here was a hostage. Stolen, he said. No one was in Tartarus willingly.

Two giant doors lay at the end of hallway. The Tudor arches vaulted high into darkness. The doors themselves disappeared into a gray mist. They were black obsidian carved with runes or hieroglyphics. As we approached, they swung open. A trail of light cut through the darkness behind them, giving no hint as to what could be inside.

Important. You're important to him. I swallowed my uncertainty. Diriel was the only one who hadn't said a word about what to do with me one way or the other. If it weren't for being with him now, I might have thought he was disinterested completely. The doors were three feet wide and, as soon as we cleared them, they closed behind us.

Green flames unfurled with a whoosh in the ceiling above. They rose into the air and spread out like tendrils to reveal a library.

"Wow," I breathed. It was a whole other world. The shelves were massive. Some spun on glass wheels as we got closer, twisting out of our path.

It would be easy to get lost in here.

"We keep track of every history in our world and yours. There are few texts from the other realms, though they are harder to come by. You'll find journals, memoirs, everything you could possibly wish or want for has a record."

"How many realms are there?" I had always wondered if there was *more* out there. Not necessarily aliens, but I never believed we were the only life on Earth.

"Thousands," he clipped. "You will be assigned several readings, but you are welcome to any texts that interest you." He stopped short of several large glass cases, filled with not just books but round crystal orbs. One of the cases shifted, making room for another one to slide forward and stop directly in front of him. Diriel plucked out a large gold book with ease, though it must have weighed at least fifty pounds by the size of it.

A table appeared between us. He set it down and began flicking through each page, his eyes zooming over each line inked into the papyrus.

"Humans are not permitted in here. While it would be best that you do not consort with them, it is not forbidden. Do not bring any of them here. Do you understand?"

I nodded.

"Good. Our texts are sacred. They were never meant for mortals. They make them sick. Some texts even have the power to kill you if you pick them up the wrong way or discard them carelessly. Even someone like you or me." He grinned at my horror-struck expression. "You do not seem like the careless type."

"I'm not. I have a broad collection of books back home. I love to read." I would have to figure out which books could harm me and make sure to never go near them. I peeked at the pages beneath Diriel's hand when he plucked me on the forehead. "Ow! What was that for?"

Blood welled at the tip of his index finger. "Now you can read them all." The jewel of blood slipped beneath the surface of his skin, completely healed.

I wiped my forehead clean. Blood smeared the back of my hand.

He let out a sigh. "What is your full name?"

"Ezra Adele Hollen. Why?"

He pulled an ink quill from the binding and scrawled my name between two others. "We keep record of all angelicas." Before I could question him, he said, "Names have power. It is good to keep track of everyone. In the event it is ever used against them, this book tells you exactly where they are so we can send aid."

"How could someone do that?"

He shrugged. "A long time ago, there was a man called Solomon who had the power to control demons. It used to be you had to have his mark or be of his bloodline, but there are ways to skirt around it, dark power that can manipulate souls."

I didn't love the idea of being added to the menagerie. "Can you control me now?"

A soft smile spread over his face when he looked at me. "Not at all. If you could be controlled, that meeting would have gone much differently." He closed the book and set it back within its place before calling another row of shelves forward. They spun like dancers. The blue glow of the fire cast eerie light about the room as it refracted.

Diriel pulled two books out and handed me one. "You might want to start with this one."

CHAPTER EIGHT: WHEN DARKNESS ANSWERS

Ezra

The book Diriel gave me was heavy for its small size and gave me a headache as soon as my fingers touched it. The cover was an intricate pattern of wings with an open fist in the middle.

The story was about the rise and fall of the nephilim. It started when an amorini by the name of Samyaza first laid eyes on mankind. On women specifically. He claimed to love them, but by the way he moved through them, it sounded a lot more like lust.

All his children were unnatural with gold skin and fiery eyes. Even those with lighter eyes seemed to burn aflame. They grew taller than any mortal and, with a flick of their hands, could bring fire to their fingertips.

After him, others flew down. Azazel, Azza, and Uzza. Their children spread like wildfire, hopping from continent to continent. It wasn't long before men started to recognize the nephilim as gods. They made offerings to them and blood sacrifices. Great pyramids were raised. Wars were started and kingdoms struck down.

For all that they could do, the fathers of the nephilim could not.

The angels became envious of their power. But instead of culling them, they simply bred more.

The world fell so far into darkness that God decided to destroy it. Heaven's gates were opened, and a great flood was poured down onto the earth. Everyone drowned save for one man and his family.

I set the book down. It was the story of Noah's ark and strange in that it was familiar but entirely different from the one I grew up hearing.

Diriel's scribbles had long since ceased. I turned, expecting to find him browsing one of the shelves.

Where is he?

"Diriel?" His name did not make so much as an echo as it was stolen by the silence of the library. I moved the book to my seat as I stood, waiting. The only sound within the stacks was my own breathing. What had been a thing of beauty suddenly became eerie.

The darkness that had been mere shadows now moved. Something scuttled in their midst across the top of the shelves.

It is nothing. It's just a trick.

I walked carefully to the desk. Diriel had been writing quickly. His fingers had flown through the pages, turning them in a blur. Some of the symbols were distorted, shaped in odd lines and dashes.

Out of the light will come a great darkness. Beneath a starless sky and bleeding sun.

Much of it was gibberish, fragments of a thought. Yet he was so intent.

Unease shifted to dread as the darkness grew heavy. I was being watched. I jerked my hand away and peered into the shadows.

Diriel's name was on my lips. No, not him. This was different. Whoever it was, was putrid. There was a distinct scent of sulfur that hadn't been there before.

Is it him?

The angel.

"I know you're there." I bit the inside of my lip as soon as I said it. Horror 101, don't call out to the darkness. I'd seen enough scary movies to know that person was always the first one to go.

"I am not trying to hide," a voice answered.

A rush of chills enveloped me as I looked for where the voice might have come from. It was a split second before he stepped out of the shadows that I realized it wasn't the angel from before. But, even as his dark hair and teak-gold skin melded from the darkness, I knew he had been hiding. How long, I have no idea. His sapphire eyes danced with mischief as he stepped into the light. Their hue matched the shade of his black braids twisting down his chest.

He trailed long fingers across the nearest shelf. They hissed under his touch, bringing a smile to his face. Deep laugh lines creased his mouth. The smile didn't suit him. It was too gentle for someone who looked like they had been cut from stone. His sharp jawline and finer cheekbones were perfectly chiseled.

"Humans are not permitted within the great library of Vélos," he said. He moved like a panther, soundlessly and with such grace. He made stalking so casual that I did not notice what he was doing until he was a few feet from me.

"I am a guest of Diriel's."

His eyes flicked down to the pen clenched in my fist. He smirked.

"And yet he has left you unattended." His gaze moved up my body, appreciating me. It made my skin crawl. I lifted my chin, not wanting to give him the satisfaction of knowing he bothered me. "Who are you?"

"Ezra," I said slowly.

The corner of his mouth twitched. He reminded me of Bishop in the way his mouth quirked, like he enjoyed smiling. It gave him a less frightening appearance. Perhaps that was his weapon.

He moved to my side and peered down at Diriel's papers. His intensity grew as he reached for a page, pulling it free as he slid it closer with his finger.

"And you are?" I asked.

His attention flitted between papers. "Don't touch me. Get off me. It hurts. *Please*," he said, the last word a hiss. "You can call me whatever you like."

My blood rushed. Every instinct told me to run, yet my feet were rooted to the ground. At this point, I recognized everyone as a potential danger. He struck me as someone who would chase me if I fled.

His brow furrowed as he flipped through the papers. I placed my hand over them and pulled them toward me. I didn't like his sudden interest in them, and the action hid the tremors in my hand.

"I believe Diriel's notes are private," I said.

"And what do you know of the *Hymn of the Sun and the Moon*?"

I stared back coolly. I couldn't think of a quippy comment to fire back.

He smirked and crossed his arms, clasping one of his wrists. He wore vambraces daggered with bone-hilted knives. I swallowed. "Just as I thought. These are not for your eyes either," he said, nodding to the side.

It dawned on me then that he was using Diriel's notes to get closer to me.

"What is the *Hymn of the Sun and the Moon*?" If I pretended to stay on topic, perhaps he would too.

"It is a myth. A story of destruction and chaos. Where Tartarus wins and Heaven falls." He slid a finger under the strap of my dress. He hooked it as I took a step back, pulling it so it fell from my shoulder. "Shame, really." He leaned toward me and inhaled.

I grabbed my dress as I stumbled back, pulling it free. My feet caught on the hem and my hip slammed into the side of the desk as he followed me. Two pointed fangs touched the bottom of his lip as he smiled.

"Where is your keeper?" he asked.

"Valen is a call away."

The stranger's brow arched. "Not Diriel?" His bright eyes noted my dress. "Ah, yes. The color of the bastard cyn. How could I have missed it? I would expect one of your beauty to belong to Bishop, truth be told. None of those other fools deserve you."

"I don't belong to any of them."

His smile went from generous to cruel. "Then you will not mind if I take you for myself."

He moved with the speed of a viper. His hand encircled the entirety of my bicep and pulled me against his chest. "Relax," he said as I jerked my arm. "I just want a taste," he hissed. He grabbed me by the hair and jerked my head to the side, exposing my neck. The blue of his eyes was lost in the shadows as he leered down at me. The blunt press of his teeth grazed my neck. Two sharp points bit harder.

I shoved my hand into his face and willed every bit of strength

I had into pushing him away. Sparks, flitting pieces of orange embers, burst across his mouth. He reeled back, letting me go.

Did I do that?

The only trace of fire was the absolute fury behind his eyes. "What are you?"

"I am someone you don't want to fuck with," I growled. Let him think the tremor in my voice was rage and not fear. Fear about what he might do to me and whatever the hell it was I had just done to him.

"Has Vélos made its own little witch?" His fingers twitched at his sides. Or, what should have been fingers. Instead, there were long black claws protruding from his flesh. They glinted in the light like iron. He inhaled again, nostrils flaring. A smile fluttered over his face. "They are shielding you. You do not even have a scent."

I threw up my hands as he took a step forward. Nothing came out of them, but the movement was enough to make him pause. He took another step then stopped, his head twisting to the side so sharp his neck cracked. A curse left his lips.

He looked down at the papers on the desk once more, his face curling in distaste. The shadows played across his features, making his eyes appear completely black. "You so much as speak a word that I was here and a bite will be the least of your worries."

By the time I blinked, he was gone. The dread was no longer there. I could not feel the weight of his eyes. Like an apparition, he disappeared.

I looked down at my hand. It trembled so bad that the papers rustled beneath my touch. I skimmed over the fine curls of ink.

Upon the dawn the gates shall be opened. Under the moon's wane all light will be swallowed. The fury of Tartarus will consume—

"Finished already?"

"Oh fuck!" I clutched my chest as I spun to Diriel.

He held up his hand. "I didn't mean to startle you."

"It's fine," I said, catching my breath. "I scare easily." I reached for one of the books stacked to the side, well away from the papers I had been so clearly snooping through. "I wanted to see what else you had planned for me. I didn't know where you had gone." Lord, don't let me sound as guilty as I felt.

Diriel gave me a wary look before nodding. "The first two you can take. And this one too." He handed me a green leather-bound book with an even thicker spine. "It is the truth of what happened in the Fall and the foundation of the five courts." He ran his hand over the scattered parchment, quickly gathering them into a stack. "You'll take the ones I already gave you as well."

"The story of the nephilim is more complex than I expected," I confessed.

Part of me wanted to tell him what had happened. About the stranger, about the sparks that flew from my hand, but how could I tell him without tattling on myself?

"When you compare it to what you learned on Earth, it will appear that way. Come, gather your studies."

He stood at the middle of the walkway as I stacked the books and scooped up what I had left on the chair.

Light cut into my eyes, making me squint as we exited onto the main street. It wasn't exactly sunlight, as the world appeared to be caught in a permanent state of twilight. But it was brighter than it had been in the library.

The damp air of an oncoming storm brushed against my cheeks

as we made our way over one of the smaller bridges. I shifted the books from one arm to the other. I stopped, adjusting the bottom book as it slipped free from the wedge of my elbow.

"Wait a minute," I grumbled under my breath, trying to push it back into place. I didn't want to find out what would happen if I offended the books by dropping them.

"Ah, I was wondering where you were," Diriel called.

I blew a stray piece of hair from my face as I looked up. My stomach dropped.

Valen strode toward us, hands behind his back and his head held high. One look was all it took for me to find the burning distaste I had for him. He dropped his hands and tossed a bag at me he had been clutching behind his back.

I stepped to the side, barely keeping my grip on the books, before it could hit me in the face.

Bastard.

Diriel gave Valen a pointed look. He stooped down to collect the bag and held it open for me so I could put the books inside.

"How is Jinn?" he asked.

The name sent chills racing across my body.

"Furious," Valen answered, humor in his voice. "He'll get over it."

"And Bishop?" Diriel pressed.

"Content."

The blood in my ears was pounding so loudly I wondered if they could hear it. At this point, it wasn't far-fetched to believe they had supersonic hearing. I shouldered the bag from Diriel's grasp. I fingered the spines of the books, making sure they were all in their proper place.

"I need to speak with you alone." When I said nothing, Valen let out a deep breath. "Ezra," he clarified.

"I don't want to hear what you have to say," I said. "Neither do I want to be alone with you."

"I'm not going to hurt you," he said slowly.

"I beg to differ."

"I rescued you," Valen ground out. "I think that speaks to my intentions."

I faced him then, my fingers curling into a fist along the strap digging into my shoulder. "Your intentions serve you. They are not for my benefit."

"You're making me angry." He didn't need to voice it. Shadows reached out to him and curled up his arms in wisps of smoke.

"What are you going to do? Hit me?" As soon as I said it, I feared it. To Hell with it, I would throw one of the books at him if he tried that again. Maybe I would get lucky and it would curse him.

Diriel cleared his throat. "And, on that note." He looked between us, his eyes lingering on me. He had the audacity to throw me a warning look. "There are other matters I must see to. I will see you again when your studies begin. Or perhaps for dinner," he added, almost a question. "Remember what I said." He nodded to Valen and continued the way we had been going.

I was at Diriel's heel when Valen stepped in front of me, cutting me off from tailing the other angel.

"Play nice," Diriel called over his shoulder.

"Move," I snapped. I sidestepped only for Valen to move with me.

"I can make your life a living hell." Valen followed me as I darted past him. Where had Diriel gone? The bridge was empty, save for a small wisp of smoke at its center.

The shadows danced around Valen, fanning out in the shape of writing snakes as he took up my side.

"I'm already in it." I tightened my hold on the leather strap and lengthened my stride. The wide-open space felt suffocating with Valen's proximity.

His face skewed. "I think I preferred the sopping heap from last night."

I spun on my heel. He was right there, a tall dark force of hard muscle and solid shadow. I took a step back only to find myself pressed against a cool wall of stone. He had herded me into a corner. My heart skittered and I cursed Diriel for leaving me with him.

"Why? Because she was more compliant? I'm not afraid of you."

That easy smirk that seemed to hang on his face turned his mouth up. "Oh, but you are. You have been backed into a corner and the only thing you can do is bare your teeth." He set his hands on either side of me, pressing my back further against the wall, his long fingers digging into the stone. He inhaled softly, his lids lowering as he looked at me. "I can smell it on you."

Fear was an enemy's greatest weapon. Courage was mine. "I bite," I threatened.

His smirk turned into a grin to reveal teeth I knew could leave a mark. His canines had lengthened to sharpened points.

"I bet you do." He let out a slow breath as he leaned away. "I came to apologize, but your ire gets the best of me." He continued to look at me as the struggle of what he should say warred within his head. It was another heartbeat before he took a step back. "I'm sorry. I lost control of my emotions and... reacted poorly."

I'd heard lines like that before. Was all too familiar with them.

And yet, there was something in the way Valen held himself that I actually believed him. Not that I would give him the satisfaction of knowing that. His head was tilted to the side, exposing part of his throat submissively. His full mouth was pursed thin.

I wanted to laugh. It was killing him to apologize to me. I wondered if one of the other cyn had forced him to do it.

The outline of my hand could be seen in tiny pink dots on his gilded skin. "I hit you first," I finally managed.

"That does not excuse my response. Will you forgive me?"

Oh, this was even better. "A fallen angel asking for forgiveness. Has that ever happened?"

At that, his eyes lit up. "Never," he said, softly smiling.

"I might reconsider burning Vélos to the ground." I felt we had reached some sort of common ground by our exchange. The color of his eyes shifted, no longer dark and angry.

I eyed him, trying to read past whatever front he was putting on. "You don't need my forgiveness. Whether I like being here or not, whether I like you or not, you've made it clear that I'm stuck."

He frowned. "I do not want you to be miserable."

"I hardly think I can be happy here." I looked around in disbelief. "You kidnapped me and hit me."

"I rescued you," he bit. He shut his eyes before slowly opening them again, their color a sunset after a hard storm. "I am trying to apologize for hurting you. I am sorry for it, Ezra. I am sorry for taking the life you had away from you. I will spend our entire lives making up for it if you will only stop behaving like a spoiled brat."

I hadn't even considered what my life was going to be like. Was I immortal now? Had I always been? And I wasn't a brat. So, I had blown up and hit him. *Maybe* I overreacted, but my life had been flipped upside down and they thought they owned it.

I wasn't going to be a slave or whore.

Bishop's words brought heat back to my face.

I looked out to the mountains, to the white structures that made

Vélos look like something straight out of a fairy tale. I couldn't forgive him, not yet. I wasn't one to hold onto grudges, but it was too soon.

"Thank you for saving me," I forced out.

He looked at me a few more heartbeats. It was easier to breathe when he finally looked away. "I will not hurt you again."

Men's words were only worth so much.

A fallen angel's even less. *A demon*, my mind whispered.

I could smell it on him. The sulfuric stench of impurity and ash. How I had missed it before is beyond me. Was there a difference between fallen angels and demons?

And how was something that was supposed to be evil so incredibly beautiful? I stole a glance. Heartbreakingly beautiful is what he was. He wasn't the pretty kind of beautiful you see in supermodels or high-class actors. It didn't compare to Killian's earthly features one bit. He had too many sharp edges. Edges that you could slice your finger on.

Valen was the picture reference of a villain. Even when he smiled, which I had seen little of, he looked lethal. Brutal and vicious.

I'd never pictured curls on a bad guy, but they worked for him. Especially the stray pieces that fell across his eyes when they met mine.

"Let us start anew," he said.

I looked at his outstretched hand like it would burn me. It felt like too much time had passed before I finally took it. He pulled me away from the wall, and I stumbled forward, catching myself against his chest. He was several heads taller than me. I had to crane my head to look at him. His gold eyes were more frightening when he was framed in shadow.

Warmth filled the space between us. Before he let me go, I could swear I saw flames between our fingers. His or mine?

"I meant what I said before. No one is going to force you to do anything you don't want. I'll kill anyone who tries."

I let out a shuddering breath. "You'd kill for me?"

He looked at me thoughtfully. "And serve their head on a platter to you once it was done." He was so matter of fact about it. As if it was the most normal admission in the world.

"Even if it was one of you?" I held my breath.

He cocked his head. "Did Diriel do something?"

"No. No, I—" I couldn't tell him. Not until I figured out who the stranger was. He couldn't be cyn, I had already met all four of them. But kings had advisors. "I was just asking."

"If it came to it, yes," Valen said after a moment.

I wanted so badly to believe him.

I clicked my nails together to distract myself from the unease building in the back of my mind. "So, now what?"

He paused. "Would you like to see Vélos?"

I had said I didn't want to be schooled, but the idea didn't seem so bad the more I thought about it. Valen was right; this was an opportunity.

CHAPTER NINE: WONDERS OF THE UNDERWORLD

Ezra

We walked what felt like the entirety of Vélos over the next couple of days, only for Valen to lead me back to his room in the evenings to continue in the morning. I knew what he was doing. The little tastes he gave me were startling but not overwhelming. I hated to admit it, but it was hard not to fall in love with everything he showed me.

Especially the technological side of it all.

The tall steeple I had seen in the hologram was the Great Hall. We passed through it, but it was so quick that I wasn't able to catch a glimpse inside. Its top was covered in stained glass and crystalline lights.

Within the human districts were smaller cathedrals alight with pristine music. There was an arcane energy within Vélos that spoke to me. It drew me in like every fairy tale I had drowned myself in.

Yet, within the allure was a foreboding darkness. Vélos was too pretty. Too magical with its lights, tapestries, and artwork. This place was not meant for Hell yet murderers and assassins ruled it.

We passed through a chamber of starlight. "I always pictured Hell to be more archaic."

"Where do you think humans get all of their ideas?" Valen's brow arched. "In another decade, there will be crafts like these." He motioned to the ships with their long wings and glass hulls that passed through the sky. "We give a little bit out at a time."

I marveled at the various ships. "Why?"

"Because if we were to give humanity our knowledge all at once, you would destroy yourselves. And that takes away the fun of hunting you ourselves." His eyes glinted as he cast me a sideways look.

Wicked creature. "No. I mean, why share this knowledge at all?"

Valen shrugged. "It pisses Heaven off."

I saw angels. Demons, Valen corrected when I inquired about them.

Fallen angels and demons were the same. Few still held onto the word angel, while their brothers reveled in being called something darker. He said the majority of Tartarus had taken to falling quickly. I noticed early on that some stank more of rot and sulfur while others had more pleasant scents. Beneath the sulfur and ash that clung to Valen was the distinct scents of sandalwood and sage. The same scents that lulled me to sleep every night.

What surprised me most was the number of mortals. They were distinguishable by appearance alone. The more attractive ones didn't compare to the demons' ethereal beauty. They kept their eyes down when we passed, veering as far out of our path as they could.

The amorini avoided us too, though they weren't as blatant

about it. I wondered if they were all afraid of the cyn or if it was just Valen that instilled the fear.

As we wandered through a market, Valen explained that it gave the humans a bit of normalcy to work. It wasn't required of them as most of them served the amorini, but it seemed to appease those who were restless. I didn't like the way he said that, and I didn't want to ask what he meant by serving them. I had already seen a few humans with chains around their throats. The most common was a collar with a ring in the center. It was clear as day that these people were slaves.

Valen pointed out that I was better than the humans. Higher quality. I cringed. I didn't like the sound of that in the slightest. Nor did I want to hold myself above anyone when I was a firm believer in equality.

"No living thing was made to be equal and so they are not," Valen said.

"We might have been made different, but saying my blood makes me more worthy than a human," I shook my head, "is a terrible thing to consider."

"I am not talking about race and gender, Ezra. I am talking about a pyramid of power. Humans are only worthy of the power granted to them, which is the size of a grain of salt. Angels are granted significantly more. And you?" He clicked his tongue. "You're above us all, darling."

Just on the outskirts of the market was a garden. Valen tipped his head in response to the question in my eyes. I padded through the gates. Who could have imagined there would be flowers here?

Their colors were vibrant hues I could not fathom. I touched one of the blossoms, trying to wrap my brain around what it might be. There was nothing to compare it to. It was a light shade with the density of a bright yellow and grew darker than emerald at its base. The bloom was held up on a long, twisting stem. It had rounded petals with rippling edges, while its leaves were pointed and narrow.

I turned to Valen. "What is this?"

"Neos. They were the first flowers to bloom after the Fall." Pride crept into his gaze.

"And its color?"

"Delen." There was a hint of amusement behind his voice.

"It's beautiful."

Beautiful. Beautiful. Everything was beautiful. I felt like a broken record every time I mentioned it and yet I could not stop.

I could feel him studying me as I moved through the garden. I approached a gnarled gate, sculpted with iron flowers and arrows set between a giant hedge wall. Tentatively, I laid my hand on it. It looked like the start of a maze. A soft touch on my elbow drew me back.

"It is easy to get lost in the Labyrinth. There is a spell on the path that we cannot break." I didn't flinch from him when the tender flare of sparks rose between us. I hadn't been able to recreate what had happened in the library, but every time Valen and I touched, light sparked. My power answering to his, he had said.

A wrack of pain hit me as he turned me away from the gate. I gripped his arm, holding onto him tightly to keep from buckling. I ignored his look of protest. I knew my skin was as red as the dress I wore, inflamed and angry. "I'm fine," I breathed, though he hadn't asked.

The pain kept me up late and made it difficult to rise. But I was more stubborn than my affliction, so I pretended it didn't bother me. I clenched my jaw, biting back the yell of agony I wanted to release.

The moment I admitted to the severity of the pain, the sooner they would rip out the wings I didn't want to believe I had.

"Ezra," Valen said softly.

"I'm fine. It comes and goes. This is just a bad wave of it." I waved my hand for good measure, as if the pain hadn't taken another sharp bite out of me.

"Let us get you to rest," he said.

I dug my fingers into his flesh as tears gathered behind my eyes. I nodded, not trusting myself to speak. Valen wrapped me in his embrace and, in a flurry of smoke and embers, took me away.

We landed at the threshold of a brightly lit room decorated with white linens and flowers.

"We thought it best to give you a place to call your own," he said at my hesitance.

The windows were sealed with glass, unlike his that were left open. And it was smaller, more intimate with a dual hearth that divided the parlor from the bedroom. My books had been arranged on a birch bookshelf and beside it was a desk with paper and two quill pens. The greenery and strange colors were what I liked most about it. It was cozy, for the cage it was.

I turned to him, crossing my arms. "You aren't worried I'll try to run away?"

"I'm right next door. If you try anything, or invite any sort of trouble to your doorstep, I'll hear it."

Of course he would. I rolled my eyes and strode farther into the room. The parlor alone was bigger than my entire apartment. Nicer too. I turned, but Valen was gone. The thanks I had been about to give him died on my lips.

Sleep evaded me that night. The pain had receded to an annoying gnawing. I strode from the bedroom to the desk, picking up one of Diriel's required reads, and kicked back my bare feet.

My attempt at reading only lasted a few minutes before I was keeling over. My scars had healed to white grueling lines yesterday. There was no pain against my flesh when I touched them. It came from under my skin, buried so far down that my bones ached.

I sat up, turning my face to the fire. Tears welled as I watched the flames. Three days ago, I had been a normal girl living a terribly tragic life. There was nothing normal about it other than my daily nine-to-five, basic meals, and gym routines. Normal people didn't kill everyone around them.

I brushed the tears away. Crying wouldn't change anything. It wouldn't take me home. It wouldn't bring back loved ones. It wouldn't change who I was. *What* I was.

The sound of an engine's roar drew my attention to the window. I watched as a craft whirred overhead with two more behind it. The smaller ships, bastions, must be an escort for the carrier. Below them, sparks flew, splattering like paint against the pastel sky. A welcoming party or celebration. Maybe both.

Watching more lights crack across the sky as the ships descended from view made my heart twist. Everything was so beautiful and strange, and yet here I was, wallowing.

I looked at the door that separated me from the hallway leading to Valen. I didn't exactly want *his* company, but I didn't want to be alone either. An incessant thorn in my side, he was still someone to talk to. The only other person I might consider speaking with was Diriel, but I didn't know how to contact him.

"Can you only hear me when I'm up to no good, or will you come calling because I'm bored?"

I waited, watching the door. Nothing happened.

"I'm going to break one of these windows and jump out of it." I picked up a candlestick to make my point. Still, nothing happened, so I set it back down with a thump.

My eyes narrowed. He had been bluffing. He couldn't hear me. I bit my lip as another wave of pain struck me. Fine. It was just fine. A walk would do me better than staying cooped up in here. Maybe it would loosen whatever was going on in my back and then I could finally get some sleep.

"Last chance before I take off," I called. I snickered, opened the door, and froze.

Valen was leaning against the door frame, his hands splayed on either side. "What do you want?" His hair was rumpled and the shadows dark under his eyes.

I swallowed.

He pushed into the room, forcing me back into it. The eerie glow of his eyes made my skin crawl as they worked over my body. It was the reflection of the fire doing that to his eyes, I told myself.

"Well? You wanted me so here I am."

I cleared my throat. "I couldn't sleep."

"You thought waking me would help?"

I fidgeted with the hem of my shirt before crossing my arms. "I don't know what I was thinking. I didn't think you would really show up. That you could hear me at all. I thought maybe you made it all up." I knew I was rambling, but I couldn't stop myself.

"What do you want?" he repeated, cutting me off.

I don't want to be alone. That unspoken confession resonated down to my very soul. I couldn't bare that weakness to him, but the longer I looked at him, the more the longing and loss built. I felt the second I looked away I would break. All it would take is a gentle push for me to shatter.

"You were right." I finally broke away from his searing gaze. "About misery clinging to me. People have been dying ever since I was born. I always thought it was bad luck, or Death. I never imagined it would have been an angel that finally met me.

"I have no one. No one is looking for me. No one ever will. The last person alive that I still love wants nothing to do with me. There is nothing for me to go back to, but I am terrified of being here. I've been alone my whole life, but now, more than ever, I feel its weight."

Valen didn't interrupt me. He stood patiently while I poured out the entirety of my heart and how much I fucking *hated* being in Tartarus despite the evil that had befallen me on Earth. It was the first time he didn't feel like a giant storm cloud come to blow me over. So, I kept going. I told him about the deaths. I told him what the angel had really done to me before he landed on the water to save me.

"I thought, how much more suffering can I bear before I break? And here I am." I waved my hand about the room.

I threw my head back to stop any more frustrated tears from falling. I didn't see him out of my peripheral before I felt the warm touch of his hand slide along the side of my neck. His thumb brushed the flat of my cheek.

"Tears are not a sign of weakness. Cry, Ezra. Mourn the life you have left behind. And when you are done, live the one you have been gifted. You have power. You have a family that cherishes you.

Nothing and no one will be taken from you. Not ever again."

He was looking at me so fiercely I thought a fire might catch. I knew he desired me in one way or another. And I knew, without a doubt, that what he said was true. Not that he could protect me from being hurt, though he would try damned hard, but that the amorini would cherish me. I recognized the raw need for me to see that in his eyes.

He was offering everything I had ever wanted. A place to belong where I did not have to constantly look over my shoulder. A family that would not be ripped away from me.

"I want to believe you. I want to trust you," I said.

"All things take time."

I turned from his hand, looking to the mountains. I yearned for everything he offered. But how could I accept it when this was a place of evil? "Is there goodness here?"

"You are proof that there is. Just as much as there is evil in Heaven. Tartarus is a dangerous place, but you have seen its beauty. I have no doubt your presence will bring more light to its shadows."

Or would my light be sucked up by the darkness? My stomach clenched. I couldn't let that happen. I wouldn't let this place win. Not Tartarus and not the angel.

Valen brushed away the stray tears as they ran down my face. His heat crept to the inner parts of me, soothing the anxiety that fluttered frantically within my chest.

I took a deep breath. Little embers flickered from his fingertips. He was watching me curiously.

"I don't want to rely on you to save me. I want to see this fire I have as you do." And not the curse it felt like.

"Is this about Jinn?"

"Jinn. Bishop. The angel… And anyone else who might think

they can control me."

Valen's eyes hardened and a smirk tugged at the corner of his full lips. "Are you agreeing to be trained?"

I threw him a look which earned me a flash of his teeth. "To be strong like you. I won't be someone's lap dog."

A low rumble rose in the back of Valen's throat. "Oh, never that." He slid his touch down my arm to my hand. He brought it to his lips. His warm breath danced over the top of my knuckles. "It would be my pleasure to teach you our ways. It'll be grueling."

"I can take it." I clenched my jaw. "So long as you keep your word."

Diriel had already given me his, but I needed Valen's. I needed to hear it from him, the one who had saved me from death. I needed to know he would keep me safe from the defilement and evil. And then, when I had learned everything I could, I would use it to set myself free. I would take as much as Tartarus could give and then I would use it against them.

Valen's eyes gleamed like jewels as he finally pressed his lips to my skin. Embers crept up my hand as he said, "You have it, Ezra."

I should have clarified that it meant keeping me safe from him as well. But I couldn't get out the words with the way he was looking at me. I couldn't slow my heart long enough to consider anything other than how fierce and terrifyingly beautiful he looked in that moment. His touch, his gaze, *he*—was a snare I could not disentangle myself from.

"It will make things easier if your wings are pulled," he ventured. He hadn't let go of my hand.

I stopped breathing and looked down at where we were connected. The pain had vanished. Had it dissipated as soon as he entered the room? Or had it happened when he touched me? I wasn't ready for *that*. Not yet.

"Another day or two. That's it."

He glared at me, but I could see the humor within the shadows of his stare. "You're a stubborn thing."

"A few more days."

He held the challenge of my gaze for a few more heartbeats. "A few more days," he agreed.

I crawled into bed alone after that. I watched Valen through the fire as he turned into the parlor. Instead of returning to his bed, he stretched out on the couch and tucked his arm behind his head.

CHAPTER TEN: IT'S ALL IN THE EYES

Valen

It was almost too easy. I had expected her to take advantage of the space I put between us, not reach out so soon. I'd felt her need and loss before she called to me. Gods, and the way she had poured out her heart! The beast inside me had writhed to break free at every sad story and heartbreak. But she wasn't a victim I could feed on.

She needed a guardian.

I stretched out on her couch, knowing full well she watched me through the flames. I wanted her to see me. To know that I was there to protect her.

She was mine.

I waited until her breath deepened before going to her bedside. Embers sparked in the wake of my touch as I ran my fingers down her arm. The light moved like glitter. There one second and gone the next.

It took everything in me to leave her. I knew if I didn't, I would break the promise I had made to her. Her blood would be so much sweeter once it had been won.

I needed to feed. Or hunt. Anything to sate my rising want.

I shook away the racing thoughts as my gums began to ache. My fangs lengthened, begging to be sunk into warm flesh and hot blood.

The Noir was just that, black and ominous. Moving portraits lined the main entrance while firelight ghosted the ceiling. The eyes of demons reflected the low light, glistening like black diamonds in the shadows. In the middle of the throng of bodies was Bishop.

The hall reeked of sex and open throats. I rarely visited, having become bored with how easy it was to feed on the willing. I enjoyed the thrill of hunting and the heady scent of fear my prey emitted just before I struck. But days like today, it was a convenient place to sate my hunger fast.

"How is Ezra?" Bishop asked, not missing a beat.

I bristled as I sat down, stretching my long legs out to lay beside him. The warm gasps of sex only intensified my need. Where had my lack of control gone?

"Well enough. She has decided to train." I cut him a look from the corner of my eye.

"Is that all?" Bishop drawled.

"It is a start," I ground out.

"So, her wings have still not been pulled." He sucked the back of his teeth with a roll of his eyes.

"It is hard enough for me to touch her without her trying to bite me." Tonight was the first time she had allowed any sort of intimate touch. My lips against her knuckles had been a risk. The way her embers had crept out from under my mouth was more than enough warning of what could happen if I pushed her too far.

"All whores have sharp teeth. Every single one comes screaming bloody murder. I thought you liked the ones that bite?" Bishop's light gaze darkened, his lips curling.

"I am surprised you would speak so lowly of such a relic."

He was goading me out of jealousy. Had the roles been reversed, Bishop would have his lips against her ear whispering sweet nothings. He hated that I had been the one to find her. It radiated off him as clear as the River Styx.

"Relic," Bishop scoffed. "I want Atticus to look at her."

I cocked my head, trying to hide the panic that surely reached my eyes. "You think Diriel lies?" Did he suspect my own deceit?

I looked up as one of the women approached us, her long legs flashing through her maroon skirts. Bruises of the same color lined her neck.

"Females do not have a place among our kind. The fact that she does suggests she can break the curse. I would like to trust Diriel, but his loyalty has always been questionable."

That is because he is more loyal to me than you.

I looked away as the woman knelt between us, catching Bishop's heated gaze. "I agree we should have someone look at her, but Atticus? Our alliance with Eurynomos is durable at best. I do not see it standing once they find out about her."

Bishop smirked as he ran his hand through the woman's long dark hair, exposing more bruises on her shoulders. He grabbed the back of her neck, pulling her forward. A gasp burst from her lips, her eyes going wide. Her nostrils flared as Bishop inhaled the air beside her face.

"It is worth the risk," he finally said. His eyes had glazed over, replaced by the sudden rise of lust.

My own breathing had quickened at the woman's heightened fear. Gods, it was a delicious scent. I focused on the smell of her instead of the prickle of fear that rose on the back of my neck. If

Atticus looked at her, he would see straight away that she was not barren. Eurynomos was only tied to us until we no longer benefited them. Even if they did not try to steal her, they would demand her.

Because of her eyes.

Blue eyes were only found in the keras bloodline. Their coloring could very well be due to her human lineage, but they would claim her all the same.

I took the hand the woman had clasped around my thigh for support. Her eyes darted to mine. I tightened my hold.

The mess of bruises was worse than I previously noted. Her entire skin lacked luster. The light behind her eyes was nearly dead. It would be cruel if we didn't help her along.

Bishop ran a talon across the woman's throat. Like fine paper, her flesh split apart in a cascade of red. I moaned. Unable to deny myself, I pulled her to me, clamping my lips to the seam and sinking my extended fangs into the torn folds of her flesh.

Her only response was grasping the front of Bishop's shirt. And then her grip faltered as she fell heavy between us. Bishop nestled his face into the opposite crook of her neck. The sound of his fangs chewing against her was so satisfying it made my jaw ache. I bit harder.

Bishop withdrew the same time I did, his mouth open and hungry. His eyes dropped to my lips. They seared into me like lightning bolts, blazing white. When he met my gaze, it was with a lustful smirk.

"Stop hoarding Ezra."

I leaned back, letting him get a better view of me. Bishop always wanted what he couldn't have.

"Afraid she won't fall for you now that I have a head start?" I ran my tongue over the corner of my lip, savoring the forgotten woman's essence. There was a time when I remembered all their names.

I kept my gaze teasing as I looked back at him, but internally I wanted to throttle him. If it had been anyone but Ezra, I would have willingly shared. But she wasn't just anyone.

"You could have her for a decade and her path would still lead to me."

"You did call her a whore," I reminded him.

Bishop reached down, digging his finger behind the woman's eye until it popped free with a wet slurp. He turned it between his fingers. The amber hue of the iris was devoid of light. All luster as dull as the woman's ashen skin.

"She will be. The whore of Vélos, salvation of the Fallen." He popped the eye into his mouth and chewed.

CHAPTER ELEVEN: A HIGHER POWER

Raguel

Somewhere near Lake Almanor, California

August 18, 2025

The lavender sky was dusted with pink cotton clouds. They sat low over the lake, clinging to the edge as night's shadows crept back into the forest.

Two males walked the shoreline, both tall and lean in their gilded armor. The first was red haired with ivory skin wrought with defined muscles. Dark red eyes, with split irises, were set within his narrow face. The sound of ruffling feathers caught the wind. At his back, neatly folded, were six red wings. Between the crimson feathers were thousands of eyes, each one flashing open and then shut, searching.

The air felt heavy, wrong. Something terrible had happened here.

His companion was red too, though his skin was a brighter gold. He wrapped his hand around the pommel of his sword, stopping short of the water where the trail stopped.

Stale blood dotted the rocks at his feet. It was the same scent as at the camp. Female, by the belongings left there.

It wasn't the blood that had drawn the males, or the distinct smell of another angelic. Not even the dead fish floating on the surface of the water were important. Those things didn't demand the attention of the seraphim, much less an archangel.

It was the stench. Rot clung in the air like a black pollute. You could practically taste it. Rotten meat, putrid fruit.

"Raguel," the male said. He motioned to the middle of the lake. "It's there."

The pale male was still, already looking in the same direction. "Stay here. Keep an eye out."

Raguel pulled a silver sword free from the sheath at his hip as he approached the veil. It was hard to miss, but the closer he got he could see the seam. Angels made tears like this when they spectered. But this wasn't quite the same. It was fractured, like broken glass.

Dark spills were pooling out of it in roils of black smog. The stench was worse the closer Raguel got.

The subtle shift in the air around the tear and the mortal world sent him stumbling back. It was not the force itself but what he saw within the seam that startled him.

"Fuck," Raguel hissed.

"Sir," the other angel called.

"Gladr, take five thrones from the Keep. Search the world for anything else like this, but keep it quiet."

Gladr approached hesitantly, his knuckles going white as he

fisted his sword. He stopped abruptly, coming up short beside Raguel. "It reeks of demons."

"Demons do not exude power outside of Tartarus."

"That's what it is though. Isn't it?" Gladr swallowed. Anything that putrid had to come from one of them. Heaven did not make monstrosities.

Raguel looked at him sharply, silencing whatever Gladr was going to say next. His gaze hardened before he let out a heavy sigh. "I don't know," he confessed. It was impossible by all accounts, but where else could evil come from if not the Fallen?

He ran his hand over the front of it, casting a thin layer of light across the bleed only for it to suck up everything he gave it. Raguel snatched his hand back, cutting his light off.

What abomination is this?

"Make haste, Gladr. You waste precious time."

Gladr turned, making his way back to the shore before specter-ing. He didn't want to be anywhere near the bleed, or whatever it was. It was wrong. Heaven help them if there were more bleeds like it scattered on the Earth.

Let this be the only one, he thought.

He cut a line through the air, breaking his own bleed between the mortal world and Heaven. But just before he stepped through, he stopped.

"Raguel!"

How had they missed them?

He closed the bleed and strode to the carcasses splayed against the tree line.

Four elk were amongst the rocks, as if they had dropped mid-stride. Their hooves were soft or brittle, oozing white fluid. Their eyes were the worst part. What had once been big glassy orbs were now crusted and, somehow, still bleeding.

"This is not a normal disease."

"No," Raguel agreed as he approached. His irises split as he looked down the shore before dropping down. He ran a pale finger over the stag's pelt, pulling it up in clumps though he hardly touched it. "It is new."

Raguel looked back at the fish sprawled across the bank.

A new disease of this magnitude was dangerous. It could mean plague. But a new plague had yet to be written. If God had not written it, then where had it come from? There was no one in Creation that could create something new than He. Demons could manipulate and distort what was already there, but they could never make something new. To even consider there was a higher power was something Raguel could not fathom.

CHAPTER TWELVE: IT'S LIBERATING

Ezra

I spent another day confined to my room with books because they refused to train me in anything physical until my wings were pulled. Staying confined, however, was my choice. It had become almost too painful to endure the long walks Valen had taken me on previously. And the books were fascinating.

Diriel had sat with me for the partial afternoon. He was a vault of information all his own. There was a boyish glint in his eyes whenever I asked him a question. As if no one had asked him such things in along time.

Was he made or born? What was it like being an amorini before the Fall? And so many other questions tumbled out of me.

But by the end of that day, my eyes were tired and strained. My head felt three times larger now that it was stuffed with information.

I grumbled as Valen set down another book in front of me.

"Really? More books?"

"Diriel told me you love to read," Valen said.

Yesterday had been a very *long* day. I kicked my feet up on the desk, wincing slightly as the pain twinged in my back. It was ebbing away slowly now that Valen was here. It was with his presence that it dissipated. "I do, but when I said I wanted you to train me, I thought we would be doing something more interesting."

He folded his arms, looking down at me with that arrogant smirk I wanted to wipe off his face. "Like what?"

I waved my hand. "Since you won't teach me to fight, maybe spells or something? I don't know. Magic? Something with fire."

Valen shook his head. "If we mess with deep magic, before you've opened your wings, it's only going to make things worse. It's too dangerous to exert yourself so early. Unless you've changed your mind." He arched a stupid full brow.

"Not a chance."

He sneered. "Then reading is all you will be doing until you are done being a brat."

I was glad to see my honesty hadn't deterred his foul mood. Part of me welcomed it. At least I knew he wasn't going to coddle me. Not that Valen was capable of expressing a softer side.

"You will find incantations and movements within. Small spells that will not trigger your power." He nodded to the book. "Memorize them now and it will be easier when we start on the harder stuff."

I flipped through, looking for anything interesting. Maybe there was something in here that I could use to set his ass on fire. I knew I had that sort of power. But as I skimmed the text, the only movements I found were wind related. One spell went as far as ripping the breath from someone's lungs.

"This is pretty dark," I said, turning to the next page that had instructions on how to make someone drown without the presence of water. "Is this how you kill people?"

Valen snorted. "Those silly spells? No. I prefer my bow and arrows."

I had forgotten he was a twisted version of Cupid. It was easy to forget when none of them flashed their weapons around. Heat spread under my palms as they began to sweat.

"Are you going to make me kill someone?"

He turned from the bookcase with a red book in hand. "Do you want to?"

"No," I said before he had finished asking. *Yes*, my mind answered.

Valen's brow arched. "Sure about that?"

There had only ever been one person I considered killing. But thinking about it and doing it were two different things.

"No," I answered again. "I'm not a murderer."

He leaned over the desk, setting the book down, and sniffed. Whatever he smelled amused him. The glitter in his eye paired with the cruel upturn of his mouth said it all. "I would never force you to hunt with me, Ezra. But I think you would enjoy it. It's quite liberating."

"I'm only learning what I need to, to control my power. I'm going to prove him wrong."

His countenance faltered. "The angel?"

"Yep."

Just because I accepted what I was didn't mean I was going to accept the judgement that asshole had laid on me. I wasn't evil and I was going to make sure everyone knew it.

The amusement shut off like a switch. There was no anger or annoyance. There was nothing in Valen's eyes as he looked back at me. He looked like he was about to say something before he turned away entirely.

"Practice a few of the movements. Once you've mastered three, you can have this." He tossed a package across the table.

I blinked. Where had that even come from?

I turned the package over. "What is it?"

Valen shrugged. "Get to studying, little bird."

Instead of practicing spells, I spent the first hour trying to break into the thin packaging. The tissue paper wouldn't tear no matter how much I dug my nails into it. I slid one of the pens along its edge, but not even that was sharp enough to break the binding. What sort of gifts do fallen angels give?

Perhaps it was better if I didn't know what it was.

The first two movements I mastered, or I think I mastered, by drawing simple lines and circles in the air. They were the only two that weren't vile. One was a spell to steal someone's voice and the other caused temporary blindness. Cruel but not deadly.

It took me a while to settle on the third. It was between the spell that stole the air from someone's lungs or one that made all their teeth fall out. I settled on stealing someone's breath. Out of the two, it seemed to have the most potential.

I stood, raising two fingers horizontally in front of my chest and then pressing them to my lips and breathing in sharply. The next step was to turn my hand and pull, like I was snatching something out of the air.

Nothing happened as I practiced each spell. Curse, I realized, as I took another inhale, tugging the breath from my invisible opponent with a sharp snap of my wrist.

The package on the table ripped. Between the thin strips of paper was a flash of red.

I clenched my jaw so tight it hurt as I pulled the—what the hell was it? There was no way this was a piece of clothing. I tossed the wrapping aside and turned the fabric.

I twisted it until I found the straps. This had to be the top, right?

I walked into the bedroom to try it on in front of the mirror.

The dress, if it could even be called that, hugged my body before rippling down my back in a small train. It had a tapered waist and open lace back. I didn't know whether to be more angry about the exposed back or the plunging neckline that cut to my belly button.

"He's lost his fucking mind." I grabbed the hem of the dress. It wouldn't pull up past my hips. What the hell?

I pulled at the straps on my shoulders. They didn't budge.

The dress wasn't coming off.

I tugged again and then tried to rip it. Not only did it not tear, but it didn't even wrinkle as I wrestled with it.

Valen was going to be the absolute death of me if I did not strangle him first.

I strode out of the room, my sandals smacking down the hallway as I made for Valen's quarters. I held tight to the front of the jacket I had slipped on. I was going to try one of those curses on him before I pummeled him. He couldn't hit me back if he couldn't breathe.

My fist was clenched so tight there was no color in my knuckles as I slammed it into his door.

He greeted me with a smirk. "Mastered your spells already?" His eyes widened as he looked down at me. His smirk turned into a lazy smile. "I didn't think you would actually put it on."

"What is this and why won't it come off?"

The smug look on his face deepened, like he had been expecting me to go off. All the clothes I had worn bared some part of my skin, but this was ridiculous. And my back. My torn hideous back would be on show for everyone to see.

"It's your dinner dress," he said smoothly.

"I am going to be someone's dinner in this. Get this off me, right now."

His brow arched. "Ezra," he purred. "Let's at least eat first."

I opened my mouth. *Did he just?* Heat flooded down my neck. I closed my mouth so hard my teeth clacked. I flung my hand up, twisting it into the motion I had just mastered to open his stupid present.

Valen's lips parted. I could have sworn a little gasp escaped them.

He chuckled. "I should have told you those spells only work on mortals or lesser angels. They won't work on me."

He caught my hands against his chest the same time I shoved him back. He pulled me into his room and held me firm. The door slammed shut behind us, sending off alarms inside my head.

I had to stop forgetting that Valen wasn't a normal man. He wasn't a man at all. He was a predator that had successfully snared me.

"Just because we had a heart to heart doesn't mean you can pull this crap with me. Got it? I will kick your ass." I jerked my hands at my own expense. His grip wasn't painful, but it was hard enough that I wasn't going anywhere unless he willed it.

"This is a token of my gratitude for sharing such a vulnerable piece of yourself." His voice lowered, the pitch smooth as whiskey.

My face was on fire. From embarrassment or anger I didn't know which. But I was going to burn up if he didn't let me go and I didn't get out of this damned dress. "I will end you," I growled.

A grin cocked across his face. "I've taken down entire armies. What makes you think I can't take you?"

I jerked again, and this time he let my hands go. I poked his chest. He blinked quickly, looking down where my nail bit into his shirt. Like he had never been poked.

"Because you have no idea what I'm capable of."

His eyes narrowed. "I intend to find out."

He looked so much like Killian at this angle, with his cocked head and crooked grin. I wondered if he knew what he was doing. Scaring and confusing the hell out of me at the same time.

"You could get hurt."

The smile faltered and his eyes heated to a hungry amber. The idea of pain excited him.

The door behind us burst open. It slammed against the back of the wall with a loud bang, making me jump against Valen. Valen stepped past me, throwing me behind him. He rested one hand on the back of his neck, a finger slipping between the lining of his skin.

A tall, olive-skinned male with wavy black hair strode in. He had scruff covering his square chin and broad jawline. Dried blood encrusted his leathers and the handles of the double swords at his back. A thin smile crept through his puckered mouth as he surveyed Valen.

"You're a hard man to find." He craned his head to peer around Valen. The corner of his mouth curled high as he saw me. "And now I see why. Had I known I was interrupting, I would have knocked."

Valen let out an exasperated sigh. "You should knock regardless." He strode across the room, leaving us in full view of each other. The male was shorter than any of the other amorini I had seen and had bulking muscles. He winked at me when my eyes came back to his head.

"Aren't you supposed to be in Eimai Theós?" Valen snatched a jacket thrown across the back of the couch. "Ezra. Andras is our emissary." He motioned to us.

"Yes, brutal business. I finished the job early though." Andras ran a hand over the front of his chest and paused, his eyes widening. "Forgive me, Lady. I'm sure the sight of blood disgusts you."

Valen snorted, sliding his jacket on. "Save it for someone you stand a chance with."

I hadn't paid attention to what he had been wearing when I stormed in. But the black collared shirt and fitted pants suited Valen. Red satin lined the inside of his jacket, a subtle complement to my dress.

Andras feigned innocence, placing his hand on his chest. "You wound me."

"I don't have a weak stomach, if that is what you were implying," I said.

Andras looked absolutely disgusting in the gore, yet somehow he was... charming. I took the sheer cover Valen offered me.

"Valen." I gave him an incredulous look. He was really going to make me wear the dress to dinner.

I clutched my jacket tighter before accepting his. The one he held had a little clasp in the front that wouldn't leave me exposed. The sheer back was distorted enough with its lace weave that it would hide the marks on my back.

"That is good to hear. You would be in the wrong place otherwise. And this isn't all that bad either. None of it is mine." Andras ran a hand down his front, cleaning the blood with his open palm. "I had a run in with a chimera. Those nasty creatures have been popping up all over the southern ridge of Eimai Theós. Did you know their bite can paralyze you?"

"I have no idea what a chimera is," I said. I shrugged into the slip, trying to hide behind Valen while I did so.

"It's a mixture of a lion, goat, and serpent. With scales and fur and all sorts of horns coming out of its heads."

"Heads?" I hoped to never run into a chimera.

Valen rolled his eyes. I didn't think he was capable of such a human response.

"If we don't go now, Andras will talk your ears off," he said. Valen ran his fingers along the cropped portion of his head, pushing the stray curls into place. It wasn't as if he had to worry about looking unkempt.

"I actually barged in here for a reason." Andras trailed us out the door. He lengthened his stride until he flanked my other side. Another wink was thrown my way when Valen hissed.

"Raguel paid Maalik a visit while I was there. He wanted to know if anyone had spectered into their territory. When Maalik pressed him, Raguel said they have been finding old bleeds, scars. But he wouldn't divulge anything more."

Valen placed a hand on the middle of my back, slowing our pace. "Did he mention who or what could have spectered to leave such a scar?"

"Of course not." Andras scoffed. "Raguel won't share anything if he thinks the information will benefit him better. Whoever, or *whatever*, it is, he has a small force looking for it. There were two other archangels with him and three powers."

Tension crept into Valen's mouth. "Perhaps you should attend dinner. The Murder are here and they can carry the information back to Eurynomos. I doubt they have heard anything in their stay with us."

"I met with Diriel first. Raum was there with him." There was a bitter tang in Andras's words.

The name alone should have told me enough, but I was curious. "What is the Murder?"

"They are our brothers," Valen said. "They are Eurynomos's most elite warriors and the trio that helped us gain the alliance we now have with their court."

"Vicious bastards," Andras clarified.

"They are keras." Valen gave me a curious look.

A shudder ran down my spine. That was all I needed to know to understand how dangerous they were. It left a sour taste in my mouth that he could call creatures like them brothers.

Andras leaned forward and sniffed. I lurched into Valen's arm. "Why does she not have a smell?"

"Probably because I showered, you oaf. You could take notes." The blood covering him was putrid. It was more rank than human blood with a distinct metallic smell.

Andras threw back his head and let out a deep laugh that rolled like waves. "Be careful, little girl. With a tongue that sharp, some- one might want to cut it out."

Valen was quiet as we made our way through the tyre. His face was drawn and shadowed. Haunted. Worry laced his entire body.

Andras continued to drawl about his fight with the chimera, how he had severed one head while the other two tried to devour him. I listened out of politeness, but I was only half paying atten- tion as I tried to decipher what stressed Valen.

A sudden creeping sense of dread crawled along my skin. What if it was me they were looking for? I didn't know what a bleed or spectering was, but what if it was a cover? What if it was me?

Valen held me back before we entered the dining hall, motioning for Andras to go ahead.

"Don't," Valen said as I opened my mouth. "They cannot possi- bly know about you."

"But the angel—"

"Would have brought them straight to our door if it was you they're looking for. He knew me. He would have known where to send them. They would not be seeking answers from the other courts." He looked past me, into the candlelit room with its musical laughter. "They have no idea you're here."

That wasn't convincing enough. "Something has you worried."

He sighed, his eyes finally meeting mine. "This matter complicates things, but it is nothing to concern yourself with." The tip of his tongue ran over his lower lip. "What does concern you is the role you're going to play once we cross this threshold."

I didn't like the sound of that either. This conversation about the angels wasn't over, but I would let it rest for now. "What sort of role?"

"This is an intimate dinner. The cyn, the Murder, and a few of our select warriors and their guests are in attendance. While I cannot make you do anything, I strongly recommend that you behave and listen to any cues I give you."

My eyes narrowed. "What sort of role are we talking about?"

The demure smile I was coming to recognize slipped into place. "The one of a well-behaved woman who knows how to hold her tongue. As far as everyone knows, you are a new soul that I took for myself. One that is completely enamored with me."

I scoffed, and that turned into a laugh. "Fat chance."

His brow arched the same time one corner of his mouth rose higher. "Don't you want to pick up where we left off?"

"You're insufferable."

He slid a possessive hold around my waist, folding me against his side. The warmth of his breath caressed my ear as he leaned down and said, "The pleasure I could give you would be far from tortuous."

My hand curled into a fist.

"Behave, Ezra. Just for tonight."

The teasing look dancing in his eyes was the only thing that kept my mouth shut. *We can play later*, they said.

The room was set up like a large dining room. Tables clothed in dark red and gold platters were scattered about the room. Crimson curtains draped across the ceiling and down the walls, though there were no windows behind them. Bright firelight hung in the free spaces of the ceiling, giving the room a sunset glow.

Warm scents of meat and bread filled the air. I didn't realize how hungry I was until I caught a whiff.

The amorini were easy to distinguish from the humans. They were all strikingly and unnaturally beautiful. Some, whose arms were exposed, were branded with wings, and all of them had a gilded sheen to their skin that glowed in the firelight. Valen slowed with me as I turned the room.

It was the same as it had been in the market.

It was only males who had the strange beauty. Only males who toyed with mortal women and what were clearly mortal men. How had I not noticed it sooner?

"Where are the females?"

Valen looked about with me, confused until realization hit. "We are all male."

My heart slammed against the wall of my chest.

Oh. Oh!

Understanding slammed into place as the weight of the meeting hit. I had seen the amorini, but it hadn't clicked.

He touched my arm as a swell of panic rose in my chest. "It is not a terrible thing."

"You're telling me I am the only female angel. Ever?" My heart pounded. They had told me what could happen to me, but I hadn't understood what it really meant. I hadn't understood the why.

"It is why Jinn tried to press the issue of you having children. He thinks your chances would be better than anyone else. It changes nothing. I thought you knew."

Bile rose to the back of my throat. The swell of blood rushing to my ears drowned out the voices around us. "How do you know I can't have children? I mean, how do you know for sure? Just because Diriel can't see me with children in the future doesn't mean–" Fuck, what was I saying?

Pin her down. Jinn's nasty words rang through my head.

The soft squeeze of Valen's hand should have been reassuring, but it only made me more anxious. Seers could be wrong, couldn't they? Bishop had made it clear what would happen to me if I wasn't barren. Oh, God.

"Ezra," Valen said. "Look at me." Glittering rage danced within the light of his eyes. He cupped my chin, turning my face to his. "If it were ever discovered that you are not cursed, my promise to you stands. Not a soul will touch you unless you will it. And if anyone ever does, I will wipe them from existence."

I looked back and forth between his eyes. He was not playing with me now.

But Jinn said I could free them from their prison. Through me, they could have the army they needed to overthrow Heaven.

"Do you not want your freedom?" My voice cracked with tears.

His shoulders heaved with the deep breath he took. "I do." His thumb ran down the side of my neck as he withdrew his caress. "You are the weapon we have been waiting for. But you are also precious, Ezra. I will not have you abused for the sake of our lost souls."

He couldn't mean that. He was *Fallen.* "How long have you been here?"

"Time has no meaning," he evaded.

"You don't owe me anything. Why would you do this for me?"

"Stop asking why and be thankful." His words were clipped. A clear sign of dismissal. He cut me a sharp look before steering us in the direction of the table. "We can discuss this later," he added quietly.

I swallowed hard, but the whys didn't stop coming. Why would a fallen angel not try for their freedom? Why had Valen been so adamant about keeping me safe? Why should I trust him?

"What's to stop you from using Killian against me?" It was a question I hadn't wanted to ask, but I couldn't stop myself. I already wanted to pretend that was who he was.

The corner of his mouth split, flashing his teeth. "Where would the fun in that be? I don't need to look like your boyfriend to win you over." He turned, his eyes smoldering. "If given the chance, I will make you forget everyone you have ever lent your heart and bed to. But I will not trick you into it."

Heat curled in the pit of my stomach. I looked away. The power of his eyes was unbearable. It felt as if he saw right through me. Saw me. And if I kept looking at him, kept pressing, I would unravel right there on the floor.

I can handle this. The angels, what I was, Valen. All of it. I wouldn't be given anything I couldn't handle.

Valen's thumb circled the swell of my hip as he waited for me to catch my breath.

I recognized Jinn and Bishop at the table Valen directed us to. Andras leaned over the back of Jinn's chair, his hands moving rapidly as he spoke. Two other males were seated at the long table, covered in dense shadows. And then Andras leaned back to reveal a third person.

Elena Rivera.

CHAPTER THIRTEEN: FROM THE INSIDE OUT

Ezra

I would recognize her anywhere. How could I not when her face had been plastered all over the news for the last year. Elena, better known as Lane, and her boyfriend, Jey, had been in a brutal car accident that involved a deer and another SUV that had totaled their coupe. The driver of the SUV said Jey had been standing outside on the passenger's side, trying to get the door open before he hit them. It was a blind curve and there wasn't anything he could do to stop.

The crime scene specialists concluded that a deer had jumped in front of Jey's car, resulting in the first wreck. They suspected Lane's door had jammed, and he was trying to open it when the second wreck happened.

What made it hit big was that Lane was never found, but her blood had been all over the car. It was speculated that Jey had run into bad luck while trying to dump her body. His family, of course, insisted that wasn't true. There was even a debit on his account for a ring he had bought. Lover's quarrel? No one ever knew and their family never got any answers.

Lane sat on top of the table in front of the males, her legs crossed out from under a purple velvet dress. One of her feet was pressed against a darker male's chest. He ran his hands up her shin absent-mindedly, listening intently to whatever Andras was telling them.

The angels probably.

Lane and I had been polite, never friends, but I wanted to run to her. A familiar face, and to find her here, of all places. I wondered if she would even recognize me.

"Do not look too long," Valen said.

"At what?" I looked away from her, startled that I might have done something wrong by recognizing her.

"The two there are part of the Murder. As far as they're concerned, staring is an invitation. I'd rather not have to slit one of their throats tonight." He held us just on the outskirts so I couldn't distinguish their conversation. "The darker one is Orias, the one with white hair is Atticus, and the third, who isn't here, is Raum."

Orias was the one touching Lane. His russet brown skin looked copper against the fire. His hair was long, knotted in various braids and twists linked with gold rings. The sparse amount of clothing he wore left little to the imagination. He had a broad mouth that was too large for his face and showed off all his teeth when he spoke.

His companion, Atticus, who was of lighter complexion, stared coolly at Andras with furrowed white brows. Beneath them, his eyes were so blue they were nearly white, translucent even. The clench of his jaw made his face appear narrow and gaunt. He leaned back in his seat, two scarred hands laid out before him.

"You're looking again."

"Jealous?" I arched my brow, giving him a pointed look.

"Not in the slightest," he mused, his eyes roving over me.

Heat rushed to my face as I nodded to Orias. "You're all so..."

"Beautiful? Interesting?" he teased.

"Something like that."

A hum reverberated at the back of his throat. "Some of it is true, other appearances are glamour. Amorini and keras are more human in their appearances. Though, keras can shapeshift while we cannot."

I smothered the smile that tried to break free. Fear was quickly turning into fascination. Would I be able to shift forms?

"I wasn't looking at him, you know. It's the woman. I know her."

"Elena?"

I nodded. "She goes by Lane."

"She's been in Tartarus a few years."

I shook my head. "No. It was just last year that she disappeared."

"A day on Earth is a thousand here."

That couldn't be. That meant—"She has been stuck here for thousands of years?"

She didn't look as if she had aged at all. She was exactly as I remembered her, small and petite with smooth olive skin and cobalt wavy hair. I'd never actually seen her hair down. She always wore it in some braided fashion, either down her neck or wrapped in an intricate style on the back of her head. She had pastel blue eyes that had always caught me off guard.

"And to think she could have been dead this whole time," Valen said flippantly.

"Everyone thought her boyfriend killed her," I said through gritted teeth.

Fuck. I thought the pain was done assaulting me. A ripple of it moved down my arms. It was only every now and then I would get relief before it came back brutally, tearing against my body.

"What happened to him?"

"He was killed in the crash, so there wasn't proof. It was just speculated because of what happened." I swallowed. "There was too much blood." Everyone thought Jey was a murderer now. Their families would never find peace.

"At least he did not live to suffer those assumptions."

How could he be so cold? As if neither of their lives mattered.

His lips pursed together. "I do not recommend speaking to her. The Murder claim she is a dhampir. Whoever the woman Elena was before is long gone."

"Isn't that a sort of vampire?" How many things in fantasy books were true?

"A vampire with witch's powers." By the tone of his voice, he didn't sound certain. "It is rumored she drinks blood and has the ability to scry."

"But you don't believe them." I hoped that wasn't true. The idea of drinking blood was enough to make me sick.

He shrugged. "I believe she is something. Eurynomos is a court of torture, they do not treat mortals kindly. Elena is one of the longest standing they have had in their keep. Her ability to scry is unusual, but not enough that they would keep her alive." Meaning there was something else about her that was far more valuable.

The illusion Tartarus had been building shifted. For all its beauty, its wickedness did not falter.

Valen slid his hand along my back, turning me into his body. His fingers lightened as I bristled. Or maybe it was my sweat against his touch that bothered him.

Lane turned her head, catching my eye. Her light eyes widened. The movement must have alerted Orias, because he too looked in my direction. The hue of his eyes was as blue as hers, slightly darker around the edges. The strike of his gaze hit me right between the eyes like a bolt. It brought up a wave of nausea.

"You will learn to do as I tell you," Valen hissed as he guided me to one of the two open seats.

"This dress certainly hasn't helped." I grumbled, sitting in the seat he pulled out for me. Bishop pulled his leg in as I slid between him and the chair. Sitting next to him didn't thrill me either.

Valen leaned down, his tight curls brushing the side of my face before he turned his lips against my ear. "You are in that dress because every eye fell to you as soon as we entered the room." His fingers ran down the inside of my arm. "I want them to know that you're mine."

"I am my own," I countered, which earned me the glimpse of a smile. A flash of his teeth.

"And that will be our little secret." He nipped my earlobe before taking the seat beside me.

Chills burst across my skin.

The conversation faltered as I adjusted in my seat. Andras was telling the males that Maalik had sent his own men to track Raguel.

"Hello beautiful," Bishop said. Unlike before, his hair was loose from a braid, only tied at the top in a knot, leaving the rest of his hair to flow down his back. "I was beginning to think Valen would keep you locked up forever."

Valen poured wine from a decanter Lane slid across the table. An innocent gesture that allowed her a look in my direction. The red liquid ran thick as it pooled into the tall, stemmed glass.

I gave her a half smile. My heart fluttered when she suppressed one of her own. She *did* recognize me.

"We're still not friends," I said to Bishop, looking for a glass of my own.

"Behave," Valen warned.

I know he isn't talking to me.

Bishop set a freshly poured glass in front of me. "It's alright, Valen. I don't mind if she has a sharp tongue. And why are we not friends?" He watched me with the interest of a wild animal.

Valen scooped up the glass in front of me, bringing it to his nose. Whatever it was, it must have passed his inspection because he set it back before me.

"What are your theories on Raguel's hunt?" Valen asked, nodding across the table.

Orias shifted. "It is a power play more than likely, an attempt to shake the courts. Consider the last time Raguel made an appearance."

"You know why," I said to Bishop. I brought the glass to my lips. The wine was lush and full-bodied. I was long overdue for a drink.

A flash of white darted across Bishop's silver eyes. "It was a mistake I am willing to pay dearly for," he said suggestively. His voice was barely audible, and it was by the slight angle of his head toward me that I even heard him.

"Get in line," I said.

The corner of Bishop's mouth quirked. "I think you'll find I am more patient than most."

Was that a jab at Valen?

I never felt when he leaned in. I was surprised to see he had draped his arm on the back of my chair. "I don't appreciate that you would think any woman is a whore."

"Oh, Ezra. Do not get ahead of yourself." Venom trickled into his voice. "Such a term is an honor. Just as touch is as anticipated as conversation." Bishop ran his free hand across my knee. "Neither are as corrupt as your world has made it."

Heat blossomed beneath his touch, winding its way up my thigh. I wondered how much trouble I would be in if I hit him.

"Excuse me, lords," Lane said. She leaned from her perch on the table, her legs dangling between Orias's strong thighs. "I believe the food is ready. Perhaps your guest could assist me in bringing it out."

Valen was mid-sentence, something about the west border, when Lane cut in. "Andras mentioned chimera. I do not want them sneaking across our borders." He threw me a look. If he thought for one second that I wasn't going to leap at this opportunity, he was mistaken. He could fuss at me later.

"Oh, it would be a pleasure." I grit as I looked down at Bishop. He removed his hand with a smile.

The weight of six pairs of eyes followed me around the table where Lane waited. She lengthened her stride, her short legs carrying her fast enough that I had to stretch my own to keep pace.

We had hardly reached the table being set with food when she turned on her heel and hugged me.

"Fuck," she breathed. "Fuck."

"I know," I said. I squeezed her tighter. *Don't let Valen interrupt this.*

"What are you *doing* here?" She forced a smile. "I haven't seen a familiar face in so long."

"I can't believe you're alive," I said.

She rolled her eyes. "Not even Hell can get rid of me so easily," she said, half laughing. She touched the corner of her eye daintily. "How long have you been here?"

"The other night. I didn't think I would ever see you again. A year ago, you were all over the news."

Her mouth twisted. "I still have nightmares of that night." She nodded to the group of males. "Have they let you in on anything? That they kill adelfis—soulmates—and the other, the weaker," she scoffed, "is left behind to suffer."

I swallowed. "Yes." That part of the amorini had been easy to forget when they had been treating me kindly. "What happened?"

"One of them, Frei, he's the one that shot me." She touched her hand over an old scar, a perfect straight line right over her heart. It stood out against her skin like a lightning strike. "Jey was driving us to a cabin when a deer sprung in the road. And then an arrow hit me." She looked at me with wide eyes. "It all happened so fast that I didn't know what had happened until I saw the feathers sticking out of my chest."

"They said he was trying to get you out, or move your body, before the other car came," I said slowly.

She bit her lip. It was a nervous tick. Her full lips would be raw if she kept at it. "Frei told me that. Told me that everyone thought Jey was a murderer. He was trying to get me out of the car, but the door was jammed and my seat belt was locked."

"Why didn't he let you die? I mean, if it's you he was aiming for."

"When the deer jumped, it threw off his shot and his arrow missed my heart by an inch. I think he knew about the truck and that Jey would die. He grabbed me a second before it hit us. He wanted to make my life a living Hell so that's where he brought me." She touched beneath her eyes again, trying desperately to refrain from crying. "I'm sorry. I didn't think I would be so overwhelmed seeing you."

"Please don't apologize for that. It's horrible what happened to you." I didn't know what else to say. My heart ached for her.

She cleared her throat. "Is Valen the one that took you?"

I caught Valen's eye. Oh, he was going to let into me later. Even this distance across the room, I could read it across every inch of his face. He was pissed.

"He is."

"It's rare to see him with anyone, much less wearing his color."

"What do you mean?" I asked, turning back to her. I rubbed my neck and pinched down the back of my arm. I tried to make it look casual as I attempted to chase away the pain that was rearing its head once more. Now was not the time.

"Red is Valen's signature. Everyone thinks Bishop is the worst, but I think Valen has him beat. Fire and ice, the two of them."

A fresh wave of chills took the place of the old ones, raising the hairs on my arms. So, that's what he meant by claiming me.

"Has he hurt you?" Lane asked, as if she sensed my discomfort.

I wouldn't tell her that he nearly hit me. Not after he had apologized for it. "No." I cleared my throat. "No, he hasn't. I don't think he means to."

"They were made for love and that is how they get you. They're all kind at first. Even Frei was apologetic for what he'd done. Until he wasn't."

The warning doesn't go without notice. But she didn't know that I was of value to them. Didn't know that they needed me. I wanted so badly to tell Lane what had happened. I wanted to tell her about what they thought I was. How would she react? I knew her, but could I trust her?

I opened my mouth and shut it. I would tell her eventually, but not now. It was too dangerous with so many ears listening in. And as much as I wanted to believe she was the spunky sweetheart from before, I couldn't discount that she had changed.

Where Lane had always been lean, she was now cut with muscle, the sharp look in her eyes now double-edged. And there was something else. Something I couldn't put my finger on that warned of danger.

Did she really drink blood?

She passed me a covered tray. "Don't eat. If you're hungry, wait until you're back in your quarters. This food is not for us."

I slid my hand beneath the bottom. "What is it?"

"You don't want to know." She juggled two additional platters in one hand and picked up a decanter of wine with the other. "Come on. If we take any longer, they'll come looking for us."

The crackle of a fire burst across my arms. I clenched the platter with a white-knuckled grip and begged to God, or whoever heard me all the way from Tartarus, not to drop the damn tray. It wasn't the pain heating beneath my skin that had startled me.

It was anger cracking through the air. I looked between the males, trying to peg which one it was coming from. My (*fuck, I hated thinking of any of them as mine*) cyn were throwing daggers to the Murder.

"Is this your newest pet?" Orias questioned as I set the tray down beside him. Lane slid part of her load to his other side before rounding the table to Andras and Jinn.

Pet?

"Beautiful, isn't she?" I turned to Valen's voice.

"I like her eyes," Orias said. "Would you be willing to part with her? I know we selected six from your harem, but she would make a nice addition."

Orias hadn't tried to touch me, but I flinched when he looked at me. I couldn't get back to my seat between the cyn fast enough.

Bishop chuckled. "We would not." His eyes followed me as I sat down.

Valen turned out his hand. I took it and sparks shot up around my wrist. Before I could jerk my hand away, he pushed our hands beneath the table. Only when the sparks died did he let me go.

"What of her eyes then?" Orias rested his chin on his knuckles.

A sharp chill ran down the center of my back. *What the fuck?*

"Her eyes are one of my favorite things," Valen said. He ran a finger along the side of my face.

My fingers curled at my side. He cocked his chin a hair, his brow rising.

Don't, he mouthed when I looked at him.

Don't what? Snap at him or hit him?

"She does not need them both to please you," Orias said. He sucked the back of his teeth, leaning back in his chair. He didn't even look at Lane as she propped herself on top of the table and lifted the lid covering raw meat.

It was fresh. Blood welled around the flesh in a dark red pool. Flesh that bore the tattoo of rose and dagger. My stomach turned. These were people. They were eating people.

"Mm, but I do love the look she gives me when I am fucking her," Valen said.

I blinked away the horror swelling inside my chest. Of the nausea that twisted my gut.

An insult was on the tip of my tongue. Valen slid his hand to the back of my neck and squeezed. It shot sizzling heat down the back of my spine. It coiled into my arms, threatening to unfurl into something greater.

Lane gave me a subtle shake of her head. I swallowed a sharp breath of air.

Be quiet, got it. I let my eyes convey how pissed I was instead.

"If you keep looking at me like that, I'll fuck you right here on the table," he said.

Valen would get an earful later.

Bishop chuckled. "Let's not rush dessert before dinner."

Orias's scowl lifted as his gaze shifted to something above my head. "Welcome."

"Forgive me," a smooth voice said.

There was an invitation beneath the pardon, one of authority. I knew that voice before he leaned down and placed a kiss on the side of Bishop's face. Quiet greetings were exchanged, and he turned, his sapphire eyes sliding past me to Valen.

Like a shadow, he moved behind me, his hand curling over the top of my chair as he kissed Valen too. Wisps of smoke coiled across my shoulders. I couldn't breathe. My gut feeling had been right. I was going to be sick.

"No apologies necessary, Raum," Valen said, his full lips smiling.

And then, the stranger from the library looked down at me. I had thought Jinn wanted to hurt me, still suspected it with Bishop wanting to do unspeakable things, but it was *his* feral gaze that shook me. Raum was someone to follow through with his threats. I couldn't control the way my breath came faster or the way sweat broke across my skin. Even as Valen's hand dropped from my neck to my arm, sliding to my hand again in question, could I stifle the fear of the male before me.

"I asked for her eyes, but they will not part with them," Orias pouted.

The stranger's sapphire gaze passed over me to the other Murder. *Say a word and I'll gut you*, they had said. "Orias, you are greedy. Let the cyn have their fun with her first." He smirked, turning to Bishop. To him he said, "You will have to forgive us for leaving. I would prefer to be home before Raguel catches Baal's ear."

Brothers, Valen had said. Raum and the cyn were close. I had suspected it, but God, I wish it hadn't been true. I felt like I was going to be sick. These males were evil. Valen was evil. He had to be if he associated with such monsters. Raum had all but admitted to assault in the library and Orias wanted my eyes because they were *blue*. The keras were monsters and the amorini welcomed them with open arms.

Atticus reached across the table, his long white fingers delicately picking up a piece of meat. His pale eyes seared into me as he peeled flesh from muscle and stuffed the thin piece of skin into his mouth. His eyes narrowed.

Was it growing hotter? My skin was no longer casually warm, its temperature increasing by the second. My chest grew tight, like a giant weight had been hefted on top of it.

"How is Baal these days?" Bishop asked.

I curled my hands into fists as my vision tapered. I needed to get out of here. I needed to get away from Raum. I needed to get somewhere safe.

"Tired," Raum answered. "The thirst for blood has gone dry in his mouth."

"Perhaps someone should take the weight of the crown from his head." Bishop ran a finger across the top of his glass. It sang beneath his touch.

Raum tsked. "Such talk is treason."

"Baal is not my cyn," Bishop said with a smirk. The music of the glass stopped as he picked it up and held it out for the demon to take.

There was nothing angelic in that pristine face. "But he is ours." He took the glass and extended it to the Murder. "To Baal's long life," he turned, casting his gaze upon the cyn, "and to yours, my brothers. May your power remain and your rule thrive."

Everyone but Andras raised their glass. He folded his arms, staring blatantly at Raum.

The graze of an unfamiliar touch brushed across the side of my face. I met the glow of sapphire eyes as I looked up. The scorch of his finger burned its way into my cheek.

And then the pain hit me like lightning. I reached out blindly, my fingers curling and locking like talons. Wine spilled across the table as my back seized, thrusting my arms forward. My spine straightened on its own, twisting my head back so I caught Raum's hateful, glittering stare. My vision turned gray and then everything went numb. The tingling started at my fingertips and spread up my arms, rolled over my shoulders and down, down, down. An inferno funneling into my very core.

I thrust from the table between the torment, shoving hard enough it forced Raum stumbling back. Shards of glass blew across the room as his glass fell from his hand.

"I'm sorry," I gasped. "I have to go."

The room spun and my stomach churned. I was going to vomit. I stumbled to the side, not wanting to hurl on anyone. The nausea crashed in waves. It hit me and then stopped and hit me again. I took hold of someone's arm to right myself. The door, the door. Where was it?

The entire room spun. Lane, who now stood on top of the table, spun like a ballerina, and the faces around her became one giant ghastly blur. The faces at the neighboring tables open-mouthed. Giant holes in their faces full of rows of sharp teeth.

I took another step, forcing my eyes to the ground, and the marble floor crashed against my knee. *Get up!*

I reached again, latching onto another arm as I was hoisted to my feet.

"I've got you," Valen said.

"We have to go. Now," I forced out. It was hot. Too hot.

I need to get out of here. I need to get out of this skin.

"Try to stand up. At least until we make it out of the room. From there I'll carry you," he whispered in earnest, slipping his arm around my waist and spinning me to the door.

"Has Vélos found another witch?" Raum called.

Hurry. Faster!

The doors opened as Diriel stepped into the room. He took one look at me, and his eyes went wide. He stepped back, holding the door open.

The pain that had been worming its way through my body finally exploded. It reached out like tendrils, igniting every part of me. I screamed. It was a sound that tore from my throat so violently it could be seen jolting through the air. It cracked apart the air in front of us like a seam, breaking our path apart.

The stone floor slammed into my knees as I fell forward. Valen gripped me harder and the fire that had been building within me unfurled. It ripped the breath from my lungs without leniency. Sweat burst across my skin.

"I can't breathe," I managed. God, it hurt. Everything hurt. I felt like I was on fire.

"I've got you," Valen said. He hoisted me into his arms. I was floating.

Every eye was on me, their faces turning into one massive blur as he carried me away. I cried out as the thing festering inside of me pulsed again. My arms cramped, my fingers stiffening once more.

Valen cursed under his breath and dropped to his knees, splaying me on the ground in front of him. "I'm going to pull your wings."

"Don't." I took hold of his wrist, clamping down for dear life.

"They're killing you," he snapped. "I did not save you to rot. They are burning you from the inside out. This is what I wanted to prevent." His eyes were so gold, burning with the intensity of the heat beneath my skin.

I tried to hold his gaze, to convey this wasn't what I wanted, but the pain seized me with a vengeance. It was too late for that. This thing inside me had taken hold and refused to let go. It wasn't going away this time. It ripped through me and tore through my ears in the form of sharp ringing.

Diriel cursed as he came into view. A dark shadow full of shifting rage.

"Cut her dress," Valen commanded. To me, he said, "Deep breaths." He lifted my face between his palms so my eyes would meet his. Fiery, angry orbs looked back.

I gripped his shoulders as he pulled me forward and the cool kiss of steel slid down the back of my dress. There was a slight pause before the knife was replaced with Diriel's hard fingers. He worked a quick pattern down the length of my spine, back up across my shoulders and elbows, and back again, dancing across my scars.

Fuck, it hurt. It hurt so much more now that they were holding onto me, the fire growing, billowing in my bloodstream.

"What are you doing?" Tears leaked down my cheeks, and I pulled myself closer to Valen in an attempt to shy from Diriel's touch. "Whatever it is, stop." *It hurt.* Why didn't they understand how much it hurt? The pain answered to them, pressing harder against the underside of my skin. Everything *burned.*

"Releasing your wings from your bones," Diriel murmured. I imagined his brow drawn as tight as his voice. Pinched with con-centration. The pattern made its way down each of my arms before coming around to my back again, where he repeated the process.

Valen closed his eyes as Diriel's touch hardened. Heat rushed from his palms into my face. It was different than what was already coursing through me. It numbed the pain by tangling with it. If this was power, it was an incredible feeling. I felt *alive*. A smile fell over my face as the rush took hold and the pain dissipated. I lit up with a nonexistent fire that burned and tongued my backside, soothing me until I relaxed against Valen.

As easy as the pain was stripped away, it came back twice as hard. It chased the euphoria and slashed into my arms, down every vertebra.

I cried out. Something shifted, sliding against my bones, scraping together like two fine edges. Fresh beads of sweat broke out across my stretched skin. The heat moving through me melted my skin, darkening it until it flaked off into black chunks.

Diriel slid his fingers beneath the veil of skin and shoved his thumbs against my shoulder blades. I screamed again. Blood streamed down my arms and chest. I could feel the flow move down my back, seeping into the fabric of my dress. I was going to die.

"Look at me," Valen said.

I jerked my attention to his command. Whatever was tearing me apart belonged to me. I could feel it then. I gripped Valen's forearms and tried to pull myself closer to him, pushing away from the havoc that was being wrought. Valen's eyes widened. I followed his gaze and realized I wasn't just pulling closer to him but pulling my wings out. Dark feathers ripped through the fine layer of ash that had become my skin. A mangled sound tore from my throat, and I fell forward as my wings broke free. His hands dropped to my waist as my weight nearly forced him to his back, his fingers sliding through the blood as he tried to get a good hold of me. His touch brought him close to my torn flesh and I cried out, fresh tears springing from my eyes.

The pain was so great that I couldn't stop shaking. I caught my breath only to scream again. My arms were wide open, revealing red muscle and ivory bone. What had they done to me? I felt air where I shouldn't, inside my back across my spine and ribs. The wings that had ached now burned like a hot iron. They were so heavy that I couldn't even lift them. Not that I wanted to. I wanted to lay there and die.

"She's beautiful," Diriel breathed.

Valen pushed back my damp hair, his eyes moving beyond my head. "Yes, she is." There was admiration in his voice. He leaned forward as I moaned and pressed his lips to my sweat-slicked forehead. He held onto me, adjusting his grip as he sat up so he could better accommodate my weight. It was unbearable. The pain. Was this how all angels were made? Through blood and agony.

Valen looked down at me and stroked my face. The ferocity in his eyes should have frightened me, but instead I felt safe. I didn't know a word to describe the way he looked at me, but whatever it was, was beautiful.

"I'm dying," I rasped.

Valen smirked. "You're alive."

My vision darkened and lightened. I think he said something about needing to move me and I groaned in response. There was too much noise to really hear his words. Voices, whispers, and murmurs spouted off behind him. The rest of the court had followed us out.

I could feel the pressure of Valen's touch as he adjusted his grip once more, but I couldn't experience anything other than the throbbing pain that continued to assault me. I gripped the front of his shirt on impulse. I couldn't move. I was afraid that a fraction of effort would finish me off. Seconds before, dying sounded quite nice, but I couldn't give in yet. All of the pain was because I had wings. That alone was something worth living for.

"Ezra," Valen said. I lifted my eyes to his.

My lower lip jutted out as I nodded.

"Good girl," he murmured as I reached for his neck and he slid his arms beneath my legs. My torn flesh protested, forcing another pitiful moan from my throat. Agony pierced deep within my gut when he lifted me. The room darkened and my head fell back. Just before I lost my vision completely, I caught sight of Raum at the front of the crowd. Smoke curled around his form. Then he was gone.

CHAPTER FOURTEEN: LIKE A MOTH TO FLAME

Valen

I laid her on her stomach, splaying her arms and wings gently across the bed and cleaning her wounds. It had been a long time since I'd seen a fledgling. I was careful with her wings, cleaning each feather of blood and ash that still clung to them. It was an intimate gesture to touch another's wings and, though she didn't know that yet, I didn't want to insult her.

How fucking beautiful.

I pushed her hair from her face and just looked. Who would have thought our salvation would come in the form of a woman? I promised no harm would come to her, but that did not mean she couldn't be convinced to do our bidding once she was comfortable enough.

The moment was short lived when reality set in. Word would spread like wildfire, and there was nothing I could do to stop it.

I cursed.

"We knew this would happen eventually," Diriel said. He wiped his hands with a wet cloth, cleaning the blood from them.

"We were to have more time. She is not prepared for what will happen. We are not prepared." It had been foolish to think we could have prolonged her reveal. A couple of days was not enough time for her to adjust. None of what had happened should have. Not so soon. I cursed again.

"Of course we are. That's why we swore an oath to her, isn't it? Ignorant as it was." Diriel ground his teeth before running a hand over his face.

I scoffed. That too had been a foolish thing, but it was too late now.

"Raum saw," Diriel said.

The weight of what was to come finally set in with that single name. "Yes." I couldn't say anything else. The utter rage that coursed through me that he had touched her, marking her as his would-be victim, set me on edge.

The keras wasn't cyn, but he might as well be for the way he ruled Eurynomos out from under Baal. The general couldn't have known what Ezra meant to us. It could have been as simple as wanting to please Orias. But as soon as he entered the room, he had homed in on her. The swift kiss he had placed on Bishop's cheek and then mine had not drawn his attention from her. The force of his power had been all over her, as if he had been looking for something.

"Have you ever seen one with black wings?" Diriel nodded to her.

I traced the outline of one of her primaries. "No," I said slowly. "What does it mean?"

Diriel shook his head. "I do not know. Her mystery continues to evolve. And her path is hard to decipher. It shifts constantly."

"There must be some sort of direction."

"The only thing that is clear is she holds a significant amount of power. Every path leads to chaos and it—" He shook his head again. "It changes by the second. I can't even grasp a thread of her future." Frustration made his voice taut.

"What is the will of her chaos?"

Diriel looked at me sideways. "She sides with us, but it is not without a slaughter. One second kingdoms fall and another it is worlds. I've never seen anything like it. Not even the Fall was this complicated."

A knot formed in my stomach. It wouldn't do us any good if we lost half of our men to win.

"Can she save us?"

Vélos.

Diriel nodded. "Yes, but—"

Bishop's presence swept into the room. The force of his rage rattled the doors and shut Diriel's mouth from whatever he was about to say. Smoke curled in his wake as he entered in a fury. It wasn't until he laid eyes on Ezra that the flick of ferocity shuddered into nothing. His nostrils flared as his hand ran over the top of his head.

"The Murder have extended their stay until morning," he said.

"That'll make Jinn happy." Diriel looked past Bishop, as if he expected the cyn to come through next. "Where is he?"

"Keeping the Murder occupied," Bishop said irritably. "It won't be long before they come sniffing for her." His nose curled when he said it, like the idea of the whole thing left a bad taste in his mouth.

"You should have sent them on their way. Raguel will be in Eurynomos soon and their absence will be questioned." I looked to the door, half expecting them to come in.

"It is better that they remain. So long as they are within our keep,

Baal does not know about her."

I could hardly fathom why the Murder wouldn't have run straight to Baal. But Bishop's confidence eased my immediate concern. I hoped that meant he had addressed our men and Ezra's reveal could still be done in our own timing.

"You should have spectered her away immediately," Bishop growled.

"That could have permanently damaged her. Ashes, it could have broken her wings and left her lame at the rate her power was flaring."

Bishop's sharp teeth flashed. "We don't need her for her wings."

His gaze lowered to Ezra once more, first narrowing in scrutiny and then softening in admiration despite his words. Hunger heated behind his eyes. His desire was so palpable it made my skin crawl.

I wondered if he had meant his promise when he swore to keep her safe.

"How did our men take it?" I asked, trying to refocus my rising anger.

"They have questions. We are lucky this didn't happen before the entire court. Once she has recovered, we will need to present her. Properly. As we should have done day one."

Diriel's eyes shifted from their natural color to white and back again as he struggled to grasp anything tangible that would tell him what we could expect from her. The fact that chaos surrounded her was not abnormal. All nephilim had the unfortunate fate of being doomed or being someone else's downfall. It was the price of being a god. What didn't make sense was the shift in which her life continued to change.

A needle of pain pricked within my chest. I brushed the front of my shirt absentmindedly, but it only amplified, turning into a numbing pain that made my fist clench.

"It is done now," I grumbled.

No sooner had the words left my mouth did Ezra stir. Her fists clenched and she let out a burst of breath as her entire body lit up.

The faint orange glow emanating from her skin wavered like flickering flames. Sweat pooled at the small of her back. A stain spread from beneath her body as her temperature increased. Her hair, that had been nearly white-blonde, was now a reddish gold. The same russet sheen that colored her hair spread along her wings instead of the blue hue they had been moments before.

"Wait," Diriel said.

I brushed my fingers down her arm. The glow twisted up my fingertips. In the same moment, the needling within my chest burrowed deeper, straining to get to my heart. I pulled my hand away, holding it in my other. The light receded, taking the strange feeling with it. The soft hum at our connection shuddered through me. It was the same note when I pulled her out of the water. It'd nearly blown me off my feet then. I knew what to expect whenever we touched now that I was better prepared for it. But it never ceased to take my breath away.

I'd never felt anything like it. Even now, I couldn't wrap my mind around the source of power surrounding her.

"Seraphim don't glow," Bishop said.

"Not like that," I remarked. Seraphim burned and had the ability to control fire. They breathed flame. But none of them glowed.

Bishop ran a finger over her shoulder, tracing the outline of her wing, but not touching it. No curl of light met his touch. No sparks ignited.

I was the only one she answered to.

I was the only one who had heard her call.

It felt like something took hold of me, grabbing me by the throat. It clenched so hard I thought I would be sick. I forced it down, steadying my breath and doing everything I could to keep the walls around my mind in check.

It wasn't just her power that was starting to manifest.

The thought forced its way into my mind, and I shoved it out. I did not want to consider what it meant because it wasn't true. It was impossible. But so was she.

The tattered flesh of her back was already mending together. Only the lower part of her shoulders was still exposed, white bone peeking out. She was healing quickly. Faster than I would have expected from a halfling.

She wasn't just a nephilim.

I moved closer to her, like a moth to a flame.

We would have to train her quickly, before any doubt of where she belonged could settle in. I doubted Diriel's vision was false, but there was the small possibility she would hold onto her faith and seek out Heaven. She needed to choose our side. Training her in our ways would ensure she fell.

What a shame it will be when her light fades.

A soft whimper escaped her lips. She reached out blindly in her sleep.

Bishop never took his eyes off Ezra. He was sat forward, crouched on the balls of his feet, his hands clasped tightly between his thighs. But I saw the tremble of his grip and knew that it was taking everything in him not to touch her.

CHAPTER FIFTEEN: POWERFUL, BEAUTIFUL MONSTER

Ezra

I sat upon a brazen throne at the head of a long set of stairs leading to an open floor of red tile. At the base of the stairs were two stone dragons, their wings spread and mouths ajar like they would come to life breathing flame. Before them, filling that giant room, were what could only be demons. Their black eyes and wicked grins looked up at me, and one by one they kneeled.

I walked down to them. Long, leathery black wings topped with curved talons scraped the ground behind my steps. Red hair fanned across my breasts, replacing the white gold it had been before. I rolled my shoulders back, flexing my wings wide as a rush of lava cascaded past my bare feet.

"Let this be the beginning of a new age! Your freedom is here!"

Fire lit the room in answer to the roar of the demons, flames climbing as high as the walls. Their glory was scarlet. They whorled together, raging and then all at once the demons, and all of the sound, were swallowed up.

The suddenness of it forced me to my knees. I dug my fingers into the stones. That image, that hadn't been me. That could not have been me. I shut my eyes to be rid of it, but vivid it remained. It was worse than what I had seen through Diriel. I could feel the power. *My power.*

Out of the darkness came the singular clapping of an applause.

"Well done," a voice said. "I knew you had it in you."

I jerked my head up. Thick fog rolled across the room, drawing the darkness closer. The sound stopped abruptly as he came into view. I noticed the purple hue of his eyes first. He was just as terrifying as I remembered.

"Do you see what I tried to protect you from?"

"You can't be here. As soon as Valen finds out—" He had rescued me the first time; he would come again. I looked about the empty room full of fog and darkness. The only light emanated from the angel.

"What? What will he do?" He laughed, the music of his voice winding through the air. "Where do you think we are?" He turned his body, surveying the expanse. When he looked at me, his eyes went cold. "Right now, you are in a sleep so deep that not even a trumpet could wake you should the whole sky come crashing down."

I swallowed. Can you die in a dream? I pinched my palm with my nails. I couldn't feel it. "What do you want?"

He pointed at me. "But I think you knew that already," he said, his mouth spreading into a grin too wide for his face. "I think we got off on the wrong foot. I'm Ariel, you're Ezra. *Now*, we are acquainted properly."

"You tried to kill me."

He rolled his eyes. "Yes, well you see why. Don't you? That," he pointed behind him, "all of that fire and brimstone is the destruction for mankind. You can't blame me for wanting to spare the world."

"That's not me." I curled my fists tight. "And if you knew anything about me, you would see that." I looked around, but the room was clear of everything. Even the dragons were gone, and the steps. There was no weapon within reach.

The angel held up both hands. "It does not matter that you went to church and sang praises. It doesn't matter that you have always been a kind person. None of your life matters because of what you are. You were wicked the moment you were conceived."

His words were a heavy blow to the chest. I wasn't wicked. I wasn't before and I wasn't now. Hot tears stifled the retort building in my throat. I couldn't speak. This hateful creature couldn't be an angel.

"Oh, don't cry. I know how upsetting it must be, but I am here to remove the weight from your shoulders." He touched his chest, smiling softly. "I admit I was a bit too rash last time. Let me take you from this place and right things as they should have been a long time ago. Please."

Right? This *wasn't* right. Ariel was going to murder me because my ancestor, not even my real father whoever the fuck he was, had mated with a woman. I was being held accountable for crimes I never made. Crimes that shouldn't even be named such.

Warmth spread over my body as I rallied my tears. The damp stains dried and what was left of the droplets went up in steam. "You are not from God," I gritted.

His eyes darkened. "Oh, but I am, you little *monster*. Do you know what will happen if you don't come with me? Famine, plague, disease. The entire world will die because of you. Do you think you are worth more than billions of lives?"

"You are a liar." Flame crackled at my fingertips. Bits of spark and ash flitted in the air around me. If I could not control my fire, I would become an inferno. I tugged on the chord of heat within my chest and the fire laced up my arms. If I was aflame, he couldn't hurt me. Ariel would never get the chance to touch me again.

I knew how to wield the fire without instruction. I gripped it like a rope and twisted it around my wrist. The end of the chord snapped through the air, cracking like a whip.

His smug face twisted into a snarl then changed again to one of the humble creatures he claimed to be. Nothing so easily manipulated could be just.

"Ah, that I am not. I confess it does hurt to do Heaven's work at times, but it is for the good of all Creation. Come peaceably and your death will be swift." His eyes followed the end of my flame.

"There is nothing you can ever say that will convince me to let you kill me. I have done nothing wrong."

Ariel clenched his fists. The light around him grew brighter and seized my fire with a violent grip. It snapped the flames away just as I pulled my hand free of them. His power cut through the rest of my flames, blinding me.

"Enough! You are the downfall of humanity."

I'll prove it to you! Let me prove it! I couldn't force the words out. Not when scalding light was forcing its way down my throat.

Ariel's light grew so bright it burned. It burned more than the flames that belonged to me. My legs fell out from under me, crushing my knees into the hard ground. But not before something cut against my forehead.

Dirt caked the inside of my mouth and white scorching heat

blew my hair back. I clawed to the surface of the light, screaming until my eyes flew open and my entire body lit with flame.

It funneled out of my mouth. It licked its way through the scorching light, throwing it back until there was enough space for me to breathe. To stand. I screamed until my fire burned Ariel away, until the only thing left was darkness.

The darkness slowly lifted as my eyes adjusted. An orange hue cast the shadows back as the flames looped and coiled around my body.

"Cool your fire, Ezra. I'm not going to hurt you."

I knew that voice.

I recognized the room settling around me with its backdrop of black mountains and large hearth. Through the gray smog that filled the room, I could see the outline of plants and white linens.

"You're safe."

I whipped my head to the voice.

It was *him*, not Ariel.

His palms were turned out, but every line in his body was rigid. I could smell the uncertainty on him as clear as the sage that clung to his skin. What did an angel have to fear from me? Powerful, boastful creatures.

Wicked monsters.

"He's here." Was that my voice? She sounded strange. Older.

The male cocked his head. Valen. "There is no one here but us."

I turned, searching for Ariel in the darkness. I could feel the torment of his light crawling across my skin.

Smoke simmered on the bed with its tangled white sheets. I ran my hands over the tops of my thighs. Cool satin met my touch. Someone had changed me into a slip.

"What are you doing here?" was the only question I could remotely form that encompassed the feelings curling in the pit of my stomach. I'd burned through the bed trying to flee from Ariel.

"Your power rattled the room. I was trying to wake you."

Unease joined the tension in my gut.

A jolt shot through me as I caught movement in the giltwood mirror that stood across the room. The reflection moved the same time I did. I took a step forward and the breath I'd been holding whooshed out of me. I knew the stranger in the mirror was me and yet, she was completely terrifying.

Wings.

I had wings.

Lashing pain no longer assaulted me, but I was sore. The weight of my wings made me tremble. They were massive. So dark they were almost vanta, soaking up any bit of light the night had left as an offering.

Those are the first things I noticed. The second was the iridescent sheen of my skin beneath crusted bits of ash and burn scars. The glow was not from my fire that curled in on itself, disappearing into smoke, or the light of the moon. It was my skin, now painted with the gilded sheen of angels and demons.

My strawberry-blonde hair held a darker shade of copper, but it was still gold, still mine. I touched a strand next to my face.

My breath hitched. She was nearly the woman in my vision. I reached tentatively to the feathered wing on my left. A broken sob escaped me. I'd missed it before, but my wings were entirely feathered. There was no membrane, no hooked claws coming out of the top. I wasn't the monster Ariel claimed me to be. I wasn't anything like the woman in my nightmare.

"You are remarkable," Valen said. He circled behind me, stopping a breadth from my shoulder. "Beautiful," he said to my reflection.

I couldn't breathe. I clutched my chest as I tried to inhale, but it wouldn't come. I shuddered as Valen placed a hand beneath my elbow to steady me. I shut my eyes and inhaled through my nose. The pounding of my blood sounded like a war drum, growing louder with each passing second.

"In the visions, I was a monster."

Valen was still there when I opened my eyes. The look of awe had not wavered. He tipped his head down, casting his face in a shadow so only the reflective glint of his eyes were visible.

"There is nothing monstrous about you. You are something Heaven fears because you are too perfect. Do not, for one second, let doubt creep into your mind and say you are not worthy. I can smell it on you, Ezra."

I swallowed as I met his eyes in the reflection. My heart hammered faster. *Heaven fears me.* The shape of my wings changed nothing.

"Heaven wants me dead," I choked. When did I start crying? Tears coated the back of my throat, making my voice thick. "Ariel was here. He tried to take me for... this!" I threw out my arms, inadvertently thrusting my wings out too. I flinched and wrapped my arms around myself. Burnt skin drifted to the floor.

His expression darkened. "The angel?"

"Yes."

There was a definite pause, but Valen kept whatever it was to himself. He shook his head. "Nightmares tend to be more real here, but he cannot touch you." He ran a finger under my chin, turning my face to his. "Look at me."

"They would try to kill me," I choked. I couldn't get everything else out. How unfair it was to be judged for something I had no control over. How fucking painful it was that I had lost everyone because of what I was. Either I had drawn bad luck to them like a plague or someone had killed them. That's what had happened to them, wasn't it? I was the reason everyone died. I was the monster Ariel said would condemn the entire world.

"And they will fail. Again and again. Heaven will never lay a hand on you."

"But, what if he is right? What if I am a monster?"

"Then you show them how sharp your claws are and how fierce your bite is." Swirls of darkness entered Valen's eyes as they lit up, burning like golden jewels. The grip on my chin sharpened as his fingers turned pointed. "Look at you." He twisted my face back to the mirror. "What is so monstrous about perfection?" His grip softened as his talons retracted. Beads of blood welled against my skin and, in the time that I blinked, they were gone.

I shook so badly my feathers ruffled. I shut my eyes to suppress the wave gathering against me.

Monster. Beautiful. Powerful. My thoughts cajoled.

I looked back at my reflection. The woman I was lay just beneath the surface of the angel.

I was terrifying, but Valen was right. I wasn't a monster. There was nothing hideous in the way my wings soaked up the light, or how my skin glimmered beneath the ash.

I ran my hands across my shoulders, swiping away the gray flesh to reveal iridescent pink skin.

"At the rate your power is manifesting, you'll be completely healed in another day or two. After that, I can show you how to put your wings away."

I glanced at Valen. I wasn't convinced he couldn't read my mind with the way he always answered my thoughts.

My chest fluttered. I was relieved I wouldn't be marred after all of this. I tested the weight of my wings, lifting the appendages that felt as if they had always been there. At my back's groan in protest, I let them fall back to the floor. I liked the idea of being able to hide them when I needed to.

I have wings.

Ariel was a nightmare, nothing more. Still, an impending dread shrouded me. There were too many shadows. So many places for Ariel to hide.

"Ariel burned me with his light, in the dream. I thought this might be from him." I ran a hand across my burnt wrist.

"Your burns are from your wings. Though, if it puts your mind at ease, I will search the room." Valen brushed the back of his knuckles down my arm.

For peace of mind, I nodded.

Valen moved about the room like an apparition. Parts of him flitted within the shadows, while in the light he remained whole. It sent shivers down my spine.

I waited, tense and ready to flee, as he disappeared into the adjoining rooms. When he returned, he nodded, telling me it was all clear. A shudder ebbed through me, exiting through the soles of my feet as the last of the adrenaline faded from my bloodstream.

"Thank you."

Valen ran his knuckles across my jaw. "Your guardian angel, remember?" The quirk in his mouth made me smirk. I turned into his hand in an attempt to suppress the laugh.

I never expected to see Valen's softer side. The fierce predator still lingered. Perhaps it was for my own sake that he refrained from unleashing that force. I was shaken enough without him adding to it.

My gaze fell over his shoulders, his very bare shoulders. Valen was naked save for loose-fitted joggers that hung low on his waist. Before I could entertain the embarrassment of being this close to Valen with so little clothes, my eyes wandered back to his shoulders.

"Where are your wings?" I asked.

Valen stiffened, the gentle caress on my face coming to a halt. He blinked slowly, his throat tightening before he said, "I don't have them."

It wasn't just admiration in his gaze; it was also envy. "What?"

"They burned in the Fall," he said, his eyes drifting to mine. "It was a heavy price we all paid." He reached out to my wing, not touching the feathers but dancing his fingers across their outline.

"Was it worth it?" The longing in his voice was what made me ask. The fierce fire flickered, giving way to raw grief. It was there in the shadow, behind the gold light of his eyes.

"If I had not fallen, I would not have witnessed you," he answered simply.

"Jinn said I was your key to freedom. You never would have needed me."

Valen's lips pressed into a thin-lipped smile. "Had I not fallen, I could not have rescued you."

His fingers found their way to the back of my neck. A soft tickling sensation stirred against my hairline, sprouting chills along my skin.

"What happened?"

The single motion of his head turning made my heart sink. "Not tonight, Ezra." He looked so much like Killian in that moment, the same look of longing. It sent a crack down the middle of my chest.

"Why not?"

His brow quirked as his playful, deadly mask fell back into place. "Because I am not good with stories, and it is late. You need to rest."

"Tell me something," I huffed. "There's no way I'm going to sleep any time soon." I wanted desperately to grab onto whatever it was he was withholding from me. My mind had yet to catch up to my body. I wasn't tired. I wanted to know more.

His eyes flitted to mine, down to my mouth and back again.

"What if I told you I wanted to kiss you?"

Heat flooded my cheeks. "What?"

The sharp edge of his mouth curved, taunting me. "You said to tell you something."

"You know that's not what I meant." I shifted my weight back. The hand on the back of my neck stiffened, keeping me still.

"Is that a no?" His brow arched. The vision of a man wavered as that of the fallen angel rose to the surface.

"Yes, it's a no." I swallowed.

The dimple pierced his cheek when he smiled. "That wasn't convincing."

"You've lost your mind."

A deep throaty laugh escaped him. "Well, that's certainly true, but that has nothing to do with my desire for you."

With the way we had been at each other's throats, I found it hard to believe that was true.

I opened then shut my mouth. The action only widened the broad line of his mouth. Butterflies stroked the inside of my stomach, making my breath hitch.

"I stink of sweat and blood. My skin is covered in ash. Who is to say I won't burn you?"

The challenge made his eyes darken. Not Killian, I reminded myself. Something darker. Something older. Neither was he my guardian angel in that moment.

"A little bit of danger has always excited me." His voice was laced with desire.

"It's a wonder you've survived as long as you have." This was a dangerous game I knew I couldn't win. But the way he kept looking at me, well, I was never one to back down from a challenge.

"Truly," he agreed. "I've never faced anything as fierce as you." He stepped closer, closing the small space between us. He tipped his face down.

My breath hitched again. I wasn't thinking clearly. I was still reeling from the trauma of my wings and nightmare. But it didn't stop me from tilting my face up. I knew he was beautiful, but I hadn't allowed myself to really look at him. Not like this.

He nipped the top of my cheek. "Get in bed."

Disappointment rushed through me. I shoved it down as he pulled away. I didn't really want him to kiss me. My emotions were so scrambled I was acting on impulse. Heat stained my face. I blinked away the hurt before he could see it. "Do you get a kick out of taunting me?"

He approached my bed, waving his hand over it so the mattress and burnt sheets repaired themselves. The haze of smoke disappeared next. A fresh whiff of sage filled the air as his power moved through the room.

"I am not a gentleman, Ezra. It is only for you that I pretend to be." He looked over his shoulder, waiting patiently.

Despite the uncertainty that tickled the back of my mind, I took his hand as I climbed into bed. He knew exactly how to shake me.

A wicked gleam danced in his eyes as he looked down at me. My heart was hammering so loud, I knew he could hear it. Knew he knew exactly what it meant.

I shifted before he moved, pulling my wing as close to my body as I could.

"What are you doing?"

"Protecting what's mine, now move."

I wiggled to the center of the bed as he pushed his way beneath the covers, not waiting for the protest on my lips.

"I'm not a possession."

The mattress dipped as he rolled onto his side to face me. Those golden eyes wicked bright. "Never," he said. "But you are mine nonetheless." He shifted, rolling his shoulders back as he settled in.

I opened my mouth, the words "fuck off" on my tongue when he said, "Go to sleep, Ezra." A command.

Valen wasn't going anywhere. And while the thought of standing and marching to the couch sounded exhausting, I knew he would probably follow me there too. Demons, I was quickly learning, were possessive creatures.

I rolled over with a huff. I shoved my face into the pillow as his warm chuckle made my face heat. Somehow, even with my back to him, I thought he might be able to see the effect he had on me.

But.

But... his heat soothed me. It coaxed away the ache lingering in my bones. It pulled the hood of my eyes closed and slowed my breath. His presence was the only part of him that touched me.

Tonight, he would stay to keep me safe. From nightmares, from angels, from anything that might hurt me. Here was the protector I had been waiting for. All I had ever needed was someone at my side to help me make it through.

Wicked creature that he was, he tucked the cruel part of himself away so I could find rest. My dark guardian angel stayed with me as shadows wrapped around me and pulled me down to sleep.

CHAPTER SIXTEEN: ALL OF HEAVEN

Ezra

The night passed quickly, the subtle change of the light behind my eyes rolling like storm clouds. Dreams and nightmares evaded me as I lolled in the total darkness, only half aware that I was still asleep. A warm embrace held me close. A shelter from the dangers that awaited me in the waking world.

Once there was a soft brush against my temple. A kind tone whispered against my skin. Heat enveloped me like a gentle caress. I stretched and pulled it closer to me, reveling in how it answered and tightened its hold.

Awareness crept in as something warm nuzzled the top of my head. The subtle scent of smoke reached my nostrils, clary sage and sandalwood.

I tensed and willed my breath steady.

In the middle of the night, I must have sought Valen. Or maybe he had been the one to pull me to him. Regardless of who was responsible, I lay pressed against him, my face in the crook of his neck while he held me in a gentle embrace. One of my legs had found its way between his. My wings were spread out behind me, the edge of one covering our feet over the blankets.

I moved slowly, careful not to wake him. It was only when I was nearly out of his grasp that I paused. A white scar lay raised in the middle of his chest. Thin lines marked his upper biceps, but it was the one on his chest that drew my attention.

It was massive and, by the thick scar tissue, it had been a vicious wound.

I ran a finger over one of the thin white lines where it tapered off above his sternum.

"Someone missed," he said.

I jerked my hand back. "Sorry," I murmured. I moved to sit up, but his arm around my shoulders tightened. They felt better than they had the night before, so the pressure of his hands didn't hurt. I just didn't like how familiar his touch felt.

I shrugged, and this time he let his arm fall, allowing me to inspect my own. The ash of my skin had been replaced with light bruising. Fragments of burnt skin were scattered on the bed, but it was not enough to account for what had been on my body the night before.

Valen sat up, eyeing me with a curious look, and brushed my hair behind my shoulder. "You've healed quickly," he said quietly. His mouth remained parted as his gaze raked down my arms. He shifted to look at my backside. He leaned back, propping himself on his arm where he gazed at me like a lion. Or a dragon, by the way he was still coiled around me. His hand had fallen to the top of my knee. "The power in your blood..."

"What?" I said as he trailed off.

Valen shook his head. "I've never seen anything like it in a nephilim. Your kind has always been powerful, but this is different. There is a chance you could be immortal."

My heart thudded. I didn't know if I wanted to live forever or not.

"Is there a way to find out?"

"Killing you. Either you'd survive or you wouldn't."

So, no.

An involuntary shudder raced down my back, ruffling my feathers. The wings looked even more beautiful in the pale light. Still vanta, desperate to soak up the light around them, but beautiful.

Valen studied me, his eyes narrow and assessing, like he was trying to crack the code of my power then and there.

I nodded to his chest. "What happened?" I asked, wanting to shift his attention elsewhere.

Valen frowned and then shrugged. "Bishop and I had a disagreement. He tried to kill me."

I blinked. "What?"

Valen twisted a stray end of my hair around his finger. "About two thousand years ago."

How old *was* he? No wonder he had called me a child. I couldn't fathom living past one hundred, let alone one thousand.

"Why did he try to kill you?"

Valen cocked his head to get a better look at me. "That would require me to tell you a story first."

I arched my brow and gave him a knowing look. "I'm listening."

Light danced behind Valen's eyes, moving in a playful arc, and then that light twisted and something haunted took its place.

I ignored the warning in his eyes. "Valen."

He looked past me, as if contemplating whether the story was worth telling, until he let out a breath and his eyes returned to mine.

"There was a cyn before us, the first of our kind, Episkopos. He was a fair cyn, but with age came carelessness. He was sent to shoot a woman, to bind her soul to her other half, but fell in love with her." Valen scoffed. "We were naïve and easily mistook lust for love. The Enemy forbade intimacy with mortals, that we defiled them with our affections. Love is not something angelica are capable of, not truly. It was only made for mortals. Episkopos didn't agree and he spoke for all of us when he spat in God's face."

"You make it sound as if you all didn't agree with the cyn. If that's so, why did God throw all of you out?"

"It was the same time Lucifer rose against Him. The Enemy thought it was another ploy to overthrow Him, that we couldn't be trusted. He threw us out when Lucifer fell." Red flashed across his sunset eyes.

"That's not fair." My voice strained. "How could judgement be cast for the fault of one?"

"Fair?" Valen's lips thinned. He twisted his finger around another strand of my hair. "Nothing about life is fair. The Enemy didn't care what we stood for. He only cared that we might turn on Him. We never would have if we hadn't fallen. He could have thrown Episkopos out and the rest of us would have stayed." He shook his head and flashed his teeth with a disgusted curl of his lips. "We realized that love was not power, it was weakness."

"So, you killed the people you were meant to protect," I said softly. Goosebumps rose along my flesh as his fingers brushed the curve of my neck with the turn of his fingers.

"Being grounded comes with a price. Once you get a taste for blood, you can't get it out of your mouth." His thumb grazed the vein pumping on the side of my throat. His fingers had found their way to the nape of my neck. Caressing, teasing.

I've a killer in my bed. A cool, calculating monster lying in wait.

Would I become cruel? Would hate fill my heart? In a way, Heaven had already done to me what was done to the amorini. Except I was being judged for the fault of many.

I focused on Valen's gentle touch. Let it ground me as I tried to slow my heart from its sudden rhythm.

God would not forsake me. I wasn't like the amorini. I certainly wasn't like the nephilim before me.

"Where does Bishop come in?" I let out a steady breath as I tried to refocus.

Valen's eyes flickered to the spot where he stroked me, before moving back to my face. "We were generals to Episkopos, Jinn and Diriel commanders after us. The four of us have always been close, so when Bishop approached us to overthrow Episkopos, he expected us to support him.

"Bishop was... is... very powerful. He rarely considers his actions before he executes them. And when he fell, he took to it the fastest. Part of me wonders if he wasn't the reason Episkopos damned us all. In any case, we knew we couldn't allow Bishop to take that power. It is a fierce weight and can lead to further corruption if wielded by the wrong source. A crown that powerful on Bishop's head would have been the loss of our people.

"A cyn's power is only lost at their death, which is given to their slayer. In the midst of trying to stop Bishop," Valen splayed his hand, "it broke between the four of us, crowning us individually."

I sat a little straighter, inadvertently moving closer to Valen as the story drew me in. To become a ruler of Tartarus, all you needed to do was kill whoever reigned.

"When the power settled, Bishop's wrath was instantaneous. And I was on the receiving end of it, being the first ranked amongst us. It was morning when he drew his arrow and shot me." A distant look crept into Valen's eyes as his gaze drifted past me once more.

Not distant; that was the look of regret idling there.

Remorse maybe.

But he had intervened to save his people....

"And then?" I pressed.

Valen shrugged. "That was it." A little twitch touched his face, not quite flashing his dimple.

He was hiding something. Not that he had any obligation to tell me all the details, but it was a bit of information I tucked away.

"And now all is forgiven?" I'd been burned more than once by people I thought I could trust. Attempting to kill them had never been my first instinct. How Valen could be so nonchalant, even if it had been years, was beyond me.

"I don't think Bishop will ever forgive me. But he accepted his fate when he couldn't kill me. Sometimes I think he missed on purpose." Valen's voice drifted. His hand rested on the back of my neck, and his other, I just noticed, was on the top of my thigh.

I held onto the breath in my chest like my life depended on it. His eyes became hypnotic, pulling me in. Pulling me down.

"What are you doing?" I whispered.

"I'm wondering what's so special about women with gold-spun hair that drives men mad," he said softly.

I swallowed.

"Tell me, Ezra, do you have the power to make an angel fall?"

Everything slowed in that moment. My wings splayed behind me for balance as I leaned forward, meeting the upturn of his face. Poised between wanting to flee from the killer beneath me and wanting a taste of what he offered. My heartbeat raced with the speed of wild hooves.

The pointed tips of his fangs peeked through his parted lips. The scent of his desire pooled heat between my legs.

Hunger rushed through Valen's eyes just before his tongue flicked across my lips.

"I think you could bring all of Tartarus to its knees."

My knee slipped across the sheets and between his legs. The hardness that met me should have jolted me back to reality, not nudged my lips against his so I could taste him again. How wickedly sweet his tongue was as it darted against my mouth a second time. I wanted more than just a taste.

"All of Heaven," he breathed against my mouth.

My eyes cleared and I pulled back.

The grip on the back of my neck tightened. "Does that frighten you?"

"I don't want to bring Heaven down."

A wicked gleam filled his eyes. His breath caressed the front of my face as it teased the space between our lips. The danger of falling under whatever spell he was spinning was so terribly close. It took everything in me to rip away from him.

"I'll tempt you yet," he said.

CHAPTER SEVENTEEN: THE MARK OF A BEAST

Valen

The Murder stood clad in black leathers and sheathed blades. Their glistening blue eyes like fine jewels set within their carved faces.

In any other circumstance, their appearance would have been handled as a threat. But they were leaving as soon as they said their piece. There was no reason to react as if it were.

They had requested a counsel before departing. A claim to pay respects to the Lady of Vélos. Or, more believably, to show face in light of the rumor that had been whispered throughout the court since the night of Ezra's reveal: there was a nephilim in Vélos. While keras were known for being cruel and calculating, they enjoyed the simplicity of being petty when it suited them.

Testing Ezra's temper and tempting her faith had allowed me to leave her without her demanding to attend the counsel. She remained with Andras, who was to keep her out of trouble and encourage the practice of meditation. She would need the discipline if she was going to have any sort of control over her flame.

Bishop was the only one of us to take a seat. Like me, Diriel and Jinn remained standing. I leaned over the back of the chair closest to Bishop. We knew better than to take this as a casual conversation.

I liked the Murder. We had hunted together more times than I could count. Had shared laughs, blood, and beds. None of that mattered when Ezra was up for debate. I'd suspected the rumor about Ezra had been Raum's doing. That he would ask for her, and by the look in his dark eyes, he was willing to fight for her if we denied him. Cursed, and curse those with eyes the color of water. But starting a rumor was low, even for a keras. I didn't believe that one of our men would have let it slip. They were too afraid of us, too afraid of what Bishop would do to them, should they cross him. Whatever Bishop said was law.

Bishop nodded. "Speak your piece."

Raum's eyes noted each of us then flicked to the empty space where Ezra might have stood. "How long have you had her within your keep?"

"Days," I said. "We had hoped for last night's matter to be taken care of behind closed doors before we presented her."

"A matter that was barely under your control," Raum said. "Your shield dropped." His eyes narrowed. "I felt the swell of her power. We all did. I would think, my lords, that you would have taken better care than to let that sort of power fester."

If we had forced Ezra in the beginning, none of this would have happened. But we could have been left with a bigger issue if she had combusted and burned Vélos to the ground.

The gentle rake of claws against my mental shield was the only acknowledgment Bishop gave that he agreed.

"It has been long dated since a nephilim lived. It is in our best interest to make Ezra as comfortable as possible. We wish to see her thrive. Or would you have had us force her to the ground and rip out her wings?" Bishop dipped his head, sizing them up. "Do you know what happens when you try to dominate a nephilim?"

"Yes," Orias said quickly.

Raum turned his head, catching his eye. Orias ran his tongue behind his upper lip and swallowed whatever he was about to say.

"Then you would know it would not bode well for anyone should we torment her. What is done is done. You did not seek an audience to discuss her power." Bishop pulled his gaze from Orias back to Raum.

"I'll rip out his throat before he takes her from us." Jinn's hardened gaze flicked to me. *"She is the closest thing to freedom we have. We cannot let her go."*

"Ezra will never leave Vélos," I answered. *"Let him speak."*

The crook of Raum's mouth twitched. "We would ask to be present for her introduction. That is, unless you intend to keep her tucked away." His voice was coy, the light in his eyes mischievous. And though his muscled body was at ease, there was a ripple in the line of his shoulders.

I didn't doubt he had been the one to let the rumor slip. For all his composure, Raum enjoyed playing games.

"With Raguel in Tartarus, it would be unwise to reveal her until his departure," Bishop said.

"Whispers of her are already scattered across the land." Orias turned his hand.

Bishop's silver eyes darkened. "I am aware." His power thrummed through the air with a crackle of energy, as if deciding if Orias was worth reprimanding or not. A quick shot of lightning wouldn't kill the keras, but it would fry him into silence. "We intend to introduce her once she has healed." He gave me an expectant look.

I dipped my head. "I would not be surprised if the bruises she had this morning are gone by the time I return to her. She is... impressive."

Bishop's brow furrowed. I shrugged. I could hardly answer the question in his eye when I didn't have the answers myself. It was one more thing to add to the list of mysteries that was Ezra.

"Enough with the small talk. What do you want?" Diriel interjected.

Orias grinned wide enough to show off all his teeth.

Atticus was the only one of them who did not betray emotion. As usual, there wasn't a trace of what was going on inside his head. His pale features were snuffed out by the shadows slithering around him. He was watching me, studying me. I tried not to let his stare affect me. Kept my mind focused on the present conversation.

The last thing I needed was for their seer to see more than we intended.

Raum turned his head slowly, too slow, like it was a chore to deign the cyn attention. His arrogance reminded me how close he had once been to becoming an archangel. Three days after the Fall and he would have been marked. Few outside the warriors had his amount of control and will. Few outside the mark of the archangel had their superiority.

It was a blessing in disguise he had fallen first.

"Will you use her for war or will you trade her for the freedom of Vélos?"

No one said a word. Only the soft exhale leaving Jinn's lungs could be heard. We had not discussed what we would do with her. Both led a way to freedom, an escape from Tartarus's heavy chains.

We had spared few men in the war between us and the angels. Our race was not bred for battle and, though we were powerful, it was nothing compared to our brothers.

I was not foolish enough to consider using her for bloodshed. Even if she would be able to snap her fingers and obliterate half of an army.

A trade had never crossed my mind. Turning Ezra over to Heaven went against every cell in my body. Heaven didn't make deals with demons. That wouldn't change despite Ezra's value.

"You overstep," Bishop said. "While we value your input, what we do with our own is not for you to consider."

Raum clucked his tongue. "You have not decided. Or perhaps you are divided on the matter." His gaze fell to us individually.

"What we do with Ezra is none of your concern," Jinn spat. The white of his eyes darkened with smoke. It spilled from his lips.

Gods. I thought he would be the easiest to control out of the lot and he was turning out to be the most erratic.

"*Dramatic,*" Diriel corrected.

"As your allies, we deserve to know what you intend to do with the greatest weapon Tartarus has seen since our Fall." Raum took a step forward, his fingers flexing over the hilt of his dagger. "Can she be bred?"

"She is barren," Bishop said bitterly.

Raum looked back at Atticus. The pale keras nodded once.

By the gods. I held in my relief. The tonic had held. As long as she continued to take it, we could hide the very thing that would be her ruin.

"It is yet to be determined if she will fight in the war when her powers have not yet manifested." Bishop smiled softly. Chills raced down my spine. I knew that smile. For all of Bishop's charm, he was still deadly. And it was quite apparent he was pissed off. He didn't like being questioned. "Valen has been… enticing her to our side. She needs to believe it is her idea to fight."

The creases at the edge of Raum's mouth deepened as he frowned.

"She is a believer, or Christian. Whatever they call themselves now." I waved my hand. There was always some new group that favored themselves the chosen ones. The change of titles didn't make them special.

The Murder scoffed.

"The irony. That flimsy belief is easy to break," Orias chided.

I nodded. "That is my hope. But the grip is tight on her faith, and we all know an apostasy takes time. As Bishop stated, she needs to believe what we are teaching her is true."

"It *is* true," Raum snapped, his teeth clacking together.

"We all believed in lies once, brother. Convincing her is no different. She must experience it for herself," I said.

"An angel attacking her was not enough," Jinn said. His face flushed as soon as the words left his mouth. We hadn't told anyone how I had come by her.

"Neither were your wings being ripped out," I said coolly. "How long did it take you to come to your senses?"

Jinn ducked his head, his attention shifting to the floor.

"An angel?" Raum cocked his head.

I nodded. "I happened upon one, Ariel, trying to murder her while I was hunting. Looking back, I think he was trying to rip out her wings first. He sliced her back down to the bone."

I'll never forget Ariel bending over her, his blade hacking. I couldn't fire my arrow quick enough. Blood had sprayed through the air like rain, misting his face with its twisted grin.

Even now, her back was a jagged piece of flesh. I'd felt her despair when she addressed the back of her dress. It hadn't been to mock her to leave her exposed. I meant for her to show off her scars, show the world that she had survived another one of Heaven's cruelties. Our white scars were tokens from the battles we had won.

The fact that Ezra had survived the angel and kept her wings was nothing short of a miracle.

Raum hummed. "Let us hope she is a quick learner. It is a shame something of that magnitude did not shake her."

I tipped my head. Ezra was clever, she would see the truth. I had my doubts that it would be anytime soon, however. The little brat would hold onto her faith just to spite me.

Orias stepped forward, holding a finger in the air. "If I may." He ignored Raum's simmering glare. "There are no incubi within your keep, is that correct?"

His question was so jarring that I couldn't answer him immediately, just stared blankly. It was an absurd question. But Orias never did anything without purpose. Even his pranks had some intention.

"You know this," Bishop answered.

"Has she been having nightmares?"

"Nightmares are frequent to mortals here," I said.

Orias stared, waiting for me to continue.

I knew the direction Orias was leading me. I didn't want to acknowledge it.

Dreamwalkers were rare, their practice long dead. Only a handful remained, Orias being one of them. For him to ask about an incubus only meant one thing. And that was that I had inadvertently lied to Ezra when I told her Ariel could not touch her.

But I hadn't smelled him. There had been no trace of the *eska*. No thrum of that holy burning power.

"Is it the one that attacked her?" Orias pressed.

They were all looking at me now.

"Is it true?" Bishop pressed. *"Why did you not tell me? If an angel has breached our territory—"*

I shut him out.

I shook my head. "She dreamed of him last night. That he was burning her." *Ashes.* Had her burnt flesh truly been from her wings, or had Ariel managed to sear her with his light as she claimed?

Fuck. Fuck. Fuck.

I wrangled my emotions, panic surging in me.

Orias ran his thumb along his brow. "His mark is here. *Eska* by the look of it." His eyes flitted across my face as he used the slur. "Strange that Heaven is dallying in the old ways." He looked over to Bishop, as if he had an answer to this, and then back to me.

I tried to remain passive, to keep my expression unreadable. Andras was supposed to be helping her meditate. That state of mind was as vulnerable as sleep. Ariel could attack her any moment.

"It is fine," Diriel said. *"I don't see the angel anywhere in our future."*

I hissed. Angels had a way of skirting visions.

"Strange indeed. I appreciate your candor, Orias, but we can take it from here. Should we need your services, we will send for you," Bishop said.

Raum watched Orias intently. By the scowl on Orias's face, there was an unpleasant exchange of words going on between them. Orias snapped his teeth together and waved his hand through the air.

Orias's light gaze darkened. "Understood. Something that pretty wouldn't want to wake ever again after I was done with her anyway."

Raum placed a hand across his chest. His vambraces caught in the light, cutting through the darkness. "Whatever you may need, we are at your service."

Calm. He was far too calm. What the hell was the Murder up to?

I hadn't noticed until then that Elena was missing. It was rare to see the Murder without the blue-haired bitch. Her absence was concerning though not unwelcome.

"Where is your witch?" I asked.

"She is to remain in Vélos. She informed me that they were friends on Earth. We thought she might find comfort in a familiar face. And who better to coerce her than someone she trusts?"

A flick of rage escaped me before I could smother it. Raum saw it, by the upturn of his mouth. He knew I wanted her dead, didn't know why, but he knew. It was why I had turned her over in the first place. To get her the hell out of my court.

"She is to be a spy," I said.

Diriel looked down at his hands clenched to the back of his chair. *"We will have to keep a careful eye on her."*

"A kindness," Bishop said. *"The women will loathe her for what she is. And you, Valen, have made it clear she will bite any of us that draws too close."*

"Have you finally tired of her?" I asked. Are you breaking the alliance? is what I really wanted to ask.

"Her stay will be temporary. For the time being, she will better serve you than us," Raum said. "I believe, with the recent events, we will be relying on each other more than ever."

To think he was returning her without Baal's consent. Though Baal had requested her himself, Elena was never out from under the Murder's shadow. For the last decade, Raum had been ruling out from under his cyn. Only those within Eurynomos and few within our court knew the truth. If any of the other courts caught wind, there would be an uproar. Not only would Raum be executed, but so would the rest of the Murder. We had cyns for a reason, and ruling outside of that crown had consequences.

The tattoos on Bishop's cheeks crinkled as his lips parted, canines flashing. But I cut in first.

"Will you tell Baal of this?" I asked.

Raum shrugged. "As far as I am concerned, the nephilim are still dead and buried." His sapphire eyes lit across mine. "Do give the little phoenix my best."

No sooner had the Murder departed through a bleed did Bishop surge from the table, rounding on me. "A fucking angel came into Vélos, into my territory, and you said nothing?" His snarl was a thunderclap, his light eyes flashing white.

I didn't flinch as he stepped into my space. "I did not believe there was a threat to *our* kingdom. A single nightmare is not worth raising a defense."

Bishop held up a finger. "If any of you catch a whiff of that bastard, kill him. I don't give a fuck what sort of wrath it brings down on us, I want him dead." He looked at the other two males, eyes ice cold.

Diriel shifted from one foot to the other as he nodded. Jinn, fucking Jinn, kept his head down, acknowledging Bishop but not daring to meet his eye. The coward.

"Giving Raguel another reason to visit is exactly what we need," I jibed. "We might as well make him a bed if your intention is to keep him here."

Bishop's lips remained curled as he said, "If you do not make her fall within two weeks, I will."

I shot him a glare. "You cannot be serious."

"I have done everything in my power to make us something more than forgotten archers. With Ezra, we can be more. With Ezra, we have power."

Jinn's jade eyes peeked from beneath his lashes. His nostrils flared with interest. With want. The chance to right a wrong.

If Jinn sided with Bishop....

I couldn't think on that now.

"No." A subtle shake of my head. Bishop paused at my side as I said, "I will make her fall, but only so that we may slip out of our hold. We are not made for war."

There was nothing but silence. Even Jinn and Diriel held their breath as the inhale of Bishop's power swelled. "Leave us," he hissed.

I held my ground as Diriel and Jinn departed, waiting for the blow, though I didn't know how Bishop would deal it. Whether it would be mental or physical. Perhaps he would wait until he had me in private to dole out his punishment. That is the way it was with him. Whichever way the wind blew, so did Bishop. His will was an ever-evolving, twisted thing.

"Ezra is mine," I said. *Mine. Ozien.* I'd been wrong to say we all had a claim to her. It might have been true then, but now... There wasn't a chance in all of Creation that I would let her go. Most certainly not to Bishop who now looked at me like he wanted to rip my heart out all over again.

He brushed his lip over the shell of my ear as he spoke. "If she cannot be bred, she will be bloodied. She is ours and we will use her, however I see fit," Bishop snarled.

I turned my face to his so that my lips grazed his cheek and lifted my eyes to his. "You speak as if you are the sole ruler of Velos. As if you have the right to change what I deem a new law."

Bishop grabbed my throat, his grip constricting. We were face to face now, his anger raising its head like a cobra's hood. "Do not mock me."

"Do not seek to rule me." I leaned into his hand, daring him to tighten his hold. What lay between us could not continue. For years, contempt had been festering. We had tried to cover it up with bed sheets and blood, but we had never really gone back to the way things were.

Bishop's eyes dropped to my mouth. "I own you." He took a step closer and simultaneously ran his free hand down the center of my chest. "Or do I need to remind you what I could have done to you? What I still can do to you."

I hated him. I hated him for everything he had done and for the hold he still had over me. The clench of my jaw was my only response as I reluctantly conceded. Acting on impulse no longer affected just me, but an entire people. Ezra too.

"Stop fighting me," he said, softer.

"I do love to bleed," I said mockingly.

The corner of Bishop's mouth fluttered. He released my neck and took a step back. "Join me tonight." There was a wistfulness in his voice I had not heard in years. He thumbed the scar on my chest before he withdrew his touch from there too.

I tipped my head back, shooting him a sly look that I hoped looked genuine. "How am I to fuck Ezra into submission if I am warming your bed?"

"Then let me come to yours."

That I had not expected. It stirred something in my chest, and I hated Bishop for it. I hated that he was trying. I hated that, despite everything, there was still a sickness between us that would not let go.

I could see the sense of power it gave him when I said, "I'll come to you." I did not want Ezra to know the roots of my relationship with Bishop, though she would no doubt be between us eventually. "After I am done with her so that you can taste her on me."

Molten delight reflected in his eyes.

As far as he and everyone else knew, I was already fucking Ezra. I had no idea how I was going to fake her taste and scent, but I'd figure it out. If I didn't, it was likely Bishop would try to kill me all over again, solely because I had lied to him.

CHAPTER EIGHTEEN: THE SPY

Lane

Lane stood quietly in the shadows of Vélos, waiting. Her hands shook, her nostrils flared. It had been a long time since she had been a guest of Vélos, one without the Murder. She had longed for decades to return, but now that she was here... gods, she was scared.

Vélos, despite it being one of the corners of Tartarus, was the safest place anyone damned could hope to find themselves. That had changed when she broke one of their rules. Every damned one of Vélos' minimal rules, in fact.

Do not love. Do not fall in love. Do not allow someone to fall in love with you.

Love.

In the nest of romancers, it was the greatest sin.

Her fingers touched the bottom of her throat. She could still feel Valen's teeth there, ripping her apart. Right before he slammed her into the ground, cracking her skull open.

"You have crossed me for the last time." He had spat her blood back at her.

She had expected him to kill her. Instead, Valen gave her to

Raum, to the Murder. To all of Eurynomos to do with as they pleased. Death would have been too much a mercy. And after what she had done, she didn't deserve that sort of grace.

She'd heard before that Baal had asked for her. But it was at Raum's side she had remained. The tyre within the black mountains of ice and blood had become her home. Her prison. There they had broken her and turned her into the thing she was now.

There was nothing left of the human woman she had once been.

She felt him before she saw him. He had an unmistakable power that gripped you by the back of the neck and held firm. Raum stepped into the corridor, his eyes skimming over the stained glass at the end of the hall. He soundlessly strolled toward her, his dark eyes drinking in her face.

"What did they say?" she asked, lifting her chin.

"I did not give them an opportunity to decline." His eyes dropped down to the duffle bag she held with a white-knuckled grip. Within were a handful of clothes, several jars of herbs and salves, and a spell book she was only to use if Ezra needed it. It had an assortment of instructions on how to care for a nephilim should they find themselves in a difficult situation.

"Orias will be in touch for a report."

Lane winced. "Not a crow?"

Raum smirked. It was disgusting how beautiful he looked when something wicked was running through his head. "After that little stunt you pulled in the dungeon?" His brow arched. "You are lucky I have allowed him into your dreams and not your bed."

"His dreams are as much of a torment," she gritted.

Raum shrugged. "Do us both a favor and do not fuck this up."

She couldn't shake the way Valen had looked at Ezra the other night. Demons were obsessive creatures. Once they decided they wanted something, it was theirs. That is who Ezra was to Valen. Even a blind man would have sensed his territorial claim a mile away.

And Bishop… had Valen not been at her side, he probably would have taken Ezra for himself. Right there on the table.

All males were disgusting savages.

But it was the two dragons she was worried about. Valen was going to make things especially difficult for her. He wasn't going to let Lane within a foot of Ezra. Not after what happened last time. She could play into Bishop's interest, but then that meant putting herself within his sights.

This was a no-win situation.

"I'm the only link she has to the other world. It won't be a problem." She forced a smile that was more to convince herself.

"There is one more thing I want you to look into," he said slowly.

Of course there would be something else. There was always a hidden agenda.

"Diriel is studying the Hymn."

Lane's spine stiffened. *The Hymn of the Sun and the Moon.*

She had been told time and again that the Hymn was a myth. But Lane knew better. Raum wouldn't have kept her alive as long as he had if it was just a story.

"If my guess is correct, it is because he thinks Ezra is the Sun. It aligns perfectly with what we know. I want you to uncover whatever it is he does. Get Ezra to help you, if you can."

Raum's eyes flickered over her body, lingering on her chin where a black crescent moon was tattooed on the underside. The mark that had spared her life.

"If Valen catches me with Diriel, it will be a death sentence."

"Then don't get caught. You are the only thing holding our two courts together. They are not foolish enough to break what they so desperately need."

"What need do they have of Eurynomos now that they have a nephilim?"

Those wicked eyes narrowed. "As is, that little girl is a ticking time bomb. They cannot afford to lose us when another comes to claim her. And they will need me when Baal catches wind of her."

"What are you planning to do about him?"

"Do as you are told, Lane." The unspoken threat of what he would do to her was heard loud and clear. "Whatever you uncover about the Hymn stays between us. Do not include it in your report to Orias."

That was interesting. First Baal and now Orias? She knew better than to question further.

Her throat bobbed. "Your wish is my command."

Raum ran a finger beneath her chin, tilting it up to meet his face as he bent down to her. "Do not disappoint me, Lane." His voice was soft, coaxing. It sent chills running down her spine and heat flooding into her cheeks.

Lane stood in the corridor long after Raum vanished. She shut her eyes as the weight of his tasks settled into her shoulders. Difficult tasks, but not impossible if she was careful. And if she really played her cards right, she could perhaps extend her stay, find peace within the white fortress with its pristine rivers and enchanted gardens.

A hard breath rushed through her lips. She was out of Eurynomos, and that was what mattered most. They couldn't touch her here. Even though she knew Orias would torment her in her sleep, it was better than the three in the real world. A nightmare would be easier to bear.

For the first time in 1,214 days, Lane allowed herself to smile.

CHAPTER NINETEEN: PLAY NICE

Ezra

The healing process took less time than expected. Even the cyn were surprised when my flesh mended by the next day. It was an adjustment to carry my wings at my back, but with patience and discipline I learned how to hold them so they wouldn't drag on the ground or scrape through every doorway.

It did, however, take a bit longer to learn how to pull them beneath my skin. They were impossibly large and, though the memory of them ripping free was quite fresh, I couldn't wrap my mind around how they were supposed to fit back beneath my skin.

"Think of it as if you're giving yourself a hug. The same way you wrap your arms around yourself, you will do with your wings, but pull them in instead."

If I had to listen to one more of Valen's bossy commands, I was going to lose it. Though, it wasn't near as bad as when Andras had been trying to get me to meditate. The emissary had rapped me across the knuckles to keep my mind from wandering.

The tug of power had been a slow draw. First a whisper and then a brush of fingertips. When the third strike of the cane broke the skin of my knuckles, flames gloved my hands. I would have shot them into Andras's face had he not been smiling like a fool. Sheer joy and something like pride had looked back at me.

Not only did I not like being told what to do, I couldn't stop thinking about Valen nearly kissing me. It was hard to empty out my mind when he seemed to always be at the front of it.

And now, he was with me, coaxing me into folding my wings on top of the south tower. At least I was no longer confined to my room. A change of scenery was exactly what I needed, despite the company.

"The sooner you learn to do this, the sooner you can walk the tyre at your leisure," Valen said.

I turned to him, nearly bumping him with the outreach of my feathers. He stepped to the side, avoiding the impact with ease.

The light in his eyes danced. "Angels are jealous creatures. I'd hate to have to kill half of my people if they decide they want to rip out your wings."

I scoffed. "It was dire that my wings be pulled and now that I have them, I can't even use them? What's the point?"

"The point is you now have access to your power, and we can start honing it." He ran his hands over my shoulders. I drew my wings together as he instructed, finding the small spaces within me that they were supposed to slide into. He stepped behind me, careful not to touch them.

"Besides, you'll be able to use them."

I peeked over my shoulder. "I'll fly?"

A smile, closed, but genuine, touched his mouth. "It will have to be done in secret, but yes. You didn't really think I'd keep you grounded, did you?"

Knowing that I would be able to take to the sky sounded incredible. I looked up, scanning the horizon, skimming my gaze over the white city. What would Vélos look like from so high above?

Valen continued. "Diriel has been assigned to your studies. Jinn and I will help you with weapons and combat training, and Bishop," Valen's annoyance redirected my attention to him, "with magic."

"Must all of you have a hand in my training?"

Valen's finger traced the back of my jaw, sliding his touch behind my ear. "Why? Would you rather I keep you all to myself?"

The rest of his fingers followed the first one down my neck and across my shoulders, while his thumbs rolled into my shoulder blades.

He was insufferable.

I nudged him with one of my wings.

"Careful with those things," he chuckled. "Our wings are sacred. Consider them your crown. They shouldn't be touched by just any-one. And you'll poke an eye out."

I rolled my eyes.

"They're also quite sensitive."

"Sensitive how?"

Valen arched a brow to which I extended my wing to him gently. The flare behind his eyes made my pulse quicken. His gaze trailed over the arch of my wing, and then he reached out and grazed my feathers with his knuckles.

Desire shot through me, running from my wing straight be-tween my legs. I gasped and jerked my wing away from him. Heat flooded my face as I glared at him.

"You offered," he said with a chuckle.

"You could have warned me."

He hummed. "Where is the fun in that? Now, turn so we can put them safely away."

Valen slipped my hair over one of my shoulders and started to massage my back. It was similar to the way Diriel had touched me when trying to pull my wings. Only this time, Valen's fingers did not slip beneath a veil of melting skin.

The intimacy of it made me want to bolt. Instead, I allowed myself to ease into his hard fingers.

"I'm working over the main pressure points that will trigger your joints to release and your bones to shift. There, feel that pop? Start pulling them in. Yes, just like that." Excitement heightened his voice.

I hissed as something twinged under my shoulder blade.

"Slow," he coaxed.

A warm breath slid down the length of my spine. It brushed against the feathers nestled there. It was not the wind that culled me but Valen's presence that sank into my bones. I fell into the comfort he offered and, just like that, as I finally relinquished my reserve, my wings slid in beneath my skin.

"Amazing," he said.

I twisted, looking over my shoulder. I turned my arms. There was no trace, no plume of feather to be seen.

"What do you say we start your training today?"

"So soon?"

Valen shrugged. "You're well enough. And it would be good to get you conditioned sooner than later."

Bitter cold and damp air greeted us as we left the tyre. The clouds had shifted to a hazy gray. I inhaled the sweet smell of frozen ground, exhaling to a warm plume of white breath.

A rocky pasture with golden grass stretched out before us. Within the fence were horses, or what I mistook for horses. The creatures had the same long spindly legs, rippling manes and tales, but their front legs had glistened with the fleshy pattern of scales. At the end, where their hooves should be, were dangerously curled talons, similar to an eagle's.

"What are they?" I wondered aloud.

Valen whistled. A couple of the animals' heads shot up. Only one answered the call with a keening whistle that turned into a screech. It tossed its black head into the sky and then down to the ground, shaking it furiously as it trotted toward us, tail sky high. At the end of its dished face was a beak. Thick whiskers outlined the curved maw. It thrust its nose into Valen's empty palm.

"This is Nashua. She is an odonnos." Nashua turned a large unblinking eye to me.

I held my hand out in response. Nashua chirped, snuffling my hand like any greedy equine looking for treats. Finding nothing, she turned her cheek against my hand and threw her head forward, catching me full in the chest.

"Feisty thing. Is she yours?" I held my hand out again to satisfy Nashua's curiosity.

He smiled. "She is."

"She's... odd." The creature was stunning like everything else I had seen, but it was bizarre enough to be just shy of beautiful.

"She's something. The odonni were here before we fell. They're strange creatures but loyal to a fault once you've gained their trust."

Strange was an understatement. Nashua's ears flicked back. I stepped out of reach, pulling my hand back as those ears flattened to her skull and she snaked her head toward me. Valen laughed, slapping the side of the beast's neck affectionately. Nashua bit at the air, her beak clacking together.

"And very temperamental," he chuckled.

We left Nashua and the rest of the odonni behind, making our way down a slope that cut through the dark forest. The wide path was lit by orbs of blue light. The canopy of the trees was dense that not enough light highlighted the trail.

Valen hadn't said anything since we entered the forest. It wasn't like him to not be starting trouble.

He was too tense, worried about something. The stress of it was in the tension of his jaw. The coals within his eyes a warm glow instead of the bright tendrils.

"What is it?"

At first I thought he hadn't heard me. He shortened his stride, forcing me to stop with him. It is a bad sign to see a fallen angel torn up about something.

"I lied," he said. And before my mind could plummet and worry about what exactly he had lied about, he said, "About Ariel."

I knew it. It had felt too real to be anything but a dream.

"I only just discovered that it was true this morning."

I worried the spot over my chest as a heavy weight fell upon it. Ariel had followed me. I was only half listening to Valen when something he said broke through my rising panic.

"He's a what?"

"An incubus. I didn't consider it because the practice of walking was forbidden a long time ago. There are so few left that it wasn't plausible."

I leaned into my heels. "How did you find out?"

"Orias is one of the last of his kind. He claims Ariel marked you on your forehead—you can't get it off."

I dug my palm into my forehead, trying to rub the invisible mark away.

"It doesn't work like that," he said.

"Then how do I get rid of it? Get rid of him?" The bastard had marked me as his. Marking me for death. Whatever the mark meant, I wanted it gone.

"By killing him," Valen answered. "His ability to slip into your dreams is unsettling but manageable."

"Unsettling? You weren't the one that was nearly burned alive last night." I continued down the path, running my hands through my hair. I made it a few yards before stopping. My stomach lurched. "Aren't incubi sex demons?"

"They can be, but it is not what they are predominantly known for. I'm not going to let anything happen to you, Ezra. I just thought you should know, should you face him again."

"Can you get into my dreams too?" How exactly was I to fight Ariel in my dreams?

"Only the incubi can do that. The only one at our disposal is Orias. Whom I have no desire to let loose on you."

At least we agreed on that. I shuddered at the thought of letting the keras anywhere near me.

Valen stepped in front of me. "Ariel will never touch you again. In the meantime, I want you to train so that you know how to defend yourself until I can get to you, should there be anything between us."

I tried to dampen the frustration building within me. At the very least, I needed to rein it in.

"Then let us be on our way so I can learn how to kick his ass. Properly, this time."

Valen didn't move. He continued to stare back at me, as if I was some puzzle he was trying to solve.

We made our way to the bottom of the tower, crossing one of the rivers, to a shiny gray building that looked like polished stainless steel. It wasn't really a building, more so a series of connecting walls, as it had no roof. No beams and absolutely no windows.

The idea of training sounded grand, until I was in the face of it. Surrounded by rows of targets and tables lined with various weapons. Blades, guns, weapons I had no idea what to call, and, of course, bows. There were at least fifty spread out before me—many black, others glistening silver or bronze.

At the end of the row of bows stood Andras and Jinn. Andras offered a friendly smile. I didn't bother to look at Jinn.

"Is it really necessary that Jinn be here?" I kept my voice down, but it evidently wasn't low enough.

Jinn tsked, grumbling something in a language I couldn't understand.

"It is. You're going to play nice, aren't you, Jinn?"

The auburn-headed amorini glowered before sliding his steely gaze to me. "I will be overseeing your training until I feel you are competent enough to take on someone of my skill. So, yes, I will play nice."

I walked down the line, to the swords and knives. Then to the guns. I picked up a pistol and held it up, the weight familiar in my hand. Killian had every single one of the guns laid out before me. I kept my hand steady as I brought the barrel up, pointing it to one of the targets across the field. Was this done on purpose? How could they possibly know?

It had to be a coincidence.

"I thought you only hunted with arrows."

I could feel the weight of Valen's eyes on me. And if he was concerned I might turn and use the gun on him, he didn't show it. "Few times do our arrows serve as protection from an enemy or sport. Other times, different weapons are necessary for whenever we cross into your world and an arrow will not suffice."

I set the gun down and worked my way over my other options. I recognized several blades: the karambit, katana, and a broad sword. Others were new to me but just as beautiful, if not more unique in their design.

I glanced back at the bows as Andras pulled one free.

"She's all yours," Valen said.

I turned. "I thought you were supposed to train me."

"If you spar with me now, I'll have you on your back before you can blink. And I would prefer to have that sort of tussle in private." Valen's smile was a predator's grin.

At least *someone* was in a better mood.

I scowled. "You're disgusting."

Valen stepped closer, putting us arm to arm. "I figured you could return the favor for what Andras did to your hands." His eyes danced. And then the light in his eyes darkened and the upturn of his mouth pulled tight. "They will show you what you need to learn while I am away. I'm going to look for any signs of where Ariel might be hiding."

Protector. Guardian.

"What will you do if you find him?"

Valen ran a thumb under my chin, letting his nail caress the thin veil of flesh. "Just as I told you."

I pulled my chin away. I hated the way he pulled me toward him, as if some invisible force was trying to push us together. I didn't trust myself around him. Not after how I had almost succumbed to him. My eyes slid back to Andras as his fingers danced around the pommel of the sword at his hip.

"I'm more fun than him anyway," Andras said, winking at me.

Andras was twice my size in bulk, but we were closer in height than I was to anyone else. I had a good chance at taking him. He might hand my ass back to me, but I wasn't totally unprepared. I'd taken basic self-defense when things started getting sketchy with my life five years ago. And only recently had I taken up boxing.

I frowned at the assortment of unfamiliar weapons lining the arena.

"Go easy." Valen strolled to Jinn's side.

"I'll be gentle." Andras cocked his head, sizing me up.

"I wasn't talking to you," Valen said over his shoulder.

I threw him an exasperated look before crossing my arms and facing Andras. "What do you want to work on first?"

We started with a basic warm-up that consisted of far too many burpees, lunges, and long deep stretches. From there, Andras selected a short sword that was heavy and well-balanced. Its weight was unfamiliar in my hand as he moved me through several parries. We moved through a few short circuits before Andras faced me directly, drawing his sword to put the little bit I'd learned to the test.

He moved slowly at first, showing me what to do and how to counter before throwing his blade against mine. By the fifth stroke, I was drenched in sweat and my arms were burning. My energy was nearly sapped and we had only just started. My pride took a nasty hit when he forced me back and I had barely enough time to block his blow.

You're training with a fallen angel, I reminded myself. The fact that I was keeping up at all should have been impressive.

I glanced to the edge of the arena where Jinn and Valen stood. Valen watched quietly.

The blade swung up and then, suddenly, my legs were above me. My short sword flew from my grasp. I landed on my back with a thud and Andras's blade at my throat.

"You're dead." He nicked me, making a jagged edge beneath my jaw.

The sweet burn of broken flesh seared into my throat. I shoved his blade away. Blood smeared on my fingertips when I wiped his mark away. "You're about to be," I growled.

Andras licked my blood from his blade. "Have at me," he said.

Foul. Each and every one of them.

I grabbed my sword and held it up, accepting his challenge.

After a couple more rounds, we switched to guns. My arms were shaking so badly that it was with effort that I was able to hold the pistol up and fire. Hitting every single target. Killian was an advocate for gun safety. After learning about my past, he was adamant that I carry a piece. Though I never got one of my own, I took the time when we were dating to join him at the range and work on my target practice.

I flashed my instructors an arrogant smirk after my sixth firing arm.

"Where is Valen?" I hadn't noticed when he left.

"Gone," Jinn said. His thin lips pressed tighter together. "You're much stronger than you look. You're doing well."

"With this, maybe." I set the revolver down.

Jinn's eyes narrowed. "Perhaps it is just luck. Switch to the bows and then we are done for the day."

The sun had made its gradual decline toward the mountains. A blue haze was being blotted out by the dark lavender and rose that painted Tartarus. In the distance was a swirl of air, white flurries on the wind. Snow on a warm day.

I wandered down the line, to the next set of targets and rack of bows. Jinn pulled out three arrows from the back of his neck.

Andras did the same as I bound my wrist with a guard. I couldn't pull back the bowstring. My arms were fucking jelly.

"Do those just regenerate or what?" I nodded to the arrows.

Jinn sniffed. "Or what."

"Don't mind him. He's a cranky old bastard," Andras said.

"That seems to run in the family," I commented.

Andras grinned, flashing most of his teeth. "Oh, you have no idea."

The bow was half my size, Andras stating that a long bow would be the best tool for me to start with. I bolted the arrow, looking down the field at the body bag that was my target. My muscles strained as I tightened my fingers over the feathers.

It took every last bit of strength for me to haul the bow up and pull the string taut. I honed my willpower on Jinn's nasty words. On those words that I could still plainly read in his eyes.

Pin her down.

I bit the inside of my cheek. Bit it until blood flowed across my tongue. I let the arrow go, fast and free. It struck the forehead of the mannequin with a thud, rocking it back and forth.

The amorini stared. Andras was the first to turn, his eyes wide with surprise and his mouth cocked into an arrogant grin.

"Jinn," I said. I threw the bow at the cyn's feet. "Threaten me again and next time that'll be you."

I didn't look back. I didn't give a damn. I was done.

Thank God Killian taught me anything about weapons. Thank God he took me to the shooting range, on hunting trips, and encouraged me to take all those self-defense classes. Thank God for Killian. Without him, I probably wouldn't have survived as long as I had. I certainly would not have just been able to stand my ground just now.

"Ezra," Jinn called.

Killian, as messy as we had been, had been good for me. Been good to me. And I had done everything to sever that tie between us because I was too afraid of what might befall him if I stuck around. It wasn't my choice, he had tried to say. And then I had yelled at him, done something stupid.

"Ezra."

I loved him. I still loved him and now I would never get a chance to make amends. I was trapped in Hell surrounded by wolves that would bleed me dry.

"Ezra. Slow down," Jinn called. "I'm sorry for what I said before. But you have no idea what we have suffered— You have a duty to us. To your cyn and the Fallen!"

Tears pricked the back of my eyes. I hurled into a sprint.

CHAPTER TWENTY: IN THE SHADOWS

Ezra

A stitch crawled up my side, but still I ran. I ran until the wind blocked out anything Jinn might have been yelling at me. I ran until I couldn't. Until my legs quite literally fell out from under me and I stumbled to my knees, catching myself on my palms to keep from falling over entirely.

Bile burned the back of my throat. I shut my eyes and breathed in, exhaling slowly through my mouth. I had to grab the base of a tree to haul myself up. Everything hurt. I was shaking so badly I didn't know if I would be able to make it back to the tyre.

Where was the tyre?

I looked back through the forest I had run into. Like an idiot, I had gone in blind. Neither Andras nor Jinn followed me.

I'd let myself get carried away. There was too much going on, Killian shouldn't have even crossed my mind. Fucking hormones.

An icy chill gripped me. I could feel the weight of eyes on me, roving. Dread as a tangible thing then.

The canopy tipped forward, creaking under the pressure of its fold. It had to be one of those assholes catching up to taunt me. I took a step back, trying to see which one it was as the canopy spread apart, revealing a massive shadow gliding from limb to limb. Long claws emerged from the tethers of darkness, stripping the bark from the tree as it slunk down.

"If you wanted to scare me, you've done it." My voice cracked.

It was one of them. It had to be. "Jinn," I whispered. I took a step back as the thing lifted its head.

Its mouth parted, revealing rows and rows of razor sharp teeth.

I ran. I had no energy left and yet I ran as hard as I could.

The trees rumbled as the shadow moved from treetop to treetop, crashing through the leafy barrier in pursuit. The darkness sprung through the limbs, snapping the branches beneath its weight like glass. I spun to the left as it clawed near my right.

Any attempt to circle back, to make that right, it pushed me farther to the left with hissing and snapping jaws. It was herding me. I knew it and still I let it. I couldn't stop. Not when its hot breath was on the back of my neck.

I took a sharp turn, trying once more to back track and then the shadow, the beast, landed beside me. Ashes and embers blew up in my face as I jumped free, lunging over a boulder to evade its swiping talons.

But my feet never hit the ground.

Everything slowed. The shadow rushed somewhere high above me. I reached up to the pink-tinged sky. Reaching for the tree that came crashing down above me. Branches slipped through my grasp, slicing the soft flesh of my palms with splinters. I finally grasped one and held on for dear life as the tree continued to tip forward.

My heart slammed against my chest, and I hooked my elbow

over a branch as the tree's fall came to a jarring halt. My feet dangled God knew how many feet above the ground.

I hooked my other arm over the trunk and kicked forward, pulling myself through the branches. The look I risked nearly cost me the hold I had purchased. The bottom was miles below.

A sharp exhale burst from my lips. I gritted my teeth, reaffirming my grip. I was not spared by a nearly brutal death only to fall to one.

There was no sign of movement from the base of the tree. Nothing moved along the tree line or within the canopies. Whatever had been chasing me was either gone or lying somewhere, quietly watching.

The tree groaned as I shuffled forward. I stopped. My fingers turned white as my nails bit harder into the bark. If I continued to move, my weight could be the thing that sent the tree over the edge. I couldn't wait around for someone to find me, though. Whatever, or whoever, had been chasing me could come back.

Ariel.

Fuck, what if it was Ariel?

Yelling for help went against every bone in my body but, "Andras! Jinn!"

I slid my leg forward, only taking my eyes off the trees once to readjust my hold.

There was no answer. There wasn't even a sound of crickets or birds, which likely meant Ariel was still in the forest. Silence meant a predator was close.

"Andras!"

I couldn't die here. I *wouldn't* die here. Not like this.

"Ezra?"

I tried to sit up, to see through the branches obstructing my view. A shadow moved in the trees. I tensed, lying flat and low as it took shape.

"Ezra," the voice came again. I caught a glimpse of his pale skin and black hair.

Not Ariel.

"I'm here," I croaked. "I'm here!"

Bishop stepped through the trees, eyes going wide as they landed on me. "Gods," he hissed. He hurried forward, looking from me and then the tree. "Hold on, I'll get you."

"I can't move any farther. I tried but it starts to tip over the edge." My chest was so tight and my arms, now that the adrenaline was wearing off, were sore again. I didn't know how much longer I could hold on.

"Where are Jinn and Andras? They were supposed to be with you," he growled.

"Just get me out of here. Please."

Bishop leaned forward, placing his hands on the base of the tree. For a heartbeat, I stared at him in horror. Like he was going to flip it up and send me over the edge. White bands of light slipped around his wrists and to the roots of the tree.

"Climb up," he said.

I didn't move. There wasn't one thing about Bishop that made me believe I could trust him. Not when he was holding my life in his hands.

"It's going to fall," I insisted.

"Yes, but you won't. I've got a hold on it, but you will have to be fast. Ezra, look at me." His silver eyes were hard as steel. "I will not let you fall."

I'd wedged myself between two limbs. I'd have to shimmy forward and climb, fast. I would need a burst of energy that I didn't have.

Bishop reached out with one of his hands, those bands of light dancing at his fingertips. I couldn't take it. Fear had me by the throat. Like a cat, my nails were buried into the bark.

"Ezra," Bishop persisted. Power trickled into his voice. The influence of a cyn commanding me to his side.

I pressed the toe of my boot from a branch behind me and lunged forward, wedging myself between another grouping of branches. The tree tipped. Bishop's body went taut as he tried to hold it, digging his heels into the dirt. I threw myself forward again, clawing and grappling to the outreach of his hand. My fingers brushed his.

Bishop leaned forward, letting the base of the tree go. He grasped my forearm and pulled. Hard. So hard I thought my arm might come free of its socket. The roots of the tree caught me across the face. The world spun as Bishop threw me onto the ground, his body falling over mine, caging me.

I let out a shuddering breath as the swell of his heat enveloped me. Felt the rise and fall of his chest move against mine.

"Are you alright?"

I pressed my forehead into his arm. The world settled around me. I was on the ground, safely held instead of falling to my death. I ran through the feelings coursing through my body. Sore muscles. A sweet pain beneath my eye, a cut probably. And a tender ache to the other side of my cheek where one of the larger branches had caught me.

I nodded.

As alright as I could be given the circumstances.

We stayed like that until my body stopped shaking. Only then did Bishop hoist me to my feet.

The shadows surrounding us were more menacing now that I

knew they could turn into living monsters.

"What happened?"

A cool wind ran its hand up my back. My shirt was damp, thick with sweat. My own stench hit my nose and, fuck. Did I piss myself? I glanced down and said a silent thanks. At least it didn't go through my pants.

Heat flushed my cheeks. I appreciated that Bishop said nothing, but I knew he could smell the fear and stench on me as I could.

"I got pissed and ran off. Something started chased me." I threw my arm out to the cliff. "I thought it was Jinn trying to scare me." I shrugged. "And then I thought maybe it was Ariel. The angel. I don't know what it was. It was big and fucking scary."

A faint crack rang out from the bottom of the cliff. Chills raced across my arms as the tree found its final resting place.

"Rest assured if it is that eska, he will be dead. Jinn should not have let you run off." Bishop's voice was ice cold.

"What's an *eska*?"

"That's what we call the angels. The closest word you have for it is cunt." He arched a brow as I balked. It looked like he might want to smile, but then his eyes fell to my face and every humorous trace vanished. He took a step forward, guiding me away from the edge. "Let's get you inside."

"What are you doing out here?"

As soon as the question left my lips, I stopped dead.

Bishop looked down at me. "I was coming to see your training when I heard you yelling."

I studied him. Felt the weight of his hand on the small of my back. My legs shook. "You sure?"

Bishop blinked, surprise filling his face. "I'll admit I can be an ass, but chasing you to your near death?" He pulled his hand away, resting it on my elbow as I swayed. "There are better ways to get you alone."

I wasn't so sure about that. Not after what Valen had told me. He seemed sincere, but weren't all demons bred liars?

"What happened at the field?" Bishop stepped forward, pressing his fingers gently to guide me forward. Shoulder to shoulder, we left the forest behind.

"Jinn pissed me off. I didn't want to deal with it." Short and sweet. Bishop didn't strike me as the kind to take sincere interest in anyone's problems. I looked over my shoulder, looking at the trees above us. Nothing was moving now.

A branch snapped. I jolted back into flight mode.

It was probably some animal. Some terrifying animal like the odonnos, or worse.

"I'll handle Jinn."

"Because that worked so well last time."

We made slow progress back to the tyre. As much as I hated it, I leaned into Bishop. I was thankful that he didn't flirt or tease. I didn't have the mental capacity to deal with whatever bullshit he might sling at me.

"I was hoping to give this to you on the field." Bishop pulled a leather wad from his waistband. "A little something for you to wear, so you won't be exposed while in the air." Two buckles flashed in the light as he extended the offering.

The interior was lined with brown satin, to match the polished leather. The hem reached my waist as I held it to my chest. The buckles fastened into a Y shape in the back. It would leave most of my back exposed so I would be able to use my wings.

A small smile tugged at my mouth. Bishop was an ass, but this was... thoughtful.

"See how that one fits. Adjustments can be made and, of course, you'll have multiple," he said.

"How exactly am I supposed to learn how to fly if—" I shut my mouth. It was ignorant to assume that because they didn't have wings they couldn't teach me how to fly. Heat crept to the cusp of my face.

Bishop pushed his arm into mine. "Because I have a secret." A mischievous glint danced in the silver pools of his eyes. I suspected Bishop had a great deal of secrets. I wondered if he knew what Valen had told me. What he had done to secure the crown I looked across his brow, but like the rest of them, there was no such adornment.

"I have wings," he said.

I waited for him to say something else to wrap up the joke. He kept walking.

"What do you mean?"

"Mine didn't burn."

A thousand questions flooded my mind. Bishop grinned and bumped against me once more, before I finally settled on one. "How?"

"I left. Only those who were cast out had their wings burned. Those of us who chose to leave kept them."

"The consequences of exile," I said.

Bishop nodded.

"So, does that mean you could go back if you wanted to? To Heaven?"

"No," he clipped.

No way he was going to give me a crumb and not give me the whole cookie. I nudged him as we made our way up a flight of stairs. I could feel my muscles trembling with each step.

I looked at him expectantly, waiting.

"Heaven does not like to lose its archangels. I was the only one of the amorini they wanted to keep. Tried to keep." He turned out his hand with the tattoo. "You will see few with the mark of the arch in Tartarus. Heaven believes it is because archangels cannot be corrupted. That whatever took hold of us must have been truly evil in order to depart."

I hadn't the opportunity to see his tattoo up close. The bands and geometric lines were intricate, sometimes twisting in a way that reminded me of a Celtic knot. I wondered what the rest of it looked like. Did it just cover his arm or was it the entire side of his torso?

"But they wouldn't take you back," I pressed.

Bishop paused as a pair of amorini past. They ducked their heads to the authority before them. One of them cast a glance at me, and then suddenly found the floor to be far more interesting before hurrying away.

"I want to make it clear that I have no desire to return. There is nothing Heaven could offer me that would make me change my mind." His eyes hardened to molten chrome. "In the event I tried to fly back myself, I slaughtered so many of their army on the way down that they would have me executed before I reached the first wall of Heaven. There were two hundred and twelve that attacked my men, and I killed every single one of them.

"I do not take kindly to any wrongs against what is mine. I protect my people."

Like the stolen crown on his head, that had been stolen from him, broken apart into three additional fragments.

He was so sure. So certain.

I swallowed. "I'll keep that in mind." I looked over his shoulders.

His wings would have to be larger than mine, which were massive as is. What color were they? "When do we start?"

"As soon as you want."

I wished we had started off with flying. Maybe then I could have flown off the tree instead of waiting for rescue. It was by the grace of God Bishop had shown up.

I slowed as I gauged where we were in Vélos. Somewhere just outside of the main tower, close to the library. "Tomorrow," I said. Better to start sooner than later.

Laughter danced up the steps behind us. Jinn and Andras crested the top, their faces close as if they were sharing secrets.

Bishop's entire demeanor shifted. "Tomorrow it is. Will you join me for dinner?" he asked. He wasn't looking at me when he asked. His entire focus was locked onto the two males oblivious to our presence.

I wanted nothing more than to sleep off the day. I wasn't in a particular hurry to have a repeat of the last dinner. Being in front of all those eyes, and the Murder again, wasn't exactly appealing. But I was starving. All the excitement had stirred up an appetite.

"Dinner didn't go so well last time."

"Unless you've another set of wings you're hiding, that won't happen again."

The laughter stopped abruptly. Jinn's eyes widened as he finally noticed us. "There you are. I was wondering where you ran off to."

Power hugged Bishop's form, brushing against my skin as he wound it tight. Jinn's cool face lost all color. Even Andras's tanned skin paled as the touch of Bishop's power extended across the room.

"I think I'll skip out on dinner," I said. I didn't know what was going on, what was about to happen, but I didn't want to stick around for it. "Thank you though." I held up the vest. "For this too, and for saving me."

Bishop looked down at me, smiling softly. "Anything for you, Ezra. Valen will be gone for the night, but I can check on you this evening. Just to make sure everything is alright."

To make sure Ariel didn't sneak in and kill me.

With Bishop's admission hand in hand with what I already knew about him, I didn't think it was agreeable. Yet I found myself nodding anyway. Bishop would be a good ally, providing I never found myself on the opposite end of his wrath.

A young woman named Clarissa brought me food after I bathed and changed into something more comfortable. I had tried on the vest to find it fit me near perfectly. There was a small pinch below my breasts, but with a little adjustment, I made it work. I practiced opening my wings and folding them back again, trying to remember Valen's instructions.

My wings slid out from beneath the leather, not catching, as they slipped from my arms and fell at my back. Folding them back was just as easy.

I invited Clarissa to stay, but she politely declined, saying there were other rooms she had to wait on. There was an indifference about her that made me feel unwelcome. Like I didn't belong here, or shouldn't be here.

Between the cold shoulder she gave me and the thoughts raging through my head, I fell into an unsettling sleep.

Fire and brimstone hounded me. Blood buried what had once been a city, the gore so dense the structures were no longer recognizable.

Something brushed against my face. Light as a feather.

The fire cooled, bending to white light encased in blue flames. I turned toward it, opening myself to it as it chased away the vicious nightmare. The flare surrounded me, pulling a sigh from my lips. This was so much better than the horror. The light moved farther down, running seamless hands over my thighs and up my body, fitting me into a tight, protective embrace.

CHAPTER TWENTY-ONE: I WANT HIS HEAD

Valen

It was hours before I caught a whiff of the angel. The scent was faint, fading quickly, just as he had. There were hints of him scattered throughout Vélos. He had concealed his scent the first time, that first dream that could have burned Ezra's room apart. He was playing with us.

I followed our border with Eurynomos and the cliffs overlooking Asphodel without any sign of him. As far as I could tell, Ariel was at the heart of Vélos. His exact whereabouts eluded me. He wasn't going to be found until he was ready.

I touched the daggers strapped to my thighs. Three taps.

"Orf, take Zakkai and Dagon to the South. Javan, you will go with Takkar. Kasiya, you're with me. Keep an eye out for Raguel and his men too. We don't want to kill the wrong angel."

"Not that it would be a shame," Javan said, flashing his rows of pointed teeth.

The other males chuckled.

"You don't think Ariel is a part of Raguel's flock?" Kasiya asked.

I arched a brow. I didn't particularly like when my men questioned me. I never wanted them to be in a position where they thought they could question my authority.

But Kasiya and the rest of our small party had been present when Ezra's wings were being pulled. They deserved some explanation, and I knew I could trust them to remain quiet.

The males split off, their bodies wound and double-edged, as they bled into the shadows. Hunting is what we were made for. That we hadn't pinned Ariel down yet was a personal insult to each and every amorini looking for him. There was not room for failure when our aim was always true.

"If he was, Raguel would have been on our doorstep already instead of searching the entire plane. Raguel seeks something, but it is not our little bird," I said.

Kasiya rolled his shoulders. "Let's hope we find Ariel before he does."

I nodded. God forbid Raguel caught a whiff of Ariel. Having a small army looking for Ezra would be a more difficult task to tackle. And I had no desire to go up against Raguel. Bastard he might be, he wasn't someone to fuck with.

"We'll find him. Ezra is the only leverage we have against Heaven right now."

We must *find him.*

The tyre came into view before I smelled him again. Purity. The scent of it hung in the air like a flower's fragrance. Light enough that it softened against the senses. Strong enough to slow my steps.

He was making us chase our tails.

Kasiya hissed.

"My sentiments exactly," I growled.

"By all accounts, we should have found him already." Kasiya ran a thumb over the scar that carved into his lower lip and ran up to the opposite brow. Stray pieces of hair had fallen out of his top knot and clung to the sweat beaded on his golden face.

"We'll find him. I want you and the rest of the flock to stay on alert. Do not be too obvious that Raguel picks up on it when he arrives."

There was no wind, yet the shift in the scent changed directions. As if Ariel was standing right beside me.

Kasiya bent at the waist. "I'll have a report in the morning."

I couldn't stop my upper lip from curling. "I do not want a report, I want his head."

A slow smile spread across Kasiya's face. "His head it is."

A rippling electric current struck me. Kasiya's smile fell, his body snapping to attention so quickly I knew that he felt it too.

A force like that meant only one thing.

An angel, several angels, had crossed Vélos' borders. A territory's borders were protected by each court's magic. It allowed us to keep track of who came and went. Made it nearly impossible for anyone to sneak in. At least we knew it worked on the angels now.

"That's Raguel," I said.

Their power moved through the land like lightning, cracking across the sky and then gone the next second.

Kasiya nodded. "So how has this one not triggered our borders? Our wards?"

"I don't know, but we are going to have to be even more vigilant." *"Stand down and return to the tyre,"* I shot through the bond. I didn't need my hunters running into Raguel's. "Have the flock meet you at the south gate. We all remain in the tyre until Raguel is finished with his business."

"Are you sure you don't want their heads?" He arched a brow.

"Not yet," I said.

Up and up I climbed the stairs that led to Ezra. His scent grew stronger. I was practically running by the time I reached her room. Only to come up short as I crossed the threshold.

Bishop turned from his place at the window. The hostility from our prior meeting was gone, the power held against him reserved, though I knew he had yet to be sated. As was Bishop's way. Hot one minute and cold the next. Never docile though, never not on the edge of snapping.

"Don't look so surprised. Someone had to keep her company during your absence," he purred.

I set my bow against the couch. A simple gesture that said I was comfortable here. That I belonged here. Bishop's mouth quirked, but he didn't say anything.

"I'm surprised she would invite you to stay." I glanced toward the fireplace that blocked my view of her.

Bishop tsked. "You think you're the only one who gets to warm her bed?" A deep chuckle, the thrum of war drums, rose from his chest.

"Until I say otherwise."

The silver in Bishop's eyes turned dark as storm clouds. All his pretty fine edges were sharper than usual. There was blood on his knuckles. Not his by the looks of it, already dried and flaking. No broken skin.

So, there was resentment lurking. It just wasn't directed toward me.

I nodded to his hands. "What happened?"

Bishop leaned his weight to the back of his heels. "I found Ezra clinging to a tree that had been thrown from the side of a cliff after

Jinn and Andras left her unattended. She said something chased her." He rubbed and picked at the blood. "I reminded them why we need Ezra alive."

Something had chased her, hunted her off a fucking cliff. Shadows roiled around me. "What happened that separated them?"

"She ran off."

"That is becoming a pattern with her." I looked at her through the flames. The steady rise and fall of her silhouette as she slept. "Any idea who was chasing her?"

Bishop shook his head. "I assume it is that angel of ours. Said it was a shadow."

But why wouldn't Ariel show his face when he had already done it twice? Another tactic, perhaps. Another reason why we couldn't pinpoint his location. Even demons were hard to track when they moved as shadows.

Bishop jerked his chin. "Get cleaned up, take the night off. I'll stay with her."

I slid my tongue across my canine. I'd been a fool to stand down to him. I wasn't going to make the same mistake again. Not when he was so close to her, and she so vulnerable. "I've decided I don't want to share what is mine."

Bishop cracked a smile. "Yours?" Venom was in the word. Sweet, hot venom that could curdle blood once it was injected.

I nodded to her. "Ozien."

"Need I remind you that everything within your possession is because I allow it? Including the crown on your head." His eyes flicked up my brow. To the invisible crown every cyn wore laced with thorns.

Bishop could turn on me the same way he had turned on Episkopos all those years ago. That thought had always been at the forefront of my mind. But he wasn't taking my crown. It was the one thing that helped me keep our people safe. He sure as hell wasn't getting Ezra.

"Get out," I said.

He tilted his head. "Is that an order?"

"It is."

Bishop smiled slowly. "Where is all this new defiance coming from?"

"Once I tire of her, you can have her. Until then, she's mine to fell." I tapped the dagger at my thigh.

"Oh, Valen, I have been itching to fight you. To have you beneath me."

"I no longer care for the view when my knees are bent to you. I do hope you enjoyed the taste I gave you the other night because it is the last you will get."

Lightning flashed within Bishop's eyes. Storm clouds rolled within their depths. I had gone too far.

"You never asked me why I was the one to find her. Why I'm here now," he said smoothly.

"Then tell me."

He angled his head, the predator he kept locked in his gaze looking back. Fire moved within the silver. "I'm going to teach her to fly."

I shouldn't have been surprised that he had something up his sleeve. Bishop was bound and determined to get close to Ezra. Teaching her to fly? Well, that was something he could give her no one else could. He had a nasty habit of putting me in my place without using the brute force he had likely used on Jinn and Andras.

I wanted Ezra to fly. She had every right to the sky. But that meant Bishop would be close to her wings, would find ways to touch them. Something that intimate was bound to make her sway.

He didn't know I was already ahead of him. That because I favored some stupid ex-boyfriend, I had secured a small spot in her heart. I saw the way she looked at me sometimes. With longing. And then there were moments when her walls were peeled back to reveal the wild lust she felt.

I returned his smile by flashing my teeth. "Don't let her crash and burn," I said. "The last thing we need is to have her grounded."

Bishop's eyes danced. "I'll be gentle."

I followed his gaze to the bed at the sound of rustling sheets. I tensed, waiting for a scream to burst from her lips or fire to flare along her skin. Whatever dreams held her were far more peaceful tonight.

Bishop slid past me for the door. "I've missed this side of you," he hissed. "Do let him out more often. It's more fun when you're angry."

I didn't deign to watch him leave. The desire to have his throat between my teeth was too strong. I don't know if I would have been able to stop before his neck broke.

The sheets rustled again. I took a deep breath before exhaling the tension coiled within my body.

Ezra stood in the middle of her bed, the sheets crumpled at her feet. A strap of her gown had fallen off her shoulder, exposing pale skin at the top of her chest. Her skin was luminous. Thrumming with a quiet power of silver flames. The glow shifted, turning the sheen of her skin to gold. I blinked. Had there been silver flames?

"Ezra, what—"

I couldn't bring myself to take another step. Not when her eyes snapped open to reveal fiery red orbs. There was no white, no pupil, just red. Burning rage.

The room went impossibly dark. The fire in the hearth was ripped free, the lanterns, the orbs floating in the ceiling, every last light went out. No wind had snuffed them out. They were gone because Ezra had willed it.

Ezra's lids fluttered as her eyes settled on me.

Her anger was a physical blow to my chest. I felt it the way an ax sank into wood. I leaned forward, slamming my palms into my knees to keep from falling over.

"Ezra," I snapped. "Wake up."

There was nothing conscious, nothing human, behind her wild eyes.

I pressed into the room despite the power that roiled against me. The last time I had woken her from a dream, her hands had been on fire, her eyes red-ringed. Her power was manifesting to the next stage.

It was too fast. Everything was too fast when it came to her. She would burn out, burn everything within her path, before she had the chance to make something of herself. Before she had the chance to free us.

"Ezra," I said. *Ashes, let me reach her.*

Her head tilted down. Soulless. That's what she was.

A flicker of fear lapped at the back of my neck, its hold like iron as it halted my steps.

Her mouth parted, the twisted music of an angel's scream winding in the back of her throat. Flames licked the inside of her mouth.

I lunged forward. "Wake up!" I yanked on Ezra's hand, pulling her as hard as I could. I released my power, enough to jolt her. The light of her skin, the rage of her eyes, winked out. Her body fell to the bed with a thud, her legs folding beneath her.

I didn't move for a whole two minutes to be sure she remained unconscious. The rise and fall of her breath deepened.

Ezra was going to be the downfall of something. Tartarus or Heaven. There was no way anyone would escape from her unscathed. I had not seen that power in her eyes since I was cast out. The seraphim came close to wielding it, but Ezra? She was an entirely different breed.

Chills raced along my body. Ariel had brought forth her flames while she slept. I didn't smell him then, couldn't now. He was going to take us all out with what we prized most.

I searched the room for him. Searched every corner. Looked beneath every rug and blanket. There wasn't a trace of him.

"Show your face," I hissed.

The only response was Ezra's soft exhale as she turned onto her stomach.

CHAPTER TWENTY-TWO: BREEDING MONSTERS

Ezra

I heard of Raguel's arrival long before Valen had the chance to tell me. His name was on the lips of every mortal. Clarissa had the biggest grin on her face when she came to my room, her eyes wide and her grip light on her cart of food. Her ringlet curls bounced with each step.

"He's the most magnificent thing you'll ever see. He puts them," she waved her hand, "all to shame."

"What's he like?" I wasn't about to pass up on an opportunity to get her to talk to me.

"He's a seraph, one of the most beautiful angels in existence. Have you seen a seraph? No? They're all red, very tall, and covered with hundreds of eyes. Sometimes they shut them to look more human. Which is nice because it makes them a little less scary to look at, but even with them, they're amazing. Raguel is... How do I describe him?" She sighed. "He's just magnificent."

I tried picturing what someone might look like with so many eyes. The biblically accurate depictions of angels came to mind, and I shuddered. I wouldn't necessarily call those things beautiful.

"Does Raguel visit often?"

Clarissa rearranged the food on the tray, moving bacon to one side and shifting eggs to the other. "No, that's why it is so exciting. Though he is the overseer of Tartarus."

I sat across from her, pulling my feet into the chair beneath my butt. "I thought the demons ruled here."

"They do, but Heaven rules over them. It's Raguel's job to make sure everyone stays in line."

I snorted. "He can't be doing too good of a job if demons can steal people whenever they please."

"That's because they're allowed to."

I sat forward. "Excuse me?"

"There are limits, but the amorini get to take whoever they want, providing their soulmate is already dead. They tried explaining it to me before, but it's all bullshit if you ask me. Some loophole they've managed to slip through."

"How can Raguel allow something like that?"

She shrugged. "It's in the contract, or agreement—whatever, the Fallen made with Heaven. It's the same way with when a good person gets cancer, or someone dies too soon. Well, those things happen to bad people too, but it always sucks more when bad things happen to good people, doesn't it? God allows Hell to interfere. Each race, or court, has their own rules to follow, own assaults they're allowed to cast. In Vélos, we get shot or stolen." She ticks the two off on her index and middle fingers.

One more thing to add to the list of things that didn't add up when I lived in the human world. What sort of God would allow something like that?

Guilt floods me as soon as the thought slides into my mind. It's blasphemy to think things like that. And yet it unsettled me to consider any sort of treaty between Tartarus and Heaven.

"Oh, one more thing." Clarissa handed me a cup of tea. I held the bottom carefully, the crinkle of paper settling in my palm. "Be careful with that. It's hot." She nodded to my hands.

I smiled stiffly. "Of course. And thank you, Clarissa."

She pulled her cart away. "Call me Claire," she said. "I'll see you later."

As soon as the door shut behind her, I unfolded the note.

I'm still in Vélos. Your boyfriend is an asshole. You can tell him I said so.

I'll see you soon.

— Lane

It wasn't exactly relief I felt knowing Lane was still here, not when she was the Murder's consort. Though the idea that I had some sort of friend nearby was reassuring. I couldn't stop the smile of anticipation.

As for the other matter, if she was referring to Valen, we would have to nix that quick. Just because he looked like Killian didn't make it so.

I hid the note in my desk before changing for training and heading to the library. I had a few hours with Diriel before the sun set and I was to meet with Jinn for training. With Raguel in the area, we couldn't take any chances of him seeing my training while none of the other humans received special treatment. We didn't know how long he would remain, so postponing my conditioning wasn't an option.

I'd woken alone, but the fresh hint of sage still wafted in the air to tell me Valen had been there at some point. I didn't find it near as creepy as I should have. At least I knew he was keeping his word and keeping me safe in the event that Ariel returned. He had left me his own note, the curls of his handwriting flawless. He hadn't found Ariel.

Candles burned beneath a large stone table where Diriel was already waiting for me. Shelves rolled on their invisible tracks in the distance, twisting in my peripheral.

Diriel's finger paused on one of the books as he looked up, his eyes flicking to Andras. I'd asked the male what had happened when he came to escort me from my room, but the only explanation he gave for the split across his eye was that he got into a skirmish.

"Did you do that?" Diriel asked me.

Andras snorted. "She wishes. She couldn't land a blow if she tried."

"Yet," I said.

Andras's lips curled. "Twenty pents says I have you on your ass in the first thirty seconds tonight."

"What's a pent?"

"Currency."

I rolled my eyes. "You know I don't have any money."

His judgmental gaze flickered. "Two drinks then."

An affordable bet.

"I just have to last you thirty seconds?"

Andras nodded. The hint of a smirk tugged at his mouth. I'd be an idiot to believe that yesterday had been Andras's best. If I took his bet, I had no doubt he would have me on my ass in ten seconds. I was confident, but I wasn't cocky enough to believe I could take him. Not yet.

"She'll take your bet," Diriel said. He winked at me, his blue eye flashing.

"Can't wait," Andras said, letting his grin take full form. He saluted me and then bowed to the cyn, hand over his heart.

Diriel said as the emissary turned, "Would you mind waiting at the front?"

The amorini's shoulders slouched. "Am I being promoted to the guard?"

"Until things settle down, yes." Diriel slid his hands up the sleeves of his shirt. The gray button-up was stretched taut over his forearms. "Kasiya and Javan are still hunting."

"You should enlist other men."

"You know we cannot."

Andras glowered. When he bowed, it was with contempt. His steps were heavy as he walked away. Somehow, he managed to slam the two giant doors behind him.

I circled the table to Diriel's side. "You know he is going to go at me twice as hard now."

"Yes, but I'm going to teach you a spell that will weaken his blows. You can't best our strength, so that means you'll have to fight dirty." Diriel nudged me with his shoulder. Devils, all of them. I couldn't help but smile.

"So, what's on the agenda today?"

He pointed to the center of the table. A large map was carved in its surface. The flames from the fire below lit up the borders of five distinct territories. The only one I recognized was Vélos, which lay at the bottom, or top of the map, depending on which way you looked at it.

"Today you are going to learn about our world and the rulers we coexist with here. In the northwest is Eimai Theós," he pointed to the upper left of the map, "ruled by Cyn Maalik. The majority of their court is made up of seraphim. They are our gods, the real rulers of Tartarus. The seraphim have and always will be the most powerful angels. It is this reason they keep their rule. Cyn Maalik, for all the horror stories surrounding him, is one of the fairest rulers of our realm. He rules with cunning and wisdom. A dangerous combination for a madman.

"Here," he pointed to a group of islands in the right corner, "is Thanatos. Cyn Nakir rules his islands of caves and channels. A strange place as it is full of light, but its inhabitants prefer the darkness the caves offer. We deal with them frequently to trade metals, ideas, and dreams. You'll see their messengers and seers when they come to collect knowledge from our texts."

Diriel slid his attention down, nodding toward terrain with a combination of mountains and plains. "Cyn Anzu abides over Asphodel. He is more gracious with who he allows within his court. Most of us tend to stick with our own race. In Asphodel, you will find a melting pot of demons. Powers, amorini, even some seraphim have been known to reside there."

"Why is that? Why do you remain segregated?"

Diriel shrugged. "It has more to do with the hierarchy of our power than anything else. Powerful angels or demons at the top and the weaker at the bottom."

My eyes dropped down to Vélos. The amorini were thrown at the bottom because they hadn't been part of the third that rose against Heaven. The Fallen shamed them for it.

"Eurynomos is ruled by Cyn Baal." Diriel's voice had grown thin. He opened his mouth then shut it. "Baal is one of the first angels ever created. He is one of the handful of archangels that fell from

Heaven. They're hard to miss, but when you see one it's rare."

The heat beneath the stone met my palms as I set them on the table to lean forward. "How can you tell an archangel from another? Are they a race of their own?"

Diriel cocked his head. "Archangels are not a race but an acknowledgment of the power and respect they have acquired. Seraph or not, they are the most revered. Archangels are not meant to sway from Heaven. It takes great devotion and love to be subjected to the responsibility that comes from taking the arc. They all bear the same banded and knotted tattoos on their left side."

I arched a brow. "Bishop told me he was an archangel."

Diriel ran a hand over his smooth head. "He thinks you despise him."

I waved my hand. It was partially true. "He saved me. Having a conversation was the least I could do."

Diriel chuckled darkly. "It is wise to be wary of him. Give him respect as your cyn, but if you can help it, don't ever put yourself alone with him." Though his words were light, there was hesitancy in his tone.

"Too late for that," I mumbled.

Diriel hummed. "Still."

"Believe me, I have no desire to get with him one on one. He has too much arrogance for my taste." His higher than thou superiority left a bad taste in my mouth. I slid my finger to the center of the table, over the giant black circle with the word Vasanistirio scribbled across its center.

"What's that? Vasa... How do you pronounce that?"

"Vasan-is-tirio," Diriel said. He drew his finger through the air. Starting with Eimai Theós, he drew his finger down to Vélos, up to Thanatos, down to Eurynomos, across to Asphodel, and then back up to Eimai Theós. It was an upside-down star. A pentagram. "It is where the most wicked of our brothers remain, bound in chains of darkness until Judgment. The power of our five courts holds the barriers together."

I looked at him incredulously. "You're telling me there is something bigger and badder down there that even the demons are afraid of?"

"Afraid? Who said anyone was afraid?" Both of Diriel's brows arched. "No. What is down there is the front line of the army that led against Heaven. Bigger and badder, yes. But it is Heaven that is afraid of them. Not us."

Diriel leaned across the table beside me so that we were shoulder to shoulder. "What I am about to tell you, you cannot mention to anyone."

I drew a zipper across my mouth, locked it, and then pretended to throw the key over my shoulder.

"There is a strong possibility that Eurynomos will soon have a new cyn. The Murder, the three keras you met the other night, have spent a great amount of time in our library. I suspect they are trying to find a way to break Baal's crown."

"Can they do that?"

Diriel tilted his head. "It is possible, but it will be a hard thing to accomplish. As I said, Baal is old. Though he grows weary, crossing him could easily be their deaths. There is too much at stake. Raum will be the one who does it. It is he who leads the Murder. But the crown could reject him. If he survives, Maalik could issue an order to have him thrown into the pit. Overthrowing a cyn doesn't come without a price."

"You did it." I hadn't meant it to come out as an accusation.

He nodded. "In an attempt to save our people from the slaughter Bishop would have led us into. Whatever Valen told you," he sighed, "does not even begin to cover the rage in which we battled against Bishop to take the crown. Episkopos was old too. I have started to wonder if it was then, in those brief seconds of battle, where Episkopos died and we were crowned, when your sire slipped through his chains."

My heartbeat skipped. "You think you're responsible... for me?"

Diriel's brows furrowed. "I do. There is only one angel that the curse of childbearing does not touch. Who could have escaped and sired you."

I swallowed. I knew exactly who he was talking about. He was all I had been reading about lately. "Samyaza."

"Yes."

"Why are you telling me this?"

"Because if the Murder succeeds, then the barrier in Vasanistirio will crack. A split second is all it will take for whatever monsters lurk below to spill out. I am wondering what other creatures will come out and spill into Earth." He looked down at me. One gold eye, one blue. "There are worse things than the nephilim. And I can assure you, Ezra, that you do not want to meet the beasts that would be your siblings."

God help me. Was Vasanistirio a portal to Earth? It must be, if Diriel said that monsters would spill out into it. That one had. My sire. Samyaza, for all the love he had for his children, or love for their cruelty, had been a wicked creature all on his own. Breeding monsters because he could. Breeding them for no other reason than to satisfy his lust and piss off Heaven.

"What do the others have to say about it?" I asked softly.

"I haven't mentioned it to them."

I couldn't fathom what other creatures lurked within the pit of

Hell. I did wonder, though, where Samyaza was hiding and if he knew anything about me.

CHAPTER TWENTY-THREE: LOVE IS A WEAKNESS

Ezra

Valen stood on the sidelines as I trained with Andras. Jinn was nowhere to be found. Andras and I worked through several warm-up circuits. Once I was thoroughly drenched with sweat, we switched to swords. I chose a gladius, being more comfortable with its length.

Andras met me on the mat empty handed.

"Where's yours?"

He nodded to me. "I'm going to give you the upper hand."

Right, because he was about to kick my ass. I chanted the curse Diriel had given me in my head. Over and over again. One that would stun Andras long enough for me to wound him. Or, if we were in battle, kill him.

"Ladies first," Andras drawled. He swept his arm across the floor.

Valen folded his arms. His keen eyes fixed on me as I palmed the blade, tightening my hold. I had one shot.

I stepped forward, the curse leaving my lips as soon as Andras's weight shifted. He said he would have me down in thirty seconds. In the first four, I struck him, his body going stiff. His eyes widened as he froze in his turn.

"Follow through," Diriel had said. "A curse like this does not last long on those of higher power. Andras may play an emissary, but he is a trained warrior. He is still an amorini, a hunter. He will not be under its influence for long."

I swung my blade up, sliding it beneath Andras's jaw. "You're dead," I said. I flashed him a cocky grin.

Time shifted forward and then the sky was spinning above me. The ground slammed into the center of my back. He had kicked my feet out from under me. "Getting tips from Diriel, I see." Andras rolled his shoulders back before extending his hand to help me up. "Next time, you might want to try cutting my head off entirely."

I let him heave me forward. "I'll remember that."

He picked up his blade and showed me a series of movements before moving in.

I repeated the other spells under my breath, the ones that would weaken his blows as we parried. Andras caught on quickly, his brow furrowing as he hurled toward me. The effort of his blows intensified, but they did nothing more than rattle me. I wasn't going to let him drop me again.

Only once did I counter Andras's charge successfully. I twisted out of his reach, barely, and slid the edge of my blade over the top of his thigh. The fabric split, revealing his bronze flesh.

I didn't care if he let me do it. It felt good.

At the sidelines, Valen's eyes danced. Pride.

I didn't last much longer after that. My muscles had started to cramp in protest. Andras ended our parry with his claws dancing over my heart. I threw up my hands, defeated.

Steam left Andras's lips as he let out a huff. "What do you say we show her what a real fight looks like?"

Valen tilted his head down, his eyes shining bright beneath his dark lashes. "Feeling cocky today, are we?"

"I want a real challenge," Andras said. He ran his tongue over his lip. He winked at me, his tongue sliding back between his teeth, and smiled.

Valen strode to the table closest to him where he grabbed a short sword, twin to mine, and then down to the racks that held the bows. He pulled two free, tossing the first one to Andras, and then strapped the other over his chest.

"Do you want to be the angel or the demon?" Valen asked.

Andras flashed his fangs. "Always the demon."

Valen chuckled. It was rare that I heard the music of his laughter. It was beautiful. Higher than the richness of his voice. "Always the loser," Valen teased.

He turned to me as I approached the sidelines. God, I hated it when he looked at me like that. Like he wanted to devour me, or worse, lay me on my back. It heated my core.

Valen lifted my chin. I braced myself as he tipped his head down and licked the sweat from the side of my face. Shock didn't even begin to describe what I felt.

My toes curled inside my boots.

"Well done," he said, a hiss trailing his words. Valen smiled as fresh heat stained my face.

Andras was the first to move. They were a blur of flashing swords and swirls of dark clothes. They moved like dancers, precise but deadly.

This didn't look like a skirmish at all, actually. Valen was vicious, raining down fury as Andras struggled to block his blows. They were both huffing steam, the fire within their hearts rising.

Andras twisted, cutting and slicing his sword through the air, but Valen met every single blow, dodging only a handful of times. He seemed to enjoy taking the brunt of the attacks. Savored it.

It was then, I realized, Valen truly did enjoy the idea of pain.

Valen's flames rose first as Andras struggled to keep up. Orange flames scurried up the length of his blade. They wrapped around Andras's wrist. Andras's brow furrowed as he retreated, running backward to gain time so he could pull his bow free. He jerked his wrist against Valen's flames that followed.

"Fucking asshole," he cursed. Andras threw up his bow, catching Valen's next blow with the limb.

I touched my fingers to my lips. Valen didn't stop. Not even as Andras faltered. Andras wasn't even attacking anymore. All he could do was defend himself. Blow after blow.

Wicked shadows unfurled at Valen's back in the form of great black wings.

They dropped their swords at the same time, but Valen was still faster. He kicked Andras in the chest, forcing the male to the ground with a loud crack.

Did he just break his sternum?

With deft fingers, Valen pulled an arrow from the back of his neck. It was nocked and aimed at Andras's chest in the next second.

Andras's hand shook as he let go of the arrow he had been reaching for. The grip on his bow was white-knuckled.

"What the fuck," I breathed.

Valen slowly released the tension from the string. "You're getting slow, old man."

"Fuck off," Andras gritted. He slapped Valen's hand to the side when he offered it. Pain laced his features as he rolled to his knees to stand. There was a definite indention in the middle of his chest. Real fear flickered in his warm eyes.

Their fires retreated beneath their skin.

"What the hell was that?" I breathed.

Valen's eyes were still simmering when he looked at me. The shadows folded gracefully at his back. But before he could speak, Andras held up a hand.

"Exactly what I asked for," the emissary said. A quiet break leaked through the air. He ran a hand over his chest, wincing. "Don't fret, Ezra."

"This is tame," Valen purred. A wicked grin still lingered at the edge of his mouth.

Andras nodded. He slowly removed his hand, his breath evening out. The indention was better, not entirely gone, but at least his chest was healing. He pulled the top of his shirt apart to look down. When he looked back up, he was smiling. "Already better."

I shook my head. "You're both insane."

"Entirely." Valen pointed to me. "Your turn."

I held up my hands. "Oh, no. I'm good. I'll take my chances sparring with Andras again."

Andras threw up his middle finger as he hobbled off the landing. At least his spirit hadn't been broken. "I'm done," he said. "Both of you fight dirty." He grumbled something else as he made his way off the field.

A quiet hum thrummed from Valen. "We'll make a game of it."

I eyed Valen warily as I turned back to him. "I don't want to play a game. I want to go to bed."

I was exhausted. A steady throb moved through every muscle of my body. I didn't have it in me to keep practicing. My hands were worn with what would be new calluses. I already had a few built up from working out in the gym. Strange that everything else seemed to heal, but that hard dry skin was something that stayed.

"We can take your lessons to the bedroom," Valen said.

"You've got a silver tongue," I said.

"Do you want to see what it can do?"

My stomach coiled and clenched. Never in my life had I reacted to a man the way I did Valen. Then again, never had I been at the whims of a cupid.

Heat had burned behind his eyes ever since he tried to kiss me the first time, but in that moment he looked hungry. Starved.

My voice betrayed me as I whispered, "No."

A devilish smile fell on his face. "You're a terrible liar, Ezra."

He had me there. I never was good at lying. Any time I told a lie, the truth tumbled out of my mouth immediately after. I hated lying. Hated the way it twisted my gut. The guilt that would weigh me down.

It wasn't that I didn't want to kiss him, it was that I wanted to do it at all. I hadn't stopped thinking about how I almost had. How that flick of a taste he had allowed me was seared into my memory forever. And that I wanted more of it.

"Is it because you see Killian when you look at me?"

"Your appearances hardly have anything to do with it." I turned away from him, intending to follow in Andras's footsteps.

"Do you still love him?" Valen moved to the edge of my peripheral. For every step I took, he lengthened his stride, until he was standing directly in my path.

"No," I said.

I tried to draw up the fire within me. Tried to remember what I had learned in mediating with Andras. At the same time, I went over the list of spells and curses I had learned.

Because the game had started, despite me not wanting to play. Shadows roved over Valen's shoulders; his body was still taut with energy. His weapons had been discarded, but it wasn't blades and arrows I was worried about. It was the swell of his power manifesting in the air between us. The heat of desire.

"Another lie, interesting," he purred. "Why did you leave him?"

An invisible flick of said power unfurled in my direction, stopping just short of my face. He was toying with me.

I needed a shield. I needed to learn how to shield. I drew up my hands, at the same time imagining an iron wall. I grew up with stories about fae and how iron was poison to them. Was it the same for angels?

In any case, I pictured it. Built it tall and thick so that nothing could penetrate it.

"Because Death followed me and I didn't want him to be next," I said.

"How noble," Valen said. He let the line of power he had been holding go. It slammed into me, into the wall I had so carefully built. The wall cracked and I stumbled, trying desperately to shove him away.

Another shove sent me sprawling on my back. I glared up at him, baring my teeth the way the rest of them did. I pushed myself up with everything I had, mentally and physically wanting to get out from under his spell.

Valen hissed. "Do not open your wings here."

I looked down, to the skin that was bulging around my biceps. *Shit.* That's not what I was trying to do.

This was a test, not a game. He was looking for my weak points and I had practically handed it over.

"Do you still love him?" he asked again.

"No," I said too quickly. I slid beneath his power, slipping under it and kicking him in the shin. He had let me take the shot. Let me take out the lie on him.

Valen's lips curled. "Love is weakness. It's against our laws to love, with a penalty of death. You indeed saved his life by severing yourself from him."

Hearing him say that only pissed me off. I knew I had saved Killian's life. But hearing those words made it feel wrong. Love wasn't weakness. It took guts to love someone. It took even greater strength to fall in love with someone and allow them to see that. To love and be loved equally was bravery. There was no weakness in that.

I let a curse slip through my lips, one to slow Valen's movements. He turned on his heel, like he could see it coming, and then promptly let fire spread across his hands. I tried to mimic it, but I was tired. I was so damned tired that the little bit I was doing was with effort.

"Do you pretend I'm him?"

Valen took advantage of the question catching me off guard. He let those flames lose, sent them winding around my throat. They had a snug fit, not threatening but—

My face heated. They caressed me, gentle and taunting.

I wished we had kept our blades for this lesson.

"You're a bigger asshole than he ever was."

"That's not an answer."

Valen didn't stop. He continued to prod me, using Killian as his preferred weapon of choice. It made my blood boil that he would be so crass, so childish, to use him against me.

Valen's eyes flicked down. They widened at the sight of gold flames dancing along my hands.

"There she is." That look of pride I had glimpsed earlier was once again dancing in the light of his eyes. "Now we know what your trigger is."

"Are you going to throw Killian in my face every time you want me to draw my fire?"

Valen's teeth flashed. "I want you to draw your fire on command. But if a trigger is necessary," he nodded his head to the side, "then it is anger you will dip into. Not Killian."

I cocked my head. Slowly, so slowly, the flames died out on my hands as realization hit me. The nephilim were said to have been angry, to have been full of rage.

"Don't look at me like that," Valen said. "I told you we would pick up this conversation again."

"What do you care? Why does Killian matter to you?"

"I do not care about Killian, but it interests me that we favor each other. I want to be certain you understand that we are different people in my attempt to know you better."

"Oh, believe me. I know the two of you are nothing alike." Even as the words tumbled out, it took me a moment to register his. To know me better.

"If you want to get to know me, you should start by giving a piece of yourself first. And don't use my boyfriend against me."

I left the discarded weapons and field behind. Could feel him trailing me until he was right at my shoulder. There was nowhere I could run in all of Tartarus that would be far enough away from Valen.

"I have," he said. "Admitting that my closest companion, my brother, tried to kill me is no small thing."

That was fair. And yet I didn't want to concede to him. I stopped, turning to face him as he took the final steps to reach me, leaving nothing but a few inches between us.

"What do you want, Valen?"

"You," he said, before the question had fully left my lips.

"I am not a prize that can be won. I am not a weapon to wield against Heaven. Neither am I a brood mare for you to fuck."

The corner of Valen's mouth quirked, his eyes darkened. "I see you as none of those things. I want you because of who you are, not what you are. Living the life you have is no small feat. Neither is surviving an angel. And while I admit that you would be a formidable weapon against Heaven, that is not my goal in winning you. I want to fuck you so you can experience the pleasure only I can give you. I want to hear my name on your lips when you are breathless and worn from my touch."

I swallowed. I could only stare at him. At his bluntness. I knew he was lying, about part of it at least. He had tried to tempt me into making Heaven fall days ago. I knew his mind hadn't changed that quickly. And yet, even if that was still his desire, that was not what we were currently talking about. He was talking about me. Not what I could do.

He wasn't talking about what I could do for the court, or for Tartarus. He wanted me for himself.

That was the real game. A game of temptation. Nothing good comes where temptation is involved. Nothing good comes from fallen angels. Especially not from one that bore the face of an old lover. A lover that seemed distant to me in that moment. So far away that I couldn't recall his name.

"Will you give me that honor?" Valen's hands had drifted to my body. One of them rested on my hip. The other made a slow trail up my neck, to the curve of my jaw. He tilted my face up.

I swallowed again, forcing the breath back into my lungs, for the dryness to leave my mouth. "You're going to have to try harder than that," I said. I had to force the words out.

Valen's eyes simmered, but when he smiled, it was genuine. The dimple in his cheek flashed. "So I shall," he answered.

CHAPTER TWENTY-FOUR: CHEERS

Ezra

It may come to no surprise that I could not sleep. I could not function properly around Valen. He was wearing me thin. Did that say more about me? That I was weak? Or did it speak more to the fact that he was very good at what he did?

A new guard had taken Andras's place outside my door. I assumed Andras had taken the night to recover after his tussle with Valen. He played off the injury well, but it had been a nasty one.

Valen had lingered at the door. "Should I join you tonight?" he asked.

"Hell no," I said.

"Well, you can't go traipsing around tonight. Not with the angels in our territory."

"The only place I am *traipsing* is straight to bed."

A ghost of a smirk touched his lips. "Ariel could return."

"You heard me the last two times he attacked me. I have no doubt you'll swoop in for a third." I shut the door in his face, not daring to look at him, at that stupid grin and shining eyes. I knew he would see right through me.

A soft chuckle leaked through the door.

"I mean it, Ezra. Do not go seeking trouble."

That had been two hours ago. I had tried a hot shower, and then a cold one, anything to shock common sense into my body. I'd never been one to have sex with someone for the hell of it. I'd done it before but swore never again. I hated the way it made me feel after. Dirty.

Some might call me a prude for that; I call it having standards. I wasn't going to let just anyone have a piece of me. I didn't have much left.

And even as I stood by those beliefs, my thoughts wandered back to Valen. I did want him. Not because he looked like Killian, but because he was Valen. He was by far one of the most beautiful males I had ever seen. He exuded sex appeal. The fact that he was technically forbidden was not lost on me.

And he said he wanted me.

My toes curled.

A good Christian girl lets a fallen angel into her bed. What's the worst that could happen? Good thing I was already in Hell.

I flipped through the pages of one of my studies, forcing my mind to swing anywhere but the male that occupied the room two doors from mine.

The first book was a thin collection of transcripts about nephilim and the study behind them being male when there were rumors to have been females at one point in time. Rumors because there was no physical proof, only stories of women with crooked wings.

If it is true females have evolved to share our ability, then the wrongness of them could be their sire's power rejecting them. No woman was ever created to bear an angel's power.

I snapped the book shut and tossed it to the side. Males were the same in every universe: sexist and obtuse.

I wondered what Killian would think of all this. He always thought I was strange, the way I yearned for something only fantasy books offered. Would he think I was an abomination now that I had gotten what I had wished for? Well, almost. Being the heir of a fallen angel and cast into Tartarus wasn't what I had hoped for. I'd always dreamed of being something magical and powerful, though.

The thought nestled its way into my head as I selected a new book and found a passage regarding Vasanistirio.

Only those of the most severe crimes remain in Vasanistirio, bound in chains of darkness until their judgement. We cannot free more than one of our brothers at a time. It is only on the Abaddon that we are able to rattle their confinements and wake them from eternal slumber. A prison within a prison, will our blood ever know peace?

Of all the creations, we are the only ones to suffer the turmoil of Darkness. We have been damned to lust for blood and shadows, having our light stripped from us. Where is the justice when humanity spits in the face of Heaven and they are called the chosen? Their light remains while ours is sucked into the soils of this land, binding us to misery.

It will not be until the last of our brothers are free from the pit that we can escape this prison. May mercy flee from the wrath of those cast from the Kingdom.

The name Uriel was scrawled on the back of the binding's interior. This wasn't just a textbook, but a journal. I flipped to the beginning, searching for anything about why the angels fell. There was nothing. Though there were no ripped pages, the accounts seemed to start in the middle of Uriel's story.

Diriel hadn't mentioned anything about freeing the chained. Perhaps the Abaddon was something of the past.

The quiet scrape of two rough surfaces sliding across each other had the hairs standing on the back of my neck. I stepped forward hesitantly, following the sound though my instincts told me to run in the opposite direction.

It was coming from my bedroom.

Something moved behind the gilded mirror. The shadows bobbed and swayed as a hooded figure moved amongst them. The figure took shape as it stepped into the cool light and slammed into the wooden desk with a gasp.

"Motherfucker."

I recognized that voice.

"Lane?"

She raised her head, her cobalt hair peeking through the hood. "Hi," she gritted, still suppressing the pain that must now be radiating in the shin she rubbed.

"What are you doing?"

"What does it look like?" She straightened, tossing back her hood, and dumped a duffle bag on the floor.

"Why are you sneaking into my room?" I stepped around her to investigate the hidden door that remained partially ajar.

"Your shitty boyfriend won't let me within ten feet of you. He all but locked me in my room, but I'm smarter than he is. I'm not going to let him keep me from an old friend."

Even though we weren't really friends, the comment made me smile. "Valen isn't my boyfriend."

She rolled her eyes. "Tell him that."

"Where did you come from?" I peeked at the mirror, to the long passageway that led to total darkness.

She jabbed a thumb over her shoulder. "There's a series of underground passages that link the main parts of the tyre."

Valen had warned me that Lane wasn't the same woman as before. I wasn't afraid, but I wondered if I should be wary. I looked to my desk where a candelabra stood. It wasn't much of a weapon, but it was the only thing I could attempt to wield within my reach.

"And you know about those how?"

Her brows arched. "Diriel showed me when I used to live here." She turned, following my gaze to the desk. She scoffed. "I could have you incapacitated before you even touched it. I know they told you that much about me. You don't have to stand there like I'm going to bite you."

My blood chilled. It was then I noticed the shadows beneath her eyes. And when she smiled, I saw the points of her teeth. They were not as extended as the angels', but they were fangs nonetheless.

"I'm not here to hurt you. I'm not even here to spy on you. Which, by the way, is why the Murder left me here. They want me to send them intel on you." She rolled her eyes again. She grabbed the bag from the floor and tossed it onto the desk. Papers scattered in the wake of her carelessness. I didn't think before darting to her to snatch them out the air, and the rest from the ground.

"Then why are you here? Not that I'm upset about it." How fast was she was what I really wanted to ask. And I don't think a spy would have outright told me about their snooping. At least she was honest about that. Not that I had anything to hide. Lane already knew my deep, dark secret.

I tensed as she unzipped the bag and pulled out—

Two bottles of wine. "Girls' night," she said. "I didn't know if you liked red or white, so I grabbed both. And the Murder left a few days ago. I'm a gift to you." She bent in a mock curtsy.

Whatever ideas Raum, Valen, and anyone else had of Lane, it was clear she had some of her own. I looked at the door, half expecting Valen to come barging in to foil whatever plan she was about to execute.

She turned with me. We both held our breath and, when the brooding cyn didn't break down the door, I looked back at her.

The mischief in her eyes grew as I sighed and pointed to the merlot.

She grinned, fishing two glasses out of her bag that were tucked neatly between a silk wrap and an assortment of snacks. She had even brought plates.

Lane poured both glasses and handed one to me. "Cheers," she said.

It was the clink of glass that finally snapped me out of my shock of her being here. A thousand years could change a person, but Lane was every bit as enchanting as I remembered her being.

She always had a light about her that drew people in. I think we could have been good friends before, but truthfully, I was too intimidated to approach her. Not that she would have been a bitch to me, but that she was too cool.

I smiled. "Cheers."

We sat in the parlor, across from each other. The silence didn't last long before her demeanor shifted. "So," she started slowly, "I have to ask. How did this happen?" She motioned up and down with her glass.

I took a breath before taking a large drink. Which she generously filled up again before I dove into my story. Whether it was speaking about it or reliving it inside my head, it became easier to think about what had happened. It sure as hell beat suppressing it.

"You should have seen the look on their faces when your wings came out." She shook her head. "I've never seen them all stunned stupid like that."

"Part of me wishes I had let Valen pull them before to save the headache this has turned out to be." I would never tell him that, of course.

"I'm surprised he let you. He has an issue with control."

I laughed into my glass, taking a small sip. "I've noticed." I tipped my head back. "He isn't too bad. He's an ass, but I've dealt with worse."

She arched her brow, a knowing look in her eye. "Oh, really." She dug through the bag, pulling out a wooden board and several bags of snacks which she laid on top. A small smorgasbord of meats and cheese.

"Not like that." The heat against my face betrayed me as she sat forward.

"Hey, I'm not going to judge you. I've been with Diriel and it was fantastic."

"Lane!"

"What?" She mimicked the inflection of my voice. "Andras too."

I shook my head. "He seems like a total brute."

"He is, which makes the sex even better." She held up her hand suddenly, cutting herself off. "Have you met any of the other girls? Do you know Hennie?"

I shook my head. "I've gone out a few times, but I haven't spoken to anyone other than the cyn. A woman named Clarissa waits on me regularly, though today was the first time she's ever spoken to me. I'm not sure whose fault that is, though. She gave me your note."

Lane nodded while I spoke. "Claire's cool. She can be stuck up, but now that she knows we're friends," she pointed back and forth, "she'll be a little bit nicer."

"Why's that?"

"We looked out for each other when I used to live here. She owes me."

I motioned to her. "How did you end up in Eurynomos? I can't imagine it is a better place than this."

She popped a piece of cheese in her mouth. She chewed slowly, like she was mulling over what type of answer she could give me. In the end she said, "That's complicated. And you're right, Eurynomos is what people imagine Hell to be, and it's still worse." She dusted her hands together and sat back against the couch. "The short version is Valen wanted me gone and Raum wanted me. Well, he said Baal wanted me, our cyn, but Raum's never let me far from his side. It was an easy solution to the problem Valen thought I was."

"Why?"

"Why Valen wanted me gone is because he is a prick. Why Raum wanted me, I don't know." She shrugged. Her body had gone stiff, like I was treading too close to something she didn't want me to know. It irked me that I had opened up to her but that she wasn't willing to part with her own secrets. She was lying.

"Valen said you're the longest standing in their keep."

"An unfortunate truth. I don't know why they've kept me alive, I really don't. So don't ask me." The last bit came out clipped.

Ok then. I knew a change of topic when I heard one.

She tossed back her head to finish her wine, a black crescent moon tattoo on the underside of her chin flashing.

I nodded to her. "I don't remember you having so many tattoos."

Flowers, dragons, and traditional patchwork marked both lengths of her arms. She turned out one arm and then the other, inspecting them. "There wasn't much else to do in the beginning. Plus, it was free. I figured I might as well finish what I started back home." She cocked her head. "Did you ever get any?"

"No. I don't even know what I would get now. I wanted an ouroboros for the whole rebirth, infinity thing. Or a dragon some-where. Seems kind of pointless now." Now that all of that fantasy stuff was real. Even if dragons weren't, I didn't think they would compare to literal angels. Not anymore.

"If you change your mind, I can recommend a girl in the city. She finished this sleeve," she pointed to her left arm that had a fantasy theme, "and a piece on my back. Speaking of, we should go into the city tonight. Not now, but in a little bit."

"I'm not supposed to go anywhere until Ariel is dead and Raguel leaves. Besides that, they've had me training all night. I'm exhaust-ed."

"You're already up this late, might as well pull an all-nighter." She flashed a wicked grin.

"If Valen finds out that I've snuck off, he will throttle us both."

"You, no. Me, he would have to catch first." Her grin remained. "The Murder might be wicked, but being with them has taught me a few tricks. I'm not afraid of your not-boyfriend."

The idea of going out anywhere sounded horrible. And yet, when was the last time I had fun? Real fun? I hadn't hung out with friends in a while. I hadn't been to a club in ages. I didn't know what sort of entertainment Vélos could offer at this hour, but Lane's optimism stoked my curiosity.

I glanced to the bedroom where the mirror remained ajar. "We can't stay out long, whatever we do. I'm not scared of Valen, but I don't want to piss him off either."

Lane jumped from her seat. "We don't have to stay long. Just a drink or two at one of the troves and then I'll bring you right back."

CHAPTER TWENTY-FIVE: DO YOU WORSHIP?

Ezra

C rave was written in bold pink neon above the door frame. The trove, another word for a club, was located on the border of the amorini and human districts. Club was an understatement to what *Crave* really was. It was the closest term I could come to describing the venue with its black walls and fuchsia curtains.

It was full of elaborate power. Music drifted through the air. A choir or orchestra, I could not tell whether mouths or instruments made the sound, rose in pitch. It was as lush and vibrant as the guests that flowed through the room. I'd never heard anything like it.

And the people. Exquisite. Some danced to the music, following the rhythm that had slowed to a seductive trance. While others hugged close to the shadows, their lips pressed against another's or fastened to a throat. But they were all beautiful in their fine velvet and something called qar that Lane explained was like silk. Others wore clothing that moved across their skin like water with crystal gems dangling from their wrists that cast sparkles across the room.

Some of the males were less human, and I decided that they must be a different race from the amorini. There were two specifically with long, slender necks that twisted when they turned, making them look more like snakes with their slanted eyes and ashen skin. A bleached film dipped over one's eyes as he took a drink from his glass. Hooked white talons clinked against the stem.

Another passed by with bronze scales and what looked like jagged bones behind his neck, horns maybe. But they weren't pointed like horns. These were too sharp, jagged.

Finally, I saw the source of the music. A male by the looks of them, with a crown of feathers about his head, fanning in a circle like a halo. Twelve eyes glittered across his face and, when he lifted his palms to the sky, another set of eyes blinked beneath his fingers. Beneath his body were four legs, shoed with hooves. Only the front were cloven.

The sudden urge to flee struck me. These angels—creatures—were equally terrifying in their glory. My breath lodged in the center of my chest.

Lane gave my arm a squeeze. "You get used to it."

My breath came out between a whoosh and a cough. I didn't have the urge to scream like some people do when they're terrified. I felt light-headed, like I would pass out any second. That would be more embarrassing than screaming.

"I don't think so," I said. How could you get used to something like that? Something that didn't register with the human mind because, in the real world, things like this didn't exist. The amorini were easier to accept because they looked human.

"What are they?"

Lane slid her arm through mine as I stared at the singer. "A virtue." She nodded to the gray ones. "Powers. And those over there with the two mouths are vens."

The vens had human faces with mouths set on top of each other, full of sharp teeth. Their bodies were long, serpentine with six arms.

I shuddered.

I ran my hands over the long dress Lane had fished out of my closet. Dark red, like the rest of the gowns in my possession. I don't know when Valen had snuck the one I wore now into my room, but I had to admit, he had good taste. Gold chains ran from the shoulder down to the waist. I had only said yes to this one, because out of all the dresses (there were at least twelve) it was the only one that had a covered back.

I appreciated that Lane hadn't said anything about the scars when I changed. My hair did a good job of hiding the traces that peeked through the arms of the dress.

Lane, of course, had come prepared. She wore a striking black gown that had a deep slit between her breasts, another up her thigh, and a short train in the back. I hadn't believed either of our dresses were anything but dinner attire, until I saw everyone else in the finery... or lack thereof.

A few wore minimal fashions, leaving little to the imagination.

A woman passed us, her eyes jet black save for the ring of her brown, nearly amber, irises. Her gaze flicked to Lane and then to the floor, which she promptly scurried across. I turned, watching her disappear amongst the crowd, her emerald gown flowing behind her.

"And she is a vampire," Lane said, speaking directly to my curiosity. "That's how all of their eyes look."

I blinked, looking to her. "But your eyes are different. They look normal."

She shrugged. "Vampires are made with an exchange of blood between the mortal and their maker and the demon possesses a piece of them. Anything that is possessed will have the black eyes." She tapped the corner of hers. "Raum gave me his blood, but he has never possessed me."

"And the part that makes you a witch?" Asking was a risk; Lane was particularly secretive when it came to her time in Eurynomos.

I walked several paces beside her before she said, "Eurynomos likes to experiment on their victims. The Murder treat me… well," she grimaced at the word, "but their curiosity is boundless. Oh, quick, come here." She grabbed my upper arm, pulling me behind two broad-shouldered males.

I looked between them to see Bishop moving through the throng. The silver lining of his clothes complemented his eyes. And when he smiled. Fuck, his mouth looked deadly. It was full of sharp teeth.

"If one of them is here, that means the others aren't far behind." Lane looked behind us. I turned too, half expecting Valen to materialize behind me and snatch me back into the shadows.

"We are fucked if he sees us," I said.

"We're fucked if any of them spy us," she said.

We slunk between the sheer curtains, moving slow as not to draw attention to ourselves, to skirt Bishop's wandering gaze. My eyes never left him as we snuck to the other side of the room, and how the women smiled at him when his attention lingered too long. They didn't seem bothered.

Maybe Bishop wasn't as cruel as he seemed. An ass, but not the angry villain Valen painted him to be. It was a silly thought to have, because of course he was still dangerous. I was just surprised no one appeared to be afraid of him.

I took a glass Lane handed me as we passed by one of the bars. I continued to watch as a woman in a silver gown approached him. Words were exchanged and whatever he said made her blush.

A charmer.

Part of me wondered if Valen was already here, tucked away in some dark corner with a lover. The thought shot a painful twang through my chest. An insolent thought that I had no business being jealous over even if it was true.

Was that why he had given me the option for him to stay? He would have known I would refuse his company.

Lane pointed to a male with the body of a snake, his scales in the pattern of a boa, to tell me he was a cherub. "They usually have three faces, but tonight he only wears one. Demons are fickle about those things. They're always changing their skin."

We settled in a private nook, sheltered by dark blue curtains, and watched the crowd. The music picked up its tempo and those on the dance floor started to spin faster. The women in their long gowns, the men in their fine clothes. And the demons in their ethereal beauty. It was fascinating. Overwhelming.

Lane would touch my arm from time to time, and it helped me remember to breathe.

"I had no idea," I said.

"Horrifying and amazing, isn't it?"

I nodded.

We gorged ourselves on wine and food for I don't know how long. Servant girls would come by with trays of food that Lane was constantly picking from, adding to the mound we already had. It was like she was starved. Maybe she had been. Or maybe it was because they didn't serve these foods in Eurynomos.

Lane would point at someone and tell me how she knew them or a loose piece of gossip she had overheard. It felt like old times. Just another night of hanging out with one of the girls.

I was tired after today's events, but being able to sit back, drink and relax with a friend, I almost felt normal. I shut my eyes, leaning my head against one of the pillows as the music changed to something far more suitable for a club, the tempo rising and falling, making my blood rush.

A laugh escaped me.

"What's that for?" Lane pressed.

"What a wild life we are living," I answered.

Her light eyes danced as she pressed her lips together. "Indeed." She clinked her glass against mine. "I always dreamed of finding a place like this. Not Tartarus, exactly, but this." She waved her free hand.

"I used to write stories about fairies and dragons. I think my first book was actually titled *Faerie Dragon Riders*." I laughed as the words fell out. "I was thirteen."

Lane gave me an exasperated look. "How original." She joined in my laughter as we replayed our childhood fantasies, comparing them to the creatures before us. She stood up, pulling me with her. "Let's dance!"

I wasn't much of a dancer, but within our small space, I moved and pretended to be a good one. I was breathless, my body slick with sweat as the air heated.

God, this felt good!

Lane was grinning, her sharp fangs flashing, when her eyes darted beside me.

An amorini with soft teak skin and short, cropped hair stopped in front of our cubby. He slipped his fingers between the veils, peering in. His eyes were gold set in a ring of red. "May I come in?" Though he asked permission, it was his voice that was an invitation. His gaze wandered slowly over Lane and then peeled away to land on me. His nostrils flared.

I stopped dancing.

Lane slowed but kept rolling her hips. "Yes, you can," she said, despite the glare I shot her.

He was handsome, but I didn't like the idea of being in such a tight spot with a stranger. I didn't care that it was their custom to be intimate. It wasn't mine. He ducked his head beneath the curtains and stepped over the threshold, his eyes still fastened to me.

"I've never seen you before."

He wasn't looking at my face, his eyes roving lazily over my body. Soft breaths from entangled partners fluttered and gasped between the slopes of the music. If this guy thought I was going to partake in similar activities, he was sorely mistaken.

"I'm new." Did he know what I was? If he kept sniffing the air, he might sense that I wasn't entirely human. I sat down, feigning boredom now that he had arrived.

He cocked his head and then swiftly turned to look at Lane. "You, I have seen. Your hair used to be pink." His eyes flitted over the top of her head, then back to me. He didn't move from the entrance. It was as if he was looking for something, but the space was so small, surely there wasn't anything worth discovering here.

"I like to keep things fresh," Lane said, slowly. She stopped dancing, her body coming to a slow halt. Her face skewed like she tasted something bad.

The stranger turned back to her and reached out, running a finger under her chin. His thumb ran over the corner of her mouth, wiping away crumbs that had gathered there. He leaned forward, Lane eagerly meeting him, and kissed her lips.

His tongue slipped inside her mouth. Lane jerked back, her body going rigid as that lazy smile returned to his face.

A ripple washed through the air and every single hair on my body rose on end. I tried to keep my face unreadable when he turned his attention to me. As he leaned in to cup my chin. If he felt the shift of power in the air, he didn't acknowledge it.

Valen was here. I don't know how I knew other than, I knew. I also knew that I was going to be in some serious heat if he found I'd snuck out of my room. I didn't even want to consider what the consequences would be if he found me with another male. Another male that was leaning in to kiss me.

I jerked my face out of his hand.

What was he doing in a place like this?

Not that it mattered.

Shove your double standards, I scolded myself. *You knew there was a possibility.*

It was in the brief moment of trying to peg where Valen was that I realized something was different about said male. His eyes had narrowed at my snub.

"New indeed."

The human form he wore was wrong, and he smelled different. The stench on his skin harsh and yet more floral than the scent of the demons with their rot and sulfur. My nose curled as it hit me. It's funny how something better can smell so wrong when you're accustomed to the worst. While he smelled good, he didn't smell right.

Lane reached for me abruptly, hauling me to her side. The male's eyes snapped to the side, following me. Eyes that split momentarily, separating to the side and up and down, looking at me with a shattered gaze.

The air around his shoulders shimmered. It traced the outline of his arms and over the top of his broad thighs. Outlines of—no, that wasn't right. They don't have wings.

The problem with standing is that it brought me chest to chest with the stranger. He took a half step to the side, obscuring my view of Lane.

"What's your hurry?" His voice was accusatory.

"Her keeper is here," Lane answered for me. She gave my hand a tug, but there was nowhere for me to go with him blocking our exit.

"And?" He slid a hand around Lane's neck. Moved his other to my collarbone.

Fires crackled behind his eyes when I smacked his hand away. "Get your hands off me. If my keeper," I used the same word Lane had, though I hated it, "sees us together, you're going to be in big trouble."

I could feel Valen getting closer, moving through the throng. I really didn't want to be caught dead with the male, but I didn't know how much worse it would be if Valen didn't find us. The best-case scenario was to remove ourselves from the situation entirely.

"I don't mind finding out how much trouble you're worth." The male shouldered Lane out of the way.

"Hey, back off!" she snapped. She grabbed his arm and hissed. She jerked her hand to her chest. If the look in her eyes wasn't enough, the blisters that spread along her palm were.

"You're not supposed to be here," she whispered. Horror. That's what that look was in her eyes. Not fear, not surprise. Pure horror.

"I'm exactly where I'm supposed to be."

I took a step back and he followed.

"Who are you?" Lane asked.

He whipped his head around. "That no longer concerns you. But your friend," he said, turning back slowly to me, "can call me Ramiel. Now get out." His voice dropped an octave for the command. A shot of power wracked across my skin. I didn't have time to register it because Lane was suddenly sprinting between the curtains, fleeing. Leaving me behind.

Disappointment, fear. It all twisted together as the male homed in on me.

She left me.

Ramiel leaned forward, bending at the waist so we were eye to eye. He sniffed one side of my face and then the other. A predator scenting out their prey.

"Back up," I said. I hated the way my voice trembled. He liked that, a smile forming between his thin lips. I hated when they smiled. Hated when anyone thought they could play on my fear. I curled my fists, looked past him to see which direction would be the easiest to evade him.

"There's no need for that," he said softly. "I think you'll find my appetites are much more enjoyable than the lot you've found yourself with."

His eyes split apart again, side to side.

I smelled it then, the power I couldn't place. And slowly, so very slowly, realized the fear building within me wasn't coming from me. It was the sheer impression of him that was driving me to my knees. I gritted my teeth as I fought it, but he was stronger, and my knees hit the cushioned ground with a thump.

It all hit me with such clarity. I looked up at his open, shining face and cowered. Everyone that saw an angel was struck with terror. I had felt it with Ariel as he pushed me beneath the water.

He was an angel. Not a demon. Not Fallen. A Heavenly host.

They'd found me. They'd found me and now he was going to kill me, and no one would be the wiser. The volume of the music had risen, the sounds of lust more insistent. This was not the way I imagined dying, surrounded by fucking.

"I bite," I said.

Ramiel ran a finger beneath my chin, turning my face up. "So do I, love. The only difference between us is that I do not bleed." His hand snaked around my jaw, his fingers digging hard into my jaw to pry my mouth open.

I willed whatever power I had within me to surface. I pulled at it as I tried to press off the ground, using every bit of strength to push through the hold Ramiel had keeping me submerged.

Valen suspected anger was my trigger, well, I was pissed. I was furious.

Get up!

A hand on my chin, another at the waistband of his pants, and yet I felt two invisible ones forcing my shoulders down, holding me still.

"Do you worship?" he asked.

Was this a joke? A test?

"Yes," I said.

"Then you know how to pray," he said, his eyes dancing.

I sat back on my heels, or tried to. I could still feel those invisible hands pushing back, holding me down. Forcing me to remain still.

"Yes," I said again.

The clink of the cinch of his pants shot a jolt through me. "Show me," he said. His fingers slipped beneath his belt.

I jerked my face one way and then the other. The web of his hand slid between my teeth and I bit down. I bit until his flesh popped. I bit until he let out a hiss and the picture-perfect image of his face faltered, giving way to feathers and multiple eyes. He jerked his hand free, his costume falling back into place.

"Not to pieces of shit like you," I spit at him.

Ramiel's eyes narrowed. "You little viper." He reached for me with the hand that I had just bit. His hand that was torn open, not a bead of blood to be seen.

The curtain flew back. One second Ramiel's hand was grazing my face and the next he was flying through the air, curtains billowing behind him as he shot down the row of secluded nooks. I surged to my feet as his force of power broke.

Fire burst across the top of my knuckles. I stumbled forward, falling to one of my knees even as someone scooped me under the arms. The fire flew up to my elbows.

"I've got you," Lane said. She hoisted me to her side as Valen stepped in front of us, blocking my view of Ramiel. She hadn't left me; she had gone for help. The relief I felt was overwhelming. I leaned into her as I found my balance.

I'd feel guilty later for doubting her.

Valen spun, his eyes dropping to my hands. "Put your fire out." The venom within his voice made me falter.

"He was going," but before I could finish, he barreled over me.

"I don't give a shit what he was going to do. He doesn't know what you are. Put. It. Out." He growled, his lips curling back to reveal sharp teeth.

Oh shit.

I swallowed the turmoil of emotions clawing up my throat, trying to snuff out the fire with them. I shook my hands for good measure, until the only evidence that was left were wisps of smoke.

Ramiel stood abruptly, throwing the multicolored fabrics from his shoulders. His face flushed as he hurried to buckle his pants. "You've got a lot of nerve interfering with holy work."

"Since when does holy work involve force?" Valen said. He let a piece of his power unfurl. It ran down his backside in smoke, drawing around our feet. It coaxed something deep inside me.

"I was only helping her with her prayers. Someone needs to carry them back to the heavens." His tongue ran along the corner of his mouth. "I'll take yours back if you give her to me."

"Mind the way you speak when you're before a cyn," Valen growled.

Ramiel's hand dropped to his waist, sitting on top of something I couldn't see. "Or what?" His smile faltered, his eyes looking to something past us.

Bishop strode forward coolly, the indifference he had exuded earlier replaced with malice. I took back what I said about him being charming. He looked utterly terrifying. "Or I will crucify you to the ground and let him rip out your wings while the entire court watches, trespasser," he hissed, long and slow, stretching out the word.

Surprisingly, no one else paid much attention to us. A few on-lookers stole glances, but otherwise people were so consumed with each other, they didn't notice the rise in hostility. The couple beside Ramiel were still kissing, still grinding against each other. What the fuck?

Bishop moved like a panther, padding quietly until he was at my other side. Lane pulled me back. Let the cyn handle this. I moved with her, and Valen turned, searing me with his gaze. Don't move, got it.

"Blasphemy," Ramiel spat.

"You come into our home under a false guise. That is blasphemy. You are to make your presence known before setting foot within our court," Bishop said. "Or have you forgotten your own laws?"

"What is one less whore to you?" Ramiel shot back.

"Careful," Valen warned.

"You may have nothing unless we permit it," Bishop said.

Ramiel's eyes fluttered in that creepy way of his. "If I said it was on Heaven's orders that I slaughtered half your keep, no one would bat an eye. No one intervenes with Heaven's work."

Golden flames touched Valen's fingertips.

Ramiel's smile was a spiteful thing. His grip tightened on the thing at his waist. On the silver hilt that flashed in the light.

"Gentlemen, what seems to be the problem?" The voice came from everywhere all at once. Behind, below, above. It rang inside my head.

With that voice, the entire court came to a jarring halt.

CHAPTER TWENTY-SIX: THE SERAPHIM

Ezra

The angel knew how to make an entrance. His gold armor cast light into every corner of the room. It lit across those scurrying to flee. Uncloaked their shadowed faces.

I was certain he was an angel. Not due to my experience but because of the six red wings folded at his back. Of the light and power radiating off him. The demons ducked their heads as he passed, eyes squinting and lips curling.

He was well over six feet tall, seven feet if I had to guess, packaged in porcelain skin that flickered every time he moved. His body was covered in red eyes. Every time one opened, another would close. They were everywhere his armor did not touch. On his left arm was a black banded tattoo, twin to Bishop's. He was magnificent in the way that can only be carved by battle and obedience. There wasn't a trace of kindness in his eyes.

The angel strode to the middle of the room. He cocked his head to Ramiel. "Speak," he said. The room vibrated with his command, making the demons hiss in unison.

"It was a misunderstanding," Ramiel said. He picked his way across the room until he was at the newcomer's side. He ran a hand through his dark locks, dissolving away the glamour that hid his identity as if a veil was being pulled away. His hair changed first, turning from black to red. Dark red as deep as if someone were bleeding. Feathers crowned his head in a halo. Then his eyes bled into their true color. The rest of his body followed suit.

At his back were broad red wings and his entire body, what was not gilded in armor, was covered in eyes.

The nausea that gnawed at my stomach was relentless.

I had been right.

An angel. One that was supposed to be good.

A warm hand slid over the back of my neck. I shut my eyes as I focused on Valen's heat. I tried desperately to shut out the buzzing of energy in my head. We weren't out of this yet.

"What sort of misunderstanding?" The angel looked to the cyn, skimmed behind them to me and Lane. His eyes noted Valen's hand on the back of my neck before settling on my face. "Well?" He was asking me.

"Prayers," I rasped. I swallowed, trying to find strength for my voice.

The angel waited.

I hardened my fear. I shot a look at Ramiel. "But last time I checked, you didn't need your hands down your pants for that."

The grip on the back of my neck tightened. I winced under the pressure of Valen's hand, moving closer to him if only to find some relief.

"Liar," Ramiel spat.

"I'm not lying," I said.

The angel sniffed the air and turned, slowly, to Ramiel. The male didn't so much as shift beneath all those eyes. His only response was to shrug as if to say, "What did you expect her to say?"

"Lies or not," the angel turned back to face our little group, "you know the consequences of laying a hand on a host."

"Perhaps Ramiel should have been forthright with his appearance. My eyes are not what they used to be," Valen said, addressing the head of the angels, swiping his fingers to those gold irises I knew missed nothing.

The angel grunted. "This matter is done with. Is it not, Ramiel?"

Ramiel forced a smile. "It is."

Fuck him. Fuck the both of them.

Angels were supposed to be saviors, protectors, and warriors. Not whatever *this* was. It was perverse and twisted as... As Ariel. Was Valen actually right? Were the angels truly wicked? Were these the creatures that made up Heaven?

Bishop gave the angel a passing glance as he made way for a set of low-seated thrones I hadn't noticed before. "What business do you seek, Raguel?" He turned and sat, the hem of his jacket flaring as he settled into the cushions.

Raguel. *The* angel everyone had been talking about.

Valen pushed me forward, moving us toward Bishop. He pulled me into his lap as we sat. Any other time I might have fought him over it. But I understood what he was doing. Appear casual and bored and the angels might move along.

Pretend to be the whore they thought I was and no one would get hurt.

Lane dropped to her knees beside us, her head slightly down, but her eyes didn't leave the angels. I sat back in Valen's lap, curling my legs up so he could slip a possessive hold between them and grip one of my thighs.

Raguel stopped a few feet away. While the eyes on his face held Bishop's gaze, the others on his body roved over me. Searching. Looking.

He knows.

Why else would he be looking at me so intensely?

I looked down at the floor, then past him, to Ramiel whose thousands of eyes were simmering.

"Have you noticed anything out of the ordinary these last weeks? Stray bleeds, signs. A stranger, perhaps?" The eyes in Raguel's face remained on Bishop while the others flitted over the crowd.

"No," Bishop said.

Raguel turned to Valen.

"Nothing strange has happened here. Though news of your search reached us long before you did. What is it?" Valen's thumb moved back and forth across my skin.

I focused on that touch. Let it ground me and begged to God (if He could even hear me from here) that the speed of my heart did not give me away.

Raguel let his arms relax at his sides. "Truthfully? I do not know. Which is why I have come here, to each kingdom of Tartarus, in hopes that someone might have knowledge of what it is I search for."

Bishop's chuckle was jolting. The music of it off-key. "We cannot help you if you give us nothing to go on."

The hard lines of Raguel's face deepened. "Not on this it seems, but perhaps you can tell me of another matter. One of a nephilim."

My stomach dropped. At the same time, Valen ran his tongue over my throat. I hardly noticed as I tried not to let the sheer panic take hold of me.

"Easy," he whispered against my skin. "Breathe."

Bishop sucked the back of his teeth. "We heard those whispers too," he said bitterly. "A false hope."

"Hope," Raguel scoffed. He grinned, flashing too-bright white teeth. "Your curse still holds."

"Unfortunately," Bishop grumbled. "I believe I speak for all of Tartarus when I say this, that if there was a nephilim it would not be allowed out into the world. It would be chained to the bed, doing what it does best in order to breed an army against you and everything you stand for.

"*If* that rumor were true, you would have to search the depths of Tartarus to find it. No one would be foolish enough to let it out."

Valen gave my thigh a gentle squeeze as my heart skipped a beat. This was for show, of course. It had to be.

Pin her down. Jinn's words rang in my head.

"Then you will not mind if we interview your harem. A rumor it may be, but it is best to be certain all the same."

Bishop shrugged. "You will anyway." He paused. "But I am feeling generous to my people tonight." His eyes skimmed along the crowd, to the mortals that huddled together. None of the music or festivities had resumed. Half looked enthralled with the host; the others were terrified. "Interview them, pray with them—true prayers." Bishop's eyes danced, silver flames sprouting beneath his lashes. "But if any of your men lay a hand to any of them, they forfeit their life to me."

Ramiel broadened his stance. "You defy Heaven."

"It is my greatest pleasure," Bishop purred.

"We do not need to touch anyone to find the information we seek," Raguel said.

Bishop held up two fingers. "And you will do it without guise.

My people have the right to know to whom it is they speak. They deserve you to uphold your own laws." He cut his fingers through the air. "Lose the glamour. All of it."

My pulse pounded in the few seconds Raguel hesitated. It felt like minutes before the angel conceded, the eyes on his arms fluttering in agreement.

He raised his hand, signaling to his men with the flick of two fingers. Nine of the males shimmered throughout the trove as their glamour fell away. Dark hair was replaced with red, smooth skin with blazing eyes.

There were too many.

Oh God, they were going to find out.

How did news of me slip? I looked up at Valen, trying to convey that we needed to leave. To run. Not that I had any clue where we could run to that the angels could not find us.

He dipped his head forward, his nose brushing against mine. It was too dangerous to exchange words. I shut my eyes and followed the flow of his breath. In and out slowly we breathed. He turned his face and slid his lips to the side of my mouth, to the very corner, and kissed me.

"I'll start with these two."

Raguel's voice jolted me out of the lull Valen had been pulling me into. I felt Valen tense beneath me before his eyes slid open, flaming.

"You can see that I am busy with this one," he said. He motioned to Lane. "She is free, however."

Lane threw him daggers with her eyes. Whatever had happened between the two of them, they seriously hated each other now. I briefly wondered if Valen had been another one of Lane's lovers that had ended badly, and that's why they were so bitter. A tinge of jealousy graced me, though I had no right to it.

Lane hopped up, crossed her arms over her chest, and said, "I'll answer whatever questions you have providing it's not that one asking them." She pointed to Ramiel.

Raguel considered her a moment and motioned for one of the other males to approach her. They moved to the side where he offered her a seat. The angel held out his hands, but Lane's remained crossed.

The angel made no move to push Lane as he turned his hands to lay over the top of his thighs and spoke in words so softly that I could not hear them.

Valen took my hand gently and slowly offered it out to Bishop. The cyn leaned forward and kissed my wrist. I jolted. A soft chuckle left Bishop's throat as he parted his lips to run his tongue in slow circles over my skin.

Valen's hand had moved higher up my thigh. "Sit still," he hissed. I had not heard this version of Valen before and it genuinely frightened me. The voice he used now belonged to a serpent.

I turned to him as he dropped his head and pressed his lips into the top of my shoulder. His eyes held mine. Valen was still there, but something else lurked within the depths of his gaze. Something hungry. Dark and wicked.

Bishop slid his touch up my arm so that my hand slid across his face and my fingertips skimmed across the shaved part of his head. His tongue swirled across the inside of my elbow, sprouting chills across both my arms.

I had never been touched like this before, let alone by two males. Beneath the uncertainty pounding through my veins was heat. I couldn't deny that the way they touched me felt good. A breath left my lips that had Bishop's eyes flicking up to meet mine. They were hard as steel.

"Now, you," Raguel said, breaking into my thoughts.

I started, turning back to Raguel. I could feel my face turn as red as his feathers.

I looked from him to the demons I was caught between.

"You can have her when we are done with her," Valen said. To make his point, he shoved my legs apart and slid his hand all the way up, until his thumb brushed against my sensitive flesh.

It was enough to snap me out of the daze they had lulled me into.

"Don't you dare," I snarled at him. Guise be damned, I was not going to be put on display in front of so many people. In front of angels.

Valen grinned. "But I so love to."

Sharp points grazed my flesh as Bishop's fangs slid free. This needed to stop. They needed to stop right now.

"Enough," Raguel snapped. "I will personally see to her."

"She is safe between us," Valen hissed. His canines had elongated. His tongue brushed the back of them as he spoke.

Raguel smirked. "As safe as Lydia, Monique, and all the others were?" He sucked in a breath between his teeth. "I remember all of their names, do you?"

An uncomfortable silence filled the space between us. Neither of the cyn spoke.

"I didn't think so. I will take her now." Raguel held out his hand, his banded fingers beckoning me forward.

A low hiss emitted from Bishop's throat, but not even he offered another comment. Because even all the way down here, angels had more power than all the kings of hell.

I wondered what would happen if I were to ask Raguel to take me home. If he would listen to my plea. One look at his stony face told me I'd never see home again if I confessed.

Valen slid his hand free of my thighs to draw a finger on the side of my face, pushing my hair back. At the same time, Bishop let my arm go. Remnants of his kisses still buzzed over my flesh.

"You will return her to me once you've finished your inquest," Valen said.

Raguel's eyes dropped to the dress I was wearing. "I will."

Valen pressed his lips against my ear. "Raguel keeps his word."

That didn't make me feel any safer as I put my hand in Raguel's and let him draw me to my feet. His power was beautifully fierce. A gracious thing that made me smile as soon as we touched. There was nothing unkind in his touch, unlike his countenance that said this was a very dangerous male. I wondered, though, if it was the glory of him that Claire had been referring to when she spoke of him.

I understood it, even as I wanted to cower from him.

I squeezed his fingers on impulse.

"Ramiel," Raguel said, his voice cool and even. "Remain with the cyn, and if you feel so inclined, perhaps you will be kind enough to take their prayers in the way you offered this young woman."

Ramiel balked, his face paling.

Meanwhile, Bishop sat forward with a wicked grin on his face. His chrome eyes slid down Ramiel's body like oil.

"What's your name?" Raguel asked.

I licked my lips. "Ezra."

"Ezra, walk with me," the angel said.

On impulse, I followed. I was practically at his heel even though I knew he would be my end. If Ramiel didn't know what I was, then Raguel might not either. He didn't seem intent on tearing me apart. He looked peeved though, annoyed that the males were hindering his search with their dramatics.

Raguel was looking for something. If that something was me, this situation would have gone differently. I had nothing to go on but my gut, and even that felt like it would betray me any second.

I threw one last look at the cyn. Valen brushed his finger over his lips. A silent command.

I followed Raguel in the wake of his grace. My heart thrummed loudly, a drum that timed my steps.

Somewhere in the background, I heard Ramiel say, "You can choke on your prayers."

CHAPTER TWENTY-SEVEN: TAKE THIS TOKEN

Ezra

"Your keeper does not trust me." The lilt in Raguel's voice sounded like laughter.

I turned, looking for Valen, but the only thing that trailed us was natural darkness. No one lurked in the shadows.

"The demons are a distrustful lot," I said. I glanced at Raguel, meeting two of the eyes on his shoulders. They blinked in response, opening a mass of them on his forearm.

"Hmm." Raguel slowed to keep up with my stride. I was a fast walker, but no way could I keep up with his long legs. "That they are. My condolences on capturing the attention of those brutes. One is bad enough, but two." Raguel sucked the back of his teeth. "You must be special."

You have no idea.

Diriel said they couldn't read minds unless there was an exchange of blood between partners. Did that go for all angels or just the Fallen? In any case, I didn't want Raguel to catch on to just how special I was. I focused on shielding my mind and lay open for any signs of someone trying to get in.

"You should ask Ramiel. He seemed to think so." My face heated at the memory, of his vile touch. Not even the amorini, handsy as they were, had the audacity to actually force me into such a position. Valen certainly knew how to push my buttons, but he didn't push himself on me. I didn't count what had happened on the thrones before the angels. That had been a show. Not an act behind a veil where no one could see us. Where no one could see the harm that might have happened.

Raguel looked down at me. "Ramiel is new to his position."

I snorted. The eyes on his wings opened, looking like bleeding slits as they narrowed at me. "So that excuses him from forcing himself on me? I thought you were supposed to be the good guys."

"We are neither good nor bad. We simply are. We do the work of Heaven as is expected of us, carrying out our Father's judgement and commandments. But what Ramiel did was outside of those expectations." He held out his arm, allowing me to step in front of him down a set of stairs that led to the river.

I realized he was leading me somewhere. A nervous prickle stalked the back of my neck. This was a secluded area, with no witnesses to hear me scream. I swallowed and made it down the first set of stairs before reaching another, watching the water grow closer.

Would he try to drown me too? *You're not supposed to be thinking about that.*

The neon lights of the taller steeples reflected in the gentle flow of water. It made the stained glass they reflected behind dance and twinkle. I took a deep breath as I dragged my eyes away from the colors and hoped I wouldn't be splashing through them soon.

"What makes him any better than the Fallen?"

Raguel waited at the bottom of the third and final landing before leading us down the riverbank, keeping himself between me and the water.

"The Fallen turned their backs on Heaven. They gave up their glory, their souls. Everything that made them worthy burned in their revolt. They are nothing like those of us who still serve."

"You know that's not what I was asking."

Raguel paused, and I stopped a few feet ahead of him. "We all face temptations. Ramiel, in the face of his, was not strong enough to resist them. I turn my eye away from my men in Tartarus so they may cleanse their impurities, so long as whatever party they seek company with is willing. Ramiel will bear his punishment at the hands of my commander tonight."

I stared at him. He had only walked in on the tail end of things. I hadn't expected him to take the word of a human over another angel.

Raguel tapped the side of his head. "I see through the eyes of all my men connected to me."

I looked at the mass of eyes on his body and then the two set within his face with their split irises. That was unsettling. I thought having someone read your mind would be invasive, but to see through them. I shuddered inwardly.

"What will be done to him?"

Raguel tsked. "You're already in Hell. I'll not give you further fuel for your nightmares." He approached a slab of broken stone, what could have once been a bench, and seated himself beside it. His massive wings splayed out behind him, resting in the dark blades of grass. A single pair fell across his chest and into his lap. As he settled back, the eyes along his skin shut tight, giving the impression of unbroken flesh.

Raguel keeps his word.

Let's hope he does. I took a breath and sat down on the slab. This put us at eye level and, I realized, that was probably his intention.

The corner of Raguel's lip twitched. The only strangeness to him was the hollow set of his crimson eyes within his face. All the others were gone entirely.

He's making himself appear human.

As human as an angel could without scaring me shitless.

"Ezra," he scowled at the mountains, "you are not made for a place like this."

"I didn't ask to be here," I said.

Raguel nodded. "No one here comes willingly. Even the spoiled on Earth that think Tartarus is the better option than Heaven come to fear and loathe it."

A spark of hope ignited in my chest. "What are you saying?"

Could he, no he couldn't possibly be offering me–

This wasn't an inquisition at all. This was something else. Raguel could be my ticket home.

"I am saying you are someone made for my Father's kingdom." A coin appeared between his index and middle fingers. He turned it, the gold shimmer catching in the dull light.

I sat up straight. "You can get me out of here?" I blurted. I didn't know whether to be joyful or scared, but the idea of leaving Tartarus was too good to pass up.

Raguel looked at me from the corner of his eye. After ten seconds, I realized that wasn't the case. My heart faltered. The hope that had flared so bright fluttered.

"If I could," he said. "But it is not the will of the fates, nor of Heaven."

Raguel turned the coin between his fingers again, moving it

across his knuckles. "I do not grant favors often to mortals, but," he held the coin out to me, "should you ever be in need, use this and I will come. I will do what I can to help you within the limitations of my Father's will."

Not a coin, a seal. I brushed my thumb against the smooth ridges of the favor. The geometric pattern similar to the tattoos of the arc, but this had three circles, two smaller ones at the top, and a much larger one in the center.

This was the opportunity I had been waiting for, and yet it felt cheap.

What good was a favor if I was still damned?

Bitterness rose within me. It burned the back of my eyelids as I shut them to keep my resentment from being seen.

I curled my fingers over the seal. "Thank you," I said. There was nothing grateful in my tone. I couldn't keep the dejection from my voice.

It's not like he would walk away if he knew what I was.

I swallowed, forcing the next question out. "What is a nephilim?"

I wanted to know what Raguel really thought of my kind. *My kind.* Strange that I felt something for my kin that no longer existed. That everyone hated them because of their sires.

It fed my rising animosity.

Raguel didn't appear to hear my question at first, instead choosing to remain silent as he contemplated at my side. It was several more minutes before he finally answered. "Abominations. They are the children of demons and women. Creatures bred out of lust and violence for the sole purpose of destruction."

The hole in my chest grew deeper. An expanding gap of ache.

"I didn't know it was possible for angels to... well," I motioned my hands in the air.

"Demons," Raguel said again. "Angels do not succumb to such sins. It is our brothers who fell who took part in human flesh." A growl hung to the back of every word. "It is no longer possible. God cursed the last of the Fallen so they would not spread the chaos to mankind."

I nearly reminded him that one of his own angels had tried to succumb to such a sin. But something told me Raguel would only reiterate what he had already told me. That there was some loophole for the angels to slip through because they had their grace.

How was that fair?

How the hell did they get to push the boundaries, to sin, yet people like me and the amorini were damned for simply existing?

I swallowed. I could feel the heat building within me as my anger rose in tempo. I shoved it down to the hole in my chest I had been trying to fill for God knows how long.

"But you think one has been born?"

"It is impossible for such a thing to happen yet stranger things have happened. While I do not believe it is possible, I think it wise to investigate nonetheless. One lost nephilim could be the downfall of Earth."

My brow furrowed. That's not what I had been told. The cyn had said I could help them take down Heaven. They had mentioned nothing of Earth. "How's that?"

"Because a nephilim would force God's hand into destroying the world sooner than when it has been foretold. That sort of corruption left unchecked would be the ruin of mankind. It would be the ruin of Heaven too, if their chaos was unleashed on the world. It would make God a liar. Which He is not."

Unease coiled within my stomach, twisting and knotting.

"What if they were good?"

Raguel shook his head. "There is nothing within a nephilim that would deem salvation."

The hole grew into a cavern. I felt absolutely hollow. There was truly no hope for me. How could there be, when a renowned archangel did not even have faith.

Wicked, selfish creature.

I couldn't agree with Raguel. There was no room for me to plead my case without shining a spotlight on myself. If Raguel knew what I was, he would kill me.

The reality crashed into me. I leaned against my knees, turning my face away so he could not see how he had wounded me.

"So, what are you really looking for?" I cleared my throat as I struggled to change the direction of our conversation. To maintain some control over my spiraling emotions.

Raguel leaned forward so he was peering up into my face. Though the eyes on his body remained closed, it felt like they were still looking at me. "You're a curious thing."

"Can you blame me? I never imagined any of this." I looked back to the tyre. Its shadow loomed over the water trickling in front of us. "Every day brings new questions."

"Do not ask too many of your captors. They spread lies, even amongst those they favor." Raguel's wings shifted on his chest. "As for what I am looking for, I truly do not know. Evil leaks into your world, rot that only comes from Tartarus, and yet Hell has no power to do such a thing."

At least I could take some comfort in knowing I wasn't the one wreaking havoc on Earth.

I studied Raguel as he tipped his face back, viewing the twisted heavens high above. I hated him. In that moment, I detested him for everything he stood for. He was wrong. He was so incredibly wrong about the nephilim. About me. And I was so fucking angry that I couldn't tell him that without dying for it.

Beneath the resentment was something that drew me to him. I wondered if it was within my human nature to like one of God's messengers.

The conflict of my affections made my skin crawl.

I wanted him to leave Vélos. To leave Tartarus altogether.

I couldn't wrap my mind around how someone who was supposed to be so noble could be so unfeeling. So closed off to believe that I had no salvation.

Heaven, as Valen had told me time and again, was a cruel place.

"One last question," I said. Raguel looked at me expectantly. His dual irises remained steady as he held my gaze. "Why did you bring me out here?"

Raguel nodded to my clasped hands. "To give you that."

I ran my thumb over the cheap courtesy. "I would ask you to free me of this place, you know?"

Raguel stood. He tucked all six incredible wings at his back. I took his hand as he offered it to me. "Perhaps when you do, Heaven's will, will have changed and I can do just that." He brushed his thumb over the back of my hand. He motioned for me to move in front of him. Back to the trove. Back to Valen.

"Could you not vouch for me now?"

"It is not for you to understand Heaven's will, Ezra. It is for me to interpret it and for you to accept it regardless of how you may feel about it."

It was not the answer I wanted. It was not the one I was going to accept. If Raguel would not free me from this place, I would find my own way.

"Besides, Valen seems to have taken a liking to you."

"What does that matter?"

"I like Valen," he said matter-of-factly.

My brows arched in surprise.

"He is more tolerable than most." There was truth in his words. The corner of his mouth tipped up one second and then disappeared the next. If I didn't know any better, I would have wagered Raguel considered Valen more than just tolerable.

CHAPTER TWENTY-EIGHT: TO HAVE POWER

Ezra

My eyes fluttered. It had been nearly an entire day since I last slept. The sky shifted colors, lightening to periwinkle pink. The moons had made their journey to the other side of the mountains.

Raguel returned me to Valen as promised, who had been waiting for us outside of *Crave*. He had been pacing like a caged animal when we approached, his muscles taut with energy. At the sight of me, his muscles uncoiled.

Music still sang from within, but it was dull compared to earlier. It seemed the majority of the white city had started to turn in for the evening. Laughter echoed down the glistening street, and I glimpsed two bodies hurdling down the road on what looked like a hover bike.

"Try to keep this one alive," Raguel said. A command was in the underlay of his voice.

Valen's eyes flashed, but his expression was coy when he said, "Oh, she's not going anywhere."

It wasn't until Valen touched me that I recognized that the flare I had seen in his eyes was desperation. Desperate to get to me, to keep me safe. A thrum of power coursed through me the instant his fingers wove around the back of my neck.

Raguel saw it. How could he have missed it with all those eyes?

"Valen," he said softly, drawing the male's attention up. "Do your kingdom a favor and relieve Bishop of his crown."

Valen tensed. "I would never betray my brother."

Raguel's gaze drifted to me. He tsked. "That's a shame."

"Do not make yourself too comfortable, Raguel. I would hate for you to get stuck down here with the rest of us." Valen slid his arm around my waist as he made a cut in the air. The bleed was tapered with gray tendrils of smoke.

Raguel's grin was awkward on his pale face. "Always so hospitable."

I barely recognized that Valen took me to his room instead of mine. I was keenly aware, however, of his temper still simmering in shadows and flits of ash. I was exhausted, though, physically and mentally, and didn't care.

I understood what Raguel had said about the nephilim, had it fed to me these last few weeks. But I still didn't want to accept it. I wouldn't.

"Ezra," Valen said softly.

I waved him off. "Yell at me in the morning." The words came out sharper than I intended.

"I told you to stay out of trouble."

"And you disrespected me for disobeying you. You don't get to do that. I understand what happened on the dais was for Raguel, but I will not be treated like one of the mindless women who fall at your feet. I am not someone you can boss around." I threw up my hands. "I didn't know all of that was going to happen. I just wanted a break from everything. To have a bit of fun."

"Fun that could have cost you your life," he snapped. "Even if the angels hadn't shown up, that is not the sort of place you should have been."

Heat flooded my face. "I was there for the drinks. Lane didn't tell me what sort of club we were going to."

"Oh, come on. You're in a court of fallen cupids where we deal in lust and love. You had to have had some idea." His brow arched as he looked at me from under his lashes. He was baiting me.

"Are you jealous that I didn't come to you?" I tracked him as he crossed the room toward me. "That's what this is. What hurts more, your pride or your feelings?"

Valen's teeth flashed. "I know you want me. Though, I think you would seek someone else's bed to spite me."

I stood my ground despite how close we were standing. The sliver of space between us a fragile barrier. "So, feelings then?"

This game between us, the pull and tug, drove me wild. Paired with the heat simmering within my blood, I didn't think I could dampen it much longer.

He trailed a finger from my brow down to my chin. "I don't have feelings, sweetheart. I just don't like the idea of someone else touching you."

"Because you'd be so good at it." Steam left my lips.

I couldn't stop myself. Couldn't stop from encouraging him. Any rational thoughts I might have had were lost to the haze of his heat. To the musk of his scent surrounding me. I was inviting him in.

"I could make you fall." He wasn't just talking about pulling me to the Fallen's side. He looked like Killian far too much and he would use it to his advantage. *Was* using it to his advantage. Even if their similarities became muddied the more time passed.

Wicked creature.

I took one step back. Valen took one forward.

"Make it so that anyone after me would be ash in your mouth." His thumb ran across my lower lip as he twisted his hand, resting it lightly over the front of my neck. "Though we both know, there's only ever going to be me. And all those before me are nothing." His face tipped down.

"Screw you." I turned on my heel. Valen gripped me hard enough that I spun back to face him with my next step. "I'm not in the mood to play your games. I'm sick of them."

"And I'm sick of yours," he growled. There was such rage in his eyes. I shifted back, but before I could follow through, Valen leaned in.

His lips met mine in a fatal swoop. His skin to mine, his scent, his heat, his taste overwhelmed me. I leaned into him, let his fingers tighten around my neck as they slid into my hair.

The first time I ever kissed a boy, sparks had flown. It had been sweet and timid. Butterflies had rushed to the pit of my stomach. The feel of his lips against mine had gone straight to my head and I thought, at the time, it was the best thing in the world.

That was nothing compared to kissing Valen. I knew then I couldn't pretend. Valen held all the cards.

I folded. There was no coming back from this.

Live sparks spun through the air between our mouths as I parted my lips to gasp. He inhaled what I gave him, taking advantage of my open mouth and slipping his tongue inside. An orange flame danced behind his teeth, answering the rising heat in the back of my throat. I arched into him, wanting more, *needing* more.

He snaked an arm around my waist and pulled me flush against him. He was an inferno. A towering wall of flame caging me against his body.

The spell was broken all too soon as he eased back.

"Why did you do that?" The breathlessness of my voice gave away my need.

"Because if something were to happen to you, I would spend the rest of my life regretting that I had not." His eyes flicked to my mouth.

I'd never tasted anything like Valen. Had never come close to experiencing the needy want that coursed through me.

"You can do it again." I swallowed. "If you want."

Valen's eyes searched mine. A low hum rumbled deep within his chest. "I want to do many things to you, Ezra." He ran his thumb over my lips, parting them. "Who do you see?"

For once, I wasn't offended that he brought up Killian. Maybe I should have felt guilty that I disregarded Killian. But I didn't care. Not when I knew this was his way of asking permission. To make sure I knew what I was doing.

"You."

The light in his eyes flared.

"Valen."

His name barely left my lips before his were pressed against mine. This was the kiss of a male who was absolutely starved, desperate to devour me. I parted for him as if I could sate that hunger.

I let him lead me back to his bed, one backward step after the other. Until my thighs hit the edge of the mattress.

The fire within me swelled. It tunneled through my blood, filling that void in my chest. Heat climbed the walls of my throat. I opened my eyes to see a flash of color dart between his lips.

I brushed my finger over his lower lip. "What is this?"

He parted his mouth so I could see the fire dancing in the back of his throat. I opened mine in response, could feel the rush of something in the back of mine answer. I closed it, my breath hitching.

"Power." The sound of his need was coarse in his voice. The hard press of it dug into my thigh as he pushed his hips into me.

If this was what power really felt like it, then I would gladly let it consume me. It was a lush. Intoxicating. I reveled in the way I felt beneath Valen's hands. I didn't stop my smile before I kissed him again.

"I'm still angry with you," he said between kisses.

"I know. Let's leave it for tomorrow." I silenced his retort with another kiss. "I want to keep doing this. Just this."

"Let me have you, Ezra."

I slid my nose against his, breathing him in. "This is all you get. Punishment for whatever you're going to dole out to me later."

His white teeth flashed in the darkness. "You harpy."

I nipped his nose. "This is all you're ever going to get."

Valen's low chuckle was kind music. It wrapped around me and sent chills racing along every inch of my body. "Lies do not suit you."

I rolled my hips into his in response. I wanted to chase this feeling, but I wanted to see how far I could push him. I had only had a little taste of power and already I wanted more. Could I bring a fallen angel to his knees?

Valen's wicked desire pulsed against my thigh as he slid me onto my back. His weight fell into me, pinning me hard to the bed.

"I don't intend to be tossed to the side once you've had your fill."

Valen cocked his head. "You think I would do that?"

"You're a master of love and lust. I'm not your first conquest. But if you take me, I will be your last."

A sinister grin fell across his face. It was delicious seeing how carnally wicked he looked when he surveyed me beneath his lashes. How utterly sexy he was when he smiled like that with one corner of his mouth higher than the other. An arrogant smile. A confident one.

"Oh, Ezra. I have you right where I want you. Mind." He kissed the center of my forehead and then slowly, so achingly slow, moved down the length of my body. His breath edged over my chest, dragging chills to the surface of my skin. Below my breasts, he planted another kiss. "Body." Lower he dragged his sinful mouth to the center of my thighs. "Soul." He pressed his lips against me. The warm breath he blew against the thin scrap of fabric arched my back.

"I have no desire beyond you." He placed his lips back on me, parted them so he could press his teeth into my sensitive flesh.

Valen was everything I had been waiting for.

I came undone. Fire leapt to my skin as I reached for his head to pull him closer. It raced across my knuckles, spreading to the sharp point of my elbows. My vision clouded as white-hot need burned through my body, consuming every sensible thought in my head.

He hummed against me, sending soft vibrations through my body as I slid my fingers through his curls. I tightened my hand into a fist in an attempt to ground myself. He ran his sinful tongue over my underwear.

"You're a devil," I breathed.

Valen eased forward, sliding up my body. "A compliment coming from you." He pressed his mouth over my hardened nipple beneath my dress. The sensation of the fabric on my skin and the heat of his tongue sent me on edge. My fire spread, delving across the top of my thighs. I could feel my blood boiling down to my toes. "The things I would do to you, Ezra."

"Not a chance," I huffed.

He slid a talon beneath the chains at the top of my dress, breaking the links. I don't know when he had allowed that part of himself to change. It should have frightened me, seeing him in that suspension between man and monster. My blood only quaked in response, growing hotter by the second.

"Tell me you're mine so I can have you."

It took everything in me to deny him. Every scrap of sanity I had left. I had never truly faced temptation until now. It wasn't even denying him to hold onto my grace or morality. I didn't give a fuck about that anymore.

I just wanted Valen to work for it. I was being held together by a thread that was fraying quickly and I didn't want to be the one who broke first. I didn't want to make it easy for him.

He chuckled when I narrowed my gaze. I arched my back as I fractured, pushing my breast against his lips. The fabric fell away as I moved, exposing myself to him. Valen held my eyes as he took my nipple in his mouth. He sucked it between his teeth, biting gently. I tightened my grip in his hair, urging him to continue while I shrugged my other strap off. He slid his palm over my other breast, kneading it while he continued to work me with his mouth.

I continued to fray as he traced one of those deadly talons over my arm. I couldn't contain the whimper that escaped the back of my throat.

He grinned, my nipple still between his teeth. His tongue flicked out as he pulled away to blow a warm breath on the other one. "Two little words and I'll do every wicked thing I'm considering."

Not yet.

"No."

"*I'm yours.* I want to hear you say it."

I hadn't even realized I had been writhing against him until I stopped. I had already given him too much. He knew exactly how to play me. Dark music left his lips as he laughed and fastened his mouth back to me.

"Not a fucking chance." I half laughed, half gasped as he bit down harder on my nipple, the sharp points of his teeth pinching. His flames rose in answer to mine. They tangled together across our bodies. The entire room that had been lit by soft moonlight was now awash in a bright orange glow.

His hand slid under the skirt of my dress. Valen shifted, turning his head to kiss me as his hand slid to my center. "They're just words," he said.

Nothing was that easy.

I caught his wrist before he could slide his hand higher. "I gave you more than I intended."

A growl rumbled through his chest, the very end of it turning into a purr as he said, "You're a generous woman." He turned his hand so that his fingers circled around my wrist in turn. "Will you not give a little more? I can smell how wet you are."

"You're *the* devil."

Valen kissed the middle of my palm. "You're soaking," he said. His eyes held mine as he spoke, begging me to fall for the web he had so craftily woven.

I couldn't fucking breathe when he looked at me like that. I knew my face was on fire, that I was blushing like a madwoman.

It was torture for me as much as it was for him. Especially when he looked so beautiful amongst the firelight. Fire that slowly receded beneath our skin. He slid to my side, albeit reluctantly.

He plucked at the scrap of my dress. "You should take this off."

I scoffed. "And give you easier access."

"To get comfortable." Steam left his lips as he spoke. A fading wisp of white rising into the air. "I'd hate for you to get tangled up in all these chains while you sleep."

"Do you have something else for me to wear?"

He looked like he was about to say something vile by the twist in his mouth, but instead Valen rose and pulled out a t-shirt from his dresser. He held it out on the tip of his claw as he approached the bed.

Why was I denying him again? I couldn't think straight as he looked down at me. Looked into me. I swear he could read my mind as I stood to shimmy out of the dress. My hands shook as I pushed the fabric and chains over my hips, letting it fall to the ground with a soft clink.

I stood in nothing but my lace underwear, allowing him to see me fully before taking the shirt from him. The glow of his eyes darkened and the tremors in my hands spread to the rest of my body.

He is so terrifyingly beautiful.

The way he looked at me. I had never had anyone look at me that way. Like he was utterly enraptured. His eyes dragged slowly from my face to the large swell of my breasts, down my stomach, to the curve of my hips and all the way to my feet. His assessment was achingly slow.

"You are the most exquisite thing I have ever seen," he said.

I twisted the shirt over my head when his eyes finally met mine. "I bet you say that to all the girls."

Valen smirked as he followed me into bed. "I haven't meant any of it until you."

My gut twisted at the thought of him being with anyone else. It was stupid. Of course he had been with other people. I had had my own share of partners. I swallowed the jealousy hardening in my chest as I turned away from him.

Valen chuckled. "Don't be jealous."

"I'm not jealous." I sucked the back of my teeth as I nestled into the pillows.

The bare skin of his chest pressed into my back as he slid in behind me. When had he taken his clothes off? Before I could wonder if he had removed anything else, I felt his hard cock press against my ass. He was wearing something, but the jeans were gone.

I bit my lip to stifle a groan.

"I can smell it on you," he said against my neck. "Beneath your wet desire. I like the idea of you being territorial over me."

He was going to be the death of me. Not Ariel, not Raguel. Not anyone or anything else. Valen would be the one to do me in. I knew it because I felt like combusting right then. He was insufferable.

I shook out what lust still clung to me, trying to rid it from my body.

"I'm not territorial. You don't even belong to me," I snapped.

It was stupid to have allowed us to get this far. It was his nature to seduce me. I had foolishly fallen for it. Not entirely, but I was close enough to the edge to know the damage I had already caused myself.

I shut my eyes tight and willed out the nasty thoughts that

sprung into my head. Of Valen with someone else. Ideas that Valen was using me for his own gain. That once he got what he wanted, I would be forgotten.

Those things didn't matter. At that moment, he was mine, if only temporarily.

I hated it and I loved it. I loved that it was his bed I was in. His arms I curled into.

"Hmm," Valen hummed. The span of his hand slid up my thigh, stopping short of the hem of my shirt. The warm blow of his breath slid down the back of my neck as he pressed his nose into my hair.

Fatigue hit me with a vengeance. A yawn ripped from my lungs. I scooted closer to him despite the unnecessary feelings trying to rattle me. He was so warm. So big. His entire body enveloped me when he pulled me into his embrace.

Darkness pulled my lids low and a quiet sigh escaped my lips.

I felt his breath move against my neck as he murmured something. I could have sworn he said, "You had me the moment you woke me."

CHAPTER TWENTY-NINE: A DANGEROUS GAMBLE

Raguel

Raguel slid to the seat beside the hearth of the guest quarters. Despite being Tartarus's overseer, it went against every atom of the angel's being to remain in the prison. But someone had to do the job. He had never once complained about an assignment.

Gladr unhooked his vambraces. "You think the pollution originated here, don't you?"

Raguel's mouth curled. "If the bleed had not been tainted, it would have been easier to follow. But I believe so."

Gladr rubbed his wrists, forcing the blood to circulate faster. "What makes you think it is coming from Vélos?"

"We should check Asphodel to be certain." Ramiel was propped in one of the corners, his arms folded across his narrow chest.

Raguel drummed his fingers over the arm of the chair. "Valen has taken an interest in that young woman you sought to fornicate with." His sharp gaze slid to the male.

Ramiel tsked. "What of it?"

Raguel's blood boiled. Ramiel was as hot-headed as they came. He had been riding the line of grace and sin since he had been assigned to Raguel's flock. He needed to be reminded of his duties.

"Have you ever seen Valen with anyone else?" Raguel held up his finger. "Outside of Bishop and the Murder. Have you ever seen him show favor to anyone?"

The angels contemplated.

Gladr frowned. "No."

Ramiel's gaze narrowed as he looked down at the floor, searching his memory.

"I saw nothing in her, was given no direction when I had her alone, but," Raguel shook his head, "there is something off about her."

"She's not the nephilim we have all been hearing about," Gladr offered.

"Of course she isn't. Females are not allotted power and there has never been one that wasn't male," Ramiel said.

While Raguel agreed with Ramiel, the angel's bitterness grated on him. He flicked his fingers out to Torah, a young power just shy of his hundredth year, and Calix, a seraph, who had been watching Ramiel just as closely. They stood soundlessly and moved to the door to await his next command.

"I don't know what she is, but I am certain that Valen is hiding something. They all are."

"Maybe he finally fell in love," Gladr offered. He smiled, half laughing to himself.

Raguel's stare bloodied. "Our kind does not fall in love. Holy or damned."

"It didn't stop their last cyn. Angels fall all the time." Ramiel pushed off from his seat and strode to the middle of the room, turning his stare toward the mountains.

Raguel watched the male closely. He wasn't talking about falling in love.

Ramiel had come from the fifth ring of Heaven. He belonged to one of the lower districts, seven or eight. Raguel had been told to give him a chance, that there was something within the hotheaded seraph to be molded.

The only thing Raguel saw now was how much closer he was to treading that line that would ground him.

"You speak as if you are familiar with the idea," Raguel said.

Ramiel turned slowly. He gave the archangel a once over. "I see things from both perspectives."

"A dangerous view," Raguel answered.

Gladr shifted back a step, leaving space between Ramiel and Raguel. On the opposite side of the room, Torah and Calix moved closer.

"Dangerous? Not at all. If you want to learn anything about an enemy, you must think like him. Be like him." His eyes flitted toward the movement. "You suggest they are hiding something. Let one of us remain. Let me remain and I will tell you exactly what it is about that woman that makes Valen tick. I'll even uncover what is corrupting Earth."

Ramiel would fall if he remained in Vélos, of that Raguel was absolutely certain. The conflict was practically written across the young seraph's face. Raguel tapped the edge of his chair.

"Ramiel, you'll patrol with us tonight," Calix said. Calix was an overbearingly large male with flaxen skin and curling hair he kept knotted at the back of his neck. His sharp face made him look more serpentine than human or angelic. He was one of the angels that always had to tell his charges to "be not afraid".

Ramiel's color paled.

I waved my hand, signaling the males to take him. "Ramiel, perhaps you will learn a thing or two from Calix tonight. It appears you need to be reminded of the way we see things."

Ramiel swallowed his pride, forcing it so far down he nearly choked on the spit of it. "I know you do not trust me after what happened tonight, but I mean well." He lowered his head, casting his eyes to the floor. "I can get you what you seek if you just give me the opportunity."

Power rose in the air like the swell of a storm. It cracked through the air like lightning, making Ramiel flinch.

"You had the opportunity to extract information tonight. Instead, you chose to try and force your cock in some woman's mouth. The next time you consider seeing things their way or taking part in their sins, I will rip out your wings myself and leave you here." Raguel flicked his gaze to Calix.

The larger male moved forward, grabbing Ramiel by the arm, and hauled him to the door. Ramiel's lips curled. He had lost this battle. Anything else he might say could very well cost him.

"A fool, that one," Gladr said when the door closed.

"A mistake if we do not keep him leashed," Raguel said. He let his power unfurl across the room, easing it out instead of releasing it all at once. "We will extend our stay a few days, search their grounds in case we missed something before going to Thanatos and Asphodel." Raguel tipped his head back against the chair.

His thoughts wandered back to the woman with gold-spun hair and flaming blue eyes. He had wanted to help her, but Heaven had said no. It was the first time he had been denied saving a soul.

CHAPTER THIRTY: A FIT OF RAGE

Ezra

The ground met my back at full force, rattling my teeth like a couple of freshly blown dice. Embers spun into the air on impact. The blow shattered the carefully built shield I had wrapped around my body.

Valen tsked. The look of disappointment on his face did nothing to my wounded ego.

Trading a few kisses with him hadn't softened his hard exterior. He was still as brutal and irritating as ever. If not more so. He seemed to enjoy taunting me. He wasn't technically hurting me with the petty blows since we were training. It grated on me all the same, and I could tell he was eating it up.

"That was a cheap shot," I grumbled.

"You had your opening," he said. "Or were you too busy thinking of kissing me that you didn't notice?"

It was a good thing I was already red and sweating. At least he couldn't tell that I was blushing. "I wasn't thinking about that."

He flashed his teeth. "Your mind is not where it needs to be. Whatever is crossing it, let it go. Right now, you need to be here. Honing that wall around your body and your mind is just as important as training with weapons. I'm going to attack you again, but this time, I want you to hurt me. Call up whatever power you can and hurl it at me."

I clenched my bow that had fallen to the ground as I broadened my stance. I took a deep breath, refortifying the wall he had perished. "I got it." My fingers tensed over the quiver at my thigh as I moved, edging the space between us as I looked for his next move.

The cyns were adamant that I learn to move with a bow. I had moved up from a forty-pound bow to one with a sixty-pound draw. I was expected to be able to pull no less than one hundred fifty pounds by the end of my training.

I moved swiftly, nocking an arrow and shooting it at him while simultaneously unfurling a lick of power in his direction. Valen snapped the arrow in half as it buzzed past his head and casually stepped over what had been a ripple of my irritation.

Then he was on me, his claws digging into my back and one of his arrows beneath my chin. I shoved away with a frustrated grunt.

Valen wasn't the most powerful of the Fallen angels, but he was old and strong enough that if I couldn't wound him, I knew I wouldn't be able to hurt anyone else. He was so damn fast and smooth about everything. It was starting to piss me off.

I had read in the old texts that the nephilim were stronger than the angels. I wondered if they knew that. If it was why they were so careful with me. Perhaps that was why he was so insistent that nothing would be forced on me. Why, despite his pressures, Valen had been so patient when it came to my power.

A power that had been coming in spurts, manifesting in shows of flame and invisible waves that would burst through my blood with only a few seconds' notice. I'd learned to expel it into the ground through the soles of my feet when we weren't in the arena and some place more public. Being able to push it out from two precise spots had its challenges. There were always scorch marks.

Valen's touch slid against me like oil. Chills burst along my skin beneath my long-leathered exteriors. Working with Andras's power had taught me that a touch from any of the amorini was an intoxicating experience. The act didn't necessarily need to be sensual for it to feel that way. With Valen, it was a whole new level of want and confusion. Especially now.

Movement at the edge of the field caught my attention as two of the other cyn strode onto the field. Bishop's long strides were smooth, while his companion had an awkward hitch in his step.

Jinn looked... Fuck, he looked awful.

I hadn't seen him since our first training session. But whatever happened had left him in bad shape. The green bruising around his eye and jaw said that he was healing, but it looked gnarly as hell.

A feeling of unease touched me. Had he gotten into an altercation with one of the angels?

I snapped my attention back to Valen as his power swelled. I called mine from its well. I harnessed it around the front of my chest, into the palms of my hands, and started to push.

Valen flashed his teeth just before he hurled an orb of his power toward my chest.

White-hot pain lanced into me, forcing the air from my lungs.

I fell in a heap, my bow flying. Again. Numbing pain spread through the rest of my body as the invasive power coursed through me. The pain honed to a single spot in my ribs.

The asshole had broken my ribs.

The numbing turned into needles. A thousand little pin pricks diving into every cell of my body. I pushed back. He pushed harder.

All sharpness dissipated as I forced my power against Valen's. It snapped out of existence entirely. It wasn't until he had withdrawn that I realized how hard I was breathing. My lungs burned with the struggle. The sharp pain in my ribs tightened.

"Did you just break my ribs?" I touched my fingers over the spot, too tender to touch.

Valen's mouth twisted faintly. "You're not even trying."

"I am," I snapped.

"I told you to hurt me." His eyes flicked to the males. "Perhaps a change in partners will motivate you."

"Hello, beautiful." Bishop surveyed me, his eyes roving over my body languidly.

I clenched my teeth so hard that they ached. I was not going to give *him* the satisfaction of sparring. I had it on good account that Bishop fought dirtier than anyone.

"Your Highness," I gritted.

Bishop's eyes glinted with satisfaction.

"Highness," I said to Jinn. Even though I didn't know why Jinn looked the way he did, I felt bad about it. The least I could do was acknowledge him. Though I didn't want his hands on me either.

I glared at Valen as I caught on. He knew I didn't like them. Knew I hated Jinn. I couldn't tap into that emotion when sparring with Valen. Not when his jabs at Killian no longer worked. Not after our heated evening together.

The auburn-haired male smirked. "Looks like you've progressed quickly."

Not fast enough. Andras and Valen hadn't let up. I had been watching them like a hawk when they battled, trying to memorize their moves and uncover their tells. Valen never made the same move twice. He was always unpredictable. Andras tightened his right fist before he kicked or thrust his blade, but I'd only noticed that twice. They were just so damned fast.

I heaved to my feet, trying not to wince as the pain gutted my stomach.

"Jinn, I want you to fight her. No weapons, just flesh."

"My ribs are broken," I growled.

"Cracked," Valen corrected. He circled to Bishop's side.

It was then I noticed Jinn was in matching training leathers. Fresh heat scorched the tops of my cheeks. I pushed the foul words I'd direct at Valen to the side. He said no more games, yet I was being presented with another one.

"I'm not fighting Jinn. I'm not fighting anyone. You just cracked my ribs, asshole." My lips curled on their own accord.

"Jinn," Valen said flatly. Boredom traced the lines of his words. Impatience.

It made me feel better about not giving into him when he was making it very apparent he didn't give a fuck about me. Valen was nothing more than a pretty face and pretty words. If they went through with this skirmish, I was going to make him pay dearly for it.

Jinn stalked toward me. His was meticulous, his guard raised. As was the height of his power. It hummed around him like a swarm of bees, the steady thrum of it echoing against my skin.

I danced out of his reach and reached for my bow. It went skirting across the ground, far away enough that I couldn't get it without exposing my back. I'd never gotten the opportunity to watch him spar, but I assumed he was as brutal as the rest. I looked for his tells, for a clench of his fists or a shift in his weight, when he punched me. One fist in the ribs and the line of his palm into my throat.

"Ugh!" The wind jerked out of me as the pain in my ribs ruptured.

Red blossomed across my vision. Red as fiery anger raised its head to my opponent. I saw a flash of Jinn's smile through the haze. There was a satisfied look in his eye. Like he had just gotten me back for something.

Oh.

Oh.

The fucking bastard. This was personal. An opportunity to get back at me for not bending to his whims.

"Asshole."

You're going to pay for that.

I held my palm against my ribs to hold them together and moved back to gain space. I only needed to keep my distance until my bones reknitted themselves. Curses flowed through my mind, one after the other. I tied them all together carefully as I tried not to focus on how much it hurt to breathe. I would kill them all for this. Bishop included, if he kept smirking at me the way he was.

I made my move as soon as the sharpness in my breath eased. I charged forward, threw my weight into a kick, and sent my foot directly into Jinn's head.

Jinn grabbed my leg, wrapping his strong fingers above my knee, and pulled me forward. Hard. My other foot slipped out from under me, forcing me to the ground. I gritted my teeth to suppress a cry that scraped in the back of my throat.

"I'm not here to play nice," he said.

Blood erupted from my nose when Jinn's knuckles collided with my face. I gasped and sputtered, spitting blood across the ground as I rolled to my stomach. There was nothing but darkness. I struggled to regain consciousness, swimming desperately toward the light.

I caught a glimpse of Valen and Bishop as I lifted my head. What the fuck was this? They had never been this hard with me before. I was half their strength and even less their age. Jinn was going to beat me into a pulp while they watched.

A flicker of fear slid beneath the red haze. I climbed unsteadily to my feet as I faced Jinn. My face throbbed. My vision faded from black to red and black again.

"I told you not to touch her face," Valen snapped. "Neck down."

"You told him *what*?" My words were sloshed as the swelling spread across my face.

His cold eyes met mine. "Break her arm," he said.

"You said you wouldn't hurt me," I growled.

Valen's mouth pressed into a thin line. "I'm not."

I pulled my arms across my chest when Jinn's glare lowered to me. He touched his nose when he smiled. "Oops," he said. I thrust my arms out, casting fire and curses to bind him. He moved right past them, kicking me to the ground again.

He crouched on his heels and flipped me onto my stomach. Stinging pain coursed through my ribs and spine. My face felt like it was about to burst.

Jinn was going to kill me.

I glanced up at Valen. Why the hell was he letting this happen? Beside him, Bishop stood with an equal reserve, his expression almost... bored.

Everything snapped into place.

Oh, Valen was a sick fucking bastard.

I knew exactly why he was doing this.

Valen *wouldn't* hurt me. A cracked rib was nothing compared to a broken nose. Valen wouldn't bleed me. But Jinn would, because Jinn was angry at my refusal to help them.

If I was angry before, I was furious now. The red of my vision turned dark crimson.

Jinn wrenched my arm back against his thigh. Something inside me snapped. *If he breaks my arm, he will break my wing.*

I twisted, thrusting my other arm beneath my body and unfurling my fingers. Fire erupted from my palm. A long spiral funneled directly into Jinn's wide look of surprise.

I moved as soon as his hold loosened. I managed to pull my leg free, kicking in the direction my line of fire continued to burn.

Crack!

The sweet sound of broken cartilage or teeth met the end of my boot.

"Again," someone snapped.

The world spun when I found my feet. I stumbled to Jinn despite it, ducking as he took a swing for my face. The pain in my nose was nothing compared to the unyielding power of fire that took hold of my veins. I took a blow to my ribs and thrust my fist into his throat. Pressure made my skin tight. It made my breath constrict.

Smoke clouded my vision, but it was not thick enough that I lost sight of my opponent. He was trying to distract me with his own fire. Ash spun beneath our fists. Blows met. Blocks were made. Jinn swung toward me and I kicked, landing my foot square in his solar plexus. He stumbled and I hit him again, charging.

The pressure continued to build until I could restrain it no more. I let loose. Fire broke from my skin, falling in gilded pieces, dripping like lava. I threw my palms up, pulling it close and then thrusting out, sending every orange and red glimmer forward.

There was a flash of emerald fire in Jinn's eyes that encouraged me. It wasn't fear. Something more delicious. A hunger I've never felt before filled up every bit of my body, mimicking his wild ferocity.

Jinn caught hold of my fire with his own and jerked me forward.

I don't know how it happened, but somehow we ended up on the ground. I drove my elbow back into his face and swung around so I was on top of him. It was his arm now laying across my leg.

I looked up at Valen. His eyes were dark, full of heat. He nodded.

I tightened my grip on Jinn's arm while simultaneously pushing my hands down. A loud crack splintered through the air and the amorini roared. The vibrations from his pain rushed into my palm. His broken arm fell limply to the ground. His other caught me square in the temple.

The world spun as I wobbled to my side, crawling away from the amorini. Blood and grime caked the inside of my mouth. I ran my tongue over the grit, savoring it as I focused on the nausea building in my gut. I forced myself to my feet as I swallowed back the lump in my throat.

I fell on him, jerked his head forward, and ripped an arrow from the sheath behind his neck. I pressed the point of it against his chest. Amorini arrows were not crafted with wood. They did not break easy. This was a line of iron that I could force right into his heart and kill him. The bladed tip sliced like butter through his leathers.

Music filled the air. I looked between the cyn, to Diriel and Lane who had taken a spot beside them at some point. They were all laughing, eyes wide, and grinning.

Jinn smiled at me.

"What the fuck is so funny?" I growled. The pressure started to build again. I gathered it into my palms, willing the fire into one spot. I'd teach them to laugh at me.

"Look at you," Bishop said with a husky undertone. "You are

fucking magnificent."

I was straddling Jinn. Blood stained the front of my shirt. I could feel the stickiness of it covering my face. Sweat coated the rest of my body. My fists were broken and shook with fatigue beneath the flames as I poised the arrow over its mark.

Ash flitted through the air, brushing against the side of my face. The cinders were mine. I lurched backward. The world spun faster and Valen grabbed my elbow, hauling me up before I could topple over. I let him take the brunt of my weight as my eyes found Jinn.

This was my fire.

Not Jinn's. Jinn didn't have a speck of flame on him. It had all been me.

He was as broken and bloodied as he made me. Well, maybe not as broken, but he looked the part. The genuine smile on his face made my heart flutter. "Well done," Jinn said. He brushed his fingers over the spot on his shirt.

I looked back down at the power that roiled from my body, dropping the arrow. I could feel it, stronger than it had ever been before. A thrumming current.

"There's my harpy," Valen said softly. There was so much pride looking back at me.

His. I looked away before I let the word settle. There were too many emotions surging through me. A fit of rage, a wild sense of hunger for power, and something more sinful as I looked into his hypnotic eyes.

I licked my lips as I settled, focusing on the power in my blood. It felt like lust. It felt magnetic. I felt high, a strong buzz leaving my head feeling fuzzy.

Jinn pulled his arm into place. The soft crunch of his bones resetting leaked through the air. He wiggled his fingers at me, the stupid grin still locked on his face.

"Holy fuck that was badass," Lane said. She pointed, looking at Diriel. "Did you see that? I didn't know you could fight like that."

Diriel grinned.

"You're all sick fucks," I said. Giddiness rushed over me and I laughed as the buzzing intensified. I laughed so hard that tears left my eyes. This was it. This was what it felt like to have power. And it was just the beginning.

"Where did you learn to kick like that? To fight?" Lane's eyes were wide with admiration.

"Killian," I said, before I could think about what it meant to say his name. I ignored the shift in Valen's attention. "He thought it would be good for me to learn self-defense... and martial arts. Said it would be good knowledge to have given my track record."

Lane let out a long whistle. "He wasn't wrong. Who knew it would actually come in handy? Jinn, that was nasty of you."

Jinn shrugged. "No one else was going to do it." His jade eyes slid sideways to me, his head slowly following. "I think we're even now."

I flashed him a bloody snarl. "Even doesn't even begin to cover it."

That spark returned to Jinn's eyes. An offer or a challenge. I couldn't tell which. Only that his look said he was agreeable to the idea of sparring with me again. It had felt good to hurt him. To get him back for what he had said about me.

It felt good to get my hands dirty.

The pain in my face set in as the high wore off. I brushed my fingers over the top of my cheeks and winced. Jinn had made a clean break in my nose, but the swelling had been instantaneous. My whole face felt like it was twice its normal size.

Valen cupped the underside of my chin. "Hold still," he said. I shut my eyes when his fingers gripped the bridge of my nose. "I'm sorry." It was the only warning he gave before resetting my nose. Tears flooded my eyes like a broken dam. If Valen hadn't snaked his arm around my waist, I might have keeled over.

Bloody fucking angels. Demons. Monsters. Every slur and curse word I could think of ran through my head as I bit my tongue, trying to adjust to the movement in my face as the healing started. The swelling slowly faded.

"You shouldn't have done that," Bishop said. There was an icy current in his tone, as frigid as the look in his eyes.

There were not many sounds in Vélos. No crickets or cicadas spun their music this far below. But the soft churring of whatever bugs did inhabit the land had gone utterly quiet.

I looked down the line of trees. On the second scan, I saw them and froze.

Two seraphim stood at the tree line. The dark shadow of their wings was the only trace that made them known in the darkness.

"Keep your head down, Ezra," Bishop commanded. "If they see your face has healed, they'll have questions."

Lane stroked her cheek. "Just tell them she's a dhampir." The six silver rings on her hand glinted in the light. "We heal quick enough."

"Doesn't explain the fire," Bishop said.

"A witch," Lane offered.

"If they saw her flames, we will convince them they were mine," Jinn said. "That I was trying to burn you."

I nodded as I ducked my head. Fuck fuck fuck.

The angels stepped onto the field. My stomach dropped as I recognized the first one. Ramiel. The other I hadn't seen yet but immediately gave him the nickname Big Red for how massive he was. He made Bishop and Valen look small, standing well over seven feet tall. Hell, he made Raguel look small.

Tattoos that marked him as an arc wrapped around his arm and throat. Several others had been inked into the side of his face to match.

"Oh goodie. This one again," Lane grumbled toward Ramiel.

There was a fresh sheen to the armor they wore. I could see my reflection in the chest of Big Red's breast plate. Blood stained the disheveled locks of my hair that had pulled free from its braid to match the crimson on my face and shirt. Dark bruising cupped the underside of my eyes.

Maybe they wouldn't be able to tell my nose was reset and healing beneath the gore.

How much had they seen? Had they been watching the whole time, there would have been more than a scout before us. Perhaps they had heard the cyns' cheers and come to investigate. But if they had seen the fire, even a brush of it on my skin, I was done for. I prayed Jinn's lie would hold if it came to it.

It was a good idea to pretend I was a dhampir or witch, but neither of those things could call fire.

Ramiel's ruby eyes touched over every head. "What's all this?" he asked.

"Just having a little bit of fun." Jinn ran his tongue over his bloody teeth for show and then spit. The wad landed somewhere in front of the angels, making their eyes narrow into slits.

"And here I thought the golden one was some sort of favorite." Ramiel tsked through his frown. The cupid's bow of his mouth puckered as he threw a smug look at me.

I loathed that he found humor in my state. He had no idea what

I was capable of. That soon enough I would be strong enough to take him down a few pegs and burn off that crude upturn of his mouth.

"She is. This is foreplay," Valen purred. He swung his head back, nodding to Lane. "She's next if you care to watch."

A whoosh of air left Lane's lungs. The tension between Valen and Lane was getting old. He was blatantly obvious with his distaste for her, but to threaten the treatment I had just received went too far. Sure, she could probably handle herself, but unless the Murder had trained her in combat, she didn't know a thing about fighting. I had barely managed to stay on my feet and was only able to do so because of the angel's blood in my veins.

Dhampirs healed fast, but what took angels minutes would take her hours to recover from. They weren't resistant to pain.

I looked at her, willing her to tell me the deep dark secret she kept buried. The reason why Valen had turned her over to the Murder. Maybe if I knew I could help her. Intervene before Valen did something petty.

Ramiel cocked his head, the crown of his feathers shifting with the movement. "As entertaining as that would be, I have to ask, when did you start training your humans? I was under the impression that Vélos was... *kind* to their guests."

Shit. They had been watching long enough to know that the tussle between us had been a skirmish. I sent another silent curse into the air. The leathers. Jinn, Valen, and I were the only ones wearing fighting leathers.

"How do you think we get them to be so well behaved?" Bishop slid his fingers over his wrist, tattooed hand on top. A subtle but deliberate reminder of what he was.

Ramiel's nostrils flared. He turned his attention to Valen expectantly.

"Is it a crime that we should play with our toys how we wish?" Valen's words came out as a hiss. I hated when he leaned into his darker nature.

Ramiel watched him a moment longer. "No," he answered. "I am merely curious of your ways and the hours of which you spend them." He looked to the sky and turned to his companion. "Don't you find it odd, Calix? While everyone else rests, the cyn are out here with their... toys." He let the last word drop like a stone into water.

The large male grunted. A few of his jeweled eyes fluttered over us. He was scrutinizing us. Crinkles tugged at the corner of his eyes on his left bicep. Long feathers sat on the top of his head, smoothed back with the rest of his hair so that they pointed out the back like spikes.

"Run back to your master. There are signs you are supposed to be looking for," Bishop said.

Ramiel's crooked smile glinted. "It is on the orders of my partner that I am here now. I believe we are very close to finding what it is we are looking for." His gaze shifted to me. All his eyes locked to the top of my head as I found something very interesting on the ground to look at.

"We will not further waste your time," a deep voice said. Calix, I assumed, because I didn't dare look up. "Our curiosity has been satisfied."

Someone touched me from behind. I looked over my shoulder to Diriel's outstretched hand. One step, two back, and then he had his arm around my waist, drawing me to his side while Lane stood at his other.

"Let's get that face of yours fixed," he said.

I grimaced.

I let Diriel draw me away while the others exchanged small words with the seraphim. Valen turned to look at me as if to say, "I'll come for you later." We could not make our way to the far side of the field fast enough. Truly, or it would have appeared we had been running. The weight of a thousand eyes followed me.

CHAPTER THIRTY-ONE: WAR IS INEVITABLE

Ezra

The cold compress felt good against my face. The open wounds and broken bones had healed. There was only a small amount of swelling left to show for my fight with Jinn.

"Valen made you a promise. He couldn't be the one to hurt you," Diriel said.

"Tell that to the ribs he broke." I moved the ice to the other side of my face.

The steady flow of voices drowned out most of our conversation. At least, if there was anyone trying to eavesdrop, they were going to have a hard time overhearing anything.

"Had you shielded the way I told you to, that wouldn't have happened."

I waved my hand in the air. "Yeah. Yeah, I know."

Diriel had taken Lane and me to *Jade Fire*, a quieter trove in the main part of the amorini's capital. Whatever drove the seraphim had something to do with the humans, so we remained outside of their districts out of caution. After said beating, Diriel thought I deserved a cold drink instead of stuffing my head full of studies. I'd knocked two back already.

I wish I had the opportunity to clean up first. I'd been able to wash most of the blood from my face, but my appearance continued to draw curious eyes. Or maybe it was the smell of my sweat.

"Told you he was an asshole," Lane said. She was nestled against Diriel's side. The cyn hid his smirk behind his drink.

I rolled my eyes.

An asshole that I had made out with and nearly done God knows what with. Being in Tartarus was starting to corrupt me. That was the only explanation I could come up with for my tolerance of the dark and depraved.

Lane jerked upright, leaning to her other side.

The three cyn strode into the trove. Their very presence commanded the room. I noticed some of the women nudge each other. Two in particular flashed their best smiles and then giggled as they passed them by to wedge themselves at our small table.

They all took their places, Jinn on Lane's other side, Bishop on my right. Valen faltered when he caught site of Lane. His movements were stiff as he sat in the chair beside me. The tension in his jaw was so tight I was sure he was grinding his teeth. We were going to have to talk about that. Whatever it was between the two of them needed to stop. I liked Lane. I wasn't about to let someone from my past life go so easily.

Bishop's warm breath ran down my cheek to my neck. Chills raced over my skin when his nose touched me. Storm clouds churned in his eyes when I faced him. Our faces were too close together. His lips inches from mine, he flashed a broad grin.

He had nice, broad white teeth and a beautiful mouth to frame them. He was pretty. He knew exactly how to use his appeal to get what he wanted.

"I'm proud of you," he said.

I looked from his lips to his eyes. My heart was racing like a horse on a track. "For what?"

Valen's warm palm slid over my thigh. The pressure of his fingers made my toes curl.

This was some territorial bullshit that I didn't want any part of. I barely had an understanding of Valen as is. I'd never encouraged Bishop, and I did not like the feeling that I was caught between them. That I was some prize to be won.

"You coming into your power. It's a beautiful thing to witness." His eyes flashed down to my lips. "I can't wait to see you fly," he added. Bishop sat back, throwing a wicked smug look over my head.

I wondered if this was how amorini courted their prey. With flattery and commentary that said "my dick is bigger". It seemed the male ego was the same in Hell as it was on Earth. Cocky and big.

Valen cut Bishop a sideways glance then refocused it on Lane who was staring hard at Jinn as he told her about everything she had missed in Vélos the last several years. Her jaw was stiff as a corpse's.

"It really is exquisite," Diriel said. "You're retaining the history of our people quite well too." He was... off. Diriel remained slouched in his seat, his finger slightly over the top of his glass, but there was something awkward in his posture that I couldn't put my finger on.

Maybe there was more to Valen's quarrel with Lane. And I suspected in that moment, that Diriel had something to do with it. Lane was trying very hard not to acknowledge Diriel.

I flushed under Diriel's compliment all the same. I licked my lip, tasting the copper tang of blood. There were no wounds on my body. Nothing that I could feel. Just the dried remnants of what had happened. "I don't particularly care for all of your tactics," I looked at Jinn, "but thank you."

Valen's thumb stroked the inside of my thigh, drawing my attention upward. Rays of sunlight turned within his eyes. So much softer was the gold of their color than the fire that usually raged there. I'm proud of you, that look said. You're magnificent.

I was suddenly reminded of the night I first woke with my wings open. He had the same look in his eye then.

A young woman with luscious black hair tied back into a low bun slid a tray on the table to pass off three fresh glasses of, well, I assumed it to be blood. Her green eyes sparkled when she smiled at the table. There was a pause in her retreat, a quick look at Valen as she tried to catch his eye.

I don't know what came over me. Be it the rising tension that fed me, or that I was still spun up from earlier, but I stared her down. Fixed her with my gaze right between the eyes. Valen's fingers hardened with an exhale from his lips.

I saw his lips curve from the corner of my eye.

"That'll be all," I said sweetly.

The woman looked at me, her eyes widening. Ah, so we were going with the whole "she didn't see me there" trick. I let heat creep into my eyes. I didn't know if I could make the fire dance in my irises the way the others could, but I imagined it all the same and hoped that even if I couldn't that it would have the same effect.

She audibly swallowed. "Oh," she said through a forced grin. "Yes. Let me know if you need anything else." The woman gave one more glance to Valen before turning on her heel.

"Now she's learning," Bishop purred. The pristine chime of his laugh was sweet music. He tugged on the end of my braid for emphasis, pulling my chin up and exposing my throat to Valen.

It was with my head back that I finally met Valen's golden eyes. There was an echo of the ancient creature lurking beneath the simmering look of unbridled want.

It was then that I knew what I wanted. My desire matched his in that I wanted him. More importantly, I wanted this. This moment of playfulness between all of us. This feeling of belonging. Of being wanted.

I sat forward, tugging my hair from Bishop's grip and looking down the amber beer in front of me.

If Raguel wouldn't help me, no one would. The amorini had been the only ones to offer sanctuary. As I contemplated it, my anger subsided about the altercation with Jinn. They were honing my abilities, teaching me to control and contain them. They wanted me here.

Valen had proved his desires again and again. Had been following through with every promise.

Diriel was right in that I was not so different from them. I had done nothing wrong in my life to condemn me, just as they had not. Yet there I was, in Tartarus, with an entire court that didn't belong here.

I knew they killed people, stole others, but who wouldn't turn a little wicked after having your wings and light stripped from you? They had been forced from a place of glory without cause. Perhaps they could change if they were free of this place. If their grace was restored, maybe they would assist the adelifis as they had been made to do.

Valen had been honest when he said what the angels would do

to me. But it took hearing it from Raguel's mouth to convince me.

I looked amongst the crowd, to the humans entangled with the Fallen. Stolen souls brimming with smiles and warm light in their eyes. They didn't just appear happy, they were happy. And, maybe, I could petition for those who weren't if I agreed to help the amorini. Maybe those could be returned to Earth if Vélos was granted freedom.

"What are you thinking so hard about?" Valen asked. He turned toward me, putting his back to the dark-haired woman as she passed by our table to serve another.

I ran my finger across the condensation of the glass. "I am thinking that I want to help you." I said it so softly that my own voice barely reached my ears.

Stillness fell over the table.

I caught Jinn's eye first as I looked up and quickly looked back down to my glass. Hope shone back like a mirror in his gaze.

"I don't want to be part of the war, but if there is a way, I want to help free you. Free Vélos."

"War is inevitable." Bishop's voice, normally rough and deep, had a softness to it.

I sighed. "Then I want to be as little involved with it as possible. For as long as possible." I couldn't fight. Even if I now understood what Heaven stood for, I couldn't find it within me to take part in bloodshed. "Tell me what to do for your people without it."

"Do you mean that?" Valen's voice was full of surprise. I was just as taken aback by the words falling from my mouth. Words I couldn't stop.

"Raguel made it clear what would happen to me."

"What did he say?"

I couldn't help but notice how quiet they all were. How intense their focus was on me. A breath was being held collectively. Any second now and the spell could be broken.

It felt like a knife twisting inside my chest as I repeated Raguel's words. I hated how certain he had been. "He said that it was not the will of the fates or of Heaven that he take me from this place."

It hurt just as badly the second time.

Valen's voice hitched. "You told him?"

I shook my head. "I pleaded as a human. He doesn't know what I am."

Bishop let out a sigh first. "Ashes."

Valen didn't blink as he peered down at me. A soft smile touched his lips. "If he has pleaded your case with Heaven and been denied, then you are truly home." Though he spoke openly, it came across as more of a question to himself. An idea he couldn't grasp.

"Are you certain?" he pressed. He wanted this as much as the others. The chance for freedom. I had not expected him to ask me.

Once more, the glass captured my focus.

It felt like a waste to be coveted in the shadows of Tartarus and to be forsaken in the light of Heaven for nothing. All my life I had been told I was important by my father, but lived a tragedy that forced me into the bleak gloom of humanity. Had I known what I was earlier in life, would I have acted differently? Would I have taken control of my life, knowing I had the power to change it? To save the lives of those falling around me?

I was a nephilim. I had angels' blood in my veins. I recognized the power. I had the opportunity to save an entire people from an injustice. I had the chance to right a wrong.

Raguel, in all his glory, would despise me for what I was if he knew the truth. Just as Ariel had said, I was not made for Heaven.

What did any of that matter when I had four cyns beside me?

What did Heaven's opinion matter when the demon beside me looked at me so fondly? Had been at my side from the beginning offering me sanctuary. Had been my guardian from the moment he landed on that black-mirrored lake.

Demon. I hated to think of Valen as such a thing. Fallen angel had a better ring to it, even if the two were the same. There was nothing monstrous about him. Deadly, yes. Dangerous. Wicked at times, but nothing I had seen for myself warranted such a slur.

I could feel the weight of apprehension as they awaited my answer.

"Yes," I finally said. I held up my finger as their collective tension started to melt. "But on my own terms. No funny business," I said pointedly to Jinn. "And just you. Just the amorini. Like I said, I want no part in the war, but I will help you any way that I can to regain your freedom." To regain our freedom.

The only one who wasn't smiling was Valen, though his relief settled around me like a warm blanket. I was giving them what they wanted yet he was troubled. He wasn't telling me something. I had grown accustomed to watching Valen when he thought I wasn't looking at him. His telltale signs were subtle. A flicker of his lashes, a flick of his nails together. Rarely did his face give way to what he was thinking.

This time, it was the pause of the brush in his fingers over my knee that told me what I had said bothered him.

I had half a mind to demand that he tell me what he was thinking.

But I didn't. I didn't have time to when Bishop kissed the side of my face. Everyone else was beaming.

I caught Lane's half-hearted smile.

"You too," I mouthed to her. I would not leave Lane behind to be forgotten or returned to the Murder. Lane would come with us.

Her pale eyes glistened.

"We should toast," Lane said. She raised her glass into the air. "To Ezra, for kicking ass and taking names."

Jinn snorted. "You know that I let her win, don't you?"

Lane elbowed him in the side. Jinn bared his teeth, but I saw the pride he had reserved for me on the field as he encouraged my power to surface.

"To Ezra," everyone said, lifting their glasses.

"To the harpy," Valen said.

"To our freedom," Bishop said.

Our group was a strange one. The dynamic of the four cyn was strange in itself. Their wisdom and age were prevalent, but right then, in that moment, they all seemed so young and carefree. Even Lane, who I knew was much older than me now, allowed a gentler, younger side of herself to shine through. Our glasses clinked together. Finally, I was amongst a people that I felt I could call home.

CHAPTER THIRTY-TWO: DRINK WITH US

Valen

My mind reeled. She would help us. I had longed for the chance of retribution for so long that I thought it a fantasy. I had dreamt of escaping Tartarus's hold for good. No more short trips to Earth. Of going somewhere new or wreaking havoc on Heaven. I had played out multiple fantasies, all of them outside of this prison. All of them better than this hell.

Yet what she had said of Raguel troubled me.

Ezra had asked to be taken from here, and Raguel had denied her. It was not Heaven's will.

What she had said had either been missed by the others or disregarded for one of Raguel's half-ass apologies. But Raguel didn't lie. He took pride in staying true to his word. He took more pride in serving Heaven.

That he had been told she should remain here truly did mean she belonged with us. That she belonged with me. But, why? Unless even the higher powers of Heaven truly did not know of Ezra's existence.

I should be as elated as my brothers. Should be the one kissing the side of Ezra's face instead of Bishop. Her face, already stained red with alcohol, deepened in blush as Bishop whispered something in her ear.

She had no idea what she had just consented to. The horror that would not yield once Bishop was free. He would agree to her terms up until the very end. Then he would reveal he was bringing Eurynomos with us. We could not abandon them, our allies that had been beside us for centuries. My chest hardened as I realized as much as I wanted to leave Tartarus, we could not.

"We have paid our penance," Diriel's soft voice whispered inside my head.

I met his eyes across the table. He knew me too well.

"We will deal with the reparations once we are free."

"Those reparations could condemn us to Vasanistirio," I said.

Diriel cocked his head. *"They won't."*

"I will not subject her to such a prison."

"You want this as much as the rest of us. Do not throw it away now because you are growing fond of the girl. It is easy, she is rare. I care for her too, but we must take this chance while we have it."

I stretched my arm across the table and flexed my fingers. *"She is a part of your prophecy, isn't she."* It wasn't a question. Diriel had come to me months ago, stating he believed he was close in figuring out the solution to our exile. *"The Hymn of the Sun and the Moon."*

Diriel's silence was the confirmation I needed.

"If you are to help us, then perhaps you would be open to becoming more like us." Bishop still toyed with the end of her long braid. He flipped the end through his fingers. A predator playing with its next meal.

"We're practically cousins," Ezra said. "I don't see how much more alike we could get considering where we're both sitting."

It was enough to pull me out of my spiral. The shift in topic that I needed to draw me back to the present before the others noticed my distraction. "Don't ever call us cousins," I said.

Ezra threw me a sly look. "You call yourselves brothers."

"The word does not mean the same here as it does to your kind. Brother is a term of affection, not of relationship. Angels are not kin."

"So, I'd be your... sister?" Her face scrunched. "No. Never mind. I can't get behind that." A visible shudder ran through her body when she twisted away from me. I could smell her embarrassment as a light sweat broke over her skin.

Ezra turned to Bishop. "What did you have in mind?"

I gave her thigh a squeeze. Playing with Bishop had its consequences, and it had been hard enough for me to keep him at bay. He was practically gnawing at the bit, desperate to sink his teeth into something soft and warm.

"Drink with us." Bishop slid his glass in front of her.

The color drained from Ezra's soft complexion. She opened her mouth, shut it, and opened it again. Nothing came out as she stared at Bishop. Her fingers flexed over the glass of ale in her grip.

A quiet hiss whispered from my lips, a warning to the silver-eyed cyn. Bishop's greed had no limits. She had given him more than he could have hoped for, but he wanted more. He always wanted more. He wanted her to fall. Consuming blood was one of the first steps to becoming grounded.

"How about we play a game instead," Lane offered. She raised her glass before anyone could object. "Never have I ever." She paused, considering the laundry list of what she had and hadn't done. I knew Lane well enough to know the extent of her crimes. "Seen a dragon."

Diriel rolled his eyes.

Ezra gawked as we each lifted our glasses. "Shut up, they're real?"

"You're between two of them right now," Lane muttered.

I wasn't sure if she had started calling us that nickname or if she had picked it up from someone else. In any case, that is what Bishop and I were known as. Silver and gold, hoarding each other, hoarding what we desired most: blood, flesh, sex, death. Whatever our desires were in that moment was what we coveted most. Or so the stories went.

I turned my focus to Ezra, less my ire toward the blue-haired woman get the best of me. She was feeling ballsy because she thought she was safe in Ezra's presence. She was, for now. "They are, though they're rare. There are rumors that Eimai Theós has one, and of course there is the great Leviathan. We have wyrms, wingless dragons here and in the southwest territories."

"Now that is something I would like to see."

"Nasty things," Diriel said. "If you're lucky enough to see one, it means you're about ten seconds from being burnt to a crisp."

Ezra turned her hand over to reveal flames idling in her palms. "I don't think that's something I need to worry about."

I snatched her hand off the table. "Eyes," I hissed.

Ezra's eyes hollowed but she nodded.

"Never have I ever killed a hydra while riding a pegasus and nearly killing myself in doing so," Diriel's mouth quirked higher as he spoke.

I scowled. "That was one time and I didn't almost die. Hydras can't shoot bows."

Bishop held up a finger. "Fate nearly made an exception that day. Now stop bitching and drink."

Ezra's open curiosity was fixated on me as I took a sip of blood. I wish she would ask me about it. About the fool's dare I had accepted all for the sake of feeling something again. It hadn't cured the numbness. I let myself smile at the memory though, of the hydra's hot breath on my neck as it tried to devour me. All the while, I was just happy to be in the air again.

I don't hear Bishop's turn but drink knowing it is probably something I did. Ezra skips her first turn, stating she needs to come up with something good. Around and around we go until we are back at Ezra.

She runs the nail of her middle finger over her brow. "Never have I ever... killed someone," Ezra said slowly.

We all drank. It wasn't an ideal game to play when we had done everything in the book. The only one who wasn't drinking, hadn't even taken a sip, was Ezra whose fingers drummed over her glass. A single tap of three fingers.

A nervous tick she had when something bothered her. Except it wasn't distaste for our nature I scented on her. I knew she hated that. Had wondered if she had considered it before agreeing to help us, of what it might mean. I didn't think she was particularly bothered that she hadn't been drinking either.

"Never have I ever *thought* about killing someone," I said.

We raised our glasses again, and this time, Ezra joined in. She threw me a sharp look. I had guessed correctly.

Jinn laced his fingers together as he leered forward. "Do tell," he purred.

Thinking about killing someone was the exact same thing as the act itself as far as Heaven was concerned. It intrigued me that Ezra was not as much of a saint as she pretended to be. There was a small chance that it wasn't just Tartarus that settled her power. Perhaps it was her becoming more comfortable within our world. Comfortable enough to reveal who *she* really was.

Ezra ran her fingers through her hair. "I had a friend back home, Katie Kirkwood." She nodded to Lane. By the sudden blotch of her face, she knew who Katie was. The tightness returned to her jaw that had started to loosen as she relaxed. "She had everything going for her, was on track to go to Harvard a year early. Had money, love, happiness. The best clothes, a brand-new Mercedes, scholarships galore. She was a golden child. And she was selfless about it. Whatever she had, she gave it back tenfold.

"She started seeing this guy, Matt. It seemed innocent at first, until it wasn't. He ended up raping her, got away with the whole thing. Six months later she killed herself because she couldn't take the shame of it anymore. Everyone blamed her for leading him on." Slick bitterness coated Ezra's words. "After everything she had done for her community, they all thought her a liar."

"That bastard is still free?" Lane's face was as sharp as the blades dangling from her ears.

Ezra nodded, running her tongue over her teeth. "I've thought about killing him multiple times. With my luck, I thought I might be able to get away with it. But of course, I never did. I've only ever been trained to defend myself, not kill anyone."

There it was. How she had restrained her nature while having the desire to kill feeding her was beyond me.

Bishop touched my fingers dangling over her shoulder. *"We have her."*

We did.

While she was the key to our freedom, we were the key to avenging her friend. Revenge for revenge. It was perfect.

I was so fucking torn.

It was all falling into place perfectly. And yet, and yet...

"We need her," Diriel said. Pleaded.

They were waiting for me to coax her. By claiming her, it was my job to bring her to her knees.

I wanted to tear Bishop's smug smile from his face. Despite my war with him, these males were my family. Ezra was a tool, a weapon that would aid us. I could not put her before them. I could keep her safe in getting what we needed though.

I ran my fingers over her arm. "Would you hunt with us?"

Ezra pressed her hand against my chest. "Don't be greedy."

I grabbed the end of her chin with my thumb and forefinger. "You don't care for our ways of retribution. So, what if we change them? Kill those that deserve it? Get justice for those who cannot."

The words came easily enough. I could not give up the hunt, but I would change. For her, I would change the way I did it.

Her brows knit together in unison with her mouth twisting. "Don't ask that of me."

"I already have," I purred. "Liberating, remember?"

Ezra sucked the back of her teeth. "I'll think about it," she said.

I smiled. "That's all I ask."

The crowd parted for several of my hunters and Andras. The emissary pulled up a chair next to Jinn and pointedly looked at Ezra, reminding her that she owed him.

I raised my hand, catching Kasiya's attention as he halted to survey the space.

The grim lines of his face told me all I needed to know. Ariel had not been found. The weary smile of the captain did little to console me. *We'll find him*, that smile said. We would. We had to.

If Ariel was waiting until Raguel and his men departed, we would be waiting for his return.

CHAPTER THIRTY-THREE: GOOD RIDDANCE

Ezra

The Great Hall was awash with light from the three moons of Tartarus. The ceiling that was made entirely of red glass refracted rays of light that faded from pink to white as it brushed the marble floor lined with golden candelabras. Hand-carved candlesticks burned white flames, its wax frozen in a constant state of drip. The room smelled of honeyed gardenias.

A better name of the space would have been the Glass Hall, as the walls (not windows) were made entirely of glass. The city lights looked like twinkling starlight.

Most of the attendants I recognized as either amorini or human. I suspected the others were another race of demon. One man in particular had two horns spiraling from his silver hair. Gold bangles were stacked one on top of the other around his neck.

There was something oddly familiar about the Hall. Like I had visited it before. But of all the places, the Great Hall was not a place I had yet seen.

I linked my arm with Andras's as I made a pan of the room

once we made our way past the initial crowd. Everyone was in fine clothing. Some of the males wore leather-fitted attire while the women donned soft silks and cashmere.

It was when my eyes found the opposite end of the room which we proceeded that I stopped short.

At the end of our path was a flight of stairs framed by two stone dragons. Their maws stretched wide, showing off their massive teeth. One looked down over the Hall while the other snaked its head low. Ivory talons dug into the floor and first few steps. Their wings were drawn back across the railing.

I followed the stone membrane up to a line of thrones. Above the thrones was a perfect circle with rays pointing out like sunlight that had an arrow shooting through it, the point heading upwards.

Diriel, Valen, Bishop, and Jinn were already seated.

Andras said something, but I couldn't hear him over the rush of blood in my ears. It was Bishop's seat I had risen from in the dream. It was those steps I had walked to when the entire court of Vélos kneeled before me.

I caught Valen's gaze in the turmoil of my thoughts as we climbed the steps. He must have seen the horror on my face by the way his brows knit together.

Andras offered my hand to Valen, a formality in the exchange. Valen's fingers entwined with mine as he pulled me forward. I'd been told it wasn't customary for a pet to be seated with a cyn while they were on a throne, but Valen was enjoying rattling things. I stood between him and Bishop; my hands folded neatly in front of me.

Bishop turned his head to me, offering a soft smile.

"You look like you've seen a ghost," he said.

"I think I have." I scanned the crowd for any sign of Ariel. There were too many faces to sift through. Even though my eyesight had improved, I could not tell the color of anyone's eyes from this distance. Still, I looked for the lavender hues I knew were lurking. "My last dream with the angel was in this room."

Valen cocked his head in my direction. I had told him everything. How my wings had been shaped differently, the molten lava, Ariel's attack. All of it. So, when his eyes scanned down the row, skimming over Bishop and Jinn, I knew what he was asking.

I reached out to the back of Bishop's chair, where his silver gaze could not see me, and tapped it. I swallowed as I clasped my hands together.

Valen glared, but he didn't say anything. He turned his attention back to the court. "Perhaps he chose this place for what it stands for." He drummed his fingers over the arm of his chair.

Bishop looked back at me. "We cast our judgement here. When the angels depart, you will witness some of it."

I looked for Ariel again, dreading that I would see him but hoping I might to finally end it all.

"Who is she?"

A woman's voice carried from somewhere below. I looked down to see two dark-haired women looking up at me. They were all looking at me. The entire court was stealing glances. I could feel their curiosity all over my face. I stood out like a rose between the black thrones with the cyn in their dark leathers. It was a mistake to have me on display like this. An arrogant, foolish move.

Before I could make a case, the doors to the Hall opened. The crowd parted for the eleven seraphim that strode across the marble. They bore gilded helmets that gave off rays of golden light. It offset their bright red features. Seeing them like this, in more finery than they had worn when I saw them a couple of nights ago, was breathtaking.

The seraphim were the sun incarnate.

The weight of Raguel's seal felt like it was burning a hole in my pocket. I rested my hand over its shape. I don't know why I brought it with me. Another foolish mistake. To bear the token of someone who did not care about me in the slightest.

I recognized Ramiel and Calix, with one other seraph, behind Raguel. Ramiel was the only one who looked annoyed to be leaving. I could only tell by the twist of his mouth beneath his helmet and the narrowed eyes on the top of his hands.

Good riddance.

Raguel's gaze lingered on me as he stopped at the bottom of the staircase. He looked remorseful, almost. It was there and gone in a blink.

He had no right to look at me like that. Not when he had the power to do something but refused to. Angels had as much freewill as humans did. He was choosing not to help me. He was choosing to abandon me.

The beast inside of me, my power, lifted its head. She stretched from her slumber, yawning as her attention swung to the angels.

I tightened her leash. I would not show them what I was now, not when we were so close to escaping their judgment. Besides, I had already made up my mind. The angels would only stand in my way.

I willed my face to become stony. I did not need his remorse. I was not the helpless little girl he thought me to be.

"Thank you for your hospitality." Raguel touched two fingers to his chest and then his chin. "Our search has proven fruitless, so we will be on our way. I would ask that if anything strange occurs within your kingdom that you would call for me."

A plea.

Raguel had said there was rot leaking into Earth. He had denied that Tartarus had such a power, but what if it was true? What if the Fallen had found a way to penetrate the veil?

"Of course, Raguel. We are at your beck and call." The bitterness in Bishop's voice was so apparent I could practically taste the acrid taste of it.

"Anything," Raguel said. He set his palm over the hilt of one of his swords as he looked at me.

I kept my face grave. You won't be hearing from me.

"Andras will escort you to Asphodel." Bishop's voice was imposing. It was a command, that Andras would go with the angels whether they liked it or not. To make sure they left our territory entirely. "He has business with Cyn Anzu."

Andras strode down the steps, the long blood-dipped cape at his back twisting in his wake. He had no such business with Anzu.

Raguel offered a closed smile as he nodded. "Then we will be on our way." He touched his fingers to his chin again.

The seraphim turned as one, parting as Raguel passed between them and followed in the order in which they arrived. Andras kept pace with the archangel as they left.

As soon as the doors closed, the entire court seemed to let out a relieved sigh. I don't remember when the tension had built, but now that the immediate threat was gone, I let out a sigh right along with them.

I'd only ever experienced court proceedings in books. It was similar in the way the cyn dealt with their kingdom. Families came forward and offered tithes. Others asked for donations, magics that could assist them in their craft.

Bishop dealt with all of them. I looked to either side, to Jinn and

Diriel, whose faces were carved still as stone. Bishop was the only one who addressed the court.

Valen's shoulders eased suddenly, breaking his spell of stillness.

"What is it?" I whispered.

"They're gone. They've left Vélos."

"Thank God," I said.

Valen cut me a glare. "Be careful with what you say here," he said quietly. He turned his attention forward, his lips sealing into a thin line.

Why wasn't he saying anything? Why were none of the other cyn addressing their people?

"Harold Nixon, do you seek a tithe or do you offer one?" It was the same question Bishop had asked everyone that stepped forward.

"Neither," the man said. He was dressed in dark green attire that, if I hadn't sensed the dullness of his aura already, said he was human from the outer city. "I wanted to inquire about her." He turned his brown eyes to me.

Bishop turned slowly, his eyes widening as if it was his first time seeing me. "What about her?"

Harold visibly swallowed. "A few of us have been wondering... Well, we never see you with human companions and, for the past several weeks, she hasn't been outside the company of at least one of you." His eyes darted to the cyn individually.

Valen stiffened. No, readied. His head angled down so that his curls shadowed his golden eyes. It had a menacing effect.

"Since when is it the business of a mortal who we choose to favor?" His voice was cold as death.

Harold licked his lips, his eyes darting from Valen to Bishop.

Bishop tsked. "Who put you up to this, dear Harold?" he

crooned, his voice like velvet and as chilling as Valen's. "Are one of your lovers jealous?"

Harold was trembling now. He clenched his hands together so hard his knuckles whitened. "No, Your Highness. Just... talk I heard in the city. Everyone is asking about her. Even yours." He said the last part quietly, quickly. As if Bishop wouldn't hear his insinuation that the amorini had started to ask questions.

"Mine?" He sent his silver gaze across the crowd. "Yes, I suppose her favoritism would make you all curious. Step forward, Ezra." Bishop held out his hand. I took it as Bishop stood, towering over me. He twisted his wrist, making me spin on the dais. I turned stiffly as he presented me.

"Ezra is what our dear guests have been looking for," Bishop purred. "Well, one of the things." He lowered his arm as I faced the crowd again. "A rumor took flight a week ago, of a nephilim having been seen. Well, here she is."

All feeling drained from my body. I clutched Bishop's hand only so my legs would not drop out from under me. Had he really thrown me to the wolves?

"What the fuck," I started, my voice breathless. His double-edged glare cut me off.

"Nephilim are not women." The voice came from an amorini, a male with wavy blonde hair. "Who is she really?"

"If she was a nephilim, Raguel would have killed her," someone else said. "Surely, the angels would have known."

More voices rose to the commotion. I could smell their uncertainty. It filled my nose with the scent of warm copper pennies, not unlike the smell of blood. The pit of my stomach turned.

Bishop held up his hand, silencing them.

"The nephilim have always been a great but evasive race. When

Heaven cursed us from bearing children upon women, we lost companions in this war against them. By chance, by fate," Bishop held up a finger, drawing out the suspense of his tale, "Valen found her when he was meant to kill her. Strange, is it not? That our children were slaughtered and the one that escaped, the one that was spared, was destined to die at the hands of the Fallen."

I laced my fingers together to hide the tremors working through them. I had never thought of it like that. That perhaps Valen had been destined to kill me. He'd said it was by chance, but what if it wasn't? What if Heaven had pitted him against me and Ariel was sent as backup? Insurance that no matter what happened, I would be killed.

As if reading my mind, Bishop spoke the same. He told the court of the angel that hunted me and how Valen had dragged me back to their keep.

"It is the Enemy that named the nephilim as an abomination. A child of His two greatest creations, some might say. Well, at least one of them."

There were a few chuckles from the amorini in the crowd.

"It is true that women do not have a place in the hierarchy of Heaven, but here she stands with the blood of a demon coursing through her veins. Think about it," Bishop hissed.

An eerie silence fell across the crowd. There were no murmurs, but their eyes upon me felt loud.

"Heaven cursed us against women. The power that flows in her veins broke through that curse and made her what she is. A weapon hidden in plain sight, for as you have all pointed out, the nephilim were male." He cocked his head toward me. "Or, they once were."

"You have seen her with each of us because we have a hand in her education as we refine her skills and discern her sire's bloodline. Ezra has agreed to help us, to help you, Vélos, and buy us our freedom from this prison."

The silence was so deafening that I had to press a palm to my forehead to suppress the headache that started to grow behind my eyes. The swell of power in the room was instantaneous. It ripped back and forth like a flag caught in the wind.

The court didn't believe.

"It's true," I spoke up, sliding my hand down the side of my neck. "The cyn have told me your story, how you were wrongfully cast out and condemned. You and I have that in common. I have been damned because of the one who made me. I want to help."

"Prove it," someone snapped.

Bishop's head jerked in the direction of the voice. A gray haze fell across his body that started to simmer.

"Any woman could stand up there and speak such blasphemy," another spat.

"I am not just any woman," I shot back.

The beast inside me had been patient. I coaxed her gently to surface, for the flames to sprout within my hands. They came readily. Orange and gold bands slid up my wrists.

"A trick."

"They're playing with us."

"Your tricks will make the other courts hate us more."

"You damned us and now this. You would kill us all!"

My heart was racing as I turned my back on the people. I caught the glimpse of fury in Bishop's eyes. His people did not believe him. The temper reflected in all of the cyns' eyes. In Valen's, there was curiosity as he waited to see what I would do.

There was no going back from this. If I did this, I sealed my fate.

Looking at Valen, I knew there wasn't anywhere else I wanted to be.

I took off my shirt. I'd been wearing the leather harness Bishop had made me as a bra. I didn't know when or if I would need to open my wings. It proved being ready had its perks.

Valen stood quickly, his hand coming to my side. "You do not have to do this," he said.

I shook my head. "I do."

A hiss swelled in the back of his throat. "Do not make me slaughter my own people, Ezra."

"You won't have to."

"Should they decide to rip out your wings, we will have no choice," Bishop answered. His eyes narrowed, but he didn't try to stop me. He needed this. They all needed me to prove that what Bishop said was true.

"Then let's hope I am right," I said. I slid my hand into Valen's at my hip. He would be my anchor.

I trained my eyes on the male before me. He was my haven, my light in the darkness. I focused on him as I worked through the muscles holding my wings in place. It had gotten easier but no less strange. One second, I could not feel them buried beneath my flesh, and the next my wings were a heavy weight pulling at my back.

A collective gasp shot through the room. Its echo reverberated across the glass, sending quieter sounds into the ceiling. I held tight to Valen's fingers as I turned, removing his hand from me but not letting him go entirely.

"I am what your cyn claims me to be, a child born of angels and men. This is no trick of the light and you are not new to beliefs, but I am real. My flame is my own." I turned my hand outward and let the fire crawl up my arm.

The vision of them kneeling before me was an overlay to the

wide-eyed expressions before me. My beast licked her lips with anticipation.

"Your cyn and I have come to an agreement. They believe that I have the power to break you, break Vélos, from your hold. I intend to set you free." I looked down my nose as the amorini scowled at my wings. Their jealousy was palpable, but so was their awe. When was the last time they had seen one of my kind?

"Anyone who chooses to work outside of our cause," Bishop said slowly, "will be executed. We have only just slipped through Raguel's fingers. One word to him and our chance at freedom is ripped away. This includes you, mortals." Bishop's voice rose. "If you want to go home, to Earth, to your families and loved ones, then you will do as you are told."

Jinn and Diriel stood, stepping forward on the platform next to us. There were quick glances of hesitation amongst the court. Then, one by one, they kneeled before their cyns.

I'd never cared for monarchs who ruled by manipulating their subject's fear, but my did it feel good when it was done in my favor.

CHAPTER THIRTY-FOUR: THE TALON

Lane

Lane ran her finger across the lines of pristine penmanship as her pen flew across the pages next to it. It was only a matter of time before someone noticed she was missing.

It was wrong to use Diriel for his research, but there was not a more efficient way of gathering what Raum needed. He would be angry if he found out, but he would forgive her. He always did.

The Hymn was just as important to her. It spoke of her, of the Moon that could control angels with the use of their true name. The crescent moon tattooed on the underside of her chin was the mark that had spared her throat the day she had been thrown at Raum's feet.

Lane stuffed the notes in her shirt, blew out the glowing orb on the desk, and slipped away into the underground tunnels.

The Moon was said to be able to open gateways to other worlds, other realms. She was the one who could lock the gates of Tartarus forever. So long as Eurynomos controlled the Moon, they controlled the fate of the Fallen. If they controlled the Moon, they could keep the door open once it was unlocked.

And the Sun, the powerful raging Sun, was Ezra. She was the

one who would open that door. Lane didn't know how, that much hadn't been discovered yet, but she knew it was Ezra. Her name was all over Diriel's transcripts.

Lane counted her steps, making a right turn on thirty-seven. The tunnels were dense with moisture. It was comforting to know, as she passed through a cobweb, that they were not frequently used. It was a wonder Valen hadn't sealed them. Unless he didn't know that's how she had snuck into Ezra's room the other night.

Lane barred her door shut once she was back within her room. Her heart raced against the pages she had stuffed there. *Thump-thump. Thump-thump.*

She kept them there when she crawled into bed. Raum had said Orias would dreamwalk to her when it was time to check in. But secretly, Lane had sent a crow to Eurynomos informing Raum that she had information he would want.

The rush of adrenaline kept her far from slumber.

She focused on the softness of the pillow beneath her head. How warm linens weighed down her anxiety. She could enjoy the luxuries of Vélos while she was here. She had earned that much.

Lane's eyes fluttered. She clutched the front of her chest tighter.

The bed dipped at Lane's feet. Her heart lurched into her throat. No matter how many times Orias did this to her, it always scared her. It didn't matter that he now crawled slowly up the bed, instead of his usual flurry of claws and fangs. This slow, precise movement was equally jarring.

Lane sat up, meeting his blue eyes that now looked wholly black in the darkness.

"I am flattered you would be so eager to see me," Orias said. "I was not due for several days." He crawled up her body until he was sitting atop her thighs, crushing them beneath the dense weight of his muscles.

"I thought you might appreciate the information I've gathered."

The moons' light lit Orias's face when he leaned forward. His hair was twisted off his neck. The gold rings hooked in the braids at his scalp glimmered.

"Where's Raum?"

Orias tugged on the neck of her t-shirt. The fabric changed, softening to thin straps of satin and bunching at her thighs in the length of a gown. "That's better," he said, his eyes lowering to her exposed skin. "He is waiting for us."

The demon took his time surveying her. She swallowed.

"You haven't fucked anyone, have you?"

Lane balked. "No. I would never. That's not my mission."

Orias's eyes snapped to hers. He smiled, pulling his lips wide apart. "But it is your nature to defy us when you get the chance. Now tell me the truth, have you fucked anyone?"

"No." Lane held his gaze, willing him to see the truth for what it was. She'd been tempted, but she wasn't an idiot. The Murder would know if she had let anyone touch her.

Orias rolled his eyes. "You're such a disappointment, Lane. I suppose I'll have to find something else to punish you for." The smile fell into an annoyed scowl. "What news do you have of Ezra?" He rolled gracefully to his feet.

She followed him, catching the papers as they fell inside the gown to her hips. She stuffed them into the band of her underwear while Orias's back was turned. Lane didn't know why Raum didn't want to share information on the Hymn with Orias, but she would follow orders. While the Murder typically moved as one, it was Raum who was their head.

Lane replayed the image of Ezra caught between the two dragons, her throat laid bare to Valen. An offering from Bishop, though she knew that the other male had her. It was clear as day that something had shifted between the two. Ezra hadn't verbalized it before Valen showed up, but every line of her body had. And the way Valen looked at her.

The very thought made her stomach clench.

"She's Valen's. Officially, I think," she clarified. "But I think Bishop is going to make a move. You know how he likes to play."

Orias blinked slowly. "I expected them to be sharing her by now."

As was usual with the dragons. Lane tracked Orias's line of thinking. They only got a piece of something if Bishop had it first. It was a setback for whatever plans they had for Ezra.

Lane shrugged. "I'm sure it will happen soon."

The room changed to a forest, to a snowy dirt road, and then to a human city. Orias loved theatrics. His show of traveling was mild compared to what he was truly capable of manipulating in REM sleep.

"I've made a talon for you. It sits on the west side of the Styx at the base of the mountains. Raum is waiting for you there," Orias said. He pointed between two skyscrapers lit by a glowing sunset of pink. Between the halogen-lit windows were the black mountains of Vélos.

She whipped her head to him. "How the Hell did you manage to sneak a talon into Vélos?"

Orias splayed his hands across his chest. "I am the best." He stopped at the base of the mountain, his eyes moving up to inspect the talon.

It looked like a mirror, tall with black glass. A sort of mist crept at its base. "I'll be waiting for you," Orias said.

Lane nodded and stepped forward, letting the spell of the incubus's creation envelop her.

Talons were created by the incubi as a way to manipulate reality in the real world. To access those of a wakeful mind. Inside, you could be anywhere. Everything was malleable to the whims of those inside. Places, food, people.

Raum had chosen a bedroom for their setting. A large bed lay in its center with crumpled sheets as if it had recently been fucked in. Glowing lights hovered beneath a peaked ceiling that looked as if it was made of starlight. The ground was black sand and somewhere in the distance was the sound of crashing waves.

Beyond that was darkness.

Raum's power hit her as soon as the wall of the talon sealed behind her. It was a force that made the hair on the back of her neck stand on end. She made another pan around the room when she saw him. The silhouette of his shadow hung to the edge of the darkness.

She raised her chin. "I have something you want."

The silhouette didn't move.

Lane hiked up the skirt of her gown, pulling the papers free. The pages ruffled in a breeze.

"Thank you." Raum's voice brushed the back of her head.

Her grip tightened on the papers as he circled to her front. The apparition before her was gone.

Raum plucked the papers from her grasp. "Have a seat." His gaze flicked quickly over her scrawled writing.

Lane sat back against the bed as he flipped to the next page. "Diriel has confirmed it then, Ezra is the sun."

Lane's mouth twisted.

"She can open the gate," he said quietly. "You can keep it open."

Raum's sapphire eyes glimmered like starlight as he looked up at her. His gaze tore through her, stirring forbidden heat in her core. The wicked glint within the night sky of his gaze sent heat unfurling across her cheeks.

"You have done well." Raum ran his fingers down through her hair to stroke the back of her neck. "Turn around," he said.

Nothing good ever came from turning your back on Raum. Lane hesitated before turning slowly.

Lying on the bed that had magically appeared was Hennie. Her soft skin stood out against the cream sheets. Her heavy black curls fanned around her head like a halo. She reached up, curling a finger at Lane, her smile beckoning.

Talons were tricky places. They only accounted for the people who were in them. Either this was really Hennie or someone else wearing her appearance like a costume. Lane's stomach coiled. The only other person it could be, if it wasn't Hennie, was Orias.

Where there were two, there was a third.

Lane glanced around the room, but there was no sign of Atticus. No trace that the third male was lurking, but that didn't mean he wasn't there.

Lane stiffened as Raum pressed against her backside. His empty hands smooth down the length of her arms. "What is this?"

"A gift," he said. He inhaled her scent, running his nose along her cheek.

Raum had stripped every single thing Lane ever had. Had flayed her of her will and desires until they were his own. He had inquired before, about everyone else she had been with. One by one they were collected from Vélos and killed in the depths of Eurynomos. Hennie's was a face that had never entered the wicked halls because she belonged to one of Vélos's guards. One of the higher-ups.

"A gift," Lane repeated.

"You continue to prove your loyalty." He slid her hair to the side, brushing his lips over her throat. "Take advantage of my kindness. You know it does not come often."

There was a sharp prick, a bit of pressure, and then Raum's teeth were buried beneath the surface of Lane's skin. Her head tipped back involuntarily into Raum's hand as he cupped her other cheek. He stepped forward, pressing his hard length into her backside.

Lane was pinned as he drank from her. Her breath came in short spurts as her desire heightened.

Raum's jaw locked, forcing a moan from her chest.

Abruptly, he ripped his fangs free and pressed his bloody lips beside her ear. "Taste her," Raum said. "Taste me on her." The gown fell to the ground without a sound as Raum's claws scraped across the front of her chest.

Lane's eyes fluttered across her old lover. Hennie's fingers moved between her legs as she watched them. Watched Raum run his big hands over Lane's body.

Lane saw the bite marks then, the bruises around her neck, hidden in the shadow of her dark hair. She allowed a faint smile to touch her lips. Hennie flashed one in return, briefly, before her eyes dropped down to the spot where Raum was touching her. He took one of her nipples between his fingers and pinched. He scraped his talons over her inner thigh with the other.

Lane stepped out of his grip, climbing on top of the bed, between Hennie's legs. It felt like her blood was on fire. Every inch of her body was hot, growing hotter.

"It's you," she said.

Hennie bit her lip as she nodded. "Crazy, right?" The playfulness fell out of her face as she looked up at Lane. "I've fucking missed you."

Lane swooped down and pressed her mouth to Hennie's. Sweet like honeyed candy. Hennie was always so sweet. She could taste the copper tang of Raum's bite on her swollen mouth. It made her hungry.

The kiss was started soft. It hardened as Hennie deepened the kiss, encouraging Lane to settle over her body, pressing her breasts on top of her.

She had missed her too. Had missed her so much.

Lane looked back at Raum. He had his cock in his hand and a lazy smile on his face that made the laugh lines in his face crinkle. He was utterly beautiful when he was in nothing but his gilded skin. The iridescent sheen of it moved like firelight as he stepped closer, sliding a hand across Lane's back.

Raum was equally cruel as he was beautiful. There was no deny-ing that. His muscles were inhuman, bulking and large and rippled when he moved. His raven hair fell over his shoulders. Though she couldn't see them, she knew the feathers on his back lay exposed like the ones protruding from the back of his knuckles.

Chills raced up her spine as she turned back to Hennie, slid down her body, and kissed the tender flesh of her thighs. An encouraging sigh escaped Hennie's lungs.

Raum's tongue swiped across Lane's slit. She moaned and turned her head, sliding her tongue against Hennie's apex. She tasted just as Lane remembered. Sweeter than her lips but just as intoxicating. She fastened her lips over her clit and hummed, sending soft vibrations jolting through her.

Hennie's thighs stiffened. She ran her fingers through Lane's blue hair, twisting them until she had a good hold.

Lane slid her fingers inside Hennie, curling them up as she feasted on her, and slowly moved them in and out.

"Oh, yes," Hennie breathed. "This is what I've needed." Her legs tightened around Lane's head as the dhampir worked her fingers faster.

It was all Lane could do to stay focused on Hennie while Raum devoured her. His long tongue curling in and out of her, making her wetter and wetter. She groaned when he withdrew, but she didn't stop as she worked Hennie.

Lane's grip hardened on Hennie's thigh as she felt Raum slide his cock between her legs. A low growl of approval rumbled in Raum's chest as he rubbed the head of his cock against her entrance. Her desire coated him, making the tip glisten.

He pushed forward, slowly, achingly slow, until he was hilted inside of her.

Lane moaned against Hennie's apex, her tongue delving wildly inside her lover.

"That is better," he said, his voice husky. "I missed how you felt around my cock." Raum pulled back and then pushed in, pressing his balls against her. It always felt like the first time whenever he fucked her. Like he was stretching her to her limits as he forced his way impossibly deep.

Hennie turned her grip in Lane's hair as her tongue worked faster over her clit. Her eyes flashed up to capture her release. She wanted to see Hennie come undone. Wanted to see the way her face scrunched right before she climaxed. Her breath was coming faster. She threw her hips up, grinding herself on Lane's lips as she chased her need.

Lane slid a third finger inside and fucked Hennie harder, pushing her over the edge. Hennie's back arched as her thighs locked around Lane's face.

Raum shoved Lane forward, pushing her up and over on top of Hennie as the woman's cry of pleasure broke through the air. He gave Lane one more thrust, then pulled out abruptly, only to push himself inside of Hennie. Lane kissed her. Swallowed the gasps that burst from her lungs every time Raum slammed into her.

Lane's face was buried in Hennie's neck when everything shifted. Hennie's smooth skin hardened with muscle, her shoulders and neck broadened. The soft perfume of her curls deepened to the frankincense of twists and knots. But it was the cock sliding up into Lane that made her realize what had happened. That Hennie was not a young woman at all but the second Murder.

Orias wrapped a strong arm around her waist and pulled her down so that he was hilted against her. "Hurry up," he growled.

Raum pushed the head of his cock against her ass.

She knew it was too good to be true. Knew that Raum's kindness had its limits. Having Hennie, even the illusion of her, had run its course.

With one hand on her hip and the other on her shoulder, Raum slammed forward.

They fucked her thoroughly, simultaneously pounding into her with no regard for anything but their own pleasure.

There was pain in their fucking, sweet delicious pain that made Lane's jaw ache. She turned her face into Orias's neck and bit down. Blunt human teeth broke his skin apart.

Orias groaned, his fingers turning into talons as he sank them into her hips. "Vicious little bitch," he growled. He threw his hips up, once, twice, and on the third time hit her so hard that her lips dislodged and blood sprayed across her face from the vein she had ripped open.

Strong fingers grabbed her chin. Orias rubbed his face against hers, coating it with his own essence, before shoving her back down to the wound.

Lane's hungry lips found her mark and she drank. She drank and drank and drank. Demon's blood was like velvet. Fine wine that cost millions.

A heavy weight pressed into her back as Raum leaned forward. His long tongue licked across Orias's face, collecting every glistening ruby.

This was how it was between them. Vicious and gory. There was no romance with demons, just bloody, painful fucking.

Lane moaned. As twisted and fucked up as being with them was, she loved it. Reveled in the perversion of being caught between the males when their bloodlust rose. She bit into Orias's neck harder, coaxing the blood to flow faster.

Faster. More. She needed more.

Raum's bite was like a gunshot to her back. His jaws locked at the base of her neck where it met her shoulder. Orias followed suit on the other side. More blood sprayed across Orias, over the pristine sheets.

They fucked her harder. Their talons sunk into her skin, the only way to keep her pinned with the blood slicking her skin.

Fuck.

"Fuck," she said aloud. Heat roiled within her; her muscles tightened.

"Let it go, Lane," Raum rasped. He pushed her down, pushed deeper inside of her as she tightened around his cock.

Orias was grunting with each thrust as he tried to outpower Raum. "Right there," he growled as he worked the head of his cock against the hard ridges of her cunt. "Right there and I am going to break you."

Lane dug her nails into Orias's shoulders. There was no thinking. No sense of time or anything outside of their cocks moving. And then, all at once, Lane burst. A cry left her throat as she seized around them. The height of her orgasm increased as they fucked her even harder.

Orias broke first. One stroke behind him and Raum was coming, pressing his hips as hard as he could into his partner's below.

"I missed our little cunt," Orias said. He licked the side of her face and thrust his hips up for emphasis. Lane moaned in response.

Raum chuckled as he withdrew. "It is unfortunate that our time together is so short."

Lane disentangled herself from them, flopping down between them as the haze of lust continued to assault her.

"Fuck," she breathed.

"Tell me you missed us," Raum said.

Lane craned her head back. "I did," she confessed. There was no denying that she had ridden out her pleasure on both of them the same time they rode her. She would feel the effects of it later. For now, it felt good to be lying in a state of bliss. They hadn't hurt her. Not as badly as they could have.

Raum slid his fingers between her legs. He looked down on her as he pressed his fingers inside, gliding his touch through the mixture of her and Orias. Lane's breath hitched as his nails scraped across her skin. Not talons, but she knew he could change that quickly enough.

"Such a good little spy," he said. He brought his fingers to his lips and crudely sucked them. A low, satisfied hum rumbled within his chest. The weight of his stare crushed her as Orias snaked an arm around her waist.

Raum kissed her gently before rising. "You will give Ezra my best when you see her." He cocked his head, surveying her while he dressed.

Lane nodded. "I will. She's growing quickly. Her power really is... something else." A tinge of jealousy lined her words.

Raum smirked. "Good." His eyes flicked to Orias. "Do not be too long," he said to the male. Then, without another glance at Lane as he walked away, he vanished. Leaving Lane alone with the second in command.

Orias slid off the bed. He reached down, snagging the gown Hennie had been wearing. He fisted it against his face and breathed in. "Still smells like her," he said and tossed it into Lane's face.

Her gut clenched. The bile rose swiftly in the back of her throat as reality came crashing around her. What Lane had not remembered until that very moment was that a person needed to be dead for a demon to steal their face.

Orias slapped her cheek lightly. "Don't look so sad. She got to come before I killed her." He grinned, so wide that all of his teeth flashed. His eyes darted to the tears brimming behind her eyes, further stretching that wicked sneer.

"Is what you do to me not enough?" She choked.

Orias pouted, tipping his head down to make his slanted eyes seem larger than they really were. "Of course not." His brows rose. "And that is why I will be back next week." His eyes flicked across her body. "To spend some time with you, just us."

Lane's heart hammered. No. No, no, no!

"Raum will punish you if you go too far," she gritted.

Orias tsked. He leaned forward, his finger pointed directly at her forehead. "Raum's the one that gave me his blessing." He shoved his finger against her skin, forcing her back, back, back. The world reeled around her in a stream of colors.

She lurched forward. The mirrored and blank edges of the talon seeped away, revealing black rock. Four white towers stood erect in the distance.

Orias had made her sleepwalk to the edge of the mountains, to the hidden alcove where the talon now lay. Barefoot and cold, she made her way back to the tyre.

CHAPTER THIRTY-FIVE: THE HUNT

Ezra

Soul ties hung in the air like the strings of balloons. I tugged at the red thread dangling above me next to so many others.

We had come to an agreement that we would hunt only those that deserved it. Murderers, rapists, thieves. It was sick to think that anyone wicked had an adelfi. That they would be deserving of one.

The thread popped free. I clasped it in my fist. I knew the person was going to be terrible, yet I couldn't bring myself to look at it. I was going to take my first life. This time, when someone died, it would be by my hand.

"Diriel has decided to remain while we hunt. Our little stunt has caused a stir and we thought it best that at least one of us remains," Bishop said.

A stir was putting it lightly. There had been absolute chaos, to the point that Valen had to specter me away. That's what it was called, when he moved us through the smoke bleeds. It was like teleporting, but more efficient.

Some thought I was a spy for Heaven. But that didn't explain my wings. No one could explain why I was the only female to have ever been graced with angelic blood.

I uncurled my fist.

This.... this had to be a joke.

I ran my thumb over the scrawled ink, flipping the tie over. The name remained the same. I glanced up to see if the other cyn had noticed, but they were busy looking at their own ties.

"I've got a serial killer," Jinn said devilishly. "Hunting the hunter," he shuddered. "This will be fun."

I grabbed Valen's arm. "What the fuck is this?" I hissed.

Valen looked down at the tie. His eyes widened. "Is that?"

"Yes."

Killian Lee Odair.

I felt like I was going to throw up. "Why is my boyfriend's name on here? Did you do this?"

Valen snatched the tie from my hand, replacing it with his own. "No. Don't say a word about it. I'll take care of it."

"Take care of it?" My voice hitched. I reached for the tie again, my only connection to the man I once loved. Still loved. What had he done to condemn him? He wasn't a bad person.

Valen caught my wrist and heaved me against his chest.

"Is something wrong?" Bishop was watching us carefully.

Valen sneered. "She's just nervous." He nipped at my vein before I jerked my hand away.

Bishop sauntered forward. He brushed his thumb over my chin. I knew he could feel me quaking, that he could smell it on me. Killian's name was like a neon sign flashing in my brain. I had drawn Killian's name. Killian. My Killian.

"We'll be with you the whole time. There's nothing to worry over," Bishop said.

I swallowed, trying to feign ignorance. "I know it's just... Sorry,"

I said.

Bishop's mouth quirked. "Don't be. This will be fun." He looked over Valen's head. "Do you have her bow?"

Valen touched his chest where two bows rested. "All ready."

Bishop nodded. "Then let's go. Shall we?"

Valen wrapped me in his arms, tucking my head beneath his chin. Just like the first time. "They don't know about Killian. I will keep Bishop from him, but Ezra, he *cannot* see him. Bishop cannot see what Killian looks like."

Who he looks like.

I nodded as smoke enveloped us. Through the flashing pain of moving from one world to the next, all I saw was Killian's name. It was a mantra in my head. The one person that got away was supposed to die tonight.

I lurched hard into Valen's chest as we landed.

I took the bow he extended to me with shaking hands. "Valen," I started.

His sharp look silenced me.

Why couldn't Bishop know? What did Valen mean when he said he would take care of Killian?

"Please don't," I whispered. Please don't kill him, I silently begged.

Bishop and Jinn were already moving ahead of us. I was so consumed in what was going to happen that I hadn't noticed where we had landed. Reno. I recognized the bright lights flashing around us. The whir of cars with their blaring horns.

Valen slid his arm around my waist as we followed the other cyn. "I won't," he said. "I won't have to unless Bishop sees him. Bishop upholds our laws with a fierce sword, where I have been lax in your affection for the male. If he sees him, if he finds out who Killian is to you, the boy will die."

I jerked my head up to face him, but he kept us moving. The line of his mouth was twisted so hard that deep lines were creased in his cheeks.

"I won't," he said again, though I wasn't sure he was speaking entirely to me.

"Good." I nodded. Killian would be kept safe. He would be the one that got away.

Valen's grip hardened. "And Ezra, don't even think about running."

Tall skyscrapers with color-changing lights surrounded us. The bustle of the city was strange. I hadn't been away long, yet something about it irked me. Like the appeal of the city life I once loved so much was an irritant.

Home. I was finally home. Not the exact place I had grown up, but Earth. And it felt wrong.

The ritz and glam was now dull. Lifeless. The air was rank with smog, piss, and death.

"I don't think that's something you need to worry about," I said softly.

"It has lost its appeal, hasn't it?" Jinn called over his shoulder. He flashed his teeth at my expression, which I'm sure was full of disappointment.

I had thought I would be excited to be back on Earth. Once I would have loved the big neon lights and, now, they were nothing but a disenchantment. As we made our mark across the city, I found myself wishing for the dark beauty of Vélos.

Brandon Stoker hadn't been caught in ten years. Law enforcement had found six of the twenty-one women he had killed. Of the remaining fifteen, they only knew of two who were missing. The others were nameless. So unimportant to society that no one cared if they ever turned up again.

I wondered if anyone was looking for me. If there was some window my face was plastered across that said "Missing".

Bishop sucked the back of his teeth. "That's not that many."

"Who has the biggest body count? You, me, or Valen?" Jinn pointed to each of the males individually but stopped when Valen threw him a nasty look.

I ran my fingers across the line of the bow strung across my chest. "You know things are going to change if I get you out," I said.

Jinn's brow arched in time with the upward crook of his mouth. "Who says I wasn't talking about fucking?"

My cheeks colored against his taunt.

"He is trying to get under your skin," Valen said.

"He's succeeding," I gritted. The only comfort, and a very small one at that, was that it kept my mind off of Killian. "You know I never agreed to fucking you," I said to Jinn.

Jinn slid a sly tongue over his teeth. "You don't know what you're missing."

We walked for several blocks before turning down a side street that led to a quiet neighborhood, as quiet as it could be this close to the city. A couple of people stood outside one of the homes, smoking. The smell of nicotine and weed made the inside of my nose itch. Weird how that bothered me more than the demons' sulfur and black smoke.

"What's going to happen to this guy's adelfi?" I asked.

Valen's shoulder tensed as it brushed against mine. "She's already dead," he said. "He started with her."

My foot skipped on a broken piece of the sidewalk. How... how could someone kill their soulmate? Valen must have seen the question running through my eyes.

"Sometimes people are just wicked, Ezra. It doesn't matter how much you love them, if they don't want to be saved, they won't be."

Bishop held his finger up in the air, the silver rings on his hand flashing under a street lamp. "No matter which side of the coin love falls, it is a weakness. That is why it is in our laws that it be forbidden within our kingdom. Loving someone will get you killed."

A sharp pang ripped through my chest. I nodded, not wanting to accept it but listening to them all the same. It's not like they had been wrong about anything else they had told me so far.

"How do you know everything about the adelfis?" I asked.

I eyed the house that we stopped in front of. A little white cottage with brick steps and a single iron railing. Plain. Simple. There was nothing menacing about it except the dark wave that rolled down the front steps like a red carpet.

"Their stories come to us when we touch their soul tie," Valen answered. I stiffened as Jinn and then Bishop passed through the front door like an apparition.

I looked up at Valen. "How much do you know about..." *Don't say his name,* a little voice in my head reminded me.

Valen's mouth twisted as Bishop opened the front door for us. "Enough," he said. He slid his hand over the small of my back as we followed the other cyn inside.

My heart hammered faster. I wondered what the soul tie had shown Valen. What he had seen of me. And what crime had Killian committed? That's what I really wanted to know.

My heart raced even faster as we approached the closed door of a bedroom. The sense of evil was heavy here. Its foreboding pounded like a bass drum.

This was all too much. My legs quake beneath me as the door swung inward to reveal Brandon laying fast asleep in his bed. As if he didn't have a care in the world. As if he had no blood on his hands.

"Will he be able to see us?" I asked.

Bishop cocked his head. "Do you want him to?"

I chewed the inside of my lip. I'd seen plenty of people die, but I'd never seen someone murdered. How much different could it be? Death was death, right?

I shrugged. "I don't... know. He should suffer something for what he's done."

Bishop nudged against me with his shoulder and grinned. "Then let's wake this bastard up."

Jinn climbed on top of the bed. He was so tall that he had to hunch his shoulders to fit under the ceiling.

"Brandon," he hissed. The voice did not belong to Jinn. Or maybe it did and came from some other part of him I didn't understand yet. It was a whisper, but loud enough that it echoed through the house, as if he had spoken behind me and directly into my ear. Chills raced across my skin.

Brandon stirred slowly and then blinked. His entire body went still as the shadow above him shifted.

I didn't know the amorini could shape-shift until Jinn dropped down onto the man's chest. One second, he was the pristine beautiful redhead. The next, he was a leathery black beast with sharp claws and fangs with a thousand arrows protruding from his back.

"It's time to wake up," the beast snarled.

Brandon lurched out of bed, his eyes as wide as his gaping mouth.

I ran out the room when Jinn thrust a clawed hand through his chest.

I barely made it down the hallway before choking down the bile. I braced myself against the wall as the burn threatened to climb its way back up my throat.

Murder was very different from any other death I had seen. A car accident, suicide, cancer—they had nothing on the monstrosity I had just witnessed.

I waved Valen off as he edged to my side. "I'm fine. I've got it."

"We're going to have to toughen that gut," Bishop said. "We have a long night ahead of us."

I nodded. "Yeah, just..." Fuck, my throat burned. And my mouth tasted awful. "It's going to take some getting used to."

There was a savage flesh-ripping sound that made my stomach turn over.

Bishop grinned as I shuddered. "This next one will be easier. She's a little thing. They always fade fast."

Jinn met us outside; the front of his shirt was spot free despite the blood covering his hands and what had been sprayed across his face. "Fuck, I needed that." He rolled his neck. *Crack. Crack. Crack.* The same sound the bones had made beneath his teeth.

I flinched when Valen held me to specter to our next target.

"Jinn was more vicious than I expected. If things take a turn, I want you to distance yourself from us. Bloodlust is a very real thing amongst our kind. Once it hits, there's really no way to stop it until you're sated, and even then, some choose to keep going."

I looked at him in horror. "You're making me reconsider helping you at all."

"It is the price of falling, Ezra. Blood is our life source. So long as we are trapped, we need it."

I looked at him and then at the backs of the other males. "You won't need it when you're free." It wasn't a question. I could not knowingly unleash them as they were.

Valen paused, too long to give me reassurance. "Perhaps," he said.

Bass blared inside of the next home in celebration of Katie's birthday. We slipped into the party with another couple. I knew they could see us by the looks on every single human face that took in the large three males. Their jaws dropped; someone dropped their beer. I didn't blame them. They were stunning.

"Mine's here too," Valen said. He lifted his chin, scenting the air. Two pointed fangs rested on the top of his lower lip.

I could have fainted right then.

"And if I'm not mistaken," Bishop said, "I believe Ezra's isn't too far after this. Maybe we should invite him over." He threw a mischievous look Valen's way.

It was too close to home. My heart hammered wildly. I couldn't help looking amongst the crowd, looking for the spitting image of the male standing next to me.

I cast my eyes over the crowd, catching curious glances and the flash of a new horror the news broadcasted on a TV in the background. There were a few guys standing in front of the screen. A blue glow obscured the concern on their faces. None of them were Killian.

This second hunt wasn't as brutal as the first one. Instead, we grabbed a couple of drinks and blended in with the humans around us, as much as angelica could blend in, before singling the woman out. Everyone was looking at the males, their eyes jumping from one to the next. The men were equally curious, but their egos were bigger by the looks of their puffed-up chests and snide comments.

Idiots, all of them. Not a single person was concerned that there were predators amongst them. Two women in crop tops and jeans approached Jinn. Their fingers were laced together, their liquored smiles glistening as they looked him up and down. As if he was a meal.

He cocked a grin before resting one hand on the hip of the first woman and touching the second under her chin. They wouldn't be swooning if they knew what those hands had just done.

I followed Bishop as he snagged his prey, a young woman by the name of Kaycee Ann who had been drinking and driving when she struck a woman jogging late at night. The victim was dead by the time first responders arrived.

Kaycee had never been caught. Mommy's credit card had her car in the shop the next morning and there had been a pact made between the two that no one else would ever find out what happened.

They hadn't planned on demons tracking her down. Given the family's track record, you'd think they would have some idea what happened to corrupt people. That the truth always came out.

In this instance, it was Bishop whispering Kaycee's deep dark secret to her seconds before he slammed an arrow in the center of her chest.

Her eyes snapped open. I saw the image he was playing for everyone else. If anyone was looking, they would see Bishop fondling the woman, her head tipped back into his shoulder as if she enjoyed it. No one could see the blood he was smearing into her skin or that he had his fangs gum deep in her neck.

Someone touched my shoulder. I lurched forward, a little sound escaping my lips. Valen smirked. "I'm going to go find him," he said.

I nodded, but Valen stopped me when I tried to follow.

"Keep Bishop distracted. And if you see Killian, try not to let him see you. It will make this whole process more difficult." Valen angled his head down so that his eyes were cast in shadows. "I mean it, Ezra. Don't seek him out and don't run."

I made a beeline for the kitchen and snagged another beer out of a cooler. "I got it," I snapped. I leaned my hip into the counter. "It's not like I have anywhere to run anyway. How do we even know that this is safe?" I motioned my bottle around the room. "Won't Ariel know I'm here?"

Valen's tongue ran across his teeth behind his lips. "Our power dampens yours. Besides, there are too many witnesses. Ariel seems to be one of theatrics. He can't risk killing you without drawing attention of his own."

I nodded, shooing him off as I took a drink. Valen's eyes narrowed, but he didn't say anything else as he left the room.

I truly hadn't considered running. I knew there was nowhere I could run that one of the angels wouldn't find me, Fallen or otherwise. I pushed the thought from my head entirely as I focused on working up the courage to kill someone.

Valen hadn't told me who I was supposed to kill. There hadn't been an opportunity when I was so consumed with worrying about Killian and the small window between jumping worlds.

I looked up as someone entered the kitchen, my heart freezing as I half expected to see Killian in the doorway.

Bishop brushed the corner of his mouth as he strode in. The metallic scent of blood crossed the room upon his entry, making my lips curl in response.

Bishop grinned. "I'm not that bad, am I?"

A small trickle of fear seeped into my conscious as the demon approached. He was too calm for my liking, having just ripped out someone's throat.

"You're a monster," I said.

Despite the flashing lights beating in time with the music, I could see his grin broaden. His fangs looked even more terrible up close. They were impossibly sharp and impossibly white. Not even predators in the animal kingdom had teeth so piercing.

"A monster who kills monsters," he said. "I think that makes me a little bit better, doesn't it?" He plucked the bottle out of my hand, his eyes never leaving mine as he took a swig of amber. His mouth twisted, crooking the black line in the center of his lip. "You couldn't find something stronger?"

"What do you want?" I crossed my arms to hide my shaking hands. He reeked of death and triumph. It was unnerving how relaxed he appeared, like tonight was like any other. For him, I supposed it was.

They were all so calm. So mild *killing* people.

"I want us to be friends," he said. "Why don't you like me?"

"I don't like Jinn either," I said.

"But I gave you a gift." He pointed.

I rolled my eyes. A gift I hadn't really been able to use yet. "Yes, and I've already thanked you for it."

He stepped closer, until he filled up my entire line of sight. "So, what's the problem?" He slid the bottle on the bar behind me as I met him the rest of the way. I wasn't going to be cornered. Bishop's eyes heated as I looked up at him, challenging him. Beneath the stench of blood was the musk of arousal.

"There's no problem, Bishop. I just think it's best that we keep our distance."

Bishop cocked his head. "Are you scared of me?"

Acknowledging your fear of a demon gives them power. But I knew I already reeked of fear. I was afraid of what Bishop would do if he found out about Killian. I was afraid of the way he looked at me, more so when he thought I wasn't paying attention. There was a desire of possession in the wake of his eyes.

But Killian. That's what I was most concerned about. Would he outright kill him? Would I somehow be punished for him? Would Valen?

Of course he would die. Valen had said as much.

I swallowed, realizing I was taking too long to answer as my thoughts hounded me. "A little," I said.

"You don't have to be." Bishop tipped his head down. That tang of blood brushed across my face as he exhaled.

Movement caught my eye beside Bishop's shoulder from the adjacent room.

Speak of the devil and he will show his face.

I recognized Killian despite the changes he had made. He had shaved his head. His hair wasn't completely gone, but the curls were. There was a silver stud in his nose that hadn't been there before. He was still handsome, still had the beautiful charm I had fallen in love with surrounding him. But something seemed a little broken about him. As if he had lost something special.

The breath in my chest faltered as I noticed his changes. Even Killian had become disenchanted.

His brow furrowed when he saw me and then his eyes widened. "Ezra?" His voice, suppressed over the music, was an alarm inside my head. "Where have you been? I've been looking for you."

Fuck.

Bishop cocked his head in the direction of my gaze. I grabbed him by the front of the shirt, pulling him against me, before he could see the man making his way for us. Before he could see Valen's likeness and rip out his throat the way he had ripped out Kaycee's.

Bishop's eyes snapped into focus, locking onto me with a flash of lightning.

"Then show me," I said. I didn't think about what I was doing before I rose up on my toes and kissed him.

There was no hesitation on Bishop's part as he leaned into my kiss. He shoved me so hard against the wall that our teeth clacked together.

"Took you long enough," he growled.

Oh, fuck.

Heat pooled against my core. I hadn't expected my body to give in as easily as his desires. I truthfully hadn't expected him to respond so quickly. Even though I knew he had been waiting. Patient as a wolf and now I was beneath his jaws.

I tensed as his hands ran up my arms and cupped the underside of my jaw, but Bishop's touch never hardened. He was gentle with me despite his hunger. His tongue slipped between my lips, sending electric tingles through my body. I leaned in, letting the tip of my tongue brush across his. He tasted *divine*. Like fresh rain.

A low purr of satisfaction rumbled in his chest.

I dug my nails into the top of his shoulders as I broke our lips free, only for him to drop his hot mouth onto my throat. The feeling of his tongue brushing the vein in my neck was sinful.

I slid my hand over the back of his head to hold him there as I struggled to regain control of myself. Getting lost in Bishop wasn't part of the plan. It sure as Hell wasn't a smart one. And yet, desire flooded me, made my eyes heavy-lidded.

Killian and Valen were face to face. The man took a step back as he looked Valen up and down. He shook his head at the image of his own flesh and blood.

Valen grabbed him by the back of the neck before he could retreat farther and pulled him into his shoulder like they were old buddies. Killian was stiff as a board. His gaze started to shift my way and I tipped my head back to feign that I didn't see him. Didn't see the way his face crumpled at the way another man was touching me. That I had moved on.

"I've been looking for you." The pain in those words cut through me like any blade would. I hadn't for a second believed someone would come looking for me. How much time had passed on Earth? How long had Killian searched for me? Why had he when I was the one who had left him?

I had hoped he wouldn't recognize me. That he would have thought my image was a trick of the light. But he knew me, as sure as I knew him. And I couldn't do anything about it.

Valen saw too. There was a flash of something sinister in his eyes and then it was gone. He said something against Killian's ear and shoved the man out of the room.

I shoved against Bishop, like I would follow them. It encouraged his hands to roam farther, to cup my breast. I slipped my fingers into Bishop's loose hair and tugged as the scrape of his fangs slid up my jaw.

Focus. I couldn't focus when his mouth was on me and his hard cock was digging into my thigh. This was going too far too quickly. My nostrils flared as the scent of his arousal heightened.

I pressed a hand against his chest when his lips found mine

again.

"That wasn't so scary, was it?" Bishop hissed as he spoke, his voice deep with lust's intent.

"I got carried away," I murmured. I didn't dare look to see where Valen had taken Killian, though my conscience was screaming at me to do so. Something moved inside me, a surge of power that strained to find the men.

Bishop ran a hand down my side, over the curve of my ass and gave it a squeeze. "It's natural to feel this way when you hunt. Gets the blood hot."

He thought I was turned on by death. The idea might have made my stomach turn if I didn't have a role to play.

"Still," I murmured.

His hard length jerked against me. His silver eyes raged like a hurricane. Bishop was the kind of male that liked to see how far he could push someone before they broke. I needed to end this, put space between us, before he pulled me over the edge with him.

He looked down my form, drinking me in. "You are always welcome to seek me out when things become uncertain," he purred. "You're young and new. I want to help you."

I could feel the heat creep up to my ears. This was not the sort of help I needed.

He smirked. "Red really is a good color on you."

I scoffed and pushed against him to slip away. Bishop turned with me, sliding behind me to pull me against his chest. "Stay. Let's have some fun," he said against my ear. His voice was pristine silver bells. There was an allure to it, an offer. I felt myself giving in, leaning into his touch as he slid the flat of his palm over my stomach.

"Are you two finished or shall we take Ezra to her kill?" Valen materialized out of thin air. It was like having a bucket of ice water dumped over my head.

Shame. Guilt. Betrayal. It washed over me with a vengeance. I hadn't even realized I had closed my eyes when I had sunk into Bishop's embrace. What the fuck was wrong with me?

Bishop chuckled. The sound of his voice deepening stirred a forbidden desire within me. I had never thought of Bishop in any other way than being a cocky arrogant prick. I had never desired him. And yet my body responded to him. Right in front of Valen.

Bishop tipped my head back and kissed me. I stiffened. I grabbed the front of his shirt to push him away again, but he was already moving, turning to Valen but not letting me go. He slid his tongue between the male's lips, letting him taste me.

I blinked.

The tension never uncoiled from Valen as he kissed Bishop back. The soft stroke of Bishop's thumb over my neck lit something inside of me. There was something possessive in the way he held onto me. In the way he kissed Valen.

"Let's go find Jinn," Bishop said. "I'm sure it'll be more fun if it's the four of us."

He gave the back of my neck a squeeze and slipped into the throng of people who parted for him like the Red Sea.

CHAPTER THIRTY-SIX: THE KILL

Ezra

Valen looked like he wanted to beat me. Hell, I needed someone to knock some sense into me.

"You told me to distract him," I said.

He kept staring.

"What the fuck was I supposed to do?"

Without so much as touching me, Valen jerked me against his chest. The sting of his power sent a jolt through my bones. "Perhaps you could have not enjoyed yourself so thoroughly while I was off doing you a favor." He still didn't touch me. He couldn't when his hands were curled into fists.

I pressed my fingers against my temples. "I didn't *want* to kiss him. It wasn't the plan. I just—I didn't know what else to do when I saw Killian. I didn't think about it. Besides, you kissed him too." I motioned up and down.

Valen sucked the back of his teeth. "What lays between Bishop and me is complicated."

"Oh, so you can kiss him but when I do it, I'm in trouble? Where is Killian? What did you do to him?"

"He's in one of the back rooms. Alive," he clarified quickly. He looked down sharply. "Don't ask anything else of me. Your lover is safe and that is all that matters."

I followed Valen as he touched my hip and forced down everything I wanted to ask him. Maybe I should have tried to distract Bishop another way. I could have spoken to Killian, told him what had happened. That I was ok.

I looked over my shoulder, half expecting to see his face in the crowd again.

"I want to see him," I said. I couldn't leave. I couldn't leave him again when he was right there. "He said he was looking for me. He should know that I'm ok."

"Ezra," Valen warned. "His life is only spared so long as he remains hidden."

"I'll never have another opportunity to see him."

"You don't need to see him," Valen retorted.

"Valen, he is the only one that managed to get away."

His teeth clacked from snapping his jaw so hard. "And he will suffer the consequences of your curse if you do not leave him behind. Every second we dally puts his life at risk. I do not know what it means for the two of us to look so similar, but nothing good can come of it where you are involved. Bishop will kill him, what part of that do you not understand? Best case it is done by my hand, at worst it will be your own. Is that what you want?"

I shook my head. I believed Valen, I did, but another part of me thought I could steady Bishop, convince him to give me this one thing. They were all cyn, surely, he didn't have that much control. That he could trump Valen's decision.

I shifted. "No, but—"

"Killian is nothing to you anymore," he snapped. "Forget him." He grabbed me by the shoulder to push me ahead.

I turned, stepping in his path. "Please, it'll just be for a second. I'll never ask anything like this of you again."

"You're a terrible liar." Valen's chest heaved. "I think you get off getting beneath my skin." His gold eyes darted over my head before he grabbed my hand and pulled me the opposite direction. We climbed a flight of stairs and crossed a balcony that overlooked the main part of the house.

I caught a flash of red hair in the crowd. Jinn, with his face buried against the side of a woman's neck.

I darted after Valen, not wanting to get caught. I hadn't seen Bishop, but in his dark clothes, despite his build, he'd be easy to miss.

The rise and fall of Killian's chest broke something in me. He was safe. Safe and unharmed from the chaos that followed me. I reached out to his hand and then stopped.

"He won't wake," Valen said. "He will sleep under the spell until we leave."

Hot tears sprung into my eyes. The sound of them plopping onto the comforter was deafening as I tried to blink them away. I slipped my hand in Killian's.

"Thank you," I said.

Seeing him brought back a surge of emotions I had tried desperately to suppress. I had wanted to believe my feelings for Killian had waned. I still loved him. Though, touching him, feeling his skin against mine, I knew I was no longer *in* love with him. That something else had replaced the feeling I had chased while being with him.

It didn't soften the blow.

"He said he was looking for me. After the way I broke up with him, I didn't think he would notice that I didn't come back. Not that I meant to fall off the face of the earth."

Valen let out a heavy sigh. "I have not altered his memory, if it gives you piece of mind."

A sad smile tugged at my lips. "Can you make sure he knows I'm ok?"

"He knows you are in a better place."

I tried not to let the edge in Valen's tone grate on my nerves. "What is his crime?" I asked, brushing my thumb over the back of his hand.

Valen grumbled. "I don't know."

I whipped my head around. "What is it?" I pressed.

"His sins did not warrant him to be hunted tonight. Not under our new conditions. I don't know how his name was drawn."

I looked back at Killian. "Who is his adelfi?"

"Ezra." Valen's voice hardened.

"Just tell me."

Valen's warm hand slid under my arm to pull me to my feet. It took everything in me to let go. It wasn't until I was standing did the dull haze of the world settle in again. That next to Valen, Killian looked no more alluring than a stranger would.

"It does not matter who she is," he said. "She's not you."

The words were a sharp stab to my heart.

He stepped back, pulling me with him, until he could spin me around to press my back into the door. "She's not you, because you're mine." His gold eyes flared as he looked down at me. I could lose myself in that glow, in the warmth and want that enveloped me. "Do you understand me?"

"I don't think you'll let me forget it," I said. This night was one disaster after the next. I hadn't expected it to go well, but throwing Killian and what had happened with Bishop into the mix made me nauseous.

Valen's mouth twisted. "Ezra," he said softly, like my name was a question. I looked from him to Killian and back again as the thing inside me shifted again. It tugged against my heart. It was too much. All of this was too much.

"I can't do this right now," I said. "Not here."

Valen grabbed the door before I could. "Not here," he agreed. "Not before they figure out I haven't killed anyone yet."

Music enveloped me when Valen opened the door. I hadn't realized how quiet it was shut in the dark. It took everything in me to step out, to walk away from Killian. But, somehow, every step became easier. The knot in my chest unwound with each step down the staircase, through the halls, and to the front door where the other two cyn waited.

I had made the decision to move forward with the amorini. I could not do that, could not accept the male at my back, if I held onto my past.

The bow was lighter than I expected, but the line of it felt stronger than what I was used to as I pulled it back. The muscles in my arms resisted, my fingers turning red as soon as the band sliced into them. It helped that my new workout routine had cut new muscles, but I was still a long way from becoming like the assassins next to me.

Matt laughed, the sharp lines of his smile cutting deep into the wide flesh of his cheeks. He turned, his eyes passing over us.

"A gift," Bishop had said. Matt had been chosen for me specifically to exact the revenge my friend could not wield six feet below.

Shooting him when he couldn't even see me felt cowardly. I wanted him to know who wielded justice's blade.

"If it helps," Bishop said, stepping next to me a few feet away. "He has had his eye on the blonde. And if the shadows around him are being honest, his intentions will be the same as last time."

I lowered the bow, my arms letting out a sweet flood of relief, and followed Bishop's general line of sight. And then back to Matt, who did have his eyes locked on her as he tipped his head back to drink from his beer can.

She was a small, bubbly girl with a shining smile. Katie used to be like that. A light that had made everyone's life better when she entered it. Kind, outspoken when it came to the defense of others. She'd been at the top of her class until she used that proud voice to tell people what Matt had done. And all those people she had stood up for? Not one of them believed her over Matt. Because they were friends with Matt. They *knew* Matt. He would never do something like that.

He had taken everything away from her. Had ripped it from her the way he had ripped her dress.

My fist clenched over the bow again. He deserved to die for what he had done.

I felt then what the amorini had been feeling all night. The clawing hunger tore at my throat. More power shifted, the creature within raising its head as I wet my lips.

"You would be saving a life technically," Jinn said.

"More than one," Bishop agreed.

They each offered words of encouragement. All but Valen. He stood to my other side; his arms crossed over his broad chest as he looked at the humans.

I looked away the same time he turned to me and raised the bow. My hands were shaking, my eyes burning with tears of rage. I hauled back the band as hard as I could until my arm was straight, aching against the tension.

My teeth ground together as I fought to stabilize my aim. This was easy. I had shot targets plenty of times before on the field. The dummy was no different than the man before me.

My gut clenched.

Did Matt deserve to die? He deserved brutal punishment for what he had done. But who was I to condemn him to death?

The arrow fell over his heart.

Let go. Just let go.

My fingers burned, eager to release the arrow in one, two—

As many times as I had thought about killing him, I couldn't do it.

I wasn't a murderer. Killing him would make me a monster. Killing him would make us equals.

I lowered the bow once more, releasing the tension.

Someone sucked the back of their teeth in disappointment.

I turned to Valen. "You said all sins were equal. Killing him is only going to prove Ariel's point."

"I also said that if you've already thought about it, you might as well commit to it. But killing him isn't a crime. Whatever Ariel tried to put into your head is." He nodded to the humans. "Are you going to let him get away with another attack or are you going to do something about it?"

Matt leaned into the blonde, whispering something against her ear as his hand skimmed over the top of her drink. I didn't need to see the tablet to know he had put one in there.

"I can do it for you," Bishop said.

I looked from him to Matt, to the bow, and then to the rest of them. They were all waiting on what they knew I couldn't do. *Wouldn't* do.

"I can't do this, but I don't condemn you," I said quickly. *Too much. Too much!* I had seen two people murdered tonight and I was to commit a third. Having been chased by Death my entire life, I wasn't as familiar with it as I thought. I did not know how to wield its blade. Its arrow.

My head felt like it was on fire. The creature within me hissed. I could feel the power swirling inside of me, begging to be released.

Bishop pulled his bow from over his chest. He looked over my head to Valen and smirked, before turning his eyes to Matt and raising the bow. He didn't let just one arrow fly. He let go three. He was so quick to draw, reaching behind his neck for the next two arrows, that his hand had been no more than a blur.

Matt was the first to fall. The man next to him the second. And then the blonde. Three black arrows protruded through the front of their chest, or their back, straight through their hearts. The remaining two couples jumped to their feet. A rattled scream lodged its way into one woman's throat as she struggled to breathe.

Panicked chatter erupted through the air.

"Bishop," Jinn said, exasperated. Like it wasn't anything other than an inconvenience that he had shot multiple people.

Bishop shrugged. "Oops," he said, his mouth curling into a vicious grin. "They can see the arrows, by the way." At the same time, the couple took off running through the woods. I could hear their heartbeats from here. Or was that mine? The loud rush of blood, the smell of it, was overpowering.

Jinn shot through the woods, moving like a panther in the night.

I couldn't breathe. Bishop had just killed three people. I knew without a shadow of a doubt that the ones who had fled weren't making it out of here alive either.

Innocent and unsuspecting one moment and then gone the next. Well, as far as I knew, only one of them was guilty of living. It didn't bother me like I thought it would. Maybe the first two murders had numbed me.

Their hunger could not—would not—be contained. I looked at him in horror. They wouldn't change. This was their nature, to hunt and to kill.

Bishop slung his bow over his shoulder. "I nicked his heart for you," he said. "He's still alive if you want to finish the job." He took my chin in his hand. Bishop looked too beautiful when he smiled, too perfect for what he had just done. "It would be a mercy if you killed him now, rather than let him bleed out. Perhaps you'll come find me when it is done."

I followed the brush of his fingertips as he dropped his hand, turning away from me to stalk the runners.

It didn't feel real anymore.

I stopped at the edge of the camp, standing at the cusp of the tree line, and looked down on the bodies a few feet away. I inhaled, breathing in the potent, metallic tang of blood.

This was a dream. Another nightmare to rattle me.

I stepped into the clearing, looking for any sign of Ariel. Where was he?

Over the crackle of the fire was the shallow intake of breath, and a soft exhale. I crept closer to it, all the while my eyes darting through the trees, looking for any sign of the angel.

Matt was on his back, his eyes wide in disbelief, his mouth parted as he struggled to breathe. Bishop hadn't just nicked his heart; he had shot him in the lung.

He was going to suffocate before he bled out.

A scream rose into the air before it was violently ripped away. I blinked.

This wasn't a dream.

Matt's eyes flickered to me as I crouched beside him. An air of recognition crossed his face as his brow furrowed. Then his eyes widened. His lips moved, but no words came out. A fish gasping for water on land.

"Ezra."

I looked up.

I hadn't realized Valen had stayed with me. I rose, looking back down at Matt. He reached toward me, a desperate grasp at the ground as I took a couple of steps back.

"You stayed," I said.

Valen was looking at me through those thick curls as he cocked his head to the side. Like I was a puzzle that needed to be solved. "Tell me what you want," he said.

I didn't know what I wanted. I thought I had and now that Matt was fading at my feet, it didn't feel as good as I thought it would. Was it because I wasn't the one to do it? I still could, technically. Bishop was right; it would be a mercy to kill him now. But monsters didn't deserve mercy.

The longer I looked at Matt, the angrier I became. How many other lives had he selfishly taken? How many had tried to fight him and failed?

I might not be able to kill him, but I sure as hell wasn't going to save him.

No one in my life comes out unscathed.

"I want to go…" I shook my head. Home. Earth no longer offered that solace. Vélos was home, but in that moment, it didn't feel like it. I didn't even feel like myself in my own skin. I wanted to remove myself before the creature hissing inside my head took over. "I want to go," I said.

I took another step back, moving in a trance, until I was at Valen's side. Matt wouldn't live. He wouldn't hurt anyone ever again. And the others?

Casualties.

Or maybe they had committed crimes of their own? I looked in the distance where I knew the prey had been caught. The amorini weren't merciful. It might be a coincidence that they killed horrible people, but it wasn't because they were out doing good deeds.

My stomach turned.

Why wasn't I upset about any of this?

The muffled inhale of Matt's breath cut into my thoughts. "You deserve worse than this," I said.

"Then give it to him," Valen said.

The line of my spine straightened as I looked at him. "I said take me back."

Valen broadened his stance. "I will. After." He nodded to Matt.

"Ez…ra. Whattt-t…fuck." Matt's words had started to slur. How he was able to still speak was a surprise. I wouldn't put it past Bishop to have laced the arrow with some sort of spell to draw out his death. Good. Let him die slowly.

"He deserves to suffer for what he has done."

"And this kill is supposed to be by your hand."

"Take me back. Now."

Valen's face curled with a temper of his own right before he grabbed me. He jerked me against his chest and gave no warning as we fell into a bleed, taking us back to the underworld.

His grip tightened as soon as we landed in Vélos and I tried to break away from him. The world was still spinning, but I didn't care. I needed to get away from him. I dug my nails into his arm and forced him away. This time, he let me go, and I stumbled a few steps before crashing onto the floor on one of my knees.

If my body ever got accustomed to spectering, it would be a blessing. I threw out my arm as I felt him come up beside me. I pushed to my feet.

I scanned the hallway, glimpsing the tall doors of the library to my left, before making my way in the general direction of the village. I needed a drink. Liquor specifically because the cheap beer hadn't done shit to steady my nerves or the speed of my mind.

"Ezra," Valen said.

"No." I kept walking. I actually had no idea where I might find a trove, but I had to get away. From him, from what the others had done. From what I had almost done and what I *hadn't* done.

Why was I so conflicted? Why couldn't I kill Matt? The cyn had killed awful people for me, Valen had spared Killian, but I... I couldn't uphold my end of the bargain. How was I going to prove to the amorini that I was on their side if I couldn't even make one kill?

Valen snarled. "Don't walk away from me."

"Or what?" I flicked a strand of hair out of my face as a burst of wind blew it all forward. He materialized in my path, a seam of smoke in his wake as he spectered in front of me.

"I'm not like you," I said. "I thought I could be, but I was wrong." That was the truth of what was gnawing at me.

Valen scoffed. "I'm disappointed in you. It doesn't pay to be good if you sit around and do nothing. If you believe in something, then you need to act on it."

His words stung. I'd never cared before whether I disappointed Valen or not, but this...this hurt.

I made to sidestep around him but he moved with me. "Killing people is not a belief I hold," I said.

His eyes narrowed. "*Being* good isn't the same as *doing* good. You think letting that boy die makes you more superior than if you had done it yourself? It makes you a coward." His lips curled back, revealing his white teeth and the sharp fangs of his canines. "Fuck whatever excuse you're about to make because Bishop shot him. This isn't about him, it's about you not avenging your friend. About not stopping that boy from doing something else. You were willing to sit by and let it happen again because of your faith. How can God turn away from you when He has already forsaken you? Do you have any idea how childish you are? How foolish?"

Who was he to act all high and mighty? This had nothing to do with my faith. That was gone. Shriveled up when Raguel denied me.

"That's not it," I ground out. "I am not a coward."

"You're a *terrible* fucking liar, Ezra. You should know by now that I can see through you."

"It's because I wanted to. I've never felt that and had the power to do something about it. I felt starved for it," I snapped. "Ever since my power woke, I have felt this thing inside of me. Like I'm waking up after a long sleep. She feels like me but she isn't. I have compromised with you. But if I fall further..." I shook my head. "I don't want her to take over. I couldn't kill him because I don't want to become the monster Ariel showed me to be."

There it was. That was the real truth of it. It terrified me that I had wanted to kill Matt. That something within my jaw had ached to have him under my teeth the way Bishop had rung that woman's neck.

I swallowed. Forced *her* down with a hard shove.

"Don't you ever grow tired of making excuses?" Valen's teeth flashed.

"I'm not making excuses."

"That power is a part of you. You cannot run from who you are. Unleash her."

This wasn't Valen. He was nowhere remotely close to the male I had spent the last several weeks with. This wasn't even the male that had spared Killian. This was the dragon I heard whispers about. The one that was all fire and rage. Golden and menacing.

Why he had chosen this moment to take out his ire was beyond me.

"Back off, Valen," I growled.

He stepped forward, forcing me back. Enticing that part of me I wanted to snuff.

"Not a chance," he said.

"What is this? Are you still pissed off that I kissed Bishop? Or is it Killian?" I shoved against his chest, forcing him to take a step back.

A slam of Valen's power sent me stumbling back farther. I clutched the bow at my chest on impulse, but it was useless. I had no arrows. They were forgotten in the quiver I had left on Earth. Not that I would have been able to string one before he relieved me of it.

"The jealous image you have of me in your head has run its

course. Stop hiding. I'm pissed that you won't let me see the real you. Every time she comes to the surface, you check her. I know there is a murderous little villain in there. A little heathen waiting to be unleashed. I saw it the night I kissed you and I can see her now."

Embers cracked across my fingertips. I turned my head slightly. I was a few feet from the library. If I could make it to the doors, I could lose him. For at least a few hours, I could wait him out until the bloodlust or whatever the hell this was fizzled out.

"Let her out," he hissed. Commanded. The compulsion shot through me like an arrow and bolted me dead in my tracks.

Heat fanned against my cheeks.

"You want to see that side of me, you're going to have to rip her out the way you tore out my wings," I challenged.

Valen angled his head so that his eyes fell into the shadows. Shadows so dark that I could not see the glow I knew burned in their midst. "Then you better start running, Ezra. Because as soon as I lay a hand to you, you're going to do exactly what I want... whether you like it or not."

My nostrils flared as I scented it. The raw need of his want, his anger, *him*. There was a feral edge in the tension of his body that made every hair on mine stand on end. Goose flesh broke out on my skin.

I took a step back; he took one forward. I moved to the side, he stepped with me. The moon cast half of his face in light as I took another step. The glow of his iris was nearly red. Hungry.

"If you touch me, the deal's off. You can all rot here." The embers flickered against the palm of my hands.

A vicious grin broke his beautiful face apart. "Run, Ezra."

My back slammed against the door as his power hit me again. So strong that it whipped the flames from my hands. I spun, shoving all of my weight into the door until there was enough of a gap that I could wedge myself through. I caught a glimpse of one of his golden eyes through the crack of the door before I turned and ran.

CHAPTER THIRTY-SEVEN: THE CHASE

Ezra

The shelves swung and locked with a loud clack, one after the other as I darted through them. I ditched the bow, not wanting it to get caught while I made my retreat.

Bang. Switch. Clack!

Round and round they spun as I ran through the path of their maze. I didn't know where I was running to, only that if I stopped something very bad was going to happen.

Bang. Switch. Clack!

I'd only explored the front half of the library. The farther I ran, the fewer lanterns there were. The glow of the lights floating in the ceiling lessened until I was running in total darkness.

A loud bang of one of the shelves sliding in the distance made my heart skip a beat. I slid to a stop, freezing on impulse, and strained my ears to listen.

I knew... I fucking knew that if Valen got a hold of me I would bend to him. If he told me to burn down the world, I would. The creature inside of me strained for him. She was clawing at the shield in my mind, trying desperately to break free. My skin was hot with fire that begged to be released.

If Valen touched me, I would become the harpy he called me.

And that terrified me.

Click. Swish.

The sound of the shelves spinning was getting closer as he homed in on me. His presence pulsed like a beacon, the thrum of it bright as if he were lit up.

"You running only makes this more thrilling for me," he said. Right beside me. His voice had brushed against my ear, but as I whirled to face him, there was nothing.

A fresh wave of chills bit into my skin. I walked faster, pushing into a light jog—heel to toe to silence my footfalls as I slid down another aisle of books, this one thankfully not on tracks. The sound of the shelves moving still came from behind, but I swore I could feel him on the opposite aisle stalking me. The pressure of his power so palpable that it took everything in me not to bolt.

I spooked easily, and if Valen didn't know that before, he did now. It most certainly was a thrill for him. Because every time I thought I saw his shadow in my peripheral, to turn and see nothing, the more frightened I became.

I don't know if in that moment I was more afraid of him or the woman I was about to become as the other side of me hissed within my mind. Yes, she purred.

I turned down another corridor, hopping down a flight of steps and into total darkness.

The sense of evil was so strong that it nearly knocked me off my feet. I stumbled back, at once regretting that I thought I could lose him in the darkness.

Fuck.

I turned around, moving lightly back up the stairs as whatever lay below watched me. I could feel their eyes on me.

Click. Swish. Bang.

That final lock of a bookcase was deafening. I stopped at the front of the railing, my heart hammering so wildly that I couldn't hear anything else over the rush of blood in my ears.

He was close. He was so close that if I moved forward, I knew he would be waiting for me. And I couldn't go back down those steps. Not when the darkness was watching me with such intent.

I chewed the inside of my lower lip as I pushed forward, looking, listening for any sign of Valen.

There was still no sign of him as I skirted along the edge of the aisles, looking down each one in search for a flash of light that would point me back to the main part of the library.

BANG!

The shelf on my right lurched forward. I was running again. Blindly, this time. I didn't know if it was Valen that chased me or the darkness, but I ran as fast as I could, no longer caring that I was giving away my location as if I wore a tracker.

The shelf in front of me spun and I ran into another shelf. I ran my hands along it, pushing.

It wasn't a shelf. It was a wall.

I turned, pressing my back into it as the bookcase rolled to the side, not spinning this time, to reveal the silhouette of a male.

Valen's scent overpowered me as he stalked forward, his head angled down slightly so that his curls fell to one side. His chin lifted as he came to a halt in front of me, placing a hand beside my head as he leaned forward.

He inhaled a deep breath and blew it out softly, stirring the hair at my ear.

"Gods, you smell delicious. Fear, sweat," he breathed again, tilting his head down, "Wet." He slid a hand around my neck. "Does being hunted turn you on, Ezra?"

Only when you do it.

I kept my mouth shut as I met his gold eyes. They were as heated as I felt, burning with so much need I could have combusted right then.

The creature within groaned with anticipation.

He cocked his head. With the movement, my clothes changed. Gone were the fitted long-sleeved top and black jeans. Like a mirage, they shifted into a crimson satin dress that cut low in the front and fell just below my knees.

"That's better," he said.

"I'm not going to help you." The lie was blatant. Why the hell was I trying to lie to him when I couldn't even lie to myself?

His teeth flashed in the darkness. "You're going to do whatever I tell you to."

"What happened to not making me do something I don't want to do?"

His thumb stroked the front of my throat. He pressed harder as I swallowed. "I no longer wish to play the part of a gentleman. You want this. It leaks through every pore in your body. From the wet slit between your thighs."

Heat roiled in my core. Ashes, Valen was terrifying. So beautifully terrifying that it made my mouth water. I knew he wouldn't hurt me, but I knew our game had officially ended.

Bishop had tried to make me feel like this, but only Valen could make me truly melt. To bend to him when I should be cowering. I'd never wanted someone so terribly.

Valen ran a hand beneath my dress, pushing the hem to the

plump of my thigh. My breath hitched as his skin met mine. When I didn't move, he pushed his hand higher and then back to the curve of my ass. He squeezed.

I loved the feel of his large hands grabbing me. The way he kneaded my skin when I knew he could tear me apart.

My lips parted when his thumb skimmed over my bottom lip. I stuck out my tongue, inviting him inside.

He pushed his thumb over my tongue, let me suck it between my lips. There was no denying the fire within his eyes. It wasn't a reflection. No cast of the sun or moon's light. This was his fire, heating and expanding within the gold depths.

I swirled my tongue over him, hollowing my cheeks until something like a groan escaped his lips.

He tugged his thumb free, running it down my chin and to my throat.

My legs parted as he shoved a knee between my legs. His eyes never left my face. There was a question there, as his hand skimmed over the top of my thigh. I spread my legs a little wider in answer.

It was over. He had won.

Raw hunger sparked in his eyes right before he kissed me.

Our tongues tangled together, tasting, prodding each other. He tasted sweet. So sinfully sweet that I thought I would melt right there. Until he slipped a finger inside of me and I moaned.

"You're soaking," he said against my mouth. He pushed his tongue between my lips the same time he shoved a second finger inside of me.

I broke our kiss to press my forehead into his shoulder.

He pushed me back, his hand splaying gently across my throat. He curled his fingers before slowly moving them in and out of me.

"Oh fuck," I whispered, breathless. That felt good. It felt so fucking good. The fire within my core tightened. The creature within writhed slowly as she too took pleasure in what Valen gave freely.

"Gods, Ezra." He pressed his thumb into my clit as he worked his fingers. The fingers on my neck hardened. A smile fluttered over my face, encouraging him. He held me suspended between pleasure and pain. The edge of my vision darkened with the pressure of his hand.

"You're mine," he said.

I whimpered, stepping on my tiptoes in an attempt to find relief against the hand around my neck as my vision narrowed.

"Say it," he said.

So, there was still one more move. One more play to be met before the game could truly be won.

I glared. "Never."

The pressure of Valen's fingers hardened inside of me. *Yes. Right there.* That's exactly where I needed him. A needy whimper left me, and I fought between grinding against him and easing the pressure on my throat. In my current position, I couldn't have both.

His fingers moved in and out quickly. Building, building. *There. Stay there.*

"Say it, and I'll give you what you want." The pressure stopped. My vision flooded with bright colors as I sucked in the breath I hadn't realized he had been denying me.

I huffed and raised my hips, trying to grind against his hand again. To entice him to touch that spot again.

"Please," I said. Begged. I had resorted to begging so quickly and I didn't give a fuck. "Please."

A sinister grin fell over his face, carving the dimple into his cheek. "Say it," he crooned. He rolled his thumb over my clit, his fingers stroking me gently.

Then stopped.

I cut him a razor glare and he chuckled. He kissed me slowly, savoring me.

He was going to keep this up until I gave him what he wanted. Two simple words.

I licked my lips. They were just words. I didn't have to mean them. I just needed to say them so he would touch me again.

He growled with anticipation.

"I'm yours," I said. And it was not the lie I had hoped it to be.

"Good girl." His kiss was soft and then hard, possessive. He leaned away to look down on me as his fingers hardened and he started to work me. I clung to his shoulders as he became more forceful. As he demanded me to release by touch alone.

I gushed over his hand, coming undone entirely with a silent scream. He fucked me harder. His eyes dropped from my face to where we were joined, his eyes glazing over.

"I love that," he said hoarsely. "I always knew you were a little sinner. Look at the mess you're making all over my hand."

I didn't stop coming until a cry escaped me. "Fuck!" I gasped.

He kept his fingers buried inside of me as I came down from my high. My legs shook. It was only when my eyes fluttered back open, did he pull himself free. He stuck his fingers in his mouth, sucking them clean.

"I'm going to eat you alive," he rasped.

Valen shoved me back. I was falling through the air, falling into nothing, and then my back landed on a tabletop, forcing a blow of air from my lips. Papers crunched and crinkled beneath my weight.

The curl of smoke from the bleed he had just pushed us through faded over his shoulder. I'd never spectered without him holding on to me. Didn't know it was possible to be pushed through space like that.

It was a passing thought as he followed me through and kneeled before me, shoving my dress over my hips to reveal the red panties I had worn. I hadn't thought he would see them tonight, but in secret I had worn them for him.

The smirk on his face parted, flashing his fangs, like he knew exactly why I had done it. "You naughty girl." Both of his hands cupped my thighs. Sharp talons scraped against my skin and cut through the fabric, tossing it to the side so I was utterly exposed.

My chest was so tight I thought I was going to burst. There was no thought in my head than how badly I wanted him. And how beautiful he looked, gazing up at me like a dragon with those burning eyes.

Slowly, so achingly slow, he kissed his way to my apex. His lips skimmed over my ankle, my calf, my knee. Higher. I needed him higher.

He placed his lips between my thighs.

I could not contain the animal inside of me any longer. Yes, I said. Yes, she agreed. Heat burst beneath my skin, moving like lava when he ran his tongue over my slit bottom to top. A low growl or purr, I don't know what sound it was, tore out of his throat. And then he slid his tongue inside.

His tongue, no one's tongue was that long. But he pushed it deep inside, flexing and curling it. I groaned, my eyes rolling back. When he did pull back, only to fasten his lips over my clit, I swear the end had been forked.

It was with his lips sucking my clit that he slipped his fingers back inside of me. He worked me thoroughly, making me gasp and moan. Noises that I didn't know I could make were ripped from me as I turned feral. I reached forward, tangling my fingers in his curls and giving him a hard tug.

He nipped me, the sharp sting of his fangs making my back arch in pain. The fire of his eyes flashed as he captured me in his gaze. "Harder," he growled.

I groaned and twisted my wrist, gathering more of his hair in my fist and tugging. Valen snarled and hardened his fingers, rubbing them over the ridges inside my cunt until something in me came undone again.

"Stop," I gasped. "Slow down. Please." It hurt so good. It was blissful pain that I couldn't take.

Valen only added more pressure. "Not until you come all over my face."

I couldn't breathe. Didn't he realize I couldn't breathe?

I jerked his head, trying to pull him away from me, but he wouldn't move. "Now," he said. His voice vibrated over my clit as he started sucking again.

A shock of his power ruptured through me and then I was truly falling. Into a void of bliss, I was shoved. There was nothing but blinding euphoria. My silent cry turned keening and then I was gushing.

Valen scooped me up by the hips as he stood, his mouth still fastened to me, as he forced my weight to my shoulders. His tongue delved inside of me as I came again and again and again. I don't know when one orgasm ended and the others started. There was nothing but him and it was so painfully sweet.

"Oh God," I gasped as he finally retracted, lowering my hips slowly. My chest heaved as I struggled to come back to my body.

"Your prayers are no good here," he said.

A flash of defiance rose in me, sparking a wicked grin across his striking face. "Devil," I said.

"In the flesh." His gaze raked up my body. The light danced on his glistening face. He was covered in me, a drop of my essence hung on his chin.

I leaned forward, pulling him against my body and swept my tongue over it. His fingers dug into the back of my head as he forced me to his mouth. As we both struggled to overpower the other.

"You heathen."

"Wicked creature." I was gasping the words. *Fuck. Fuck, this was amazing.*

He hummed, the rumble deep within his chest, a smirk spreading across his face. To make the point of my words, he dug his talons into my skin. I didn't even flinch when they broke my skin.

He was sinfully beautiful even as he let his other form slip through. The gold sheen of his dark skin shown beautifully against the glow of firelight. Gold rings in his ears. Gold eyes. Valen was indeed a treasure. A forbidden star, but something sacred all the same.

I ran my hand down his chest, savoring the way his muscles flexed beneath my fingers. I hesitated to stop. There would be time to savor the rest of him later. Right now, I needed something else.

I cupped him through his pants. He was hard as steel and straining against the denim.

"Careful," he growled.

I squeezed him, just a little bit. Enough to let him know I didn't have any intention on being careful. "I want more."

He leaned forward to take my lower lip between his teeth. "You're greedy, harpy."

"I am," I breathed.

He kissed me. Our tongues danced together. I could taste myself on him still and that only made me want him more.

"There is no going back once I fuck you," he said.

I nodded.

"Ezra," he said. I snapped my eyes open, not remembering when I had shut them. "I am not going to stop. Once I have you, once you are wrapped around me, I will not stop. There is no changing your mind. No pleading me to slow down. Once I take you, you belong to me. Fully."

This wasn't just the fallen part that wanted desperately to consume me. This was Valen, the male who had saved me from the lake.

I nodded, sealing my fate. "I know," I breathed.

Killian didn't cross my mind in that moment. The night's events were a distant memory. Not even Raguel's abandonment or Ariel's jibes could tear me from this moment. There was only Valen. If what was happening to us now was the result of bending to him, I would gladly fall.

I pulled the button free at the top of his pants, pulled down the zipper. He helped me shove them over his broad thighs. The way his muscles roiled as he stepped out of them made me groan. I swung my gaze to the center of him.

The size of him.

I swallowed.

Valen kissed me. "We are made different from humans. It'll hurt at first." He took my hand and placed it over his length. It wasn't just the little barbs covering the base of his cock but the actual heat that poured from him. Hot iron. "And then you'll be in bliss."

"What are they for?"

"To hold you in place, so you cannot get away."

Hysteria tickled the back of my mind. I had felt him before, but

I hadn't *really* felt him like this, skin to skin. And no way I had ever imagined he would be as large as he was, like my mind had been downplaying him from the beginning for my own sanity.

There was a large gap between my fingers as I stroked him, down, down, down, and then up again. Tiny pinpricks laced across my flesh.

"You're going to break me," I said.

He brushed his nose against mine. "Yes," he hissed. "You'll thank me for it."

He inhaled as the speed of my heart increased. I re-tangled my fingers in his hair with my free hand, holding his face against mine.

I flicked my thumb over the smooth head. He pushed forward, sliding within my palm. I let my fingers relax and move down to his balls. Full and tight. He wanted me as badly as I wanted him. His eyes narrowed when I squeezed him.

I grinned and slid my fingers back up his shaft, encircling him again. The barbs scraped my skin, but they didn't hurt. In fact, the more I moved my hand, the softer they felt. Or maybe it was my hand going numb. I squeezed him tighter.

"Ezra." My name was a plea on his lips.

I lifted my hips as I brought the head of his cock down to brush it over my entrance. I tensed at the stinging pain that lanced through me when the head of his cock slipped in. Despite my intake of breath, Valen groaned, thrusting his hips forward, sliding out and over me in an attempt to seat inside of me. He rubbed against me, coating himself with my heat while I continued to work my hand down his length, making sure he was good and covered.

"Promise to put me together at the end," I said breathlessly.

Valen nudged his lips against mine before pulling back, catching my eyes with his. What I saw there made me twist my hand and slide down his shaft, with an encouraging stroke. There were too many promises in those eyes. Promises I didn't want to consider.

I slid my hand away as the head of his cock found my entrance and he pushed.

CHAPTER THIRTY-EIGHT: OZIEN

Valen

I had tried to push her, to force her to fall one last time in an attempt to prove to Bishop that I was on his side. To prove to myself that I was the demon I had been forced to become. But as I hunted her through the library, I knew I could not, would not bend her to Tartarus's will. I would gladly continue to rot as I had for centuries, if it spared the light that flared so beautifully beneath her skin.

Nephilim don't glow like that. Not even the seraphim had the hue of molten silver in the vein of their flames. Not like her.

The possessive need to consume her, to truly possess her, was a beast within my blood. She was mine.

Mine.

Mine.

Ozien.

I knew before sliding into Ezra that there would be no going back. I knew the moment I tasted her. She had spoiled all other pleasures for me when I kissed her.

Her body tightened as I slid the first few inches of my cock in. I placed a hand on her stomach, trying to ease her breath.

It took everything in me not to fuck her like I wanted to. I breathed, trying to control my waxing desire.

"Good girl," I encouraged.

Her brow knitted with pain; a sight that made my cock stiffen. She was so tight. Ashes, she was so fucking tight and hot and wet and perfect. I might be kind to her, but that did not abash my demented cravings. I wanted to break her. And though I hadn't responded to her, I would put her back together... only to break her all over again. Mine to use as I pleased.

"Fuck, you have to stop," she said, her eyes snapping open. She looked down where we were joined. I was only halfway inside of her. "You're too big. It's too much."

"No stopping, remember?" I pressed closer to her, still sliding in slowly, as I offered her my throat. "Bite me," I commanded.

Her breath came as a sharp hiss through her teeth. Her nails dug into the top of my shoulder, into my scalp, carving crescent shapes into my skin. I thrust my hips up, shoving in another inch, before she listened. Her blunt human teeth bit into my skin. It was only when her jaw was fastened tight, did I shove the rest of the way into her hot little cunt. My hips slapped against her ass with a loud smack of flesh.

A cry tore from her and she tightened around me. The scent of her desire flooded my senses.

I had smelled the tea on her breath that morning. Even though I knew she was safe, something in me broke as her pussy squeezed my cock. I ground into her as if I could break through the little bit of safety I had secretly provided her. I surged forward, fangs first, into her throat.

Her skin welcomed my teeth with a quiet pop. The rush of her blood over my tongue made my eyes roll back into my head and I dug in harder, tightening my jaw and pushing my hips down until I was pressing so hard into her, her breath quaked through her teeth.

Never in my life had I tasted the blood of a halfling. If angels' blood was divine, then Ezra's was grace itself.

A low feral moan tore from her throat as she threw her head back. I could feel a fresh wave of wetness coat the length of my cock as she squeezed around me.

"That's it."

She jolted, the whites of her eyes flashing as she tried to look at me despite my lips still being fastened to her as I drank. Forming a bond that allowed access to each other's mind was easy. All you needed was an exchange of blood and an intention.

"Blood," she said.

"A blood bond," I confirmed. I uprooted my fangs, sliding my tongue over the wound that sprayed into my mouth. *"Now you are wholly mine."*

Her blue eyes were wide as she met my gaze, and then looked to my mouth where I knew her blood still glistened.

"Then you are mine." Her thought was hesitant, like she wasn't sure that mind speaking would work. Or that she had won me.

"Yes." I moved my hips back, and then forward again. Slowly to let her adjust to me before I gave in to the beast writhing inside of me. I could barely leash my desires as it was. Neither my talons nor fangs would retract.

Her tongue darted over her lower lip. Her eyes fluttered as I eased my way back inside of her. She lifted her hips up, meeting me. A flash of pain made her mouth twist, but it didn't stop her from pulling back as I withdrew and throwing her hips up to meet me as I thrust forward.

"Good girl." "Good fucking girl," I said aloud. I pressed my fore-

head to hers as I concentrated on every little thing. How incredible she smelled, how she tasted, how she felt. It was glorious.

She nudged her nose against mine and I met her kiss.

"More," she said.

I groaned in answer. I slid one arm around her waist and held her firmly by the top of her shoulder as I gave in and fucked her like the monster I was.

I could not get deep enough, could not press myself close enough to her. I was obsessed with Ezra and I wanted to consume her. I had longed for this for so fucking long.

She was the closest I would ever return to Heaven. She was an answer to a prayer I had pleaded so long ago. Fucking her was my redemption. Possessing her was my salvation.

I felt the drop. Realized it too late. Realized it and fucked her harder.

Mine.

I fell hard, crashing into her again and again until I was blinded by the rise in both of our flames. Red, green, a flash of silver. Where our lips met was a wildfire.

"Valen!" Her back arched as I shifted my hips, rubbing the head of my cock over the hard ridges of her cunt. My name was a release on her tongue.

I loved the way she came around my cock. The way she tightened and pulled me deeper inside of her. Loved her voice as she cried out. Her cry turned louder, turning into a scream, and then a song. An angel's song.

She had our music.

Her head tilted back as she looked up to the ceiling, exposing the slope of her throat.

My fangs were beneath her skin once more, my tongue coaxing

the blood to rush into my mouth. Hot and luxurious. There was nothing finer.

Her fingers tangled in my hair, holding me close as I drank. Her legs wrapped around me as I pounded into her. And finally, there it was. Her release came and I dove over the edge with her, slamming my hips down into hers, pinning her to the table of now ruined transcripts.

I released her neck, savored the way her blood flowed across her skin. I moved my hips forward, slowly, as I came. I ground my hips down, wanting to be as deep inside her as I possibly could. Even though my seed wouldn't take, I didn't want to waste a single drop.

She held me tight, wrapping her arms around my torso as her pussy milked every last drop of cum out of my balls.

Her skin was flush with embers and sweat.

I fucked her again that night. Fucked her so hard that I knew everyone within our tower would hear us. I wanted them to hear how good I made her feel. No one else would ever be able to make her sound like that.

By the time we were finished, we were both covered in enough scratches and blood to look like we had come from battle.

"What have you done to me?" she breathed.

I hummed, fingering the puncture wounds on her throat. I grinned, remembering how she had dug her nails into my face and kissed me when I was fucking her with her legs over my shoulders. I could still feel the bite of those sharp claws.

"Unleashed a hellcat, evidently."

She swatted my shoulder. "I've never…" She blushed, and then her eyes narrowed into devil slits. "I've never wanted to tear into someone like that."

I kissed her. Ashes, I could kiss her for the rest of the night and be perfectly content. She tasted like honey. Her mouth, her blood. Every taste was intoxicating.

"Liberating, isn't it?"

Her eyes hadn't released from their glare. "I suppose this means you're going to be an even bigger pain in the ass."

"That depends, do you want me to fuck you there next?"

From her chest up she turned blood red. "Don't even think about it."

"Too late," I said. I nipped the top of her cheek.

"You don't get to fuck me there unless I get to do it to you first."

"Ok." I grinned as she managed to turn another shade darker. She hid her face behind her hands. "It's too late to hide from me now, sinner. Who knew a proper church girl like you would be so dirty?"

"I hate you," she said.

I hummed, pulling her against my chest. "Maybe, but you love the way I make you feel. I could take you again right now and have you saying all sorts of dirty things." I slid my hand over her stomach, over her hip, and squeezed her plump ass. She had so much of it. Even in my large hands there was so much more to grab. "What did you say earlier? To fuck you harder with my big cock? That you wanted me to get deeper." I kissed her. "To ruin you."

"Shut up," she hissed.

I chuckled as I nuzzled her neck. I slid my palm over the front of her thigh and shoved it between her legs where she was still soaking wet with need and cum and blood. "I should fuck that filthy mouth of yours next."

Her chest heaved as I slid a finger inside of her. "Valen. I can't. I literally can't go anymore." She giggled, short and breathy as I stroked her softly. "Please. Just let me rest for a little bit."

"I'll let you rest for the night, but in the morning...."

She groaned under her smile. She was so fucking beautiful when she smiled. She was a star with the way she glowed. I pulled my finger out of her and stroked the swell of her thigh.

"How are you not exhausted?" She leaned her head back as I breathed along the column of her throat that was covered in fang marks.

"I don't want to miss a second with you."

Her eyes fluttered under my kiss. "I'm not going anywhere," her voice drifted as fatigue settled in.

I ran my nails along her scalp, helping her along. No, she wasn't going anywhere. I wouldn't let her.

She tugged my arm against her chest, pulling me closer as she drifted to sleep. "Good night, guardian angel."

The smile that passed over my lips spread on its own accord. I would never let anything happen to Ezra. Ever.

CHAPTER THIRTY-NINE: FREE FALLING

Ezra

Cold wind filled my lungs as I took a deep breath. I ran my finger under the hem of the flight harness to steady my nerves. I leaned over the edge of the tower. My hair whipped wildly about my face, obscuring my vision of the vivid landscape.

"I have a fear of falling," I said after a beat. Some nephilim I was turning out to be.

The tower was impossibly high. We would learn rather quickly if I was immortal or not if I could not use my wings properly. The thought made my stomach turn. I took a step back.

Valen was somewhere below, but being so high up I couldn't place him. He had made a joke about being there to catch me if I fell. If only he knew how clumsy I was and that falling was likely to happen.

Dark storm clouds rolled in from the west, their blackness muddying the soft pastel sky I had grown used to. I could smell the heavy rainfall from here. The thunder of it a quiet boom.

"The drop is the hardest part. You have to trust yourself, trust the wind beneath your wings. If you believe you will fall, you will," Bishop said.

Bishop pulled off his shirt, revealing a leather tunic twin to mine, and hard lines of carved pale muscle. He looked like a sandstone statue with smooth, unblemished skin. The tattoos on his hand stretched to his shoulder and slid across his chest in geometric shapes and knots. The line of his lip drew down next to the mark of the arc, tucking beneath his vest and disappearing below his waistband. My face heated as I wondered exactly how far down that line ran. And did his archangel tattoos follow it?

"If you can stay in the air for more than five minutes, I'll let you see the rest of it."

My eyes snapped to his face as he approached me. I could feel the blood rising up my neck. "That doesn't entice me to succeed."

Bishop's eyes flashed as my hair snapped in front of my face again. "Turn around," he said.

I scowled but did as he instructed.

Chills darted along my skin as he began sectioning off my hair. The wind fought him, but Bishop's deft fingers caught any pieces of hair that tried to fly from his grip. I should have known better and tied my hair myself. His nails scraped over my scalp, sending another wave of chills crashing beneath his touch.

"It should entice you to see an archangel when they are most bare," he said softly. Even over the maddening wind, I could hear him. As if he was right in my ear, though I knew he still stood straight behind me. "Not many are allotted the privilege."

"Your attempts at flirting fall on deaf ears," I said.

Bishop chuckled. "What must I do to slide into your good graces?" There was a hiss in the word slide. Cheeky bastard.

I looked over my shoulder to find him tying the end of my braid, his silver eyes watching me from beneath his lashes. "Haven't you heard? You've been bested."

Darkness flashed in his eyes. "I like a good challenge, and in all my years, I've never lost." The braid slapped into the middle of my back when he let it go. He brushed his shoulder against mine, winking.

I swallowed my rebuttal. Bishop never had a chance. Not when Valen had been there from the start.

Arrogant prick.

"Just shut up and teach me how to fly," I snapped.

Bishop smirked before dropping his arms and thrusting his wings free. Four giant dark wings that covered the landing in shadow. Their dove gray coloring suited the storm clouds in his eyes. They were darker at the top, a shade that reminded me of gruella by the way they faded to his primaries. He took a step back, flexing them. They had to stretch twenty, maybe even thirty feet wide.

"Show off," I grumbled under my breath.

I followed suit and opened my wings, letting them rest gently at my back. They were so much darker, so much smaller.

And he had four of them.

"Do all amorini have four wings?" I asked.

He flexed his wings once more before tucking them at his back. "They did."

Right.

Bishop jerked his chin forward. I stepped up to the edge and took a deep breath. I wanted this, and yet I was terrified of what might happen should I fail.

"Remember what I told you on the way up here?"

I gave him a sideways look.

"Don't forget to breathe."

Bishop slammed his palm into the middle of my back, sending me sprawling through the air with a scream lodged in my throat. A scream that wouldn't come as the jolt of the fall ripped my breath away.

He pushed me. He fucking pushed me off and now I was falling. *Fucking fuck fuck.*

Instinct took over as I twisted my body and thrust out my wings in an attempt to right myself. A strong wind caught the underside and forced them back. I clawed through the air, trying to level my body with the ground as it rushed to meet me. I forced my wings out again, pushing them down then up.

A warm updraft caught me, pushing me high into the air, just above the trees. My breath caught and I gasped as the wind held me suspended.

I flapped my wings. I was gliding through the air. Another flap.

Unable to contain myself, I let out a squeal of excitement.

Oh my gosh!

Flying.

I was flying!

Being embraced by the wind is unlike anything I have ever experienced. The way it held my wings aloft as if they were weightless, as if I weighed nothing. How it tugged my long hair, tangling the lose strands of my braid together.

I turned up, gaining height as I made my way back to the tower.

A rasping stream of laughter poured out of my mouth. I reached out, wriggling my fingers through the clouds. My fingers slipped right through the cool mist.

A dark blur leapt from the tower as Bishop dropped down. Pictures and stories of angels do not do them justice. He was magnificent, shining bright and silver, dark and chrome. His four wings beat powerfully at his back. I couldn't have looked away from him if I wanted to. He was beautiful.

He threw me a smug look. "Comfortable?"

No words would come through my ragged breathing, so I threw him the meanest look I could muster. When I could speak, it was to shout, "I could have died!"

"Yet here you are." His wings rotated forward, buffeting me to the side with their gust.

He danced out of my grasp as I reached for him. I followed, climbing higher and higher. We didn't level out until we were well above the clouds. Glimpses of Velos peeked through the mist—bright, beautiful, and vibrant. The white city was glorious. All of the lights twinkling below us looked like the stars of Earth.

Bishop's upper lip curled. "I want you to follow me down so we can practice landing. We'll start with wide circles, gradually getting lower. Once you're about ten feet off the ground, I want you to start pulling your wings in and bank to your dominate side. You should land easily on your feet. Just make sure to tuck your wings against your back so you don't accidentally trip on them."

I nodded. "Ok."

I watched Bishop take the first few circles down before I tried following him. I teetered on the wind, my heart skipping as the sky threatened to drop me. He made it look so effortless.

I turned, pulling one of my wings slightly as I dipped inward, gliding down in his wake.

Ok, this isn't so bad.

I leveled out once more before going again.

Slow and steady wins... the... race...

I turned down once more, my heart skipping with anticipation. This wasn't bad at all.

A large upsurge of warm wind scooped me up, forcing me high into the air. I thrust out my wings too quickly, trying to flap against the wind, when the entire world started to spin. I was overcompensating and now, now everything was flying past me.

I was falling!

"Tuck your wings!"

Bishop's voice boomed like thunder from somewhere above me. I twisted, trying to see where he was through the tears stinging my eyes. I pulled my wings in and felt the speed of my fall increase.

He scooped me from the air, but we were already too close to the ground. His wings wrapped around my back to take the brunt of the force as we impacted. My head snapped forward, smacking into his and then back down to the soft cushion of his wings.

"Umph," I groaned as his weight crushed me into the ground.

Bishop leaned back, freeing his upper wings so that they curled over his back.

I looked at him, between us, and then peeked back at the field we had landed in. A wave of giddiness flooded my blood and I laughed. I couldn't stop laughing as the rush of adrenaline coursed its way through my body. I had flown. I had fallen, but that didn't matter because for a few minutes I had been airborne.

His breath caressed my face when he laughed with me, the sharp points of his canines peeking from under his upper lip.

"You didn't have to be so dramatic declining my wager," he said, his teeth still flashing.

He had a beautiful smile.

"Fuck your wager. You shoved me off a tower."

I pulled my eyes from his mouth to find his own gaze pulling away from my lips. When our eyes met, a hot thrill shot through me and I reflexively gripped his forearms. Our heavy breathing was the only sound between us until he tipped his head down, closing the sliver of space, and everything went still when his lips met mine.

It was sweeter than I remembered, kissing him. He tasted of whiskey, dark and fiery. There was no tang of blood to give me pause this time. When I opened my mouth to catch my breath, his tongue slipped inside.

I dropped my hands to his waist and slid them up his side. In response, he stretched one of his arms out, lowering himself so we were chest to chest. When my hands brushed his wings, he let out a muffled growl before breaking away. He turned his face into his shoulder and a very apparent shudder ran through his body.

"Shit," I said, breathless.

What the actual fuck was wrong with me?

He didn't turn his head, but he gave me a look from the corner of his eye.

"I didn't mean to touch them."

Bishop helped me to my feet, his eyes looking past me. I turned, but there was no one there. My heart dropped at the thought that Valen might have seen us.

What the fuck am I doing?

I touched my lips. I didn't even remember wanting to kiss Bishop, just that I had done it. It was as if my body had a mind of its own. Guilt made my heart heavy.

"Valen told me they were sacred. I don't know what I was thinking," I blurted.

"I'm not offended," he said. "The gesture is as intimate as it is sacred. If I allowed you to continue, it wouldn't be flying we would be practicing today."

I stared at him wide-eyed. "Fuck's sake," I said under my breath.

He grinned. "Keep it up and you'll see the rest of my tattoo."

I shoved him. Bishop's smile broadened.

"You know I'm with Valen," I said.

He shrugged. "Who says you can't be with both of us?"

"No," I said.

"Why have one cyn when you could have two? All four of us?"

Bishop didn't give me an opportunity to respond before he started giving me instructions on how we would take off from the ground. It was like a switch had flipped inside his head and it was back to business.

I tried to focus on lifting my feet off the ground, but I kept coming back to what he said.

I was familiar with how intimate the amorini were. As much as it had riled me at first, I had grown used to the idea. But having that sort of invitation caught me by surprise.

Contemplating it didn't do anything to shake the weight expanding in my stomach. The amorini might be accustomed to sharing partners, but that wasn't something I had ever done.

I wanted to pretend like nothing had happened between me and Bishop, but I couldn't even look at him without my face turning cherry.

Meeting Valen's gaze had been an even bigger challenge. He met us in the field a few minutes after I had learned to take off from the ground. And I knew as soon as he looked at me that he knew.

I felt like I was betraying Valen. As far as I knew, he hadn't been seeking out someone else's bed. How could he when he was warming mine every night?

He was waiting for me in my chambers that evening after I had showered. I tried to scrub every trace of Bishop from me, but still I felt dirty.

"You're playing with fire." Valen stood beside the hearth, his arms folded across his broad chest.

"I don't know what you're talking about."

Valen tsked. "I know my brother better than you ever will. What did he do? Call you beautiful?" His head cocked to the side as he tracked my movements. "Mmm, not that. We have all named you such."

I didn't look at him. Couldn't by the guilt that was threatening to consume me. I walked back into the bedroom, to hang my vest in the closet. I felt him enter the room behind me, his shadows pooled across the floor, wrapping languidly around my feet.

Valen purred. It was something akin to a growl, but softer. "He kissed you." Silence and then, "And you kissed him back."

My hands were shaking so hard. I hadn't meant to kiss him. I really hadn't. It just happened.

My silence was damning as I let my tortured thoughts assault me.

"Was it more than a kiss?"

"No," I said quickly. *Fuck no.*

"You're a very naughty girl, Ezra. I do hate when you lie to me."

I swallowed. "I didn't mean to kiss him. And no, it wasn't like the party where I felt I didn't have a choice. I just... I don't know."

I felt him approach me, though I refused to face him. "Bishop is beautiful in his own right. He exudes sex, does he not?"

My chest was heavy. Any second and it would cave. It felt like Valen was right behind me and, though I didn't want to face him, I was more frightened of leaving my back exposed to him. I turned slowly.

His eyes were shining orbs. "Answer me," he said.

"Yes."

"He knows he cannot have you so he has been using his charms and power on you."

"He… what?" I hadn't felt like I had been influenced. Thoughts of him never tracked my mind when we were apart. But when we were close, my mind wandered. That's when it hit me. All the times Bishop had touched me, I had wanted him.

"He's charming me? Is that how you seduce your victims?" Anger bubbled in my chest.

"The attraction has to be there for it to take root."

My eyes narrowed. "Is that what you've been doing to me?"

Valen's mouth quirked. "I have no need for tricks to take what already belongs to me." Venom made his voice thick.

"Then if you know he charmed me, why are you angry at me?"

"I'm not angry," he said slowly. So slow that I knew that he was, in fact, angry. "Touch, kisses, sex, they are all as common as an exchange of words here. It is to be expected that you partake in the ways of your new home. There is no shame in it." His eyes fluttered down my body, lingering in certain areas, before he met my eyes again.

"Then why do you look like you want to strangle me?" I licked my lips. His eyes followed the movement, growing more heated.

Valen closed the small space between us, taking my jaw in his hand. I winced under his strong grip.

"Get on your knees," Valen said.

I blinked beneath furrowed brows. "Wh—?"

"On your knees," he repeated, his voice harsher.

I shook my head in his grip. "Why?"

"Because when I claimed you, I had no idea the hold you would have over me. How delicious you would be." He tipped his face down, his nose brushing my skin. The warm flick of his tongue brushed my jaw. "And I have decided I do not want to share you, Ezra. Not even for a kiss. So, now, you must be punished."

"Perhaps you should tell your brother to keep his hands to himself." I winced harder when his grip tightened.

"I will deal with Bishop accordingly. Right now, you need to worry about yourself." It was the same voice he had used the night he hunted me through the library. A new weight was added to my chest. This one not of guilt but anticipation.

I met the ground with a huff as heat coiled in the pit of my stomach. Valen still held onto my chin. His thumb brushed over my skin.

I didn't take my eyes off him, though I knew what he presented me with. I could feel the heat radiating off him like a furnace. The scent of his desire was the smoke billowing around his body. I didn't take my eyes off him as I reached up and undid his pants.

Valen pushed his pants over his hips. He held his cock in front of my face. With his other hand, he lifted my chin again, so the head was poised at my lips.

It all happened in a matter of seconds and, already, I was soaking wet.

"I hope you enjoyed that kiss," Valen said. "Because my lips are the only ones that will ever be touching you from now on. Now, open up so I can fuck his taste off your tongue."

Just like that, I was a puddle. I had a mind to shoot something back at him, but my desire for him won out. I opened wide and slid my tongue on the underside of his cock.

A wicked gleam dashed in his eyes. "You should know, this is for my pleasure." It was the only warning he gave me before shoving his cock between my lips. He worked the first few inches in, letting my jaw get accustomed to his girth, before working deeper, trying to force himself farther. The barbs scraped the thin skin apart.

I grabbed hold of his thighs and pressed against him, trying to slow his thrusts. Blood and precum swabbed over my tongue. As fucked up as it all was, I loved it. I loved the way his head was tilted back slightly, his eyes cast in shadow as he watched his cock move in and out of my mouth. How carnal he looked with his hair falling around his face, the way the building sweat made the golden sheen of his skin glisten even more.

The soft sounds he moaned made my toes curl.

Valen might have me on my knees, but he was at my mercy.

I let my teeth slide over his sensitive flesh. He hissed, his eyes turning two shades darker. "You'll be in bigger trouble for that."

I narrowed my eyes and let my teeth slide across him again.

Valen took my head in both of his hands and thrust forward. Between his size and the force of his drive, my jaw cracked. My eyes widened as my stomach dropped. Fuck, he really was going to break me.

"You better not," I warned.

Valen grabbed me by the back of the head and forced me down so that his balls were pressed against my chin. I dug my nails into his thighs as air was denied from me and sharp unbidding pain erupted through my jaw and throat. Tears blurred my vision.

He groaned, holding me hard even when I slapped his thighs. I was going to suffocate if he didn't let up. Dying by cock wasn't the way I imagined I'd go.

He pulled me off his shaft and looked down, his eyes feral and wicked. Behind the beast was something else though. I nodded.

"Again," I said.

His chest heaved as he parted his mouth to speak.

"I'm fine," I rasped. "Now fuck me."

Valen's teeth flashed and he fisted my head down back over his cock. He let out a long, deep moan that made my pussy drip. I knew I was soaked through my panties, and if he kept it up, evidence would seep right through my pants. I wanted to grab my nipples, then shove my fingers inside of myself, but I couldn't let go of him with how hard he was fucking me.

He pulled back, allowing me barely enough time to catch my breath before shoving the length of his cock down my throat. His hand encircled my neck, gripping it hard.

"You look so pretty taking my cock. Feel how I'm stretching you." He purred. "Gods, Ezra. You're so fucking perfect."

I moaned. I was too gone to lust to even mentally respond.

He didn't last long after that. I grabbed his ass and pulled him against me as his cock stiffened. He came with a loud groan, swift and hot down the back of my throat.

I fell in a heap, my chest heaving as I gulped air like water.

Valen stood over me as he took off his shirt. His muscles flexed with the movement. "Don't ever let Bishop touch you again. I don't care what it's for. The others know better, but he will not hesitate to try."

I swallowed, nodding. "Yeah," I gasped.

He jerked his chin forward. "Now take off your pants."

I shook my head. "I can't," I swallowed, "breathe. You've gotta give me a minute."

Valen sneered. "All you have to do is lay there, princess. It's my turn to make you come."

As Valen devoured me like his own personal feast, making me come more times than I could count, I had no doubt in my mind that he was mine. That there wasn't another woman that could drive him as mad as I did. If he was truly a dragon, then I was his gold. I cursed Bishop for trying to put any other thought in my head.

CHAPTER FORTY: A FAIR TRADE

Ezra

Thick smog clouded my vision. Tears leaked from my eyes as I blinked, trying to rid the poison that had found its way within them. Burning ignited within my lungs every time I breathed. Every breath felt like it was going to be my last. It hurt so damn much to breathe. This wasn't smoke or pollution, it was something else. So putrid and rotten, I didn't know what to call it. The air held a horrible sense of wrongness.

I tugged my shirt up over my face to catch my breath. I recognized this place from a vacation I had taken to Charleston one summer. There was no aroma of the fine cuisine or seafood. Hell, even the smell of horse piss that had stained the streets had been obliterated. What once had been a lively strip of bars and shops was eerily silent. Bodies lay fallen across the sidewalks, between abandoned cars and slumped over dinner tables.

I saw the glimmer of her dress first, then her face. Beside her was another woman with flashing red hair and a pink satin dress. Their mouths were locked into silent screams. Boils covered their skin, marred what might have been pretty faces. What flesh hadn't burst or been chewed off by rats was black with decay.

My stomach turned, and I with it, as I tried to find anything else to look at to keep from vomiting.

There were bodies everywhere.

Music still pumped into the streets from the clubs lining the strip. Whatever happened had been sudden and violent.

"My, my, my. What a busy little bee you've been."

My fingers trembled over my lips as I looked for Ariel amongst the cadavers. Movement slid across the neon pink lights within the nearest club.

Ariel was wearing a fitted gray suit. He ran his hand over the collar as he stepped over a man decked out in clothing that made him look rich but had probably been as broke as the rest of the patrons littered around him.

"How does it feel, being the face of a revolution?" He spread his hands as he stepped into the street. He was only a few feet from me, but it was too close.

"Have you been in Vélos this whole time?"

"How else do you think Killian's tie was pulled?"

"You asshole. He could have died!" Anger thrilled within my veins. Killian would have been Ariel's last victim, the final piece that would tear me apart. I shook my head in disbelief of his abhorrent hunger.

Ariel shrugged, at the same time he swiped his palm over his shoulder. The royal hue of his eyes became frosted when he narrowed his gaze. "What is he compared to those you have destroyed? How could you do something like this? To your own people?" He motioned to the fallen bodies.

"You know I didn't do this. I have neither the will nor the power for it. What do you want? Really." I touched my hand over my thigh that had been bare before but was suddenly adorned with daggers.

Ariel's lips curled. He surveyed the space between us, his gaze roaming over the bodies, and then to the smog that clung to the air. "I want to become an archangel. And you, well, you'll take me right to the top."

"What are you?" I asked slowly. In all of my studies, I hadn't come across any mention of purple eyes. There were shades of blue that mimicked the hue in the keras, but nothing quite so distinct.

Ariel touched his chest. "I'm new. Something the lot down here wouldn't be privy to. I'm what the keras were supposed to be, before they got off track. There's some still in Heaven, but there was a need for a more compliant race. One that wouldn't be tempted to fall when doling out their punishments."

I scrutinized him with a narrow gaze.

"I'm a tithe."

I snorted, my mouth furling back with disgust. "An angel that collects payments from sinners for their crimes." I studied him, the way his eyes glimmered as I guessed correctly. "I have made no such crimes that would warrant punishments befit for the keras to dole out, much less you."

Ariel slid his hands into his pockets. We were standing in the middle of the street now, two bodies the only barrier between us. "Oh, Ezra," he pouted.

"Tell me, isn't acting outside of Heaven's will a symptom of falling?"

All amusement vanished from his face. "I can assure you it is the will of all Creation that you wind up dead."

That's not true. Not technically. Yes, I was condemned for what I was. But Raguel had looked me right in the eye and told me otherwise. If I was supposed to die, he would have done it then. He would not have left me behind.

"That's not what Raguel said."

Ariel's grin twisted into a grimace. "Semantics. And don't think I don't know about your little trip the other night. How did it feel holding someone's fate in your hands? How does it feel being the rot of mankind?" He splayed his palms out to the scene around us.

I had the first dagger free and flying through the air by the time I reached for a second. It passed through thin air, clattering against the window of the club.

A cold hand wrapped around my face and Ariel's other arm ensnared my waist. "I won't be letting you get away this time," he hissed against my ear. Hot pain erupted through my center as a silver blade protruded from my stomach.

Heat and holy fire erupted along the length of the sword and I screamed. I screamed so loud that it lodged in my throat as the air was ripped from my lungs.

I jerked. The dream snapped back to reality as I surged up from the bed and the moons' light scattered across my vision, revealing golden eyes looming back at me. I gasped, a single hand going to my stomach as I focused on Valen's burning gaze. His face, gilded and sharp, looked deadly leering over me.

"Ariel," I breathed. The pain needled its way into my gut, but as I pulled up my shift, there was nothing there. No wound, no blood.

Valen took a sudden hold of my shoulder. "Be still," he hissed, his voice as sharp as the blade that had pierced me.

The fire of his eyes burned with the intensity of a dragon's scales. The edge of his voice was deadly. I froze, my muscles coiling.

His eyes flickered from my face to the place beside it. His beautiful, gorgeous face split apart into that of a hateful, feral beast. The snarl that left his lips had me throwing my hands up to block his blow.

A sharp pain erupted in the back of my head. Valen's fingers dug their way through my hair, diving deeper and deeper, pulling my head back and popping the vertebrae in my neck.

"Valen!"

Oh God, he was going to kill me. Perhaps he had seen what Ariel had. Or maybe he knew I couldn't give him what he desired and so he was done. Done with me.

I slammed my fist in his direction, but he dodged it, not letting his eyes off—he wasn't looking at me. He was looking at something tangled within my hair.

He pulled again and, this time, something heaved against the back of my head. I turned, trying to dislodge whatever he had such a tight hold on.

My heartbeat raced as he continued to pull, the veins in his throat standing out. His teeth bared and sharp.

The glimpse of the pale hand in his grasp made my heart slam into my chest. I lurched forward the same moment Valen pulled again, pulling the hand out of my hair. The pain that flashed across my back was instant, blinding, as I snatched my hair and rolled the opposite direction.

It was like watching a horror film as the hand turned into an arm and the arm turned into a male. At some point, the person stopped fighting and lunged at Valen, sending the three of us sprawling onto the hard floor in a tangle of limbs and fury.

Valen was on his feet first, stalking to the pale figure with its light hair and menacing lavender eyes.

Ariel whipped his head around, eyes flashing.

Valen was on him in an instant, his hand encompassing the entirety of his throat. "How dare you," he snarled.

The angel smiled. It expanded until his face split apart and he began to laugh. He did not even try to pry the fingers gripping his throat so tight, bruises blossoming beneath them. He only laughed.

"Took you long enough to notice."

"Do not mock me, walker." Valen's body rippled with rage.

"I found her first. I have every right to her," Ariel said.

Valen answered, his voice strangely calm. "She was mine at her first breath and yet you would defy your own Maker's laws."

"I would rectify them! I have been honest with her, but have you? Does she even know what she is?"

Valen was too close to Ariel. He didn't see the silver blade the angel was inching his way. His fingers curled around the hilt.

"Valen!"

It all happened too fast. Valen's face transformed into a hideous monster, his nose elongating into a mouth with razor sharp teeth. The tips of his fingers curled into hooked black claws. And then Ariel was sliding the blade across his chest, splitting his gilded dark skin apart with a single red line.

Burnt flesh's stench filled the air. Valen's transformation faltered as he took a couple of steps back. He caught Ariel's second blow with his hand. The blade burned into his palm as much as it cut the flesh.

"Fa-har!" The curse barked from my throat. A simple thing. One that would bide Valen a quick distraction.

Ariel chuckled. "Those only work on demons." His bright teeth flashed in the dark.

"That's exactly what you are." I reached for the beast inside of me, jerked her awake to shake the power loose.

I reached for Ariel. My hand fell through the air, but flames sprouted from my fingertips and wrapped around the angel's wrist. I pulled, snapping his arm out. How had I done that? It was enough to throw his blade arm out of line. Valen sank sharp teeth into Ariel's neck. He thrashed his head from side to side, spewing blood into the air.

Ariel jerked his wrist free of my flame.

Darkness filled the air. The rank stench of it burned my nostrils. It made the pit of my stomach coil. I flung another band of fire out and watched as it coiled into smoke, dissipating into nothing.

Ariel shook me off as if I was but a mild irritant.

Valen stumbled back. Blood riveted between his fingers as he clung to his chest where Ariel slashed him a second time. He bared his fangs and the monster beneath his skin broke his face apart. The angel was overpowering him. It showed in the sway of his steps. But the flame behind his eyes was brighter than the hunger that glowed in the depth of Ariel's purple hues. And this time, when he fell upon him, it was carnage.

It was dark; the faint light of the night hid most of what happened. There was a swirl of smoke, burnt and tattered wings spread in the air, and claws cut through pristine white skin like silk.

Ariel's scream curdled my blood. Yet I couldn't take my eyes off him and the havoc Valen wreaked. Red spray splattered across my face. Its metallic flavor burst across my tongue.

Valen was a formidable fighter when his rage took control, but so was Ariel. They were matched in skill and, before I knew it, Ariel had Valen on the ground.

No.

Valen had been winning.

Ariel sunk the tip of his blade into Valen's chest, marking the line of his scar.

I had felt my power stirring for weeks now. Had seen it in the flames that danced over my hands. Had tasted it whenever I kissed Valen. But as I saw Ariel standing over Valen, the point of his sword sliding deeper into his chest, it felt like a dam broke. Like whatever had been suppressing my power cracked.

It funneled out of me in a torrent. I didn't think as I launched myself at Ariel. Didn't consider that I was still a novice when it came to fighting as I homed in on the dark power I had only felt in my dreams. Strong bright flames raced down my hands and uncoiled like a whip. I threw the line of flame out. This time it held. Fire fastened around his neck, and I pulled the angel into my chest.

Ariel's eyes went wide in surprise as he slammed into me. Then narrowed. He raised to his full height to look down at me, his face alight with my fire glowing around his throat. The flames were ripped from me, snuffed out the moment he took hold of me.

I called to the fire, but his touch—no, his power—constricted my throat.

"A fair trade," he said. "How sweet of you to sacrifice yourself for him." He wrapped his arm around my waist. A bright light emitted from his skin, burning, agonizing light. "How poetic."

A bleed appeared behind Ariel. He fell back, pulling me with him as we spectered into darkness.

CHAPTER FORTY-ONE: DON'T FALL

Ezra

I twisted in Ariel's hold, his kratiste. My arms were trapped within Ariel's embrace. The line of my flame stuttered to life, but it did not burn him the way his touch did me. His mouth was not open in silent agony like mine was. I couldn't breathe. I couldn't breathe, and Ariel was taking me somewhere to finish me off.

I dug my nails into his chest, sinking them as deep into his skin, through the fabric of his shirt, as I could. I did not have fangs. I was not a demon. But that didn't stop me from anchoring myself against him before I sunk my blunt teeth into his neck.

Blood gushed into my mouth as my aim hit true. I should have recoiled from the hot liquid pooling down my throat. I should not have dug my teeth in harder so that the blood would flow faster.

Valen's blood had been dull in comparison. This was life. Rich, beating, glorious life. In it, I saw galaxies, worlds stacked on top of each other and running parallel to others. Faces of a billion beings that my simple mind could not comprehend. Languages raced through my mind. Creation surpassed everything I had been taught. It was vast. Endless.

The real world tumbled around us as Ariel tried to pry me off. I dug in harder and scratched at his face.

"You evil," he snarled. His movements became desperate when he could not dislodge me. I wasn't going to let go. If Ariel was going to kill me, I was going to take him with me. Bleeding him was the only thing that made sense in that moment. Drinking him dry was the only thing I cared about. I chewed and swallowed. Chewed and swallowed.

He hooked his fingers into the side of my mouth and ripped me away from his throat. The images stopped flying by me in time for the real world to rush by, and to the tree that came up too quickly in my line of vision before I crashed into it. Branches snapped under my weight as I fell to the ground, the bark leaving angry tears in my skin.

I hit the ground with a hiss of pain. Blood burst behind my teeth. I ran my tongue over my lips to catch up every last drop. Mine, Ariel's. It was delicious.

A jolt of power cracked through the air.

"Where are you?" Valen asked.

I licked my lips again as I stumbled to my feet, looking for a landmark. Fuck, I had a massive headache. My vision blurred then sharpened.

"Somewhere in the forest. It's colder here." There were small flurries of snow on the ground. Strange. It didn't snow in Vélos.

My heart quickened. *"Eurynomos. I think."* That wasn't good, but it wasn't awful. Eurynomos were our allies. But only the Murder knew what I was, and I didn't think introducing myself to an entire court, under these circumstances, was a good idea.

"I'm coming. Where's Ariel?"

There was no sign of him in the dense shadow of the forest. I couldn't smell him if I wanted to, not with his blood coating my face. The hairs on the back of my neck rose. I twisted, ducking on instinct right as a blade cut where my head had just been.

"I was going to grant you mercy," the angel snarled. He clamped a hand over the side of his neck. "I am going to strip you down piece by piece and then leave you scattered across the entire continent."

"With me," I shot back. *"Hurry. Please."*

The weight of Ariel's anger grounded me. Not even the scent of his blood clouded my judgement as I felt his divine power rise. All those times I dreamed of Ariel, he had been playing with me. The graze of his words and sword had been no more than taunts. My palms broke out with sweat as I readied myself, tensing as his power grew.

He was going to obliterate me.

Fear is a funny thing. It can make or break you, forcing you to make the decision to fly or fight.

Good thing I could do both.

I straightened, letting my arms fall to my sides. Three flying lessons were all I needed to get off the ground.

I could get away. Ariel would not be stupid enough to fly with me in enemy territory. If he was, then let someone see him and strike him down.

"Ezra, do not fly!" Valen commanded. He sounded louder, closer.

Before I could twist the straps of my dress down, Ariel charged me.

I should have run. I should have been faster.

Ariel hit me with a blinding white light that momentarily stunned me, and then he was pulling me into his embrace, enveloping me with his wings that weren't there before.

Everything burned.

My hair caught first. Boils blistered across my skin next.

I screamed.

"I will be the savior of humanity," he hissed in my ear. "I am your end. No one will remember you. Your name will be forgotten at the next turn of the wind. You are dead, Ezra Hollen. Finally."

His touch, his light—it all fucking burned.

I thrashed in his embrace when my skin began to melt. Melt, not peel, in sizzling globs.

The next scream that broke from my lungs was a war cry. It circled up, spinning higher and higher until a loud crack, like a bomb exploding, shattered the air around us. It ripped through Ariel's light, tearing black holes into it that burst like paint spatters.

I didn't stop screaming until a series of cracks broke around us.

Ariel stumbled backward, letting me crash to the ground.

The vision in my right eye was gone entirely. The edge of my vision in the left was blurry at best.

Ariel looked around, his nostrils flaring as the reverberations of my scream continued to tear through the air.

"Stop this," he said. "Stop it!" He spun on his heel as the echo of my cry stretched higher. He spun the other way as the world around him began to crumble. He threw out his light at the cracks in the sky, only to have it sucked through those cracks. His breath hitched, coming in short and fast bursts.

Something slammed into Ariel, cutting off his rising hysteria. The scent of warm blood bursting through the air stung my nose.

Valen stepped in front of me, his bow laced with an arrow. It was so much like the first time that for a brief moment I thought I was dreaming. That this could not possibly be real. Me at Valen's feet, bleeding. Ariel, at the end of his arrow, snarling. Only this time the angel was beaming with holy power in the form of hot blue and purple flames.

I blinked, willing the fogginess of my good eye to go away. I was healing too slowly. Ariel's light was poison.

I forced myself up on my elbows and shook my head. Get up.

Ariel twisted the blade he fisted. He pointed the tip at me. "Do you see now what rot she is?"

Valen moved forward, angling the end of his arrow higher, sighting over Ariel's head. "You should have left us alone," he said quietly. So deadly quiet that it froze my blood. "Forgotten all about her. Because of you, she will be condemned."

"She's an abomination! You're not even supposed to be here, surely you know the evil. Look at this!" Ariel threw his hand up. I followed it to the cracks in the sky and air around him. It looked exactly like a cracked LED screen. Fragmented with bits of color and big black pieces of void.

What is that?

It was in the moment of Valen's hesitation that Ariel struck. It was a subtle turn of his head to look at the broken air, when Ariel spectered directly in front of him and cut his sword down. Valen threw his bow up, blocking a blow so hard that it cracked through the air, making his arms shudder.

Get up.

I slid a knee under me. The world spun. Ariel and Valen moved so quickly that, amongst the stirring forest, it made my stomach turn. I shut my eyes.

I brushed against the darkness inside of me. It was there still, wounded and bleeding. One more burst. I needed one more burst to draw Ariel's attention to me.

Green and orange flames twisted through the air, silver swords and black claws. And then, with the same brutal light Ariel had inflicted on me, Valen was on the ground again. Blood burst from his mouth.

No. "Valen!"

Ariel threw a knee into Valen's back. He slipped his fingers to the slit of his neck and crudely ripped out one of his arrows.

No no no no no.

I dug my nails into the black earth. My burnt hands frayed at the knuckles. The monster inside of me lifted her head. There was still a little bit of fight left. I blinked again as the vision in my eye stitched together. Hair spilled across my face.

Ariel was not going to kill him.

He was not going to take him from me. I wouldn't let him.

Shadows spilled out from my palms like oil. It flowed freely now, like a tap had been left open. Where they spread across the ground, rot followed. I whispered to my fire, urging it forward, to consume everything it touched. The more I let out, the farther I fell into my power. I rode it down. A soft humming started in my head. It shook the blood in my veins. The beast licked her lips. Yes, there was one fight still left.

"She's falling," Ariel breathed. He pushed the arrow deeper into Valen's back. To the amorini, he said, "Too bad you won't be here to see the extent of it."

Valen pushed up on his palms, trying to shake Ariel off, but only managed to drive the arrow deeper. His face skewed with pain. Ariel shoved him back into the ground.

"Ezra! Don't!" Valen barked. Spit flew through his gritted teeth as his face was pressed harder into the dirt. "Do not fall."

I heard them both but it didn't register. Whatever they were saying didn't matter because Ariel was killing Valen and I would not have him taken from me.

"Don't fall!"

A plea. A prayer.

A slashing line of power struck across the center of my chest. I called on the ancient beast that had been born into my blood. The raging power that tried to stall me had claws. But its claws were not sharper than mine. Its will was not stronger than mine. It was not more powerful than the blood my sire gifted me.

Heaven had damned me, and I was going to give them a reason for doing so.

I fell so far into my power that, when I hit the bottom, my breath stuttered. Hues of vast colors fell like rain from my palms. From my pores, crystallized gems bled.

I pulled up, pulled my power so fast and so hard it made my head swim. Up, up, up from the grave it had been buried. I ripped the ground apart, embedding dirt beneath my nails as I rose, pushing to my feet. The skin of my arms peeled away as my wings opened behind me, draping at my back in a pillar of smoke and ash.

My lungs burned with brimstone, with the curse that they had made me. The power against me had stopped, now resorting to banging. Calling on me. Begging me to stop. Faster I pulled my power, urging it to my palms where I could wield it true.

A wicked, nasty burning erupted within my core and burst across my entire body.

Ariel jerked back as bright flames billowed out of my palms. He fell to his ass then stumbled to his feet in the blink of an eye. The arrow in Valen's back forgotten, only halfway in. His eyes widened, his mouth gaping in horror.

"You cannot wield that power." Ariel's voice was broken with fear.

White and silver. Vicious and cold. The flames thrashed along my body in a manner that fires do not move. They coiled and slithered. It was wild. Untamed. I couldn't hold them much longer.

"You wanted a monster, well now you've got one," I snarled. I let the heat of my rage unfurl. Let the source of my power hurl toward Ariel like the arrow he had tried to drive into Valen's heart.

Ariel's shock made him slow. He dove out of the way, but not before the fury of my flames caught up his wings. He screamed.

Angels and their music are a beautiful thing. But when they scream, it sounds like a car crash, the shattering of windows. The cry of defeat when a loved one is lost. It was agony.

It took everything in me not to cover my ears from the horror of it. I winced, pushing myself forward as I followed him, letting the flame take me by the hand and drive him down.

He spun behind a tree as I let my flames barrel after him. I would burn this entire forest down to get to him. I would burn this entire fucking realm so long as he died in the process.

I pulled my flames in slightly as I crouched next to Valen. His breath was shallow. Blood pooled from his mouth, his nose. Even his tears ran red. I ripped the arrow from his back, fisting the bloody shaft so tightly my knuckles whitened. "You're going to be ok," I said.

I slipped my fingers into the snow and fallen leaves and willed my power to move forward. Fire skirted across the ground. Find him, I commanded.

This sort of power was dangerous. It was heady, delicious. It was unlike anything I had ever imagined. With this sort of power, I was unstoppable. I would call my flames back. Eventually. Once Ariel was dead, I could think about relinquishing it.

"Ezra." Valen's voice was coated in blood. He shifted until he was on his knees, swaying. His eyes fell to my hands, to the colorful stones still leaking from them.

I bared my teeth, shaking the remaining gems from my skin. "Not yet." I couldn't give up this power yet. I whipped my head in the direction Ariel had fled. "Come out, you coward!"

Valen stood and caught hold of my wrist before I could step away. It was like I had been struck by lightning. Something grounded me as he held onto me, his grip growing tighter as if he felt the surge too. He looked at where he held me in shock, at the flames encircling his arm. His nostrils flared as the flames licked up his arm.

"They won't hurt you," I said. I didn't know what sort of power I wielded. But I knew I wouldn't hurt Valen and so what came from me would not either.

"Ezra," Valen said. His voice was growing stronger. Within it was reverence.

I touched my free hand to his face. "Consider us even," I said. A life for a life.

A smile flitted across his face, but it didn't reach his eyes. There was something else beneath the wonder of his gaze. Something I could not decipher as I leaned forward to kiss him.

I kissed him hard, drinking him in to quench the billowing thirst to save him. Salt and iron tears bled between our lips. His hand snaked around the back of my neck as he pulled me against his chest, crushing me against him so hard that my neck cracked. I didn't care. It didn't matter because he was solid beneath me, his strength returning. Valen would live.

"I couldn't let him take you from me."

Valen touched my hand that was still on his face. "There isn't a force in all Creation that will part me from you."

I forced a smile. "And I, you."

Valen's eyes shifted past my head and I turned with him, listening. There would be time for soft words later. If Ariel retreated to Heaven, it would all be over. It would not just be one angel we had to face but an army of them.

Valen leaned against me as we stood, his breath swooping low. He licked a stray tear of blood from his lips. "I'm fine," he said. "He's close."

"Then he should come finish what he started!" I shouted into the abyss of the forest. Ariel was dead. I knew it. Valen knew it. He knew it. He had underestimated me, thought me as weak as the day he dragged me out onto the lake.

"What has Vélos been up to all these centuries?" The voice hissed around us, moving like the wind. I tensed as Ariel's voice brushed over me, the wrongness of it making my skin crawl. "Do you seek to bring on the Abaddon? Have you stolen Prometheus?"

Valen put a hand out, stopping me in my tracks. He took a step forward so that I was slightly behind him. I still gripped the arrow I had pulled from his back. Between that and my flames, it was the only weapon I had.

"How do you kill an angel?" I asked.

"Cut off their wings and then cut off their heads." His eyes snapped to the side as he searched for movement. "As soon as you see him, force him to the ground."

I nodded.

The sound of metal sung through the air. Valen jerked me forward, pulling my face from the air Ariel's blade had slashed through. I toppled over him, twisting onto my back and throwing up my palms, shooting silver flames into a second blade that curved down upon us.

I let my wings unfurl, let them push me off the ground as I pulled

Ariel toward me so I could pin him beneath me.

Ariel's teeth gnashed together. He released his own fire of red and orange, a flash of blue, but they did nothing to tamp my flame.

Ariel threw up his sword, cutting through the air, and spectered a few feet away. He moved quickly and thrust out his two white wings.

Valen snarled. He snatched his bow from the ground and reached back behind his neck, nocking a long black arrow.

Ariel surged through the canopy of black and white trees. His feathers battered the branches as he struggled to climb past the claws of the forest. It's wasn't until he broke into the sky that Valen let his arrow fly.

The arrow whistled upward, straight into Ariel's spine between his wings. His arms flailed outward and, then, he was falling. Dark red flames caught his wings as he crashed down.

"Angels don't burn," I said, rushing forward with Valen as Ariel's descent cast him away from us.

"Demons do," Valen snarled. He loped ahead, another arrow at the ready. It was bolted in Ariel's throat before the angel hit the ground. A third and fourth set went into his wings as he landed with a loud smack on his front.

I let loose the rein of my flames. They wrapped around his limbs like chains, stretching him out into a seven-pointed star.

"What have you done?" Ariel jerked his face back and forth as his wings burned away. "What-wh-?" His words no longer forming, instead coming out in sharp, winded breaths.

Valen tore off a piece of Ariel's shirt. He wrapped it around his palm, knotted it at the back, and jerked one of the silver swords from its sheath. "Hold him."

"Yes," I breathed. I was tired, but I was not so spent that I would lose my grip. I couldn't. Not yet. Just a little bit longer. I poured more of my power into the flames to prove my point. Relished in Ariel's guttural agony as they tightened around his throat.

Valen stepped over Ariel, placing a foot on either side of his waist. "That day on the lake, you were trying to cut out her wings," he said. He flipped the blade in his hand. "Allow me to return the favor."

Ariel's scream was the sound of a loved one dying. Of a short life being ripped away.

Valen dug Ariel's own blade into his back. He thrust it hard and deep. This was not the slashing Ariel had done to me, the torture I still bore on my back. Valen was precise with the cut, clean. He carved out the first wing, tossing it to the side while it burned and smoked.

"Stop!" Ariel's voice rasped. Blood flowed freely from his back, so dark it ran black. "Please, not my wings! I'll let her go. I'll do anything!"

Valen thrust his blade beneath his shoulder blade. Ariel screamed again. Valen leaned forward, putting his face close to Ariel's. "You ask mercy from the wrong creature, for I have none." Valen twisted the blade, severing Ariel's second wing from his back with a sickening crack. This one he took his time with.

I couldn't take my eyes off Valen as he worked through the bone. At the terrifying beauty that washed across his face as he ripped each wing free.

His eyes flicked to me. In answer, I released Ariel.

The angel crawled to his wings. His hands shook as he reached for one. His sobs were terrible sounds, wracking his entire body.

Valen followed him, his head bent in the way predators do when they're about to make the killing blow. I picked my way to his side.

To look down at the miserable creature that had hunted me my entire life. That had nearly succeeded in parting me from it.

Nothing.

He was absolutely nothing.

How pathetic that something so powerful could amass to the tears and blood that lay at my feet.

As another twisted sob tore out of Ariel's throat, I was reminded that Valen had this done to him. Had lost those beautiful wings in the Fall. For no reason other than he was an amorini. Cast out and burned for what he was.

I could see he was remembering it too. How the fire within his eyes guttered.

That light shifted once more. Valen flipped the knife, that now extended into a sword, and brought it down on Ariel's neck without a sound.

The angel's screaming ceased.

The sudden silence was too much. I inhaled, not remembering when I had stopped breathing, and let out a sound. Not a sob or moan. Something animalistic.

Valen whirled toward me. I smiled. It was done. It was finished. I took a step forward and everything around me shuttered. My flames blew out as I fell into Valen's arms.

CHAPTER FORTY-TWO: PROMETHEUS

Valen

Ezra's breath was shallow as I rested my palm over her chest. She had used too much of her power too quickly. She was inexperienced with the force she wielded, and it was likely that it could kill her. Was killing her.

The burns on her face weren't healing. Ariel's holy light had done that.

I wrapped her against my chest. I couldn't heal her. Archangels were the only ones entitled to that power. Bishop was coming, but he wasn't moving fast enough. The others were close behind, Jinn and Diriel.... and the Murder. They would have felt us crossing into their borders.

The entire court would have seen the absolute rage Ezra had unleashed.

I could possess her. Give her a piece of myself so I might heal her. It was the only way demons could alter life. But contorting her soul like that, I couldn't. Even if it saved her, I would be defiling her.

"She's dying." I let the words trickle through the bond that connected me to the others.

A choked sob escaped me as I looked around us. The veil between Tartarus and Earth was torn to ribbons. It was such a thin space that separated us from the humans, but a stronghold that had never broken no matter how hard we had tried. We had clawed, screamed, burned our way through every part of Tartarus trying to break free.

We had the fury of tens of thousands and yet all it had taken to break it was the wrath of a woman scorned. One terrifying scream from a nephilim and it had shattered.

I twisted my fingers into her hair as her breath deepened to another level.

"Stay with me," I said, my lips against her brow. "Stay with me, harpy." I looked back to the sky, to the broken veil, and said two words I never thought I would utter again.

"God, please."

Please save her. Please don't take her from me.

A loud crash blew the snow apart in front of me as Bishop crashed to the ground. His pale face was flushed and his silver eyes wide. He took one look around before he landed on Ezra and fell to his knees in front of us.

"Give her to me," his voice broke.

My grip tightened before I passed her into his arms. "He burned her and then she fell. She crashed too hard and too fast." I tried to force the pain from my voice, but I couldn't. I couldn't lose her when I had finally won her.

Bishop laid her on the ground between us. He touched his palm to the side of her face, the other to her chest. His piercing eyes were so focused on her I thought they might sear holes through her flesh. It could not have been more than a minute, though it felt like hours, when his lashes finally fluttered.

"I've got her," he said firmly. He let out a shudder. "It's not death that has her. It's something else."

I rose to my knees. "What?" I snapped.

Bishop's jaw snapped shut as Diriel and Jinn slid across the snow in a flurry with their bows notched.

"The Murder tried to intercept us," Jinn said, gasping.

I looked to them and back to Ezra. "Put your weapons away."

"They are dressed for battle," Diriel hissed.

I nodded. "And we are not bringing them one. Do it."

Ezra's flesh began to mend. Fresh pink skin threaded together beneath the blood, dirt, and ash. Her chest rose with a deep inhale. Slowly, her hair grew longer. It had darkened to another shade of burnished gold.

Bishop looked up. "Those from her?"

I followed his line of sight to the silver flames burning the trees. "Yes." I nodded to the veil. "So is that."

"We're so fucked," Jinn said as he threw his bow across his chest. "If Baal doesn't kill us, Raguel will. This is it, isn't it? What Raguel was looking for?"

They were all looking at me.

"I think so. I didn't think it at the time." Car lights flashed across a highway through the veil. "But it must be. It was her scream. She must have ripped a hole in the veil when I rescued her."

"We're fucked," Jinn said again.

"No, we're not," Bishop growled. "No one is taking her from us."

The Murder's arrival was not as quick and sudden as the cyns' had been. It was soundless, like a ghost floating across the snow. It was the shadow that spilled down from a cluster of trees that was not on fire that gave us any warning that they were here. The shadow twisted, morphing into the pale keras.

Atticus stepped into our circle of carnage, his nostrils flaring.

More shadows bled into the surrounding forest, then Raum and Orias and two more generals I recognized were there.

Raum stopped short, holding his fist up to halt whoever lay behind him. I have never once smelled fear on the male.

It seeped from his pores as he looked at the bright silver flames of Heaven.

One by one the others noticed it too. Tension roiled through their bodies, the weapons in their hands becoming their shields. Any second and someone might bolt. Demons are not afraid of much. Only that which can surely kill them.

Atticus picked his way across the scene until he was standing over Ariel's body. He kicked the head so that it rolled to the side, revealing the wide purple eyes.

"Start talking," Raum hissed.

I entwined my fingers with Ezra's before addressing him. "The incubus tried to take her. Our fight landed us in your territory."

"Incubi do not wield Prometheus," Raum snarled.

"Angels do," I evaded.

Atticus had turned to inspect the flames. He reached out tentatively with a scarred hand and recoiled when one of them brushed his fingertips. He let out a pained hiss.

"An angel who was in the early stages of a Fall," Orias said. He moved beside Atticus to take the male's hand and inspect the fresh burns. He frowned and curled Atticus's hand into a fist.

They hadn't burned me. I blinked. Prometheus hadn't burned me when she touched me.

"His wings wouldn't have burned otherwise," Orias said.

"Not even with this," Atticus said, nodding to the flames. He stepped forward, leering into the tear in the veil. His breath hitched.

Ezra's chest rose again, a pained sound whistling from her lips. I tightened my grip on her.

"We'll get her back to the tyre," Bishop said to me.

Raum stepped forward, his hand resting on one of his favored daggers. "You are not going anywhere, and most certainly not with her. What has happened here is an act of war."

Bishop's lips curled the same time mine did, but he was faster to speak. "This war is not between us. Valen finished it before an army could come down. Where are your thanks?"

Raum cocked his head. "That girl has brought Heaven's fire to our land. There is no alliance between us when she can bring down the Enemy's wrath at her beck and call. If you think Baal is going to turn a blind eye to this, you are mistaken. He readies an army as we speak. How long have you known?"

"Baal has no power here," Bishop snarled.

A thick wave of tension filled the air. Now was not the time to call Raum out.

This would damn me. Would damn us both, but perhaps it would direct their attention elsewhere. "She fell," I said.

"She did?" Bishop removed his hand from her face as the rest of her skin healed. He kept his other on her chest, keeping the flow of his magic tied to her.

I nodded. "She might have wielded this, but she fell first. There were no signs of it before just now." Liar. I saw the flash of silver when she stood in her bed fast asleep. I saw it in her eyes whenever I pushed her too hard. It had always been there, quietly lurking.

"You are coming with us. Get up," Raum said. He jerked his chin to the Murder.

Bishop and I rose at the same time, readying, but blocking their way to Ezra. The world tipped to the side. With all the adrenaline pumping through my veins, I had forgotten that I was still bleeding.

"You lay a single hand on her and I'll cut it off," I snarled. "We are cyn and you will not command us like dogs. Have you even noticed what she did?"

Raum's lip tugged up. His sapphire eyes flickered to a place beside my head.

"Look," I commanded.

Raum's mouth twisted into a sneer and then stopped. Everyone was looking now. At the tears in the veil that lay just beyond the flames.

"You are going to let us walk out of here. You arrived to find nothing but the aftermath of a battle that resulted in the death of an angel... and access to Earth."

Orias looked hesitantly at Raum as his hand fell to the longsword at his hip.

"She fell. You have your gateway to humanity," I shot through our bonds. I didn't want the others to hear. Just the cyn of Vélos and the Murder. They were the only ones that mattered.

Crows landed in the trees, settling above the other warriors with their masked faces. Raum had brought a small army with him.

"We are still your allies," Bishop said. *"Imagine what she can do once this power is harnessed. Ready for that war, in which she can aid us."*

My jaw clenched. Ezra would not set foot on the battlefield.

Raum smirked. "You know Baal will hear of this. Of her."

"You're going to tell him," Diriel said.

"I am," he said sharply. "Enjoy her while you still have her."

My fist was flying through the air before I could think. My knuckles struck the center of his jaw with a loud crack. Raum stumbled back.

He held up his hand as Orias drew his sword. Diriel and Jinn had nocked their bows.

Raum grinned. "Atticus, take one of the wings back to Cyn Baal. Let him know the threat has been disposed of…" His voice trailed as he looked at me. Cold and calculating. Raum was an absolutely ruthless bastard. "That it resulted into tears of the veil. And that there are traces of a nephilim."

Atticus twisted, going up in a billow of smoke before shifting into the creeping black bird that clawed and flew between the tree tops.

"Bastard," Bishop hissed.

Raum shrugged.

"Don't touch her," I snarled as Bishop bent over to scoop Ezra into his arms. I ignored his cool gaze and shouldered him to the side.

I lifted her against my bloodied chest and held her tight. Even as I bared my fangs, though, I did not shove Bishop off as he wrapped an arm around me. He knew as well as I, in my condition, that I might fall. I let him pull me into his kratiste. Watched as Diriel and Jinn spectered ahead of us.

War was coming. I saw it in Raum's dark gaze as the smoke billowed between us. He would not let Ezra go. Once Baal knew of her and the jewels of her eyes, he would demand her. And, if by some slim chance the keras let us be, Heaven would bring down their wrath and dissolve the Fallen they had cast out so long ago.

CHAPTER FORTY-THREE: LET IT DIE

Ezra

I was suspended. Floating. The water was a warm cocoon that held me in a gentle caress. I moved my fingers back and forth in the water. Traces of raw power throbbed through my aching body. There was a mask over my face that I pushed back. I was in a tub, or pool. It took a moment for my eyes to adjust to the light the salt rocks emitted.

The space felt like a void, but I could feel him.

"Valen." My voice sounded strange underwater. It lapped against my ears as I spoke.

A shadow within the darkness moved in my peripheral. "I'm here," he said.

I reached up, straining my fingers through the black to feel him. The light was bright enough to light the water itself, but I couldn't see anything past the shadows.

His fingertips brushed against mine, sliding over my palm then wrapping around my wrist. I pulled, urging him closer to the water.

Valen slid into the light, his hair disheveled despite it being pulled back into a knot at the top of his head. Stray curls had escaped their band and framed his face as he leaned down to wade in the water beside me. His dark clothes molded to his body as soon as the moisture hit them.

"I'm here," he said again. He slid his hands beneath my head, his fingers tracing the bare skin of my shoulders, and pulled me against his chest.

Something had happened. Something terrible.

There was too much tension in the soft touch of his fingers, too much of it in the air.

"What did I do?" I asked. I didn't like that I couldn't see him. I twisted in my suspension, ignoring the way he tried to halt me so that I could face him.

"Go slow. Let the Styx waters do their job," he said.

"What did I do?" I pressed.

"Nothing," he said. He ran his fingers along the frame of my face. "Nothing wrong," he clarified.

I let my hand trail down his neck, to the center of his chest. "I thought he was going to kill you."

A sad smile tugged at Valen's mouth. "You need never worry about me." His chest swelled as he searched between my eyes. "You, though. You need to be more careful. I don't know what I would have done had something happened to you." He slid his other hand out, his fingertips gracing the edge of my wings.

"I wasn't going to let you go."

His fingers trailed higher, touching more of my wings. Even in the darkness, I could see the question in his eyes. When I didn't stop him, he continued his exploration, moving languidly, pulling soft sighs from my mouth.

All at once we reached for each other. He pulled me hard against him and I dug my nails into his skin. It was not until I was flush against him that I realized I was naked.

He pressed his face against mine, slid his forehead and nose hard into my skin, and breathed me in. He kissed me, his mouth desperate.

I reached between us to claw at his pants. We nearly died. Yet here we were, both safe and sound, a little bruised up but alive. I needed to be closer to him.

Something had happened when the silver flames tore out of me. A shift in my soul, a fracture to some hidden part of myself. Whatever it was left me starving. It left me wanting more. More of life. More of Valen.

"You need to rest," Valen said, but he didn't stop me as I wrapped my hand around his length. His fingers explored my wings, encouraging me. "Ezra," he grunted as I slid his cock inside of me.

Death had chased me my entire life and I had finally won.

I won my life. I had won the cyn beneath me that was coming undone with every stroke of my pussy around his shaft.

Our fucking was not sweet, it was not slow. It was passionate and hard. Quick as if the danger still lurked in the shadows. I came fast with Valen right behind me, forcing himself up so hard that he pushed me out of the water.

I clung to him, locking my thighs around his so he remained inside of me.

A surge of emotions welled within my chest. I finally understood the shift in my heart as Valen kissed me. I had been fighting it for weeks now, telling myself that whatever this was between us wasn't real. That it couldn't last.

But it could.

The battle with Ariel had proven that.

Love was not a weakness. It's what had saved us.

"I love you," I said through our kiss. "I love you."

He eased back, nudging my nose softly. "Shh."

"Valen."

"Ezra," he warned. That's when I felt it. The stiffness of his body.

I leaned back. Embarrassment, rejection, it hit me hard. "I," I started. "I'm sorry. I don't expect you to feel the same. I just... well, it's true." But did he not love me back? I didn't imagine this bond between us. It was real.

Suddenly it felt awkward to have him inside of me. I pressed my hand on his chest to shift up, to feel... nothing. Absolutely nothing. His heart did not even beat for me.

"I thought you felt the same."

Valen's hands slid to my waist to lift me off. I scrambled to my feet, swaying in the dark pool of water. Water so deep I hadn't even known because Valen was there. I wasn't afraid with him at my side, but now, as he looked everywhere but at me, I felt like I was drowning.

My heart slammed against my chest.

"Even if it wasn't against our laws, angels do not feel love. I don't. *I can't.* What we have is something special, but it will never be love. I could kill you for even saying such things. I should."

I looked at him, dumbstruck. "I know you care about me."

"Stop, Ezra."

I shook my head and reached for him even as he moved to stand. "No, you stop. What happened? Is it my power? I'm still learning. You can help me control it. Did something else happen with Ariel?" I wracked my memory, trying to draw up any detail that would tell me why he had changed.

He had been afraid of my fire. I saw it in his eyes as he looked down at my hands as the gems fell from them. As the flames licked against his skin.

"It's—" He shook his head, fastening his pants angrily. "I do care for you, but I don't love you. You don't have an adelfi, remember?"

"You said…" What the fuck was happening? It felt like my entire world was crumbling beneath me. I finally had one good thing, one beautiful thing, and it was withering in front of me. Ariel was dead. I had won. And yet… I was still losing. I could feel the ground falling beneath my feet, threatening to pull me underneath the glass surface.

"We are possessive creatures," Valen said. "I claimed you as mine, as a possession. A lover, a…" His voice trailed off, but I saw the word clear as if he had spoken it.

"Don't you fucking dare," the pain came through my voice, solid as if he had made the blow with a knife. The tightness in my chest constricted, forcing nausea into the pit of my stomach, the breath in my lungs to become lighter. I felt dizzy as I stood, staring after him as he climbed from the pool.

"A whore, that's all I am to you? You fucking liar. Don't walk away from me!" My voice echoed through the chamber.

Valen's shoulders stiffened. He turned, looking down on me. The water dripped from his clothes, making a soft pit-pat sound as they fell against the stone floor.

"You call me a liar and you cannot even look me in the eye to reject me. You said…" Tears and rage contorted my words. "You said nothing in all of Creation could part us." I remembered that. He had made so many promises and whispered kind things.

The corner of his jaw flexed as he swallowed. "You seem to have forgotten what I am. I am not just an amorini, I am a demon. Neither of those things take kindly to having something of theirs taken away. You mistake my infatuation with love, which is forbidden," he growled. He rocked back on his heel, his lips curling in distaste.

"Whatever you feel for me, Ezra, let it die." His eyes skimmed across my wings. "I'll be back for you once you're well."

"Valen!"

I surged up from the water, not caring that the movement hurt and dragged me down. Pain ravaged me from the wounds his words had inflicted.

But he was gone, vanished into the darkness in which he was made.

CHAPTER FORTY-FOUR: THE HYMN

Ezra

Days bled into weeks. Nights felt longer when all I did was toss and turn. I didn't dream anymore. There was no trace of destruction and chaos to haunt me now that Ariel was dead. Not dreaming was equally torturous.

I ate, but barely. At some point Claire stopped bringing me tea. In fact, she had been replaced entirely by another woman, Sita, with warm brown skin and light blonde hair. A stark contrast between the two with her welcoming smile and crinkling blue eyes.

"What happened to Claire?" I hadn't meant it to come out as sharp as it did.

"She's been reassigned. I'm your lady now." There was something off-putting about the woman. Claire and I hadn't been particularly close, but I had grown used to her. I didn't like change.

I frowned. "Claire used to bring me tea. Would you make sure I get that in the mornings?" I didn't know if the tea really had anything to do with calming my nerves, but it had stopped weeks ago and that's when my anxiousness returned. Or perhaps it was all due to what Valen had done.

The last time I saw the coward, he had been on the back of an odonnos in fitted clothes and tall riding boots. Andras and two escorts from Eurynomos had flanked him. I didn't see his face beneath the dark helm. He barely even glanced my way when I stepped onto the field before he was gone. I watched the four horsemen on their ill-footed steeds canter into the depths of the forest.

That had been two months ago. Two months of grieving that turned my heart bitter. Losing him might have been easier if he was dead. Sometimes I wished he was. Other days, I tormented myself with the guilt of wishing such a thing.

I had been told he had gone to inform the other courts of what had taken place. Talk of war had bloomed across the continents and the cyns of Vélos wanted it to be known that I was not their enemy, but an ally. I knew it was more than that when Andras returned without him. Valen was avoiding me.

War was coming, but it wouldn't be amongst the Fallen.

I was so numb to the idea of it that I no longer argued with Bishop when he spoke of how I would aid them. The cyn had broken it to me, of what I had done in the fight with Ariel. How my scream had shattered the veil between humanity's world and ours.

"A harpy indeed," Bishop had said.

"Don't call me that," I had snarled. The name stung like a bee's needle. I didn't need someone else calling me that.

His light eyes had glimmered. I didn't know if I hated Bishop more for prodding me or continuing with his flirts and taunts. At least I knew he didn't pity me.

It came with a crashing realization that I had been what Raguel had been looking for. Scouts had been sent out through all five courts. After weeks of searching, another tear had been found, leading to a black lake tucked somewhere in the Californian mountains.

The place that started it all.

Tartarus was bleeding into Earth. Ariel had been right; I would be the fall of humanity. I would be their end. Except no one had been brave enough to cross over into Earth. Many still thought it to be a trick devised by Heaven. And I, a nephilim, was still a forgotten myth to some.

I was as much of a myth as the Hymn of the Sun and the Moon. A prophecy where Tartarus rose from its depths and Heaven came crashing down. Raum's words came back to me in the eerie memory. I had forgotten him mentioning it.

So, when the words unfurled in the texts before me, I could barely keep the burn of bile from the back of my throat. A lick of anger, a knot of dread. Flicking emotions assaulted me so frequently now that I could hardly control my flames when they burst across my knuckles. Red and orange lashings that encased my hands like lace gloves.

I looked at the texts before me now. At all of the meticulous notes Diriel had been working on since Valen found me. He believed in the Hymn, that there was a way to free the Fallen and win the war against those who cast them out.

Lane had her nose in another book, her eyes eating up the pages faster than her fingers could turn them. Ever since the incident (as I liked to call it), she had been more on edge. Or maybe I hadn't noticed how tense she could be now that Valen wasn't around to distract me.

I'd noticed a bruise on the back of her neck last week, but when I inquired about it, she brushed it off as rough foreplay. She hadn't met my eyes.

There had not been a single word from Eurynomos.

I watched Lane and, very slowly, looked down at the text before me.

She will bear the mark of Solomon below her chin
A half-carved moon branded by the angels
And she will speak their name and their will, will be hers
With the voice of Heaven she will speak

"You're the Moon," I said softly. The crescent had been tattooed on the underside of her chin as long as I had known her.

Lane stilled. Diriel stopped what he was doing too, his pen coming to a sudden halt.

"That's why Baal never killed you. They know of the prophecy." I looked at Diriel. "I'm right, aren't I?"

Please, say no.

She looked at Diriel before she met my eyes. I saw him nod from my peripheral. "Yes," she said softly. "It's not Baal who believes in it though, it's Raum. The others think I'm some pet to him. Atticus is the only one who knows. He's not ever mentioned it to Orias."

My heart fell into the pit of my stomach. She had known this entire time. She wasn't just a spy they had left behind; she was the other piece. With the sun and moon together... what? What sort of picture would the puzzle make now that we were together?

"Why?"

Lane shrugged, her eyes darting back to the book in front of her as she tried to throw her guard up. "Orias has a big mouth. His ego is twice as large. Perhaps Raum thinks he would take matters into his own hands. Contort the prophecy somehow." She shook her head. "I might be the moon, but Raum only tells me so much."

She was lying. I could smell the stink of her sweat from across the room. I could hear the thrum of her pulse quicken.

My jaw clenched. "Raum mentioned it, the first night I met him." I looked at Diriel. "He was here, while you stepped away. Is that why he left you here? To see if I was the Sun?"

Lane wasn't looking at me now. I wanted to see if she would own up to it now that she was caught.

Was there anyone I could trust? I had let her in, confided in her. Had shown her my flames, both gold and silver. All for her to report back to Raum.

"Yes, but I told you before I wasn't going to tell them anything. I haven't. You're my friend," she said, slowly meeting my eyes. She flinched as her stare met mine. Good, I hoped she felt the dagger's edge of betrayal I was feeling too. "I haven't betrayed you." As if she knew my thoughts. I focused on putting a shield around my mind. I didn't know how dhampirs' powers worked, if they needed a blood bond to read minds. How could I when Lane kept everything to herself? And why would she talk when I gave everything up so freely?

"I've given Raum pieces, but not the whole truth. The last thing I want is for you to fall into their hands. And selfishly, I have no plans of ever going back."

"You won't," Diriel said quickly.

Steam bubbled behind my lips as I maintained control over my emotions. "Why do you think Baal doesn't know?" I asked.

"Because Raum intends to overthrow him," Diriel said.

Right. I had forgotten about that too.

I nodded and looked back down at the texts before me.

The woman who was the sun sat upon the throne of the underworld

An eighth star was added to her crown

At her back were giant black wings. In her eyes was the Fury of Hell.

Ariel had been right. The visions were ingrained into my memory. Diriel had said I wouldn't become the monster. But here were the texts that proved it.

My mouth went dry as I tried to focus on the words. I tried to ignore the weight of betrayal weighing on my shoulders. It grew the further I read—about the destruction I was said to unleash on humanity.

With her left hand she commanded the stars to the earth. Beneath her rage the world burned.
Her gaze turned to the next world where she sent a new army. On it went that I saw worlds fall beneath her fury.
The stars praised her name, "O Great Sun, How you have saved us! Glory be to your shining light!"
But then a great darkness fell upon her as the Moon raised its sword.
From out of her mouth of vengeance, a war cry that parted the oceans.

There were notes scribbled between the verses. Signs to look for when coming across the Sun. That she would be an orphan or abandoned. She would have an angel's blessing. (Blessing was crossed out, the word blood written over the top of it.) She would be bound to the depths of Hell, condemned like those who fell before her.

Was it getting hot? It felt like I couldn't breathe.

The Moon was the Sun's complete opposite, mortal and human. She would bear the gift of Solomon in that she could control the angels and demons by the power of their name. She would pass beneath the eyes of many before she was discovered, after she too was abandoned. Both women would be stripped of everything so that they had no ties to the world they were born into. So that they could serve the Hymn and free their brothers.

Both the darkness and the light would have the power to move through Creation. The Sun could open the gates, and the Moon could lock them and control their rulers. Those who were not killed in Heaven would be confined to the bowels of darkness which the Fallen had been cast. Together they would become the queens of Tartarus.

Bitterness welled within me. I felt the heat behind my eyes as I struggled to grasp onto anything that would ground me. I truly had fallen that day I saved Valen. Was this what would really happen? Would I destroy worlds and... Lane would help me?

"It says nothing about Prometheus in here," I said, my voice hoarse.

"That is something I have had a hard time understanding. I'm not sure how you called it to you, that you are still able to wield Heaven's flame. It doesn't make any sense," Diriel said. His face pinched together like he had tasted something sour.

I pressed my palms into the table as I leaned away to keep them from shaking.

I had been chosen—no, fated—to bring down everything I knew and believed in. There was nothing I could do to stop it.

Maybe it was a shame that Valen hadn't killed Killian that night. At least he wouldn't have suffered the destruction raging toward him. He would have truly been free. I thought back to what I had seen on the TV that night. Clips of a plague. I remembered the boils on the women's skin in my last dream with Ariel.

Me.

It was all because of me.

I never wanted this.

I couldn't stop it.

"If you'll excuse me," I said stiffly.

"We are going to try and do this with as little casualties as possible," Diriel said.

I stopped. "If Tartarus's poison doesn't kill the humans first, you will. I don't need to have met the other courts to know their hatred for my kind. For Heaven. Don't lie to me. Either of you." I looked at them both. "I'm quite full on them already."

CHAPTER FORTY-FIVE: TRUE RELIGION

Ezra

I tensed at the soft rap of knuckles on my door. I'd been cooped up in my room so long, I wasn't quite sure if it had been hours or days that past. I knew remaining tucked away was doing more harm than good, but I hadn't wanted to face anyone when I was still quietly stewing on the discovery I had made about the Hymn.

No one had tried to bother me. They must have gotten to Sita because not even she said much. She'd tried at first, but when I'd done nothing but respond with a frosty glare, she resorted to silence.

I jerked the door open, a haughty remark dying on my tongue when I met Bishop's surprised expression. His hand was still raised in the air, his knuckles curled.

"Oh," I murmured.

A sheepish smile laced with the edge of a sneer tugged at his lips. "Expecting someone else?"

I followed his gaze as it made a slow run of me. I took a step back, paused, and turned away. Bishop hesitated at the open door before stepping over the threshold, his tall riding boots glistening.

"I wasn't expecting you." I don't know why I let him in.

Bishop surveyed the disheveled room. I took the opportunity to look at him while his attention was elsewhere. His shirt was unbuttoned to the bottom of his chest and tucked into black pants. It wasn't until he was at my back that I realized he wasn't looking at the room but circling me.

I shifted under his stare. "What do you want?"

A low hum sank in his chest. "Unfortunately, I am not here to seduce you this time." He clasped his hands behind his back. The door swung shut behind us with a thud.

The corner of his jaw ticked when my heart beat faster.

He knew.

He knew... Ashes, how did he find out? Did Valen tell him? Was it Lane or Diriel? Did *they* even know?

"Sit with me." Bishop turned his hand out to the couch.

I tried to remain aloof as I lifted my chin and walked past him. But I knew he could hear my heart, knew he could smell the fear carving a pit in my chest. Certainly, he could smell my grief.

I glance toward the windows. Would he catch me if I ran? Where would I go?

He looked down on me as I took my seat. "Do you know why I'm here?"

Because I fell in love.

"No," I lied.

The muscle in his jaw tightened again. "What happened that night?"

"You'll have to be more specific–"

Bishop's cool gaze bore into me. "I want to know how you called Prometheus."

It took me a moment to register what he was saying. So, this wasn't about the crime I had committed? Why did this feel like an interrogation then? Like I had done something *wrong*. His sharp gaze hardened the longer I didn't speak.

Chills raced across my flesh. I'd never sunk that far in my power before. I didn't even know I could. Nephilim were rumored to be stronger than the angels, but with my bloodline so muddied and my skills lacking, I doubted I would ever match my brothers' power. Much less my sire's, whoever he was. It had been months and we were no closer to determining who he might be.

"I don't know," I said.

"What did you feel when it happened?"

Fury. Unbridled, relentless fury. "Rage," I answered. I could still see the arrow being shoved into Valen's back. Of the shaft sliding beneath his skin, into his heart.

Bishop took a deep breath. His eyes flicked to the ceiling and, slowly, he sat down beside me. "And?" he coaxed.

I was terrified he was going to take Valen from me. I saw that he was killing him and I couldn't imagine my life without him. And then I lost him anyway...

I wish I had a silver tongue so that I could have lied. Instead, I twisted the truth. "Ariel had taken everyone from me. He forced me to isolate myself until he could finally kill me. I wasn't going to let him take everything I had gained by being here. I fell into it. Into the pain that has haunted me from birth. I chased it, roped it against me and rode it back up with the intent that I would kill him."

Bishop's scrutinizing gaze didn't falter as he searched my eyes for answers. Diriel had tried to press me on how I'd managed it, but I hadn't wanted to talk about it. A sense of unease laced within me as I wondered if he could smell the missing truth.

"Prometheus is fire sent by Heaven gifted to a handful of angels. It is a rare gift that few are granted. There are a small hundred of archangels who can." Bishop leaned against the back of the couch. He cocked his head as he studied me.

I leveled my gaze with his. "Are you accusing me of something?"

Bishop's mouth quirked. "Should I be?"

"Are rage and Heaven close siblings?"

That cracked a smile across his face. I nearly breathed a sigh of relief. "At times. This is not an interrogation, Ezra. I am merely trying to understand what happened."

"You know as much as I do. I didn't even know about Prometheus until Diriel told me what I had done."

Bishop ran his nails over the shadow of his chin. I'd never seen him with stubble before. I hadn't even considered how the rest of them had been affected by what I'd done. He looked tired.

"Can you do it again?"

I let out a nervous laugh. "I don't know how. Wouldn't that be dangerous?"

Bishop shrugged and cocked his head the other way. "Prometheus is a curse to the Fallen, but if one of us can use it, I see no reason why we cannot take advantage of it."

"What can it do?"

"It can destroy worlds. Or, as evidenced by your scream, tear through the veils that keep us trapped here."

I flinched inwardly. I'd promised I would help the amorini, but knowing I had inadvertently helped the rest of the demons twisted my core into knots.

"I'd like to test it. See what you're truly capable of," he said softly, leaning forward on his knees. "Helping us is the right thing to do. You see that now, don't you?"

Begrudgingly, I nodded. I couldn't shake the feeling that it was wrong that I had fallen. That I had made a grave mistake.

"Will you let me guide you now?"

Tension roiled within me. There had to be a catch. Something that Bishop wanted in return. I didn't believe I wasn't owed some sort of punishment for falling in love with Valen. Not that he knew, but there was *something* off. Hell, even if he wanted me to wield Heaven's fire, I felt that too would come with a price.

"What do you want?"

Bishop's expression was unreadable. "To be friends."

"And?"

A flutter of power skipped through the air. His face remained composed as he said, "Stay away from Valen. Do that and I'll not have to punish you."

My heart stopped.

I knew it. I fucking knew it. Tension twisted up my throat, making it harder to breathe. "He isn't here," I said. "And even if he was, I have no desire to ever speak to him again."

"And why is that?"

We looked at each other. One waiting for the other to concede. I cursed myself for not being able to leash my emotions the way he could. "You know why," I ventured.

Bishop ducked his head. His silence was agony. I wish he would say something, and at the same time I was terrified of what would come out of his mouth. "We have very few laws."

"I know."

"I like you, Ezra. I want to make that clear outside of the fact that I need you. That *we* need you." He lifted my chin with the touch of his finger. It was ice cold. "But I am cyn and I must uphold those laws. If anyone catches wind of what has happened, I will have no choice but to make an example out of you."

The knot in my stomach tightened. Once more, my breath hitched. The inside of my mouth suddenly felt dry and stale. "What would you have to do?"

Bishop pinched my chin between his thumb and index finger and smiled. "We will not worry about that, as it will not come to it. Because you no longer love him, do you?"

I shook my head.

"Answer me."

"No." Tears ran down my face. I didn't know when I started crying and hated that it was in front of Bishop that my walls crumbled. "I hate him," I said. "I didn't mean to. I am not accustomed to your laws yet, but I am trying. I have *been* trying."

Bishop ran his knuckles over both sides of my face, swiping the tears away. "And that is why I am giving you grace." The chill of his touch slipped below my skin. It made my jaw ache and my neck stiffen. "Your punishment will be light." A sinister smile crinkled the lines on his face when I flinched. "So long as you tell me in detail of the rage you felt when you ripped a hole in the world. Tell me how much you hate him."

The sentence I served for falling in love with an amorini was to relive my fall again and again and again. I screamed violently, breathlessly as my throat turned raw. It felt as if someone had raked their claws down it. I fell in a shaking heap at Bishop's feet and sweet pain ripped through my skull.

I fell into that well of power searching for the silver flames that evaded me when I needed them. That was Bishop's punishment. To make me wield Prometheus so that we could learn how to harness it.

Every time I tried to pull my power up, I could feel his beneath mine encouraging me, trying to help me claw back to the surface. His presence was a boost every time, but no matter how hard I tried, my flames remained golden.

My gut clenched, threatening to relieve me of what little I had eaten. I dug my nails into the ground to steady my shaking hands.

"Again," Bishop barked.

He had mockingly told me this was tough love. I might have believed it had I not seen the glint of satisfaction in his eye when my pained scream tore a small rip in the sky. Whether it was because I could tear through the veil without Prometheus or that I was in pain, I wasn't sure.

We had been at it for hours. My throat and lungs were spent. I couldn't scream anymore if I wanted to.

"I can't," I said, barely a whisper. I eyed him through the twilight haze.

"You can."

"Maybe they were Ariel's."

Bishop shook his head. "Valen saw them in your hands."

I hated the way his name wounded me. As if the wound had ever healed.

"I can't," I said again. I pressed my palms into my thighs as I sat up. My head felt like it was on fire, so I dropped it between my knees.

A warm touch settled across my back. I leaned my head back into the comfort. I was so tired I didn't flinch when I felt Bishop's hand slide on the outside of my thigh. I blinked lazily and looked down where he was crouched in front of me.

"You can. I know you can," he pressed. "But I will give you a break. I have been too eager, and the last thing I want to do is burn you out."

It wasn't exactly an apology.

I took his extended hand with a grunt as he helped me to my feet. Breathing in to do something as simple as standing hurt. I was used to feeling sore after physically exerting myself, but this was a whole new level of discomfort.

"I need time, Bishop. I know you're fucking pissed off at me about Valen. Him aside–"

"I know," he interjected. "Like I said, too eager."

"I will get us out of here. That hasn't changed." It wasn't a total lie. I believed the amorini had been wrongfully cast out, but I was angry at them for their lies. And now that Eurynomos had access to humanity, I didn't know how I was going to free *just* the amorini. How was I to stop everyone else from leaving?

Bishop slid his arm around my shoulders, and I allowed him to take the brunt of my trembling weight as I leaned against him.

"Thank you," he said softly. He ran his fingers through my scalp and down the length of my braid.

I took a deep breath and breathed him in. They all had the power of fire, but Bishop always smelled like it. The scent had always given me comfort.

I tipped my head back to look at him. I smiled softly.

"You should come to service."

"Service?" He had to be joking.

"Did he never mention it to you?" Bishop frowned. "I always wondered why I never saw you."

"What sort of service?"

Bishop hummed. "A pleasure service."

I eased back and cocked a brow at him. "Bishop."

"You don't have to participate. Come and watch. Sit with me."

I opened my mouth to refuse when his expression softened. My tongue flicked over the back of my teeth as the words died on my tongue.

"It's important. To me," he added, his face reddening, "that you be there. Things have changed, Ezra, and I think it is important that you show our people you want to be here. That you care for them."

I was more surprised Valen had kept the services hidden from me this long and that no one had brought it to my attention sooner. Nausea rolled in my core. A pleasure service was certainly what it sounded like. Had Valen kept it from me because he participated?

The weight of Bishop's gaze weighed down my shoulders. I rolled them, trying to ease the tension and anxiety. Before I could think better of it, I was telling him yes, albeit reluctantly. His eyes lit up like Christmas morning.

There were only a few hours before service was to start, so I had little time to wash and change. I selected a black dress of ruched mesh fabric that had a slit up one of the legs. In my haste, I twisted my long hair up and brushed copper shadow across my eyelids and cheekbones. I painted my lips in a shade of dark red. I was done with thirty minutes to spare and alternated between pacing and sitting once my heels started to dig into my feet.

By the time Bishop retrieved me, I was a nervous wreck. I'd finally said yes. I didn't know how big of a mistake I had made until I opened the door and saw him standing there in his unbuttoned green shirt tucked into black leather pants that gripped his strong thighs. His hair was left unbound and fell over one shoulder.

The dark cloak that was tied about his throat outlined him like dark wings. Coal lined his eyes that made his silver eyes pop like starlight. Silver rings flashed across his knuckles when he turned to offer me his elbow.

Had he always been so striking?

Even as I felt the unwanted draw to him, I couldn't forget how hard he had pushed me and the simmer that had been in his gaze earlier.

"Don't look at me like that," he said.

"Like what?"

"Like you're afraid I'll bite you."

I snorted. "I know you bite."

He flashed his fangs, making my point. "Only if you ask me nicely."

I rolled my eyes but allowed myself to smirk. It wasn't exactly a smile, but it was something. It felt strange to banter with him when I felt like I was teetering on the edge of his good graces. The idea of danger thrilled me.

Service was held in a chamber set off from the Great Hall. It shared the same glass walls as the Hall, but instead of clear, it was all pink. It was like looking at a church through rose-colored glasses. There were pews and an alter with the amorinis' symbol of two cupped hands with an arrow at their center lofted below the ceiling.

On the stage stood an amorini. At his feet were a man and woman. All three were naked. It looked as if the humans were praying to him. Their knees dug into the hard floor while their faces remained upturned to the demon.

The familiar sounds of sex murmured beneath the low melody playing through the air.

Bishop pulled me into one of the pews at the back of the room. My heart sped up as I followed him down the aisle and noticed the pews were actually beds. We skirted up the side aisle, past entangled couples until we were at the front of the room, where everyone could see us. I could feel the weight of their eyes on me.

I swallowed thickly.

"Relax," Bishop whispered.

It was impossible to relax when I felt so exposed, though I knew we were probably the most clothed people in the room. "That's easy for you to say."

"What about this makes you uncomfortable?"

I turned to him. "Everyone is having sex," I hissed.

"And?"

My brow furrowed while his countenance remained open and patient.

Bishop nodded to the stage. "Look."

The woman had risen to her feet where she was kissing the amorini while the man remained on his knees and was kissing the length of the male's cock. My face was on fire. It was a wonder I didn't burst into flames right then.

"In your world, sex is something so many are made to feel ashamed of. Lust is a sin that your preachers tell you will damn you to Hell. When in fact, sex is and has been one of the most glorified acts of worship. You feel and give with your body, mind, heart, and soul. It is selfless."

"Heart," I said mockingly.

Bishop tipped his head down. "Love is for fools. Lust is for the wise. Lust allows you to explore all the possibilities of the flesh and spirit without being rooted to one person. It gives you power, over others and over yourself. It's freedom."

The amorini knelt on the stage, pushing the woman down with him. His lips were fastened to hers when he pushed his knee between her thighs and the man moved behind him. The man ran his hands over the amorini's hips.

I wanted to look away, and at the same time I couldn't. I was embarrassed, but as Bishop's soft voice whispered in my ear, I wanted to fight it. Why was I embarrassed? Just because this wasn't normal for me didn't make it wrong for them.

The three were still kissing, their hands roaming. A bead of precum dripped from the man's cock onto the amorini's skin. I looked down at my hands as my chest grew tight. Bishop slid his hand between mine. I was keenly aware of how big he was pressed against me. How much stronger and more powerful he was than me. How dangerous he was.

I imagined what it would feel like to have Bishop's hand slide around my throat the way the amorini slid his around the woman's.

I blinked.

Spells, Valen had said. I blinked again through the haze as a woman's soft release filled the air.

"Do you think you have power over me?" I turned to Bishop. "I know you want it, but I wonder, do you think you have it already?"

"Have you ever been worshiped, Ezra?"

His question caught me so off guard I didn't notice his deflection. "Of course not."

Bishop hummed, a deep thrum that reverberated against my core.

"Do not look away," he said.

"Bishop," I started to protest.

"Do it." The command in his voice sent a simultaneous flare of excitement and fear through my veins.

I turned my gaze slowly back to the stage.

I didn't look away when the amorini slid inside the woman and started fucking her. I didn't look away when the man slid into him from behind. Their three bodies pushed and pulled, their skin glistening more as the heat rose in the room.

Something slammed against the back of our pew followed by a low moan.

I didn't look away when Bishop slid his hand up the slit of my dress and pressed his hand to my bare thigh. He might as well have touched me on a more sensitive area because as soon as his heat melted into my skin, I thought I would come undone.

The spell of the service was intoxicating. At some point, the shame of what I was watching left me and I became completely enraptured by the trio on the stage. They had switched positions, the amorini laid on his back while the male sat astride him, his head thrown back and eyes heavy-lidded. The woman straddled the amorini and reached back to slide the man inside of her.

I'd seen porn, but this wasn't that. The way they moved and kissed and touched each other, it was art. I understood what Bishop was trying to show me. It was sexy and beautiful and, though it might be against their laws, the three of them looked entirely in love. Enraptured with each other as their skin grew red and hot with need.

Bishop hadn't moved, but I swore I felt hands moving over my body. Hands that ran through my hair, over my breasts, and slowly, so slowly, traced their way up to my slit. I could feel fingers stroking me through my panties.

I blinked heavily as I tried to catch a glimpse. Bishop's hand remained on my thigh, and his other was somewhere in his lap.

Was this him or part of the service?

The trio had changed positions again. The amorini pulled cuffs that I hadn't noticed were dangling from the ceiling and clasped the man's wrist. Only when he was secured did he enter him from behind. The man grunted, his arms straining against the biting leather. Still on the ground was the woman with her legs spread wide as she dove her fingers in and out of her pussy before them.

"Is this how you worship?" I asked. My voice sounded strange, breathy.

"And how I like to be worshiped." Bishop's pupils were blown out, completely void of their silver light when I looked across at him. His upper lip was slightly puckered, a sign that his fangs had slid free.

I couldn't take my eyes off his mouth. The black line that ran down his throat was calling my name. A small part of me said it was wrong to be here, to be wondering if he would taste as good as last time now that he did not have blood on his tongue.

"Whatever you're thinking, do it," he said.

The invisible hands cupped both of my breasts and squeezed gently. The distinct slapping of flesh grew louder. I turned my head, catching two women astride a man or amorini, I couldn't tell. They were locked at the lips, one sitting on his face and the other over his cock, their hips working furiously.

I looked back to Bishop. Was I worried about something before? Wasn't there something about him I shouldn't forget?

Those full lips parted into a grin. Sharp teeth glistened in the light.

I reached out and ran a finger over his fangs. There was a sharp pain and then a drop of blood welled to the edge of my fingertip. Before I could pull back, Bishop's hand had encircled my wrist. He held my finger out and held my eyes as he swiped his tongue over the drop.

He moved at the same time I did. Our lips crashed together and he had me hoisted and sat on his lap in a single move. I grabbed the back of his head while his broad hand spread over the span of my back.

I kissed my way down the line of his tattoo, leaving red smears in my wake. Bishop tilted his head back, exposing his throat to me while he reached between us and slid his hand between my thighs. There was nothing between us but unbridled need. I ground against him, rubbing against his hard cock straining beneath his pants.

He let out a frustrated sound and shoved his hand between us. I fell against his chest when he pushed his fingers inside of me.

"I knew I could make you drip," he said. "You're such a fucking tease."

"I'm sorry," I said.

"Sorry?" Bishop grabbed the back of my neck and jerked my face into his. His fingers hardened. My mouth went wide when his fingers plunged in and out of me viciously. "Show me how sorry you are. That you would wait so long to let me fuck you."

No words entered my head. There was only terrible pleasure building behind his fingers.

"You don't look sorry." His grip tightened until I was looking at him. Then I was falling into the dark pools that were his eyes.

"I- am," I forced.

While Bishop's fingers continued to punch into me, a vibration of his power moved against my clit in a steady thrum. He felt so good.

"Prove it. Come for me. Come for your cyn," he commanded.

Blinding lights swam behind my eyes. The ringing of silver bells burst in my ears. I came violently and with a scream at the back of my throat that ripped free as I gushed over his hand.

The light shifted to a deep tangerine. I looked around lazily, the stage and its performers coming into view again. They had finished. Their bodies were slick with sweat. The woman's face was covered in cum that the amorini licked off hungrily.

I looked over at Bishop and...

We hadn't moved.

My stomach dropped. The vision had been so elaborate. So real. *What just happened?*

He looked down at me with an arched brow. His hand was still poised on my thigh. "What do you think?"

There was no stain of lipstick on his skin. His hair wasn't mussed where I had run my fingers through it.

I looked back to the stage where another woman was approaching the amorini. She stripped the sheer robe she was wearing. It slid to the floor with a hiss. The amorini's cock twitched as his eyes slid down her full form.

I had just imagined Bishop roughly fingering me to climax. My stomach turned and I felt the horrible burn of bile rise in the back of my throat.

What the fuck *just happened?*

"I think I've seen enough," I said breathlessly.

The room suddenly felt too small and I was too aware that I was soaking wet between my thighs. The lust that filled the room must be doing something, or maybe it was all of the amorini together that was making me feel this way. Whatever it was, I had to get out of there before I did something stupid.

Bishop dipped his head.

We exited the other side so that we walked down the middle aisle. Heads lolled to the side as we passed. The amorini touched their fingers to their lips amidst their pleasures, a sign of respect to their cyn. If my arm had not been hooked with Bishop's I would have bolted.

I rubbed my throat. It felt dry and raw.

I swallowed.

CHAPTER FORTY-SIX: MY VALENTINE

Ezra

I stood in the middle of the arena, the line of the bow pressed against my lips. I let out a slow breath and let my arrow fly. Its whistle echoed through the air, flying like the wind until it struck the dummy's head, 240 yards away. Six arrows in total fanned out like a jagged mask on the mannequin's face; another cluster sprouted from the chest. I was ridiculously good at this. Too bad there was no one around to see it.

I tapped my fingers anxiously over my bow. I should be putting these skills to use.

A strip of skin tore off my lip as I chewed it. Before I could determine if what I was about to do was a good idea, I grabbed a fist of arrows and stuffed them into my quiver.

Just because I couldn't do it before didn't mean I couldn't do it now.

I had nearly worked up the courage to convince myself that I could kill someone who deserved it when I came to an abrupt halt in the Room of Souls. I hadn't expected to find Bishop and Jinn there. They were looking up at the soul ties, pointing at them to select their next pair of victims.

Bishop had been his normal flirty, but arrogant, self since the worship service. I'd been too embarrassed to tell him what I had seen and he hadn't questioned why I had been acting so strange. By strange, I could hardly look him in the eye without picturing the vivid scene we'd committed in my mind and turning three shades darker. He always bore an amused expression like he knew something. I was thankful he never asked me about it.

He'd taught me a few new spells and I'd been able to create two pockets of space where I hurriedly stuffed my bow and arrows before they could see them.

Two twin braids framed his face when he looked down. "To what do we owe the pleasure?" he purred. He twisted a red chord around his index finger as he looked at me with a tilt of his head.

It had been three days and I still couldn't act normal around him. "I was looking for Jinn," I blurted, my eyes snapping to the other male. "To see if you wanted to go hunting."

Jinn arched a brow. "Are you still going to ask me?"

I looked between them, at their leathers and long black bows. It wouldn't be wise to go now, not with both of them. My gaze slid to Bishop. His expression gave nothing away, but I knew he was hoping I would join. He hadn't pursued me harder, but neither had he given up the chase.

Bishop was simply biding his time. Waiting for an invitation.

I knew what he offered, he had all but spelled it out for me the other night, but I wasn't in a hurry to be tossed to the side again. Not so soon after. I was furious at Valen, but fury did not heal the vast wound he had left. The wound that continued to fester the longer he was away. Bishop only complicated things.

"Where are you heading?" I asked instead.

"A little town outside of Tokyo," Jinn answered.

Killing wasn't the answer to my problems. It would only push me closer to the edge of darkness. But I needed to do something. I needed a distraction.

No, going with both of the males, being caught between them when the bloodlust hit, was not a good idea.

I dipped my chin. "Maybe another time." I turned on my heel, focusing on each step so it did not appear that I was running. I didn't know what I was doing. What I was trying to do. I was numb and angry.

It felt like I was being torn in multiple directions.

I was angry all of the time. So fucking bitter that food no longer held its flavor against my tongue.

Angels truly are made of pain and agony.

A warm flow of air brushed against my backside before I felt the touch to my shoulder. I turned and looked up at Bishop.

"Come with us," he said.

For a brief moment, I considered giving in. Giving Bishop what he wanted so that I might forget what Valen had done to me for a few minutes. Perhaps it would chase away the ache within my bones.

Involuntarily, my eyes dropped to his mouth. A slight quirk tugged his full lips into a hopeful smirk.

"Another time," I said. I met his eyes, silver and electric. "But if you aren't back too late," I shot a glance at Jinn, "maybe we can get a drink."

I could feel Jinn staring at us as I met Bishop's eyes again. The weight of his question bore into me. Why him? Why had I gone to seek Jinn? What game was I playing?

I don't know, I wanted to say. Perhaps it was the danger they both offered that excited me.

"We won't be gone for more than a couple of hours," Bishop said. He tugged at my braid. "Don't start without us."

I smiled, a genuine one this time, though it was soft. "Better be quick about it then." I threw another look at Jinn before leaving. My heart hammered in my chest as I made my way to the closest trove I could find. I was playing with fire.

I wondered if I would be able to withstand Bishop's burn.

Lane wriggled in Andras's lap as he whispered something against her ear. She snorted, covering her mouth before she wriggled again.

Andras wrapped his arms around her waist and pulled her against his chest.

"Andras," she hissed.

"Get a room," I said.

Lane rolled her eyes. She pushed Andras's arms down and leaned across to me. "I'm glad you decided to come out tonight. I was getting worried."

I was still angry with her, but after she found me sobbing in my room one night, I felt a little less resentful. She finally told me what happened. Valen had cast her out of Vélos after finding her and Diriel entangled in each other's arms, sweet words passing between their lips.

"I fell in love with Diriel. He said he loved me." She had looked pained then, as if mentioning it had brought her right back to the moment. "Valen brought me within an inch of my life. Baal had asked of me and Valen stopped denying him and sent me off. He thought Baal would kill me, like they do with the rest of the harem sent to Eurynomos. The amorini can love, they just choose not to."

I ran a hand over my face. "You think Valen was lying?"

Lane bite her lip. "Not necessarily. I think it was a game to him.

I thought he did care for you, could have sworn a blind man could see it but...Valentine is his real name. Don't tell anyone I told you that because it'll be my head. He has done it before, letting humans fall in love with him and then killing them. You're just lucky you're an asset to the Fallen."

Valentine. A stupid fucking name for a stupid fucking male. It reminded me of the way he had described Eros. Childish and insolent. A cruel, wicked cyn.

"There are far worse you could have fallen into bed with," Andras said. "Valen isn't all bad. He helped you come into your power. Hell, without him you might be dead."

I snorted. Letting Ariel kill me would have been a favor.

"What are they doing here?" Lane asked, her voice tight.

I followed her gaze to the entrance where Raum and Orias stood. Raum ducked his head as he walked down the steps into the trove, Orias behind him. Atticus followed.

"Speak of the devil and he shall show his face," Andras said. I could feel him looking at me.

My heart stopped.

Valen walked in next, clipping close to the back of Atticus's heels.

"Shit," Lane whispered. "We can go. Come on, Andras. Let's all go to Devil's Maw or back to the tyre. We can watch a show."

I couldn't take my eyes off Valen as he passed through the room. My heart was beating again, so fast I thought it would explode out of my chest. I felt like I was going to be sick.

Valen looked the same but different. His hair had grown longer, the curls reaching the top of his shoulders. The sides were braided and twisted back with leather. But it was his face that drew the harsh difference. He looked aged and worn. More brutal.

A warm hand grabbed my shoulder. I flinched.

Andras squeezed. "Let's go," he said. "Unless you want him to see you like this."

I slapped his hand away and stood. I didn't want to run. I had every right to be here. But seeing him made my legs weak. It brought up every moment between us until the last one.

The four males invaded one of the cubbies across from us. Two women entered not long after, their bodies clad in sheer periwinkle fabrics. I couldn't take my eyes off them. Not even when the woman with long dark hair straddled Valen's lap.

"Let's go," I snapped. I couldn't watch but neither could I look away.

"Andras, you go out first. We can slip out behind you," Lane said. She threaded her fingers with mine, squeezing tight.

Hot tears burned the back of my eyes.

Valen was kissing Orias. His hand was wrapped around the larger male's throat as the woman grinded against him.

All the hurt heated within me. I cast a glance about the room, briefly noting how many people occupied the trove. A lot of people would die if I let my rage unfurl.

The woman stripped off her top. Valen broke his kiss from Orias to lean toward her as she lifted her breasts to his face.

I rushed out of the trove as the first traces of fire caught hold of my skin. Everything was a blur as I jogged down the street.

I blacked out. I must have. One second, I was running and the next, I was bent over trying to catch my breath, my throat raw like I had been screaming.

Andras and Lane weren't anywhere to be found.

I stumbled to the side, turning slowly to gather my surroundings. I had a memory that Valen might have seen me as he looked over the woman's shoulder. There had been surprise in his eyes.

I pressed a hand to my head.

"They said I might find you out here."

I gritted my teeth. "Not now," I snapped. I started moving. As long as I was moving, I would be fine. And in the direction far away from Valen.

Bishop's warmth enveloped me as he circled in front of me, cutting me off. He took one look at me and smirked. "I suppose you're not still up for that drink tonight."

I opened my mouth to fire something back. I had nothing. I was drained. The heat on my tongue had fizzled out.

Bishop frowned. "Let me escort you back to your room," he said softly.

"I don't need your pity." I made a move to shove past him but Bishop grabbed my arms and jerked me in front of him again.

"You don't have it. I know what happened," he said.

I stiffened. Bishop was supposed to be the worst. Valen would play with his victims; Bishop just enjoyed killing them.

"I don't expect your feelings to fade overnight. It's going to take longer for your angelic blood to overpower your humanity. I told you before that I want to help you."

His thumb stroked my arm. I hadn't seen this side of Bishop. Still cool but oddly soft. It made the hurt shift inside of me. I took a deep breath in an attempt to hold it together. I wouldn't let him see me cry.

"Let's go." Bishop didn't give me a choice as he slid his arm around my waist and guided me back to the tyre. He told me about their hunt, asked if I had ever seen Tokyo. When I said no, he described it to me, that for a place on Earth it was interesting with the neon lights and fast cars.

As we reached the front entrance, Bishop turned me in the opposite direction of my room.

"Where are we going?" I'd been through this wing, but truthfully, I had never explored it.

"Valen has guests tonight. I didn't think you would want to be privy to that."

What I had seen had made me sick. But the thought of him fucking someone else made me even more sick.

"Amorini are not monogamous," Bishop once told me.

Maybe Valen had been with other people before and I had been too blind to see it.

Bishop opened a black door that swung into a large room of eccentric decor. Like most of the rooms, there was a fireplace, large windows, and Victorian furniture. But this one had a different flare, more menacing yet inviting. It didn't make sense.

In the next room was a glimpse of a large bed.

"You can stay here tonight. I have other business to attend to this evening, so I won't be here." I turned to find him watching me. "There's a cabinet full of liquor and blood over there," he jutted his chin. "Help yourself to anything you want."

I scrunched my nose at the mention of blood. I was still refusing that, despite the lingering craving I got for Ariel's blood now and again. "Is this your final ploy to get me into your bed?"

Bishop smirked. "Can I not show you kindness?" When I didn't respond, he rolled his eyes. "Of course I want you in my bed, Ezra, but as I said, I won't be here. It's comfortable. Take advantage of it. This offer doesn't come along often."

I smirked. The offer had been on the table the entire time.

"Where will you be?"

"I have a meeting with Raum." He waved his fingers in the direction of the liquor cabinet. "Make yourself at home."

"You know Raum knows about me, right? About the Hymn?"

Bishop nodded. "It is why I am meeting with him. To prevent any interference from Eurynomos when it comes to you. Things have changed between us, but your safety comes first."

The fact that he still considered my feelings at all when he spoke of the war and the Hymn spoke volumes. Bishop had always been harsh, but at least he was honest. With Bishop, what you saw was what you got.

I reached for him as he turned. Bishop's fingertips locked with mine before our fingers intertwined. An electric current thrummed between our palms.

"Thank you," I said softly.

Bishop hesitated then leaned forward and pressed a kiss to the top of my head. "That's what friends are for," he said. He let my hand go before walking out the door.

CHAPTER FORTY-SEVEN: BURN IN HEAVEN

Ezra

Comfortable was a fucking understatement. Bishop's bed was the most luxurious and ludicrous thing I had ever been in. Twenty people would have easily fit in it. I took a sip of wine and set it carefully on the end table. I shimmied out of my boots and pants. I crawled between the sheets, to the middle of the bed, and flopped down with a loud "umph".

It smelled of him. Of course it did, but his smell on the sheets was overpowering. Divine. It heated my blood. Bishop was like a summer thunderstorm in the mountains. The scent had always made my mouth water.

I wondered if this was another one of Bishop's charms to try and tempt me into his bed… I guess it had worked.

How many other women had he lured here? I immediately pushed the thought away. That was a path I did not want to go down. Besides, it didn't matter. I didn't like him. He was a fuckboy. Women would kill to have Bishop look at them the way he looked at me.

The way Valen used to look at me.

I scoffed and crawled back to the edge of the bed, snatching the glass off the table.

I finished that drink and then I had two more.

The sound of running water woke me. I shifted, leaning up on my elbows as I looked around. Where the hell was I?

It hit me all at once and I froze. Bishop was in the shower and I was still in his bed. It was my plan to wake up early and sneak out before he returned. When you lose track of how many drinks you've had, it makes it easier to sleep in.

"Shit," I hissed. I was halfway to the side of the bed to get my clothes when the door to my right opened.

"You snore like a cerebos, you know that?" Bishop walked out with a towel around his waist, another he wrung his long hair with.

Bishop was sin in physical form. His tattoo *did* go all the way down his leg. And the line on his mouth I imagined went all the way down too. His flesh glistened as steam rose off its surface.

"A wha–? I do not!" I hurled a pillow at him for comparing me to the three-headed demon dogs that ran wild in the hills. And to hide that I had been staring.

He dodged it, his broad white teeth flashing as he smiled. "You do. I could hear you down the hallway when I came in."

I rolled my eyes and hopped off the bed, snatching my pants from the floor.

"Well, you were right, your bed is comfortable." I pulled my jeans on.

"You're welcome to use it again."

"Another meeting?" I raked my hand through my hair. Ashes, I hated the way he was looking at me. Where were my boots?

"No more meetings. Not for a while," he said.

I did roll my eyes at that. "So, you'd be in it this time."

"Is that such a bad thing?" He tossed the towel to the side. His black hair was long and thick. Wet, it fell in soft waves over his chest.

"Help me find my boots." I crouched to look under the bed. Had I kicked them under there? "Aren't you teaching me new spells today?"

I jumped when he approached me. He slid his finger into the air beside my head and pulled out my muddy hiking boots. "I'm going to teach you how to use the pockets around you. How to store items and pull from your inventory."

He held the boots by their laces in front of me.

A sharp wave of heat hit me, but this time it didn't come from him. He wasn't touching me, so I knew he wasn't influencing me either. For the first time, I noticed how attractive Bishop was. The black of his tattoos and hair was stark against his pale skin. It was beautiful. *He* was beautiful, sexy even, if you forgot how arrogant he could be.

I took the boots. "You and your games."

He grinned. "Go freshen up. I'll come get you and then Diriel can have you after that."

I slid past him and turned before giving him a mocking bow. "Yes, Your Majesty."

Bishop's eyes smoldered. "I do love to hear those words on your lips." He reached down to the towel at his waist, but I was already walking out the door by the time I heard it fall to the floor.

I shook my hands as I walked back to my room in an attempt to shake off the nervous jitters working their way through me. "Ezra, you're angry and hurt and fucking confused. Don't even think about it." The fact that I was even considering giving into Bishop's desires was insanity. But isn't that what you do when you have a broken heart? You find the worst, sexiest thing and make a shit ton of mistakes with them.

"Think about what?"

My blood froze. Valen leaned against a tall column. His arms were folded across his broad chest. His eyes blazed like wildfires.

"None of your business," I snapped. I kept walking. My façade was crumbling. I hadn't expected to see him, but I knew there was a chance I could run into him; this was his hall too. Seeing him gutted me.

"You are my business," he said, trailing behind me.

No the fuck I'm not.

"Where were you last night?"

"I'm surprised you noticed I was missing. What with you being gone two months and your face in some bitch's tits." *Stupid. Now he* knows *you're still hurting.*

"Hmm," he hummed, stepping in front of me to block access to my room. "Jealous?"

Yes.

Stubble had grown across his face. There was a new scar on the underside of his eye. That and the one on his palm from the angel's sword were the only ones that stood out. I knew his body was lined with more. He looked the same but different.

"No, actually. I feel sorry for her. For both of you. Now if you'll move, I have to get ready."

He slid to the side as I stepped forward. My skin was on fire at the thought of brushing against him, my stomach in knots. But he didn't touch me. I heard his inhale as I walked by, cursed the chills that broke over my skin because of it.

"I told you to stay away from him." Venom trickled into his voice.

A harsh, broken laugh burst from my lips. "I don't give a fuck what you think. Especially when *you* get to fuck whoever you want," I gritted. I tossed the door behind me.

"You fucked him?"

"Maybe." Let his imagination run wild. Let it devour any peace he had and rot his sanity.

"You still belong to me," he growled.

I whirled on him, catching the door before it could close. "I don't belong to anyone, but most definitely not you. All you've done is ruin my life. You had your fun, but it's over now."

"I get to ruin you however I see fit, Ezra. My time away from you has only whet my appetite." He leaned against the door jam, his face cool and menacing. This wasn't the Valen I had grown to know. This was the demon beneath, vile and wicked. The one that had rescued me in the water and then left me in darkness. His eyes dropped to my chest. "I bet I could reach for your heart right now and you'd let me take it."

Turmoil raced upward. Ashes split in the air around me.

"Burn in Heaven," I said and slammed the door in his face. I took three long strides into the middle of the room and clenched my fists while I told myself not to cry.

CHAPTER FORTY-EIGHT: ON MY HONOR

Raguel

Kaza, The Second Circle of Heaven

Screams battered through the speakers. There were so many voices that it sounded like white noise or light rain hissing through the orbs. Their shelled appearance twisted back and forth as the cries of terror came again and again.

The screens flashed with macabre. Blood and black pollution touched nearly every corner of the world. It was spreading quickly, moving through the veins of the land like an unfettered wildfire. It was in the water, the crops, the animals.

It burst along flesh in the shape of yellow-filled boils. It blinded eyes with small scales crusted over like sand.

The screams were the worst of it. The abruptness of it as it scattered across the earth. The sudden bursts of air ripped from the human's lungs when panic ensued and gunfire followed. The wailing of children whose parents were suddenly snatched by death. Or the parents who found their sons and daughters lying dead in the street with no apparent cause.

It was madness. The amount of horror… There had never been anything like it.

It.

Raguel didn't know what it was. It was as if sin had been made a soul and was wreaking havoc like a raging dragon among those who did not bend. But even that did not suffice because those who were lost were felled in kind.

Raguel watched as the bees fell from the sky. Then the birds. Watched as the cattle and crops withered to dust. The beasts of the oceans turned their bellies to the sky, turning the dark blue waters red.

His nostrils flared as he looked at every pixel down to the mili-dots that made up someone's pore. Where was it coming from?

He felt the counsel judging him. Sabriel and Gabriel at their head, waiting for an explanation that would never come.

"You found nothing and this is the result," Sabriel said.

Raguel's eyes shifted to the large male.

Sabriel gleamed gold, his skin more ornate than many of the angels within the seven circles of Heaven. His hair was so red it looked like a polished black stone. The gems of his eyes flickered, roving over Raguel as if Tartarus's overseer were hiding something.

"A rumor of a nephilim, that is all," Raguel reiterated for the third time. His jaw ached from clenching so long.

"Perhaps one lives," Sabriel's counterpart said. Gabriel drummed his long fingers over the arm of his seat. He cocked his head, looking at the screens.

"I was beside you when we slaughtered them and their kin. The demons were cursed to be sure their offspring would never rise again. It is not possible for one to exist," Raguel said.

"Then what is the cause of this?" Sabriel threw his hand out to the screens. He thought he was so high and mighty up there on his throne, looking down on everyone as if he were a cyn.

"I have not found its source yet. But I will." He had tried to explain that the poison mimicked the rot of Tartarus, but that was out of the question. Tartarus didn't have that kind of power, Sabriel commented. Exactly, Raguel had said. But skeptic as he was, what else could it possibly be? Not even he believed it to be entirely true, so why would the others?

Raguel was one body; he could not be everywhere at once. And the Fallen were clever. Perhaps they had found a way to bleed into humanity.

"I want you to go to Michigan," Sabriel said. "There is a girl I want you to find."

Raguel's brow furrowed. "A girl?" What did a girl matter when the entire world was falling apart? "Do you believe she has something to do with this?"

"It is not your place to question me," Sabriel quipped.

Raguel pressed his tongue to the inside of his cheek. It wasn't his place to challenge the hierarchy. But he didn't want to go on another goose chase and return empty handed.

"She could be the nephilim everyone is talking about," Gabriel said.

Raguel openly balked. "Women cannot bear our power," he started.

"Leah Jo Corrine. You are to find her; ensure she is alive and safe and then report back to me. From there, I will figure out what to do with you."

Raguel's teeth scraped together. *Why don't you go have a look yourself?* he wanted to bark at them. How was he supposed to lead his men when they gave him nothing to go on? Was she a nephilim? Had something changed in the laws to allow such an abomination?

"On my honor, Sabriel." Raguel placed an open palm to his chest. A sign of respect to those of higher power. The only difference between Raguel and Sabriel's power was the distance of space between them. Raguel took pride in upholding the Maker's laws and ordains, but something about the archangel Sabriel had always rubbed him wrong.

Maybe it was because he thought he could handle the position better. Or, perhaps, it was simply because he didn't care for the male's holy arrogance.

Raguel had challenged the male before. Sabriel had only smiled.

The doors to the council chamber were nothing more than dark beams of light that blocked out sound to the outside corridor. A twinge of energy ruffled his feathers as Raguel past through the lights. He strode down the white walkway, his feet not making a sound but the breath of his lungs sent an echo in his path.

Another beam of light and he was before his men. He jerked his chin to the guards standing before them, their lasses, a heavy weapon that mimicked a broadax, stood tall at their backs like menacing banners. The smaller blade on the back curved into the shape of a crescent moon.

Raguel's gaze skimmed over his flock. Gladr, Torah, Calix, Ramiel, Uriel. Six. His flock had dwindled to six as punishment for having not prevented the rot of Earth. For not knowing what evaded the entire realm. It only further solidified his growing fear that whatever this was came from Tartarus. For it was the underworld that he oversaw, not the empire of men.

The archangel strode through the clouds, letting his flock trail behind him. He would go to Michigan, but he would do it on his terms.

Kaza was one of the main cities in the second circle of Heaven. The first was where the Trinity resided, overseeing everything below His eye. But Kaza acted as the first circle, dealing out orders, fulfilling prayers, and executing judgement.

It was a vast land of knowledge and wealth. The Golden City, some called it. In the distance, hiivas burst across the sky. The light tendrils dancing amongst the clouds like fireworks. This was no time to celebrate. Perhaps another world had been created and was a success, but Earth was falling.

"Ramiel," Raguel called.

The seraph lengthened his stride until he was at his shoulder.

"You want to prove yourself." It wasn't a question.

"I do," Ramiel said.

"You and Calix stay behind and find what you can on a Leah Jo Corrine. She's a human on Earth."

"And where will you go?"

Raguel smirked at the edge in his voice. It was the same tone he had just used with Sabriel.

"I am going to find her. I am to assure she is well, nothing else." He stopped walking, turning to Ramiel. "I want you to figure out why."

Ramiel's lip curled. "We should be going back to Tartarus, not searching for some child on a dying planet."

Raguel nodded. "You and I finally agree on something. Find what you can and, when I return, we will do just that." He looked at the other three. "The rest of you are with me."

A bleed slid through the air before Raguel. He stepped through, leaving enough space so the others could follow him through. It might be a mistake sending Ramiel after the information he sought. It was a risk to trust an angel on the edge of falling. But Raguel had faith. If he didn't, who else would?

CHAPTER FORTY-NINE: PLAY DIRTY

Ezra

Valen wasn't even looking at me. Hadn't looked at me all night. And I would know because I couldn't keep my eyes off him.

I'd found my way back to *Crave*. I was becoming a regular. A regular who didn't partake in any of the extracurricular activities. As far as troves went, it was the nicest. *Devil's Maw* was more of a dive bar, but no one visited there. Everyone liked to come to the trove with the bright red walls that moved with lithe bodies to sultry music. I shouldn't have continued my trips to the trove, but drinking was about the only thing keeping me sane. It dulled the ache constantly rolling through my veins.

A woman with bronze skin and satin black hair sat beside Valen. She had full lips and a small, sharp nose. And her body was one Aphrodite would have killed for, with plush soft curves that Valen couldn't keep his hands off. It was the same woman from the other night.

I looked away. Is that what he liked? I wasn't short in the department of curves, but I was nothing like the woman leaning into him now. Nor did I have her stark beauty. I'd been told I looked odd on

Earth, still pretty but odd. Like there wasn't something quite right about my face and height.

Perhaps I was just as strange to Valen's appetite and that was why he had discarded me.

Jealousy's iron flame flicked against my chest. I'd been an idiot to think he had genuinely cared about me. And why would he? He was thousands of years old where people like me would be nothing more than a memory in his lifespan. A blip, as he had once said.

Still, I thought I had been special to him. I thought I'd been more than a tool to wield.

I took a long drink from my glass, looking anywhere but Valen when the woman shifted into his lap. My gaze drifted across the room, sliding across Jinn and Bishop who were in conversation.

Bishop looked right back at me.

I held his gaze for another two seconds before I slowly continued my span of the room. My heart hammered. "You're playing with fire," Valen had once told me.

I had learned to love the feel of a fire burning against my skin. I let the flames dance over and between my fingers. I only tested my silver flames in private. I didn't want anyone to know that I still had access to them. It wasn't the force in which Bishop tried to have me wield them, but it was something.

I hadn't been able to hold onto Prometheus. Any time it made an appearance, it was gone within the next blink. Sometimes I wondered if I imagined it coming back at all.

I let a sliver of silver leak into the orange glow as I contemplated what it would be like to be burned by Bishop. He had done a good job of getting under my skin.

Friends. I smirked. I had guy friends and I knew guys who wanted to be "friends". Bishop couldn't fool me. But that was part of the fun. He hadn't hidden his nature. Hadn't tried to spare my feelings in discussions that might upset me. Bishop was real.

I took another drink and, when I looked back, Bishop wasn't looking at me, but he had a smirk on his face that said he saw right through me.

The loud scrape of a chair skidded beside me. Andras plopped down, pulling the decanter from my table to his side.

"It's wine," I said.

He arched his brow. "Am I not allowed to drink it?"

"No... I... Don't you drink blood?"

Andras arched his brow. "I do, but I also enjoy drinking alcohol when I am in dire need of it."

You and me both, I thought.

I held out my glass for a refill. Andras cracked a smile. "You know, our drinks are not the same. You might be a nephilim, but enough of this will still knock you on your ass."

"That's the point." I waggled the glass.

I felt the pressure of being watched and looked up to find Bishop's gaze settling over me again. He answered Jinn, not taking his eyes off me.

A swirl of heat ran through my core. I had slept in his bed the last three nights. He hadn't made a move, hadn't even slept in the bed with me, but I knew he was waiting. I had an open heart that was still bleeding. He was the shark circling, waiting for me to tire.

I don't know why he wanted me other than maybe I presented a challenge. I had seen him with multiple women. Men too. I'd even seen him with the one Valen currently had his teeth in, gnawing at her neck.

Fuck, my stomach was in knots. Why was I doing this to myself?

I took another drink.

I wasn't going to be another notch in a belt. Not to another one of them.

"I can smell your jealousy from here," Andras said.

"You're sitting right next to me," I countered. "And I'm not jealous."

"Really? Because Valen was all over you before and now that he's not, you seem a little sore about it."

"Drop it," I said.

Andras chuckled. "Don't get mad at me. If you want to get back at him, you're going to have to play dirty."

"Dirty how?" I asked, turning to him.

"Well, you could make out with me and see where the night takes us." He laughed halfway through as I rolled my eyes. "Am I that unappealing?"

"None of you are unappealing and you know it. Besides, I don't mess with guys my friends have been with. And getting back at him by hooking up with someone else is the last thing I want to do."

"Why?" Andras asked.

"What?"

"Why?" he repeated. He cocked his head. "Sex is our religion. You know how we worship. You're one of us now." He nudged his glass into the air. "You should partake in it."

I rolled my eyes. "I've been to one of your services and I have no desire to go back."

Before I could elaborate, he said, "If you don't want me in your bed, then maybe you should take advantage of the male's you've been sleeping in."

"Andras," I hissed.

He shrugged. "It's not exactly a secret. I'm just surprised he hasn't fucked some sense into you yet. And I know he hasn't because you wouldn't be pining."

I scowled at him. "I thought Valen was your friend. Aren't you supposed to be on his side?"

"He is my friend, but so are you. And your mood swings annoy me. Do something about them and forget him."

I scoffed into my glass. Andras had been the most carefree I had seen him this last week. With the other courts in discussion with what to do about me, he wasn't exactly needed outside of Vélos.

I glanced across to Valen and found his eyes turning from me just before the woman kissed him, capturing his attention.

My face scorched. Why was I sitting here torturing myself?

"Do it," Andras said.

"You're as bad as Lane," I scolded.

He chuckled. "Who do you think I learned it from?" Andras leaned in, lowering his voice. "You don't even have to do anything with Bishop, but leaving here with him will get a response. We have heard you've been staying with him, but no one has seen it. I know Valen. I don't know what is up his ass, but he has never been as captured as he is by you. So, if you want his attention, get Bishop's."

"Getting Bishop's attention isn't the problem," I murmured. I watched a couple of dancers twirl on the floor in front of us. I could feel Bishop looking at me. He deserved an award for his patience.

I looked up as Diriel approached. He waved off one of the servers that approached. He pulled out the seat to Andras's left but paused when he looked at me. "Am I interrupting?"

"If you consider Andras trying to convince me to bed Bishop to get back at Valen important," I answered.

Diriel's eyes widened. "Don't do that." He whipped his head to Andras. "That is terrible advice."

The emissary shrugged. "I think it's perfectly reasonable considering he looks like he is about to take Sarah over the table." Andras nodded in their direction. I couldn't look. I knew it was only going to get worse. "She might as well get even. That is, unless you're volunteering." He leaned back to look at Diriel. "She already turned me down."

"If anyone were to even touch Ezra, Valen would lose his head," Diriel said.

I set my glass down. "Hold on. So, he gets to do whatever he wants but if I do it, he is going to have a problem?" *Oh hell no.*

Diriel's brow furrowed and Andras grinned.

"Double standards," Andras said. "And Valen contending with Bishop would be something I'd like to see again."

"You're an idiot," Diriel hissed to the rogue. "Them contending is what got us into this mess."

"I'm bored. This little lovers' quarrel is the most fun I've had in weeks." Andras winked at me.

Diriel ignored him. To me he said, "It's not like that."

"That's exactly what it is." I risked glancing over again and, sure enough, Valen's face was buried in the woman's neck, blood running between the cut of her breasts. Her hips moved against him.

No way was I going to let him rule me while he got to do whatever he wanted. I turned my attention across the room, to Bishop. His head was tilted back, his eyes half lidded as he looked up at a woman propositioning herself. I let a subtle wave of my power skirt across the room.

He turned and I flashed him a smile.

If I knew him as well as I thought I did, he would see it as the invitation it was. There was no other alternative. I traced my lower lip, remembering the way he had caught it between his teeth the first time he kissed me. "Finally," he had said.

I was going to give Bishop exactly what he wanted.

Another ten minutes went by and, when Bishop still didn't come to me, I decided to leave. I certainly wasn't going to go to him, and I was done torturing myself with Valen.

"I'm going to bed," I told the males.

Diriel looked up at me as I stood, his face twisting in what could only be described as pity.

"Let one of us walk with you," he said.

"I'm fine."

"You drank as much as I did, and I know you were drinking before I sat down," Andras countered.

I wasn't going to admit that I had drunk more than I could handle. It didn't matter when I was going to crash as soon as my head hit the pillow. I winced. If Bishop wasn't going to approach me, I supposed that meant I needed to go back to my own room.

It would be fine. I would be able to sleep through whatever ruckus Valen caused.

I hoped.

"No. Thank you." I leaned forward and kissed him on the top of his head. I paused. He paused. "I'm fine," I said at his confusion. My face flushed and I ducked my head from Diriel's questioning look and turned right into a wall of muscle.

Strong hands caught me around the shoulders.

Bishop let me go as soon as I was stable enough to stand without swaying. Which I only managed when I leaned my hip into the chair.

"Are you leaving?" he asked, his eyes dancing.

"No," Diriel said at the same time I said, "Yes."

The cyn looked between us and then to the empty wine glass

behind me. "I was coming to join you, but I won't keep you if you're turning in for the night."

Blazing, irrefutable anger struck me across the back of the head like a mental slap. Bishop must have felt it too because even he flinched. He looked past me, and I followed his eyes to Valen. Sarah was still kissing him and yet his eyes were focused on me.

It was the only thing I needed to spur me into making what was probably the worst decision of my life. Or maybe the best.

"I'm not tired," I said.

The blatant invitation brought heat to the silver of his eyes, turning them to dark chrome. "I know a place," he said.

Andras hissed. He rubbed the side of his head. "Actually, Ezra." But I didn't stick around to hear what he had to say. I didn't want to hear another one of Diriel's protests.

I slipped my arm through Bishop's and let him lead me back to his room.

CHAPTER FIFTY: BEST FRIENDS

Ezra

The door clicking behind us felt like a lock sliding into a latch. Bishop leaned against the door, assessing me like a predator.

"What do you want, Ezra?"

I crossed the room to the liquor cabinet. "Another drink to start." I pulled out two glasses, but as I reached for one of the decanters, he laid his hand over mine and moved it to another. I swallowed and grabbed the neck, pouring whatever it was into the scotch glasses.

"What else?" he said, his voice a hiss as he took one of the glasses from me.

"I want what you want," I said. "To be friends."

Bishop smirked as he sat on the lounge. "Friends?" There was an eerie reflection in his eye as the fire from the hearth danced across his face.

"Best friends."

Mischief gleamed in his eyes. Ashes, he was beautiful. Why had I never paid him attention before?

"Are there any advantages to being *best* friends?"

I ran my tongue over my lower lip. I really hadn't thought this through, on how I was going to handle him. I thought I had all the cards, but Bishop was already a step ahead of me.

"Maybe." I slid my index finger over the rim of my glass, contemplating. Did I want this with him? It didn't have to be consistent. It could just be for the night.

He cocked his head. "You've been sleeping in my bed, but now you're afraid to sit next to me."

Not a question. I was. I'd already made this mistake with one of them and I was terrified to do it again. I might be dumb, but I wasn't stupid. I had been paying closer attention in court and to the way people treated the cyn than when I first arrived. There might be four crowns in Vélos, but Bishop ruled. Everything would be different with him.

"I'm not like him," he said.

That much had been clear from the beginning. "I never thought you were."

"Do you want to know why?"

I nodded and took a seat beside him.

"Because I am not going to play games with you. None that concern your heart, at least. There will never be any love between us, but there will be passion. I will not toss you to the side like a common whore. You won't be a cyn, but I'll treat you like royalty. How does that sound, princess?"

Direct and honest. "This feels like a transaction."

Bishop shook his head. "I know what I want and what you deserve."

I took a sip of my drink. It was lush and full bodied. I took another drink. I'd never had anything like it. It had a flavor to it I couldn't place, had probably never tasted before in my human life.

My eyes narrowed. "You kill people for falling in love. Is it because I'm a nephilim that you haven't killed me? Why you still haven't punished me?"

Bishop slid a broad hand over my thigh. "I already told you. You're young and I want to teach you our ways. I'm a forgiving man, Ezra, and I see a world of potential in you."

"How kind of you."

His fangs slid free when he smiled. "Would you like to see how kind I can be?" I focused on his mouth. On the tattoo that ran across his lip. To the slow circles his thumb made on my thigh.

As enticing as he was, something stilled within me. The glint in his eyes told me that if I went all the way with Bishop, I would never truly be free of him. I could see the desire to conquer, to possess. I'd known men like him all my life.

But I wanted to feel something I knew only he could give me. He could dull the ache in my heart and maybe then I could begin to heal.

"Yes," I said. "But just a taste."

Bishop's eyes darkened as he cocked his head. "I'm a hungry man." A slow smile spread across his beautiful face.

I clinked my glass against his and prayed he didn't see the way my hand shook. "You'll have to learn to pace yourself." I pressed the rim of the glass to my lips, catching another whiff of the heady substance.

Bishop fingered the bottom of the glass and pushed up, tipping it back so that I had to drink. As the lush liquid pooled into my mouth, I realized what it was too late. My eyes went wide even as I swallowed it, emptying out the glass entirely.

"Delicious, isn't it? It's not quite as good as an angel's, but it satisfies the hunger all the same."

My head buzzed with thickness; my senses clouded. I watched in slow motion as he took the glass from me and leaned forward.

Watched as I slipped out of my body and tipped my face up to his, to the blood that waited behind his teeth from the sip he had just taken.

I watched in horror as he pressed his mouth to mine and fed me that blood and slid his tongue into my mouth, encouraging me to swallow.

The whole experience was out of body and yet I felt his skin on mine. Heat pooled into my stomach as soon as his lips explored mine. A haze came over me and I leaned into him, kissing him back. I let him suck my tongue into his mouth.

I slid my hands through his hair and pushed him back to straddle him. He grabbed my ass, pulling me hard against his hips as his mouth assaulted mine.

The sliver of me that looked from afar was screaming. "Don't," she shouted. I shut my eyes, ignoring her and savoring the way he touched me, the way he kissed me. Bishop was different. It was not a pleasant experience and yet I could not stop as our kisses grew more urgent.

"I'll not be satisfied with a taste," he huffed against my mouth. He pulled my hips forward and back as he worked me over his hard cock.

The buzzing intensified to a sharp ringing in my ears. Something about this was supposed to be wrong and yet I melted against him. The heat in my stomach simmered between my thighs and I ground against him of my own will.

Bishop's hands snaked beneath my shirt. The feel of his fingertips against my skin was razor sharp. As soon as I was free of mine, I pulled his shirt off. I traced the small, detailed lines of his tattoos with my nails. It was even more fascinating up close. The twists of knots and hieroglyphics were entangled within the geometric symbols.

"Beautiful," I said.

"You are."

I met his devilish grin with one of my own. I traced the line on his lip down with my finger, sliding it down his abdomen to the waistband of his pants. Bishop was cut like fine marble, his skin so pale he didn't seem real.

Valen was like that, dark sculpted muscle of lethality. My brow furrowed at the thought of him. Bishop must have sensed it because he took the opportunity to kiss me again. I leaned into his mouth and let him chase all thoughts of Valen away.

Something slithered up my leg and wrapped around my calf. It tightened with the grip of a snake. I broke our kiss to look back... at the black leather bind wrapped around my leg. The end of it had a sharp, hooked end that glistened like the head of a knife.

Bishop purred against my throat. "I'm going to show you what it's like to be with a demon."

I noticed the other subtle changes then. How his nails had turned into talons, and his fingers were longer, darker.

I crashed back into my body as I realized what was about to happen.

I stared numbly at the hand on my bicep as he licked the slope of my neck. I turned my head down again as the tail tightened and it coiled its way up to the middle of my thigh. This was wrong. Not just at him changing, but what we were doing.

A sharp sting bit into my neck. And just like that, I was sucked back into his warmth, into the haze of the lust boiling in his blood. I leaned into his bite, his claws and tail forgotten.

A whoosh of air swept through the room. Bishop's head snapped up. Crimson blood coated his lips as he looked behind me.

"I was hoping you'd join us."

Jinn stood in the entryway, his nostrils flaring at the sight before him. That's all I saw before the room spun and I fell against Bishop's chest. I clung to him as his hand slid up my back, the other beneath my bra to cup my breast. The room melted together.

My gosh, the incessant ringing wouldn't stop.

I reached between us to unfasten his pants. I needed to be closer to him. I needed to feel him inside of me. Bishop lifted his hips to assist me while simultaneously trying to rip my pants down. It was a difficult task in our position, but I don't think either of us were thinking clearly. Need was the only thing driving us.

"As much as this sight pleases me, there's been an issue," Jinn said hoarsely.

"Let it wait," Bishop groaned. "I think you deserve a taste for your loyalty."

My hand brushed against his large cock straining beneath his undershorts and he let out a deeper groan. I slid down his body and kissed his length still covered in fabric.

"We just received word that emissaries from the other courts will be arriving tomorrow. Atticus has remained in Eurynomos's stead," Jinn said. I watched him from the corner of my eye as I continued kissing Bishop. He looked pained, his pupils blown out and his jaw clenched.

Bishop grabbed my head abruptly and shifted so that I lolled to the side. The ceiling was spinning before me now. Slowly, slowly it wound down, coming back into focus. Bishop's shadow loomed over me, his pants hugging the middle of his hips.

"What?" he snapped. The word shattered through the air like lightning.

Jinn eyed me from the corner of his eye. "It would appear Eurynomos is not satisfied with our prior arrangement."

Bishop ran a hand over his face before muttering a string of dark-language curses. "Where is Atticus?"

"The Noir."

The words had hardly left Jinn's lips before Bishop was striding out of the room, his shirt clenched in his fist as he jerked his pants up. He stopped at the door abruptly. "Make a bond yourself, but do not fuck her until I return." Bishop ran his hand over his chin.

I sat up lazily as the ringing edged in my mind. I pressed a hand to my temple. What the fuck? The room flickered as Bishop disappeared through the door like an apparition.

Jinn stepped in front of me, his tall riding boots glistening. Something warred within him, I could see the fight for control even in my daze. "You're a mess," he said.

I scowled at him. "You're." I hiccuped. "What?"

"And drunk," he said through curled lips. Jinn mumbled something before reaching out. "Can you stand up, at least?"

I pushed his hand off me and tried to stand and swayed, catching myself on the back of the couch. My head felt like it was on fire. I didn't even notice when Jinn pulled me against his side. Chills burst across my skin and I let out a frosty huff.

He was so warm. I hugged closer to him, pressing my cold nose into his chest.

"Fuck," he mumbled. "How much of his blood did he give you?"

I grasped his forearm. "I didn't drink his blood."

"No? Then why are your eyes frosted over. How much blood did you drink?"

I wrapped an arm around his waist to better hold myself up. The rich flavor of the drink still sat heavy on my tongue. "I was drinking with Andras and then..." It *had* been blood Bishop had given me.

But his?

"He bit me," I said.

"Yes," he said. "Come on, let's get you out of here."

Make a bond... Had Bishop just made a link to my mind?

I stumbled against him as he turned us. "I need to go to bed."

"That's where I'm taking you."

I snorted as he led me from Bishop's room, whatever worry I had been stressing over already forgotten. "Oh, so you finally get what you want." I tripped over my feet and stumbled into his side again.

"I hate to disappoint you, but the sordid image you have of me isn't accurate," he said bitterly. There was no warning before Jinn scooped me up and tossed me over his shoulder.

"What are you doing? Put me down!" A cool breeze slid over my back in place of where Bishop's warm –cold– hands had been. My shirt was somewhere discarded on the floor behind us.

"I'm taking you to bed. Your bed," he clarified and jerked the back of my pants up to cover my bare skin.

"I don't want to go to *my* bed."

My stomach churned as I twisted. Jinn's grip hardened on the back of my thigh. Heat slid from his touch into my bones. It dove into the cold that held me in a firm grip.

The room spun again.

I'd been drunk plenty of times, but it felt nothing like this. There was something festering beneath my skin, a deep ache in my core that would not be shaken. Perhaps Bishop had woken something inside of me. Or maybe when he fed me his blood, he had seeded something.

The idea would have been scarier were my mind not fogged.

"Are you going to join me?"

Jinn sucked the back of his teeth. "Let it go, Ezra. I have regretted what I said to you for a long while. And while I do not expect you to forgive me for it, I'm sorry. I'm not joining you. I don't even want you. Not anymore," he added more quietly.

"Why? Is it because I can give you what you want without having to fuck me?"

"Something like that," he grumbled.

"That's not a real answer."

There was a moment of silence as he jogged down a flight of stairs and then back up another set that led to the tower I had been avoiding. I gripped his hips as I sat up, watching the hallway grow farther and farther away, drawing me closer to the one place I didn't want to be.

"No," he said. "I'm going to meet with Bishop to do damage control."

"For the courts?"

"Yes."

"Are they really going to start a war with V—Vélos?" I smacked my lips together as the word stuck to my tongue. The longer Bishop's blood sat in my mouth, the thicker my tongue grew. The flavor was becoming stale.

"If it means getting to you, yes."

I snorted. "So now you're 'Team Ezra' because you don't want anyone else to have me? Typical."

Jinn slapped my ass playfully. "I was always Team Ezra. I just didn't know how to show it before."

I laughed at that. The fit of giggles took over until my stomach hurt. "Ugh, you've got to put me down. This hurts and my head is killing me."

"We're almost there."

"And you weren't team me. You've been team... ass. You're an asshole."

"And you're a brat," he shot back.

There was no force in the punch I slammed into his back.

"Do you have any idea what would have happened had I not interrupted just now?" he said quietly, nearly a whisper.

Obviously, but why did he sound strained about it? I couldn't think straight, though I tried my best to see past the fog in my mind.

"What are you doing?" I would recognize that double-edged threat of a voice anywhere.

I shifted so I could peek around Jinn's arm. Valen was standing at the end of the hall. He looked different upside down. He wasn't as threatening.

"He's taking me to bed," I said with a hiccup. "I'm a big girl, I can walk."

Jinn hoisted me higher, shifting my weight so he could get a better grip on me. I was keenly aware of his broad hand splayed across my upper thigh. How his heat seeped into me was different. They all had the same fire, but each level was different, like it mimicked their power. I thought I felt a tremor in his touch.

"Put her down," Valen growled.

"On second thought, keep me up here, Jinn." I pointed forward and then back toward Valen, to the door he was standing guard in front of. "And take me to my room."

Jinn didn't move. "This is not what it looks like," he said.

"What does it look like?" Valen asked coolly.

Jinn's hand slid up my thigh as he shifted to drop me to my feet. I slid down his front, clinging to his shoulders in case my body decided to collapse in on itself.

"She got drunk and I'm taking her to her room."

"How gentlemanly of you," Valen said.

"Yes, he has turned out to be quite the gentleman, hasn't he?" I tapped the underside of Jinn's jaw. "You had me fooled."

Jinn's green eyes flared. *Stop playing with me*, they said.

"Ezra, come here." The command in Valen's voice awakened something inside of me. I made myself stand straighter even though my head swam.

"No."

Valen's brow arched. A flare of his power swelled in the air.

"Go," Jinn said against my ear. "He is likely to have my head if you don't and I'd very much like to keep it."

"Why don't you go?" I shot back at Valen. "Jinn and I were having a nice chat until you came along and ruined it. No one wants you here."

The flare of power skittered through the shadows. Valen strode forward, smooth as a wolf, head tipped down, muscles bunched. He was ready for a fight.

I didn't give him the opportunity to touch me before I grabbed Jinn's hand and pulled him with me, forcing him to trail behind me as I walked past Valen and into my room. Jinn came to a slamming halt at the doorway. I looked down at my empty hand as he snatched his away.

"I've done what I needed to," he said, running his tongue over his lower lip. "Valen," he said, turning to the male blocking his exit. "You should come too. I expect your insight will be appreciated in light of what will happen tomorrow."

Valen stared at him. I could tell when a private conversation was being had.

I scrutinized Jinn as the fog lifted inside my head. He was behaving as a gentleman and, for the life of me, I could not figure out why.

Anyone in his position and character would have taken advantage of the situation. Yet here he was, trying to protect me.

It's another act, my mind contemplated. *Another ploy to draw you to another one of their sides.*

Maybe.

Valen jerked his chin.

Jinn ran a hand over his fitted green shirt. He looked back at me. "I'll see you tomorrow."

Wait, he was leaving? He was giving up just like that?

I took a step forward as he slid into the shadows, leaving me alone with the last person I wanted to be with.

We stood staring at each other for what felt like an eternity.

Emotions I didn't want to face came surging to the surface. I couldn't look him in the eye without remembering the way they had cut into me when he denied me. It was too much for my fragmented state.

Valen's nostrils flared as he reached out a hand.

"Don't," I said.

He looked at the space between us, a sliver that felt like a canyon. His mouth twisted as he struggled to find the right thing to say. There was nothing that would shorten the distance he had created.

"Did you mean what you said to me in the Styx?" I don't know why I asked. Perhaps I had a sick pleasure for torture.

Valen's eyes lowered when I finally braved to face them. His lashes fluttered as he looked at my body. His eyes darkened as he drank in the red scratches Bishop had left behind.

I'd forgotten I wasn't wearing a shirt, leaving Bishop's markings entirely exposed. The bite on my neck suddenly throbbed.

Valen's jaw clenched. "I thought you were smarter than this."

"Don't deflect with insults. It makes you sound like a narcissist."

Valen's eyes glimmered when he finally met my glare.

"You don't get to fuck around and not suffer the consequences of discarding me," I said. "For someone as old as you are, you're acting like a spoiled child that wants something only because another kid has it. Get over it."

Saying it made my stomach turn. It made me picture him being with someone else. It made me face the reality of what I had almost done with Bishop... and that I hated it. I hated what Valen had done to me. I hated that I had sought out Bishop to get back at him. Jinn was right, I had no idea what I was doing before he interrupted us. It was all one disgusting mess that had my stomach in knots.

Valen took a step forward. I took a step back. He herded me deeper into the room until the door slammed behind us. "I am not going anywhere, Ezra. You will never be rid of me so long as I live. I will haunt you for the rest of your days."

I shook my head. "No, you won't. Because if I know one thing about demons, it's that they don't have any power unless you give it to them. So, get the fuck out of my room and back to your whore's bed before it grows any colder."

One second, I was facing him and the next I was slammed against the wall. I grunted as his hand encircled my throat, his eyes blazing like an untamed wildfire. His skin on mine completely ripped away the fog in my head. He flooded my senses, overrode whatever buzz had seeped into my bones. I saw him with such clarity that I nearly burst into tears from the surge of emotion.

"Perhaps it is your bed I intend to warm," he said.

"The only way that'll happen is if I set your ass on fire," I growled.

Valen smirked. His eyes fluttered from my face to my heaving chest. He released his hold on my neck and slid his fingers down to the crease of my breasts, centering his touch over the thrum of my heart.

"Take it," I challenged.

Valen's jaw ticked. "I already have it." He cocked his head, looking at me like the greedy dragon he was. "Stop trying to give it away to someone else, because I'm not giving it up."

I didn't move as he stepped away. It was as if he had branded me to the spot I stood, welding me in place.

"You told me to let my love for you die." I swallowed, forcing the words from my throat even as my chest tightened. "I advise you to do the same. Snuff out your obsession and move on. You'll never get me back."

Valen chuckled. "We'll see about that." He turned, pulling a cape of shadows with him that encased the room in darkness. A fire rose in the hearth in a blaze. It made his eyes look like golden jewels as he looked down upon me before he left, leaving me awash with the sense of an omen.

If he had meant to scare me, it worked. But I would not let fear ground me into submission.

I showered and rinsed my mouth out more times than I could count. None of it did anything to wash away the marks Bishop had left me with, or the guilt that weighed me down for a crime I had no fault in.

Sleep evaded me. I was all too aware of the male in the next room over.

CHAPTER FIFTY-ONE:
ALL THAT'S MISSING IS A CROWN

Ezra

"A ball?"

Lane twirled around the room; the periwinkle dress held to her form as she danced. She held it out in front of her. Her bare feet moved steadily across the tiles and then to the fur rug where she made another spin.

"It sends a message. A ball is more formal but less threatening than a council meeting. The other courts believe Vélos wants a war. Vélos wants to show them the only war we seek is with Heaven."

I suppose that would have been well and good if that didn't require me to wear a dress. I fingered the satin fabric of the dress in front of me. I still hadn't come to terms with my role in this war. I was starting to accept it, but just like finding out what I was, I wasn't given much of a choice. It was written and so it would come to pass.

"Aren't you going to open it?" Lane nodded to the box at the foot of my bed.

It had been there when I got out of the shower that morning and I wasn't exactly in the mood for gifts. Whoever it was from, I banked their intentions were far from pure.

"I'd rather not."

She hung her dress on the wardrobe. "Well, I'm curious enough for the both of us."

I waved my hand at her as I looked through the closet. Red. Red. Red. Every dress was bloody fucking red. Even if they hadn't been, none were appropriate for a ball.

"Oh," she purred.

"What?" I looked back.

She held up the box and, peeking between the red tissue paper, was golden embellishment. She pulled it free, letting the long gown fall to the ground.

"It's stunning."

It was long-sleeved with a subtle high collar. The sides were cut out along with an exposed back and short train. It was stunning with glistening material that reminded me of stingray skin. Its color was not metallic and gaudy but closer to morning sunlight. It refracted and glittered with every turn.

"Whose color is it?" I asked.

Lane shrugged. "I don't honestly know. I think you should wear it though."

I reached past her, sliding my fingers through the box to see if there was a note. Nothing.

"I don't think taking gifts from someone unknown is a wise idea," I said.

She nodded to the closet. "So, you'll wear one of those instead?" She scoffed. "I didn't think so." She wriggled the dress in front of me. "Come on. You have to try it."

I chewed the inside of my lip. I didn't have many options and there wasn't enough time to run into town to search for something else. "Fine," I sighed.

The dress was even more beautiful on. It hugged my body perfectly. The white scars carved into my back stood out like tattoos but, looking at them, there against the gold and across the muscle of my skin, gave me a sense of pride. I turned the other way, catching a faint red glow in the gems of the gown. When the light caught it, it looked like firelight.

There were seams along the arms that made my heart flutter. I knew that if I pulled them apart, I would be able to pull my wings free without the dress falling. Whoever had made this had done so with intention.

"Ok, we seriously need to figure out who is behind this because I need one. You look like a goddess."

Lane looked like a goddess herself. The light blue of her gown paired well with the cobalt of her hair that she had curled and pulled to one side. Hers was embellished along the bodice, while the skirt was left unadorned. Its shimmer when she moved glided like water. Her signature needles that hung from her ears were paired with hoops lining the arch.

"So do you," I said.

Her eyes crinkled when she grinned. "All of Tartarus will be talking about us for weeks!"

I smoothed my palms over my thighs. They would, but I had a bad feeling that wasn't going to be a good thing.

I tightened my grip on Andras's arm as we neared the entrance of the Great Hall. Lane walked breezily on his other side, her head lifted high. Any other circumstance and I might have shared her enthusiasm.

The cyns were waiting for us in their black-trimmed tunics and fitted pants, all trimmed with their signature colors. Diriel's vest was detailed with dark blue threading, Jinn in forest green, Bishop adorned in silver, and Valen in death's red.

Bishop strode forward, taking me into his arms. I tried not to flinch at his touch. I couldn't, not when a warm sensation spread over my skin. "You could be a queen," he said.

I flashed him a soft smile. Now that I knew what he was doing, I knew how to pretend.

"All that's missing is a crown," Valen said.

Tension filled the room, ripping the air out of my lungs. I pressed a hand to my chest and forced a more genuine smile at Bishop. The silver-eyed male stroked the side of my neck where his fang marks remained.

"Perhaps we will find her one before the end of the night," Bishop said.

Jinn and Diriel shifted, their stances broadening. Valen, on the other hand, remained aloof, his expression bored despite the blatant animosity roiling off him.

I smoothed my palms over the front of my thighs. "Can we get this over with? Save the dick measuring contest for later." I took my place behind Bishop and Valen. The back of my neck prickled as Jinn and Diriel took the space behind me. They would be my guards for the evening.

Andras had assured me on our walk that nothing would happen to me. That the emissaries were only here to take notes and report, not to attack.

Valen leaned over to whisper in Bishop's ear. Whatever he said released the tension in Bishop's shoulders. The male turned and smiled at Valen before kissing him on the lips.

I don't know how I never noticed it before, this ease between them beneath the layers of contempt. Valen and Bishop were a strange combination, but as Bishop looked at his counterpart, I could see the raw affection he had for the male at his side. I'd never seen them together intimately, but that didn't mean the rumors never reached me. Valen had been with me since I arrived, but now that things had shifted, would they go back to the way they were? Is that why Valen wanted me to stay away from Bishop? Not for my own safety, but because he claimed him.

Ashes, I hated angels. I hated demons. I wish I could have fallen into any other story.

We approached the steps leading to the Great Hall as someone announced our entrance. Every eye lifted as we strode down. I kept my chin high as I followed the cyns to their thrones where I would stand behind them for all to gawk at. As a trophy and a target.

But we never made it to the thrones. We were approached almost immediately on our path by Zephyr, Eimai Theós's emissary, and his entourage. The tall seraph bowed low, lowering every eye on his body.

"Forgive my urgency," he said, "but Cyn Maalik bade I be the first to lay eyes on her." He remained low until Bishop motioned him to rise. The seraphim believed themselves to be of the highest order and ruled as such. Seeing one show such respect to the cyns surprised me.

I suppressed the smile that tugged behind my lips.

"We expect no less from Maalik. Ezra," Bishop said, extending his hand to his side.

I swear my arm tingled as it brushed against Valen's when I stepped between them. I tried to ignore his presence, how strong and powerful he felt beside me, and let my smile unfurl.

"May I?" Zephyr extended his hand. A soft tap to my shoulder told me otherwise. Seers could see just fine without touching someone. Making contact only made their visions clearer.

I laced my fingers together. "I know it might be strange having lived in Vélos, but I am not big on touch. You may read me, though."

Zephyr's mouth quirked. "A wise one. You are right, I do not need to touch you. I have seen all that I need to and know that Cyn Maalik will be quite pleased with you." The seraph's many eyes passed along the cyn. "We have not seen one of ours so fair in a long time."

I cocked my head. "Excuse me?"

"Zephyr," Bishop said. "You overstep."

The male bowed. "I only mean an angelica is so rare. For if she was a seraph, you would have given her to us a long time ago." The seraphim behind him murmured in agreement.

A grin spread across Valen's face. "Surely," he said. "Enjoy the evening, Zephyr, for I am sure we will see you again before the night is done."

"My lords." To me, the male touched his fingers to his lips. "My lady."

Bishop moved us ahead where we were intercepted by another emissary from Thanatos. Haffa, I believe his name was. His skin was night sky black with raised notches along every bit of open flesh. Stacks of gold rings lined his fingers. A silver tattoo of a siren with sharp pointed fins slid out from under his short white hair.

"That is a fine dress."

I clenched my jaw. Valen hadn't tried to speak through our bond since his return.

"It is."

He smirked before turning to greet another guest, not an emissary but another amorini with jet-black hair and eyes to match. The red thread of his tunic caught the light and shifted to gold.

I blinked, thinking it was a trick of the light. The dragon embroidered along the shoulder of his attire color-shifted just as my dress did. Red to gold. Gold to red.

"You bastard."

A smile burst across Valen's mouth, but he didn't acknowledge me as he continued on with his conversation.

Bishop reached across, placing a hand over Valen's back and pulling him into the conversation with Haffa. Ashes, I hated this. It was bad enough that tonight was about me, but I couldn't even stew properly without my emotions clouding my judgement.

Around us, a small crowd gathered, but beyond that people were dancing. Humans had been allowed to participate in tonight's event. They were as finely adorned as the demons, their gowns and tunics glittering and flowing with their movement. It was a nice change from the usual sensual gatherings that took place. Everyone looked so elegant.

I snagged a glass of champagne from a passing server that was promptly plucked from my hand and set back on the tray. Jinn glared down at me.

"You have no idea the things that are at play here. We cannot have you getting sloshed and having a repeat of last night," he chided.

I wanted to forget everything about last night. "I know exactly what is at play. I'm at stake and you all don't want to lose me."

Jinn's brows furrowed when he opened his mouth then shut it. He shook his head. "Can you dance?"

I looked back to the floor of dancers. "Not well," I admitted.

Jinn extended his hand. "It's just like fighting."

Dancing was only like fighting in the sense that there are certain moves you must master in order to execute the next step. Of which I did terribly. The first two times I stepped on Jinn's toes, I thought he would sock me right there on the dance floor. The third time, I couldn't help but laugh as literal steam pooled out of his ears.

"You asked for this," I said, touching my hand over my mouth.

"If you would stop fighting me and let me lead," he grumbled. "How are you so good on the field but here you're worse than a newborn foal?"

I straightened my shoulders and positioned my hands in the air like a mannequin. "You're right. I'm purposefully making this difficult. But it's only to get back at you."

He pulled me against him and stepped back. I followed him, sidestepping when his thumb tensed on my hand and moving back as his fingers dug into my waist. Subtle gestures that guided me through the steps. He was a good lead. I wasn't surprised by it. Jinn was an incredible instructor. We might have our differences, but he was formidable in his execution.

"As I said, there are things at work here you do not understand. Things I cannot tell you. Look at the words presented to you, at the roles we all play. It's all an act for something much larger. This is the only warning I can give you, Ezra. You must be careful."

The hem of my gown spun around my ankles as he twirled me out. I twisted back into his arms, my back against his chest as he led us backward, before spinning me out again.

"What are you talking about?" I asked. The tempo of the music increased and so did we.

"Nothing is what it seems. Neither are the people around you," he said.

I followed him a few more steps until the music slowed and finally came to a lulling halt. I looked up at him, trying to find the answers within his green eyes. "Why can't you speak clearly?"

He opened his mouth and I leaned forward, eager to hear whatever secret he held.

"May I cut in?"

I met Diriel's eyes that crinkled when he smiled.

"You're welcome to her, but she's likely to scuff your boots," Jinn said, releasing me. He was getting good at evading conversations when they became too serious.

Dancing with Diriel was just as tense as it had been with Jinn. Having the emissaries here had set them all on edge. I felt the bulk of a dagger beneath Diriel's breast as I placed my hand over the front of his tunic. I knew that they could protect me, but I couldn't help but feel that an even bigger bomb than the one I had set off was about to drop.

"Do you know what Jinn was on about?"

"Jinn likes to speak in riddles," Diriel eluded.

We fell into step with those around us. Diriel lifted his hand and I raised my palm against it.

"And you evade me too," I said. "It seems you are all keeping a very big secret."

Diriel's hand slid across the back of my neck as we approached an amorini and his partner before trading off. My heart fluttered as the other male circled around me, sliding his hand over my waist, but then I was back with Diriel.

"You know I cannot keep anything from you."

"You kept what I was to yourself."

Diriel frowned. "I wanted to be certain of it before I said anything. It was not my intention to leave you in the dark. I planned on telling you, but the angel set things so far off track that I could not foresee." Diriel pressed his forehead to mine as our dance came to a halt. "I will never fail you, Ezra. Please do not see my tardiness as such."

I touched the side of his face, holding us there as we exchanged breaths. Diriel had become a good friend. The stab of betrayal I had felt when I learned of the prophecy had pulled the rug out from under me. I leaned into the kiss he placed on my brow.

"How can I stay angry at you?" I said, meeting his two-toned eyes.

"Simmer for as long as you need." He matched my smile, his straight white teeth flashing between his full lips taking the weight of the moment off my shoulders. If only for a moment.

I moved through the rest of the evening on Bishop's arm. He took Diriel's place and kept me at his side. I harnessed my power like a shroud, blocking off any spells he tried to cast on me so that I might bend to him. The only time my power wavered was when he kissed me and I rose to meet him.

His eyes glimmered as he thumbed the marks on my neck.

"Keza is Asphodel's emissary," Bishop said. He touched his palm to his chest in greeting to the gray-skinned male who approached us. "I hope the long travel was not too hard on you."

Keza had a long spindly neck that made him look serpentine. Wings stuck out the back of his head, framing it like a feathered halo. His yellow eyes were reptilian, complete with a second white lid. "Long indeed," he said. He turned his strange head to me, dropping it down so he could look me in the face. "No one said it was a girl. Bah! Cyn Baal must be losing his mind. This is no threat."

My eyes narrowed. I was not an it. "Heaven would disagree, though I am not a threat to your kingdoms," I said.

Keza blinked in surprise. "And it speaks for itself."

"Ezra is quite capable," Bishop said. "She is powerful, make no mistake, but there is no threat against Tartarus from her or us."

Keza's wide mouth twisted, revealing rows of sharp teeth. "Cyn Anzu will still see her, but I have no concern. Perhaps you can bring her to the planes."

Fat chance.

The corner of Bishop's mouth tugged. I schooled myself before the shock could reach my face. Could he read my mind now? I hadn't drunk directly from him, but I wondered all the same that because I had consumed his blood, and he mine, if that had truly created a link to our minds.

Clouded memories of the other night had surfaced that morning. I was glad the long sleeves I wore hid the chills that suddenly raced across my skin. I was more frightened than angry at what he had done.

I felt him on my right. The familiarity was almost painful as he glided to my side.

"Ezra, will you dance with me?" Valen asked.

I looked at the hand Valen extended to me. Everyone was watching. What sort of message would it send if I danced with all of them but him? I could do this.

"I think I've worn her out," Bishop said.

I'd been breathless by the time he let me rest. He wanted to make a point with me, to show off that he had the nephilim and not anyone else.

Valen's expression remained impassive. "Good thing I am the last one she has to dance with. I won't keep her long."

A flicker of irritation flashed across Bishop's eyes. It was in the tick of his jaw when he nodded. He grabbed my hand before I could leave his side and pulled me close, kissing me again. It was the first time his mouth tasted bitter. That the taste of him turned to ash.

A warmth unlike any I had ever known enveloped me as I touched Valen. I couldn't breathe as he led me to the center of the room. The moons had not completely taken over the sky, so the sun's golden light spilled a path for us to the ballroom floor. It felt natural touching him. I could feel myself falling all over again even as the voice inside my head screamed at me to run.

Moving with Valen was like the flow of a river. Swift and sure, a force to be reckoned with. I knew every inch of his body. I anticipated when he would move and followed him seamlessly. In turn, he played me effortlessly.

We didn't speak. There were too many bitter words and heartache stored in my heart that I knew nothing good would come from opening my mouth. I was thankful he didn't taunt me as he had the last few nights. But ashes, the way he looked at me. Like he would devour me right there and didn't care who saw.

It brought heat to my face as he drew me closer, pressing my body flush to his. My breath caught.

The scent of his raw desire flooded my senses. I could feel it pressed against me as we spun across the floor, not even a sliver of air between us.

Murmurs swept across the floor, whispering over the song someone had started to sing. I opened my mouth as the heat intensified between us. Valen's mouth parted to reveal flames on the back of his tongue.

My grip tightened on his shoulder. I felt his fingers dig into my waist. He could deny it all he wanted, I could hate him forever, but neither of us could deny the fire that bound us. Never had mine answered to another. Not even a tendril rose for Bishop. And I bet he had tried. With all of his spells and charms, he had tried to call me to him and it hadn't worked.

Valen's fingers slid through the seams of my dress's sleeves, parting the fabric.

"Open them," he said. "Let them see what you truly are."

I hated him. I feared what the emissaries would do if they saw them.

I trusted him. I gave him a small nod.

Valen spun me, spun me so fast that I broke contact with his fingers, and ripped my wings free.

The crowd lurched backward as I spread them to their extent, flashing the ebony feathers in the face of those who had lost theirs. Orange flames burst across the underside of my dress and licked across the marble floor, turning my dress bright red.

I caught sight of Keza's wide eyes as I turned back to Valen. There was a sharp tug between us that had my feet flying to him. I tucked my wings in as I met his hands and let him pull me across the floor that was now laid bare to us.

In that moment, I forgot about the crowd. I forgot about what he had done. I forgot about the horror that lay on the horizon.

In that moment, there was only us. For the first time in months, I let myself truly smile.

He made me feel alive.

He had broken me and there he was, pulling me up from the grave. His fingers tangled in the back of my hair as he pulled our faces close. It took every bit of strength within me not to kiss him.

Valen grinned. The movement caused his lips to brush mine. A new wave of heat brushed over my face. My stomach fluttered at the sight of him. God, he was beautiful. He was everything.

That's when the sharp sting hit me.

"Don't do this to me," I said, breathless. The moment he kissed me, I would fall back into him. I was at his mercy.

Valen slid my hand in his behind his neck and pushed me back. I spread my wings parallel to the floor as Valen bent me over as the music reached its final crescendo.

A pale glint caught my eye.

Crouched in the rafters was the other emissary I had not missed. Atticus was crouched in the shadows, still as a gargoyle. His hands and feet were hooked with claws as he leered over the banister. He was so high up I doubt anyone else had noticed him.

Looking at him then, it was the first time I had ever seen the male smile, and it was utterly terrifying. His narrow face spread too wide, revealing elongated fangs that cut over his lips.

Valen pulled me up, obscuring my view of the demon. I pressed the side of my face to his as I struggled to catch my breath. That's when I noticed how quiet it was.

I jerked away from Valen as the cold stares finally hit. Fire danced at both of our feet. Sweat glistened over Valen's brow like dark gems. I turned, pulling my wings against me as I looked for some sort of exit, a rescuer.

The amorini had gone deathly still. Confusion spread across the mass and then the murmurs started. Some of the humans had started to back pedal from the floor.

A loud applause started. "Magnificent!" Zephyr called. His entourage followed, their eyes darting across the crowd as tension spread.

The music started up again with a hesitant strum. The voices increased, but some of the amorini walked back to the floor as if pretending everything was normal.

The seraph circled me before coming to an immediate halt. "If you fight half as well as you dance, I will be in awe." He grinned as he extended his hand into the air. "Eimai Theós will not war with Vélos. I have seen what I needed to and, truly, Ezra is the Salvation of the Fallen."

I couldn't match his smile. He got all of that from a dance? This had to be some joke I was missing the punchline to. Again, my eyes darted to the crowd and their questioning, accusing eyes.

It wasn't just any dance.

I looked back to the floor, but Valen was gone. Even the monster in the rafters had disappeared.

The only one left to congratulate me on gaining the alliance was Bishop, whose eyes bore his wrath like lightning.

CHAPTER FIFTY-TWO: AND IT ALL CAME CRASHING DOWN

Ezra

There is nothing more frightening than being on the arm of an enemy. I don't know if Bishop had been mine all along or if he had become my opponent during the dance. I adorned his arm the rest of the evening, but it felt like I was chained to his side instead. Something had changed. There was no kindness in his touch when it lingered on my neck. The hold was possessive.

When I told him I wasn't feeling well, he looked right through me. I knew he saw the lie, but I was too afraid to be with him any longer. Zephyr and another seraph had his attention, so I knew he couldn't come with me. Not yet at least.

I pressed my lips against his cheek. "Come find me later," I said.

His eyes lightened as he traced the curve of my jaw. "I will. There is much between us that needs to be finished." He brought his thumb up to my mouth where he pulled my bottom lip down. I bit it softly.

I threw a sheepish look over my shoulder to the other males. "It was a pleasure meeting you."

Zephyr touched his lips. "The pleasure is all mine. I hope your recovery is swift for I do wish to see you fight before we go."

I nodded, bowing to Bishop before leaving the room and praying it didn't look like I was fleeing.

A strong grip encircled my forearm.

"Keep walking," Jinn said. I looked up at him and noticed Andras trailing behind us, his hand resting on the pommel of his sword.

"I don't need an escort," I said, but didn't fight to break away from him.

I felt the lingering trace of darkness following us to my quarters. By the time we reached my tower, I was a bunch of muscle waiting to sprint at the first sign of danger.

"What's going on?" I asked.

"The stunt you and Valen just pulled might have cost us our alliance with the other courts. The bastard should have waited," Jinn said.

My brow furrowed. "It was a dance. I danced with all of you. And Zephyr enjoyed the show. Isn't Eimai Theós the one we should be worried about?"

Jinn shook his head and tapped his fingers to his temple. "I'll explain later."

"Andras?"

The male wouldn't look at me as Jinn ushered me into my room.

"Stay here and do not leave," Jinn said.

"Hey, wait a minute." The door slammed in front of my face. The unmistakable shift of power made my blood run cold. I pulled at the handle.

"Jinn. Andras! What the fuck, guys!" If I was in danger, I didn't want to be locked in my room. I knocked on the door and called for Andras again, but there was no answer.

I pulled in my wings as I paced the room, replaying the last dance. I groaned into my hands. Whatever we had done had been bad. That was the moment Bishop had changed. I'd never seen such a look in his eyes, but I recognized it from my time on Earth. When a man is angry, they get a special glint in their eyes right before they rupture. How Bishop had maintained his composure was a testament to his control.

The entire crowd had gone cold.

My eyes slid across my bedroom wall to the tapestry that hung there. I chewed the inside of my lip before padding to it. I'd never asked Lane how she had gotten the door open, but I knew it was still there. I pushed against the stone wall until part of it gave way.

I knew Bishop would stay true to his word and finish what we started last night. I didn't want to be here when he came searching. I feared the demon he would unleash on me once he had me bare.

I slipped into leather pants and a long-sleeved top before digging out a cloak and dagger. My hand hovered over the bow tucked inside my wardrobe. It would be too bulky to carry, and I didn't know where I was going, just that I needed to get out of my room quickly.

I belted the dagger and slipped into the secret passage. I pushed the door closed behind me and waited. When I was sure no one would come barging after me, I made my way down the dark tunnel.

I held orange flames in my palm to light the way down the slope. There were strange markings along the walls. The hieroglyphs were similar to the Egyptians' work with human bodies and animal heads. Other symbols I'd never seen before. I followed them down, but there was no story to them, no tale. Or maybe Diriel had not gifted me to read the language.

I walked until I reached a fork in the path that split off into four different directions. I tried to picture where I was within the tyre, if I was at its center or had split off past it and beneath the forest. I should have kept better track.

"Eenie, meanie, minie....mo." The fourth path it was.

I trailed my fingers along the walls, letting my fire catch the markings. I stopped dead.

Beside one of the markings of an angelic being with the heads of a cattle, dog, and goat were claw marks. Embedded within was a piece of fingernail.

I jerked my hand away in horror.

I pulled my cloak tighter around my neck as I searched the wall for other signs. There were no bones on the floor, no other sign of a struggle. But I could feel the weight of something terrible hanging in the air.

I didn't see the shadow until it was almost on me. The soft smell of sage was the only thing that stopped me from sliding the dagger across Valen's throat as he emerged from the darkness.

Valen touched the end of the dagger I held toward him.

"What the fuck are you doing here?" I breathed.

"I could ask you the same thing," he said. "There are ghosts in these halls."

That wasn't true. Ghosts weren't real. Those on Earth were demons that slipped through the veil. To haunt or taunt people with false images of their loved ones. It was one of the first things Valen had taught me on our strolls. Before I had my wings.

I swallowed. "I asked you first." Even though I didn't believe in spirits, this place felt haunted now that I had found a fingernail in the wall. I wasn't going to let him scare me.

"I'm here for you," he said.

"Why?"

Valen's teeth flashed. "You know why."

I tightened my grip. "You don't own me, Valen. Why do you insist on harboring me? You *broke* my heart."

"Not well enough," he said.

I scoffed. "Fuck you. I'd say you have no idea what you've done, but I wasn't the first. I know all about you, *Valentine*. Do you keep their hearts in a jar locked away in your closet?" I was seething and I couldn't stop. There was too much pain and pent-up energy I hadn't truly been able to release. Now that I was in front of him, it came out full force.

I pressed the blade against his throat.

If it was a shock that I knew his real name, he didn't show it. He lifted his chin, exposing the muscular slope of his neck to me. A clear shot. "I don't deny my crimes before I met you. You, however, were never meant to be a casualty."

My hand trembled as I fought the urge to slice the knife into his skin. To bleed him the same way he had bled me.

"You pulled me out of death's grasp. You gave me the opportunity to be someone new, to be someone powerful. You said I was a miracle and built me up. And then you abandoned me to return and torment me. I will not tell you again, I do not belong to you. You cannot come waltzing back now that someone else has me."

Valen's eyes darkened. "Bishop doesn't have you. But the more you give yourself to him, you'll find yourself a prisoner."

"Like you're any better."

"Everything I have done has been to safeguard you. Everything, Ezra. Everything Bishop has and will do is for his own gain. You think he wants you for you? He wants you so he can control you. Your power, your gifts. He plans to extort you until there is nothing left. War is not the only thing you should be worried about."

I shook my head and sunk my teeth into my lip. "You know, you did some good for me, I'll admit that. But don't pretend you're any better than him. I know Bishop is wicked. I've seen it. At least he never pretended to be something he isn't." I don't know why I tried to stand up for Bishop when it was him I was running from. I just didn't want Valen to be right.

Valen's face split apart in a pained, snarling grin. "You think the Bishop you know is real? Do you have any idea what is happening up there right now?" The laugh that leaked out of him made my blood run cold. "Let me tell you a story and then you can judge me. It wasn't until recently that I learned the truth of it myself."

He jammed his first two fingers into his chest. "He did shoot me. While he fought to kill Episkipos, *my cyn*, the first amorini, the three of us tried to stop him. Episkipos was so badly injured by Bishop's rage alone we knew there was no saving him. Either Bishop would bear the crown or no one would. Someone needed to lead us. So, the three of us tore our cyn apart in hopes that one of us would kill him before Bishop did."

Valen's voice was thick with emotion, his teeth bared as if he re-lived the memory. "When the crown broke upon our heads, Bishop erupted. The power of an archangel is a mighty gift. It strikes the soul when wielded appropriately. When he struck, the entire sky fell. The stars winked out. He knew I was the one who led Jinn and Diriel to fight against him, so it was me he went after. He shot me, pinned my wrists to the ground so he could cut open my chest and rip out my heart."

I stared in horror. I didn't want to believe it, but how could I not when I had never felt Valen's heartbeat? It had never been in his chest. All those times I had laid against his chest there had been silence.

Valen ran a hand over his head. "It was only recently that I learned the truth of our fall. That Episkipos did fall for Rachel, the golden-haired human destined for another mortal. He didn't just fall for her, though, she fell too and their souls bound. It was never he who went against God. It was Bishop. Their name is one and the same, all he had to do was steal his face. Bishop who damned us. It was the venom of his words that condemned the amorini to fall."

He held my gaze as the story fell together. I shook my head. "What are you saying?"

"I have speculated for a long while that there was more to our fall than I was led to believe. You being what you are, your scream waking me, it shook that which I had suppressed. You woke me from a slumber I thought I would never stir from.

"Those gems that fell from your hand, they're rainbow obsidian. A rare gem formed when adelfis fall."

Something shattered and a startled sob broke from my chest. I pressed the edge of the dagger harder against his throat. Blood slid down the length of the blade as my hand shook.

"When their souls bind," he said softly.

She's falling.

Don't fall.

I shut my eyes as hot tears bit into the back of them.

"I said what I did in hopes it would sever the bond. To protect you. At least until I could find some place safe for you. I knew that when Bishop discovered the truth of you, he would finally kill me and then I couldn't protect you. So long as he has my heart, my hands are bound."

My heart staggered against my chest.

"What else have you lied about?"

He inhaled, and it looked like whatever he was about to say next would gut him. "You're not barren."

The dagger clattered to the ground.

"What?" My voice was so small I hadn't thought I'd spoken aloud.

"The tea you've been drinking, it's a contraceptive."

I didn't know what to touch on first. Ache and anger boiled within me. "So instead of telling me all of this when you had the chance, you run away for two months? And you think showing up now, laying it all out that what... That I'm supposed to understand? That I'll forgive you?"

The boil spilled over. "What the fuck, Valen? You're my..." I couldn't bring myself to say it. Deep down, I knew it. I think I had known it, that I was creeping closer to the edge where I would lose myself in him. But when I finally gave in, he had ripped it all away from me.

I couldn't breathe. I leaned against the wall, sliding my hand over the markings and digging my nails into the grooves to hold myself up.

"What happened with the dance?" I looked up at him. "The entire crowd went still, Bishop looked as if he could kill me, and Jinn locked me in my room. What have you done?"

"I didn't run," he said softly, teeth bared. "I've been a prisoner to Baal in Eurynomos. And that performance we just put on showed my people the lie we have been living."

CHAPTER FIFTY-THREE: SHE FELL

Bishop

Two Months Prior

A flurry of messages had been coming and going from Vélos. So many Andras had to pull from the guards to help carry them all to the cyn. The entire expanse of Tartarus had heard about Ezra. The female nephilim that Vélos was harboring. As if she was some criminal.

If she was not Fallen herself, Bishop would have treated her as such. Prometheus was Heaven's fire, something he had been able to wield a long time ago. It was the one thing that kept the prisoners of Vasanistirio chained in their abyss. No one could climb in or out without burning entirely. It wasn't just flesh and bone that would burn in the flame but souls too.

Bishop had been surprised to see Atticus reach out and touch them. Perhaps he thought he was immune to Prometheus now. He was one of the few who had survived the flames, the scars on his hands evidence of it.

Cyn Maalik was demanding an audience. Cyn Nakir had threatened to call upon Raguel if she was not killed. Cyn Anzu had been quiet, more than likely waiting to see what decision would hold so he knew who to correctly support. Asphodel was far removed from the other courts and, as such, kept to themselves.

Cyn Baal, on the other hand, was quietly fuming.

You understand as well as I that Prometheus is an unwelcome weapon but perhaps we can use it to our advantage. Already my men have started to explore the tears of the veil the nephilim left behind. We may be able to cross over to man's world soon. Accept my invitation to Eurynomos so that we may stop this war between us before it has begun. I have been told she has the eyes of my blood. That I am keen to see.

"Give her up or we will wipe you off the map" is what the letter said in short.

The letter went up in flames between Bishop's fingertips.

The amorini finally had something everyone wanted. He wasn't about to relinquish this bit of power after being snubbed for so long. He was surprised by the response to her. The Fallen should have been more supportive. Did they not remember the power the nephilim had? The destruction they raged over mankind?

Bishop quietly fumed and plotted in his room. Ezra was in the salt chambers still healing. He had managed to reverse the damage Ariel had inflicted and what Prometheus had done to her, but it would take a long while before she was well again. Already, five days had passed. Each time he visited, she remained motionless. Every time Valen had been there, pacing like a caged animal in the shadows.

There was a temper with him too. A flare of power that made Bishop's blood hot and his hunger raw. He had grown bolder as of late, and that was starting to get beneath his skin. The last few reminders Bishop had given him of his place had only seemed to sharpen Valen's teeth.

Bishop fingered the still healing bite marks on his throat. "They won't take her from us."

Valen had looked at him with burning eyes. There was so much tension flowing through his body, it had been hard to read him. "I'll burn anyone to the ground that tries."

Bishop pulled the band from the end of his braid, freeing the long twist of his hair. So would he. He would kill anyone who tried to take her. Who even looked at her wrong. He had waited long enough to have her; he would be damned if another cyn swiped her before he had his taste. Before she was bred and molded for war.

He shouldered into his bedroom, stripping his shirt and pants as he went.

An icy chill swept through the room, the flint of ash hot on its trail. Bishop turned, surveying the empty space.

No, not empty.

There in the corner was a silhouette. It reclined in the leather chair. Only the edges of the male's frame and the reflective glint of his eyes could be seen.

Bishop's teeth flashed. "Come to steal my crown instead?"

The shadow purred with laughter, then tsked. "I have no desire for yours, brother. I told you war is coming and you deny my cyn's requests. I cannot hold him much longer."

"You should already bear his crown."

"Patience," the male hissed, "is a virtue."

Fire erupted from the hearth, blanketing the intruder in an orange glow that did nothing to dampen his menace. Raum's fists were clenched, his arms stretched out over the back of the winged-backed chair.

"I'm here to sway you."

Bishop strode forward, standing directly in front of the keras. "I'm not giving you Ezra. She's mine."

Raum's brow arched. "Are you certain? I could have sworn she was Valen's."

Bishop's nostrils flared. "I have allowed him to toy with her until she fell. I needed to be sure he could sway her to us since it is his attention she sought. Now that she has," he tipped his head, "I am no longer inclined to wait."

"Oh, she fell," Raum said. The way he said it made Bishop's skin crawl. He held Bishop's gaze a second longer and extended one of his hands. He uncurled his fingers to reveal small rainbow gems.

Bishop looked at the stones, his pupils dilating.

A thousand questions were on his lips. Raum smiled, the laugh lines in his face creasing. "They were buried in the snow, likely where they first landed when the angel tried to take her. Only a few yards away, but we missed them the first time, what with the break in the veil and Prometheus."

A quiet fury settled over Bishop as he extended his hand. The small gems were heavy in his hand as Raum turned them into his palm. The keras kept one, fingering it. "I have seen them in your bow, but I have never had the chance to inspect them up close. Rainbow obsidian." Raum hummed. "I thought your kind could not fall. That Episkipos was some silly little bedtime story."

"Do not speak of things which you do not know," Bishop growled.

The rage was growing quickly, filling his senses. Raum could smell it, reveled in it even. And then, suddenly, Bishop erupted. He spun, casting the gems across the room in a fit of lightning and thunder. Fire burst across the ceiling as his fury unleashed with a loud roar.

Raum sat back and smiled. "I told you he would betray you."

"I gave him everything," Bishop snarled. "I let them keep their crowns, their lives. And he takes this from me?" The stone pillars framing the windows cracked, the glass walls splintering.

"She fell," Valen had said.

A lie. A bold-faced lie, twisted within the truth. She had fallen, just not the way she was supposed to. Valen had too.

Before the amorini fell and they sought to bind the souls of the adelfis, one of the telling signs that the arrow had struck true, that their souls had aligned, was the rainbow obsidian. A rare gem, rarer now that an adelfi never found their other half, that formed and hardened when their souls intertwined.

Adelfis. Valen was her adelfi.

It was Episkopos all over again. It went against everything they stood for. Everything *he* believed in. They were better than love. They were more than the foolish *gift* Heaven had bestowed the mortals.

They were stronger, more powerful than love. *Better.*

Bishop let out a roar that shook the room.

He leaned down and threw the large table decorated with skins and wines across the room. He was a storm, whipping and whirling, tearing everything in sight.

Raum watched. He drank in every drop of sweat that bled from the cyn. His teeth sharpened as Bishop's roars grew louder, his human form constantly flickering until the seam of flesh could no longer contain the demon and a giant black beast was pacing back and forth across the room. Its long tail lashed angrily behind it, the four feathered wings clamped to its spine rigid.

Raum slid from his seat and circled the beast. "I still stand with you, brother. Before the crest of the third moon, I intend to wear Baal's crown. Until then, we need to satisfy him. Give me Valen. Just for a little while so Baal may take out his wrath on him," he coaxed. "Apart from him, she is just another girl. A weak-minded woman you can bend to your will. She will be susceptible to influence now that she's had an angel's blood in her mouth."

Bishop swung his massive head to the demon, keeping one dark eye on the male as he continued to circle. "This will stay Baal's hand until I have won the throne."

Bishop hissed, the sound reverberating through the room. "What is to keep you from demanding her once you rule?"

Raum slid his tongue over his lower lip. "I do not need to demand her when you are going to let me take her. It can be in your bed for all I care when I do. The only thing I want is the child I breed into her."

Stillness fell across the room. So quiet that not even the air moving in and out of their lungs could be heard. A crackle of electricity popped through the air. Then another. The slow swell of power made the hairs on Raum's body stand on end.

Bishop's lips curled back, revealing rows of teeth that would tear through the other demon's flesh if what he was insinuating was true.

Raum held out the rainbow obsidian. "Your dear brothers have been lying about that too."

There was an explosion of smoke and lightning as Bishop charged Raum. His rage flashed across his vision, blinding him. But Raum was gone. The only evidence he had been there at all was the rainbow obsidian scattered across the floor.

Bishop slid his hands through his hair. He needed to compose himself. They would feel his rage, both of them would, but not before he got all of the answers directly. Perhaps it was a mistake.

He licked his lips as he strode to the far tower. His lashes fluttered frantically as he tried to stifle the fire lighting behind them. He hesitated, reaching Ezra's door first, and stepped back on his heel to knock.

"Oh," the woman said. Claire.

Bishop's brow arched.

Claire stepped back, flinging the door open and bowing. "Forgive me, sire. I didn't expect you."

Bishop stepped into the room, his gaze panning.

"Where is Ezra?"

Claire audibly swallowed. "I believe she is still in the salt chambers. I was told to ready her quarters for her return. Perhaps she is coming back tonight?"

There was nothing out of the ordinary. All of the books Diriel had left her to study were appropriate. Journals and texts of the Fall, of their people. There were even a few about magic. Bishop's nails raked over the front of the covers.

Diriel could not have known she wasn't affected by the curse. Atticus had been in agreement that she was barren. There were no children in her future. Something had only recently changed.

An assortment of foods lined the table. Bishop walked down the line, bringing each to his nose.

"May I help you search for something?" Claire offered. Her eyes shifted to the plates.

A whiff of a bitter herb filled the air. Bishop paused, his eyes skimming until they landed on the tea kettle. He flipped the lid and brought it to his nose.

"What is this?" he asked, turning.

Claire stood slowly, clasping her shaking hands in front of her. At least someone still had the good sense to be afraid of him. Her body swayed as she looked at the pot.

"Tea."

"What *kind* of tea?"

Claire swallowed again. "Leake root," she said softly.

Leake root.

The name seared through his patience. Leake root was a contraceptive. It was used on the harem should the men and women tangle, but had been used in another lifetime when the curse did not lay between women and angels.

"You are not to give her anymore of this. In fact, you are no longer Ezra's lady. You're being reassigned."

Claire's eyes widened. "But... yes, sire. I was only doing what Cyn Diriel instructed."

They had betrayed him. *This* was how they had hidden it. How Atticus had not seen anything. They had known and kept the knowledge for themselves. Was it so they could have her first or to protect her? Was Jinn in on it too?

They were protecting her from you.

Bishop's teeth ground together. How long had they been plotting against him?

Bishop nodded. "As you should. You are to send someone else to take your place, I don't care who. When you are done, go to my quarters."

"Have I offended you?" she asked softly.

"Greatly."

Claire's eyes welled with tears. Her bottom lip jutted out. "I have been loyal to you," she started.

"My patience is thin. If you run fast, perhaps I will have changed my mind by the time I get to you."

Claire spun on her heel, a sob breaking through her chest as she darted down the hall.

Bishop poured the tea out the window and let the pot shatter to the ground below.

He chewed the inside of his lip, fighting the urge to tear apart her room. Did *she* know? Bishop lounged across the couch before the hearth.

It didn't matter now. She wouldn't be getting one drop of the plant ever again.

He ran his first two fingers over his lip.

He remembered their first kiss. How her eyes had darted to the side right before she grabbed him and pressed her lips to his. How later, Valen and Ezra had slunk upstairs. He had expected them to follow him out, but when they didn't, he had gone searching. He watched from the shadows of the crowd and waited for them to come out of the room. He thought he had gone to fuck her, to kiss his taste out of Ezra's mouth.

Ezra hadn't been flushed. Flustered, but not moused like Valen had taken her.

Valen had been hiding something then too.

Someone had said her name before she kissed him.

There was one more thing to do. Bishop pushed off from the couch and spectered to the chamber below the cathedral, where the soul ties were kept.

It was customary to keep track of every soul they killed. It was one in the long list of rules in the agreement the amorini had with Heaven. They could kill an adelfi, but they must keep record of them.

Bishop flipped through the pages, searching for the date they had taken Ezra on her first hunt.

Brandon Stoker – Jinn Calvantai, Cyn

Kaycee Ann Reeser – Bishop Sorrinse, Cyn

Matthew Foster – Valentine Erosa, Cyn

Killian Odair – Ezra Hollen

Matthew had been hand selected, but the others had been drawn at random. Who was Killian and why had Valen switched with Ezra? He hadn't thought anything of it at the time. He wanted to see her kill, had wanted to see her dirty her hands, but had been too caught up in the bloodlust to question anything. Had been too caught up with the feel of Ezra's body beneath his.

"I've picked that boy for her, Matt. Perhaps after her first kill, she'll want to add another."

"Or enjoy us tearing him apart for her," Jinn had offered.

The dark-skinned male had smiled, flashing his fangs. Ezra was never supposed to get Matt's tie. Valen had switched them.

Bishop leaned away from the table. He looked across the ties hanging from the ceiling.

"Let's see who you are, Killian Odair." Bishop slammed the book shut.

Claire was kneeling at the foot of his bed when Bishop returned that night, her entire body trembling. If she had been smart, she would have run. Hidden somewhere until he forgot about her. Perhaps she thought he would forgive her. It wasn't her fault about the tea; she had only been doing what she was told. But Bishop was not a forgiving male.

He waited for her to look at him, to get a glimpse of the evil that stalked toward her. Then he was upon her, a blur of fangs and claws. A blood curdling scream rose into the air, then another. She screamed until her throat was relieved of her.

What was left of Claire's body lay scattered across the room.

CHAPTER FIFTY-FOUR: A BROTHER'S DECEIT

Valen

Reno, Nevada

Two Months Prior

The bar was lush with the sound of drunken stupor and music pouring out of a broken speaker. The live band consisted of a tall, spindly man clad in denim with an acoustic guitar. His companion, a stout fellow with an acoustic of his own, was draped in a gray hoodie two sizes too big. The crowd cheered as their song finished. Their music sounded as good as they looked.

I made a quick scan of the room, following Bishop through the throng that crowded the sticky floor. This wasn't our usual hunting grounds. In a place like this, we stood out. I preferred hunting discreetly, but he had insisted we remain in view.

My stomach was in knots. The pain in Ezra's voice as she yelled at me replayed over and over in my head.

Let it die.

It was what I had been telling myself the moment I fell for her. One of us falling was enough to condemn us both. But her crashing down with the heat of Heaven's fire and the gems that pooled out of her pores had been what would damn us for eternity.

She couldn't know. No one could know. They would kill me and then who would protect her? Once Bishop knew the truth, he would ruin her.

I would find a way to make amends later. If she wallowed in her pain long enough, she would become angry. She would hate me.

Perhaps it would be enough to sever the bond.

I sidled next to Bishop as he slid onto the bar stool, flashing a grin that made the woman next to him blush.

"Hey cutie," he said.

"Um, hi," she breathed. By her doe-eyed stare, she'd probably never had someone like Bishop approach her. If she trusted her instincts, she would have run. Her heartbeat pummeling against her chest was sweet music to the predators beside her.

She wasn't who we were here for. But all the same, Bishop might decide to kill her. Why not? It would be easy. She was already melting at his feet.

I nodded to the bartender as she approached. At least she tried to stifle her shock. Her heart rate sped up and ah, yes, there it was. Fear.

"What can I get you?" She forced a smile.

Good girl. At least she had good sense to be afraid.

"I'll take a gin old fashioned and a bourbon for my friend." I smiled back, trying to keep the wolf from my grin. We weren't here for her either.

"You know I hate that shit," Bishop shot, momentarily looking away from his would-be victim.

"They don't keep blood on tap," I shot back.

I handed the bartender a fifty when she came back with our glasses. "Keep the change."

Pop music blasted over the speakers as the two men from the stage walked off for a break. A young couple ran out onto the floor, inspiring a few others to follow them to dance. I looked at each of them, searching. I couldn't tell which one Bishop had a tie for.

Ten minutes ticked by and then twenty. I didn't understand the point of just sitting there drinking cheap liquor and listening to grating music. Bishop and I didn't hang out. Our time together was either violent or lustful, or a mix of the two. Amorini were only allotted a few hours in the mortal world before growing sick, the call of Tartarus becoming unbearable. It was agonizing, and I didn't want to wait around to see which symptom would start first. We were the only Fallen who could tolerate the separation from Tartarus for any length of time. All others would crumble in a matter of minutes.

Some demons managed to slip through, taking root in a host, but it didn't last. Tartarus owned them and so to Hell they must return.

"Who's your friend?" one of the woman's friends had piped.

"Jake," Bishop turned, flashing his arrogant smile.

Ah yes, mortal names. I resisted the urge to curl my nose at the simplicity of it. I looked nothing like a Jake.

"He can be a bit shy," he teased.

"I'm Charlie," the girl said. "Are you new here?" She looked between us.

"Just visiting," I answered. I looked past her.

"Please tell me you did not drag us all the way here to toy with these

women." I let my annoyance trickle into Bishop's mind.

"What about you ladies?" *"I've brought us here for someone much more interesting,"* he answered.

I frowned as I took another swallow of my drink. "Excuse me," I said. Charlie's face fell as I moved past her, weeding my way through the crowd. I wanted to get this over with. I wanted to get back to Ezra. I couldn't shake the feeling that something would happen to her while I was gone. That whatever happened, it would be because of me. Because of what I had said. Because I had left her.

I fucked up. Maybe there was a way to tell her the truth and keep her safe. Maybe now was the time to take Bishop's crown.

I shut my eyes to steady my racing thoughts. I would finish this hunt and get back to her. I would figure it out from there. I just needed to be with her.

Ashes, I could practically smell her.

A cool trickle of uncertainty eased its way down my spine.

I *did* smell Ezra.

It was old. So stale it had probably been several weeks since she had been here. I tensed, following her scent like a bloodhound to—

A man leaned over his drink at the end of the bar, his fingers swiping through his screen. Dread rushed into the room like a night wind. I should have killed him. If I had taken Killian's life, he would not be subjected to the horror to come.

"Ah, I see you finally found him." Bishop's amusement only cautioned me.

"What is this?" I feigned.

"Why don't you tell me?"

I turned to Bishop. There was nothing playful in his gaze as he met mine. I knew that look. I had seen it before he ripped out the throat of an enemy. I'd seen him eat countless hearts of our own men that had wronged him right after that bitter, fury-filled look filled his face.

I couldn't bring myself to approach Killian. I had never been afraid to face anything and yet I was rooted to the ground.

Bishop rammed his shoulder into mine in the time that I blinked. In the next, he was seated next to Killian. "Hey man," he said. Friendly, but not as cheerful as he was with the women. "What's your name?"

Killian turned, his face silhouetted against the harsh lights behind the bar. "Killian."

My stomach turned.

"I'm Bishop." He nodded to me. "And this is Valen."

The entire world fell out from under me when Killian faced me. He looked just as surprised the first time he had seen me. It was still a shock to see how similar we looked. Killian's brow furrowed. "I've seen you before."

"Have you?" Bishop turned to me in surprise.

"And you," he said, glaring at Bishop.

Bishop's face split into a sinister grin. "Is that so? Funny, I don't remember ever meeting you. When was this?"

"At the party. I recognize your tattoos," Killian said bitterly.

"What was I doing?"

"*Enough,*" I said.

How did he find out? How could he possibly know? I'd been careful. Ezra and I had not been bonded long enough for anyone to even suspect.

As my fear grew, I tightened the reins on the tension pooling through my body. Bishop would make a move. I would just have to be faster.

Killian's eyes flicked to me. His skin paled. I'd grabbed him seconds before he had been about to rip Bishop off Ezra. I'd threatened to kill him if he made a sound. I think he was remembering that now. His scent shifted the same time his pupils dilated.

Killian's face hardened.

Now is not the time to play the bigger man, you fool.

"If you're here, I'm going to assume she got bored with you too." Killian scoffed. "I got the message the last time."

"What message?" Bishop pressed.

Killian gave him a funny look then glared at me. "That you would kill me if I kept looking for her. That I needed to let her go."

Bishop grabbed Killian's jaw so hard his fingers made divots into his skin. Killian flinched, trying to pull out of his ironclad grip. A curse slurred through his lips. "I wondered why she clung to you when she should have chosen me. I thought it was because you found her, that it made her feel special, or something ridiculous. But it's really just because you look like this scrap of a man." Bishop looked at me. "Her would-be adelfi."

"Our appearances are a coincidence," I said.

"He was her tie and you switched with her." Bishop's nails bit into Killian's face. "He is supposed to be dead."

Killian gripped Bishop's hand with both of his as he tried to pry him off. "Get the fuck off," he hissed through his twisted mouth.

"I made the calculated decision to let him live so that she would trust me." My head was abuzz with the increase of power swelling around us. I ran my tongue over the roof of my mouth as it dried completely. "To ensure that she would fall. Which she did."

With a twist of his wrist, Bishop snapped Killian's jaw. The man let out a mangled scream as he fell to the floor.

"You would lie to my face." Bishop spoke softly and yet the volume of his power was striking. Time came to a screeching halt. The music and loud voices cut off like a switch. The dancers became motionless; drinks were fixed mid-pour. Every single person was frozen save for the three of us.

Killian's body seized. One hand held his jaw shut while the other pawed at his throat. He heaved forward as a cough wracked his chest.

"I'm not lying," I said.

I didn't move as Killian clawed at his throat with both hands. I wouldn't back down from Bishop. Not this time.

Bishop leaned against the bar. Most demons' eyes darkened when they were angry. Bishop's turned white. The silver irises frosted like a winter's storm.

My power wove within me. I pulled it forward quietly, guiding it from the depths it rested. I had been biding my time, trying to find the right moment to strike Bishop down. I was a fool to think there was ever going to be a perfect moment. Like always, he was three steps ahead.

Killian slammed his palm into the ground, breaking my focus. Blood spewed from his mouth as he coughed again. His nails raked red trails down his throat and, with a horrific wheeze, Killian hurled. Thousands and thousands of gems burst from his mouth. Glittering rainbow obsidian stones scattered across the floor, coated in blood.

"Let him go," I said coolly. He didn't deserve this. Ezra was right; he was supposed to be the one that got away. The one who lived. I took a step forward. "He has nothing to do with this."

"Surely, he does. It's like looking into a fucking mirror!" Bishop's voice cracked across the room, shattering every glass.

Killian screamed from the gaping hole in his mouth.

"As if it is a crime to bear the face of another."

"A fucking stand-in is what he is. It was the same with Episkopos and that boy," he spat. "As if God or Heaven ever gave a shit about us."

"Enough," I snapped. "Yes. He was a stand in. He was placed in Ezra's life where others would fall, until I could find her. Though I had no idea of her existence until I took her from Ariel."

"How dare you," Bishop snarled, rising from his chair. "After everything I have done for you."

"You have done nothing but hold us hostage while you rule as a tyrant," I seethed. There was no coming back from this. I had faced Bishop once and lost. Losing this time only resulted in death, and it wasn't going to be mine. I couldn't lose Ezra. Not when I had just found her.

"I thought killing Episkopos would have rot the seed he left behind."

"You cannot change fate," I shot back. "You cannot change what has already been written. You tried and failed when you killed Rachel, when you corrupted Episkopos before killing him. Try as you might, you cannot manipulate true love."

"You do not know the meaning of love, you selfish fucker. It is because of love that I do not kill you where you stand and take back what you stole from me. What all three of you traitors stole." Bishop's power was magnanimous. It was easy to forget we were not equals, not even with the bit of the cyn's power I had drank. Not when he was an archangel.

"You forgot the meaning of love long before you fell. What you feel for me is obsession."

Bishop's lips were so far curled that there was nothing but exposed gums and sharp teeth. "You will break the bond and then you will step aside. If you do not, I will rip out her wings." His mouth fluttered into a sneer.

"You would not dare," I seethed.

"I will ground her. And after she is done bleeding, I will rip out her heart and put it into a box that I will throw into the pit of Vasanistirio so that you may never regain it."

I flinched. Grounding was one of the worst things to befall an angel. That was why all of the Fallen had their wings burned. But to rip out her heart? It was a gamble if it would kill her or not. My kind could only be killed in the heart by either being struck by an arrow or having it consumed. But someone else, they could live eons without their hearts before they started to age. Having her heart thrown into Vasanistirio, however, meant Ezra would live out her days in utter torment, screaming. God help her if she was immortal.

"I have sat by idly, allowing you to play cyn," Bishop continued. "Flaunting your stolen power. You do not get her too."

"Ezra is not yours to bid."

"Neither was Episkopos's power yours!" The rattle of broken glass was like wind chimes at his roar.

"You would have damned us all. We stole from you to save Vélos. If it were up to you, humanity would have been killed."

"If it were up to me, I would have led us to victory—"

"And slaughtered us too. You have always wanted too much. You destroy everything you touch. And fitting that you are the only one unscathed by your sins while the rest of us smolder. And now you would threaten the one saving grace blessed to us for your selfish desires. Your jealousy knows no bounds!"

"I deserve her. I have worked for everything only to have it ripped from me." He paused, his chest heaving. Flames had found their way across his knuckles. They steadily climbed their way up his hands. "You know me, brother," he spat. "I keep true to my word. If you do not break the tie with her, you will both suffer for it."

A wave of power struck the center of my chest. It cracked down across my shoulders, forcing me to my knees. I caught myself with my palms, fighting every bit of him until my arms gave out and my face hit the floor.

Mere seconds ticked by but it felt like minutes. Hours. Sharp ringing blasted through my eardrums, a side effect from a force of power greater than my own. Blood trickled out of my ears. I could feel the wetness of it spreading to my eyes. I gritted my teeth.

A shudder ran through me as the power receded.

Bishop crouched over Killian before grabbing his hair and jerking his neck back so far, his vertebrae cracked. I sent my power around the man's throat. His dark skin slid apart like a tear in paper. A dark waterfall of blood riveted down his throat and pooled at his knees.

Bishop's head snapped in my direction.

"Better a swift death than to be killed by a monster," I said.

Innocent. Innocent of any crime. Innocent of being Ezra's adelfi and he was dead by my hand. I had promised Ezra I would spare him, and I had. It was for her I even killed him at all. Bishop would have dragged his life out until the very last thread had spun out. He would have done it before her, and that was not a horror I could allow her to bear.

"I'll kill you," he hissed.

"I suggest that you do, because I'm not giving Ezra up." In a flash, I unleashed my power. It knocked Bishop through the bleed I had opened behind him and sent him reeling right back into Tartarus. I followed him, an arrow in my hand that I slammed down toward his chest.

Bishop grabbed the tip of the arrow, his eyes wide with shock as I bared down on him.

"I'll be taking your crown too."

His surprise only lasted a second before he erupted, sending a burst of black lightning through my body. It burned my skin and ripped the breath from my lungs.

I let the change take me, allowed my talons to unsheathe and the hook of my tail to snake free. I slid every natural blade I had into his body and then I sunk my teeth into his throat.

Bishop's fire and lightning continued to assault me. Blood burst from my eyes and nose. It spilled across my skin as he tore me apart. I clawed at his chest, tearing for the heartbeat that thrummed like a battle drum in my ear.

A sharp pain slid into my gut. Horrible pain that gouged my eyes. I had suffered this before, and I would do it again. I had to. There was no room for failure when it was Ezra's life in the balance.

A slicing pain shot into the center of my chest. A pain that could not be real. Blood, both his and mine, erupted from my mouth as I jerked my teeth free.

"I'll do it," Bishop snarled. "I'll destroy you."

I blinked the blood from my eyes to see my beating heart clenched in his fist, between the arrow-tipped claws we all wore. It stilled my poisoned claws embedded in his chest.

His breath was shallow beneath the crackle of his power.

"Bow to me. Release her. Do it and I'll not kill you."

My claws and hook remained within his skin as I stared at it.

I had searched everywhere for my heart. To the deepest parts of Tartarus and to the tallest mountain in Eimai Theós. I'd allowed myself to win back Bishop's trust in the hope he kept it close. For years I had found empty compartments and chambers. It didn't matter now where he had hidden it, there it was in front of me. I could take it.

If I took it, it would change nothing. Ezra would still be at a monster's mercy. Worlds would fall. Her world. Things could not go back to the way they were. The only way was forward.

Slowly, my eyes slid back to my brother's face. "I am a prisoner to you no more." I sunk my teeth into his throat and pushed all of my weight and power into the center of his chest. His claws pierced my heart, ripping all sense and feeling from me but the pain of the true death that was upon me.

Tears mixed with the blood in my eyes as I thought of Ezra. That I had finally found her only to have her ripped away from me. There was a brief second where I considered letting go, because if I was dead then no one would be there to protect her. Not even Diriel would be able to stand against Bishop, though I knew he would try.

But I knew. I fucking knew I could take Bishop with me. It would save her. It would save my people.

I felt the thorns of the crown searing into my skull as he tried to rip mine from me and the weight of his bore down on my head as I tried to steal his.

A blinding white force struck me across the back of the head. My mouth was ripped free of Bishop's throat, and I was knocked back into my human form, ten feet away from him.

Colored splotches dotted my vision as I rose to my hands. Three figures stood over Bishop, one of them stooping down to assist the male.

"Traitors," I snarled at the Murder.

Raum tsked. "The only traitor amongst us is you." He swiped his finger in the blood pooled in the middle of Bishop's chest and stuck it in his mouth. "I told you Baal wanted him and here I find you trying to kill each other."

Bishop rolled to his side. Cracks leaked through the air as his chest started to mend. Blood dribbled out of his mouth and nose. His limbs were shaking, his muscles spasming. His light eyes were white when they landed on me.

"He won't give her up," he said.

Raum slid an arm beneath him and hoisted Bishop to his feet. "He will. Once we are done with him, he will have to."

I'd been privy to a few of the Murder's tortures. Those had not exceeded the tales that circulated Tartarus. Keras were known for their livid cruelty.

My lips curled. "You would turn me over, betray your own brother, for what? Ezra? She is mine, and if you think you can steal her, you are a fool. They," I jerked my head to the Murder, "will take her from you and then someone else from them if she is not killed first. You stupid fool."

Bishop's jaw hardened. "She's mine and so is Vélos. I suggest you use your time wisely in Eurynomos and think about what your life is worth. You will bend to my will or I will relieve you of yours."

I had nothing left to throw at him, but I sent the last wisp of my power at him anyway, snapping it across his face like a whip. Bishop's head jerked back as a fresh red line of blood spit his cheek apart.

"That is enough," Raum growled. "Take him to the chambers," he said to Orias.

I dug my fingers into the black ground. I cast a quick glance around us, to the forest and black mountains. The Murder had been waiting for us. This had been Bishop's plan all along.

Bishop cradled my heart against his chest. It was there. Yet I could not reach it. An amorini without its heart is a slave to the one who owns it. So long as Bishop possessed it, I would be forced to do his bidding.

I snapped at Orias as he grabbed me. While I was turned, Atticus grabbed my other arm, hauling me to my feet. His shadows slipped around me, binding me in a cocoon of darkness. I could hear the quiet hum of a ship's engine somewhere in the forest. I'd been so focused on Bishop; I hadn't noticed it when we landed.

"You have two months to fix this," Bishop said.

Raum looked back at him coolly. "Need I remind you we have always cleaned up your messes? We will break him." The keras's sapphire eyes danced in the morning light. "And then we will break him some more."

CHAPTER FIFTY-FIVE: DARKNESS CALLS

Valen

Eurynomos, Tartarus
Two months prior

In the dimly-lit chamber, I was laid across a cool metal table. Cold iron bound my throat, wrists, and ankles; it burned divots into my flesh. It stank of rot and putrid decay. My only company for the first three days were the screams that broke through the obsidian walls. That and the rats I could hear scurrying somewhere below me.

No food, water, or blood was given to me in those first days. Perhaps they thought it would make me more compliant. Something as simple as starving would not dull my senses. It sure as hell wouldn't kill me.

It didn't matter what the keras did to me, I would live so long as Bishop held my heart.

I had never considered the possibility of being at the mercy of the horrors that resided in Eurynomos. The Murder oversaw me that first week. Raum and Atticus would stand in the back corner and watch as Orias went to work.

The torture began slowly. My nails were ripped off, the rings in my ears were torn out. Gradually, it increased. Orias slid a razor-thin blade through my skin, carving flesh from muscle in thin, nearly translucent strips. He hung them above me on a wire.

In the moments of torture, I fantasized how I would cut Bishop apart piece by piece. How the red of his lips would pale as I bled him dry. And then I imagined how sweet it would be to finally kill the Murder that had been a stain on my kingdom since they set foot within our borders.

Raum hummed a song in the darkness as Orias worked.

"I've never heard you scream," Orias said. He flicked the spiraled knife in his hand toward the light. He looked down on me with those soulless blue eyes and then slid the knife into my stomach, and twisted. "Will you sing for me?" He jerked his arm back, ripping my intestines from the puncture wound.

I clenched my jaw, fighting the scream that clung in my throat. A garbled grunt came out instead as I ground my teeth together.

"Oh, come on, that's not the right note." Orias slid the knife in again. Twist and pull. Stab and twist. He did it until my insides were spilled across the lower half of my body. As punishment for my silence, Orias left me like that for two days. Rats crawled over my body and picked apart the tender flesh with their jagged teeth.

When the Murder returned, it was to piece me back together, only so Orias could tear me apart all over again. Atticus's scarred hands worked diligently as he reassembled my mutilated body.

"I hope you understand the magnitude of destruction that is

going to fall upon your heads when I get out of here," I said.

Atticus smirked, but as usual he said nothing. Silent as a ghost.

Orias looked over from his place next to Raum. "If you were anything other than an amorini, we might take that threat seriously." A mischievous grin touched his broad mouth. "Look at you, Valen." Orias thrust out his bottom lip in a mock pout. "You're nothing."

"Come closer, Orias, and say it to my face."

A low hiss emitted from the keras.

Raum chuckled.

Orias leered over the table. His hair twisted across his bare shoulders. The gold rings that linked across his scalp danced in the dim light. This close, I could see the silver dragon skin that adorned his throat and engulfed his jawline. The flutter of a smile touched my lips.

"Surely you do not wear the scales because you are afraid of little ol' me."

Orias's eyes flared. "I have no fear," he said.

The iron cuffs sizzled against my skin as I leaned into them. I waited until Orias was a few inches from me before snaking out my power and pulling him against me, sinking my teeth into his cheek. I clenched my jaw as he reeled backward and tore the flesh of meat clean from his face.

Orias screamed.

I slipped the meat over my tongue and swallowed it down. The rot turned my stomach over, but it was substance. "You should have worn it higher," I said.

A silver flash past through the air as Orias's longsword came down and sliced clean through my legs. My back arched as the blade buried into the steel below me. I ground my teeth together as the cry Orias had searched for threatened to break free.

Raum grabbed Orias by the shoulder and threw him back. "We are to be precise. Go clear your head," he barked.

Orias's hand remained cupped over the side of his face. Blood trickled down his forearm and coated the front of his chest.

Atticus trailed after the male, his footsteps soundless as his light was swallowed in the darkness.

All that remained was Raum, his eyes unblinking. He was always watching. He had missed nothing, and I could tell he was still calculating.

"Does Baal know of your betrayal?" I asked.

Raum's brow arched. "Betrayal?" The demon let the word hang between us. Somewhere in the distance, someone wailed. "I live to serve my cyn, something you would do well to learn yourself." His eyes trailed down to where the sword lay buried. With one hand, he jerked it up, earning a grunt from my throat. He held it above me as he moved to where Orias had been minutes before.

"Tell Baal," he whispered. The edge of the sword hovered over the collar at my throat. "I will not stop you."

I held his eyes and slowly looked away.

Raum chuckled. "That is what I thought."

Baal would never believe his most prized warrior would betray him. Not from an amorini who would say anything to escape their hold. The truth of the words would not matter.

Raum slid his palm over my mouth, pressing my lips so hard into my teeth I couldn't open it, though I tried. Steep, smoking darkness filtered into my nostrils. It burned the back of my eyes and cut off my air. I jerked against him as the smoke pulled up my past sins and twisted them into wicked visions before my eyes.

"Bishop has promised me her first child," he said. "I have not decided if I will keep it for myself to raise or gift it to one of the others. What do you think?" he hissed. "The possibilities are endless. Perhaps I will be lucky and get her with two."

Each movement was agonizing as I fought against my restraints. Each shock of pain heated my rage. I was going to kill him. I was going to kill every last one of them.

The smoke stripped apart my sanity. I chewed the inside of my mouth, trying to bite my way to his hand to make it stop. To rip out the depraved things that dripped from his lips. I pulled at my power, but whatever he was doing suppressed it.

Raum grinned and pushed his hand harder. The dark magic encased me, winding its way through my body, my soul, and wrung me until the scream I had been holding so tightly was ripped from me.

My suffering was all consuming, a white-hot blaze that tore me to shreds from the inside out.

"There it is," Raum breathed. "I knew I could make you sing."

The insidious poison took everything I was and stripped me bare.

I don't know how much time past before I came to again. It was when I inhaled that I realized something else was wrong. My shackles had been removed and I was lying on my stomach. I gripped the side of the table as a wash of pain clouded my senses and let out a sound only an animal could make.

They had tried to pull what was left of my wings while I was passed out. What I saw in my peripheral still made my stomach turn, and I leaned over the side to vomit yellow bile and blood. My ribs were broken outside of my back in the form of two bloody wings.

The image of Lane past across my mind's eye. I knew what lay within the walls of Eurynomos and I had abandoned her here to hold onto my throne and my crown. To live the lie I had been fed.

Diriel had not been her adelfi, yet I had been blinded by the emotion I felt toward him, at what would happen had Bishop discovered an ounce of affection between the two. I could not give up my brother, but the woman could be replaced. I'd abandoned her to save him. I'd given her to the torment I suffered now.

I bet she would be laughing if she could see me now.

"I hear you've been causing trouble," a voice flitted through the grate of the doorway.

Chills that had nothing to do with the temperature shot across my skin. Baal had that effect on people. It had been rumored that he was really the devil with his lush voice and steely contempt.

"Come now. You usually have so much to say." The cell door opened without a sound as the Cyn of Eurynomos stepped in. Like usual, he was clouded in darkness. Bits of flame flashed beneath his feet and dark swirls of galaxies moved in the blackness.

"Do you know why you're here?" Baal asked.

I didn't say a word. Not that I could. My throat was raw from screaming.

A row of glistening white teeth cracked across the darkness like a Cheshire grin. A pale hand reached out of the darkness and slid across my face. He trailed a long finger down the length of my back. It slid down across my hip, down my ass, and continued down the swell of my thighs.

"You should have told me about the girl. As her adelfi, perhaps we could have come to an arrangement." Baal paused in his exploration to curl back into the shadows. "Perhaps we still can."

Baal would never lay a finger on Ezra.

"Ah, there is that fire."

Embers flitted through the air as my power struggled to light. I eased back to the center of the table as Baal stepped through the darkness clouding him. The horns on his head had grown longer since the last I had seen him, ode to his age.

The starlight of his eyes glistened with the thousands of tears he had stolen. "I always thought you were too good for a crown. A male that walks the line of the light is a male unworthy."

I followed him down until his dark head was bent before me. Baal kissed me on the brow, his lips a pale blue.

"You are wise, Baal," I rasped.

A slow smile spread on the cyn's face. "I am. I have lived lifetimes very few can dream of. I have seen worlds live and die. Heavens made anew. Hells burning for eternity in every universe."

I clenched the metal beneath me with sweat-slicked palms. "Ezra has already given you what you desire. She has opened a doorway to Earth, making way for your rule and destruction."

Baal's eyes glimmered.

"She has given you freedom."

Baal sighed. He ran a gentle thumb over the side of my cheek. "Freedom no longer suits me. I desire more than that. I ask you again, do you know why you are here?"

I ground my teeth together.

"You are here because your inelegance has not been tested. It is apparent by your bond with the nephilim and betrayal to Cyn Bishop that grace flows within your blood. How you have managed to retain it all these years is... fascinating. You are quite the performer, Valentine. Or should I call you Eros?"

My blood froze. If my heart had been in my chest, it would have stopped beating.

Baal slid a book from behind his back. *The Book of Names.* "I had Raum retrieve it last time he visited. Selfish that you would keep something so precious to yourself. You amorini, too lowly to be great and too proud to level yourselves with the rest of us."

Names are sacred to angels. They hold power. And God help the soul who was at the will of anyone who owned an angel's true name. Demon or a host.

"You know Bishop is not fit to rule," I started. The words bubbled in the back of my throat as Baal flipped through the pages.

"Shhh," the demon crooned.

"Baal," I growled. "You do not know the mistake you will make if you go after her. Take what she gave you and be done with it. You can take Bishop's crown for yourself for all I care. Do not fly so high that you are burned again."

Baal didn't so much as acknowledge me. He turned another page, his eyes skimming until he found what he was looking for.

"I hate to do this to you, Valen. Even with your wings in Heaven, I always saw such great potential in you."

Baal slid his thumb over my brow. "Let me show you the fate of Ezra Bree Hollen." The demon pushed me into a sea of darkness and there I dreamed.

I dreamed of Ezra and all the fates that stood before her. It was those dreams, those vicious nightmares, that finally broke me.

She was on bloody knees with Baal before her, dark shadow wings spread at his back. She clawed the ground in an attempt to flee, only to be caught and pinned beneath him.

I saw the children she bore used and murdered. I saw her bound to a cross as flames licked at her feet. A feral scream ripped from her throat, the cry of a banshee, of the harpy I had named her. It was her scream that ripped mine from my chest.

Again and again I saw her tormented while I remained trapped in utter Hell unable to stop any of it.

There was no end. When one vision ended, another began. I could not say if I was trapped there for years or a few minutes. It continued on until sweet darkness enveloped me and I slept. I slept and slept. I clung to the nothingness so that I might not relive any of what I had witnessed.

Soft lips pressed against mine. A gentle touch ran through my hair.

"Wake up," she said.

My lids fluttered up to see Ezra's bright face. She flashed a worried smile.

"There you are."

I lurched from the bed.

My room.

One of the three moons' faces shed its light across the marble floor. It cast a soft glow against Ezra's pale skin.

"You were having a nightmare," she said. "It took me forever to wake you up."

I skimmed my fingers over her face. Sparks skirted beneath my fingertips; her warmth bled into me. I grasped the back of her head and pressed my forehead against hers, holding her there as I came down from the dark.

"You're ok. I've got you," she said softly. Her full lips slid over the top of my cheek.

I breathed her in as I angled my head to survey the room once more.

I had torn it apart when I had denied her. I had ripped every cloth and tapestry to shreds. The columns had been black by the time I was done, the stones singed. I'd had a mind to tear apart the entire tyre before Bishop intercepted me.

This wasn't real.

Perhaps they meant to soften me before dealing another blow.

I shut my eyes. This wasn't Ezra's face pressed to mine.

They didn't know what I had said to her before I was taken. They couldn't. As far as everyone knew, my soul had tied with Ezra's and we were in love. They didn't know I had left her broken.

I faced her slowly. It looked so much like her. I looked for any trace of the incubus that was playing the part of my adelfi.

"Little phoenix," I said.

Ezra smiled. "I hate when you call me that."

I slid my hand around her neck and stroked it softly. Her skin was smooth, soft as I remembered it. I knew how easily it would break against my teeth. Would her blood taste the same as it did in the waking world? "I never call you that, love."

Gods, she was beautiful, even this false image of her. The knit of her brow was nearly perfect.

But it didn't soften the blow as I sunk my hand into her chest. It did not dull my claws as I gripped them around her heart and ripped it free.

The world of golden light and pristine smiles contorted into the mass of horrors I had lived a lifetime of and then that, too, was ripped away.

I fell to the floor. Blinding cold pain ruptured through me as I landed on my back. The wings of my ribs were still cracked open, but even in pain I laughed.

Baal stumbled back into Raum's waiting arms, clutching at his torn and bloody chest. Beside him, still gripping his forearm, was Orias, his other fist pressed to his forehead.

I shouldn't have laughed, but neither did I try to stop it as music slipped through my cracked lips. "You shouldn't let others walk with you, Orias. Someone might get hurt."

The demon's lips curled. A stray blood tear ran down from the corner of his eye.

"Do you fear the amorini yet?" I gasped as darkness clutched against my chest. It ripped away the insults I would have said.

Baal's fingers still worked over his gaping chest. The devil of the darkness growled. The seams of his mouth parted to his ears when he spoke.

"Again. Put him under again," he snarled.

And again, I witnessed years of Ezra's grace being stripped from her.

CHAPTER FIFTY-SIX: I MADE YOU A PROMISE

Valen

Ezra's back slid down the wall before she fell to the floor in a heap. I followed her down. Her mind was a whirl. Thoughts of me. Anguish for Killian. Her breath came in deep, controlled gulps.

"I'm sorry," I said.

Her eyes shimmered as she blinked up at me. "Sorry?" she choked.

"For Killian. It was the only way I could spare him. I made you a promise that I would not kill him, and I did. It was only so he would not suffer." I cut my tongue over the edge of my teeth. "Bishop would have tormented him much the way the keras did me. He would not have survived it."

She pressed her hand to her heart. When I reached for her, she didn't stop me.

"Valen," she said, her voice a broken whisper. "I am angry, hurt even but," she choked on her tears again, "how can I be knowing what they did to you? What you endured...." A guttural sob tore through her.

"I'm fine," I lied. I couldn't bring myself to share all the other horrors I had left in that cold, dark dungeon. Not when I was unable to face them myself. What she didn't know couldn't hurt her.

My breath staggered as I pulled her into my arms. Saints, it felt so good to have her within my embrace again, to smell the real her. I breathed in her anguish and tears. I had longed for the way she smelled while in the bowels of Eurynomos. I had longed to feel her skin against mine, her heat intertwining with my fire. I held her tighter as her arms snapped around my shoulders.

"I would do it again. I made you a promise that I would keep you safe."

I splayed a palm down the back of her hair as she shook her head, her sobs shaking her entire body. I ran my nails through the silky strands of her golden hair. Slid them over her scalp and down until she was ready to look at me.

I brushed a thumb over her cheeks, brushing away her tears' trails. Her face crumbled, but instead of letting the fresh wave of water go, she took a deep breath. "How did you get out?"

My harpy had always been a perceptive one.

My mouth twisted at the thought. "I suffered worse things than I can tell you. It was only when I gave into them that Baal loosened his hold. It was only when they broke me that I would be free to return to Vélos. To be returned to Bishop."

Ezra's hair fell forward as she shook her head. "You didn't

break."

I ran my palm down her face. "I thought I did... Holding onto you was the only thing that kept me from falling into the hold they tried to lock me in. But they had to know that I gave you up, that I would be malleable to Bishop's will."

"Why does Bishop care so much? Not about me, but you? You've ruled at his side for so long now. I don't understand." Her fingers had found their way beneath my shirt sleeves. It was a small gesture that would make my heart swell had I had it. She wanted to be as close to me as she could.

I sat down in the dirt, spreading my legs on either side of her so she was still shielded by my body. She let me take her hands in mine. They were so small. Her fingers long and slender. Strong and deft enough to use the finest of bows.

She had been weaker when I found her. In my absence, she had grown into a strong woman. I admired the veins in her hands, the muscles that cut into her arms. She would make a fine archer if our people were ever returned to their glory.

"Bishop's entire existence has been about control. Over our people, the throne, me, and now you. After our fall, we became lovers. It started happening with most of our men. We had never desired anything of the flesh before, but grounding changed something within us. I hated him. I hated him for killing Episkopos, for forcing his blood onto our hands. I hated that he had my heart. Despite our laws, that he created, I think Bishop started to love me. Not in a real romantic sense, but infatuation. He became obsessed.

"He's never been right in the mind. If it were not for the color of his eyes, I would think he a keras that had been misplaced. When he shot lovers, he was harsh about it. His adelfis would always fall too fast or too hard. Often finding each other only for one or both to die in a sudden tragedy.

"It happened enough that it became a pattern. I remember those days vividly. Specifically, I remember the day I finally worked up the courage to ask him about it. Bishop had shrugged, saying human lives were short and that they were fortunate to have found each other at all.

"I should have said something, but I was a fool then. I thought that perhaps it was God's will that Bishop's adelfis die. I was born in the matters of the heart and thought I did not have the wisdom to interpret what was happening or that it was above my conscience, and yet..."

"You knew something was wrong," Ezra said softly.

I took a deep breath as I met her light eyes. I didn't know when my gaze had drifted to the corner. To the nail marks of the humans we had first locked down here. In those early days, they had been turned loose and hunted for sport. As a way to say "fuck you" to Heaven. But we didn't have the full story then. We never had.

Guilt's familiar touch worked its way through my gut. I had been so angry then. My rage consumed me and, without a second thought, I had fed it the blood of thousands of innocents.

"Baal told me the truth of our fall. That he had gifted Bishop the ability to shift shapes. I didn't know keras could do that, gift their powers to someone. Bishop went in place of our cyn and spat in God's face." I shook my head, trying to make sense of it all. If it were true, that Episkopos and Rachel were adelfis... What had Bishop truly said to cast us out? Bits of the story still came in pieces between images of torment. Of Baal's wicked teeth and the gleam of Orias's blades.

"He could have been lying," Ezra offered. I knew not even she believed the comfort she tried to give.

"No. It is the only thing that finally feels… right. To know that my brother had been conspiring with the Fallen all along pains me. And then I think of all the crimes I have committed since being cast out. Of the innocents I hunted and tortured of my own will. As if it would satisfy the anger that raged within my blood."

Shadows swirled around me as the tension in my muscles threatened to snap. I was tired. I was so damn tired and fucking angry.

"You didn't know."

She flinched when my eyes snapped back to hers. "I made the choices I did, knowing they were wrong, Ezra. Do not try to soften my crimes when I willingly committed them." I swallowed, looking her over. The sharpness of her gaze met mine with an edge as fine as the blade she bore at her hip.

"What?" She shifted her back against the wall.

"I wish I had half of your control back then."

Ezra's lashes fluttered as she turned away. "I don't know about that. My control has started to dissolve. I don't know what I believe anymore with this prophecy, after Ariel. Fuck, what I almost did with Bishop." A heady scent of shame wafted off her skin. "I was trying to get back at you. Had I known…. Fuck, Valen."

"I had to make you believe what I needed them to. Baal started sending men through the veil and I could not rot a second longer in Eurynomos without knowing what was happening to you. I couldn't reach you. Whatever wards they have in Eurynomos blocked me from speaking to you through the bond."

"That first night you saw me with the Murder was to ensure their spells had held."

Her brows furrowed. "What sort of spells? What did they do?"

I waved my hand. "A compulsion spell that would keep me

entrapped to their desires, that would bind me to their will and Bishop's. Done correctly, it'll last a lifetime, but you also need the prisoner's consent."

Ezra's mouth quirked slightly. "And you lied."

"It broke as soon as we entered Vélos. I had planned to speak with you then."

"Except I wasn't there," she said softly.

"No."

A blush darkened her cheeks. "After what you had said, and the women..."

"The women were pawns. What you saw was the extent of it, though I am sorry you had to witness it at all. I wanted to tear them apart because they were not you."

Soft scratching came from somewhere above. I lifted my head, looking for rats or some sort of wraith lurking above our heads. Perhaps it was footfalls coming from way above. I was never easily spooked, but recently the shadows had started to take new shapes and it was hard for me to determine what was real and what wasn't.

"And Bishop?" she asked.

I cocked my head down, keeping an ear trained for any sign of unwelcomed guests.

"Has he touched you?"

Her words twisted where my heart should be. It was not a jealous question but one of quiet rage. A sense of pride fluttered in my chest that she would still feel any sort of possession over me. That she would care at all.

"I think you know the answer to that," I said.

I watched her carefully as a red light flashed through her irises. On the edge of her left eye was a flash of silver, there and gone as she turned her head away from the light. The quiet scent of her rage should not have heated my blood the way that it did. It made my cock twitch with feral hunger.

I brushed against her mind. Images of Bishop telling her sweet words while he ravaged me flashed across her mind. Her stomach churned at the memory of the kiss Bishop and I had shared earlier. As she wondered what else we had done in private. He's been playing us both.

"Do not make yourself sick." The images she painted made my words bitter.

"Get out of my head."

I bowed my head. "It is nothing I have not endured before. It will be the last, however. I mean to take Bishop's crown and free my people from his tyranny."

Ezra drug her fingers through her hair. "You can't do it without your heart."

I disagreed. If I failed to live through the battle, Jinn and Diriel would be left to stand, and I knew they would do the right thing. They would lead our men. I'd nearly taken Bishop before, only this time I had no intention of dying. I would see him through and keep Ezra. "I have no intentions of getting it back before I end him."

Her face skewed. "So, you'd risk the chance of him killing you again? Make me lose you a second time? For good? I don't think so."

I couldn't help it. I smiled. Ezra had turned into quite the viper. It irked me that I was probably the cause of it, but the fact that she had sharpened her claws was good for her. All her smooth edges had been refined to polished blades.

"You'll not lose me."

"You're right, because I'm going to get your heart."

It felt like a cavern had fallen between us. She didn't know what she was saying. I sure as hell wasn't going to let her anywhere near Bishop again if I could help it. "He will only give it up if he knows he has no other move. And that'll be with an arrow in it."

She licked her lip as she stood. The space between us was filled with cold.

I followed her. My shadows churned around her feet, testing her posture in the event she might make a run for it.

"He knows how angry and hurt I am over you. I can ask for it." She swiped a stray tear from her face. "I'll make him believe he has me and then I'll run. But not before I have what belongs to you."

"If you manage to ever lay hands on it, you might as well keep it." I cupped her chin so the moons' light would wash over her face. The white sheen was iridescent against the gold of her angelic skin. "But I cannot ask that of you. I've been a prisoner to him and Tartarus for a long while. I think I can manage a little longer until you're away. Let me not fail you, Ezra."

Ezra's brow furrowed. "You said I didn't have an adelfi."

I hissed at her swift change of topic.

I slid my free hand over her waist and drew her to me. "I lied."

"Did you know when you found me?"

"No. In truth, I was too blinded by what you were to acknowl-edge the possibility that there was something more to you waking me. Ashes, Ezra, you did wake me. I have been lost to the darkness for so long I did not ever think I would wake. I don't know for certain when I knew what you were, but I knew we were in great danger when I fell for you in the library. I knew that if you ever chased after me that we would be damned."

Her red lips were parted. I slid my thumb over that beautiful mouth, so soft and inviting.

"After the hunt," she breathed.

"I was supposed to make you fall, but I couldn't do it. I couldn't break the light of your faith when it shone so bright. Ezra…" It hurt to swallow. "Will you forgive me?"

She turned her head away. Tension built up like a coiled spring the longer she went without saying anything. "I don't know if I can."

I had expected nothing less, yet it still pained me to hear.

"Not yet," she added softly. "I… You killed him, Valen. You promised to keep Killian safe, and it was by your hand— I hate you for that. And I am angry for hating you. There's no denying there's something binding us together. My feelings over the last few months do not overshadow what you suffered for me. Or the torment you faced before me." As she spoke, her fingers slid up the front of my tunic. Wisps of gold fire slid beneath her palm.

I could deal with her hating me so long as she kept looking at me with that glorious fury in her eyes. So long as she was *looking* at me, I didn't give a damn. It gave me hope.

"I'm conflicted," she confessed.

I leaned into her palm, willing her scorch to tear a hole in my clothes so I could feel her on my skin. I needed her to replace the darkness that had seeped into my bones.

The lick of her flames wrapped around my neck, tipping my chin up with a brush of their heat.

The red glint returned to her eyes. I could smell the desire on her. To tear me apart or fuck me, I couldn't tell which. Both would be welcome. A shadow fell across my gaze as I dug my fingers into the small of her back, begging her to sink those long nails beneath my flesh.

She curled her hand against my chest and pulled me down.

Her kiss lit a fire in my belly. I forced her back against the wall as her teeth bit into my lip, into my tongue when I tried to taste her. Her nails were sharp as daggers as she clawed the back of my head.

"You make me feel," she gasped.

"Yes," I breathed against her mouth. Ezra was the closest I would ever return to Heaven. She was life's breath to my soul. I did not deserve her, but I would gladly take whatever she would give me.

Her blunt teeth tore into my lip. "I'll kill you myself if I ever see you with another woman."

I groaned as she thrust her hips against my hard cock.

"And I'll kill anyone who touches you that is not me," she growled. "They will all die for what they have done to you. Every last one."

I hissed as her burn finally met my flesh. Sweet pain shot through my nerves. Fuck, my harpy was perfect.

"Please," I begged.

"I hate you for your lies," she seethed, her voice growing thick with tears.

"I know." I ripped the top of her shirt, exposing the base of her throat and shoulder so I could plant my lips to her sweet flesh.

"I hate you for... killing him," she forced out. Her head tipped back as my fangs brushed against her.

"Forgive me," I breathed.

"Never." Her hands dove to the front of my pants. I caught her wrist as her fingers laced through the buckle.

Red and silver flashed in her light irises. She was utterly terrifying in that moment. It only fed my perverse desire to have her, to be ruled by her. I didn't want to hold her off, but I knew she would regret fucking me in the middle of a damp tunnel come morning. Her emotions were a wildfire I did not want to tame but soothe.

I felt it the moment the thought crossed her mind. She thought back to the River Styx when I had tried to stop her then. To the rejection that followed swiftly after. I felt her withdrawing, her walls going up.

I snaked my hand around the back of her neck. "Don't you dare," I growled. "My pause is no rejection, harpy. I want you to punish me for how I have wronged you. Slipping inside of you will only be a reward."

Those cold eyes hardened. "Rewarding you is the last thing I want to do... but you deserve some relief. I am not so angry that I can overlook what you suffered because of me. For me." Her eyes fluttered to my lips, then across my eyes.

I was on the edge of a cliff. The only thing that stopped me from falling over was the firm grip she had on my collar as I dangled over the chasm.

"I am yours to do with as you please," I purred. My throat was hot with want. My gums ached where my fangs had elongated, pulsing with the desire to feed. To bite into her flesh so that I could properly taste her. "Let me taste the pain I have caused you."

"Kneel," she said.

When I hesitated, she flashed me a devilish grin. Ezra was a real brat when she wanted to be, and I fucking loved it. She was a harpy through and through.

I slid my hands down the back of her thighs as I kneeled before her. I pressed my lips into her thighs as I looked up.

Her fingers tangled in my curls as she ran her nails across my scalp. The tenderness did more to me than she would ever know. I wanted to be bloodied, and yet her touch stilled that part of me.

"Feast on me," she said.

Of all the things—

There was no hesitation as I drew her pants down to her ankles.

Ashes, I ached for her. My cock strained against my pants, but as much as I wanted to pull it free and fist myself to her, I wouldn't. This moment was hers.

I slid my tongue up the inside of her thigh and followed the path with soft kisses. I did the same to the other, letting my tongue split and lengthen. Chills spread over her flesh, encouraging me to taste more of her.

I shoved her legs as wide as the restriction of her pants would allow. And slowly, so very slowly, I licked across her slit. The sharp inhale of breath was a javelin to my chest. I gripped the plush curves of her thighs so hard I knew her skin would bruise. She might be in command, but I was going to leave every mark I could. She was mine.

"Here?" I asked and licked her again.

Ezra rethreaded her fingers in my hair. "I said feast."

I could see the reflection of the light burning in my eyes in her own right before I buried my face between her thighs.

Ezra tasted like sweet golden honey. Her nectar dripped down the back of my throat as I worked my tongue in and out, forcing soft moans from her lips.

Her flesh broke apart to my teeth like fruit, blood bursting across my tongue as I worked at the vein in her thigh. I had tasted from the women upon my return, but I had not truly fed. How could I when they all tasted like ash in my mouth compared to my adelfi?

My adelfi.

Mine.

Ozien.

I slid a hand to her ass and squeezed as I sank my fangs in deeper, earning another deep moan that nearly pushed me over the edge. As her breath heightened, I ripped my fangs free.

"Tell me how much you hate me," I said.

"I *hate* you," she gasped.

"Again."

"I hate you," she said through bared teeth.

I licked at her slit. "Now tell me how much you love me."

Beautiful silver light filled her blue eyes.

I did not wait for her response before I thrust my tongue back inside of her. I held tight to her ass and, with my free hand, pressed my thumb against her clit.

"Valen!"

I fastened my mouth to her. My fangs pierced her most sensitive flesh as she tightened around my tongue. I worked over her hard, wet interior ridges, coaxing her to the edge with me.

"Fuck. I love you. I fucking hate that I love you!"

Those three little words let loose the feral beast within me. I bit down hard.

Ezra was undone. Her fingers pulled firm against my hair as she bucked against my mouth. I pulled her hips forward and back, encouraging her to ride me, to chase the high that rained over her.

Sweet honey and warm blood flooded my mouth as she peaked, her voice straining into a silent keen as she found release.

God, she was bliss.

Nothing would ever part me from her.

Not ever again.

CHAPTER FIFTY-SEVEN: WE'RE ALL DAMNED

Ezra

The sun cut through the white clouds covering Vélos. A foreign chill crept through the air, as if signifying a great change was about to befall the land. To be certain, change was coming. I could feel it as I crept back to my room last night through the still locked door.

I'd insisted that Valen not follow in case Bishop was waiting for me. It had taken a lot more convincing and twice as many bites to his perfect lips before he complied. Bishop might be angry, but he wouldn't take it out on me. Not if he thought there was still a chance at winning me. Or that's what I told myself. Valen had told me a slew of other stories of Bishop's horrors that left me second guessing.

I'd been an idiot to get as close as I had to Bishop.

A horrible realization hit me that the vision I'd had at the service might not have been a vision at all. I hadn't told Valen, but as he spun his stories, one was almost kin to mine where a woman had been cast under a lagnia spell. Lagnia, or lust, spells were rarely cast as they used more energy and often had violent consequences. In Valen's story, Bishop had used one to compel a girl to be more compliant to his will after he shot and killed her husband. The spell allows the caster to mold not just their body, but their mind to whatever they want. The side effects were an unraveled mind, loss of time, and a more willing partner.

I was going to kill him. The more I learned about Bishop, about what Valen and the others had endured, what the fucker had been trying to do to me, the angrier I became.

I couldn't sleep. I only managed to get a couple of hours' rest before I gave up and sat by the window to watch the sun take the moons' place.

I promised Valen I wouldn't go after his heart. But he had lied to me, so I owed it to him to return the favor. I knew I could get it, I just hadn't figured out how. Every time I imagined getting close to Bishop, it was so I could wrap my hands around his throat and choke the life out of him.

I'd have to be careful. The cyn was on edge, and anything slightly out of line might be the thing that pushed him over.

I was going to kill him for what he had done to Valen.

I flicked my power out, trying to draw on the silver flames, but the only fire that filled my palm was red and gold. Useless.

A soft rap of knuckles on the door drew my eyes away from the horizon.

"Come in."

Andras opened the door to my room, letting Lane creep in before slamming it shut and bolting it behind her. Her eyes went wide as she looked back.

"Well, that was rude," she said.

I met her halfway, embracing her. I hadn't even thought of

what would become of her, but seeing Lane made me fearful. She squeezed me back.

"I'm alright." She held me at arm's length. "But how are you? They locked you up? It's an absolute shit show out there."

"What's going on?"

Lane sat opposite me on the couch, drawing her knees together. Her eyes darted to the door before she leaned forward. "Do you know what you did? With Valen?"

I nodded. "Valen told me last night. He told me everything."

Her eyes narrowed. "You *saw* him?"

"In the tunnels."

Lane's eyes darted to the door again before she cursed. "The court is in an uproar. They're demanding answers to questions that Bishop won't answer. No one has seen Valen since your little stunt. What did he tell you?"

The accusation of her tone made my lips curl. "What happened wasn't a stunt, it was a challenge. He showed them that... that he is my adelfi and I'm his. Something about the way our flames intertwined and how they answered to each other. That's why everyone is so angry or has questions. It's not supposed to be possible."

I watched as color leeched from Lane's face. I could see the simmering of coals light behind her eyes.

"And Valen didn't just leave. He has been a prisoner to your cyn."

Lane's eyes widened. "What? No... What do you mean he's been a *prisoner*?"

I ran my nails through my hair and then I told her everything. I watched as her olive skin paled. The beds of her nails were red and torn by the time she finished chewing them.

She sat back in silence, trying to process it all. "What the fuck," she said, her voice shaking.

"I know."

"The fucking prick." It didn't sound as near of an insult as I'm sure she meant it. Lane touched her fingers to her mouth before she dropped it suddenly to her lap. "You know, I always wished he would go through what he abandoned me to. It doesn't taste as sweet as I thought it would. They do horrible things, Ezra. Horrible, wicked things." Her eyes were bloodshot as she looked up at me.

"You never told me what they did to you," I said softly.

Lane spun the silver ring in her nose before she dropped her hands again.

I didn't think she would tell me, but confessing Valen's tale must have moved something in her.

"Think of every bad thing that can happen to someone. Every. Thing. That is what they did. They bled me. They raped me. They beat me. They starved me. They gave me fucking diseases," she spat. Lane slammed her palms into the couch and dug her nails into the cushion. "They haunted me. I couldn't dream because they tormented me there too. They stripped me of everything that I was. And then, when I thought there was nothing more they could possibly ruin me with," she waved her hand over her body, "they made me this. For fun," she said with a mocking laugh. "Dhampirs need blood to survive. Without it the blood in our veins will boil. We are not vampires so we do not live forever, but we are given their same constraints.

"I am one of their longest standing because I withstood their torture. It became a game to the Murder. How strange that a woman, something so fragile, could withstand such violence.

"Raum stumbled on the Hymn when he was looking for a way to overthrow Baal. Then it all made sense. Why I could withstand them, why he could not part with me. I was the lock to one part of the puzzle he had been searching for. All that was missing was the key." Her eyes darted to me.

A new crack had torn its way through my heart. I restrained the tears gathering behind my eyes. How could they do this? How could such evil exist?

"What's worse? I'm not the moon."

I blinked. "But you are. That's why we are together." I motioned between us.

"Fate is a cruel mistress. It took you coming here for me to discover that what Raum made me is a lie. That he made a mistake." She tapped the underside of her chin. "'She will bear the mark of Solomon beneath her chin.' There is a mistranslation in the text. It is not a *svedis* mark, but an *alithis*. A *true* mark. All I have is a tattoo," she said, her voice breaking.

I took her clenched fists into my hands.

"They're going to kill me when they find out. I've been able to trick them with the use of some names, but that's only because I threatened those demons first into giving them to me. Into playing along. The second Raum finds out, I'm done. Together, you and I, we are supposed to bring down humanity, Heaven—we are to bring down all Creation. And I can't do it. Even if I could, I don't want to."

I squeezed her hands tight. "Lane," I said, trying to slow her hysteria.

"They are an evil that the devil himself would fear."

I thought it had been fear in her voice, but it was malice. Poison dripped from her words. She had suffered so much to not be the one thing that kept her alive.

"If there is a way for you to free the amorini, you need to do it and do it soon. There are good males among them. You and I have met them."

I laced my fingers through hers and sat against her shoulder. I didn't know how to tear through the veil and there wasn't anything in Diriel's research that instructed me how to do so.

I thought back to the night Ariel nearly killed Valen. If I had known he didn't have a heart, would I have fought for him as I did knowing he wouldn't have died? Yes. Of course I would have. Seeing any harm come to him set my blood on fire. "Don't fall," Valen said. A smirk pinched my mouth. He was right, I had damned us.

It was seeing him beneath that arrow, my fierce guardian angel, that had awoken my rage and fear. Two twisted, sickening emotions that made my muscles quiver. I ground my teeth together.

In the moment I thought I would lose everything, I had dropped.

I sat forward.

When Ariel had dragged me out onto the water... "My scream," I said. "I think it's my scream."

Lane sat back to get a better look at me. "What is?"

"When Ariel nearly killed Valen, I screamed, I let loose," I motioned over my chest, "everything within me. All of my rage. And when he tried to kill me on the lake, on Earth." I turned to her. "Raguel said it appeared Tartarus was bleeding into Earth. He was right. I must have ripped through the veil when Ariel tried to kill me the first time."

"You called Prometheus then too?"

"No, but I must have torn something. Right? That's what Raguel was looking for."

Lane toyed with one of her long-pointed earrings. "So where is the other tear?"

I shrugged. "I don't know. Unless this is something else Diriel has been keeping from me."

"He hasn't mentioned it to me."

Fucking hell, this was brutal. There were too many parts and far too many enemies.

"And Raum? What has he said to you, little spy?"

Lane pursed her lips. "He intends to use you to tear more seams throughout the land so all of Tartarus can pool into humanity. He planned to use me to open the gates to other realms. You would help get us there and stave off any advances to anyone who might stand in the way."

"He must not have gotten the word that I'm not on his side."

Lane shrugged. "They've all been banking that you would fall. It doesn't take long for those trapped here to fall apart from God."

I hadn't even contemplated where I stood in my faith. I'd told Valen I was conflicted, and that was still true. It was hard to break a belief you had grown up in, but in the face of everything, every lie—my faith dwindled. I was one half of the heart to a prophecy that had been lost or never gifted to mankind to begin with.

I studied the woman beside me that was to have been my counterpart. If she was not the moon, who was? Was she safe or locked away somewhere? Had she even been born yet?

"Oh, and he wants you to break into Vasanistirio."

Her statement ripped me from my thoughts. I stared at her in horror.

"My thoughts exactly," she said.

"Is Bishop in on this?"

"I doubt it. By the sound of it, Bishop just wants to be in control of what he thinks is his." She cocked her head. "Raum won't tell Orias about the Hymn, and those two are thick as devils. That being the case, it's unlikely he would mention anything to Bishop."

Every hair on my body stood rigid. Something about that didn't add up. Raum's schemes were bigger than I could have imagined. But if Bishop didn't know, did Raum mean to steal me? And how did he intend to accomplish any of this with Baal still alive?

It tracked, at least. If someone didn't want me dead, they wanted to use me.

My blood ran cold. Bishop knew I wasn't barren. That thought had completely evaded me until now. He had known the entire time I had been in his bed...

A shudder made my stomach curl.

They all knew.

I looked back toward the window. I hadn't even thought about flying off until now. No way those idiots locked the door and didn't set other wards. If Bishop knew all that I could do, he wouldn't be taking any chances.

I was completely and utterly fucked. I would be, literally, if I didn't come up with an escape plan.

"It seems we're all damned unless we can stop them. Eurynomos has to fall and Bishop with them," Lane said.

"That might halt things for a time, but everyone knows about me. This petty war between courts won't stop with Eurynomos."

Lane's light eyes narrowed. "I would rather take my chances with them than spend one more day with any one of those creatures in the black mountains."

I tapped my fingers one by one. "So, first we escape. Get Valen's heart. Round up the good amorini and figure out how to tear another seam in the veil, close said veil and all the others once we are on Earth. Stay there or figure out how to get to another realm. Oh, and try not to get killed by the Murder, the other cyn, and Heaven while doing it."

Lane threw back her head. "Sounds about right. Sure you don't want to try and face them all head on?" She flashed a fanged smirk in my direction.

"Fuck, I need a drink."

Lane clapped her hands together and jumped off the couch in the same motion. "That I can handle."

"Are you ok?"

I turned to the book Lane had open in front of her. I wanted to look at the mistranslation she had mentioned. Perhaps she was the one mistaken. I had no intention of fulfilling any fucking line in the prophecy, but if I could prove that she was the moon, then at least she would be spared.

"Peachy," Valen shot back.

"What's going on out there?"

"The emissaries are still here. They wish to see you perform."

"What sort of performance?"

"They want to see you in action, to see if you're truly able to wield Heaven's fire."

"I can't."

"Having you perform will bide us more time until I can figure out how to get you out of here."

Silence.

"What about you?"

"I may have started a war." He sounded smug about it. I could picture the dimple cutting into his cheek. *"But there is nothing to*

be done about it until the other courts leave. Our people have questions that Bishop is refusing to address. The court won't push him, not until the emissaries depart. To show further weakness with a divide in the cyn might encourage the other courts to rule us, if not remove us entirely just to get to you."

"Peachy."

Valen's music laughed through my head.

"Lane is with me. I think Raum means to steal me."

There was another long pause. I looked up from the pages and glanced at Lane with her furrowed brow and cobalt hair.

"He won't lay hands on you. None of them will."

"Yes, well, that doesn't mean they won't try. She's not the moon, but they don't know that yet. So, unless we can come up with a solid plan quick, it sounds like we are all screwed."

"Focus on getting ready for your show and let me handle the rest."

"Valen."

"Ezra, trust me. And don't do anything foolish."

I felt him withdraw, like a door quietly closing—

Banging open.

The door to my bedroom burst open, making Lane and me both flinch. Bishop preceded Jinn and Diriel. I half expected to see my adelfi walk in behind them. I tried not to look worried when he didn't appear. He had sounded fine through the bond a moment ago, so he couldn't be bad off. Right?

Lane stood abruptly in front of me as if she meant to protect me.

I stood with her and slid my fingers across her back. *I've got this,* I tried to convey.

I had to act quick.

"It's about time you showed up," I spoke as Bishop's lips parted to speak.

He cocked his head. "Excuse me?"

Careful, Ezra, you don't want to be too aggressive. Remember he is a loose cannon, I told myself.

"I've been locked up all night. You said you would come for me. Thank God Lane was granted access."

Bishop's jaw ticked in time with his fluttering lashes at his enemy's name. Oh, that was interesting.

"I have been in counsel with our guests. Half of them want you dead while the others are trying to bargain for you. I locked you up for your own safety." The cyn glanced over my person and then to the table where Lane and I had been hovering.

I crossed my arms over my chest. "You're right," I said, lowering my gaze. "I know there are things at work I don't understand, but I hate being left in the dark, especially when they concern me. You let Valen parade me around the dance floor like some fool and then locked me up with no explanation. What was I supposed to think? You all treat me like I am some piece of property."

I was very good at pretending to be a spoiled brat when I needed to be.

"Why didn't you come see me when you were done?" I pressed.

Bishop tipped his head to the other males. "Will you give us a moment?"

Diriel motioned to Lane. I tapped her back when the dhampir didn't move. "Go, we don't both need to be in trouble for something we didn't do," I grumbled.

The three of them moved back toward the main door. Bishop slid his fingers over the table as he halted in front of me. He was a tower of lethal muscle and fury. I could smell it on him, strong as melted silver.

His pewter eyes flitted between mine. I looked back at him coolly, waiting for an explanation. All the while, I let my rage for him simmer. My hands weren't big enough to wrap around his throat. I'd need to figure another tactic if I wanted to kill him.

"Has Valen been to see you?" he asked softly.

"Of course not."

Bishop's brow cocked.

"He hasn't and, if he did, I would have made sure he left with a knife in his chest."

Bishop didn't budge.

"Is that why you didn't come see me? Did you think I fell back into his hands?"

"Yes," he said. "Your dance was quite... enchanting. It made me angry seeing you with him that way. After the promises you made to me, I didn't think you would deign touch him again. When I could not get away, my mind wandered."

"Imagine being on the other end of it. If this is about my wings, I didn't want to open them. He threatened to torment me if I didn't. The whole thing made *me* angry." I finally looked away from him. I twisted my fingers together. "I waited for you all night."

Bishop's gentle touch lifted my chin. For the first time, I acknowledged when his spell hit me. It wound around my wrist and slowly climbed its way up my arm. From there, it spread like ivy until my entire body was shrouded with envy and hot-blooded lust.

"I'm here now."

I willed every trace of hatred for him from my face. It was by God's grace I managed it. The fury that churned in my belly, to gut him, to flay him for what he had done to Valen, to his people, what he was planning to do to me. The ill fates were endless as I slid my fingers across the shaven part of his head.

"You said you would treat me like a princess. You told me you weren't like him."

"We are nothing alike." Finally, he spoke the truth. Dark blue clouded the backside of his silver irises. Bishop surely would have been a magnificent force had he not become the rot that stood before me.

"Is your heart truly broken?"

I placed Bishop's hand over my chest. "Can you not feel it bleeding?"

The spell tightened its bind around my wrist. Against any will of my own, I tipped my face up, willing him to kiss me, wanting him to. The monster that lurked within me prowled at the back of my mind, fangs and claws flashing, daring him to take the bait.

Bishop pressed his lips to mine.

I slid my arms over his shoulders and crossed my wrists behind his neck. The urgency of his spell intensified. I parted my lips and slid my tongue between his. His sharp teeth scraped along the flesh of my tongue, making me stiffen and his arms tighten on my waist.

Four sharp fangs pierced my tongue. I flinched the moment it happened, right before he crushed me against his chest. I opened my eyes in alarm, but Bishop wasn't looking at me. Instead, he kept his eyes closed and sucked the blood straight from its source.

Diriel and Jinn had their backs turned. If Lane was still present, I could not see her behind their builds.

Fine.

Let the bastard drink.

I slid my hand into his mohawk and held him there. With my free hand, I let my flames skirt out as they dove into the compartments on his person. I let them dive into each invisible box, searching. My hands slid to the front of his chest, earning a low growl.

Bishop released me, his lips slick with spit and blood. "I would have you now," he said.

There was no time to respond. Not when darkness blew into the room, suffocating the need building between me and the archangel.

The fourth cyn strode in, his fingers adjusting the button on his jacket's sleeve as he looked us over.

"Ah, I see you've got our whore ready," Valen said. "Are we going to get this show on the road or continue to let our enemies extend their stay?"

Dark shadows wove around my body. This might be a show, a long-drawn-out play, but I was going to make Valen pay for calling me that word.

I could see in Valen's sinister grin that he knew that.

The spell around my body tugged me aggressively.

"What's going on?" I looked between them, trying not to give away that what Bishop was doing was starting to suffocate me.

Bishop turned his icy glower toward me, though I felt his attention was still directed to his competition. "The court wishes to see you perform. Get changed into your leathers. We are to start within the hour."

I pouted as I drew a long finger down the front of his attire. The satin hissed under my nail as it glided down to the end of his tunic, over the leather chord that wrapped around his waist and slid underneath to the top of his pants.

"There will be time for that later," he purred. His eyes narrowed into a cat's slit as he threw a look at Valen. Even if he did suspect Valen of betraying him, he had no idea I was in on it. This was something I could work with. I needed it to work if I was going to get Valen's heart.

I threw a nasty look at Valen. "Try not to fuck things up this time and stay out of my way."

All their eyes were on me, as if collectively holding their breath.

The dark amorini sneered, his gold eyes flashing. "Seems you have no better hold on her than I did," he said.

I scoffed, turning before their bickering turned into a bloody mess. The tension in the air writhed like a snake, winding back into a strike.

Bishop caught my arm as I turned. "Put your harness on."

My brow furrowed. Everyone had already seen my wings. I thought it to be too dangerous to fly.

Angels are jealous creatures.

Lane followed me into my bedroom as I quickly changed. Her eyes met mine in the mirror as she laced the back of my harness, her mouth stretched into a thin line. I knew she could feel it as well as I, that something terrible was going to happen in these next few hours. I just prayed that whatever happened, we would all come out alive and well on the other side.

CHAPTER FIFTY-EIGHT: I BESTED AN ANGEL

Ezra

The sun's heat against the black leather seared into the thin layer of my skin. I ran my finger under my collar in an attempt to stretch the material so I could breathe easier. What was supposed to be a day's performance had turned into three. The longer the emissaries remained, the tighter the tension wound amongst the amorini. All hell was going to bust loose; it was just a matter of when.

I had barely slept between sparring and searching for Valen's heart when I was not attached to Bishop's hip. He might as well have put a collar on my neck the way he dragged me along wherever he went. His paranoia had grown to a new height. The only good that came of it was that he did not try to fuck me. For the time being, he was too worried someone else was going to steal me and, perhaps, that Valen's spell had been broken.

Valen still portrayed himself as Bishop's dutiful villain. His cold exterior toward me did not crack. Neither did he falter when Bishop touched him. As angry as I was, I could only imagine how Valen must be raging.

Just now the two were seated on thrones overlooking the small arena. Bishop's possessive touch ran up Valen's thigh.

I shut out any ill thoughts I had of the situation. Bishop and I had exchanged blood multiple times now, and I wasn't confident he couldn't hear my thoughts.

"Why the performance with the dance?" Bishop asked.

Valen hummed and cocked his head back to meet Bishop's gaze. "You are asking me just now? I thought you knew."

"Tell me," Bishop hissed.

"Because I knew it would piss you off and that you would finally see me as your competition." A sly grin spread his full lips apart. Behind the smile, I recognized the malice that coursed through his blood. "I was right. And don't act like you don't enjoy my brutality. You weren't so angry the other night when I had you on your back."

Bishop's eyes flickered with a subtle hint of amusement. "I quite enjoy this new you, but the lack of respect not so much."

I turned my attention to the small crowd to clear my mind of their conversation. I could only handle one thing at a time. The first two days had been outside, where my training had taken place in the beginning, but this morning had been moved to a small area encapsulated with pearl-white stones.

"Perhaps too many eyes are on her," Zephyr had suggested when my silver flames did not make an appearance.

Prepare to be disappointed again, I mused silently.

The privacy didn't stop people from spilling outside, flooding the streets and alleyways.

Jinn and Diriel took their seats the same moment Andras tightened the strap of my harness. My eyes watered before I could read their lips as they spoke to the two cyn presiding before them.

I hissed. "I need to breathe."

"She hasn't had need to fly this entire time. Relax, Andras," Lane bit.

"Better to be safe than sorry." He pushed his thumb into my ribs, making me suck in air, right before he tightened the second buckle. It made me feel like a horse getting her girth tightened before a long ride. I wanted to whip around and bite him.

"Save it," Andras said through his teeth. "You're fighting one of the seraphim today. I wouldn't be surprised if it is Zephyr himself."

I slid my arms into the leather jacket Lane presented me with. The arms were fitted with what appeared to be dragon scales, a design that matched the boots that cut off at my knees. I'd been fortunate enough to spar with Andras and Jinn the last couple of days. I knew how they fought, and perhaps that was the issue.

"They want to push me," I said.

Andras gave me a clipped nod. "Eimai Theós breed warriors. There is a reason they are the hierarchy of Tartarus. We have trained you to the best of our abilities, but be prepared for any-thing."

With everything I had read about the different angelic races, their courts, their beliefs, and their powers, if my competi-tor wanted to catch me off guard, he could do any number of things—such as trapping me in my mind for a second, to feel like an eternity of agony, to imploding everyone around me, leaving only two of us standing.

"Great," I mumbled.

Wind blew against the back of my head, threatening to undo the plaits my hair had been twisted in. It raked chills down my spine, despite how warm it was in the arena.

I looked over every face in the crowd. Scanned every window, banister, and shadow. Colorful light spilled across the floor from the stained-glass ceiling. I followed the pool of color to my sparring partner. Not Zephyr but another seraph that went by the name of Baako. He was taller than anyone I had ever faced before.

Baako was at least seven foot three with light marble skin that bound large chords of muscle.

"Did they have to pick the biggest one?" Lane whispered. "He's fucking huge."

"Don't let his size distract you," Andras said, walking me to the floor. "You will be lither and can move in spaces he cannot. He is fast, but you have to be faster."

"Is that all?" I drawled.

Andras shrugged. "Don't get killed."

I snorted. "Zephyr seemed intent on wooing me, so I think we are good on that front." I skimmed the faces of the crowd again. Unease flooded my system. "Atticus is missing."

My companions looked with me. Lane's pupils dilated as her search became more frantic. When she met my eyes, I knew she was wondering the same.

Is this it?

Was this the moment Raum would strike?

Or was Atticus's absence merely a coincidence?

The keras had been present up until this moment, always hiding somewhere unlikely. There was a chance he was still out of view. Just yesterday, he had been hiding in the shadow of a woman, in her literal shadow, before moving to a young boy's frame to nestle in the small pool of darkness his body cast. I knew in my gut he wasn't here though.

"If he is up to something, I know his tricks. I'll find him." Lane darted into the crowd before Andras or I could stop her.

The male gripped my shoulder. "Do not let that distract you either. You know how Atticus likes to play. I'm sure he is watching, waiting to throw you off when he decides to show himself."

A powerful force washed against me as I blinked away the burning in my eyes. It was time.

I nodded to Andras as he stepped back, allowing me to take the floor with Baako. The male was even more intimidating as he ate up the floor.

There was no introduction, no flashy announcement, before we moved, the first steps of our dance initiated the moment we made eye contact. There was no need for one when I had been putting on a show for them every day of their stay.

My mentors had taught me well, but it was evident there was still more for me to learn when Baako threw out his hand, funneling a jolt of power so wild that I landed straight on my back. A flicker of fear shot through me as I felt his steps approach. I let the monster inside me push me to my feet as his blade sang forward. Stone and dust burst like a fountain as it cracked beside me.

Baako grinned, flashing gold-tipped fangs as he pulled the blade free. "You are not used to fighting someone as powerful as me."

My sword sang against his. The muscles in my arms screamed as he bore down on me. I did not have a good hold at this angle.

"On the contrary," I gritted. "I bested an angel. Your little power doesn't intimidate me."

Sometimes I never knew when to keep my mouth shut. This was one of those times I should have swallowed my pride and kept the snide comment to myself.

Baako's grin fell, and he tossed his sword to the ground. "Let me show you my power." No sooner had the last word left his lips before a sharp, slicing pain entered my head. I dropped my own blade in favor of clutching my head. My mouth opened in a silent wail as tears burst into my eyes.

Somewhere in the distance, I thought I heard Zephyr say Baako's name, but I wasn't sure. Not when the pain intensified and began winding its way down my spine.

The beast within me panicked. She whirled about, twisting and biting at the source.

"Focus."

Ashes, it felt like he was severing my head from my neck.

"Ezra, focus," the voice came again. *"What he is doing is not real. Use your fire. It does not matter the color of your flames. Use them. Now!"*

I pulled the monster free from her cage the same moment she pushed against the door I had locked her behind. Flames spewed out clumsily, spilling across the floor like oil. I caught site of Baako's blurred form and sent them scattering to his feet.

The male grinned again, side-stepping their hunger and forcing another ring of power around my neck.

He might not kill me, but he would bring me to death's edge. It's what he was doing now as he tried to force me to my knees, the sharp pain tightening every time I struggled to breathe.

I snapped the chord of fire inside of me, the one he had not seen behind him. It arched up then skirted through the air, marking him across the forehead and jerking his face to the side. The harrowing pain evaporated the moment his eyes were torn from me.

I didn't waste a moment as I scrambled to the hilt of my sword and took up the gold blade to crash it against the dark flames he met me with. My fire devoured his as the monster within my blood fed. I became her as I evaded and attacked him simultaneously. This was not just a sparring of blades but of minds. Baako's power was great, and he was doing everything he could to bring me to heel with it.

"I am the rot that destroys the land," he said.

"I am the rain that heals it!"

Baako pushed. He drove forward, not once backing down—even when I inflicted pain upon him.

I threw the tip of my sword into the ground and let out a burst of fire power. The firewall expanded around us, rising above the crowd like a giant wave.

"Fall."

I could feel the foreign power writhing within me. The monster, the harpy Valen had named me, flashed me a bloody grin. My power expanded, the flame's heat intensifying as I dove into the well the she-beast had carved into my soul.

"Dive fast and hard."

I did.

I bore Baako's lashings as he struck at my flames, at the tender memories I had locked away in my mind he tried to bring to the surface. His storm battered me as I flew down, calling upon the darkness within.

The air was ripped from my lungs.

One moment I was in darkness, expanding, and the next every bit of breath in my lungs was gone. Every lick of fire went up in smoke. The crowd exploded into silence. Hands flew to throats as the expulsion took hold.

When it came back, it was with a vicious, terrifying roar that shook the earth.

BOOM!

Glass, stone, and bodies went flying.

The force of the gale threw me across the room. I clawed at the crumbling sky as I tumbled. My back slammed hard into one of the stands.

The air ripped from the room again.

I gasped uselessly. Heat stained my face as I felt it turning red. Darkness bled into the edge of my vision. Beyond that, everyone was doing the same thing that I was. If they were not on the ground struggling to breathe, then they were stumbling toward an exit.

Baako was on the ground, clawing at his throat, the eyes of his body twitching like a broken mechanism.

A harsh whooshing sound rose in the distance. I turned and folded my arms over my head as I braced for a second impact.

Something sharp and hard slammed into the center of my back.

I sucked in another stretch of air and let out an agonized cry. Moans and gasps of pain filled the air.

"Archers," someone gasped. "To your posts."

It was Bishop's voice that made the orders. It was he who I had heard in my head the second time as he encouraged me to fall. Not Valen's who had encouraged me to focus. It struck me as a fleeting thought. I could not think on that now, not when we were under attack, and I was surely the prize. Dead or alive.

I could not see him or any of the other cyn through the haze of dust. Even the floor where Baako had been was now covered in a thin layer of white.

I pushed against the stand in front of me, but whatever was behind me wouldn't budge.

A loud crash came from across the room, chilling my blood. Stone. It was stone against my back because the arena was crumbling. I pushed again, forcing my power and fire into it, but I was still catching my breath. They don't tell you that you need to breathe when you're struggling to stay alive.

"Valen!"

I craned my head back, but the room was a mass of darting bodies. A quick blip of darkness snuffed out the light as a shadow flew overhead.

Flew.

Is that a fucking—?

"Dragon!" someone screeched.

Fire careened through the ceiling, blasting what was left of the canopy into a million burning smithereens. The metal frame and giant drops of gold splashed like molten raindrops. Screams rose into the air like sirens.

I pushed as hard as I could against the rock and hard place I was stuck between. Shadows and ash flitted around me as I struggled until finally, finally! the rock behind me moved.

I crawled forward to waiting hands that reached from the other side.

Zephyr pulled me to my feet. A nasty gash had split his skin from his chin to his upper lip. His men bore wounds of their own, red blood crying into their flitting eyes. Baako was amongst them, his battle with me done for the moment as he gripped his sword, his eyes on the sky.

"Ezra!" My name was a war cry over the turmoil.

"Come with us," Zephyr said. "We must leave now, quickly. Maalik will give you sanctuary."

I didn't listen as I strained to see through the haze where Valen's voice had echoed.

"Ezra!" he bellowed again.

"I'm here!"

"Find her," someone else said. Bishop, I think.

The hand around my bicep tightened.

"Let go," I snapped.

The male's face skewed into a snarl. "Your kingdom is under attack. Let us help you."

Embers of fury burst from my hand as I threw my palm into Zephyr's face and shot a torrent of flames. Fuck the consequences of attacking a member of an outside court.

"I said let me go!"

The seraph stumbled back, his eyes wide with shock. "We are not behind this," he seethed. He still had a hard grip on me, but with his final words, it softened. He let me go, turning to his men. "This battle is not ours. We retreat to Eimai Theós," he commanded.

I made it a half step in their direction before the screaming outside intensified and the entire world around us exploded.

A body, or perhaps multiple, was hurled against me with the force of a cannon. Zephyr and Baako flew past me. I was only able to latch onto Baako's outstretched arm before the wind blew me too and we were falling. I buried my head against Baako's chest as we fell amongst the rock and rubble. It was his face I saw, looking up in sheer horror, as the pillar we had crashed into fell upon our heads.

CHAPTER FIFTY-NINE: WHATEVER IT TAKES

Ezra

Not even in death can screams be silenced. I could hear them in the distance amongst the rumbling of falling buildings and the rush of wind that carried the dragon across Vélos, tearing the kingdom apart.

I could see nothing in the darkness that surrounded me. I felt Baako's strong arms around me, but their heat had faded. I tentatively brushed my fingertips over his forearm. Wetness met me, the flicker of an eye. Alive then, but barely.

I let out a shuddering breath as I realized I was alive too. Once again, I had escaped death's clutches. My nose brushed against something cold and smooth when I turned my head. My heart slammed against my chest. The pillar.

We were buried.

It was one of my biggest fears next to falling: being buried alive. My breath hitched as I reached out—I couldn't reach. The stone was mere inches from my body. I let out a hiccuped breath when I moved my toes. My legs were wedged, but at least they were not paralyzed or broken.

Fire lit across my hands. I pressed against the hard surface, my horror tangible as I saw nothing but white stone.

"Where are you? Where are you, Ezra?"

I wriggled against the seraph, but he didn't budge. "Baako," I said. "Baako, wake up."

No answer.

A soft groan came from somewhere to my left. I shoved my arm across my body to direct my light in his direction.

The seraph was one of the warriors. His head rolled back as his face scrunched in pain.

"Hey! Where's Zephyr?"

The male's eyes opened on his cheek. "With us," he said, his thick voice coming out in a rasping whisper. "Somewhere," he said. He rotated his body, looking around. Flames sparked in his hands as he tried to assess the situation.

"Ezra!"

I'd never felt the full extent of the bond. When Valen tugged, it felt like I was being pulled through space. My body pressed against the cold stone in front of me involuntarily.

"Buried," I said, unable to keep the fear from my voice. "We are buried."

"Where is the sharpness you showed earlier?" The male growled. "Do not go losing your mind from being buried alive. Zephyr!" He pushed up, freeing one of his legs and then turning to work on freeing his second.

I shut my eyes. *"One of the pillars fell on top of us. We're trapped."*

"Who is with you?"

"Zephyr and his men. I can only account for two of them. I don't know what happened to Zephyr."

Another tug against the bond surged through me. Valen was coming. I could feel his urgency as he drew closer. His power overwhelmed me when I felt him somewhere above. I could not contain the tears flooding my eyes as I heard sharp claws scrape on the other side.

"Breathe, darling. I'm right here."

I slapped my palm against the stone as words failed me. I took hold of Baako with my other hand and willed him to wake up. As soon as Valen freed us, we would need to move.

The other male grunted. Dark blood coated the leg he pulled free, the eyes upon the skin no longer moving, instead gouged and oozing. Behind him, a face caught in the light. Red eyes full of terror forever frozen in death. My stomach churned as the seraph saw it too.

"I'm right here. We are going to move the pillar. We can't hold it long, so you'll have to move at the first opening you see."

The seraph could not move out of his awkward crouched position, but at least he was free. Unlike the male that had been buried beneath him. "Zephyr!" he barked. This time, his voice was strained, the pain evident as he twisted in the other direction to find his companion.

Sweat-slicked fear permeated the shadows around us.

Stone scraped together as the pillar above my face moved. Scraps of light pierced through the shadows.

"Zephyr!"

"Be quick, Ezra."

My heart slammed against my chest. "*We can't leave them trapped here.*"

"We don't know who is behind this yet. We are still under attack and need to move quickly."

"Here," a voice groaned. The seraph whipped his head around at the same time I did. at Zephyr's broken voice.

The light grew brighter.

"Move toward the light," I said.

I twisted, trying to free my feet from where they were twisted with Baako's. I found purchase on a flat surface and yanked, pulling Baako against me.

I could see through a small crack. My heart thundered in my ears as I weighed my decision. I would either have to crawl over Baako and leave him and the others, or I could try to pull him with me.

An impossible feat to carry him, but I was a nephilim. I could do this.

As soon as the crack opened a foot, I moved, climbing over Baako, wincing as my boot skidded down his shoulder. I twisted and hooked my arms beneath his shoulders and pulled. I scooted back, found my footing, and pulled.

"Hurry up!" I said to the other male.

"I see light," Zephyr groaned. "Where is it?"

"Ezra," Valen snapped.

I looked back to see him peering down at me, his face slick with sweat and gore. His eyes flicked to his side and then back to me as I struggled to pull the large male with me.

"Let him go." The snarl that left his lips would have given me pause any other time. We didn't have time for me to save someone, but I couldn't let Baako go. Not when he had braced me from an impact that might have killed me.

"Help me," I shot back, my voice breaking as wetness coated the back of my throat.

"We can't hold it," someone said. In the distance, another boom sounded.

Valen cursed before diving toward me. He slid on his belly, wrapping one arm around my waist, pulling as I scooted. Together, we were simultaneously making progress, using short bursts of furious energy to escape from being crushed.

The other male had crawled to where Baako and I had fallen, his eyes darting frantically for any sign of Zephyr whose panicked voice was rising.

Valen hauled me free and, as soon as I was clear, two other males jumped in to pull Baako out.

The seraph's head whipped toward me. "Wait! Please! Don't!"

The pillar fell with a loud exhale as the stones settled.

Pain sliced through my core as Valen's hands slid down my legs, looking for any breaks. He turned my face to meet his. Golden fires burned within the depth of his gaze. Desperation stared back at me, but beneath it was something ancient and cold. The cruel demon Tartarus had made him pulled me to my feet, ignoring the distant plea of Zephyr who remained trapped while his companion was forever silenced.

I looked down at Baako who remained unconscious at my feet, the slow rise and fall of his chest the only tell that he had survived his men.

"Death moves swiftly in war," Valen said, drawing my eyes back to him.

I swallowed the knot in my throat and nodded.

His eyes darted between mine. *"These men will not be your friends. Baako might have saved you, but it is for Eimai Theós's gain."* "We move now," he said out loud, turning to face the six males who remained.

I took in a deep shuddering breath and nodded again. Valen flicked his fingers toward a pair of cherubs. They stooped low and carried Baako between them as we slunk over the ruins.

"Take the injured and humans to the tunnels. The rest of you, gather your bows and swords and be ready. Whoever commands the dragon is not yet finished." One of the amorini nodded before darting off, his boots crunching against the broken glass. One didn't need to be quiet when there was so much destructive noise filling the air.

I stayed at Valen's shoulder, letting the brush of his heat against my arm steady me.

We made it to the front of the arena before a dark shadow fell overhead.

Valen held up his fist and we pressed into the shadows.

The soft chuffing sound of the dragon entered the room before its massive head did. The pale gray of its scales paired well with the damage it had wrought. Two pairs of color-shifting blue eyes, one stacked atop the other, were fitted on the side of its head, hooded by blue spiked scales. Those eyes looked like the depths of the sea in a storm, whipping in a torrent. Its neck was long and slender, crowned with a white mane. There was surely more of it, but that was all that could fit within the small space.

Fast footsteps carried across the other side of the room, drawing the beast's attention. Golden fire lit the inside of its maw as it opened wide, aiming at the two women who had made a break for the exit.

They didn't even have time to scream before they went up in flames.

The dragon lifted its head, an irritated hiss leaving its ash-encrusted lips as something outside distracted it.

"How do you kill a dragon?" I whispered.

"With another dragon," Valen answered just as quietly.

Fuck me.

"I share your sentiments," he said.

We waited until the dragon retreated, thrusting off the top of the arena with a mighty thrust as it took to the air. Its body was long and serpentine. It was a wyrm, a dragon without wings, yet it could fly. Its four legs tucked into its body as it slithered into the sky and then twisted suddenly, aiming for the ground below. Its mouth widened and it let out a rain of fire, molten heat cascading like lava.

I moved as Valen did, making a break for the entrance.

Vélos was burning. The clear water of the river and falls ran red. The tyre and its four pillars were charred. Bodies lay scattered about the streets. I stumbled with the males as we moved toward the direction of clanging swords and sounds of exertion from battle.

As we crested the top of the hill, we came to a full stop. The amorini were easy to distinguish with their armor of crimson, but those they faced made our numbers look small. Black-leathered bodies rushed the amorini, cutting them down like birch made to be tender.

"Take him with the others," Valen told the cherubs. They heaved Baako higher onto their shoulders and darted into the closest building. I didn't hesitate as Valen pulled me in the opposite direction.

Valen cupped my face as he pulled me into the shadows.

I took in a shuddering breath.

"Are you alright?"

My brow furrowed before I knew what he was asking. I shut my eyes and nodded. "I am, yes." I acknowledged the darker part of me that still lurked. She had never fully dived back to her resting place, instead choosing to remain at the surface, ready for anything. "My fire is ready." I opened my eyes to meet his gold. "Who is it? Asphodel?"

"We don't know. Their armor is unidentifiable. They are known to have firebreathers, but this one is riderless. Which means it is one of the four in disguise."

"To not draw the eye of another to our aid."

Valen nodded. He brushed his thumb over my jaw, taking my hand with his other.

I tipped my head up as his turned down.

The kiss was brief and yet it held all the love he had not voiced.

I pressed back against the crumbling wall. The rank stench of sulfur mingled with the charred air. Valen's grip on my hand tightened.

"Take the tunnel in your room and make the first two lefts. It will lead to a door that will take you to the maze. Whatever power reigns the gardens will keep you safe."

"How do you know? You said you cannot break its spells."

"I believe it is a place Heaven left when this prison was created. It can deceive us, hurt us, but not you."

"And what are you going to do?"

"I am going to help my people. Now is the chance for me to take control, even if it is battling someone else before I am to face my brother."

I swiped my tongue over my lower lip. "I'm going with you."

"You are going to hide."

"I can better serve you, serve this kingdom, if I am not hiding. I have the power—"

"Power untamed. We know what you are capable of, but you do not know how to wield it fully. I felt you falling, Ezra. Not for me, but to the darkness as you faced Baako. I could not hear what Bishop said to you, but I felt him there in your mind. I can only assume he was pushing you toward damnation."

His eyes flashed a merciless red. A color I had seen everywhere on him but his eyes. "You cannot fall."

"Heaven has already forsaken me. What does it matter if it will give me more power? If I can help you?"

"I will not lose you. Whoever this is, they are here for you. The second they get their hands on you—I can't let that happen. I will not." The flash of his teeth was stark against the grime on his lips. "This is not your battle."

"You just said they are here because of me. And if not them, then someone else." I had a chance to make a difference. This was an opportunity to show Vélos and anyone else what I was capable of. The emissaries had asked for a performance. I would give them one, and it would be my best show yet.

"Listen to me," Valen snapped.

I blinked at the hardness of his tone.

"You are everything, Ezra. If you fall, we are lost." He thrust his hand out to the ruins. "All of us. You have the ability to wield Prometheus, a gift granted by Heaven. Only messengers can wield Prometheus. The fact that you can is no mistake. If you fall, that will be stripped from you. There will never be a chance for you to gain access to Heaven."

The monster in me unfurled. I felt the shift of my wings beneath my bones. What he was saying didn't make any sense.

"Raguel gave you something. Did he not?" He nodded to where my hand rested over my thigh. "Ever since he departed, I have seen you worrying over your pocket. What is it?"

Cotton filled my mouth as I tried to process what he was saying.

Amongst the clouds, the dragon swirled. It made a figure eight through the four pillars and then swooped down over the town for another waterfall of fire. The screams had stopped, but the sounds of battle had only increased.

"A token," I whispered as I watched the dragon turn once more. Only this time it opened its maw, scooping men into its jaws and crushing them. Black arrows now tipped its snout like whiskers, but everywhere else they hit only bounced off.

I fumbled the coin out of my pocket. "It was a favor should I ever need one."

Valen's brow arched. "Don't you think now is the time to use it?"

"He couldn't take me then. It wasn't Heaven's will."

"Fate has changed. Make him promise to keep you alive before you turn it in."

I rubbed my thumb over the top of the coin.

Valen cupped my chin. "Go to the maze and call for him. When this battle is settled, I will come for you."

My heart hammered wildly. We were out of options and, as brave as I wanted to be, I was no match with untamed power.

"Valen," I said, my resolve cracking.

"I love you. With all the soul I have left, I love you. Do this for me so I may return to you and show you how much." His lips moved against mine as he spoke.

I leaned into his kiss as if it would be my last, forcing our teeth to scrape together with the rawness of my desperation. I had just gotten him back. The thought of losing him all over again tore me apart.

Hearing those three words fall from his lips sent a surge of movement through me like the change of a current. The rush of his power, of him, met me head on. Though our souls had bound the night the rainbow obsidian fell from my hands, it felt like I was falling for him all over again. Our sins were forgiven in that one little kiss. One little kiss that held the weight of many unspoken promises.

Static spread over my skin right before the hairs on my arm stood erect.

"I knew it!"

We broke apart at the crack of lightning. A bolt of light streaked across the pastel sky.

"I fucking knew the spell was broken," Bishop snarled. He stalked forward, his shoulders taut like a hunter about to spring on its prey. "How did you do it?"

The fallen archangel bore no wounds that I could see, but his face was smeared with blood. As if he had relieved someone of their throat with his teeth. The essence of life coated the front of his laced tunic. The twin braids hanging over his chest dripped with gore.

I made a move to step forward, but Valen was faster, taking the space between me and Bishop. "Love covers over a multitude of sins," he said with a mocking tone. "Ours is no match for your darkness."

"Bastard," Bishop snarled. Light glimmered behind his head. There and gone in a blink. What was that?

"I used to believe that. But our Father is merciful, is he not? Otherwise, this bind would never have been made. Is that what drove you mad? That a bond between humans and angels was granted?"

Bishop's lips curled. "I am far from being mad. What drove me was my ambition to be better than what we were called to be."

Valen's muscles roiled. "And is it your ambition that has unleashed this bloodshed upon us?"

Bishop's bloody face fell. "This?" he snarled, throwing out his hand. "You think me so evil I would destroy my own people? Our people?" The snarl struggled to remain as he fought to bury the pain in his light eyes. "I am trying to save them, but I cannot do it without you. Diriel and Jinn are in the south staving off the head of the army. You know the four of us are stronger together than apart and yet here you are, defying me once more." A white ring entered the frame of his irises. "I need you at the front."

Valen had been a general beneath Episkopos, and a fine one at that. Both he and Bishop had led small armies when they first fell, staving off the rest of Tartarus before they learned of the necessity of their existence on this plane.

"Did you come to find me or her?" Valen asked, his voice smooth and even.

Bishop's eyes flicked to me. "Both. I need you to hold the line for us. The men will listen to you."

"And Ezra?"

The line between Valen and me was so brutally taut I thought it might snap. Roils of anger, uncertainty, and blatant fear was cascading through the bond as he contemplated his next actions and those of Bishop.

"I am the only one who can get her away. The tunnels have crumbled, the gardens are on fire. Vélos is not safe, not so long as that dragon remains," Bishop said.

Dark black shadows hung at Valen's back, giant black wings of rage. He stood between me and his rival. His brother. His lover. His conqueror. He was risking everything for me.

No, not just for me. For his entire kingdom.

Which was worth more?

Bishop looked from him to me, to the invisible chord that tied us that was alight with an unyielding fire.

"I can get her out of here," Bishop repeated. "You know I care for her as much as you do."

"You will never care for her the way I do," Valen said, so lethal you could have sliced a finger on the edge of its threat.

When the swell of Valen's power brushed against mine, I flinched. There was so much hate and violence within him. Blinding rage that had been building for centuries.

Beneath all his darkness was love. A bright flame no longer suppressed by false laws and made-up sins.

"No," Valen said.

"We are under attack because of her," Bishop snarled.

Valen didn't budge.

He wouldn't move. He didn't trust Bishop; he had no reason to. But I knew I could. What Bishop said was true; he did care for me. Bishop might hoard me, tuck me away where no one but he could find me, but he would ensure that I was safe.

I had a stronger will than Bishop's obsession, and so did my adelfi. He could not best us.

"We can settle this between us once she is safe," Bishop added.

"Don't look at me. I don't want him to know we are communicating. I'll go with him. It'll give me a chance to find your heart while he is distracted. Stay behind and protect your people. Take the throne as you should and, once things settle, once I have your heart, I'll let you know where he has taken me."

I moved to Valen's side.

"This is not about us," Bishop said. "Not right now." A spark of hope flashed in his silver eyes when I took a step forward. "If we lose her, we lose everything. Think of our people."

"I have grown tired of when I am spoken for." I raised my chin. There was only one way Bishop could get me out of here. I pulled my wings free, stretched them forward and back, before settling them against my shoulder blades and extending one against Valen.

The line of tension in him rumpled. A cyn, so strong and powerful. My adelfi. My love. It was not within him to stand down.

I wanted to tell him to bear the load a little longer. Just a little longer and we would make it through.

"I will raze this world and the next if anything happens to her."

Bishop's jaw tightened. "I do hope you save that temper for our return. I'd like to feast on it."

Bishop extended his hand to me as he unfurled his four gray wings.

I looked back at Valen. "I'll see you soon." I spread my wings, let them take up the small space between the three of us.

Valen took my hand, slinging me back against his chest. He kissed me. Hard and desperate. That love I had caught a glimpse of before had been a grain of sand compared to this. This was a furnace. His need and desire and absolute love threatened to consume me.

Before I could grab his face, he withdrew. "As soon as this evil is cast out, I'll be right behind you." He slid his lips against my ear, breathing me in as he whispered to my mind. *"Bishop does not mean well, he never has. The moment you are out of the dragon's sight, call on Raguel. Do not let him ground you, for I fear you may be trapped where he intends. If time does not allow you to call on Raguel, flee. Do whatever it takes until I come for you."*

I bit the inside of my lip as I took Bishop's hand.

A fresh wave of screams rose in the distance. Valen couldn't come with us. He couldn't be the one to protect me, not this time.

There were too many who needed him. Though he wouldn't voice it, I knew he realized this was an opportunity to prove to his people his power over Bishop, that he could lead them.

"Ezra, promise me."

"As soon as the dragon is out of sight," I answered.

I launched myself into the sky as Bishop pulled me beside him. I didn't look back at Valen, lest he saw the trace of the lie in my eyes. I wasn't going to give up on his heart, not when I was so close to the prize.

"Whatever it takes."

A tug finally urged me to look back at what had once been Vélos.

The dragon rose on its mighty haunches. It twisted around the east tower, winding up like a spiral until its head bore down on the rest of the tyre. The muscles of its body tightened, tightened, and with a fierce roar the tower twisted free, sending it to join the rest of the ruins.

CHAPTER SIXTY: THROUGH FIRE AND ICE

Ezra

We flew fast and hard. My wings and back burned with exertion I could not afford to feel. I knew to stop would be my death or worse.

In the distance was the roar of the great beast.

No, not the distance. The dragon was close.

Bishop swooped over me. "Tuck your wings."

I didn't ask, I just did. I could feel our demise growing closer. Not even my fear of falling could stop me as I let the wind take me. The drop in my stomach was timed perfectly as the beast's head appeared from the clouds, maw aflame.

Bishop wrapped his arms around me as we dove through the sky and spectered through the expanse with one stroke of his wings after another. On the fourth drop, he tipped his head down. "Be ready to fly again." That was the only warning I got before he let me go.

I thrust my wings out again and chased him up, up into the white clouds, not daring to look behind me to see how close the dragon was. If it had stayed with us at all.

The rotations of Bishop's wings grew slower. "We have to fly higher," he said, his breath straining.

Was he hurt? Was I mistaken and the blood on him was his?

"Where are we going?" I called.

"Some place they can't find you." He was definitely panting.

A white wall of mist rose out of the air even as we cleared the dense clouds that hung over the top of Tartarus. It cut off the snow-capped mountains and land below. I couldn't see anything save for my fingers stretched in front of me. The sharp air cut through my wings, throwing me higher. I folded my arms over my chest.

I wasn't used to flying in such strong winds, and they battered me from side to side. The light flutter of free falling hit my chest every time a fist of wind hit me.

"Bishop," I yelped.

"I'm here." He flew beside me, his wing brushing mine. "It's a storm. I had not thought the winds would be so strong. We will have to head back down."

I nodded, not registering his words until I was already dropping altitude. "What about the dragon?"

"I spectered us enough that if it is still following us, we have lost it for now."

I flew beneath him, slightly behind so I could ride in his wake. The farther we dropped, the darker the clouds became, taking on a strange blue hue.

I looked up at Bishop. Now was probably not the best time to search for Valen's heart, but when would I get another chance? How much time did I have before we got to wherever it was he intended? I rotated my wings so I could catch the warm air and rise above him.

I was certain the glimmer I had seen behind his head before was the chamber that held Valen's heart. Call it a woman's intuition, but it had flared at the height of his anger. He had reached for it once before when he meant to kill Valen; perhaps he had thought to then.

If I tried to go for it now, Bishop was likely to incapacitate me to get me to our next stop. I was too valuable to be killed, but that didn't mean he wouldn't hurt me.

Bishop looked up before I could make a decision. "Come back down. I'm going to specter us once more."

Fire curled around my hand as I took aim for the compartment.

"What are you doing?" His teeth flashed as he lifted upward.

I struck, firing the heat of my anger to what I hoped were the hinges of the hidden door.

Bishop spun out of my flame's reach, fury on his face.

A large black mass burst from the clouds directly behind him. It curved up and through the mist. "Bishop!" I screeched, but he was already moving, his wings slinging him to the side as the form hurled past him and slammed into me.

I had only a second to register the thing was a net before it wrapped around my wings, drawing them back in a violent angle. Heavy weights spun together, locking with a loud clack.

"Ezra!" Bishop twisted, his eyes wide with horror. He flew down after me, his wings clamped firmly to his back. But I was faster, the weights pulling me swifter than he could fly.

I screamed as I fell. I reached for it, for Bishop's outstretched hand, my fingers clawing through the air to gain purchase on anything. On *something*.

I couldn't reach the net. I couldn't even pull my wings in to grasp it. And whatever it was made of burned. It was cutting its way through my wings, and I couldn't stop it.

I was falling too fast. The fire that burst from my fingertips and lungs swirled out in the rush. The net was too heavy. All I could see were the thick white clouds and then the bottom of the mountains as the mist cleared all too quickly.

The ground slammed into me. My skull bounced forward the same time my wings snapped under my weight. My mouth was open, but I couldn't cry. Not when the cold ground broke apart and pulled me into a drowning abyss.

Ice.

It was frozen solid ice that gave way to my rupture.

My nails skidded across the underside of the ice as I struggled to hold on. Every time I opened my eyes, the cold water burned them, forcing me to close them once more. It didn't matter that I called my fire when I was submerged in its opposing element. I was going to drown.

The weights at my back dragged me down, leaving me to gape soundlessly at the fading surface.

Something brushed my wings, a sharp pain lacerated my joints, and then I was being dragged upward. Back to the cold wind and hard ground. My scream came out in a rush of foam as the net cleaved to me and severed the main joint of my left wing. I was still heaving when I was dropped on top of the ice. A strong wind smacked me in the face, forcing me forward to wretch the water that had seeped into my lungs.

Males, all of them. I could smell the demons through the harsh cold before their boots came into view, closing in on me. My reddened fingers dug into the ice as I looked up.

"What a fine catch you are," Orias said, dropping to a crouch.

Another came up behind me, and this one I knew instantly. I hoisted myself back, gritting through the pain, until I was pressed against Bishop's legs. The male stood rigid as I clawed for purchase, trying to hoist myself up his thighs so I could stand.

Six silhouettes of odonni melded from the shadows. Four remained mounted while a fifth rider strode forward. Raum spread his hands out. "Welcome," he said.

My hands stilled. I looked up at Bishop's placid face. His skin was like porcelain. It was so white beneath the blackened blood that he didn't appear real at all. A living statue come to life. His lashes fluttered as if he just remembered me and looked down. His light eyes moved from my face, to my tangled wings.

Why was he just standing there? Why wasn't he fighting them? Or helping me get free?

"You didn't have to shoot her down. I was bringing her to you."

My mouth fell open.

Raum tsked. "Cyn Baal has grown tired of waiting on you to uphold your end of the bargain." Raum's eyes narrowed into slits as he looked down on me. "I can tell from here she's not been bred. What have you been doing for the last two months?"

"We both know it is you who rules Eurynomos. You have been doing so under his nose for years. I told you to cause a distraction. You have left Vélos in ruins!"

"What?" I breathed. The cold wind numbed the coarse pain that moved through my wings. I focused on the chill as I tried to rise, but even a subtle movement shot piercing daggers down my spine. "Bishop," I said.

"You will look to him no longer," Raum said sharply, like the crack of a whip.

"Bishop!"

The cyn looked down on me. His hands clenched into fists and he took a single step back. The little warmth he had provided was like a shield being slung away.

"Do you want to tell her, or shall I?" Raum pressed.

No one tells you that fear has a taste. It can be sour, bitter, spicy, sometimes even sweet. All four flavors burst across my tongue, flooding my senses one after the other in a vile mashup as their words enshrouded me with the weight of dread.

"What have you done?" I croaked.

He refused to break his gaze from Raum.

"When it was evident Valen could not be controlled, Bishop came to us requesting a favor. A high request after what we had already done, after all Baal had done to bring Valen to heel. In exchange for you, we would give him back his kingdom." A sly smile fell over Raum's face. "And we shall. You never made it clear on how you wished it to be returned to you."

"I trusted you," Bishop snarled. "You would make me the cyn of ruins."

"You still bear your crown, do you not? Kingdoms can be rebuilt. Consider our mercy upon what is left a gift."

"You will leave me with nothing!" Bishop's rage echoed across the tundra, clapping like thunder.

"What you have does not even belong to you!" I did not know if it was me or the monster within that screamed it. My throat burned as the heat of my power tried to wake. I shook my head. "You have destroyed your people, your brothers. For what?"

Bishop blinked in surprise before his beautiful face contorted to the demon he had always been. "None of this would have happened if not for you. You were never meant to be his. You, Vélos, the crown, it was always meant to be mine."

"At what cost?" I choked.

Bishop opened his mouth to speak and then closed it.

Orias's broad smile flashed in my peripheral.

I had expected Bishop to do something with me, but not this. I never imagined that he intended to turn me over to the Murder, to Eurynomos where those who entered died. Except I knew they wouldn't kill me, not until they got what they wanted. My breath hitched as I tried not to think about what was going to happen.

Orias ran the back of his knuckles down my face. The cluck of his tongue scolding, as if I had done something wrong.

Snow fell upon Raum's face as he looked to the sky. To the dragon that materialized from the thick white coverage and landed across from us. The weight of its body made the frozen lake shudder. The boom of cracks refracted around us.

"Ah," Raum breathed. "There he is."

Orias pushed me back into the hard ground as I jolted forward. "You stay right there."

The end of the dragon's tale lit like the wick of a candle, going up in flames as it walked toward us. The slender build of its serpentine body rippled as the fire grew and condensed into a giant black shadow. The smoke churned across the monster's face, covering it entirely with darkness. What came out of the other side drew out a pained whimper from my lips.

Atticus ran his gloved hand over the front of his dark tunic. The flash of his leggings beneath the skirt he wore were soaked in blood as were his—those were gloves of gore, not leather. He flicked out his hand, casting a bit of flesh into the snow. He smoothed his white hair next, leaving pink streaks in his locks.

"Did you like the show?" He grinned, flashing rows of sharpened teeth as the shadow of his dragon remained.

Bishop stared at him, dumbfounded.

The pale keras licked his lips, savoring the moment. I had often wondered if he was mute. I wish he had kept his mouth shut.

"Half of Vélos remains. Fifty men remain, per your request," he tipped his head to Raum, "to be our eyes. I did you the courtesy of leaving two towers standing." His nearly white eyes slid over Bishop like oil, roving him from head to toe and back again. "Less someone suspects you were behind this."

"I am to choose one other to rule with me." It wasn't quite a question. Bishop was scrambling as he tried to maintain his stolen power in the wake of those much cleverer than he.

"Kill them all for all I care," Raum said. "I do not think I need to tell you to start with Valen. We also granted you that courtesy, of keeping all three of them alive so you could repair your broken crown."

My heart hammered wildly. He could do it now. I saw it in the glimmer of his eyes, in the gleam of the chamber beside his head. Bishop could end Valen now and his men would not be the wiser upon his return. It would solve at least one of his problems. His eyes widened when he looked down at me, finally realizing why I had attacked him.

An obnoxious popping sound smacked through the air as Atticus sucked his finger clean before moving onto the next. "Jinn is barely alive, if you cannot stomach parting from your beloved yet. Though, I think he is the only one loyal to you."

Bishop's long lashes fluttered. The tight chords of muscle were wound tight beneath his hardened skin. "Call your men from my land. Now," Bishop seethed.

"I am not going to do that. Because, as of this moment, Vélos belongs to us. You will hold the crown as is required by the laws of

Tartarus, but in name it will be Eurynomos. You belong to us."

Lightning cracked between the two demons, splitting the ice beneath me. I shifted back onto my heels, wincing as I was reminded of the pain that lacerated my wings. The cold and shock were keeping me numb to what I knew would be excruciating once the adrenaline wore off.

"I will not be a slave to you, who are beneath me. I can turn you to ash where you stand. You are speaking to a cyn and you will treat me as such." Bishop was an animal pushed to desperation. A creature like that is dangerous, when they are forced to act. Fight or flight. Only one of them could do both.

Raum's countenance didn't falter. "You have made many a slave to you. I do not believe it will be hard for you to follow in their footsteps."

Cold wind battered my hair from its braid. It lashed about my face as the snow flurries increased. I dug my nails into the ice and willed the heat of my core to ignite.

I searched for Valen, following the bond down until it grew faint. There were no tatters or frays, but it was hardly there. Was he ok? Had something happened?

I looked at Atticus who simply smiled back at me, like he knew exactly what I was thinking.

"Eurynomos has me. Bishop has betrayed you; he has sacrificed all of Vélos to Eurynomos."

There was no response.

"Run if you can hear me. Take who is left and leave Vélos."

Hatred flared amongst the group like a furnace. Its heat did nothing to ignite the flames within me.

Bishop's eyes fell on me. There was a glimpse of the so-called care he had mentioned to Valen reflected in them, framed in pity's glistening stare. He didn't care for me. He was not sorry for what he had done. He was just sorry he had not made his mark. Like every time before, Bishop had reached too high and failed.

"A slave I will never be," he answered, his voice gruff. "But if it is you who leads Eurynomos, you have me as an ally. Do not let Baal get his hands on her."

Raum's sapphire eyes danced with darkness. "I will do what I can to spare her from his appetites."

Not theirs.

Rot and sulfur and lust, it mingled amongst them. Bishop had given me to the wolves, and the beasts were feral. Unlike him, they would not hesitate. Neither would they be kind like Valen. I would be slaughtered for their own pleasure.

I reached for the coin in my pocket, the soft indention of its shape a mild comfort. Slowly, I wedged my fingers into my pocket until I could feel the cool press of it against my fingertips.

"I am Ezra Hollen and I call on you Raguel to fulfill your promise. Rescue me. Spare me when you find me, but rescue me now." I mouthed the words that were caught up in the wind and carried past my captors. *Help me. Help me. Help me.*

Bishop tipped his head, resigning himself to a fate he would not have to suffer. He spared me one last glance before he turned his back.

"Where do you think you are going?" Raum called. A slow grin spread across his face, cutting deep laugh lines around his mouth. The look raked chills down my spine that had nothing to do with the cold.

Bishop's shoulders tensed as he looked over his shoulder. Long talons curved into his wrist as he clenched his fists.

The cyn turned slowly, tipping his head down as a shadow cast across his face. "We made a deal," he hissed.

"We cannot let you go unscathed."

Bishop's entire body trembled.

"What will your people think when you return without the nephilim? Unharmed. Surely, you would have fought to keep Ezra." Raum's lips curled back, revealing rows of sharp teeth. The sight of it compared to the twin fangs made my blood run cold. "Someone of your power would have to be greatly wounded to have fled without her."

Bishop was seething. Lightning rippled through the air as he struggled to control his rage. "You dare threaten me." A roll of thunder boomed in the distance.

Raum shrugged. "If you want to be believed that you were attacked, then you will take your wounds without argument."

Bishop looked between the keras, as if one of them would come to his aid. Raum was right. No one would believe him if he returned without me, pristine and holy as the day he fell. It was well known the Fallen hated him for it. And the keras were no different in their animosity. Alliance or not, purity did not have a place in Tartarus. It burned like hot coals in Raum's eyes. Fell to the smug line of his mouth when he knew he had won.

"Eska," Bishop spat.

Orias stood swiftly. The pommel of his long sword glinted at his back before he pulled it free and passed it to Raum.

"You wound me," Raum said blandly, fisting the blade as if it weighed nothing. "I will let you decide which wing it is."

Bishop's wings ruffled as he pulled them against his back. Once more, he looked at each of the keras and then, his eyes fell to me. Still curled at their feet, I didn't pity what was about to happen to him. I hated them all, but he deserved this. He deserved more than losing one of his wings for the hell he put me and his people through.

"I'm sorry, Ezra," he said. The tension eased in his right wings as he let them unfurl.

"You will be," I said. "If there is ever a day after this that I lay eyes on you, I will kill you."

Bishop's nostrils flared at my vow. His head tipped to the side and his lips parted like he meant to speak.

Raum heaved the sword. There was too much power behind the swing for him to only be taking one wing. Bishop must have seen it too, because as the sword came down, he turned and sank all of those nasty sharp teeth into the side of Raum's neck.

There was a flurry of feathers and crimson mist through the air as they spun. Bishop's top wing fell to the ground. The sword was halfway through the second when he finally let Raum go and stumbled back, slipping in his own blood.

A pristine gray wing lay bleeding between them. Raum fisted the sword with one hand and clamped down on the side of his neck with the other. Seared flesh wafted in the air, but even that was not more potent than the scent of Bishop's blood.

Bishop's head snapped in Orias's direction as the demon slunk forward and snatched the wing. "A little souvenir to add to our collection." He sneered.

"Bastards!"

"Now you are like the rest of us, brother." Raum removed his hand, inspecting the sticky blood that coated it. Half of his neck was covered in ash and crusted red. It was a wonder Bishop hadn't ripped out his throat. "Fly back home lest your sacrifice be in vain."

Someone hoisted me from the ground, pulling a broken sound from my throat. Bishop's countenance fell and, for a brief second, he looked almost regretful for what he had done. My life, and all those he had left behind, for the sake of power.

Bishop launched into the sky, into a bleed that burst overhead.

CHAPTER SIXTY-ONE: EVIL WAS HIS NAME

Ezra

The creak of leather was a constant irritation to my ears as we rode across the frozen terrain. My position on the back of the odonnos made it hard to breathe. With my hands bound with my wings, I could not shift my weight enough to breathe. Neither could I intentionally fling myself from its back as Raum had made sure my binds were nice and tight, to keep me from falling.

The tall male was saddled in front of me, his broad shoulders in line with his hips and heels, marking him an experienced rider. Feathers peeked from beneath his gloves that held the reins loose. Everything about him and the keras that followed us was relaxed.

And why shouldn't they be? As far as they were concerned, they were untouchable. No one had any proof they had attacked Vélos.

Yet.

"I can feel your stare burning a hole in my back," Raum said.

I kept my mouth shut as I looked at the others, the ones I could see from this position. Orias had ridden ahead of us to ensure the path remained clear. Atticus and the rest of the band took the rear.

The pale keras winked when I caught his eye.

Could they all turn into dragons, or were certain shapes only allotted to some of them? The scent of my fear tinged my cheeks with heat. I had no clue if my call to Raguel had worked. I doubted Valen had heard me either, remembering that he said he couldn't reach me before when he was in their territory.

I swallowed thickly. It wouldn't be long before the truth came out and Valen came looking for me. I had faith in my adelfi, but I worried what Bishop would do if he managed to get his hands on him. If he would be a man and face him before he put an arrow through his heart.

"God, please hear me and keep him safe. Spare him."

A shudder rippled across the demons in unison.

Raum chuckled. "That name has no power here. Your prayers are futile."

It had some power though. It had affected Bishop much the same it did the keras. Whether I still believed didn't matter. Names had power and the name of God was a sharp blade.

I held Raum's ocean stare as I said, "God has not forsaken me." The tick in his jaw was the only trace that the power of his Creator affected him. It gave me a flick of hope. Perhaps my faith had not been misplaced when I was condemned.

The tension in his jaw stretched into a smile. "He forgot about you a long time ago."

"He never forgets."

Raum's eyes narrowed. "I think you have done enough talking."

We rode a couple hours more into the cold. At one point, Atticus trotted forward to toss a blanket over me before falling back into place. An unexpected gesture from a creature I knew felt nothing.

My adrenaline had worn off long ago and my wings screamed in agony. My jaw ached from clenching it so hard as I struggled to choke down my pain.

Raum reached back, palming the swell of my ass as the odonnos lurched forward to climb the steep incline of the rocks before us. I grunted with each hop across the stones. Around one of the bends, I glimpsed an iron railing gutting from the side of the mountain. The higher we climbed, the more the dark kingdom showed itself.

The stories of Eurynomos did nothing to prepare me for how cruel it truly was. Its walls were made of glistening obsidian encased by a dark mountain. Every tower was a sharp point. Like giant black swords, they pierced the churning storm clouds above.

It was the screams that echoed around me as Raum lifted me from the odonnos that turned my stomach, though. Every single one a desperate cry for help. They cut through me like shards of glass, piercing one after the other. The hammer of my heart wasn't loud enough to drown out the anguish.

"Like music, is it not?" Raum looked down on me.

I bit into the metal gag he had forced in my mouth when I refused to stop my prayers. The piece on my tongue held a spike, and if I screamed it would shoot out the back of my head and anchor to the outside of my scalp. The measures of my immortality had yet to be tested, so despite the tension of power within my throat, I refrained from adding my cry to those being battered.

But when the moment was right, and this gag was removed, I would shatter every single one of them.

My core had thawed and the coals of my power were starting to warm.

Raum hoisted me to his side as I stumbled. The weight of my wings dragging behind me was becoming too much, too painful. He held me close as we climbed the steep incline of a path leading to an adjacent tower set within the face of the mountain. Flames peered back through windows cut into black rock. Little eyes to the heart of Eurynomos.

By the time we reached the end of the landing, I could no longer stand on my own. My entire body shook with fatigue. The smell of my own fear was so rank it burned my nose. It was a wonder I hadn't pissed myself already. I couldn't use what little strength I had left to fight him as he lifted me into his arms and carried me the rest of the way.

Death was not my purpose. Not when I had the power to bear more nephilim. I would need my strength to fight them later. I would die before they could set their intentions on me.

Orias pushed the two double doors before us open. The muscles in his back flexed as he shoved them, and he strode forward with the arrogance of someone who had won a battle. In a way, he had. They all had. I was the biggest prize to be won in this war.

The Hall was smaller than that of Vélos. The keras did not need the space as the only people they hosted did not make it through the night. No one visited Eurynomos.

I dug my fingers into Raum's neck as I found new strength at the sight of the throne with its steepled back that pointed obscenely to the ceiling and the fragment of bodies it was made up of. Amongst the flesh were sharp points of swords and bones that fanned out the back. At the base of it was a heap of black fur.

The black mass moved, lifting its head and turning its two beady eyes in our direction. I'd never seen a bear as large as the one that curled at the base of the throne. Its nose twitched as it scented the air and then looked back at its master who sat, legs spread wide, with a lifted sharp chin.

Baal Ukai was what I had always envisioned Death to look like. He was the creature I had thought hunted me throughout the years. Tall, pale, so wrongly human—like the skin he wore was a costume, stretched over broad muscles. Long bull-like horns lifted from the raven black waves of his hair. Above his ears another set of horns, that of a ram, curved outward. The cyn of Eurynomos had the infamous blue eyes every keras had, but these were full of starlight. Galaxies of deep purple that twisted into thousands of nebulas. So dark they could have been the depths of the ocean. Tartarus's darkest night.

His beauty didn't go beyond those eyes. The standard angelic attractiveness was there, but it was surface level. Barely that. There was something so undeniably wrong about him.

He lowered his starry gaze to me.

If the devil was real, this was him.

Little legs crawled across my skin. Something scratched the back of my neck. I jerked my head to try and shake off the touch. It intensified as Baal continued to stare. My nostrils flared, and I shifted in Raum's arms again, trying to break free.

"If you are so anxious to meet your new cyn," he said, and promptly dropped me to the ground. I fell on one of my wings, gasping as the shards of my primaries cracked beneath my weight.

When Baal moved, he was darkness incarnate. He slunk forward, his body graceful in its wrongness as he stepped over his large pet. Rotten shadows spread in the wake of his steps. At once they surrounded him so he was invisible, and the next moment they would shift, like waves in a hurricane and he was revealed.

"You brought her." His voice was as deep as his night, but softer than I anticipated. Its eerie smoothness sent my heart racing.

"As promised," Raum said.

Baal's eyes flicked to Raum. The thick veils of shadows at his shoulders coiled in serpentine bodies. "And Vélos?" He reached for me with glinting black nails, the tattoo of the arc glistening with them along his arm.

Leaning away from him only pushed me into Raum's legs. I had nowhere to go. I looked wildly past Baal's stilled hand, to the apparitions that lurked in the darkness. To the keras that stood solid amongst them. *This* was Hell. This is where lost souls came to die. Because surely, death was the only escape from the horror of the screams climbing through the air and the soulless eyes of the damned that looked through me.

"Bishop will be the only cyn left come the third sun."

I whirled to face him. "What?" I slurred around the gag.

He flashed his teeth. "You did not think we would let them live after this, did you? Your and Valen's affair has started a civil war. If in three days Bishop has not restored his crown, we will take the fragments for ourselves." He nodded to Orias and Atticus. "A gracious gift from our cyn for our loyalty." Raum tipped his head forward, his wavy raven hair falling against his jawline.

I stared at him in horror. Bishop, so desperate for what he thought he deserved, would destroy everything. It had been what Valen and the other cyn feared. It was why they had taken part in Episkopos's death in the beginning. To save their people from this madness. Now, it had come full circle. It would be so much worse not having the other cyn there to balance out Bishop's madness. Bishop, who was now at the mercy of Eurynomos's will.

Baal crouched in front of me, turning his head to survey me.

Drool fell over my chin from the gag and still I held it high. I pulled my head from Baal's reach too slow. He caught my jaw with his sharp nails. He ran his thumb over my lip, swiping a string of drool and sticking it into his mouth.

The cyn's eyes fluttered. I pushed against Baal's hand as I tried to find my feet, tried to move away from the monsters crowding me.

"Delicious," Baal said. Embers flashed across the stars of his eyes. His eyes moved across my wings. "I cannot wait to savor the rest of you."

I managed to get my foot out from underneath my butt. I put the rest of my strength into the bottom of my foot as I pushed forward. I knew as soon as my foot was flying through the air that I would regret my actions. My kick landed square in Baal's face.

I called my fire from its depths. It moved at leisure, not fast enough. Not fast enough!

Not yet, it yawned. The creature within me... She wouldn't wake! Still frozen from the cold depths, she curled back within.

Baal swiped at his unbloodied face. He looked down at his fingertips and rubbed them together. "Oh, the things I am going to do to you," he said. Calm. Unfeeling. This male was a psychopath.

Raum hauled me to my feet as Baal rose to meet us. His towering shadow loomed like a reaper ready to sow.

The bear was snarling from its place on the dais. With its head lifted, I could see the thick gold collar around its neck. Gold caps covered its canines as it spit another raging growl at me.

Not yet. Do not fight them yet. I didn't have any strength left. I was fading quickly. My fire wouldn't come to the surface. What *good* was it if it didn't listen to me?

A forked tongue darted between Baal's lips. "I respect the war within you, little angel. But there is no future in where I do not get what I want." He stepped forward so that he had to look down at me from the bridge of his nose. His long lashes brushed against the high angle of his cheekbones. "They tell me you have not been able to wield Prometheus again. A shame, as your fire is no good here." His shadows slithered around the flames cracking across my hands. They twisted around the orange tendrils and choked them. Choked them so hard that I felt it within my chest when they were snuffed out.

"Remove her gag," Baal said.

Raum tipped his head. "I would warn you, my cyn, that she has the tongue of a harpy."

The nickname was ash on his tongue. There was no feeling when he said it, though hearing that word made my heart ache. It instilled a new wave of fear as I wondered what had become of Valen.

I would have felt it if he were dead. This tie between us was stronger than the grave.

He would survive.

Valen would come for me.

Baal flicked his long fingers. Raum twisted the lock free from the back of my head. He fisted the silver gag and took a step back. I might not be able to call my fire. I might be broken. But I had enough defiance left in me to stand against them.

I swiped my tongue across the drool on my chin, gathered the wad on my tongue, and spit it right in Baal's face. The thick spatter smacked his chin. I flashed him an arrogant smile.

A crack of lightning shot through the air. That's what I thought had happened. That a loud storm had suddenly erupted within the tyre.

I blinked. Black. The stone floor. Blood in my mouth. Black

again.

A high-pitched keening shrilled in my ears as my entire body convulsed and I heaved. Dark black blood marked the floor. The floor that I was now splayed across.

Baal had struck me so hard he had thrown me across the room.

I blinked as my body shuddered and my vision tapered.

Muffled voices grew closer and suddenly my head was ripped back. My scalp burned beneath Baal's fist as he tried to jerk my hair out. That's when the pain hit me. The side of my face felt seared, and all the fight I had moments ago fled as I let out a broken sob. Beneath the pain was wetness.

Had he blown out my eardrum? He pressed his lips to my other ear, the one that wasn't in excruciating pain. I couldn't hear him through my crying. He shook me harder before he bit into the shell of my ear. Sharp needle pain assaulted me.

"I am your cyn now and you will show me respect," he hissed. "Any sin against me will be punished." Baal shoved me to the ground so hard that another crack ran through my good ear. One that came from the bones in my face. "I think time in Valen's old quarters might help her learn a few manners."

Someone hoisted me from behind. Orias, I think? All I saw was long dark hair before the room spun before me. I tried to put my feet beneath me, but my legs gave out. They dragged me by the arms that became unbound, tugging my broken wings behind me.

"Ezra," Baal called.

My captor halted as dark shadows pooled across our path. A wall of smoke billowed to my right. The only sign that Baal was amongst them was the reflective glint of his night sky eyes. "Welcome home," he said.

CHAPTER SIXTY-TWO: CIVIL WAR

Valen

The smoke of burning stone wafted through the air, casting a thick haze over the pink-hued sky. Dragonfire was one of the few things that could burn through rock, and every part of Vélos was on fire. Moans coincided with the crackling of fire in the streets. The screams of the dying had gone with them, forever blotted from Creation and memory. It is said that if a mortal dies in Tartarus, then it is there their soul will remain. None of the humans were meant for this prison, yet we had selfishly brought them here to suffer with us.

The blackened body of a young man lay just out of reach from an amorini that had been reaching for him seconds before the dragon's fire had consumed them.

There was no sign of the wingless beast now. With its departure, the army had retreated into the shadows. From somewhere in the forest or mountains, there was no trace of where they might have gone or to which they had come from. As if they were made of smoke.

The dragon had left so suddenly, launching into the air, that I knew what it chased. As much as I yelled to Ezra and Bishop, there was no response.

Every cell in my body lit up. I came to a sloshing halt in the mud. Thanatos controlled the wyrms, but shadow magic, though we all wielded it, was a gift best wielded by the keras. Darkness incarnate.

My breath came up short. Surely Bishop was not fool enough, angry enough, to have called on them to his aid. To sacrifice our entire court. To sacrifice her.

The loud brush of feathers of a crow echoed in the air. It landed on top of a pile of rubble down the hill, its beady glass eyes un-blinking as it cocked its head, surveying the ruins. The army had not disappeared into the billowing smoke.

I turned to the dark forest. The canopy was thick with shadows and evergreens. But on the lower branches, I could see them. Black spindly feet clinging to the limbs. Glassy eyes peering through the needles.

I kept turning, skimming the rest of the skyline viewable behind the ruins. They'd never left, but I couldn't let them know that I knew.

It felt like the world would drop out from under me as it spun like a murky kaleidoscope. I shut my eyes to stay my dizziness as nausea filled my gut. If Ezra was in Eurynomos... I had not told her of the true horror that lies within their fortress. There were no words in any language to describe their true wickedness. I had been honest with her about everything except what I had endured. Parts of it were still sealed from my memory, blank spaces where they had worn me down. I could not stomach to tell her the truth.

An involuntary shudder ran beneath my skin.

Bishop would not hurt her. If it was pain he wanted, I would be the one to bear it. But if they had been attacked?

The crunch of gravel summoned my attention to Kasiya. The

male tore a glove from his hand, then the other. He looked drawn, exhausted as the rest of us as we dug out those buried beneath the rubble and accounted for the lives lost.

Kasiya was one of the few men I trusted and had been the first I confided in upon my return from Eurynomos. He had quietly laid rumors around Vélos of the unrest that lay between the four cyn. And the night of the dance? He stoked the flame as the court questioned their loyalty to Bishop and his word. My performance with Ezra had been the spark to a fire a long time coming. Kasiya had been the wind that fanned its flames to life.

"You look like hell," he said.

"You're no fucking better."

Kasiya grunted. He ran a knuckle over the scar on his face. "Only thirty lost."

Only.

We shouldn't have lost anyone. We stayed out of the other courts' way, abided by the laws that governed us. It was the way of demons though. If someone had something they wanted, they would use hellfire to get it.

"Have their pyres built."

"Already begun," he said. "We will light their fires tonight."

I nodded and threw a quick look toward the forest again. "Ready our men while you're at it."

"Sire?"

"Bishop has not returned, and it concerns me. I intend to speak to those who are able to attend the funerals." I ran a hand over my head, my curls snagging from their plaits when they caught on my rings. The ring on the middle finger of my left hand caught my eye. The signet of the downward arrow and sun all four of us wore. It weighed my hand down like stone. "There is war on the horizon, my brother. Let us not be caught unprepared a second time."

"And Ezra, my lord?" Kasiya held his breath.

"With Bishop."

The male tipped his chin to the side. "This is it then."

"This is it."

"Shall I go to her?"

"I need you here with me. There are eyes in our forest."

Kasiya slid his fist over his chest before bowing, but not before I saw his gaze slide to the dark trees where our enemy waited.

I had a small sliver of hope that Bishop would bring her back. That he would rather flaunt her in my face than hide her away. Or perhaps it would be Ezra who returned alone with my heart safely clutched against her chest. This attack had jarred me. They were alright. Ezra was alright.

The Great Hall was unscathed save for a few singe marks on its exterior. I worked a hand over my chest as I stood at the entrance. There was no turning back. Everything changed the moment Ezra's scream woke me. That moment had led me to this.

I stepped into the Hall.

Four thrones stood pristine on the landing. I looked down the line of them, contemplating the weight we each carried upon our heads. It would be easier if the crown was whole. Divided, our power was restrained, chaotic only in the sense that we could not wield it fully. I didn't need all three remaining parts to do what I must. I would not end Jinn and Diriel's life unless they stood against me.

My fingers slid over the top of Jinn's throne. With a flick of my wrist, I tossed it to the ground, slinging it down the stairs. I did the same to Diriel's and, last, I stopped at mine. Second in command, second in appearance. I hurled my throne to the bottom of the Hall where it splintered into six broken pieces.

The crown had served as a collar, binding us to him despite the power that had been gifted to us. It had taken years to heal from Episkopos's death. That's something they don't tell you when you steal a cyn's crown. How your body becomes infected with poison, rotting you from the inside out to determine if you are fit to rule.

All four of us had passed, but it had taken time. The first of us to mend had been Bishop, of course. The lightning affinity of an archangel was as remarkable as it was deadly. Where we had been bedded, Bishop had sat upon the throne that rested beneath my palms.

I leaned my head back as I took his seat.

It all rushed over me like a great wave. I could not stop the tears that filled my eyes, or the unyielding pain that took me as the memories took hold and dragged me beneath the surface. There is an expectation for males to be strong and unfeeling. There is a higher one for angels, who are barred from emotions entirely.

The sting of a burn upon what was left of my wings was as clear as the day I was cast out. Smoke billowed up at my feet, encasing me as more tears fell. I was falling all over again. From Heaven, through the death of Episkopos, and the battle it had caused. Through my love with Bishop and his cruelties. Through the punishments he had executed on Jinn the first time he nearly loved a woman and ripped off her head, before thrusting the male to the whims of the monets, a vile sub race that knew only pain. Then on Diriel who he had trapped in darkness for over a decade with the screams of mortals as his only companion. To those who remained that were swiftly ended or their lives dragged over hot coals to satisfy the cyn's displeasure.

We had been beaten, tortured, and bloodied for something we

did or solely because it pleased him. It often pleased him that we join him in his sins. And I had. Better to be the one wielding the sword than at the point of its blade.

There were countless memories that flashed before my eyes, blinding me.

I screamed into the void.

I let the fire of my existence surge forth as I pummeled down into the depths of darkness that had claimed me.

Lifetimes of sin, of lies, of betrayal.

In the midst of the darkness was silver. The flash of light that was the hope of my people.

"Ezra." Her name was hoarse on my tongue.

I opened my eyes but could see nothing through the smoke and flames that cocooned me. I reached for her through the bond and there was... *nothing*. Absolutely nothing. I dug my claws that had curled into the top of the chair.

I should have felt something, but she wasn't there.

I looked to the heavens. Was that laughter I heard?

There was not a place in this land I would not find her. Our souls were bound by the will of Heaven, of the fates, and by our love. We were unbreakable.

Thirty pyres stood tall in the field. Thirty amorini raised their bows and shot flaming arrows toward them. The wood caught, washing the crowd with a muddied orange glow. The eyes of predators reflected white in the light. Those of the humans reflected the twisting flames.

Diriel and Jinn stood on either side of me. Kasiya and Andras flanked them with two more warriors on either side. Though Andras had never been named a warrior, it was for his bravery in this recent battle that I had given him rank. A new scar slid across his face, making it twin to one that already marked him. He had said it would make the women love him more, but there had been no mirth in his words.

This day had affected all of us.

Diriel had lost sight of Bishop and Ezra soon after they flew away. I had caught his eyes throughout the night shifting to white as he searched for them, but by his lack of voice, they were yet to be found.

Liquid gurgled in Jinn's lungs every time he breathed. The male had suffered a harsh blow when a building collapsed on him. His gait had been uneven, but he stood stoic as though the pain he went through was nothing.

The crack and pop of moisture leaving the wood snapped through the air. I inhaled, breathing in the thick smoke and exhaling a cloud of steam.

"My cyn," Kasiya said softly.

I blinked.

Kasiya had stepped to my right shoulder, his gaze open and waiting.

I lifted my chin, turning my gaze back to the pyres. "Though a crown rests upon your brows, I ask you, Diriel and Jinn, to step down as cyns of Vélos."

A jolt of confusion swept down the line.

"While the crown brought us together in the beginning, it has also been a constant divide. I no longer support our rule as four."

"You mean to take the throne," Diriel said softly.

"I have taken it."

Diriel's brows knit together. He ducked his head, but not before I saw the white in his eyes as if he hoped to find his answers in the future.

"And if we don't?" Jinn asked.

I felt my guard move closer. My guard that would hold Diriel and Jinn at the flick of my will so that I could remove the crests from their heads.

I looked slowly to Jinn. He was so much paler now, his skin nearly translucent. His spirit had always been as fiery as his auburn hair. I could exhale now and blow out that flame if I wanted to. "I'll kill you," I said. "I will not allow Bishop to rule us another second. If you stand in my way, I will take what I need to overthrow him."

By now I knew the rest of the court was listening. My voice was quiet, but those closest to our outer ring could hear, and whispers travel rather quickly.

"I do not want to hurt you," I said. "Forgive me for ever dragging you into this."

Jinn's eyes glistened, but by the twist of his mouth, I knew it was in anger and not relief that they did.

Diriel's fingers brushed against mine. I laced mine with his, not taking my eyes off Jinn until the male finally lowered his eyes with his head to follow.

"We are at your service," Diriel said.

"We are," Jinn spoke just for my ears.

I twisted my hand from Diriel's and clasped his wrist before I stepped forward.

"Legion." The name to summon our horde rattled the men to attention. Even the humans blinked from their red and swollen stupor. "It comes with a heavy heart that I must confess you have been lied to and that I have had a hand in twisting that lie. What has befallen us today was a reminder of that, and I can stand by no longer as I will not allow you to suffer for my sins." I motioned to Diriel and Jinn. "*Our* sins.

"It was not Episkopos that led us from our grace, but Azazel, crowned with a new name when he stole our cyn's crown. We had been led to believe that Episkopos had gone mad, and we tore him apart, devouring him for being the root of our damnation. In turn, the lust for revenge tainted us, spilling into you, feeding you our rage.

"So, let me tell you the real story."

Two days passed before the smoke finally left Vélos. Two days passed without a single word or trace of Bishop and Ezra.

I slid my knee into the mare's gut, cinching the girth around the odonnos's belly tighter. The mare reached back with a clack of its beak.

"Nashua," I scolded. I ran my hand down her neck.

The clink of tack drew my attention over my shoulder. Kasiya held the reins to a sorrel gelding. "You didn't think I was going to let you go alone, did you?"

I ran my right hand across Nashua's neck once more. It was perhaps a foolish task, what I was about to do, searching for Ezra and Bishop on my own. Where there was one, surely there would be the other. As much as I hated Bishop for what he had done, there was still a small part of me that worried something had happened to him too.

"If I may speak freely."

"You always do," I said.

Kasiya let a moment of silence pass until I finally looked at him. His face looked grim. "I do not think it wise that you would leave after so quickly usurping the throne. Our people... They want to trust you, but the shell you dropped on them has brought in a dark cloud upon their minds. It is going to take time for them to accept the change. Leaving might set them back."

"I know," I said. "But I cannot sit here not knowing what has happened to Ezra. We have spies within our forest and so I can only assume the worst."

Kasiya's mouth twisted. His gelding pawed at the ground, his talons ripping the soil with impatience.

"Then let us find her and return home quickly."

"I have asked much of you over the years."

Kasiya's lashes fluttered. "You are not asking me for this." He turned and mounted the gelding.

I sent a silent thanks to the gods, to the Creator if He could hear us from down here, and mounted Nashua.

Kasiya and I had gone on many hunts and patrols across our time. Eventually those faded as my duties became more twisted to align with Bishop's. I hated that it was the circumstances we were under now that brought us back together. As we rounded the bend, my stomach lurched and, if I had my heart, it might have beat a little faster.

Doon, Hermes, Abasi and, at the end of the line, Diriel. The four sat atop their geldings in shining leathers. Bows were fitted across each of their chests with swords and axes tied readily on their saddles or at their hips.

"Jinn is to hold the throne until we return, where you will assume your rule as our cyn," Diriel spoke. Red paint lined his brow beneath the helmet he wore. Battle markings.

A small band of six. This was better than riding alone, but… "We ride to Eurynomos in search of Ezra," I said. "As there has been no word or sight of Bishop, we can assume they have been killed or captured. I think we all know Bishop would make it a hard feat to do either, and I have not felt Ezra's passing. We must be prepared for anything.

"At any point should we come across Bishop, you are not to interfere." I looked them each in the eye, slowly and pointedly. "His crown is mine."

Diriel nudged the black gelding forward. "I at least get to hold the fucker down when you tear out his heart."

I turned with Diriel so that we were side be side. "It is the least I can allow," I said.

Diriel tipped his head down and slammed his fist against his chest. "A fair ruler you will make," he teased, but I knew there was truth in his words. "Now, let's go get our girl."

CHAPTER SIXTY-THREE: IN THE BELLY OF HELL

Ezra

Orias dragged me through the tyre by my wrists. The joints popped and snapped beneath his grip and my shoulders went next as he hauled me down so many flights of stairs I lost count. I could not keep the tears from my eyes. Not when he was ripping me apart.

My wings took the brunt of it all, shielding my body from the broken fragments of the ground while they were torn to ribbons.

"Stop! Please stop!"

He was going to rip my wings off. My arms would go next.

Down and down we went until he finally let me go at the top of the final flight and pushed me over the edge. I felt every single step, every sharp corner and blunt surface until I crashed into cold tile.

The tall male cocked his head as he watched me writhing at the bottom. "You're not as powerful as they say. Look at you." He walked down, one step at a time. "Did you know they're afraid of you? You're nothing."

I was still panting when he grabbed me by the hair, jerking me to my feet. A guttural groan was forced from my chest. Every little bit of movement shot into my still twisted wings. I couldn't push against him, not when he was pushing into my wings, breaking apart what was left of them.

"It's not so bad. You'll have a little piece of him with you tonight." Orias's dark chuckle turned my skin to goose flesh.

The smell of evil slammed into me.

I gripped hold of the doorway as Orias tried to force me into the cell. In the middle of the room was a black-stained steel table. Above it on a wire chord was flesh. Valen's flesh. I could smell him. I could smell the fear and agony he had suffered and the complete evil they had unleashed on him.

Blood. Piss. Shit. Cum. Tears. Pain. It assaulted my senses and twisted my gut with a violent wrench. I heaved forward and spilled the entirety of my stomach on the floor.

"Fuck's sake," Orias cursed. His palm slammed into my back, and I fell forward.

Iron hot pain shot into my nails as two of them caught on the stone, freeing them from my fingers. I registered it right before I fell into my own vomit and the flesh they had left behind of my adelfi.

The sound of a door banging. Laughter, sweet gentle music broke my resolve.

The sound that left my throat was not human. It wasn't even a scream. It was the beast within me come alive as she unleashed a horrific awful sound as I saw what they had done to him. Valen had lied about their torture to spare me. He had looked me dead in the eye, so stoic and brave and *sure*.

He had come back as if it had been nothing. This was not sin. This wickedness did not have a name.

How had Valen survived?

How?

I shut my eyes, but it did nothing to chase away the smell. It didn't wash the vile taste from my mouth.

I was not going to survive.

My breath hitched. I couldn't breathe. I couldn't breathe! My eyes flew open as I took in short, quick breaths, but it wasn't enough. It felt like I was suffocating. I clawed at my neck as the putridness forced its way down my throat.

I could feel his memories. Was that possible? I could feel the shudder of his screams around me. I could feel their laughter. I could hear it.

I clamped my hands over my ears.

I dug my head into my knees.

I still couldn't breathe.

I couldn't stop the wailing that tore from my soul.

They hadn't tortured me yet. They hadn't hurt me at all since they had locked me away. And why would they? When I was surrounded by the horror of what they had done to Valen.

Rot. Pain. Tears. Hate. Anguish.

His fear was as fresh as the day they bled him. It had been hard to stomach the story he gave me, but seeing it was so much worse. Especially now that I had all the fine details of what had really happened.

God... I did not deserve him. Fated or not, no one's love should have to endure such pain.

I had quietly distanced myself from God. I had stopped praying entirely after what I thought was my fall.

I shuffled to the farthest corner from the door. I brushed the rotten skin and fragments of bones to the side, making enough space for me to kneel. I bit the back of my tongue as I found my knees. There wasn't enough space for me to settle without tearing further into my wings. The pain in them alone threatened to make me pass out again. They were hot with a growing infection that wouldn't heal while they remained broken.

Words came out as broken sobs. No prayer touched my tongue. All I could do was cry. Each harsh intake of breath assaulted my chest with a heaving blow.

I didn't pray for help because there was none. I didn't pray for forgiveness because I deserved none.

I prayed that God would see me for who I truly was. I prayed for anyone to see me and to know this was not what I wanted. That if there were more like me, children born with an angel's damning blood, that we would be forgiven for a choice we never had the opportunity to make.

The stories of the kingdom in the black mountains of the north with their snow caps do not skim the horror of which Eurynomos truly was. Before, I might have believed my past trials of losing loved ones and being treated unfairly a great suffering. What a very selfish and human thing to believe. Death was not the axe's blade I had always believed it to be, but a gift. Death would have been a mercy to anyone within Eurynomos.

Screams. I heard screams in the distance. Someone begged for them to stop.

I didn't know how many times I blacked out and came to. I slipped between the veil of life and death. Not my death. It evaded me no matter how hard I prayed for it.

I'd never known such darkness to exist. When I woke again, there was no light. The blue glaze of Eurynomos had faded. I could only make out the faint outline of the metal table. Everything was lost to the void. Not being able to see made the smells that much worse. At least my sense of smell was almost burned. I'd been there for hours or days, I didn't really know. It was not long enough to get used to any of it.

I sat up slowly, keeping my back firmly pressed against the wall and wincing the whole time doing it. My body ached. My wings felt like they were on fire and in ruin. My knees were tight. My legs were screaming at me to stretch. My bladder was just as loud. I needed to piss.

I felt down the bond to find nothing but stillness. I couldn't feel anything anymore. I bit my lip to a flood of tears that threatened to spill. He was ok. It was this place that was blocking us. Nothing more.

Valen was alive and he would come for me.

My mind was at war with itself. There were moments I wanted to die. It would be the only way to escape what the keras had planned for me. Others, I wanted to live. To find a way to survive this and make my way back to Valen. I wanted to survive. To fight.

Fuck, everything hurt. My body. My heart. My head. It felt like I was on fire. I rubbed my hands over my face, scratching an itch that wasn't there.

I shut my eyes and shoved my fist into my pocket. Valen would come. Raguel would come. Someone would come for me.

I froze.

Where was the token?

I shoved my hand in my other pocket and back into the first, fumbling madly for Raguel's coin.

"Shit." I felt around my butt and legs. Where was it? Where was the token!

A small whimper left me when my fingers skimmed something mushy and damp.

"Looking for this?"

I stilled.

The darkness.

I held my breath as I followed the darkest parts of it until I met the searing orbs in its midst. There were two pinpoints of white staring back at me. They blinked. A flash of starlight and then white again.

The shadows shifted as a hand lifted. Between their fingers was Raguel's token.

"Does he know what you are? Raguel? I imagine he does not if he would part with something so precious." Baal stood, the only inclination that he had been sitting was the sudden change in the height of his eyes.

There was no sound as he moved. His presence buffered even the screams I knew echoed in the hallways.

"I have been watching you sleep. You speak in your dreams. Did you know that?" I cowered as the shadows lifted, revealing his pristine face. "What do you dream of, Ezra?"

I bit the inside of my lip to keep them from trembling. Do not show fear. Do not give him your fear. My nostrils flared as I tried to trick my mind against everything I felt.

"You do not want to tell me?" His horns glinted in the pale light he had allowed back into the room as he cocked his head. "I have ways of finding out. Orias is an incubus." A smile fanned over his wide mouth. "All of my men are skilled, but I find his talents to be particularly useful."

Baal turned the coin between his knuckles. "Do you dream of being rescued by the angel? Or is it your dear lover?" He ran the token down the side of my face, one side and then the other. "Or is it me you dream of? Of all the violent tortures I am going to inflict upon you."

My eyes snapped to the twisting galaxies.

Baal grinned. "They don't have to be dreams." He flicked his fingers so that the coin disappeared. He caressed me with his clawed touch.

I jerked my face away.

"Speak, Ezra. Let me hear this voice that had the power to rip a hole in my kingdom."

If me being vocal is what he wanted, he wasn't going to get it. I kept my mouth firmly shut. If I knew my scream would tear another hole into the veil, I would have given into his request.

If I could find the tear, I could escape. Valen said Baal had started sending his men through, which meant it was possible to leave this world behind entirely. I could escape.

Baal's eyes slid past my face to the ruin at my back. He reached for my wing. By the time I realized what he had done, it was too late. I jerked forward, away from his touch, right against his chest. I froze when he smiled, those sharpened teeth so close to my face. The heat of his rank breath made me gag.

His touch was revolting as he spread his fingers through my feathers. A low groan slid through his parted lips. He was no longer looking at me, but them, the gnarled and twisted bones. Abruptly, he grabbed my forearm with his other hand and fisted my feathers with his other.

It was painful and vile. My stomach lurched, threatening to spill what was left within.

"Stop!"

Baal cocked his head and he slid his hand down, caressing my primaries. "Why would I ever want to stop?" He grabbed hold of my wing and pulled it forward so hard I fell flat on my back with a mangled moan. Tears sprang into my eyes.

Baal was massive. He looked like a giant when he leered over me, placing himself between my legs. The hand on my arm pinned my shoulder.

"Please," I said, my voice choking.

Shadows and smoke billowed around his face when he brushed his nose against mine. "Tell me what you dream of," he said.

"D-death," I stuttered.

The cyn smiled wide, so far that it split across his cheeks. "Fear not, Ezra, for I do not intend to kill you."

That's what I was afraid of.

I could not conquer my fear when he was so close and I was in a compromised position. War is scary, but it does not affect you from across an ocean when it is not your home being obliterated. Disease is heartbreaking, but how much does it truly hurt when it is not your heart tearing in two? When you read about someone being terrifying, you never know the truth of those words until you are in the face of them.

Yet, somewhere in the recess of my mind was a voice. A silent command for me to harden myself in this monster's presence.

"You should."

A thick lock of hair fell across his shoulder as he bent his head down, turning his ear toward my mouth.

"You should," I repeated, my voice stronger this time as I willed myself to rally. Just one more try, Ezra, the voice whispered. I licked my lips, the tip of my tongue brushing against the shell of his ear. "Before *I* kill *you*."

"I am immortal," he said, turning his face back into mine and sliding his long nose up the side of my face.

The fire that had curled into the palms of my hands was weak. A brush of glowing embers. My fingers passed through the darkness as I reached for him. Baal was standing over me once more, the soulless eyes the only trace of his physical features standing out.

"I believe our guest needs a bit more conditioning."

Two keras strode in, both with wavy short hair. Their only difference were the freckles that scoured one of their faces.

"Strip her," Baal commanded.

I couldn't fight them. I tried, but I was too weak and broken. All I could do was writhe as they ripped apart my clothing. They bumped and jarred my wings in the process, not caring what pain it caused me.

I stood shaking, bent over the metal table. The demons' heat was sweltering and yet chills stood erect on my skin.

Smoke swirled past Baal's face. It draped across his shoulders and moved down to his feet. His lustful gaze roved over my body before snapping to the two keras standing at the front of the doorway. "Hand me the iron."

One of the males passed him a long pole with a twisted shape at the end. I strained against my position, but I couldn't move. Baal's power held me against the cool metal as he brought the branding rod in front of my face. I watched as it shifted from black to bright red as it heated in his grip. A crow's face atop two crossed swords glared back at me. He was going to mark me with the house seal. His seal.

Ash and wisps of my power crackled through the air, but none of it did any good to release me. I couldn't even open my mouth to tell him to stop. Tears ran down my face as I pushed against him, trying and failing to free myself.

"Shh," he crooned, sliding my hair over my shoulder to expose the back of my neck. Pressure encased my mouth as the heat grew closer to my skin. White hot agony ripped through me as the iron seared into my neck. Burnt flesh filled the air. And try as I might to scream, I could not thanks to his power sealing my lips shut.

I bore it all in silent, suppressed torture.

There was a crackle of burnt flesh breaking when he pulled the brand away.

"Turn on the screen," Baal said, nodding to the far wall. A clear box of glass slid down from the ceiling. It flickered and showed an image of the room I now shivered in.

I could barely see through the tears and sweat pooling in my eyes. I swallowed when I saw Raum and Orias hauling in Valen's limp body between them. Atticus followed and strapped iron cuffs on his neck, wrists, and ankles. The image paused to a still shot of Valen, his gold eyes wide and unblinking.

I looked at Baal in horror.

"Let this be a lesson to what will happen to you, should you show me any further disrespect."

One of the keras leaned in to close the door as Baal exited in a whirl of smoke. Upon his exit, his power released me and I fell to the floor with a broken sob. And then the film began, and I saw firsthand everything they had done to Valen.

The moments I was awake were the ones that I suppressed. I crawled into the darkness of my mind where I couldn't hear the singing of metal against bone or Valen's screams. When the keras came in to leer at me with their shining blue eyes, I forced myself to think of the ocean. Of the water I had been so terrified to tread, and prayed that I would drown in them. I didn't want to wake up anymore. Better to be lost in the abyss than feel the waves of horror that crashed against me.

There were two months of footage of what they had done to Valen. Two months of torment that they left running day and night.

A mask had been fitted over my face when I tried screaming. It had been sheer agony that ripped my voice clean and shook the bones of the tyre. I'd finally had the power to call out and they had shut me up before the flame had exited my mouth. There were twin spikes hovering over my eyes that brushed my lashes whenever I blinked. The funny thing about immortals is that it takes longer for the eyes to heal. I'm not sure why. But the next time I tried to scream, when my throat had healed from the raw and bloody mess they had turned it into, the mask penetrated my eyes. It was hard to tell how much time passed when I was trapped in the dark. Not that it mattered. Being blind did not end the sound of Valen's torment.

I no longer called out to God. I stopped hoping Raguel had received my pleas. I did not think of Heaven at all in those few days. How could such things that claimed to be good exist when there was so much evil around me? They had forsaken me, and so they became a distant memory.

My stomach growled. I could only eat when a blade was at my throat. And if I refused to eat the flesh and blood they presented, it was forced down my throat by one of the guards.

I ran my tongue over my canines, touched the points that had begun to sharpen.

Once you get a taste for blood...

Those words sifted from somewhere in the past.

Valen. I forced myself to watch what had been done to him. What he had suffered because of me and what we were together.

I remembered how he saved me from that fateful night on the lake. I think a part of me had known then he was the half of my soul that was missing when I reached for him through the smoke and embers. That night and all the others we had shared seemed so far away. I carved his face in my mind each time I closed my eyes so I would not lose him to the image *they* had made him.

He would come for me. Where all others had failed, Valen would not.

CHAPTER SIXTY-FOUR: A DEAL WITH THE DEVIL

Ezra

Feathers fell between my fingers as I glided a touch through them. One by one, they fell. Day by day, I lost what I considered to be my crown. They had been rotting since the iron chains pulled me from the sky. The open wounds had healed, I wasn't bleeding, but my feathers fell away all the same—revealing bony flesh beneath.

The slide of a metal bolt being drawn back made me curl my hands into my lap. I didn't want them to see me mourning over what they had lost long ago. It would be one more thing for them to hold over my head, to taunt me with.

I shifted, sliding my legs beneath me in case I needed to stand up quickly. I was so sore and beaten that I didn't really believe I had the energy to stand up to anyone.

I knew it was Raum before I scented him. He was the only one that visited me regularly. I never saw him, but I could feel him on the other side of the door. His shadow moved toward me, his silhouette cutting through the darkness.

I tracked his movement through the slits of the mask until he stopped in front of the gate.

He chuckled. "Even with all that iron between us, I can see your eyes burning. I do love the way you hate, Ezra. It suits you. I expected you to break weeks ago. Yet here you are. Seething." His grin broadened, creasing the laugh lines in his face. "It is quite beautiful."

Raum knew how to get a rise out of me. I could feel the fire needling at my fingertips. I wasn't in the mood to be blinded again, though, so I contained it.

"I have a proposition," he said.

I kept my mouth shut, waiting. Offers didn't come without consequences. He had nothing to bribe me with. I was the prize. Everything I had witnessed and, so far, shouldered, shook me to my core, but it also made me incredibly angry. If Raum wanted something, he was going to have to be very persuasive.

"I know you tire of this. Beneath all that fire is a young woman who seeks to rest." I tensed when he opened the gate. "Help me dethrone Baal," he said, walking in.

There was a long pause between us as I waited for him to follow up. What did he say? There was a distant memory of the cyn and Murder at a table. Bishop mentioned someone should take the weight of Baal's crown.

I smiled through the mask despite myself. "He is no longer weary, is he?"

"He has found new life," Raum agreed.

"What did you expect? That he would thank you for me and hand the crown over?" I shifted, kneeling back on my calves, and looked up at him. "You're a bigger idiot than I thought."

Raum's eyes narrowed. "Do not be so quick to insult your only ally. With Baal gone, your torments will end before they even begin."

Liar.

I could not rid the sound of Valen's scream from my mind, when Raum had forced that putrid darkness within him. Or the way his eyes had looked so empty once Raum had finished.

Raum would keep me for himself. There was no real freedom when it was offered by a demon. But having to deal with one of them instead of multiple would be an easier task to manage. Dealing with just Raum would give me an opportunity to focus on other things. To escape. It didn't matter where I went as long as I got out of this literal Hell.

"What do you want?"

Raum watched me with that eerily cool gaze. "Distract him. Nothing too obvious to tip him off. I presume you can target with your scream."

"My powers are gone. Even if they weren't, I haven't been able to use Prometheus again. It was a one-time thing."

"For your sake, I hope that is not true."

"It doesn't matter. I can't scream with this on." I tapped the chin of my iron mask.

"I will make sure it is off when the time comes."

I glared. "I want it off now."

"I do not think so."

Raum's eyes fell from my face to my wings. "Your wings should have healed by now. Do you know why they have not?"

I watched as he made the motion to stroke them. I prepared myself for it, but his fingers only grazed a hair's breadth above them. It seemed some of the Fallen still respected that an angel's wings were sacred. There was reverence in his stare that had not been there before. There hadn't been an ounce of it in Baal when he grabbed hold of me.

I tightened my lips. He was baiting me. They weren't healing because whatever was in the net had ruined them. They weren't healing because they had not been reset and every battering I took only agitated them. Or maybe it was whatever barrier separated me from the rest of Tartarus, that kept me from speaking to Valen.

I had enough pride to bite. "They are not healing because you left me to rot."

"You are changing," Raum said. "Your wings are not rotting, they are molting." The laugh lines around his mouth creased. "Look for yourself."

When I still didn't move, Raum dropped his touch to my feathers. I jerked on instinct. Sparks of my fire flitted through the air.

He spread his fingers between the feathers under the curve of my left wing. "Look."

A thin piece of translucent skin lay beneath. The red hue was a stark contrast from the black feathers. My fingers took the place of his. I stroked the thin veil softly. It was velvet soft and tender. Chills spread across my arms as I explored this foreign part of myself. I thought it had been torn flesh before so I hadn't really paid attention. I didn't want to pick apart how badly my wings were broken.

Raum eased back, sitting against the metal table as he watched me.

I searched the rest of my wings to find the stretch of membrane that lay beneath. My heart lurched as the image of me before the court of Vélos flashed across my mind. I skimmed over the top of my wings in search for the hooked claw that... that was forming beneath the skin. It was hard like bone, but not tender like the rest that were broken. On the other side, what I had thought to be broken bone was a sharp hook that had sprung free.

"There is a story of three women who bore the wings of a dragon. The Eirini. Furies. Your world has this story. Do you know it?"

I had heard about the furies in a Greek history and mythology lesson, but that was as far as my knowledge about them went. "Not really," I said quietly. "I know they're a myth."

He hummed. "It seems there is truth in it. It is said that furies are born out of rage and violence, that only in complete anguish can they be unleashed." He cocked his head. "I imagine your time in the cell bred that trait into you. Or was it there all along?"

"Does this mean I'm not a nephilim?" I swallowed thickly. Was I to be charged yet again for being something I had no control over?

"You are many things. Nephilim. Fury. Eirini. Forsaken. Phoenix." The last word came out as a hiss.

Each title felt heavier than the last.

"This will interest Baal. Tell him. Show him your wings."

I snapped my head to him. "Baal has touched my wings once. I do not want his hands on me again."

Raum ran his thumb over his lower lip. "Which would you prefer, him or me?"

The curl of my lips was my answer.

Raum smiled. "You will find I am much more pleasant than he is. With your help, we can be rid of him entirely. Will you help me steal his crown?" He looked at me from beneath his long lashes.

Raum was beautiful, there was no mistake, and I could feel the draw of attraction toward him even now. I wanted to tell him no and yet the word would not leave my lips. Instead, I said, "Why would I help you when my fate remains the same? Will you not rape me and keep me a prisoner still?"

"It is not rape if you are willing. Neither are you a prisoner if you choose to serve me."

"You give me no choice," I spat.

Raum shrugged. "I can be kind, Ezra. My hands will be the only ones that touch you while Baal will let not just us but the entire kingdom ravage you for the mere pleasure of your screams." He leaned forward, his palms pressed into the dried gore on the table behind him. "He will bleed you until you are nothing more than a husk, a wisp of the woman you were made to be.

"The fate laid out before you, aiding us in the war against mankind and Heaven, does not change. As is the fate of your children. Do not look so disgusted. The nephilim were gods once. Your children will be gods. Just as you are a goddess." The last word came out as a hiss.

He said it with such belief. There was a genuine softness in his voice that would have made a lesser woman believe he spoke with the kindness he bribed me with.

"I don't want that. I do not want gods for children. I do not want to war with my God." My conviction made my eyes wet. The words had fallen out of my mouth, and now that they were out there, I knew at least part of it was true. The small thread of faith I still had was frayed, but it was there. "I want my freedom. I want my adelfi."

The corner of Raum's jaw ticked. "Neither of those is an option."

"You ask me to bargain with nothing for me to gain but a looser collar."

"I am giving you a choice," he growled.

"I have never been given fair choice," I shot back.

"Humanity's concept that life should be fair is intolerable. Life is not fair and neither are the gods that created it. Your fate was written before you were born and so you must see it through." His eyes snapped up to the cell door. A shadow fell over his shoulders and Raum thrust away from the table entirely before crossing the room.

"You're jealous. Humanity was given a choice to serve while it has always been expected of you, of the angels." I cocked my head as his body went rigid. "You hate us, don't you?"

Raum smirked. "What will it be, Ezra?"

The enemy of my enemy is my friend. It made me sick that I was even contemplating helping him. I didn't even know if I could. I knew what my triggers were, yet I hadn't been able to call up the flames, much less Prometheus, my entire time here.

Raum didn't need me to overthrow Baal. It would be a good excuse to use me as a scapegoat if the court questioned him. But his ambitions were greater than that. He would use me as the Sun as was told in the Hymn.

"What are your conditions?"

"There will be a performance at the end of the week. It is a ritual to feed our men when their blood grows too hot. You will be at Baal's side in a private suite of the coliseum. I suggest you take that opportunity to call down Prometheus as it is the only thing that will hold him."

I stared at him, dumbfounded. I was starting to think all demons were mad. Being imprisoned for as long as they had, it was no surprise.

I fingered one of my wings. I was glad they were large enough to cover my nakedness from him, not that he seemed to care one way or the other. There were too many gears turning in his thick skull. "And what's to stop me from using Prometheus against you if I am able to wield it? Why should I not take Baal's crown for myself?"

I hadn't thought of it. The words came out faster than my mind could keep up. Killing a cyn honored their murderer with their power. If I could steal Baal's power, someone of his age and talent, I'd be unstoppable. They'd never be able to touch me.

Raum's brow cocked. "You could not stomach the price of the crown. As for Prometheus, you will not use it on me. I am your ally, but I will happily oblige in being your enemy if given the opportunity. You do not want to find out how cruel I can be, Ezra."

"I am sure I will find out regardless." I looked to the screen where Atticus was carefully stitching Valen's stomach. I didn't bother asking the question I already had the answer to. I'd never see him again if I took Raum's deal.

Raum crouched before me. "Do we have a deal? You do as I ask of you and no harm will come to you."

Taking down Baal was one less enemy. One less in an army of thousands. My stomach turned as I made one more fatal attempt to reach out to Valen. Like every time before, there was only silence.

I couldn't wait on Valen to save me.

"I'll think about it," I said.

I tensed when he reached behind my head. There was the jarring sound of iron scraping against itself before the mask fell from my face, landing painfully close to my bare toes.

I let Raum take my hands as he pulled me to my feet. Heat rushed to my face as he tipped his head down to inspect me. My body had withered and was covered in grime. It did not keep the spark of lust from out of his eyes.

He snapped his fingers.

A wash of sulfur filled the room when Orias and Atticus walked in. A burst of white fog left my lips when I tried to back away, but Raum wouldn't let me go. His large hands cuffed my wrists.

"Prepare her for Baal. He has requested her presence this

evening," he said.

I dug my heels into the ground when the males grabbed my arms. "You liar," I seethed.

Raum tsked. "Be a good girl, Ezra, and do not give my men trouble. They have my permission to punish you should you do so."

"I thought I wasn't for Baal."

"You are not. Take it as a sign of trust that I removed your mask. We all have a role to play. Assume yours."

I shoved against the beast inside of me. I pushed hard, but it was if she wasn't there at all. As if she had disappeared like all the others, abandoning me. I could not escape without her. I could not fight back if I did not have my fire.

Raum hummed softly. "That graceful spirit of yours will be the death of you."

CHAPTER SIXTY-FIVE: WORSHIP SERVICE

Ezra

Abhorrent screams filled the kingdom of Eurynomos. Screams of the dead and dying.

They had taken me to a private room. Moments came in bits and pieces of Orias pinning down my thrashing naked body while Atticus reset and bandaged my wings. They had forced an iron bit into my mouth that chaffed and burned my lips.

By the time they finished, I was nothing more than a trembling, sweating mess.

I hadn't screamed. As much as I had wanted to, I didn't. What good would it do if my powers were gone?

What had they done to strip me of them?

A warm blanket fell across my back, making me flinch.

I jerked forward and stared into the sharp face framed with cobalt hair.

"I'm sorry. It's me." Her soft voice was hoarse, like she had been crying. Lane's face was drawn, her eyes red and swollen. "I'm sorry," she said again.

"Where are they?" The words were coarse on my tongue. It felt like my mouth was full of sand.

"It's just us," she said. "I'm to help you clean up."

From the corner of my eye, I could see the bandages they had wrapped around my wings to keep them in place. Hooked claws rose over the top of each like menacing scythes.

It had been torture, but they hadn't tortured me. I was surprised they had tried mending me at all. I planted my palms beneath me as I rose up. Atticus had been meticulous. I had seen enough of what he had done to Valen to know that every bone had been set into its proper place. Even the silk scarf holding his mendings in place was finely wrapped.

The room was a faded, dull gray. It had a bed, a small mantle with a burning fire, and a pool that pressed against a solid glass wall. Outside of that wall was roiling darkness. Lightning flashed within its murk, revealing the outline of a building.

"How'd you get out?"

Lane slid her arm through mine as I found my feet. I grabbed hold of the blanket she had tossed over me and clutched it to my chest. As if it could shield me.

Lane swallowed. "One of the soldiers found me when I went looking for Atticus. I didn't make it a block from the arena before someone grabbed me. There wasn't anything I could do. I tried to get away, to warn you, but they had me halfway back to Eurynomos by the time Vélos started to fall." She took a deep gulp of air. "I didn't think they would be foolish enough to actually kidnap you. Not with all the emissaries there."

"They didn't." I pressed my fingers against my temples. The inside of my head felt like it was on fire. "Bishop gave me to them in exchange for Vélos. He said he was flying me to safety and they…"

My power had been ripped from me the moment the net encased my wings. It had burned some sacred part of me. Perhaps that was why the Fallen's wings were burned. The fire that they wielded could also strip them of their power.

"They shot me down," I whispered.

Lane's eyes widened. "And now they have put you together again."

"They kept me below, where they had Valen. I saw what they did to him. Is he here?"

"No," she said quickly. "No. Whatever they showed you would have been from before. A crow flew in a few hours ago. Vélos is in chaos, but Valen lives."

I slapped a hand over my mouth as a sudden sob hiccuped out of me. Tears welled in my eyes. He was alive. Alive!

Lane rubbed my arm through the blanket. "He's ok," she said.

"I can't feel him here. I thought he was gone." I slid my finger across my nose.

"Eurynomos is an impenetrable fortress. Nothing goes in or out unless one of the keras wills it. Not even soul bonds. But he's ok, Ezra. Valen is ok."

"So long as Bishop has his heart, he won't be. He is at his mercy."

Lane's lips pursed together. "Well, he hasn't killed him yet, so there must be a reason. Here, let's get you in the water. Get this filth off you."

I let her help me down the steps into the pool. As soon as the warm water clutched me, I let out a high-pitched sigh. It felt good, but as the darkness peeled up to my thighs, I tightened my grip in her hand. "I can't swim," I said.

"It's not deep."

"It's how Ariel almost killed me. And they shot me over a frozen lake."

"They—fuck, Ezra. Here." Lane held tight to my hand as she reached across the floor to grab a couple of bottles. "Just sit on the steps and I'll help you. Can you spread your wings on the floor? Yes, like that. Does it hurt?"

The warm water eased the ache that had set deep in my bones. It penetrated the last bit of reserve I had and shattered it to a million pieces. Lane didn't stop me, or try to tell me everything was going to be alright. Lies would not be a comfort in this hell hole.

I cried as she poured oil into my hair and lathered it. I cried as she washed the dirt and blood from my skin.

Her fingers brushed gently against the brand at the back of my neck. I heard her swallow. "I have one too," she said softly. "I guess this makes us sisters now."

A forced laugh broke between my sobs.

She turned my face to hers, her eyes shining with unshed tears. "You will endure. You will overcome. They start by trying to break down your mental barriers and then the real torture comes. You're strong, Ezra. I saw the fire within you when I met you all those years ago. Do not let them snuff it out." She wiped a cloth over my face.

"I have no power here," I said.

"That is what they want you to think. They want it to be a trigger that only they can pull. Valen overcame them. I have endured them. Now it's your turn. Bend if you must, but do not yield to them. Endure and hold fast."

She pressed her forehead to mine as I slumped forward.

"Whatever it takes," I whispered.

She nodded against me. "Whatever it takes."

I didn't recognize the woman presented to Baal. I'd been given a veil of a dress, so sheer that it left nothing to the imagination. My breasts, hips, waning muscles, and scars were on full display. The blue hue of Eurynomos cast a strange glow across my skin, highlighting my cheekbones and bare shoulders like a neon light. The gilded brush of my skin was almost unidentifiable beneath the cool tone.

I wanted nothing more than to crawl into a hole and hide from the eyes I could feel stripping me bare as we made our way through the Hall. I kept my chin raised high despite the heat that stained my entire body from embarrassment. The Great Hall of Eurynomos was draped in black billowing silks. Behind them were black-glassed mirrors, dark windows that reflected writhing bodies and feasting mouths.

My hands were firmly clasped together to steady the tremors that ran through them. Chains of fear slowed my steps as Baal's blue gaze slid down the line of my body.

Spread across the dais, enshrouded in silks of black and gold, he looked like a renaissance painting. Gold paint ringed the base of his horns to match the line that ran down his chin. The Murder surrounded him along with six other guards and three human women. The women all had gold collars about their necks that matched their painted skin.

Lane brushed the back of her knuckles against mine as our guards came to a halt before the cyn.

Lane slid down to the ground, the gold beads of her dress tinkling. She gave a sharp tug to the hem of my dress before I did the same. Never once had my cyn demanded that I kneel to them. Baal certainly didn't deserve it.

"They said the nephilim could not be tamed." Baal's eyes narrowed into a challenge. I felt something move within me. I nearly breathed a sigh of relief, but I didn't want him to know the darkness inside of me had returned. Awakened.

It twisted and turned the longer he looked. It called to him.

No, he was calling to me.

"All females are easily swayed," Orias said. He slid his hand between Raum's thighs as he looked down on me. "And broken."

"Are you broken, little dove?" The silk at Baal's waist slid down as he leaned forward, revealing the hard cut of a V in his lower abdomen.

I pulled the darkness inside of me close. I didn't want him to see what I was capable of. Neither did I want to test his patience after he had thrown me clear across the room with a single slap.

Baal chuckled. "No, I do not think you are. I do not mind a challenge." He waved his hand, beckoning me forward. "Come, it is time for worship."

The demon pulled me to the ground. One of my knees slid between his legs and my wings thrust up stiffly, shadowing us. A red ring of fire encircled the light irises. As my shadow fell, the fire faded to a dull burn. It gave me the sense that Baal was far more frightening in the darkness than he was in the dull light.

Those same eyes flickered to my wings. A low hum rumbled in his chest as he shifted his legs so that I was seated between them. My bound wings draped across his back.

Baal pushed my long hair back, exposing my throat. "I hear you enjoy services," he hissed. "Your prayers have rattled my abode."

His lips stroked the side of my neck with every word. His hot breath made me tense, knowing that behind it were sharp teeth that could rip out my throat.

Six tall shrouded beings approached the dais. A crown of thorns hovered above their heads encased in blue flame. As they came to a stop, they lifted their hands, all stained black as night, to the sky.

"I pray no more," I said.

"Not to the Enemy, but you will to me."

From my peripheral, I could see Raum watching me. I knew now was not the moment he had asked me to strike. But when Baal slid his hand across my stomach, I so desperately wanted it to be. My power coiled and flicked in answer.

The veiled subjects parted for a nude woman painted in red. Runes of a darker shade were carved into her skin. What looked to be scales covered her legs. On the side of her face and the top of her hips were thin membranes... No, they were fins. Sharp, pointed fins that flared as she moved.

As she kneeled, all those before the dais did the same.

She bowed her head to the floor, rose up, and lifted her hands. She did this six times before she stopped and looked to Baal and let out the most chilling sound I've ever heard. Her voice rose high, higher, until it felt like my hearing would break beneath the volume, before the sound circled down again and slipped into a melodious, yet ominous, lullaby.

Chill bumps raced across my skin. Raum chuckled, his music adding an eerie undertone to the woman's. Baal's laughter joined next as his hand lifted higher, skimming the underside of my breast.

"She is a siren," he whispered against my ear. "The markings on her body bind her to this form and to me. All our services begin with her voice. Beautiful, is it not?"

Hauntingly so. "Yes," I said. Even if she looked terrifying, the music was lulling as if the sound of her voice was a spell all its own.

The court's voice answered next, their baritone notes giving balance to her lilt voice. Those on the dais with us lifted their heads and joined in. Raum's eyes were closed as he sang the next verse. Orias rested his chin over the top of his partner's head as he sang too. As I turned, I saw Atticus was doing the same, his scarred hands pressed together in prayer.

Dread pressed a hand to my shoulder. Its talons curved into my skin as Baal pulled me against his chest.

"Laek y al mi gorro, Baal."

The phrase rose into the air as the demons began to chant.

"Laek y al mi gorro, Baal," the cyn whispered into my ear. "All hail the god, Baal."

I couldn't breathe. Oh God, I could not breathe. I struggled to sit up, but Baal wouldn't give me an inch. His teeth pressed into my skin as he smiled.

"Pray with them," he said.

The siren moved her hands, writing symbols into the air as her voice rose higher once more.

The congregation raised their palms to the sky. As the siren made a swift cut in the air with her finger, so too did a red line appear on the wrists of the people. Blood spilled down their forearms.

"Laek y al mi gorro, Baal," they chanted.

This is blasphemy. This... this is evil.

"Let me go," I said. The darkness within me was chaotic, wild. I could feel my power being pulled in two directions. It burned the underside of my skin. It grew warmer where Baal's skin was laid to mine as he slid one of his hands up the underside of my skirt.

"Are you not a believer?" Baal purred.

The heady scent of spiced blood filled the room. Red rivulets pooled toward the siren.

"No," I said. Not in this. I could never believe in something like this.

The siren's voice faded, the congregation's turning into a soft hum behind her. She bent down and scooped her hands in the pool of blood before her. Slowly, she rose and padded toward us, her bare, scaled feet making a soft grating sound on the stones.

I had no choice but to lean against Baal as she drew closer. His hand clasped down on my thigh as he leaned forward, nestling me into the crook of his shoulder as he tipped his head up to the woman.

Only when the music in the room had faded entirely did she speak. "Cyn Baal, we offer you our blood in thanks. We ask that you would have mercy upon us and continue to guide us. It is through you that our divinity may be reclaimed and through you shall we have it." Black film flicked across her eyes as she looked down at him. Carefully, she tipped her fingers toward his eager, open mouth.

Baal drank and drank. Even when I knew her small palms could not hold so much blood, he still drank. When finally her palms ran dry, she pulled away and kneeled.

"I accept your offering," he rumbled. "Go forth now and bare message to the world that I am your god. Let this world and the next see my power in the blood that you will shed. My children," Baal raised his hand, "my blessing is upon you and upon the food that has been so carefully prepared for you."

"Amen!" The voice was universal, as if it had been one giant voice that spoke and not the thousands in unison.

Had I not been paralyzed in fear, I might have done something. Run. Unleashed my power. But I did nothing. I could not do anything under the weight of what had happened, what was happening.

Six more veiled beings entered the room with a group of humans behind them. Men, women, children. Children. Sweat coated my body as I stiffened and fire rose to my fingertips.

"There she is," Baal purred.

I turned to him as the fire made its way up my arms, highlighting his face with a sinister glow. "Stop this."

"How do you think we have survived down here?" Baal caught my throat with his other hand and, suddenly, he was twisting around me. He coiled and curled until he had me pressed upon my back, leering over me. "We feast on darkness, ash, and blood. Before the amorini, it was the blood of our brothers. Ah, you did not know that, did you? That they provide nourishment to the world from their harem."

I bared my chattering teeth. "Trying to turn me against them, against Valen, isn't going to work. You are a monster with or without them. It is not by fear that I am going to serve you."

"How do you think you are going to survive?"

"I am not Fallen." And yet I could feel the tug. This horrible pull between light and dark even as I knew what nasty creation the darkness would make if I gave into it. I had seen it. I could hear it in the quickening breaths of the demons as they salivated. I could smell their need, my own core heating.

Baal grabbed my face. He forced his index finger and thumb between my lips. "Your fangs say otherwise."

"You forced me." I snapped at his fingers he curled away.

"Exactly," he hissed. "I have power over you. I am your god and you will bow to me by my force."

There was no denying the fear that coated my sweat. I was terrified of the beast before me. And when the screams started—ashes, when the screams started—I could not look away from him. He was terror, but I knew to look away from him would be so much worse. Tears flooded my eyes as the crunch of bone and tearing of flesh filled the air. Garbled pleas saturated the air.

"I am your god," Baal hissed. The lower half of his body coiled, his muscles flexing like a snake's. "Say it."

I shook my head. "No."

The screams had given way to obscene sucking sounds as the demons started their feast. From the corner of my eye, I saw the guard slink down to the rest of the court, their bodies twisting in the shadows. All but three moved. I could feel them there, trapping us in a triangle.

The hard press of Baal's cock slid up my thigh as his hips roiled against me.

Oh God. This was how it was going to be. He was going to take me just like this, amongst the horror of his kingdom. And I was too afraid to do anything. I'd never been stuck like this, but he was so overpowering, so fucking terrifying, that all I could do was remain pinned.

Baal's smile grew into a sneer that ran from ear to ear.

"Shhh," he hissed through his teeth. "I will have you, but not tonight. Tonight, we worship." He leaned down and pressed a kiss to my forehead, teeth to skin. "Hear how sweet their prayers are." He ran a claw down the front of my dress, splitting it apart. He slid his hand back up my thigh and spread over my center, just below my belly.

Flames rushed to my skin. They engulfed his hand, but they did not burn him. Baal's fingers stroked the hair between my thighs before he lifted them to his face. My fire danced along his curled nails before he inhaled. The golden light swirled into his nostrils.

"Do not bring her before me until she is pure. When I have her, I want her wings to be intact."

Raum stood and bowed at the waist. "Forgive me, my cyn. I only wished to please you."

Baal sucked the back of his teeth as he coiled back to his seat on the lounge, his eyes darting at the massacre before him. "How could you ever disappoint me, Raum?" He jerked his chin forward. "You are dismissed."

Raum bent down, taking my tense body into his arms. The Murder moved as one. Orias and Atticus, for as large as they were, made their way nimbly down the steps. Lane followed with them. I kept my eyes on the dais as Raum carried me through the gore. But in the reflections of the giant black mirrors, I saw the carnage.

Baal remained on the landing, his legs and arms spread wide as he basked in his service.

By the time Raum set me down in my room, I was shaking uncontrollably. Our companions remained outside the doorway, their predatory eyes reflecting the light. Raum slid his fingers under the straps of the dress, pushing them off until I was standing naked in front of him.

"Yes," I whispered.

Raum cocked his head. "Yes?"

"I don't know how I'll do it, but yes."

Orias leaned into the room and pulled the door shut, leaving Raum and me alone. I looked up at him with tear-filled eyes. There was no going back after this. I knew giving Raum what he desired was a choice I would regret for the rest of my life, but he did not compare to the evil of Baal. Nothing and no one could ever compare to Baal.

I could reason with Raum. I could look him in the eye and withstand him. Baal, as helpless as I felt to admit, I could not.

Raum grabbed hold of my elbow as my legs started to shake.

"You are to debilitate him, not kill him. You will renounce your past life and give service to me. In turn, I shall guard you, keep you from what he would have done to you tonight had your wings been whole."

I nodded. "Yes."

"Whether Valen lives or dies, you no longer belong to him."

My eyes snapped to his. What he was saying was impossible. Valen and I were made for each other. "I am going to kill you for what you did to him."

Raum brushed the top of my cheek with two fingers. The laugh lines of his face cut a deep crease. "You can try."

"You will not go unpunished."

His fingers dug into my chin. A flick of heat reflected against the gems of his eyes. "As I said, little phoenix."

I would make his suffering great, but in the heat of what had nearly happened with Baal against what Raum was offering me, I had no choice. I could lie along with them. I nodded.

He tipped my chin up. "To make a deal, our kind typically deals in sex." The laugh lines of his face deepened when he smirked. "But let us seal it in a kiss instead. For good faith."

I hated him. I hated every single one of them.

God, forgive me for my wavering faith, but if You are there, give me the power to best this. Give me the strength to overcome this evil.

My prayer fell on deaf ears.

My power stirred to meet Raum as he tipped his face toward

mine.

No, I couldn't do this. There was another way. I just needed time to figure out what it was. If I called Prometheus now, I could burn this entire place down.

I tugged against the fire burning in my blood just as Raum's lips met mine. He took advantage of my open mouth as I gasped and slid his tongue inside. I flicked my tongue against his as if to push him out. Raum's tongue retreated only so he could pull mine into his mouth and suck.

He caught my hand before my slap could land.

He cocked his head. "You taste like honey."

"Fuck you," I growled.

Dark shadows filled his eyes as he looked down my body. Desire filled the space between us. "You will," Raum said, and stepped back into a bleed with only the heat of his gaze for company.

CHAPTER SIXTY-SIX: THE VOICE

Ezra

That night, I dreamed of a starless sky and black sand beaches. Gilded bodies were cast upon the shore in armor of bronze and flesh. I walked amongst them, my wings trailing behind me, caressing the faces of those fallen.

"Ezra."

The voice was a whisper.

CHAPTER SIXTY-SEVEN: FALLEN GODS

Valen

The road to Eurynomos was long and quiet. Every now and then, I saw movement overhead and would track the crows that followed. Six all together. Unless it was the same one playing tricks, shadowing in and out of the branches.

It would have been faster to specter on foot, but it was nearly impossible to do so with the odonni. They were too dense and heavy to specter, and we needed them to carry our food and gear. Our stops were brief to allow the animals to rest when white salty sweat had gathered at their withers. I was pushing us hard, but we did not have time to waste.

That had been weeks ago.

We had made good time, but it was not fast enough. It was just a hunch that they had flown this direction. The crows were the only reassurance I had that we were on the right path.

What was that?

I held up my fist.

"Do you hear that?"

It sounded as if something was being dragged through dirt and leaves. Something big and heavy. Not a demon, then, or it would have been soundless. I pulled my sword free of its sheath before urging Nashua forward. I heard the others do the same, metal sliding free from leather.

Something white flashed beyond the trees. It was cold here, colder now that we were nearing Eurynomos's borders, but there had not been a trace of their snow yet.

Kasiya trotted past me, scouting as we neared the small grove ahead.

He pulled up on his mount abruptly, jerking too hard on the bit as he turned to face me.

In the grove, stumbling from left to right, was Bishop. His entire body heaved with exertion; his sweat made his gilded skin glisten even more beneath the rising golden light from above. He was bloodier than the day he left, his clothes unchanged, unwashed.

And then I saw them.

His large gray wings were what I had heard. Barbs and leaves were tangled within his feathers.

I urged Nashua forward as panic took hold. I looked behind him, searching for any sign of Ezra. Bishop's eyes fluttered as we broke through the tree line, his light eyes gracing each of us. The corner of his mouth tugged upward and then he crashed to his knees.

"You are a blessing for sore eyes," he breathed.

Kasiya went galloping past Bishop, Doon right behind him as they fanned out across the grove, heading for the next range of forest. "Ezra!" they shouted. Her name was lost in the shadows, but still they called.

I jerked against the chord but, like every other day since Bishop had flown off with her, I could not *feel* her.

Diriel's eyes were white as he too surveyed the field.

"Where is Ezra?" My throat was thick. I knew she was alive, but something had clearly gone terribly wrong. Bishop was missing a wing, a second hanging on by the measly tendons and flesh that remained.

Bishop's eyes narrowed as he looked up. His mouth twisted before he said, "I am hardly well."

"What happened?" I snapped.

"Why do you look at me as if I have done something? And why do you come with a small band? Where is our army to attack them?" His fingers dug into the ground beneath him to steady himself.

Bishop wouldn't look at me. He was looking everywhere but at me, and that's when I knew. I was certain who had her then. I looked once more across his back, to the bloody and broken wings.

"Who did this?"

"Eurynomos has betrayed us," he snapped. "They shot us down over the lake and cut my wings. I couldn't stop them from taking her. I tried."

Liar. Wicked fucking liar.

"What lake?" Diriel asked.

Bishop hesitated as the lie he could have easily maneuver out of unraveled.

"Coctyus. The dragon chased us—"

It dawned on me that Bishop had known all along. Coctyus was on the way to Eurynomos. There was no other path that would have led them over the eternally frozen lake had he not already been heading for the black castle in the mountains.

I could hear the drone of his lies speeding up, though I did not listen to the words. I had been through this before, when he had come to me to conspire against Episkopos. Fervent and rapid, he had bid me to support him in his cause.

"Tell me," I said slowly, "brother, how we have had an alliance with the keras for years and they have never wronged us. Tell me, that after you threw me into their claws to be tortured, that they would turn on Vélos. No, that they would turn on you." Fire crept into my gaze as I looked down upon him. Rage funneled into my blood, heated it, coaxed me to spring from my saddle so I could bear down on his throat and dig my claws into his heart.

"The moment you left with her, the army turned to ash, the dragon hot on your wings."

"The dragon *chased* us," Bishop hissed.

"Where is Ezra?"

"Where do you think she is? Look at what they did to me!" Bishop threw a hand out to his broken wings.

Fire crackled beneath my palms. I could not hear anything else he was saying. Eurynomos had Ezra. Of all the places he could have taken her, he had given her to them. I'd been a fool to think Bishop would keep her safe. I had bet that he would hoard her, but never did I imagine he would send her to such horror and despair.

"You let them take her."

"How could you?" Diriel was staring numbly at Bishop. I could see his lashes fluttering as he blinked back what could only be tears. "She was one of us... the key to freedom, our kin. How could you?" Diriel's eyes were flashing, his breath short as he looked for any trace of her or her future. The vein in his temple stood erect.

"I fought for her after they shot us down," Bishop growled. The muscles wound tightly beneath his skin roiled. "We had a dragon upon us."

"You fucking coward!" I jumped from my saddle and strode toward him. Fire lit the grass beneath my boots.

Bishop's body jerked as he looked up at me. Surprise, confusion, and then anger flashed across the silver of his eyes.

Bishop was the force of a mighty gale, a hurricane. He had the power of the arc buzzing within his blood that could shatter an army, but he was no match for the brutality that was the keras. If it was the Murder he had met with, of which I was certain, he was certainly no match for all three of them who had been bred in violence while Bishop had only learned it. They were war while he was but a battle.

Then there was Baal, the oldest of the angels made at the dawn of the first Creation. The devil himself would cower at his feet. Baal, who had all the time in the world, who would draw out Ezra's suffering until our Judgement.

"What did you say?"

"You didn't fight, you fled. Just as you fled during our exile that you caused. If I know one thing, it is that Baal is not a liar."

Bishop's breathing halted. Just like that. There was no more struggle in his next inhale, no tremors running through his hands. The odonni tensed beneath their riders, backing up and pulling against the reins that held them still.

Bishop stood faster than I could blink. "I can kill you here and now. One bolt straight into your heart and you are done."

Baal had shown me everything. Every conversation he had with Bishop before our fall, every spell he had taught him. I let the agony that Baal had inflicted on me flood through the bond I shared with Bishop and shoved him back with it.

His hand flew to his chest, his eyes glazing over. Dark clouds rolled across the sky, scattering the golden light of the sun in different directions.

My lip curled as I met his challenge. "Do you know what is more dangerous than a living threat? A dead one. Make a martyr of me, if you will, but our people know the truth. They will never again bow to you. I made sure to tell them of your sins before I left in search of Ezra."

Bishop's eyes flashed to the riders who now circled him. "What the fuck have you done?"

"Vélos is mine. You have been exiled from the kingdom you drove into hell and I mean to restore us to our glory."

"*You,*" he snarled.

"Does Baal have her or did the Murder take her?"

"You cannot take Vélos," he snarled. Bolts of lightning cracked amidst the dark clouds. "Everything you think you have is mine." Energy buzzed through the air as the force of his power swelled.

I heaved my sword up the moment Bishop moved.

Bishop swung his talons up, and the next moment he had shifted into the horrible, wicked beast we all were. Beneath the costume of angelic beauty was a monster. Another price for falling.

Blade met talon and teeth as he lunged at me with such fury.

I spun from his reach and slid my blade across his side, cutting across his ribs and thrusting my sword into his belly. I pulled back and dove it into the dip of his hip as he turned.

Our last dance had begun.

CHAPTER SIXTY-EIGHT: HEAVEN UNLEASHED

Ezra

Ezra

The viewing platform was at least twelve stories high, far enough from the ground that we could see everything but not be caught up in the thrall of the raging crowd. The arena was alive with voices. Murmurs rose between the shouts of triumph and groans of displeasure.

I followed my escort to an ornately carved lounge. Furs and feathered drapes were cast about in the shape of a nest. Silver decanters of wine or blood were spread over the floor within arm's reach. In the midst of it all was Baal. He tipped his head up, the movement sinister with his horns tipping back into the shadows that slid off his hair.

The bear was chained to the corner of the room. The silver collar around its neck was covered in what looked like diamonds. Its ear flicked in my direction, but it didn't so much as open an eye.

The cyn's eyes narrowed, his pupils dilating as he took me in.

Slowly, a smile spread over his inhuman face.

"Welcome, Ezra. It is a pleasure to have you join me."

I didn't move, couldn't move. My feet were frozen as I looked from him to the large window to the clear glass floor that dropped off like an infinity pool. There were other guards, a few seraphim, and cherubs lurking in nests of their own, but with Baal's eyes on me it felt like we were the only two in the room. A terrible sinking feeling pooled in my gut.

"Come here." His whisper echoed as the compulsion slid over my skin like oil.

I let out a shaky breath as I stepped forward on trembling legs.

I placed my hand in Baal's long fingers. He was ice cold. I'd been touched by cold before, his this was so unnatural that I thought he might actually have the power to turn me to ice.

His blue eyes of starlight slid past my shoulders as I stood motionless, waiting for some other command. Lane had unbound my wings that morning. Though the bones were healed, their appearance was still unsavory. Thick tufts of feathers still clung to the membrane that lay hidden beneath. As Raum instructed, I left them open instead of pulling them beneath my skin like I so desperately wanted to.

"Your wings have healed," he said, giving me a gentle pull so I dropped to my knees.

"Yes," I answered, not quite looking at him. It was unnerving how beautiful and scary he was at the same time. I'd never known someone who could be so striking force such terror into anyone by the sheer sight of them.

Baal slid one of his long nails down the shaft of a feather. I stiffened, but no ache came as they relaxed down my back. "Beautiful." He plucked at one of the feathers and then smoothed it down quickly after.

Both touches sent a hot coil to my belly.

Baal's fangs flashed. "There will be more time for that later."

Just like that, the heat fizzled out as stark cold fear flooded my senses.

The door slid open to the Murder. All three in matching black leather. Beneath the trim was a subtle blue glow, the same that bore down on the rest of Eurynomos. They glistened like gems when they moved.

Raum's hair was sectioned off into a top knot. Three braids ran across his scalp, diving into the twist of hair. It left the feathers on the back of his neck exposed, something I had not noticed before. There were several smaller ones behind his ears, more jagged so that they looked like spikes. The daggers on his vambraces shone like obsidian.

Orias, for once, was wearing a shirt. I'd grown so accustomed to seeing him wearing next to nothing that I did a double take. His broadsword was strapped to his back and a red axe rested at his hip.

Atticus bore no weapons that I could see. But the pale male looked as lethal as his companions. He remained close to Orias's side as the three males approached us and bowed before Baal.

Raum dropped to his knee as Baal held out his hand for him to kiss. He laced his fingers through the cyn's when the demon smiled.

"What have you in store for me today?" Baal asked.

"Do not command me to tell," Raum answered. "It will ruin the surprise."

"Give me a hint."

"A bloodbath," Raum hissed. The lines of his face creased as his sapphire eyes darkened.

"Delicious," Baal purred. He rolled his head toward me and tugged Raum's hand with the gesture. I stiffened when he placed Raum's hand over my breast. Heat flooded my body, replacing the cold as a flash of embarrassment and anger touched my skin. "Just a taste," Baal said, squeezing his hand so that Raum's nails bit into my sensitive flesh. "Give me a good show and I'll invite you to our bed this evening."

My head snapped to the cyn. If he only knew the taste Raum had had of me, he would not have been so abrasive. If he knew, I had it in mind that he would have ripped out Raum's throat knowing his best warrior had sampled me before he had.

Still, he baited my temper.

Raum slid his hand to my other breast when Baal let go. I willed daggers through my eyes to the keras. He grinned and pinched my nipple between his thumb and forefinger. "It will be the event of the century," Raum's eyes held mine as he spoke.

Baal chuckled, and Raum let me go, turning that broad grin to the cyn he was promising to end.

Was it hot in here suddenly? It felt like I couldn't breathe. Sweat pooled beneath my scalp.

"I await your performance," Baal said, extending his hand.

Raum rose and stepped back between Orias and Atticus. The three bowed in unison.

Raum's eyes slid to me before he turned on his heel. The other two males followed, but Atticus paused. It was a brief hesitation that his eyes slid to me and jerked his chin. A quick nod and then he was gone.

My nostrils flared as I refocused my attention to the coliseum. I didn't know how I was supposed to do this. While it felt like Baal and I were alone, we were not. If by chance I did take down Baal, what was to stop the other witnesses from acting?

Atticus must have seen something I could not. I looked around the room, searching for a weapon, only to find them strapped to the guards. And what was I going to do about the damn bear? I had been a fool to accept Raum's deal.

"What is going on inside that head of yours?" Baal crooned.

I cast him a nervous glance. At least I didn't have to hide my fear around him. Being confident and cocky probably would have set him on my track. Being that I was genuinely terrified of him, and no doubt reeked of it, would work to my advantage if I ever figured out how I was going to kill him. I'd be lucky if I could maim someone of his age.

"I'm wondering what you have planned for me." It wasn't a lie. It had been a constant thought. Along with what would happen if I failed to incapacitate the cyn. What sort of fury would he unleash on me then?

Baal tugged me into his lap so that my wings splayed behind me. I stiffened but let him adjust me so that I was sitting between his legs with my wings folded around us. God, I hated his touch. I hated the smell of putrid rot and sulfur that leaked from his skin. It was with force that I swallowed the bile burning its way up my throat.

"There are many. It has been a long time since I've had a nephilim. While I am eager to feel the inside of one again," he slid a palm over my thigh, "I do enjoy the way you squirm beneath me." His mouth fluttered to show off his razor-sharp teeth again. "Do I not call to you? My darkness to your chaos?"

Breathe. I would not survive this if I let my emotions rule me. If I was going to best this demon, I needed to be patient. I needed to bide my time and figure out his weakness. Then again, if he had one, wouldn't Raum have found it already?

"Your darkness does," I answered honestly.

A smile tugged at his lips. Absentmindedly, he looked out at the arena where the fights had already begun. Rather, one had concluded. Guards dragged away the fallen bodies. Once they were clear, fresh bodies were presented. Amorini, a seraph, and two other angels I could not determine.

I swallowed when the Murder stepped into the arena. The crowd's voice rose into the air. There were thousands, if not millions, in the stands. The keras were a large race, much larger than I had originally thought. I hadn't even seen the half of them the other night when so much of the Hall had been shrouded in darkness.

Baal trailed his fingers over the top of my wing. Heat twisted my stomach and struck a nerve between my thighs. I clenched my fist at the response I had no control over.

"It has been so long," he said.

Baal was no longer looking at the scrimmage but my wings. Longing filled his gaze as he retraced his touch, sliding it higher to the crooked claw that rose over the top.

"I never saw one with these." He twisted his finger over the top, pressing into it until I heard the soft pop of skin as it broke. He rubbed the blood between his fingers, inspecting it.

"Perhaps I'll use them on you." I swallowed thickly as soon as the words left my mouth. I was envisioning them buried within his chest as I stabbed a knife through his heart.

Baal's mouth crooked. "I have an appetite for pain that you have not developed a taste for, little dove. By tonight you will know its flavor, though." The back of his knuckles slid across my feathers and then to the sensitive membrane beneath.

I bit my lip to hide the sharp intake of breath as another wave of heat washed over me. I couldn't do this. I could not sit by idly and let him do this to me. Was I supposed to wait for some signal from Raum?

He was in the arena now, moving with elegance that did not suit his size. Yet he had mastered all of the steps. His blade clashed against the smaller one the seraphim gripped. With a twist of his wrist, the sword was buried in the red male's chest, tucked safely beneath the collarbone.

There were three large screens above the arena and every single one of them zoomed in on the male's wide eyes as Raum thrust downward and exited the tip through the bone and straight into his jaw.

The crowd applauded with a frenzy.

"What is this?" Baal said. He slid his fingers through my feathers, splaying the entirety of his palm against the thin skin.

I pulled my wing away. "They're still tender," I feigned.

Baal sat up, grabbed hold of my wing, and pulled it out. Small red veins ran through the membrane and disappeared into the feathers still holding on.

Baal's pupils dilated. His nostrils flared as the heat between us warmed.

"Let go," I snapped.

"Hold your tongue," he said, pulling a feather free. He looked at the tip before he pulled another one, and another one.

"Stop," I growled and shifted to my knees as I slid off his lap.

He wasn't listening to me. How could he even hear me over the sudden roar of the crowd? Ashes, I could smell his musk as he grew more fixated.

Everything was moving too fast. He was going to tear me apart and then... and then.

No. That wasn't going to happen.

I wouldn't let it.

I stood and grabbed Baal's wrist and twisted, forcing him down on his knees. "Don't touch me," I growled.

The quiet murmurs of the room went silent. The roar of the crowd on the outside was a dull drone. The blood in my ears, the crash of bloody waves, was far louder.

Baal surged forward, knocking me back a couple of paces. "You will not speak to your cyn that way. Kneel, girl." Baal's power assaulted me, forcing me to stumble back as the invisible force ripped through me. Wetness blurred my vision, but it was not tears that fell from my face.

I shook my head.

I would be dead after this. If I was not, I knew that I would wish it. The surge of his evil that swelled in the air assured me of that. It forced chills to my skin; it took my breath.

This was fear.

But I would not be a slave to it.

Baal hit me so hard that I flew across the room, smacking into a couple of patrons' feet. They pulled them up as dark shadows raced across the floor to me. Outside, the crowd's cheer rose higher.

Baal shoved his knee into the middle of my back, grabbed a fistful of feathers, and pulled. I let out a cry of pain and tried to shake him off, but he was stronger. Baal was so impossibly heavy that I could not even rise an inch from the ground.

"I have never seen wings such as these," he breathed. He pulled more and more of my feathers free, stripping me of the little crowns that hid the horrible vision beneath.

"These wings," he said.

"Stop!"

Baal splayed his hand over the membrane. His groan matched the moan ripped from my throat. This wasn't right. His touch was intimate. His touch brought on a forceful wave of lust that was not his right to take. I dug my nails into the ground as he did the same with my other wing.

"What a fine mare you are. Something new and horrible." Baal flipped me over, folding my left wing beneath my body. His eyes roved over the one still outstretched, over the claw that hooked at the top. He followed that trail until he got to my face.

"I am afraid you cannot keep these."

"What?"

"I want them."

Of all the things, this is not what I imagined he would try to take from me.

"No," I said.

Baal cocked his head. "No?"

"You can't have them."

Baal grabbed me by the cheeks and hauled me forward. "You belong to me. That means every inch of your body is mine to do with as I please. But just for your impudence, perhaps I'll fuck the holes in your back first after I've ripped them free."

The thing inside me uncoiled. Slowly, she stretched her lithe body, scales gleaming like a snake's as she moved. It had been weeks of silence from the power, from the monster within.

I pushed off my wing still tucked to the ground and slashed a handful of claws in the face of the cyn. I was a burst of ener-gy—fiery, hot, and spitting. I wanted to see the stars of his eyes wink out.

Baal whipped his head from side to side as I caught him in the face. But my attack was short as he grabbed hold of me and forced me to the ground once more, slamming me on my stomach.

The more I fought, the more anxious the beast within grew. She started to pace, her nails sharpening on the cold walls of my core.

"Fight me," Baal said, his voice like fire in my ear. "I prefer a bitch who bites back. Makes their screams sweeter when I take them."

Cold steel slid up the center of my back. I was thrust back to the moment Ariel had thrown me on the water. To the chill of his blade as he hacked into me, trying to cut out the very things that made me what I was.

Through the glass floor, I could see the Murder fighting. All three were covered in blood. The coating on Atticus's skin made him stand out like a red beacon. He was fast and sure, his blade moving so quickly you could not actually see it cutting through the air. Orias and Raum fought side by side, their movement intertwined like dancers. Precise and bloody. There was so much blood it would have been hard to recognize them had I not already known who they were. Raum waded through a patch of gore as he approached an amorini and cut the male in half before he could raise his weapon to block the blow. I didn't know it was possible to cut someone clean in half like that.

The crowd roared as the touch of steel pierced my skin.

I felt Baal's attention snap past me. Half of the arena was on fire. It rose like a tidal wave at the command of Raum's raised palm. Then it crashed down with the close of his fist and fell onto the demons that tried to flee.

The beast within me purred. Her nails dug into the ground as my hands stretched out to steady the tension that threatened to shake loose. I would not become part of this slaughter. I sure as hell wasn't going to be one of its victims.

"Get off me," I said.

Baal leaned forward, his blade still pressed against the base of my wing. He kicked my thighs apart and settled himself between them. I gritted my teeth as a fresh wave of fear hit when his forked tongue snaked across the side of my face. "What was that?"

I focused on the fire blazing. On the screams being consumed by its fury.

Wakeeeee uppppp.

The voice hissed like a snake within my mind. Not mine, but hers. The beast's. It had taken me this long to realize that we were one and the same and that the only thing that had been suppressing my power was me.

Heat crept to the center of my palm.

Baal chuckled and slid the blade beneath my skin. It kept my wing locked out, allowing him to touch it without worry that I would snap it closed.

An angel's wings were their crown. They were sacred and intimate. Heat pooled into the bottom of my stomach. It boiled its way up my intestines, working slowly as it gathered its strength. The lust that Baal tried to extract from me was not stronger than the utter rage that spread through my bloodstream like poison.

I drew upon every death that had hounded me. The pain of Ariel hunting me. To the night Valen had almost been ripped from me. To the moment I had crash-landed on the ice, separating me from him forever.

"I said get off me!"

Sweet pain erupted from me. It burst from within as my power ripped free and cut deep as Baal's blade tried to relieve the wing he had pinned down.

The room burst apart. Baal flew across the room, his large body slamming into a nest of keras, sending them scattering in different directions.

I was on my feet in an instant, my wings thrust wide as venomous shadows surged toward me. I tore through the darkness, ripping it apart with the fire that poured from my fingertips.

A flash of white moved through the rippling darkness. There was nothing beautiful about Baal now. His rage had taken on a physical form, contorting his face into a wicked beast made up of fangs and snakeskin. His jaw unhinged as he came for me, the smoke wings at his back spreading wide to mimic the shape of bat wings like my own.

In my peripheral, the others cowered.

The cyn made a horrible sound that bellowed deep in his chest. "I am going to suck the life from your bones. Once I am finished, I will burn you before our children, right before I make them gods of the world."

Evil. This was a true creature of evil. If the rumors were true that he was the Morningstar, I believed them. That only made what I was about to do so much sweeter.

Twin bolts of energy shot down over my shoulders. It pressed upon me with a force as mighty as a storm. As furious as the rage of injustice.

"Your rot will never touch me." I held my power close and then slowly pulled it back until it was as taut as an amorini's bowstring.

The blue light of Eurynomos darkened as the clouds above swirled together. The blue light shifted to purple and everything was cast in a lavender glow. I pulled the power harder and tore the entire sky apart as I pulled down in all directions, that force of power that belonged to me. Only me.

Baal's hand shot out, sending a rope of green flame and thick shadows. It slammed into my chest, and I let that arrow of fury fly. I let the entirety of my rage loose in the scream that ripped from me.

Silver light met rampant darkness and everything exploded.

The force of the explosion knocked me back. Glass shattered into thousands of glittering shards, tinkling together like silver bells as they crashed to the ground. Screams wailed like sirens, rising high and low as the Fallen burned.

I forced myself to my hands and feet, jerking the silver flames around my wrists as I readied for another attack. The silver swirled around me, billowing like a giant funnel as it ripped through the room and caught up everyone around me.

Black smoke and white dust flung through the air. In the midst of it, I saw shadows writhing. Some darted for an exit while others flailed. A cherub fell to the ground at my feet. He clawed his face as silver flames consumed it.

A spark of hunger flitted through me as I moved through the burning demons. Their screams overpowered the roar of the crowd from the coliseum. Burnt flesh stung my nostrils.

A wave of nausea forced me to my knees. I fell and stumbled forward, trying to remain standing. I would not burn out the way I had before. I could not.

Where are you?

I vaguely got the sense that the reason I could not hear the crowd from outside was because they had gone silent. That whatever Baal and I had just done had stolen the entire show. Or perhaps the billowing of flames was too loud to hear anything at all.

There was a heap of darkness in the far corner of the room. Behind it was cracked stone where Baal's body had smashed against it. The shallow rise and fall of his back was the only distinction that indicated he was still alive.

I slipped out of the funnel, moving slowly toward the bulk. I slid a silver band around his neck and pulled, twisting the male's body over.

Baal's chest was wide open, split apart as if he had been struck by lightning. The marble of his flesh was blackened to a crisp.

The starlight of his blue eyes was nothing but sizzling black coals.

I waved a shaking hand over him, but the cyn didn't move.

Footsteps pounded into the room. I was already winding up another bolt of power, stepping back into the funnel, when I turned to see Raum slide into view, the dark and pale keras hot on his heels.

The sapphire light of his eyes went wide as they fell to me.

I fisted the string of power the same moment he took a step forward. I slammed my fist into Baal's chest, sending another surge of fury into the pit of his soul.

Atticus darted past the males and jerked me from the flames. He pulled against me so hard that my vertebrae cracked and my wrist snapped in his palms. His palms that had caught fire and were creeping up his arms. I didn't let go of my line of power barreling into Baal.

The only way I could ever beat them is if I wore a crown.

Atticus flipped me over and something thin and hard wrapped around my neck with a sharp jerk. My power cracked to a stuttering halt as I struggled to breathe. I clawed at the cord around my neck as I tried to get my fingers beneath it. Atticus shifted, sliding his knee between my shoulder blades and pushing down while he pulled up on my throat.

My vision darkened and, from my peripheral, I saw the silver funnel retreat. The purple hue began to fade. No. No!

I reached for it but...

But...

I couldn't grab hold of it. I couldn't grasp hold of anything as the light of the world darkened.

Heat encased me and then everything went numb.

"Cyn Baal has been attacked! Send aid!" someone was shouting. So far away. Underwater.

Darkness pulled me under.

CHAPTER SIXTY-NINE: JUDGEMENT

Valen

Bishop moved within a cloak of smoke and fire. Lightning crashed at my feet but never struck me. Either because I was too swift for him to strike or because he sought to tire me.

One second, a terrible leathery beast was upon me. The next, it was a male in human form hauling a sword down. The obsidian rainbow hilt glistened in the flash of white light within Bishop's grip. I swung my sword up, sharp edge to sharp edge. The impact rattled my bones.

The light in the sky shattered. Sun, moons, and stars were ripped apart as a gale ripped through the land. It proceeded the rupture that tore through another one of Bishop's impacts, ripping apart steel and flesh one and the same.

I stumbled backward, my sword flying from my hand as the ground began to shake.

A black crack of lightning tore across the sky. City lights and satellites blinked through the oblivion; galaxies turned against each other. The entire sky was being torn apart.

In the distance, the source of its destruction flashed like a beacon.

Ezra.

I stood motionless as I watched silver light careen through the sky once more. The pastel sky turned purple, glazing over with a lavender hue.

Prometheus funneled from the sky in the form of a pillar of fire, its billowing light so far away, and yet it was so close. Ezra was right there. I knew that it was her. Even if I still could not feel her, I knew that it was her.

"Gods," Bishop gasped. His sword arm dropped as he turned to stare at the beacon.

I needed her. This war with Bishop would last a lifetime, but Ezra. Ashes, she could burn out. I didn't know anyone who could wield that sort of power, not even when I was in Heaven had I known one to call the flame of that magnitude.

I didn't think of what my leaving my people behind a second time might mean. I turned and ran for Nashua. I was within the saddle in a split second.

"Valen! Wait!" Bishop slid in front of my mount, his palm raised. "That... it's not her. No one can do that."

"Move," I snarled.

"It is our Judgement!" The white rage of his eyes had softened, revealing the stark fear beneath it. I should have driven an arrow in him then, but as the light continued to pour from the sky, all I could think of was Ezra. And how something terrible was about to befall her.

"May it be swift," I said, jerking the bit against the odonnos's mouth. "For if you still live upon my return, you are a dead man."

Kasiya was shouting orders over the roar of the distant fire. I saw the males running to their mounts, but I did not wait to see if they would follow.

I ran. I flew fast and hard as the odonnos's hooves and talons took us the rest of the way to Eurynomos.

I could feel the force of an army chasing me down, but I did not take my eyes off the flame.

God hold her. I'm coming.

An odonnos pulled on either side of me. Kasiya and Diriel pushed their steeds into the ground. I slid my hand through the air, cutting a bleed that we could specter through. This might kill the odonni, forcing their dense bodies through such trauma. "Forgive me, Nashua," I said. I did it again and again, through forest, rock, and snow.

I felt her. As soon as we crossed Eurynomos's borders, I felt her.

Fire, fury, and rage.

CHAPTER SEVENTY: A HOLY BLADE

Ezra

Death had a taste of me and spat me out. I had longed for relief my whole life and it denied me.

My golden hair covered my face. Through the strands, I could see blue and gold light. The clank of chains slid across the ground as I rolled to my stomach. They had bound me.

"We should have done it then."

"There was no time!" Raum snarled. "I need Baal's crown."

"That was the peak of her rage," Atticus said. I think it was Atticus. His voice sounded gruff, different. I'd only heard him one other time, so I wasn't certain. "That is the force we needed to turn her."

I peered at the three males that stood on the edge of the room. Raum. Orias. Atticus. The Murder. My demise. The hate that radiated off them was a flame I welcomed.

"What are you boys squabbling about?" My voice sounded different. Older and calm. Too calm even to my own ears.

I sat up with a groan. Everything hurt. The sharp taste of copper filled my mouth. I smacked my dry lips together, working the flow of blood leaking from my gums.

They had chained me to the middle of a stone ring. Wrists, ankles... wings. They had clamped rings through the top of my wings, prostrating them over the ground. Tears welled in my eyes as I snapped my attention back to them.

Raum licked his lips. "I made you a deal."

"A crown sounded better than a collar." I ran my fingers across the bruising I knew lay on my throat. I flashed him a bloody smile.

"A crown you are not worthy of." Raum cocked his head. "Your kind always was greedy. Wanting more than they deserved."

"You're no different. Baal and Bishop could be your true brothers for as much as you boast about how much you deserve. All of you." I cast a glance at Orias and Atticus.

Orias slid forward, his chest expanding with an agitated hiss.

They were awful creatures, but they did not instill the same fear in me as their cyn. Besides, I had burned that motherfucker near to his death. I'd have done it if they hadn't stopped me. If they had been a few seconds later, I could have killed him.

I could kill them.

"I'm here, Ezra. I'm here."

The voice slammed into me so suddenly—

Valen. Valen was coming for me.

I couldn't think when he was speaking so clearly. Had I gone mad?

"You are not mad, harpy. I am coming for you and I have every intention of burning through Eurynomos to get to you."

I blinked the tears away, shaking my head. I couldn't let the Murder know—oh ashes, he was coming!

"We turn her now."

Turn me? Raum was sorely fucking mistaken if he thought I was going to fall now. Now that help was on the way. Now that I knew

I could control the power. Now that it had answered me when I needed it most. Now that Heaven's fire belonged to me.

Behind him, a screen flickered on. He pointed toward it as an image of a snowy forest appeared. "Two hours ago, our wards notified us that our borders had been crossed." Odonni were barreling through the thick snow. Six terrifying masses. At their head was Valen, his face drawn and blood spattered. I recognized Diriel beneath his hood flanking his left side. On his right was a guard I had seen often, Kasiya. They were right there with him, charging forward.

Every single one, the odonni included, looked exhausted. One of the animals stumbled, its rider jerking hard on the reins to keep it moving.

Beneath the screen, a door opened where a keras soldier dragged Lane in. Her face was bloody, split apart at her brow and lip. The jewels in her ears and nose had been ripped clean out.

I sat up. What was this?

"Valen, something is wrong. They know you're here."

"I know they do, but I will not abandon you. Hold on a little bit longer."

"I can see you. They have me chained up... somewhere, but there is a giant screen and I can see you. Valen, for the love of God, turn back before they—"

"You once told me you were never given a fair choice. Allow me to present you with one." Raum motioned to Orias who strode toward Lane. She was so small compared to him, even more so when she cowered. The demon was a lethal wall of battle, his muscles flexing with anticipation.

I could hear Valen calling to me in the recess of my mind.

"We discovered something, when Baal sent scouts through the

veil. Even with Tartarus leaking into your world, we are still vulnerable to Heaven's power over it. While we are able to rule, we cannot remain. We cannot take root. We have a theory that a human host will solve this issue."

I looked from Raum to the screen to Lane. Lane let out a whimper when Orias hauled her to her feet. "Demons... you already possess people. I've seen it," I said.

"Those possessions are no more than a projection. We are not truly within a body when we take it."

Orias trailed a finger beneath her tear-stained jaw. What did she have to do with all of this? What were they—? No.

Raum's wide grin spread across his beautiful face. "Now you are catching on."

"Let her go!"

Raum held up his finger. "Careful, Ezra. I said I would give you a choice, remember?" He prowled forward, stopping just shy of the length of my chains, should I pull them taut. He leaned forward and lowered his voice to a whisper so only I could hear. "I know she is not a part of this prophecy." His lashes fluttered as he stood back up. "And, therefore, no longer of use to me."

"She is!" I looked to Lane who was trying her best to keep her chin lifted. Her chin that was dripping with tears. "She is your moon and I am... I am your sun."

Raum cocked his head as he studied me. "You are." The muscles in his shoulders rolled as he twisted his neck. "Here is your choice, Ezra. Choose Lane and I will spare her from possession. I will let you keep her as a pet should you choose. In sparing her, I will send an army upon Valen and what remains of Vélos." The screen flickered to show an army of keras, each armed with bows and the black arrows of the amorini. How had they gotten the bolts? How had they gotten so many?

"I know Valen does not have his heart, but that will not stop me from slaughtering his men and tossing him into Vasanistirio where he will suffer in agony for all eternity."

"You fucking devil!"

Raum didn't miss a beat. The light behind his eyes sparkled as my temper rose. "Or, spare your adelfi. Choose him and I will let him live. But then Lane." He turned out his hand to where she trembled in Orias's grasp. Whatever the demon was whispering in her ear had broken through her resolve. "Lane gets to be the first to test our little theory."

"Don't," she said. Even as she said it, I knew she hoped for more. Hoped that I would choose her. "I do not want to live another moment with them. Being with you in Vélos was a small reprieve. Please, Ezra."

Choose me. We could fight them together. I could see it in her shimmering eyes, despite the contradiction of her words.

The screen flashed to a different angle as a snow storm bore down on Valen and his loyalists. In the trees, clouded in white, moved their enemy.

"You have thirty seconds to decide," Raum said.

"Don't do this, Raum. You already have me chained here to take what you want," I spat. Do not take them too.

Raum tsked. "I am giving you a kindness by giving you a choice. So, choose, Ezra. The girl or the cupid. You cannot have both."

"You will give me neither! You have told me my fate. This is not kindness you dangle in front of me. It is cruelty. I will give you what you want. Spare them!"

"Fifteen seconds," he said.

"You can have it. You can have a child with me! I give it freely!

Please!"

"Ten."

"Raum!"

"Oh, fuck this." Orias jerked Lane against him. He clamped both of his hands on either side of her face and pressed his lips against her open mouth as she inhaled to scream.

"Wait!" I lurched forward, but the chains remained firm. I looked from the screen and back to Lane and Orias as he began to dissolve. His body rippled and faded around the edges as he—as he forced himself into her mouth. I could not look away as he slunk his way into her body, making her throat and chest swell. Her limbs and torso twisted until the entirety of the shadow of his smoke had filled her up completely.

"Lane!" I screamed.

She stumbled forward and turned, her body swaying from side to side. When she blinked, the blue of her eyes was gone, replaced by total and utter darkness. The black orbs reflecting back like two giant stones of obsidian.

A bleed appeared behind her and, with a twisted grin, she stepped into it.

"Valen. Run! Run! Run!"

"I'm almost there, darling," he answered, breathless.

Nononono!

Why didn't he understand? Why wouldn't he listen? Where was Lane?

It was only a few minutes before Lane reappeared, her body convulsing and bulging when she stepped back through the bleed.

Her fingers trembled over her lips then her head. "Hurts," she rasped. "No room. There's no room." Her voice broke apart as she shook uncontrollably.

A male groan escaped her throat, intertwining with the rising panic that was her voice.

Oh God.

"Get out." She ran her nails down her face. "No room." Lane stumbled to the side, her black eyes flashing like prey.

"It is a tight fit," Orias hissed through her lips. One of her hands slid down her body obscenely.

In another flash Lane's eyes widened, so wide they might have been white had she not been consumed. "Oh my God, get out of me!"

Her tongue raked across her lips. "As you wish," Orias hissed, but it was her mouth that moved. She looked wildly around the room until her eyes landed on me. A fleeting moment where she begged me. A fleeting moment before her face twisted into a horrible, terrible grin.

Her body twisted, twisted and broke apart into a thousand bloody pieces as Orias rose out of the gore. He flicked a piece of flesh from his shoulder like lint. "She was right, there was no room. We will have to choose those closer to our size. A man, perhaps. I think it'll work, though. I could not feel the poison of Earth while wearing her skin."

I blinked.

I blinked again.

Lane was gone.

Just like that, she had been standing there and then it was just Orias. Bloody, glistening Orias.

Lane, who had been stolen from her love and forced to the will of devils for thousands of years, was gone.

"Your time is up and you still have not made a decision." In an unspoken command, no doubt one that shot through a blood bond, Raum sent a message that changed the tense image on the screen into a flurry as the masses in white fell upon the six amorini.

"Valen!"

A crack of energy shot through the air as I reached for him and sent a wave of power down the line of our bond. I watched his odonnos rear against one of the keras. How Valen fell back into his saddle and then lurched forward as the odonnos fell on its talons and he cut the keras down with a sword.

An arrow caught him in the shoulder.

They would maim him, wound him enough to drag him to the pit. And the others... An arrow caught Diriel in the throat. He cut it off and sliced in a downward motion to the two keras that were trying to haul him off his mount.

Something within me cracked.

"I am going to burn Eurynomos to the ground. Take your men and run."

Valen whirled as if he were looking for my voice. He pushed his mount forward from the fray but was met with a wall of bodies that forced him back. The odonnos's head snaked to the side, its beak snapping wildly.

I felt the familiar tingling of fire as it coursed through my veins.

A shock of Valen's power rose up to meet mine.

"I am with you."

"This could kill you."

"I am not afraid of your fury. Unleash your wrath."

Raum faced me fully, his muscles tensing as the power continued to build. The force came swift from above as I fell down into the well of my power, crashing to the bottom so I could pull it down into the empty space.

Light and darkness collided as I pulled them both within me, pulled up everything owed to me.

Raum sneered. "You think your God will answer you this time? You just failed one of His children. Like everyone else who comes into your life, Lane is dead because of you. Heaven has seen you for the horror that you are. Why would they answer you now?"

I wanted to clasp my hands over my ears, but the shackles wouldn't budge. On the screen, a keras sliced an amorini's head from their body. Valen had arrows impaled in his back and shoulders. Blood coated his lips.

They couldn't die.

Valen couldn't die. But he was slowing. He was very clearly struggling to keep himself upright.

Raum approached me, his beautiful face twisting into a cruel mask. "You're going to kill him next. Valen's blood will be on your hands, and then who will want you?"

"Stop," I hissed. I pulled at the power, but it wasn't enough.

"God forsake you. You are nothing. Do you hear me? You are nothing to Heaven but unwanted. You were never going to have a place among the angels."

My nostrils flared as his words penetrated me deeper than a knife ever could. He was right. I had failed. Was failing as Valen's men fell into the snow.

Raum chuckled. "You weak woman."

On the screen, the colors of the sky shifted. There were other powers outside of Heaven. I'd felt it briefly when Bishop urged me to it, had dipped my fingers into its darkness on accident on other occasions.

I was a child of angels and men who had been both blessed and cursed by Heaven. There was more than just Prometheus that was owed to me. I was Fallen. That meant their power belonged to me too.

"Shut up," I said.

"Ezra?" Valen's voice was hoarse.

"Heaven refuses to help you. It is not enough, is it? What will you do? What can you do but let them die?" Raum taunted. His voice was a whisper, as if he was right in my ear.

My lids fluttered as I teetered on the edge of a void. I felt an expanse of darkness within me. I reached out blindly, feeling to anything that would answer. I needed more.

A surge of power brushed back.

It sent a shock through my bloodstream. I reached forward and toppled over the edge.

The room dropped out from under me as I fell within myself.

"Ezra. Ezra!" Valen was shouting at me, but I was in a free fall, diving too fast that I couldn't stop if I wanted to.

I could not see the world around me. There was no screen, no Murder, no chains around me. There was only darkness.

When I finally crashed to the bottom, green flames burst from beneath me. This. This was it! This is what I needed. Raw, untapped power created by those full of rage.

Muffled voices were shouting at me. Taunting me.

I wrapped the bands of power around myself, slipped them over my body like a second skin, and rushed from the pit I had found them.

"Don't fall! Ezra, don't! I'm here!"

The flames bore me up. I jerked forward as I slammed back into my body, my hands ablaze with silver and green flames. Prometheus and Hellfire, they both belonged to me. Their sharp colors bled from my feet, pooling across the floor. They funneled over the ceiling, encasing the entire room in vibrant, wicked light.

On the screen behind Raum's head, I could see Valen running. He was screaming, cutting down everyone who stood in his path. My name was a war cry on his lips. An arrow bolted through his throat and Valen was falling.

I lurched from the ground, arms, legs, and wings straining against the chains as I let out my fury unfurled into a scream and shot everything I had at Raum. In the same moment that I rose to my feet and lunged forward, a blade slid across my throat.

I never saw when Atticus moved behind me. I didn't see him at all until his scarred face was staring down at me, the thin line of his blade dripping with my blood. The blade that he held with gloved hands that smoked beneath his grip.

A holy blade.

The flesh of my neck split apart like paper, and a surge of blood spilled out before the force of his blow knocked me to the ground. Above me, I saw the silver power retreating and the green flames of the underworld blow out like a candle. The sound of a wet paper bag gaping was the only thing I could hear.

It was hoarse and noisy.

The fire, silver and gold, stuttered as I tried to hold onto it and struggled to breathe.

The beautiful music of Raum's laughter chased me into the darkness.

CHAPTER SEVENTY-ONE: I AM WITH YOU

Valen

The funnel of light returned to the sky from the kingdom above. Heaven had answered. I saw the shift in the sky as an arrow sank into my shoulder, nearly forcing me off the back of the odonnos.

"I am going to burn Eurynomos to the ground. Take your men and run."

Her voice was right there. Right in my ear, but I could not see her. I urged the gelding forward, pushing him against the warring bodies that cut us down. I was not going to run, not when I was so close to her. I could see the mass of the tyre just through the trees.

I gave to her that which I had kept hidden. I slid the stolen power of Episkopos down our bond, aligning it with hers as she drew upon the holy fire.

"I am with you."

"This could kill you," she said softly, fiercely.

"I am not afraid of your fury. Unleash your wrath."

A force hit me from the right side. I flew from the odonnos's back as it was ripped from me, torn away by a giant bolt. We were a small band against the hundreds that warred for Eurynomos, but that number was nothing when we had burning rage pumping through our veins.

I saw the light in the sky shift from lavender to... a more royal hue to green flames.

"Ezra?"

God, no. Please no.

What had they done to her?

"Ezra. Ezra! Do not fall! You are saved! Do you hear me? Do not fall. Heaven has not forgotten you."

"Ezra!"

A bolt shot through my throat. I crashed to the ground as the sky turned dark. She was pulling from the wrong source. Ezra, for all her power, was no longer calling on just Heaven to wield Prometheus, but Hell.

I broke the arrow and pulled it free.

My sword cut through the neck of a keras and straight through the heart of another. The keras were skilled, bred into the violence in which they wrought. I had been molded to it, forced into its grasp, and Hell, if that wasn't just as deadly.

I could still save her.

The ground was soaked with black red blood, the snow spattered in glistening rubies of it by the time we finished.

And then the bolt struck me.

I stumbled back into the snow as the force of it ripped through my chest. I gasped, sliding my hands over the empty space. There was no bolt, no arrow.

No.

No!

"Ezra!"

Pain lacerated my throat. I couldn't breathe. I couldn't fucking breathe and neither could she.

Kasiya slid to my side, his hands roaming over my chest that I clawed at. "There is no wound," he said.

Diriel's body shook. "Gods," he gasped, his eyes going stark white. "They've..."

Don't say it. It wasn't true. They couldn't.

"Ezra! Harpy, answer me!"

I felt the brush of her against my mind, her fingertips there along my soul and then gone.

"No," I rasped. "To your feet now."

Diriel stepped in my way, his hand shaking as he held it in front of me. "Valen," he said.

"She is right there. I am not leaving without her," I snarled. I shouldn't have let her go. This was my fault. I had thought Bishop would save her from the attack and, instead, he had killed her.

Ezra was...

"Valen," Diriel said, his voice hardening.

I jerked Diriel's collar in my fist. "I gave you an order, Diriel. You will obey your cyn." Strong hands jerked me from behind, but I did not let go of Diriel. "We are not leaving without her."

We could not.

Ezra's death slithered through my blood like poison. I fell to my knees as the venom took hold and severed the soul tie. My stomach lurched and I fell to the side as colorful gems blew out of my mouth. The rainbow obsidian glistened and then turned to ash, sizzling into hot coals in the snow.

I grappled for the gems, looking for any that had not spoiled. But every time I opened my hand, there was only black soot.

They were gone. Every last one.

Just like her.

Ezra was gone.

CHAPTER SEVENTY-TWO: AFTER THE BEES

Raguel

Marquette, Michigan

Leah ran her fingers through her dark hair. It snagged on the tie she had it bound in. With a frustrated sound, she ripped the elastic band out and vigorously knotted her hair in a new ponytail.

On the screen of the TV flashed a fallen bridge. She flipped the channel to a bombing in Italy. Each channel bore some new horror. After the bees had disappeared, the plagues started and war became rampant as humans struggled to maintain some sort of control as their world slipped through their fingers.

"I never thought we would live to see a day like this," she said quietly.

The male came up beside her, James.

He ran a firm hand over her shoulder. "We prepared for this though. We'll be ok. Nothing is going to happen to us."

Leah's thin brows knotted, and her lips paled as she continued to stare at the newscasters. "James," she said quietly. She dragged her dark eyes away. "You know I don't believe in God and stuff... but do you think.... this is it? The end?"

James slid his hand down her arm as he crouched in front of her. "It's the beginning of something new. It's scary but— Leah, look at me. I'll never let anything happen to you. You know why?"

Her small body tensed with enough stress to fill the small house they called a home. "Why?"

James flashed a sharp white smile. "Close your eyes," he said.

"James," she said, exasperated.

"Just do it, come on." He squeezed her hand.

Leah scowled and shut her eyes.

"No peeking," he said.

James pulled out a silver ring from his pocket with a shaking hand. Raguel could smell the uncertainty and fear from where he stood in the hallway. It was foolish for such sentiments when their world was dying, yet Raguel allowed himself to appreciate the simple gesture. He cocked his head as the man took a breath.

"Open your eyes."

Leah looked from the ring to James and back again. Her mouth opened, but no words came out.

Her tan skin flushed bright red. "James," she breathed.

"I know the world is going to shit, but I wouldn't want to face it with anyone else. We have conquered so much together. This is just another storm for us to weather."

Tears filled Leah's eyes. "You've got fucked-up timing," she choked.

"Will you marry me, Leah?"

She nodded as her lips twisted together and tears spilled down her freckled face. "Yes. God, yes," she breathed.

They kissed. And as the adelfis tangled their hands in each other's hair, laughing and grinning between the kisses, the invisible red chord that tied them flared.

Gladr mused. "I've never understood humans and marriage."

"It's a gift from our Father," Raguel said with a smile. The world had changed drastically in the last year. It touched him that humans still found the beauty in destruction. It was fortunate that the two had found each other without the help of an amorini. A rare event that many had died without experiencing as many more would.

Humankind lived their life never having the opportunity to meet the mate of their soul. Leah and James had happened upon it by chance.

He watched as they crouched on the floor, looking for the ring that had been discarded when Leah launched herself at James. The young woman found it beneath the entertainment center and held it up with a crooked grin.

James slid it on Leah's fingers, and a fresh wave of tears flooded her eyes.

"Who are you?" Raguel asked. He had spent weeks studying the young woman but nothing apparent stood out about her. There was nothing extraordinary that would warrant Heaven to watch her so closely.

"I do not foresee much more happening in the life of this woman," Raguel said. "Perhaps fate has graced them, and they will make it out of this destruction that befalls them. Let us return home and see what awaits us."

The journey to Heaven happened in a flash. The golden warmth of the city was a welcome warmth against Raguel's face. It was within the sanctity that he felt most whole, though it was often his duty to remain in Tartarus to oversee the cyns who ruled the pit of darkness.

As soon as they landed, Gladr split off in search of Ramiel. Raguel still had his doubts about the young male, but if there was a secret to uncover a truth, he trusted Ramiel to find it. Riding the line seemed to have its perks.

Ramiel's normally smug face was grim when he met them in the pentelic white Room of Whispers. This space was not often used, as the angelica did not believe in keeping secrets. But by the look on Ramiel's face, Raguel had chosen right.

"What's your report?"

"That girl you were sent to look after. Leah? She is an heir of Solomon," Ramiel said.

Raguel stilled. "His bloodline was eradicated in their year 1232."

"Clearly an extension of it was missed. But that's not all." Ramiel turned to Calix. "Do you want to tell him or should I?"

Calix's mouth twisted. "It's about the girl Valen had at his side."

"Ezra," Ramiel cut in.

"What about her?"

"She's the nephilim."

"That's impossible," Raguel snarled.

"And she's Valen's adelfi."

Raguel looked at Calix, but the large male didn't blink. He was as grim as Raguel felt. Angelica were not female.

Raguel's red cape fluttered behind him as he turned. The sole of his boots moved soundlessly as he paced. There was a story of a female nephilim, but it was so unlike the gods that had ruled Egypt it was thought to be a myth. The creature was never found. None of them were. Where stories were spun of women with wings, only frail minds and hopeful smiles could be found.

It couldn't be.

White lights flashed through the room, making the stark brightness of it almost blinding. Raguel shielded his eyes as he exited the Room of Whispers, the males trailing after him.

There were screens all across the city. The largest of them spread horizontally across the bridge they faced. Images of Earth flashed on the smaller screens, but it was the large screen that held his and every other's attention.

Darkness swept across the earth, washing every living thing with boils. The boils inflated with puss, swelling so large that they made the humans unrecognizable. The animals looked like a deformity of their species. There were so few left and, just like that, they were gone, bursting at the seams.

One by one, humanity fell. One body after another with a soundless thump.

Other images changed as more and more plagues revealed themselves.

"There you are!"

A young cherub came to a stumbling halt in front of Raguel. "I have been looking... everywhere... for... you," he gasped. He held out a reader, a small device that transcribed messages.

I am Ezra Hollen and I call on you, Raguel, to fulfill your promise. Rescue me. Spare me when you find me, but rescue me now.

Help me. Help me. Help me.

Forgive me that I didn't tell you.

Please help me.

Help me.

Help me.

Help me.

The messages ran so far down the screen, like she had been chanting the two words over and over again. Calling to him, begging him to help her and he had not answered. Anger tinged Raguel's cheeks as bright as his hair. Anger that she had lied. Anger that he had not been here to answer her. To save her.

Where had she... He got to the bottom, to her last message. The prayers had come from Eurynomos. His stomach coiled at the memory of her shining face and at the horror that would befall her, surely had befallen her, in Hell itself.

"They've gotten through the veil," someone said.

Raguel's head snapped up.

"High to low," another cursed.

Raguel dropped his hand to his side as he stepped forward.

On the big screen, a man was lying in the street, his entire body twitching as a tendril of black smoke coiled out of his nostrils.

The crowd had gone silent. No one moved as the man's body convulsed once more before he slowly sat up. He ran a hand over his face, testing it. As if it was not his own. Raguel took another step forward as a terrible sense of dread filled him.

The man's eyes flashed open, revealing obsidian black orbs.

"He's been possessed. Almighty, they have gotten through," Gladr whispered.

Ramiel stood on Raguel's other side, his eyes wide with shock as the male on the screen rose from his position and looked around before motioning to someone else. Another male with jet black eyes.

Raguel looked back down at the screen clutched in his palm and the cries for help that screamed back at him.

CHAPTER SEVENTY-THREE: WHAT WONDERS

The Fury

Blood. It obliterated my senses like a thousand fireworks all going off at once. Different shades of crimson filled the back of my eyelids, bursting like blood vessels waiting to be tasted. The scorch of its scent burned the back of my raw throat. I could hear it too, its rich pumping through my veins sounded swift like a river.

I needed it.

I ran my hands over my face, imagining it covered my body. I wanted to dig my claws into it, to feast on anything that kept it prisoner from me. I wanted to taste its vengeance, its grief, its *rage*.

The absence of the lush wine burned.

Everything hurt.

As my eyes opened, I was met by three things. The reality that I was dead, or perhaps I had died, before waking was the first to strike me. Another life had been gifted to me. A radiant, hungry life that made my teeth ache. The second were the three pairs of blue eyes staring back at me. All male by the smell of them. Covered in musk, sex, and blood. That smell was the third thing that made my belly lurch. A lush, slick scent that watered my dry mouth. Hunger clawed at my throat again, demanding to be quenched.

I locked eyes with the male closest to me. Within his burnished face was authority. He was beautiful with his raven black hair, pretty even, with his defined features. Feathers spread at the nape of his neck, several more twisted in those thick locks.

"There she is," the male purred, his sapphire eyes dark and wide. I had a sense that I should know who he was. Fear and anticipation made my stomach flutter. What would he taste like? I ran my tongue over my lower lip as I traced each dip of muscle with my gaze.

I kept him in my peripheral as I rose to my hands to get a better look at the other two, equally beautiful, males. The first was porcelain with blonde, nearly white hair, with his hands clasped at his back. His light eyes, so blue they were nearly translucent, flicked to the first, and then to his companion, before settling on me.

I looked to his companion. The russet-skinned male rolled his shoulder, slipping out of a leather jacket that fell with a wet smack to the floor. He was covered from head to toe in blood. I looked down at my hands that were covered in it. I flexed my fingers. It was mostly dry across my knuckles. Within my palms, it remained sticky. I dabbed my fingers together, watching the way the thin lines stretched and broke.

"How do you feel?" the first one asked.

I felt everything. I could feel their anticipation as tangible as the air I breathed. There was uncertainty too. But the feeling that I questioned the most was the sexual hunger that wafted off the male beside me.

"Alecto," he said softly.

Was that my name? I felt as if I should remember something,

or perhaps this was the way one was made, curious and new and whole. I didn't know who I was. I felt so... alive! My skin buzzed with electricity that filled the charged air. My eyes found his lips as I spoke. "Hungry. Strange." A dull thrum resonated in the back of my head, low and consistent.

There was a surge of something great that moved within me. Chaos was its name. It roiled in my blood, pumped through my heart faster than it ever had before. I could taste the power of it. Could feel the dull sense of a burn as it kindled.

"I can help you with that." The feathered male held out his hand. "Do you remember me?"

His words snapped me out of my contemplation. I paused as I reached for him. I hadn't noticed the large wings attached to my back until then. Bits of feather clung to them, as if they had been plucked. No, that wasn't the right word.

Molted.

The few feathers left were hanging on by a thread. Beneath them were membraned wings, shimmering like black velvet. At their top were large, hooked talons that glistened the same. I blew out a breath, sending a feather shuddering from its pore to the ground.

Someone let out an exasperated huff. "She is like a child."

My gaze panned back to the darker of the three and the annoyed look plastered across his face.

"No, she is not," the white-haired one said. "Look at her eyes."

The first male touched his fingers to the underside of my chin, lifting my eyes to his. "Seraph eyes," he said. "The stories of them being closely related are true then." His fingers slipped down the side of my throat to a strand of my hair. He curled a red lock around his finger, inspecting it.

"We have about ten minutes before she understands her power, if those stories are correct. Insulting her, Orias," White Hair addressed his companion with a hiss, "is not something you want to do."

Orias's lips curled, revealing a broad line of white teeth. "I wasn't afraid of her before and I'm not now. I will say, she's much prettier with the new wings. And the blood does wonders for her skin." He stepped forward, his bare feet leaving a trail of red in his wake. "You always have looked delicious in red," he said, leering over me.

"Alecto," the first one said. "Do you know who I am?"

I did know him. I knew all three of them, but I didn't understand why or how. They looked dangerous, and yet I didn't get the sense that I should fear them. Not even with the way their eyes roved over me. I was something they coveted. The first one had such longing in his eyes, a plea for me to remember.

I leaned forward and inhaled him. Ashes, he smelled divine.

I let him take my hands, drawing me to my feet. His eyes washed over me as I stood, taking in the expanse of my wings before settling back on my face with wide admiration.

"I am Raum, your adelfi." He was gentle when he spoke. Familiar.

Another language came to me then, the flow of words jolting and quick. I winced as the influx of it hit me.

"Ozien," I said softly.

I leaned into his warmth. His muscles rippled beneath me, coiling like a snake in response to my touch. A protective hold that enveloped me like a lover.

"Mine," I said, finally recognizing the word.

Raum smiled, deep laugh lines cutting into his face. "Yes," he said. He was so elegantly beautiful.

Orias's deep baritone of a laugh cracked through the air. "What were you saying, Atticus?" He gave White Hair a mocking grin.

Atticus, the pale one, wore a tight frown.

The smell of death was beneath Raum's skin. A fresh death. Fresh always tasted better.

I pressed my nose to the underside of his chin. He smelled good. It burned into my senses, flooding my mouth with water. My gums ached, the front where my canines were more painful than the rest. I flicked my tongue to the curve of his flesh. Raum let out a harsh breath in response, his arm around my shoulders flexing.

"Take what you need," he said. His long fingers ran through my hair, cradling the back of my head.

I kissed his throat. His gilded skin shimmered beneath my parted mouth as flames licked across my tongue.

"Raum," I heard Atticus say. A warning. His voice sounded far away. "Raum, you need to let her go now."

I swiped my tongue across his skin for another taste. Delicious. Back and forth I switched from tongue to lips, trying to feel him. Trying to get a better taste of him.

My teeth hurt.

I kissed Raum harder.

"Bite," he commanded.

"Raum," Atticus hissed.

"You'll get your turn," Orias chuckled.

I nipped at Raum's skin. Once, twice, and then I bit, with blunt teeth. Raum winced as I chewed on his skin, struggling to release the sweet essence that called to me. His hand fisted in my hair as he pulled me back.

"Use your fangs," he hissed. He snapped the air in front of my face, his own sharp teeth flashing.

I bared my teeth and snapped in return. I tongued the roof of my mouth, then the front of my gums, searching for fangs I could tear him open with. Two small holes, on my upper and lower gums. The source of the pain in my face.

"Let the hunger lead you," Raum guided.

Heat barreled up my throat as he spoke. That clawing hunger was going to be the death of me. I gave into my wild appetite as the ache intensified in my mouth. What could only be my fangs slid free from their sheaths.

As soon as Raum loosened his hold, I struck.

Sweet, luscious, luxurious warmth filled my mouth as my aim fell true, tearing open the vein at his throat.

Raum grunted but held me close still. "Good girl."

Images burst across my vision as his blood flooded my tongue. I ground my jaw against him, working that delicious life source free. Agonizingly beautiful memories of pearl gates and golden streets flashed before my eyes. Large metal birds shared the skies with angels. Yes, angels. That's what he was.

What I am.

Smoke and fire. Blade and battle. The images pummeled forward as I locked my jaw around his throat.

More. I needed more.

Strong hands gripped my wings, only to let go with a curse.

"I can't touch her," Orias growled. "Fuck! Fuck, my hands are burning."

Raum held onto me, his fingers curving into talons as I refused to let go. He wouldn't be able to bleed me before I got what I wanted. Through the haze of the battle was a box. A flimsy little thing that would not keep me out. I tore through the shield surrounding it, devouring that which he kept sacred. All those little secrets he kept tucked away. That he thought he could hide from me.

The sound of tearing flesh and blood splatting across my face spread as he ripped me free of his throat. Gaping puncture wounds locked eyes with me, enticing me to another drink. This hunger would make me an animal if I did not rein it in. I tore my eyes from those spouts and met the sapphire stare baring into me. I saw him for what he really was. Who he was. A creature of darkness and infinite power. A creature of ambition and chaos. Will incarnated that would not be changed.

His face jerked as I latched hold of his chin, drawing his face before mine until our noses brushed. The flash of fear in the oceans of his eyes excited my tongue from my mouth. He did not bend to his terror but twisted it so that it became a leash around his fist as he pushed our mouths together. He licked up his blood, slathering my face with his scent.

"My golden sun," he breathed into my mouth. "What wonders you shall perform."

AUTHOR'S NOTE

It took me eighteen long years of writing and rewriting this book before I was finally happy with it. Eighteen years and she is finally here! Originally titled My Valentine, Ezra's story was to be a romantic tragedy. I am thrilled with how it has evolved and connects seamlessly to my Revelation series, making this story bigger and badder than ever. Ezra's story has always been incredibly special to me, as it dives deep into the power of faith and love and the struggle many experience when searching for them.

I have so many people to thank when it comes to writing this book. First, to everyone who doesn't believe in true love. Your doubt in it and distaste for Valentine's Day is what initially inspired this story. To Kaylee for listening to me gab about my ideas at work and saying "You need to write that story." I'd always kept my stories to myself, but one day I felt vulnerable enough to share this silly draft I had stashed away on a floppy disc. It was your encouragement that led me to pursue my love for writing. To Tara, for being the best roommate and sister I never knew I needed. You have been a huge blessing in my life and I'm so lucky to know you. To Kendall, you are an absolute gem. Thank you for reading my work when it was raw and riddled with errors. Your input quite literally saved me from writer's block numerous times. I love that through my stories and our love for books, I have found a wonderful friend. To Heather for being a light in my life with your love and wisdom. It is an honor to be able to call you my friend. And most importantly, to God for guiding me out of a loveless relationship and guarding my heart until I can be so blessed to find my adelfi.

ABOUT THE AUTHOR

ALLISON PAIGE'S novels are inspired by her dreams and night-mares. Her stories shed light on villains and the darker side of what it takes to make a hero.

Allison loves traveling with her camera, particularly in the Irish countryside, and has several ongoing projects she writes out of her home in Charleston, South Carolina. She fills her spare time working with animals of all types and is a fervent advocate of bee, ocean, and wildlife conservation.

www.authorallisonpaige.com